A Room

YOUVAL SHIMONI

A ROOM

TRANSLATED BY MICHAEL SHARP

DALKEY ARCHIVE PRESS

Originally published in Hebrew as *Heder* in 2006

©2006 by Youval Shimoni
Worldwide Translation copyright ©2016 by the Institute
for the Translation of Hebrew Literature

First edition, 2016
All rights reserved

Library of Congress Cataloging-in-Publication Data

Names: Shimoni, Youval, 1955- author. | Sharp, Michael (Translator)
    translator.
Title: A room / by Youval Shimoni ; translated by Michael Sharp.
Other titles: Heder. English
Description: First edition. | Victoria, TX : Dalkey Archive Press, 2016.
Identifiers: LCCN 2015040713 | ISBN 9781628971330 (pbk. : alk. paper)
Classification: LCC PJ5054.S453723 H413 2016 | DDC 892.43/6--dc23
LC record available at http://lccn.loc.gov/2015040713

ILLINOIS
ARTS
COUNCIL
AGENCY

Partially funded by a grant by the Illinois Arts Council, a state agency

The Hebrew Literature Series is published in collaboration with the Institute for the Translation of Hebrew
Literature and sponsored by the Office of Cultural Affairs, Consulate General of Israel, and New York.

Dalkey Archive Press publications are, in part, made possible through the support of the University of
Houston-Victoria and its programs in creative writing, publishing, and translation.

Dalkey Archive Press
Victoria, TX / McLean, IL / Dublin / London
www.dalkeyarchive.com

Cover: Art by Eric Longfellow
Typesetting: Kari Larsen

Printed on permanent/durable acid-free paper

CONTENTS

"In that Empire, the Art of Cartography attained such Perfection that the map of a single Province occupied the entirety of a City, and the map of the Empire, the entirety of a Province."

(Jorge Luis Borges)

THE LAMP

1

From a distance the fire could already be seen, around and above it an immense night sky with no avenue or groves on its periphery to protrude their treetops toward it; there were only plowed fields whose furrows were previously swallowed up by the dark and now revealed their nakedness in the glow of the fire. And the police who arrived in their patrol car from a nearby suburb, and the doctor summoned from his room by the female medic, and the female medic herself, stood illuminated by it, gazing at it as it grew, soared and swayed to and fro, a gigantic rustling yellow treetop shedding sparks, spreading clusters of them into the night, as if all the stars in its depths had been spread by a fire such as this, in which a man is burning.

But when the Renault travels the road, an old white Renault 12, bumping over potholes, its shadow traveling at times in front, at times on its side and at times slipping away to spread itself flat beneath the wheels, as if the driver, whose own shadow is swallowed by that of the car, wished to flatten his paunch under those wheels – when they roll and skip over the partially cracked asphalt, worn down and wary of soft shoulders, the fire will have left nothing but a large blackened stain, a

few remnants and a mound of ash. By then
the sun will have ascended like the pupil
of Cyclops' eye, blinded and searing, or
like the filament of a globe to which this
entire dome, whose edges are charted by
the horizon, is as a glass pear.

And then there's the investigator, after
all an investigation is required. It won't be
the first time that questions are asked and
answers demanded in order to prevent a
recurrence of such an event. He'll stretch
his arm toward the window handle on
the right, turn it a few times, and a breeze
from the hidden sea will enter through one
window and exit through another, and
for a brief moment the old car and some
nameless uprooted bushes out there are
strung together, just as it'll string together
the buildings across the empty fields after
he'll pass them: low white buildings all
cast from one mold, and in front of each
one, blue and black signposts. It'll string
together all the rooms except for the one
that has been sealed.

But first the investigator will have to
turn into a small side road onto which
eucalyptus trees cast their shadows here and
there according to the capricious whims
of the wind and the sun, all their trunks
painted white to serve as a pale backdrop
for the ants that scurry up and down them
like black angels on a ladder whose top is
in the sky. He'll soon have to slow down so
as not to expose the Renault's questionable
breaking power, coming to a complete halt
before the rope stretched across the road
in an arc from the sentry post to a pole on
the other side, stopping it before this loose

white rope along whose entire length there is nothing but a lone ant crossing as if it were an acrobat waiting for the sentry to cheer, even though his eyes are shut and his head inclined forward – he'll have to stop and blow the horn.

And to wait. And to blow the horn again. And to observe how the little black ant is startled and loses its grip on the grain, it'll watch it from the rope for a moment longer as if from a bridge when the grain falls to the asphalt and is immediately swept away in all its greyness, if it would not already have been swept away by the wind: it came from the sea and crossed all its waves and islands and whales merely in order to sweep part of this road at the sentry's feet, to ruffle the few hairs left on his head by the barber at the base and to slip between his eyelashes, puffing up behind them white dreamlike sails or sweaty tennis skirts, and in order to rustle the faded eucalyptus leaves on its way to the bend of the road, to the empty fields and the mound of ash, while the investigator blows his horn again.

And he waits. And he watches the sentry's features pull themselves together, his black pupils rising up in the whiteness like the heads of people rising to leave a cinema as the lights go on, or leaving the closed and sealed room in which the short film will be screened for him – a film about which the police had told him and about which the female medic had told them and he had discussed watching it with the master sergeant and the master sergeant promised to notify the sentry. Look here, he can phone to check it out if he doesn't believe it. Is there a telephone here? Yes there is, here's the wire and here's the handle, he can turn the handle and ask the operator for the officer on duty or for his clerk if the officer is out, or for the female medic; and he will tell them that he, the investigator who spoke to them this morning about what happened last night under their very noses, has arrived. But he hasn't arrived yet, the room hasn't been sealed yet and the fire that grew and soared, shaking branches and yellow leaves, is still contained in its place like a hidden root, a mere seed.

It's now afternoon. And if the director of the short film were to film the investigator, he might show him from a bird's eye view, from the back of a genial, fat-bellied wild goose whose feathers smoothed down by the wind are grasped by Nils Holgerson's legs, his small hands clasping its neck, his face freckled like Shechter's as a child, his pockets bulging like his as well. But it's not Shechter who will watch the investigator, but rather the investigator who will watch him.

And if the master sergeant were to film him – turning the telephone handle himself, pressing the button on the side of the earpiece and talking to the operator (yes he wants to speak with the officer on duty, yes he's speaking from the sentry post, yes the sentry is next to him, a bit sleepy but alive and well) – he would show him from the height of treetops, from which apples peek out with blushing faces, and he, the master sergeant, stretches his hand out and gently inserts them into the sack that he's been given as a regular member of the kibbutz. But it's not the master sergeant who will watch the investigator, but rather the investigator who will watch him.

And the actor, who calls himself Miki Le-Mic on cards that he distributes at birthday parties, if he were to film the investigator it might be from the level of a bench – a park bench on an avenue whose treetops are lit by the morning sun and their foliage spread out leaf by leaf. He would film him silently listening to the voice on the line, holding the mouthpiece at a distance due to the smell of garlic and bringing it closer again in order tell the earpiece that yes, he had already arranged it that morning, yes, that's what he was told, precisely, and he's come especially. What, hadn't they heard what happened last night?

And the two actresses, who would not have come to the base had it not been for the short film (whose one and only redeeming feature was making it possible to see how this death took place in the background), they would film the investigator not from a stage, but from a window with a view of an entire city, its empty streets, its deserted sidewalks, its flashing traffic lights. From there they would show him listening to the earpiece, kicking a small stone, glancing at his watch, looking at the sentry whose head once again is about to droop. But it's the investigator who will watch them both from the sealed room to which at long last he's permitted to walk; yes, to walk, not to drive. He should kindly park outside like everyone else. Yes outside; with all due respect to the investigation, a civilian vehicle cannot enter here, by order.

And Merav, yes that's what she's called, Merav, who together with the master sergeant makes instructional films for the soldiers on the base, as if five whole levels of rank and almost twenty years and a family did not separate them, if she were to film the investigator – parking his Renault by the roadside, closing the car door gently because the sentry's head has fallen forwards (there are no sails there between his eyelids, but rather the hems of white skirts that for a moment fly up above naked private parts) – she would not film him from high up, but rather at eye level, standing if he stood, sitting if he sat, lying down if he lay down and thrown to the ground if he were thrown to the ground.

For the time being he is still on his feet, and if the bags under his eyes are darkening, perhaps they've been hung there simply by the hours of sleep that have eluded them (he was awoken in the middle of the night and told to begin an investigation, the boss's secretary spoke in bedroom tones in a voice he already recognized, and conclusions by evening please, and no waffling this time, bottom line, was it or was it not an accident?).

And the lighting technician, whom the actor sometimes referred to as Eran-the-lighting-man, as if he were one of the cartoon characters that he impersonated for children, if he were to film the investigator it would be from the scary height of a diving board or from the crane that can be seen in television programs rising through the studio, hovering and circling with the cameraman seated on its edge like a pilot; and its movement would not be slow, but a swift and decisive plunge leaving nothing in its wake, the movement of a great exploding missile.

But the investigator, who will be watching him, stops for a moment, looks right and left and walks on. In the shade of the eucalyptus trees there's no tap with water for him to wash his face with before watching the film; just a few blue and black tin signposts with letters in white, "the base is your home, look after it," or "it's better to lose a moment in your life than lose your life in a moment," or "should they ascend to heaven, I'll bring them down from there." He advances slowly as directed; straight ahead all the way to the dining hall and then left to the end. There he should see the clinic's signpost, yes, the room just across. What, the female medic didn't tell him? With her running off at the mouth didn't she tell him everything?

A stumpy fire extinguisher leaks outside the clinic, but the investigator turns to the office with sealed windows opposite, opens the door and enters: a large flabby man, sweaty from his walk, two dark stains already spreading from his armpits.

And Joe, Joseph or Yossi, yes, that's what he was called, when there was still someone to call him by his name, the soundman who recorded everything – scenes from the silly short film that the master sergeant filmed as a memento – he would film the investigator from an unchanging height: not increasing, not decreasing, not moving. He would show him from a lizard's eye view, a likeable little lizard whose feet clutch the whitewash, the floor its sky. Under them the investigator sits down on an office chair with a soft sigh of relief, which only the lizard hears.

In front of him there's a small monitor that has been prepared for the viewing and that will soon cast his reflection before him: tired, thirsty, the sacks under his eyes like those into which last remains are gathered. But as he turns the machine on – "call me with the slightest problem, all we need is for something to go wrong with the video" – his pupils tense. Maybe everything was filmed in the background, step by step, as the police had told him, as the female medic had told them: and perhaps everyone's pupils lit up when the clusters of sparks spread into the night, flying everywhere, ascending and gliding, as if the stars above them once nested in such a fire, in which a man is burning.

2

"Isn't it true it wasn't here yesterday?" asked Na'ama.

(It was the second day of shooting and the sack covered Shechter's head, and he was already familiar with each and every fiber and was aware of the smell of jute as he was of his own smells, which changed as the days passed: the vapor of his breath, the smell of his teeth, his saliva, his sweat and other odors to which he could not put a name, they too were compressed into this sack of whose outer appearance he had no idea: not because it had been placed over his head like the head of a prisoner he saw in the war, but because it was woven from the very air itself, a weave so gradual that it could not be felt until it was complete, like the changing shades of the sky that only when ended does one say: night.

Shechter knew these voices by heart too, at times in front, at times behind or above, seeping in like river water into a sack of drowned kittens, a river larger than the Yarkon and not muddy, but crystal clear with floating sheets of ice and Donald Ducks in sailor suits gliding amongst them. The voices seeped into his sack and their flow stopped there, pressing against his face and crushing him with the two or three questions they had to ask him, after which he would be released to do as he pleased; as if the fibers had not been pierced and then mended themselves inside his face like a kind of skin, new, thick and coarse, where somewhere beneath lay the real Shechter. That's what he called him, despite the fact that this one here was completely real, even more real than the other, since he still moved and breathed and spoke: as when previously for example, he told the two female soldiers to start preparing for the shoot since they didn't have much time to waste. Yes, in case they hadn't noticed, but he's sure

they had – that's how he spoke to them, in what he thought
was their language, quickly trying to add a little smile so that
he wouldn't sound like one of their commanders, but the
smile was pitiful and did not rectify matters.

Through the fibers Shechter could see their young faces
drawing away from him and blurring, like faces on a station
platform, and their young bodies, all curves, arched toward
his hands and arms, limbs of which he was now aware only
momentarily on some crowded and rocking bus, such as
the number 5, where he thought any second he's liable to
perpetrate one of those acts that would land him in some
marginal newspaper column reporting criminal offences.
They could have been his daughters had he married at twenty,
but he did not marry at twenty, nor at thirty, and it's been a
while since he last changed his bed sheets or swept the dusty
corners of his apartment or fixed a leaking faucet whose parts
he once could proudly dismantle.

He still measured time in minutes and seconds and weeks
then, while now the hot dry days return so fast that it seems
like only a month ago that he placed the fan back in storage.
The rains too hasten their return, dragging with them new,
hot, dry days that fall straight after, as if from the very same
clouds. He's been drinking milk straight from the carton
without having to worry about entertaining a lady who
might want instant or Turkish coffee with milk, someone to
ask from the kitchen, how much sugar? And to memorize her
answer for future reference and to tell her from the kitchen,
whose cupboards haven't been changed since the building
was built, that she doesn't need saccharine, no way, and that
she should choose a record because you can die waiting for
this electric kettle to boil.

He wouldn't have uttered a sentence like that now, even
if some woman had come to see him, because in his mind he
could sometimes sense such a death, not only when lying in
bed or dozing off in an armchair like an old man, but also
while standing in the kitchen preparing himself an omelet
or a vegetarian schnitzel. The life force would go out of
him then like the lightest of breezes in which dust particles

momentarily twirl and quickly fall, or would last heavily like a long convoy of refugees made up from start to end of old Shechters leaving his body laden with packages, pushing old prams brimful with blackened pots and cardboard suitcases with beaten triangles on their corners, like the suitcases in his parents' apartment placed in storage, one case inside another, like raggedy Russian dolls, the last one's womb filled with a musty smell, which time had planted and erased. Not one of those Shechters stopped to look back, as if the one sleeping in bed or dozing off in an armchair or standing in the kitchen was like a ravaged city not to be looked at, like one of the cities he once saw with his very own eyes.)

"Isn't it true it wasn't here yesterday?" Na'ama asked again.

(At that time Shechter was still a combat soldier, more or less: he rode in a command car, delivering food to squadrons or cleaning materials for armored carriers, and whenever he arrived the soldiers were glad to see him and told him that if he didn't look after them who else would? The regiment? The division? As far as they were concerned they could all drop dead. From the command car Shechter would speak to them in the kind of language everyone used: those sons of bitches, if you're not one of them they wouldn't even piss in your direction, or: who are they anyway, that's how he spoke to them, that Shechter.

Now he did his army reserve duty on a home front base, and instead of those soldiers, whom when he passed on the street hoped they wouldn't recognize him, he was faced with the two actresses from the force's entertainment group and the actor who studied drama at university, in the same building where Shechter in his youth had studied film; and the lighting man and soundman, who like him were both on reserve duty, and the master sergeant who was in charge of the video unit and who brought the equipment in his rickshaw – a rattling, chugging three-wheeled motorbike that the soundman said wasn't called a rickshaw in the orient, but rather a "tuk tuk" owing to the noise it made, tuk-tuk.

The two actresses, who in the entertainment group performed bits between songs, actually enjoyed the jiggling ride, giggling like schoolgirls when the rickshaw hit a pit in the road, especially the plumpish one whose name was Na'ama. Her dark hair was swept back into a small ponytail wrapped in a black velvet band. Her face showed vague remnants of past spots, which nobody would have noticed had she not repeatedly busied herself with them. She would take a small round mirror out of her army issue bag and check them to make it clear that she wasn't trying to deny their very existence on her cheeks, she would speak to them while applying makeup: yes, no doubt about it, they grow faster here due to the heat of the lamps. "Here, look at this one for example, you weren't here yesterday, isn't it true it wasn't here yesterday?")

Shechter kept quiet and let the master sergeant answer.

"Just leave it alone," said the sergeant, "believe me no one can see anything, even with a magnifying glass no one would see."

(It's been three years now that the master sergeant has served as a cameraman, ever since ending his stint as NCO in charge of safety on the base. From a short course held in Tzrifin he learned how to point a camera in various directions, how to record sound, how to light and how to edit clips of the big brass paying a visit, or the corps' entertainment group performing on the base, or a failed attempt to hit a moving target on a shooting range, to which he could always append an old clip of a MiG fighter plane exploding. And he was, as everyone said, a golden boy with golden hands, until things went wrong. When he first joined the video unit, he amazed everyone by building shelves for the cassettes and a table for the editing equipment – "If I had to wait for a favor from someone like the quartermaster, everything would still be lying around and nobody doing anything about it, why should anyone care?" And the actor, who had already appeared in a number of student films, remarked that the sergeant filmed in exactly the same way that he drove his rickshaw, veering to the left then to the right and suddenly braking, without taking into consideration all sorts of nuances. He spoke the word nuances with a mocking grimace indicating to all that it was not a word he would use, but rather some young Scorsese from film school who couldn't fart without nuances and concepts.)

"Believe me," the sergeant said as he peered into the second camera, "even if I zoomed right in you wouldn't see anything, don't you trust me?"

"It's not that I don't trust you," replied Na'ama and fell silent but still examined her cheek in the mirror.

"In the end I'll be the one who's insulted," said the sergeant, "you can even ask Shechter if you don't believe me." Shechter nodded his head while Na'ama looked at him through the mirror. "You're not just saying it?"

"What do you mean?" he answered, "Gidi's incapable of telling a lie."

(In fact after he moved to the home front base their relationship was still unclear: the regiment in which he had served was considered a combat unit by the corps' standards and Shechter had left it before reaching the age of thirty, a long time before he began to notice the fibers being woven around him from the air. It seemed to him that the sergeant was convinced that he had been placed in the new unit by some strings having been pulled. Later, and much to his surprise, they took a liking to each other and when the sergeant saw Shechter's name in the credits rolling at the end of some children's television program he was watching with his daughter, he began to respect him the same way he respected anyone whose name appeared on television or in the newspaper be it in a positive or negative light. Two years after the sergeant turned from being an NCO in charge of security into a cameraman, he and Shechter worked together in perfect harmony: the sergeant weary of his commanders on the base – "it's not just the officer quartermaster, it would be okay if it was just him, the trouble is that it's everyone, they're all a bunch of shits" – and Shechter weary from all his battles, those waged in reserve duty and those that took place beyond, in the wide expanse that the sergeant called "civilian life" in a special tone of voice, since to him it was a vast and limitless domain that encircled the tiny planet that was the base. The sergeant appreciates Shechter not complaining about his lack of skill, while Shechter, even if he doesn't admit it to himself, appreciates the sergeant remembering his name on the credits that continue to run at the end of the children's program, only because someone has forgotten to remove it.)

"Pick up the phone for even the smallest problem" was written on a note stuck to the VCR, but everything is running smoothly, the picture is sharp, the voices clear and the investigator has already crumpled the note between his fingers.

"Should we rehearse?" asked the sergeant.

Long and tired-looking eucalyptus leaves could be seen through the window whose pane reflected the lips of the second actress pursing them a few times before opening them to ask if they weren't too red: what did they think? Her lips were full, puffed and fleshy, smeared with lipstick they looked as if raw flesh had burst through the skin, wild and glowing.

(Kinneret[1] was her name and whenever she seemed down, the actor would ask her what the state of her water level was. She served in the force's entertainment group, and like Na'ama was one of those who stood on the sidelines or in the second row lending vocal accompaniment to the stars of the group, sometimes even without words, just long oohs. They were backup singers, who even if they have affairs, it's with male backup singers, and this status left them completely unspoiled by the affectations of stardom. They were satisfied with the simple joy of having affection showered upon them each time they appeared at some base or outpost, and learnt to be content with the random applause that sometimes came their way, like falling leaves from a bouquet thrown at the star performer. Bouquets were not thrown their way, but after the show everyone was invited to dine with the camp commander and his officers, and once, last year, she

---

1 Hebrew name for the Sea of Galilee

was asked out by a cadet pilot. She told people her boyfriend was a pilot; he told people his girlfriend was a singer. One night they went out as a foursome – the cadet pilot brought along for Na'ama a friend who had dropped out of the pilot's course and was now trying out for an elite unit – and after the movie they all went to the friend's apartment on one of the small streets off the square. It was hot and the cadet pilot and his friend took off their shirts, remaining in their bright white vests looking like two overgrown boys. They spoke about the movie, listened to a record and drank beer from a fridge packed with beer cans. The girls added harmonies to the music with their high voices, they all drank more beer, and the cadet pilot's friend told Kinneret that he was crazy for her lips and wondered what flavor her lipstick was. The cadet pilot asked Na'ama if she wasn't hot in her uniform; it was hot and empty beer cans were rolling on the floor.)

"First of all, say something," the soundman requested, "before we start the rehearsal, just so that I can set the volume level." He spoke in a quiet, low voice and bent over the recording machine, wearing a faded denim shirt that emphasized his tan. His long fingers turned the dial, setting the needle to the middle of the gauge.

"Valium?" asked the actor with a raised brow.

"Aren't you tired of that joke already?"

"Valium," the actor repeated opening the door to the inner room, an overgrown boy with a square jaw ill-suited to his chubby cheeks. "What wouldn't I give for one tablet, everything I own, half my kingdom for a Valium." His thinning brown curls almost reached the lintel and the door with a poster stuck to it closed quickly behind him.

Kinneret turned to the soundman, noticing that his temples had begun to grey: "What do you want us to say for you?"

"It's not for me, it's just to check the recording."

"Okay, not for you then, but what should we say?"

"Something nice," the soundman replied from his corner.

For a brief moment she looked at his tan and then faced the window, and while gazing out she narrowed her eyes and began to sing in sweet hushed tones.

"I shall not slumber nor shall I sleep-"

"Do me a favor, anything but that song," said the soundman. Kinneret smiled but continued to sing:

"Should they ascend to heaven, I'll bring them down from there-"

She sang the next verse, and for a moment, when she dropped the guttural enunciation and cheerful vigorous rhythm, it was almost pleasant to the ear. In the window opposite her was the sky of a winter nearing its end, a grey sky whose delicate hue did not conceal rain, but rather a pure bright blue, which appeared from time to time above the tops of the eucalyptus trees.

"Do you know what I'd like to do most now?" she asked, having finished the song.

"No," replied the sergeant, "what would you like to do?"

"You wouldn't let me anyway," she answered. The actor came out of the inner room, letting the door slam behind him, and in a deep voice, which he sweetened like a cavalier in a play of old, said, "What won't they let you do Kinneret honey, there's nothing I wouldn't let you do. My kingdom for one drop of you."

Kinneret looked at him for a moment and turned away.

"Believe me," said the actor waving his large hands in the air, "until this base is privatized nothing will ever get done here. There's no toilet paper, no newspaper, only water and plenty of it. What do they want to do, drown us? As if there aren't enough other ways to die."

The lighting man asked him what he had used instead.

"Pages from my diary," he answered, "why not, after all doesn't Miki Le-Mic keep a diary?" At once he produced an imaginary notebook from thin air, opened the covers and leafed through it with a saliva-moistened thumb and began to write in the air with the tip of his finger: "Monday, got up, got dressed, washed." Dropping his finger he glanced at them explaining with much pleasure that a limousine hooting had woken him. "A limousine, why not, don't I deserve a limousine ten meters long with a window separating the driver from the passengers?"

(Up till then the actor had done his reserve duty in one of the offices on the base, and when he once appeared at a troop party, which Shechter was asked to film, he seemed to him a comedian of the worst kind; the kind who specialized in a-Persian-an Iraqi-and-a-Georgian-are-stuck-in-an-elevator-the-Persian-says... But later he was surprised by the skills the actor had acquired through his studies and by his sad sense of humor, which at times made Shechter laugh in spite of himself, so long as it wasn't cloaked in some cheap wisecrack. If one day the actor were to be accepted by a theater, under the guidance of a real director, the kind that directs three-act plays, not shorts like Shechter, who long ago abandoned his dream of directing a full-length film – he might turn into a truly fine comic actor, and unlike Shechter, for the sake of his livelihood he will know how to utilize even the drivel he was forced to put up with. For the time being a deck of his calling cards was attached by a clothes peg to the rearview mirror of his rattling ex-rental Autobianchi, and the cards were engraved in festive lettering: "Miki Le-Mic, Special Events and Happy Occasions"; that was how the actor financed his tuition fees, and every time he gave someone a ride, even to hitchhikers whose taste was totally unknown to him, he would draw a card from the deck and present it to them, who knows, maybe they would meet on some future happy occasion.)

"Hasn't anyone here been driven in a limousine?" asked the actor. "By a chauffeur? Forget about keeping a distance, I said to the chauffeur, turn down the window man. I want to talk to you. It's about this girl, I said to him. I don't know what I'll do if she doesn't come back to me. I'll go crazy without her, off the rails. What did I do to deserve this, what?" He looked at the actresses whose backs were against the window. "What are you looking at me like that for? I'm not talking about you." His gaze moved slowly from their black Reebok sneakers that only vaguely resembled the permitted army issue shoes, up to their eyes that looked back at him; overly made-up, not for the film but because they still applied makeup with the joy of young girls dreaming of looking like the women on magazine covers.

"So what if you're in a group," he said, "big deal, wasn't I in a group? No, I wasn't in a group. Did I want to be in a group at all? Yes, I wanted to be in a group. Boy did I want to be in a group, I would have sold my soul to be in a group, my kingdom to have been in a group. And why wasn't I accepted? Because I had no personal recommendations? Nobody to pull a few strings for me? Maybe because I'm just a nobody from a poor neighborhood. No, it was just because oh boy did I sing out of tune. I made the piano keys jump." In the same effusive manner with which he spoke, he plucked a transparent microphone stand from thin air, adjusted it to his height, removed the mike from the stand and began to sing with great feeling in a high-pitched nasal voice:

> *"Snow is falling on my town,*
> *falling all night long lelong-ong ong-lelong . . ."*

He kept hitting an imaginary key, "what comes after this?"

Shechter, who listened to him but did not answer, was looking through the window at the tops of the eucalyptus trees and their calm leaves.

(Twenty years ago, during the basic artillery course, he was ordered to patrol a different grove, one next to the training ground below. And on leaving it he suddenly saw a clear and vast sky arched above him, with not one fiber of the sack, a sky that turned bluer and bluer as evening fell. The treetops, the cannons covered by tarpaulins, the silenced generator, the ugly quartermaster store and the armory, all grew dark and dim, transforming into black shadows long before the sky itself darkened at a gentle, determined, leisurely pace, impossible to follow. All was still, and that

Shechter, who waged war over the use of his first name ever since the end of basic training and refused to answer to his surname, heard the rustling of the dry leaves around him and smelt the smell of the sea that the wind carried, and thought that he wouldn't have minded continuing this guard duty for another two hours or even two or three whole years, it would all eventually pass, after which he would travel to Europe, perhaps never to return. That's what that Shechter thought. The generator had not been turned on yet and a lightplane landed on the airstrip on the other side of the fence, vibrant and rattling, yellowing in the last light like some sort of angry wasp. It looked like one of those planes from old war movies that were shown to scout groups, other than its being yellow, but soon it too dimmed and darkened, fading like embers.)

"Let's maybe hurry up," the sergeant suggested.

The actor turned his gaze from him to the girls. "Come on girls," he said in a lively voice, "get into character, no, not like that. Who ever heard of getting into character with gum in one's mouth?" At once he began to imitate for them a girl chewing enthusiastically: squeezing a wad of gum between her teeth, rolling her tongue around in her mouth, open then shut, bursting wet bubbles as she crushes the gum between her molars.

"Do you know what frustrated me most as a child?" he asked. "No, really, the thing that most frustrated me? I couldn't blow bubbles. That's what frustrated me the most at the age of six. Can you imagine what it's like being frustrated by a Bazooka? What happiness could it have been?"

In his soft voice the soundman asked again if they would speak into the microphone, but Kinneret had already blown a rosy, transparent, trembling bubble and promptly sucked it into her cavernous pink mouth.

"We used to collect the notes in the wrappers," said Na'ama. "Didn't you use to collect them?"

"They were called fortunes," said the actor still moving his jaw. "If I only knew I was going to land up here, believe me I would have thought twice about growing up."

(Shechter and his friends used to collect picture cards of football players from Israel and abroad, from Stelmach[2] to Pele. Once in a while his father would also take a look at them and one evening asked him if he had a picture of Stanley Matthews, because that was what his parents had called him before he was born: Shechter, this grown man whose body had become completely cumbersome, was once ensconced inside his mother's belly from where he would kick like the legendary footballer, Sir Stanley Matthews, his tiny hands reaching for the thin lining of her stomach and the vast world on the other side.)

"Fortunes," Kinneret said. She moved closer to the poster on the wall, standing in front of it tall and erect like the female soldier photographed there with the slogan above, "Soldier, improve your appearance!" The soldier showed off her uniform proudly, but someone had blackened in one of her front teeth and she seemed to be smiling at Kinneret from the wall, an evil smile.

"I wonder where they dug her up from," said Kinneret.

(The pink bubblegum balloon had already been buried in the depths of her mouth: she shut it, after all even saliva is contagious.)

She straightened a crease in the poster and smoothed the skirt on the soldier's shapely thigh. On the right was another poster showing armored cars racing over desert sands leaving pillars of dust in their trail – the investigator doesn't see them in place anymore – and on the opposite wall a yellowish sheet in the form of a scroll with singed edges whose emblazoned letters declared: "The world stands on but three things: love, love and love !!!" The exclamation marks were thick and emphasized with an added red outline. Through the window, beneath the streaked shadows of the leaves, were two soldiers wearing the white epaulets of prisoners, one wearily pushing a large broom while the other dragged a trash can on wheels.

"Have you noticed?" asked Kinneret, suddenly stopping. She was chewing again (with a closed mouth, each spray of saliva is contagious). She asked if they had noticed that you

---

2 Nahum Stelmach, a famous Israeli football player

don't see Arab street cleaners anymore, only Russians and always blonde, men and women, it's really weird.

"What exactly is weird about it?" asked the actor.

On the wall opposite her now was a sheet of Bristol board that someone had tried to make look like a scroll with singed edges. Innocent childlike handwriting appeared above faintly ruled pencil lines: "Before my boyfriend left he said to me-" Kinneret stopped chewing and with precise and formal diction began to read the lines written on the sheet that had been hung there in defiance of the military posters: "Cats always land on their feet. You have to envy them, my boyfriend said before he left, because they don't howl with pain."

The sergeant asked if we had to hear the whole thing, God knows we're running late.

"They never shrink in a corner, my boyfriend said," Kinneret continued to read in the same serious and plaintive tone, the kind used for assemblies and ceremonies: "and howl with pain. My boyfriend did not see my face, I did not show him my suffering, I did not show him my grief. I did not sob, but after he left I shrank in a corner and howled with pain." She traced her well-manicured fingertip slowly along the black edges of the sheet. "It's actually quite nice," she said and turned her finger to see if it was stained, put it in her mouth and sucked it briefly.

(Blackening the insides of her lips, her tongue, saliva, throat, stomach, her womb and its contents. She smeared her lips first with intensely bright lipstick, like the women on the cover of *Vogue* or *Elle*, which her mother used to buy in bulk. When she stopped and threw them away, the only place Kinneret could leaf through them was at the dentist, when she still dared to go to dentists, before she began to stay away from doctors' rooms, hospitals, clinics and pharmacies. How was she to know they would be filming opposite a clinic?)

"Did the female officer write that?" asked the lighting man. He was short and well built, his hair cut like a Marine, his fleshy lips ready to grin while his eyes surveyed the others to check if they were laughing.

"No way," said Na'ama, "I've read that before, years ago."

"She also knows how to read," said the lighting man, "all in all a talented girl," and quickly sought out the actor's eyes.

"I'm not even going to bother answering you," said Na'ama. "D'you really think you're funny?"

(She had read it in a children's newspaper back in the fifth grade: but now that time seemed long gone, though she can still feel it in her fingers, Na'ama, how they would pass each other small folded notes containing proposals and matchmaking plans for her friends, notes that she kept in one of the drawers in her room in a file that her father brought her from his workplace, when he was still working. Out of all the notes there was one particularly dear to Na'ama, one that neither she nor any of her friends had written. She had found it in the school grounds, in a far corner where they used to go to smoke, lying on one of the benches that the boys had made in woodwork class, a dry eucalyptus leaf with tiny blue letters written on it: "Hannah Feygiss, 414958, please call me." In Na'ama's eyes it was lovelier than any other note or letter she had ever read before or since and for a long time she thought about that girl; she didn't know who she was or in which class she belonged, a girl who dared to write her name like that on a leaf and wait for someone to find it; Na'ama also thought about that tree, a large eucalyptus, like one of the eucalyptus trees here; as if its seed had been brought from Australia to sprout, grow and bloom, just so that Hannah Feygiss could inscribe her name on one of its leaves for someone to find and call her up and say, "Hello Hannah, I found your name on a leaf.")

"That officer's actually really a sweet girl," said the sergeant, "even if she didn't write it. We tried to persuade her to take part."

"What did she say?" asked the lighting man still trying to turn the butterfly screw on the lamp. Rust had caused it to stick and the lighting man, after spraying it, pressed against it again with the fingers and muscles of his hand.

"She didn't want to," answered the sergeant, "she said she's camera shy."

Again the lighting man tried to force the wing of the butterfly screw and the spray, murky with rust, seeped out of the grooves.

"But in the end," said the sergeant, "that's what gave the idea for the script. It's just as well she didn't agree. Can I help you with that?"

"No," answered the lighting man, "it'll loosen in a second." **(Let's see if you are a man.)**

Through the window, above the treetops, a grey cloud made way for a patch of pure blue sky, as if it had been sprayed from the canister and then evaporated.

"Let me help you," said the sergeant.

"No no," answered the lighting man **(let's see let's see)**. He sprayed the lamp's screw again, which had now become slippery and even murkier with rust.

"There's no shame in accepting help," said the sergeant.

"But I don't need it," **(let's see)**. A dirty drop hung down from the screw, becoming elongated.

(And the pungent stinging smell of chlorine rose and the water diminished below him and his father turned his gaze from the women tanning their bodies on white towels: **let's see if you are a man**. He could still turn around and climb down the slippery waterlogged rungs, water that dripped from bathing costumes and hairy bodies, but the board quivered beneath the soles of his small shuddering feet as if it tried to shake him from it, not toward the pool, which was a very distant small shiny rectangle, but to the vast sky above him. **(Let's see if you are a man.)**

Through the window, where the two prisoners could be seen again, the beating of the trash can's wheels sounded as they skipped over pits in the road.

"That officer," said the actor after returning his gaze to the room, "the blonde with the blue eyes? What would I do with her? I'm mean really; do I need a blonde in my life?" – he looked from Na'ama to Kinneret who were still gazing outside

– "an ear to hear me out is all I need, blonde or brunette, as long as she's got an ear." The lighting man, who seemed to be waiting for some spicy joke, asked him if he meant a blonde on top and a brunette below and when he grinned he was careful to avoid Na'ama's eyes. No one seemed to be in any kind of a hurry; either it was according to plan or due to a kind of languor or sense of distraction, which was evident in all their actions: perhaps they were tired at the end of a day's shooting or perhaps they had been like that earlier.

"You've got a one-track mind," said the actor. "I know that age, oh boy do I know that age, just about the most screwed up age of all, believe me. And I've seen a thing or two in my time. God, I'm pleased I've passed that."

(In the town to which he had come from a housing project, there might not have been railings on which to sit and whistle at the girls – really whistle, drawing air in with all your might, as if the girls would be sucked in with the air – but there was a kiosk on an avenue where a few layabouts would stand and pass remarks on every girl who crossed the road and speak to the blind man about the Maccabi and Hapoel football teams while waiting for customers to come – for a whole month the actor studied his ways when he still dreamed of playing Tiresias or other blind characters – how he would reach out his hand to the exact spot where they had laid the coins down and give them exact change knowing just from the rustle of the paper which newspaper they had taken, Yediot or Ma'ariv.)

"Believe me, my entire kingdom for adolescence."

(Only when he received a note would they help him by saying: "It's a ten, Ovadia" or "twenty" or "one from the lottery, Ovadia," when someone laid down a hundred note as if it had just been won from the nearby lottery stand. And every time they took out cigarettes they would tap them on the box, shake the tobacco and stick them to their lower lips, just like the layabouts from the housing project from which he had come and layabouts from all the other towns: towns of this country whose buildings start to crumble a short while after they are built, like cheap décor, and ancient European cities where marble horses stand upright in the squares for hundreds of years: my kingdom for a horse.)

Outside between the streaks of shadow, one of the prisoners bent down with a large dustpan in his hand and the other prisoner swept small piles of dust and cigarette butts into it. Maybe every night they were kept under arrest in the base detention room, or maybe they were waiting to be transferred to a military prison – the investigator does not know – for the time being they are being kept occupied with cleaning and maintenance jobs.

Na'ama, who had been watching them through the window, turned to face the room. She glanced at Shechter, waiting for him to hurry them up to prepare for shooting, but when he remained silent she turned to the Bristol sheet on the wall. Slowly she again read what was written between the singed edges, she became serious for a moment and quickly asked in the cheerful voice of someone posing a riddle if anyone knew a song about cats. Deep in the window the prisoner tapped the dustpan, pushing the sand into it.

"From *Cats*?" said Kinneret.

The prisoner, still bent on his heels as before, dragged the dustpan backwards while his friend swept the remnants of the pile into it. A cigarette butt spilled over, which the stooped soldier immediately flicked into the can with his middle finger.

"Not from *Cats*," replied Na'ama, "it's too obvious from *Cats*; it has to be a Hebrew song."

"Good shot, Ezra," said the standing prisoner from outside, "believe me, another week of this and you'll be signed up by Maccabi." The prisoner named Ezra stood up straight. His dark blank face now against a backdrop of eucalyptus trees, and from within their foliage the sun emitted softened rays of light before the dusk. "Come on dude," said the other prisoner. The first one did not answer as he bent down again to pick up another cigarette butt, which he also flicked into the pan with his middle finger.

"The sun is rising in the skyyyyyyyyy"

Kinneret began to sing.

"Mother se-eeeends her son Yossi-
go and fetch a bottle of milk
Go quickly and don't forget,
Yosiiiii-"

She sang in a very precise high-pitched voice and both
prisoners watched her from the road, one clutching a broom,
the other a dustpan.

"Yossi strolls up the avenue
and suddenly he sees,
what's this,
a pup ta-ni-na-na-"

She emphasized the word pup, to which the sergeant
quickly retorted that the song was about a puppy not a
kitten, as if this was the sole reason for their being gathered
there. "What do you mean a cat," he said to her, "where did
you get that from? I've got a good head for that sort of thing,
if only I could have used it at school."

(He could even remember, the master sergeant, who wrote
the words and music and who sang the original version, yes,
the Roosters sang the original version. But what about the
time when his wife first brought him to the kibbutz, when
he took a shower at her place and began to sing? Across from
him was a window shielded with a mosquito net and on the
other side eucalyptus trees like the ones on the base, above
whose treetops you could see the hills of the Golan and
the white dome of Mt. Hermon, so close you could touch
it – she asked him about those old songs, didn't he think
they were schmaltzy? They were still asking each other all
sorts of questions like this one, since they weren't really that
well acquainted: what songs did they like, what landscapes,
what movies, and if they liked their salads finely chopped

or chunky? But he didn't exactly know what schmaltzy was, really, does anyone know the exact meaning, not roughly, but exactly? He fell silent, and when the stream of water suddenly weakened he could hear a bird chirping outside and thought to himself that the real country was right here, they didn't have to sing about it, the kibbuztniks; they could hear it just like this, from the window of a shower.)

"rising in the skyyyy-"

(In the boy scouts den, there was a sheet hung with a drawing of a smiling sun or an infant taking steps beneath it, freckled like Shechter the boy, which became wrinkled and would flap with each breeze as the verses of the song were projected onto it, the verses appeared in place or turned on their sides or upside down: there would always be some disobedient slide standing in defiance at the end of the projector's beam and there would always be some boy who would climb on the bench and turn his head upside down to make the others laugh, even that Shechter who was called Noam, climbed onto the bench in his sandals and turned his head with all its freckles upside down to read: ʎʞs ǝɥʇ uᴉ ƃuᴉsᴉɹ sᴉ uns ǝɥʇ.)

(And after each furlough, when the sergeant opened the rickshaw, straightaway he would smell that smell of the army: not the smell of lawns or plantations and not the smell of the geraniums, which he grew in his wing at the base, making a drip irrigation system for them from an old hose pipe whose entire length he perforated – where else would he get one from, the quartermaster? But instead the smell of hangars and grease, or the stench of toilets or their Lysol and lime disinfectants: it was just as bad, really no difference at all. Next to the fence was a tree, behind which the sergeant would urinate, a eucalyptus whose trunk was wide enough to conceal him and whose rustling leaves were enough to conceal the ugly sound of the urine, and sometimes a bird would peek out from the leaves and chirp: a bulbul. It had a yellow belly – a delicate kind of yellow – the color seemed wondrous to him, and the delicate chirping and the enormous strength it was endowed with to cross the entire sky right away.)

(It rose above those trees and over the empty fields and the buildings of the suburb and the years; and Shechter the boy walked at the head of a column of children in khaki shirts and short pants, their edges folded back over pockets swollen with apricot pits: they advanced along the banks of the Yarkon as if they were en route to discover the source of the Nile, with rucksacks on their backs and rolled up blankets with which to make Bedouin tents whose sheets they'll tether to eucalyptus trunks, and the rays of light in the foliage had not yet dimmed like the light seen through the fibers of the sack.)

"Mother se-eeends her son Yossi-"

"Kinneret's right," said Na'ama. "There is a cat in it. We once almost performed it with the group, don't you remember?"

"In a new arrangement," Kinneret said, "with synthesizers." She went back to chewing, stopped, her lips parted (the pink fetus was born, conceived, cracked open; chewed limb by limb).

"Well done," said the tall prisoner from outside, who had been listening to the song the whole time and applauded with the dustpan that he took from the other prisoner. "Wasn't that good?" "Good," said the other prisoner, "but why does it always have to be depressing songs?" "You're always depressed," said the tall prisoner.

"He's always depressed," he explained to them all from the road. "Ever since I've known him he's been depressed, right Ezra?" From the foliage a bird chirped, took flight and glided.

"Is that you Weintraub?" The sergeant approached the window. "What about those plugs I ordered?"

"Plugs, that's what's on your mind, plugs? Can't you see the mess we're in? Tell him Ezra."

"How much longer do you have?" asked the sergeant from the window.

"Two days," answered the prisoner called Weintraub from the road, "but who's counting." Above him the eucalyptus trees rustled for a moment and fell silent.

The noise they made was also recorded, and a piece of masking tape is still stuck to the VCR like a ridiculous plaster, as if the investigator came to investigate an injury not a death. "Pick up the phone for even the smallest problem," that was what was written in the note left for him, but everything is in working order and the entire room was captured by the wide lens of the reserve camera: that's what the female medic told the police, that's what they told him on the night, and in the morning she herself told him over the phone, before he left home and got into his car.

The prisoner with the dustpan bent down at the side of the road to pick up a cigarette butt that had missed the can.

"Looks like you're getting scared," Weintraub said to him, "You've turned chicken Ezra." "You're the big hero," said the first prisoner whose head could be seen from the window again, "but when Abudi comes he'll come down on us like a ton of bricks." "Let him come," said Weintraub, "right Gidi?"

"Tell me," said the sergeant approaching the window again. "Are you looking for trouble on purpose, not that I care, believe me I don't, just fix the plug first."

(The sergeant simply couldn't understand why Weintraub, someone from a good family, educated and everything, someone who also lives in a good area, right, not out of town with lawns that you can't see the end of, but certainly in one of the best parts of town, is always getting into trouble like some degenerate from the area from which the sergeant came, an area that produces the type that the army is only too happy to get rid of, that's if they turn up at the recruitment center at all. Sometimes he would try to imagine this Weintraub's house to himself, thinking of the room that he must have had since he was born, and of the quiet of those areas where no noise reaches, not of cars and not of buses and certainly not garages, and how that room remains empty each time that Weintraub is in detention or placed under arrest. Isn't it a waste?)

"You didn't bring me a new one, at least fix this one."

(And didn't he know what the soundman really thought of him, about his unprofessionalism? He knew very well, despite how quiet he was, not saying anything, what, didn't the sergeant himself know that there would be sound distortion? Sure he knew. But the sergeant enjoyed saying that, "sound distortion," and enjoyed saying there would be "low light" when there was not enough lighting, and "white balance" when adjusting the picture's shades; all these terms he learned in the course at Tzrifin but would not have known how to use had it not been for the soundman, the lighting man and Shechter: "My reserve duty personnel," he would say when requesting them for a few days of reserve duty, but say it not with the authority of a commander, but rather being proud of these colleagues who'll be arriving from the wondrous realm outside the planet that was the base.)

"Making such problems, the soundman will curse me afterwards. He's already cursing me now."

(It's true that his wife also came from out there, but she was born on a kibbutz and after moving to his place in town, most of the time she stayed indoors, enjoying being a mother and housewife like one of the women from the place where he came from. "I just like being at home," she said about the two-and-a-half roomed apartment that he bought with a mortgage, "without everyone poking their noses in my business," and through the living room balcony door the neighbors' balconies could be seen with plastic shutters missing a few slats, and some blackened by the fumes from the buses that passed below.)

"Don't tell me you don't, even if you're keeping it to yourself."

"No need to get carried away," answered the soundman. He had earphones on his head and had already fastened the faulty plug to the socket with a piece of masking tape so that it would not make a noise.

Kinneret looked at his long tanned fingers and asked him what his name was. "It's just that for two days the whole time I've been hearing 'soundman, soundman,'" she said, "but what's your real name?"

Across from her, in the opposite corner of the room, the actor placed his fingers on his head like a cockscomb or a crown of feathers. "Still waters," he answered quickly before the soundman could reply, "like a Red Indian name, not so?"

"No," answered the soundman quietly, "actually my name is Yossi," and the recording machine's gauge needle quivered in front of him. "What, are you kidding?" asked Kinneret. The soundman nodded slowly.

"I've also got a Red Indian name," the actor announced and moved the fingers above his hair as if the feathers quivered in the wind.

"Hurry up and don't forget
– Yossiiii-"

Kinneret began to sing again, elongating the last syllable of the name for as long as she could.

The actor stretched his fingers and shut them tight: "My name is bells and whistles, or the sound and the fury."

"My successful boy-"

Kinneret stopped singing and from the road the prisoner with the dustpan lifted his head toward her. "But you're not a boy," she said to the soundman and looked again at his dark tanned fingers and the pale stripe left on one of them where a ring had been removed.

"Who said I was a boy?" answered the soundman. "It's been a long time since I was a boy." He stood up straight and removed a roll of masking tape from the door handle, tearing off a strip that produced a ripping sound.

(The type that doesn't need suntan lotion, that doesn't fear wrinkled skin or skin cancer or something far worse whose name Kinneret didn't even dare to think of – instantly she stopped chewing, and the rosy fetus in her saliva was silenced – someone who is wooed, seduced, like the boy she saw last summer on the beach, maybe a student. He was lying on the sand, lying on a towel for two, lying on his stomach and reading from a folio exercise book and didn't lift his head toward his girlfriend as she came out of the water. She was wearing a tiny black tanga just like Kinneret's and didn't lie down on the vacant spot beside him, but stood over him with her legs apart, dripping water on his neck, on his shoulders, but he didn't lift his head from the pages. She opened her legs wide apart and walked over him, dripping on his back, dripping on his buttocks, and still he didn't lift his head from the pages. She knelt down on him and very slowly glided over one of his legs, slid on his thigh, brushed up against it, moistened it with her tiny tanga, shifted on it, shifted further until Kinneret herself could feel the stiffness and warmth of the thigh.)

"No one here's a child anymore," she turned to the window, "tell him Na'ama."

The soundman tore off more of the masking tape that again made a ripping sound.

"Can we start already?" asked the sergeant.

"Just a second, I can improve this a bit," the soundman answered. "Anyway we have to wait."

"We've missed the food," said the sergeant, "let's at least shoot something. Not for the army, screw the army, just so that we don't feel we've been wasting time. Believe me, what kills me the most," he stood up above the second camera, "is the feeling of having wasted time."

"Better to waste a minute," answered the soundman, "and be sure that it'll turn out the way it should." He tore off another strip of masking tape, again producing a firm vigorous sound. "You can even ask the director."

Shechter nodded his head.

(In some old film that had been shown in the faculty where he studied, a woman stood at a window and shut it and sealed the space between the window and the sill with masking tape, exactly like this, and knelt down and blocked up the space between the door and the floor and stood up and plugged the keyhole and went to the gas stove and turned on the gas.)

"Apart from that," said the actor, "the masking tape suits your movie, no?"[3]

(In the bathroom of the apartment in which Shechter has been living for the last decade there were remnants of masking tape on the windows, which he was too lazy to scrape off, since anyway nobody but him saw them or would see them, even though he once bought a special scraping implement. The shopkeeper commiserated with him: "believe me it's better than spray. It costs less and you can change the blade for the next war, I don't make any profit on these kinds of items"; on his right was an advertisement for a revolutionary drain opener, which he then also bought, but he didn't buy white paint for the doorframe despite the fact that the paint was peeling away bit by bit.)

"My movie," said Schechter, "one would think, it's not even a short."

(Like the shedding of an old skin the masking tape dropped to the floor when he removed it from the doorframe, revealing the color beneath as it had been in his grandmother's time, a murky shade of yellow like the color of old photographs in which Shechter the baby was murky and yellowed: lying on his back spread out on the lawn, or clutching his father's finger, or staring with wonder at something too enormous to be captured within the jagged edges of the photograph. The boy who sat with his father in a boat sailing on the Yarkon was also yellowed, holding an oar and trying to row through the muddy waters as if on the Mississippi or the Orinoco; his mother photographed the two of them from the boat's bow and his father cried: "Be careful not to . . ." and in the wide open mouth in the picture all his teeth were still there, the look on his face as formidable as the looks of the people about whom he spoke. They were rowing toward the cascades of the electric company, which to his father was a world unto itself: not only because it was from there that all his small joys and all his anger were derived, but also because of Rutenberg,[4]

3   In the 1991 Gulf War there was a directive to seal a room with masking tape as a precaution to a gas attack

4   Pinhas Rutenberg, founder of the Palestine Electric Company

once a daring Russian revolutionary, a dauntless man of distinction, and because of his predecessor, Thomas Alva, the genius in whose memory, on the day of his death, the whole of the United States dimmed its lights for a minute. It was a marvelous spectacle that Shechter's father never tired of relating, even though he had never visited America and had no inclination to do so: an entire continent with all its skyscrapers and all the vast farmlands of the south were darkened for a moment in commemoration of the man who had given them light.)

"The movie will barely be fifteen minutes long."

"How come?" asked the lighting man from behind the lamp. He tilted it slightly, focusing the beam of light that had turned blue from the cellophane.

"Don't blind us," said Na'ama.

"Actually, blue would suit you," answered the lighting man.

"Compliment your girlfriend, not me."

In the windowpane she could see her cheeks, her chin, her forehead; she pushed a curl of hair aside, put it back in place and turned her head. In the distance between the eucalyptus trunks on the road to the base, a long and old American car with a winged trunk was advancing.

"Isn't that your parents' car?" she asked Kinneret.

"My parents? Now? What are they coming now for, my mother's never on time."

The beam of light, which was suited for daylight tones, turned everything it touched blue: the posters, the table, everything that fell in its path.

"Wouldn't you girls like to be in a blue movie?" the lighting man asked with a wink to the actor.

"Definitely not with you around," answered Na'ama.

"I thought we we're getting along well together?"

"Get on well with your girlfriend," she replied returning her gaze to the window.

(But in the editing room he screened a clip from the show for her and juggled with all the effect buttons he was familiar with from his regular army service here: at times he enlarged one of the figures, isolating its head or one of its body parts, striping it with stripes, squaring it with squares, circling it with circles, and for a moment the group looked just like one of the groups from the video clips on television, groups whose members' names Kinneret knew and whose posters were stuck on the wall above her bed. In the editing room, around which a few meager geraniums grew, Na'ama told him that she didn't mind him playing around with it, to each his own toys, as long as it's not the part of them dancing in leotards, that's all she needs – for him to get to the part of them dancing in leotards. The lighting man fast-forwarded the cassette to them dancing in leotards. Na'ama said that she didn't mind as long as it wasn't her part. The lighting man fast-forwarded to her part. She sang the end of a rhyming verse and was immediately swallowed back into the line behind the soloists, but the lighting man returned her to stage front allowing her to repeat the rhyming end of the verse where he then froze her, enlarging her head, her body, her small breasts, striping her with stripes, squaring her with squares, circling her with circles. In the dusky editing room she looked like one of the stars of "Top of the Pops" as she leaned against the cassette cabinet that the sergeant had built. Eran's fingers touched the buttons as if playing an instrument and her body slowly thawed, fraction of movement by fraction of movement, shifting and hovering toward the back of the stage. Afterwards she and Eran went outside and sat down on the paving; they leaned against the wall of the editing room and dangled their legs over the small geraniums that the sergeant tried to grow there. The setting sun bathed the tiles in a pale orange light, before disappearing behind an asbestos awning and turning toward the small airstrip as if intending to land there between the crop spraying planes, and Na'ama took out a small mirror from her purse and looked at her cheeks. The lighting man grabbed the bag from her lap, she tried to catch the strap, he pulled it away, she said to him, "you thief," but he had already managed to turn the bag inside out and empty its contents. A bunch of keys rattled, two telephone tokens rolled away, a lipstick fell on his lap and a Bazooka wrapper dropped as well. "When I was small," the lighting man said to her, "this is how I used to go through my mother's bag." The light that fell on his short-cropped bristles turned his scalp to a shade of honey, and he stuck his hand into the bag and lifted it up on his fist like a hand puppet. "I also used to rummage through my mother's bag," said Na'ama, "but you don't know how to rummage through a bag," and she quickly reached for the strap that swung in the air and grabbed hold of it. He pulled, she pulled, he drew her toward his body and Na'ama said, "stop it you thief."

[A honey-colored rectangle of light sailed on the paving like a raft whose only survivors were the two of them, and Shechter, who at the time was swallowed up by the darkness of the editing room, heard himself mutter in a low voice: "I also used to rummage through my mother's bag the same way," like someone who's already started talking to himself – one of the Shechters to be, whose omelets he'll prepare and eat straight from the pan, who'll take out black olives from a tin can with his fingers without placing them in another container, despite the warning on the label, just as in Paris he didn't remove the ravioli but cooked it in the tin can in the hotel on a small gas cooker, which he placed on the sink, masking the hiss of the gas with the sound of running water – on the small patch of grass in that wing of the base a sprinkler drizzled a rusty drop, and he could still recall the handbags that his mother would wear out a month after they were bought, and the dark inside of the bag, which would be poured out with the contents and evaporating on its way out, and the smell of the old leather, and the faint smell of his mother's sweat, and another smell to which he could not put a name, which was perhaps the smell of dusk, that same dusk itself that lay between the folds of the curtains in his room, that hid under his bed at night, that nested in his shoes, but here was warm and fragrant to his nostrils. He heard them laughing.])

"You didn't answer me," said the lighting man.

"About what?" asked Na'ama.

"If you would take part or not," said the lighting man, "in a blue movie."

Again the actor came in from the next room; he shook his shoulders for a moment until they slackened as if the air had been let out of them. "Tell me," he said to the lighting man, "don't you have anything else in that mind of yours?" Through the window one of the prisoners lifted the rake, balanced it on the palm of his hand and took a few steps forward until it collapsed and fell, hitting the asphalt.

"That Weintraub," said the sergeant, "he's a good guy, but always screwing up. Wherever he goes, he always screws up. He could have already been made sergeant if it wasn't for all the stuff he gets up to. A good guy, a good home, who knows what gets into him?" The treetops shed small rays of light onto the road, which the wind moved slowly like the scales of a very lazy lizard, and from the foliage a bird chirped, a chirp as delicate as a shaded leaf.

"This base is actually okay, it's nice here," said Kinneret.

"Yeah?" said the sergeant. He fanned the second camera with small rubber bellows. "Even my wife says so and she grew up on a kibbutz and lived on a kibbutz for most of her life."

The actor asked if on his wife's kibbutz they whitewashed the trees and if there were prisoners who raked the grounds.

"It's impossible to have a serious conversation with you," answered the sergeant, "everything's a joke with you." He blew air again and gently wiped the lens with a small piece of flannel.

"But I am being serious," said the actor. "Is it my fault that whenever I open my mouth everyone laughs? Well not everyone. Once I appeared at some Smurf's birthday party. Boy did he cry! It started to get on the nerves of the neighbors on all the floors. In the end his father gets up, this huge guy, makes me look like Mickey Mouse next to him, grabs me by the collar and says, 'For your own sake, Miki Le-Mic, either you make my son laugh or else I hurl you down below, that'll get a laugh out of him.'"

"You see," the sergeant took another look through the camera lens, "you're not capable of being serious. Believe me, you're a hopeless case."

(Because children's birthdays, that's completely different, something else entirely. They spent maybe half the night just decorating the apartment with all sorts of balloons and paper chains, the master sergeant and his wife, and in the small hours they were still sitting and filling packets with all kinds of candies and charms, the cost of which they don't even want to think about, but he wanted her to be happy, the little one, that he shouldn't come to the nursery school on his furlough and find her sitting in a corner watching everyone with those large eyes of hers that any second will bring tears to his own as well; that they shouldn't tease her anymore, that they shouldn't laugh at her because of his rickshaw, yes, which amongst all the other parents' cars, even the ordinary Subarus, looked like something made from Lego.)

"He traumatized me," the actor clutched his throat, "I was once a normal guy, don't get me wrong. Lucky for me there were trees down there otherwise I would have been a goner."

"A hopeless case," the sergeant shook the piece of flannel.

"Yossi
strolls up
the avenue"

Kinneret began to sing, but when the soundman lifted his head to her she fell silent (the chewing gum fetus between her teeth was crushed and murdered: and promptly went down her throat like a drainpipe).

"and suddenly he sees, what's this,
a little sparkling harmon-ic-aaaaaaa"

Again she fell silent.

"Did you stop because of him?" the actor raised his eyebrow at the lighting man who was expanding the beam of light. "So what if he's looking for songs with smut, smut

without songs he doesn't look for? Take a long hard look,
maybe in the pockets? The bag?"

"He's already looked there," said Na'ama.

(At the time just two telephone tokens had rolled out,
a rattling bunch of keys, but he didn't open the small side
pocket. That's all she needed, Na'ama, for him to open the
small side pocket. Those fingers of his, which played before
on the editing table and moved her body little by little,
searched her bag later. And when they got up from sitting
– the sun had already passed over the asbestos awning and
lit up the windows of the small control tower on the airstrip
– they were of the same height: eye to eye, nose to nose,
lips to lips. But he was fattish, and fat was something she
had enough of herself. She also didn't like his laugh and his
wisecracks, all those childish smutty remarks. So what if
he had a nice name, one that even suited hers – Eran and
Na'ama – there were plenty of boys with nice names, walking
along the street in front of her, or sitting across from her on
the bus or coming and going on some other street without
her knowing they existed in the world at all and drawing
closer to her day by day, hour by hour, until they would
meet one morning, or one afternoon or one night: any time
would do, even right now. Eran even told her, unashamedly,
that he's getting married next month: two years older than
her and already getting married to his girlfriend from junior
school. "So what," he said, "if it's no good – we'll close up the
business." And the actor said: "Believe me he's right, the only
thing you can't cancel is a funeral." But the sergeant's clerk
– Merav or Meytal, she had the kind of name that totally
confused Na'ama because it was so unsuited to her – said
that she was sure that he actually loved his girlfriend a lot:
otherwise he wouldn't speak about her that way at all, yes. It
was only to save himself from getting hurt.)

"He just doesn't know how to look."

(And once on a bus, in the middle of the ride Na'ama
heard someone say something similar: "Take it from me," he
said to the girl sitting next to him, "a guy who really loves

you won't tell you. A guy who tells you just wants you for your body, not for you. I'm just telling you this, Osi, 'coz I care about you." But the sergeant's clerk was well-spoken and had lovely black eyes, which when she got excited suddenly shone above the spots that she didn't try to hide like Na'ama or that girl. Na'ama was on her way to her sister's, and a dark-haired boy got on the bus with pita bread that gave off the pleasant aroma of meat and browned onion rings. And the girl who was already seated said to him that she has to be careful of fried foods because that's what harms her skin the most, fried foods, everything fried, liver, onions, french fries, everything. The boy was silent for a while, maybe he looked at her – Na'ama couldn't see his face – and suddenly in a quiet voice, and with complete conviction, he said, "You'll see, it'll be okay, Osi, I guarantee you it'll be okay. You'll see." The bus driver blew his horn, opened the door and shouted at the driver who was travelling on his right, and the girl said: "There's not a thing I haven't tried, I swear I've tried everything." She did not say this with bitterness, but rather with a calm acceptance, still the boy who hadn't started eating the pita bread yet, again tried to encourage her. "Come on, you weren't always like this," he said to her. "Don't I remember you from school? Of course I do, with the smooth skin you had. Believe me, Osi, at school, if it wasn't for Cheli I would have been your boyfriend, not hers. I swear, Osi, I would have been your boyfriend." For a while the girl was silent, Na'ama almost turned around to look at her – and then in her quiet voice she asked: "Really? Are you serious?" And from her seat Na'ama wanted to shout at her: yes yes yes, he's serious. Can't you tell how serious he is?)

Shechter turned his head from the window to the room, half of which was bathed in blue lamp light. "What now?" he asked.

"I'll give them exactly five minutes before I start to make a big noise all over the base. No, it really gets on my nerves," the sergeant answered, "you close a deal with someone, even put it in writing, with copies, and when you come to film it's like they're doing you a favor. This one's doing you a favor by giving you his office, that one suddenly needs his car for something, and what gets me the most?" he said to Shechter, and outside the prisoners were sinking stones into the trash can. "You'd think I was doing this for myself, but they're the ones who got me into this. All of a sudden the recruitment movie's not good enough for them. You'd think that that's why they're not getting any new recruits. And now if they don't get any, who do you think they're gonna come down on? Why's it like this, Gidi? Why's it like that, Gidi? In the end they know everything. What, don't I know them? I could write a doctorate on them."

Lucky, yes, lucky they didn't take him along on defensive alert day. They were easily capable of taking him along on defensive alert day. And then when would they have started filming? They'd never have started, never. Didn't they pull that trick on him last year? Sure did. Actually it was two years ago, last year there was a war on and all of a sudden everyone's his friend. And what friends. Buddy my buddy; they remembered he was once in "ABC"[5] and wanted him to explain to them what the difference between mustard gas and nerve gas was. Does baking soda help or not? Maybe he's got a few spare gas masks? Not for them, what do you mean for them, just for the kids. "All of a sudden," he said, "all those shitheads become nice guys, what, can you refuse them? How can you tell them no?"

(At the time he sent his wife and the little one to her kibbutz in the Upper Galilee, and at night he would sit in the apartment in Holon and watch television alone or look at stills he had taken of them with the camera he brought back from the base without permission, before he bought his own private camera, with points. Far, far away, beyond the nylon sheets and masking tape and the shutter, which he had replaced himself, were those paths with towering pines on both sides and the little one riding her tricycle between them with such joy, that if it was only up to him they would have moved there long ago. Immediately after the siren they would

---

5 Atomic, biological, chemical warfare

phone him, if they could get their hands on a telephone, and didn't even tell him that his voice sounded funny because of the mask since the line was so poor anyway. As for him, what more did he want, just to hear the little one's voice say to him: "Didi? Didi?" Yes, instead of Gidi, that's what the little one called him, and not daddy, until even his wife began calling him that: Didi.)

"So does baking soda help or not?" asked the actor. He walked round and round the room with his shoulders held high, once in a while reaching out to one of the objects – the poster, the Bristol board, the small cupboard – and running his finger over them as if inspecting the cleanliness of soldiers' barracks.

"Are you asking me seriously?" the sergeant asked.

"Absolutely seriously," the actor answered, "I'm always serious." At once he ran his finger over the lamp's screw and pointed out the rust stain to the lighting man.

"Commander, it's because of the rain," said the lighting man taking his cue and looking him in the eye to make sure he had answered appropriately.

Outside, through the window, in which a streak of clear sky was spread above the treetops, a small stone struck plastic immediately followed by another striking tin.

The actor, who turned to the table, touched the telephone lying there. He inserted his finger into one of the holes of the dial, examined it, lifted the receiver and peered into the holes in the mouthpiece as if checking the barrel of a rifle at inspection.

"suddenly he sees
a smaaaall eleph-aaaant pup strolling-"

He sang, and outside another stone struck the tin can. "Won't you sing along with me Kinneret?"

"No," Kinneret answered, "I'm through with being a singer."

The actor held the receiver like a microphone. "One-two, one-two," he said into it, tapped it with his finger twice, exhaled and began to sing again.

"a smaaall herd of elephants is strooooooolling"

(But there were no elephants there, not there nor in the place where the zoo once was. From the apartment that he rented in Tel Aviv you could see the grand City Garden building, and the head of the house committee said that she still remembered the roar of the lionzsh at night: what a thing, to hear lionzsh roaring next to your home. In his housing project they only heard cats howling and the rolling of backgammon dice in the Romanian's café, and some television set blaring, and sometimes, when all was still, you could hear the small stones that the crazy woman threw against the sky and that would drop and fall on the roofs of motor cars.

"a small line of cars is traaavelling"

Battered work vans, pickup trucks with makeshift coverings at the back, lorries with The Salad King or Rafi Movers or Moshe Renovations written on them in peeling letters, and one black BMW about which the children would quarrel over which of them the Daddon brothers would let wax and polish. The local youth center that was built for them held no interest and after a year looked like it had been inaugurated along with all the housing project buildings from the time of the large immigration. One after another the stones dropped on tin roofs spotted with rust and on tattered tarpaulin covers, and in a thin wailing voice the crazy woman shouted: "Gott im Himmel!" The first time when she took the stones from her worn out handbag and the second time after they fell, as if that Gott im Himmel threw all her stones back at her. And his father, had he not sunk into the television armchair, holding the remote control with all his might, not just holding it, but clinging to it as if it were the key to the land of happiness – would get up and peek through the slats of the shutters, his thin shoulders shaking beneath the soiled shoulder straps of his vest. He barely changed it once a month, only when he went to the prostitute from the Romanian's café: the same layabouts were there just like the ones by the kiosk on the avenue, and each time his father got drunk, he would have to drag him home by force, a small boy and someone who looked like the grandfather he never had. One night when he finally got upstairs and went inside, he began to shout down at the street in the voice of an old man in the language of an old man: "Gey schluffen, Clara, bitte, gey schluffen," and at once a stone hit a shutter and fell to the courtyard. It's been a while since grass grew there – a house committee and a gardener, such things were unheard of in the housing project, not to mention a marble horse monument, even in Tel Aviv that was unheard of – couch grass grew there in winter, chrysanthemums in spring, thistles in summer and the smell of sewage all year round.)

The actor replaced the receiver. "No," he said and blew dust from his finger toward the sergeant as if blowing a kiss, "because after a week the rag with the baking soda stunk to high heaven, we almost suffocated just from the smell of it."

"Do you have to talk about the war," Kinneret asked, "don't we have enough troubles without that?"

"And it's such a nice day today," said Na'ama. She drew near to the window, and on the road, which appeared again in the distance between the eucalyptus trunks, the American car was no longer seen: just a crumpled newspaper lay there, which the wind rolled up and blew away: spread out, read, became bored with and discarded.

"I can see you're not doing anything," Weintraub called to them from outside, and the other prisoner threw another stone at the black and blue striped iron post.

"You just mind your own business," the sergeant said from the window.

Carefully Weintraub stopped the trash can and balanced it delicately as if it were a child's pram. "Come on, Gidi," he said to him, "if you're also gonna start talking to me like that then I'm really through with this place." He bent over the trash can smacking his lips at it.

Above him the eucalyptus branches shook off the specks of light that clung to them, and in a moment they all flew here and there until landing in the foliage again like a flock of tiny birds. For a brief while Weintraub sang to the trash can and then fell silent. "Tell the singer-" he said, but tilted the trash can again and began to push it slowly and the words were swallowed up by the sound of the rake. It was dragged from behind, skipping over the asphalt and scraping against it.

(Nibbled at him, leaving her white teeth marks.)

"A singer?" Kinneret said to the asphalt, "I'm through with being a singer."

(In the war she could almost visualize it in black and white: Kinneret Biran, star of the group, cut down in the bloom of youth, felled, or gone up in smoke; but no smoke went up, all the fumes did not go up, on stage they crawled, curled, twisted, wrapped round limbs that had no space between them for even drops of sweat. Her father would grow a beard; a beard would suit him. With the hat that he received from the fans he would look like a cowboy in a western: Clint Eastwood. Kinneret Biran who was a promising rock singer *died* and joined the air force entertainment group. Ever since, the music world has lost its greatest talent *died*. Her father would grow a beard; her mother would dress in black: she liked to dress in one color anyway. Yes, *died*. That's why Kremlin's Children split up, because she *died*. They couldn't find anyone to fill her shoes *died*. She was Kremlin's Children. And if she didn't fare that well in the air force entertainment group it's only because died anyone whose father isn't a somebody can forget about being promoted. *Died*. And isn't her father in show business? Her father's a wedding singer *died*, and during the past year in seaside cafés as well: quite in demand, but still a wedding singer. Dresses like a star perhaps *died*, but still just a wedding singer. He doused himself with so much aftershave lotion that her mother asked him every night if it was for new female fans: those who shoved bills into his pockets, and not just pockets, he knows where else. *Died*. That's how they met. At a wedding, her mother *died*, after all the Besame Muchos *died* asked him if he knew any Hebrew songs. He silenced the group with a well-manicured hand, took the microphone from its stand, brought it close to his mouth until it almost touched his lips, looked around at the tables until all was silent, even the cutlery fell silent, knives did not cut, forks did not prod, and said: "the next song I dedicate to the girl in purple.")

"Look who's coming," said the actor. He returned his gaze to the window and at the same time ran his finger over the lines that someone had carved on the small cupboard to count the days left until their discharge. "Your clerk. And she's gonna tell us that there're problems. Right Merav?"

In the entrance of the opened door stood a petite dark-haired girl whose short hair was not combed in any particular style, just strands of hair on the sides swept behind her ears so as not to fall in front. The khaki uniform she was wearing was slightly too big for her and hung loosely on her gaunt body, and in her right hand, on which a telephone number was written in ink, she held a file bound by an elastic band.

"Who's making problems for you honey?" said the actor. Merav ignored him and placed the file on the table.

"You know what gets me the most?" she turned to the sergeant. "What really gets me is that she's sitting there painting her nails. Just for that we have to wait, for her nail polish. Ever since the new personnel aide arrived you can't say one word to her, not one word."

(One by one she would've pulled them out, one by one, slowly; she should have been a fashion officer not a welfare officer: only once during all her service did Merav ask her for something, only once, and the welfare officer did her a favor by listening to her; and that time she really did need something, when her grandfather almost died.)

"The new personnel aide," said the sergeant, "will keep her for a month at the most." He directed his words to the lighting man, who had placed blue cellophane on the second lamp and fastened the edges with pegs. "That one's screwed half the department. Don't you listen, sweetie. Next thing your parents will be claiming I corrupted their little girl."

(As for Merav's parents, they barely came to see her, even for the ceremony at the end of basic training: in the end they rented the taxi of the Arab in Jaffa, bringing three picnic boxes containing half the house, her mother transferred all her love into food, in place of all the words she couldn't say. "Is that what your family's always like?" they asked her later in the tent. "That all the women do is cook? Don't misunderstand me, I actually think the whole family thing's nice." They also brought a Mashbir department store plastic bag with them, one of the old bags that her father kept in the kitchen cupboard folded one on top of another, filled with loquats from a tree. Afterwards the whole tent dined on fruit and food, a tent of twelve girls with whom she had absolutely nothing in common, suddenly all became her friends. They started to ask the names of the dishes, as if she were some Bushman or Hottentot they had recruited specially for research, in fact they were surprised she didn't want to cook them.)

"Don't worry, you're not corrupting me."

(During basic training she almost shaved her head like she had always wanted to do, if only she had more courage, if she had been born into a different family, a different neighborhood, a different country: Ireland. Like the singer she once saw on television, a bald-headed singer singing straight from the gut, not like the ones here, she sang from the place from where it's impossible to ever lie, where the butterflies flutter, for anyone who has butterflies: with her it was a colony of restless bats like the ones that flew over the loquats at night, taking off and diving above the tree that grew from the drainage, transforming all the filth to sweet yellow fruit each spring. They arrived, parked the taxi with precision according to the white lines and began to pour out endlessly, just like in one of the actor's elephant jokes. Right at the end her sister Smadi and her husband got out; she got out slowly and for a while looked at the whiteness of the line. Until evening the two of them sat with everyone without exchanging a word between them, without looking at each other, careful not to be left alone together.)

"I was born where you were born."

Inside the drawer of the table the actor found a pen, removed the refill from it and blew into it as if it were a whistle. "How's that?" he asked the soundman, "does it sound okay in the earphones?"

The soundman was no longer bent over the recording machine but stood across from the window with the disconnected earphones on his head. In front of him, across the road, the diminishing afternoon light sparkled between the eucalyptus leaves and glowed here and there from the wings of the gnats that were circling, and against the sun, whose outline you could already look at directly, they seemed to be flying toward a light bulb.

"No one's paying any attention to me," said the actor.

"We can hear you only too well," answered the soundman still watching from the window.

(A mosquito flew around and dived, buzzing unashamedly, and the woman who was once his wife – when he had yet to become a soundman, a thousand years ago, thousands – tried to catch it in her hands above the Mickey Mouse figures on the lampshade: she clapped her hands, turned them over and checked their emptiness. "Where are you, you little bastard," she said to the mosquito, "you're not going to bite my baby, do you hear?" And when it was crushed in her palms, through the thin material you could see her breasts jiggling, full of milk.)

"Even without earphones we can hear you."

(But at the tip of India, south of Madras, he once saw a completely naked Jain who had tied a handkerchief over his mouth and nose so as not to swallow or inhale any insect: he saw him on his first journey by train in which he traveled for thirty-six consecutive hours, and a month later, in Bangkok, he lay in a hotel room, which was damp from the monsoon rains, and through the rips in the mosquito net saw the fan circling above him, slow and rattling, and through the screen door were the shadows of painted girls who stopped and called out to him, "hey mister, you want fucky-fucky?" and their lean thighs sashayed against the dusty lattice. Only out of the cities, in villages and on the islands, when at last the rattling of the tuk tuks and the hooting of the trucks, on whose backs was written PLEASE HORN between faded arabesques, fell silent, was it possible to hear the buzzing of the mosquitoes; but they were many and with each one that he succeeded in crushing on the wall – a wall of stone, a wall of clay, a wall made of reed mats – before the bloodstain dried he was already stung by another.)

"The soundman's waiting for the sunset so that he can record it," said the actor and blew again into the dismantled pen.

The soundman, who was bent over the recording machine again (there was only one who heard the sun setting and the moon rising and the clouds floating and the mist of the ocean filling them with the smell of seaweed and fish), lifted his head: "Instead of whistling, speak."

The actor looked at the window for a moment, then straightened his shoulders and with a harsh guttural enunciation addressed the rounded sun above the treetops: "Tomorrow and tomorrow and tomorrow, creeps in this petty pace from day to day, to the last syllable of recorded time." He fell silent. The lighting man looked at him as if waiting for a joke to follow, but the actor just tucked his chin into his neck, which gave the appearance of a double chin, and in the Russian accent of a Habimah Theatre veteran continued to recite: "And all our yesterdays have lighted fools the way to dusty death." He took a bow toward the window, and another one, and from the road the prisoners, streaked by shadows, applauded.

And someone as yet faceless said: "Tell me are you deaf or something?" And the investigator – from the corner of the ceiling the little lizard sees how the skin of his scalp shines through his thinning hair: and the small monitor he's watching reflects his flabby features with the dark bags under his eyes into which all the remnants of the scenes will seemingly be gathered – turns his head to the right. The gap that the door had opened wide is already slowly narrowing and is closed; and a redheaded girl dressed in a white coat over her uniform is now approaching the table behind him. "For maybe a quarter of an hour we've been trying to get you on the phone," she said and over her eyes small round glasses glimmer in a thin frame – was it with her that he spoke this morning? For a moment he finds it hard to connect the deep feminine voice that he heard on the phone to the small figure in front of him – "didn't you hear?" She lifts the telephone receiver, listens, hits the buttons on the base; listens again. "They've hung up," she says, turns the dial with her finger and lets it go. "Someone from your office was looking for you, she didn't say what her name was, wanted to know what happened." The ponytail into which her hair was gathered swings with each and every movement of hers, jumping with joy in front of his eyes as if to defy their tiredness (in the middle of the night the boss's secretary called him and in bedroom tones said to him that he would have to investigate: and no bullshit this time, get to the bottom of things fast. A: what happened exactly. B: who's the guilty party. And C: good night to him in his bed, because he's sleeping only with it now, no?)

"That's just it, not much is happening," the investigator said from his chair, "they filmed virtually everything except what we need." It seems to him that her freckles are reddening but perhaps it's the light that's altering their shade, the little light that still filters through the sealed windows. "At least for the meantime," he quickly added so as not to offend her, after all she told the police about the filming, and the police told him, and in the empty expanse around the base – an expanse with no trees, no wheat, no thistles and two white herons soaring above for a while, not landing – perhaps the wind left a pinch of dust that had not yet dwindled away: a man was burning there in the night.

3

"How was that?" asked the actor.

"Okay," answered the soundman.

"It sounded okay to you? Going that way to their dusty deaths?" The actor blew again into the pen he had taken apart.

The lighting man grinned and looked at the bluish shadow cast on the table by the telephone. On his left, above an old newspaper, Na'ama lifted her eyes and asked who knows a European capital city with five letters the third letter an *r*.

"Warsaw," Kinneret turned from the window. "Does it fit?" And at once the actor asked if they wanted to hear jokes about Poles.

"We're sick and tired of your jokes," said Na'ama, "Warsaw's got six letters not five."

(She once read in the newspaper about people who have an obsessive impulse to make everyone laugh the whole time, about what causes this impulse, what it indicates, what it compensates for. She was already planning to study psychology after her army service if only they would accept her, and her mother said it wasn't a bad idea: maybe she would succeed in putting some sense into her nutty sister? That's how she spoke, Na'ama's mother, about her sister, and after a while suddenly lifted a floured finger to the corner of her eye, leaving a white mark there, and the tip of her finger glistened. The time after the army still seemed to Na'ama so far away that she found it difficult to imagine; it was much further away than some performance in Eilat or the Golan Heights, those hours before on the bus when one tries to imagine how many soldiers there'll be and how they'll react to the songs and the sketches and whether the acoustics will be good. All those questions would arise the moment they sat down, each in his regular place, the soloists in front and the musicians at the back. The bus was painted khaki and on its side the name of the group was written in curved white letters, and when they were seen from pavements or cars you couldn't tell from there who was a star and who wasn't, who had a whole solo and who only sang one verse like Na'ama; who was sure of himself, and who trembled as if at some school assembly when the principal finished his speech and she, Na'ama, had to begin reciting a heroic song from the War of Independence: "And the land grows still, the red eye of the sky slowly dimming." Facing the receding scenery in the window – the shining plains of the Arava or the silvery fish farms that grew smaller as you ascend the heights – from their seats they all dreamt, the stars and the non-stars, that they would light candles for them or at least matches, and that they would join in and sing all the words with them, words that actually said nothing of the things that Na'ama really wanted to say. And they dreamt that they would be called back to the stage again and again and that they would also be invited to a festive dinner with the officers, and that they would be chatted up, she too, Na'ama: "You sang one verse," they would say to her, "and it was the nicest one of all, we just couldn't see your pretty eyes from the auditorium." The red eye of the sky.)

"I actually had a joke on the tip of my tongue," said the actor. "It's just that for a second I wasn't paying attention and away it went with my tongue." He tapped his head with his finger. "That skull," he recited, elongating the vowels, "had a tongue in it and could sing once."

Yes that's how it is, he said: he's simply falling to pieces since his girlfriend left him. Perhaps his neighbor's right, actually a Polish woman, she's always telling him: "You gotta get married, doesn't matter who with, straightaway a girl will get all that nonsense out of your head."

Na'ama, who lifted her head from the crossword, said that's exactly what her mother says about her sister, only without that accent – a dimple formed in her cheek, but at once she sealed it and returned her gaze to the newspaper: a European capital with five letters the third one an *r*.

(Her sister once had a boyfriend who was an artist that no one but her sister had ever heard of. It's already been three years since they split up and she still hasn't recovered. And what now? She's already past thirty and still not married, as if life waits for someone, that's how her mother spoke. She lives in a rooftop apartment on the noisiest street there is, that's to say one and a half rooms on the roof, but you've got no idea how much money she throws away on it. In summer they whitewash up there, in winter cover it with tar, and all the time they're hanging and taking down washing right in front of her, she already knows everyone's bras and panties. On the first of each month her sister would record a new message on the answering machine, maybe someone will call by mistake and fall for her just from those words that she left there, or would be captivated by her voice: yes, even she knows full well that such miracles only happen in the movies. And then in the movies it never happens to girls who look like her, never. "The heart aches when you hear those messages," her mother said and her finger still glistened, "like some message in a bottle, and all that just from her being on her own." Three years on the roof above all those shops, one has to know, even Na'ama, that being in the group is all very well and good, it even gives some pleasure, she's not saying it doesn't, even her father enjoyed the performance, that's to say before what happened. After all she knows when he gets excited about something even if he doesn't show it. But what can you do with it afterwards? Become a singing teacher? Give drama classes? And that's at best, or do you become an art teacher? – Not her sister, it's beneath her to teach children after having an artist for a boyfriend, an artist, he didn't sell one picture – so she knows very well what all those dreams come to. Yes, very very well. You know what they say about child wonders; the wonder goes, the child stays. So if they're going to tell stories about all sorts of new stars, okay, why not. She's willing to hear, but let them come again in ten or twenty years' time. What, didn't she also have dreams

of her own once? Didn't she? From here to eternity she had.
"Why're you looking at me like that," she said to Na'ama then,
"everyone has," and lifted the cutting board to the edge of the
frying pan sending pieces of chopped onion on their way to
the bubbling oil.)

"They're also always saying that to my sister," said Merav.

"Didn't your sister get married?" the sergeant looked at her
from above the second camera. "In a hall with everything?"

"I meant before that," Merav explained, she crushed the
piece of masking tape she was rubbing between her fingers
with the tips of her nails.

(As for Merav's parents, either they pretended not to see
or they really didn't see anything with their small eyes that
became even weaker from watching over too many children
who grew up too fast. Who saw anything at all? Perhaps her
grandfather saw, but with him it wasn't possible to know what
he really saw and what was seen only in his head, he would
leave his grey eyes slightly open even when he slept, so that
the angel of death wouldn't come and catch him unawares:
first he would comb his hair, then put on his grey striped suit
and summer shoes with the air holes, and then he'd get up
and go out by himself, just as he would go to all his friends'
funerals, and to the grandchildren's weddings and the great
grandchildren's circumcisions. And just the way he'd walk on
Allenby Street down to the sea, when he was still able to walk.
She was sitting in the bridal chair that was decorated like a
queen's throne, her sister Smadi, in the gown that Claudine
sewed for her according to a pattern from abroad, she really
did look like a queen – "how white suits her skin!" said the
neighbors, "and her hair so lovely" – she sat there and a long
narrow red carpet was spread on the marble floor from the
decorated entrance right up to her. Laniado had spent a
fortune on the hall he built and her little sisters ran all around
it, stopping suddenly in order to slide, happy as she had once
been at weddings. They skated over the white marble here
and there like Russian dancers on the ice, smiling at everyone
they bumped into who lifted them up with a smile, until
Moshon arrived with his buddies: only someone who'd rather

be blind didn't see; only someone who'd rather be deaf didn't
hear the motorbikes before that. From the way they walked
you could already tell it was clear they'd downed a couple of
beers, and from the end of the hall, at the entrance decorated
with wild flowers and white ribbons, from the edge of the
red carpet he said: "How much do you bet I'll do it?" He
didn't wait for them to answer and didn't linger next to the
monitors of Cohen Productions, but moved forward on the
narrow red carpet in his black leather boots from which studs
sparkled and passed her grandfather and the bar with bottled
drinks and glasses and mounds of fruit that no one had yet
touched and came close to her sister Smadi and stood in front
of her and looked at her and bent down toward her face and
kissed her lips hard and fast with a sucking kiss.)

The lighting man tilted the lamp and its beam now lit up
the ceiling. The shadow of the telephone disappeared but the
reflected light was not enough to illuminate the table. The
lamp was aimed downwards and its doors, which had become
heated, opened **(let's see you)** until the cellophane loosened
from one of the pegs and the entire rectangle of the table shone
(let's see if you are a man). The lighting man replaced the
cellophane. The spray muddied with rust still poured from the
lamp screws making them slippery to the touch.

(His toes slipped, his shoulders, his whole body, but he
continued to climb **let's see if you are a man let's see let's see
let's see** and stepped onto the quivering board and saw his
father far down below looking at him from there and calling
to him, and he wanted to jump, not to him and not to the
glistening pool but to the dim hard flooring around it so he'll
see he'll see he'll see.)

"We'll give her seven more minutes," the sergeant lifted
the leather cap of his watch to take a look. "I'm fed up to the
back teeth." The stretch of road bound by the window was
empty, and besides the rustling of the eucalyptuses nothing
was heard from there.

"Do they still say that?" the actor asked. "That – I'm fed
up to the back teeth –?" That one was around when he did

basic training, he said. "And – everyone's getting laid while you're getting screwed – is that still around as well? Don't listen, Merav. Only Kinneret's allowed to."

"There was another one," said the soundman from his corner, "actually quite a nice one. They used to say: the-world-is-dead-gone-are-the-seas-all-the-fish-climbed-up-the-trees."

"Do they still say that?"

The sergeant nodded above the second camera and Kinneret turned her gaze to the window.

"That welfare officer," said the sergeant (it's not that he had anything against her, at least not in the beginning, now he just doesn't know what to make of her. He's not at all one of those who say: "give me a minute to talk to someone and straightaway I can tell what kind of a person they are"; he already knew very well, the sergeant, that first impressions are deceptive and sometimes second and third ones too, and sometimes you can live with someone your whole life and still not really know them. Yes even that much. For example his wife, what did she seem like to him in the beginning when he saw her for the first time at the hitchhikers' station in a group of soldiers? And what did she seem like to him the day after that when she stood there again at the end of the line, totally despondent? And what did she seem like to him inside the rickshaw when the road works rocked them both and she suddenly began to laugh? And what did she seem like to him on her kibbutz when he was there with her, and also when only hearing her voice on the phone from the apartment in Holon, the cordless phone in the little one's room? She changed the whole time, every day, every moment; when she got up she was one woman, and after showering she became another, and on returning from the city she was a different woman, and when she told the little one a story she changed again, and at night, at night it was impossible to know her at all), "it's just gone to her head. She knows the commander thinks well of her. Don't think she's the little good girl, good girl my foot. That one's a snake, a snake. With her everything eventually gets to the commander of the base."

(As for him, he wouldn't have cared about her at all had things not got complicated with the commander of the base about the camera; up till then who didn't he get praise from, even from the commander of the base. Because before then, this base really wasn't all that bad for him: the paths, as they say, already knew his footsteps, and the trees seemed almost like the trees on his wife's kibbutz, if you didn't pay any attention to the whitewash and the emergency vehicle shed or the dummy missile brought from Sinai, Sam 2 or 6, long before anyone here had heard of Scuds. Once a year, just before corps celebration day, they would also paint the missile with the corps colors, blue and black, just the way they would paint the doors of the quartermaster store and the transport office and the armory. Because as far as they were concerned, if they had enough paint, a spare gallon or so, they would have painted the leaves on the trees as well.)

"So why do you bring me someone like that?" asked the actor, "couldn't you find someone else from the group?"

"What for," said the sergeant, "she'll hardly be seen for a second, only when she catches you inside. Besides which they'd never give me anyone else. They did me a favor by giving me these two, believe me they had me down on all fours."

"I believe you," said the actor. He looked at him through the aperture of the dismantled pen as if with a captain's telescope.

The investigator rolls the film.

The lighting man entered the room again, shaking his hands and drops of water glistened for a moment in the bluish lamplight. He approached the small cupboard, bent down and opened the little tin door. From the depths of the cupboard he took out a roll of coarse toilet paper and wound it round his hand a couple of times. He wiped his hands with it, crumpled the remaining paper and threw it into the wastepaper basket.

"Give me some too," asked Na'ama, and after a while blew her nose sheepishly. She put out her hand again and the lighting man let her pull the edge of the paper until he stopped the roll with his hand.

"You're a stingy one," he said to her, "after all you've got Kleenex in your bag. What, didn't I see?"

(But before, he just turned it inside out like a little boy, not even noticing where the lipstick fell and how it stayed there for an instant; at the last second she managed to catch it before it rolled toward the geraniums. Drops fell from the sprinkler and glistened in the soft afternoon light; but her sister didn't water like this sergeant, she let everything wilt and put out cigarette stubs smoked down to the filter on what was left. She put them out crushing them one after another, and still asked Na'ama if she knew those signs, the ones they put on plants in offices, "I am not an ashtray." Well this window box happens to be one. That's especially what it was made for.)

The lighting man, who bent down again, suggested that Na'ama come with him to the base canteen: in any case it'll take a while until they begin.

"It's on me," he said to her while replacing the roll in the cupboard, "but if you want to, then chop-chop. Otherwise those guys from the course will finish everything. No, not in a minute," – she hesitated for a moment – "now. Chop-chop."

(She didn't like that, Na'ama, the way he said chop-chop to her: let him speak to his girlfriend that way, chop-chop. Never ever show someone that he's everything to you, her sister said, never ever. Take it from me. Because when he starts thinking that, you can start forgetting about him, take it from me. Her sister's boyfriend shaved his head completely, didn't even leave bristles like the lighting man or the cadet pilot. Every morning he clogged up her sister's basin, every single morning, didn't miss one morning. And why did he shave? Just to conceal his baldness. Had he stayed with her till now, not that she needs him, what do you mean, good riddance, not a day goes by that she doesn't thank God, not a day, really, not an hour goes by, he would have made some little pigtail at the back for sure. Yes, like all those bohemian bald-headed guys, so that no one should mistake them for clerks or something. When he still lived with her sister he once drew her naked in charcoal on rough paper, brown wrapping paper full of crease marks, and made her out fatter than she really was. If someone had drawn Na'ama like that, she would have been deeply insulted, maybe even cried. She cries so easily, that's the kind of heart she's got, attached straight to the eyes. But her sister said that it was actually very feminine and that real men, not pretty boys, real men just love it; they're crazy about having something to grab on to. The two of them were sitting on the roof across from the sheets waving like huge wings, and her sister, who put her leg on the withered window box, grabbed the flesh of her thigh and pinched it over and over and over until all the blood was drained from it.)

"I don't feel like it," she said.

In the sky, above the treetops, a few wisps of downy cloud floated. They moved there slowly like loops in the tail of a kite hidden by the doorframe, as if on the far side of the eucalyptuses stood a boy, in his hand a small piece of wood around which the string was unraveling, fold by fold.

"What are you looking at?" asked Na'ama.

Shechter turned his gaze from the window. The beret stuck in her epaulet pulled her shirt back, revealing a small, white, delicate section of rounded shoulder. He looked at it for a while, until she sensed his gaze and moved away.

"Wait a second," she said to the lighting man, "Bring me something anyway, take some money."

"I'm not going on my own."

"Do as you please," she turned to the window.

"What'll you give me if I go?" the lighting man sat on the chair back to front, spreading his thighs wide on both sides of the back rest. He wheeled himself over to her, his shorn head at the level of her small breasts.

"Oh oh," she said, "you making demands." For a moment she looked at the bristles and suddenly put out her hand to touch his head, letting them prick her skin. "First bring something," she said.

In the window the wisps of cloud continued to float, downy, delicate and whirling.

(With the assertive voice of a director of feature films – the director he did not become in his youth and would never be – he should have told them that they would start shooting immediately, but in the window, from far and wide, the transparent fibers were gathering, intertwining, interweaving and turning a turbid shade of jute, and through the sack Shechter imagined hearing the investigators' voices again, asking over and over, the way they must have interrogated the prisoner, what was he looking for here and for whom, and no lies, do you hear, no lies: and he repeats his name to himself, Shechter Shechter Shechter, with each utterance erasing the boy who used to fly kites made from reeds picked by the banks of the Yarkon. For three days the sacks weren't removed from the heads of the soldiers of the elite unit as well – that's what the guard at the airport in Paris told him – they were beaten, deprived of food and water and not allowed to sleep, having been forbidden to give anything away other than their name Shechter their rank staff sergeant Shechter and perhaps their army identity number two two one six two two four: that number now sounded like a long forgotten telephone number to his ears, and on the other end of the line stood Shechter the new recruit, who shaved only to speed the growth of his fluff. Behind him stood Shechter the tourist, who left the remains of his beard in the basin of a cheap hotel in the Latin Quarter, and two days later was already traveling in a command car through the ravaged streets of some coastal town or another; he couldn't remember which, the wreckage looked the same, as was the stench that rose from it. And before this, where had he been? In a European capital five letters the fourth an *i*.)

"So what are you looking at?" asked Na'ama.

"At that plane out there," he answered. Out the window one of the crop spraying planes that had been stationed at the nearby airfield was circling above the fields, emitting a greenish cloud from its bowels.

(It was old-fashioned, like the plane that turned yellow above him twenty years ago, when he was on duty in the grove of the lower practice area; and perhaps the same pilot was flying in it, but you can be sure now with a paunch and thinning hair; and when he gets out of his plane after landing, he no longer jumps but slowly and carefully goes down the plank stairs with a rail: an elderly pilot who no longer dreams of flying Boeings across the sea and bringing them in to land in distant capitals that wink at him from the night, but a crop sprayer will do for him; and afterwards he walks wearily to his car, a small box-like car, not like the one in the distant road that was momentarily seen and then quickly hidden by the eucalyptus trunks.)

"Are you sure it's not yours?" asked Na'ama. "Long, with wings at the back?" she turned to Kinneret from the window.

"Absolutely sure. They're never on time, no way."

Na'ama turned to the Bristol board. With the tip of her finger she touched the singed edges, walked to the poster, and on the soldier's white cheek left a black mark like some kind of pimply rash.

"A limousine?" asked the actor, "like mine?"

"Yours is an Autobianchi," the sergeant called from the inner room. "Some limousine."

"A horse," said the actor. "I have a horse. A kingdom for a horse. Richard the Third sold it to me. Second hand."

"What are you talking about, limousine," Kinneret said. "An antique that hardly moves."

In the window, which has been sealed since last night, the entrance gate to the base cannot be seen, nor the white rope tied loosely there, nor the investigator's car that is parked outside: just an old Renault, and due to its age and worn down tires from all the kilometers traversed, by necessity or otherwise, no one would bother stealing in the city, but here, would it be enticing to soldiers leaving the base? Would they break into it? Make it disappear as if it hadn't become a part of his body.

The sergeant came out of the inner room.

"Eran the lighting man is going to the canteen," the actor announced to him.

The sergeant dried his hands on his trousers. "You're not going anywhere," he said. "What do you mean 'why'? I'm off to fetch her in the rickshaw right now."

(Not that it would suit this welfare officer to ride with him in a rickshaw. Ride in a rickshaw? Someone like her? With a master sergeant? But it will be enough for him to park the rickshaw across from her office for a minute, not just a minute – a second, for her to shoot out of there right away like a rocket: that's all she needs there, a rickshaw, really. That someone should think she's got something going on with master sergeants.)

The soundman, who was taking a look at the newspaper supplement that Na'ama dropped, put it down on the table. "Tell her in the east it's called a taxi special."

"Isn't a rickshaw something someone pulls along by himself?" asked the sergeant. "Like you see in the movies, what do you call him?"

"A coolie," answered the soundman in his quiet voice. From above the crossword, stained by the round prints of a coffee cup, he explained that it was only in Calcutta that there were coolies and that in all other places they use three-wheeled motorbikes like the sergeant's. "Delhi, Bombay, Varanasi. Bangkok? Madras? Goa? Just like this one. Also in Kathmandu. Same thing." For a while the foreign names rang through the space of the office, resonating, lifted on high, raising golden pagodas, as transparent as the wings of the insects that the sunlight gilded in the window until they became blurred in the foliage of the eucalyptuses. From their depths a bird chirped and for a moment it sounded like a miniature prayer bell whose tongue was as fine as a hair.

"What other places have you been to?" Kinneret asked. The door slammed and a moment later the rattling of the rickshaw pulling away was heard. "My brother's just come back from there. He came back really tanned, even more than you."

(But as for her, she had sea and sun here too, and everything he did there she could do here with whomever she wanted, whenever she wanted, wherever she wanted. On the sheets on the carpet on the table on the floor on the wall on the stage, until fear got hold of her and sunk its teeth in. It was only in the sea that she had never done it, right in the sea, with the movement of the waves back and forth, like she once saw and only years later realized what she had seen. At the time she was crawling on the sand with an orange plastic spoon, and from the sand she picked up pieces of Bamba[6] that had fallen from a packet and become dotted with grains as if with sesame seeds. Someone called out – called out from afar and their voice was distorted in the wind – "Kinneret" – she lifted her head. "Don't go near the water." She went near. Tiny tongues licked her feet and hands. She giggled and more came, fingerlike and tickling. Chuckling. They dotted her with droplets and suddenly pricked and annoyed her; one stole a piece of Bamba: the Bamba floated on the water, darkened slowly and sank. She stretched out her hand to catch it: a small yellowish fish, sesame-like, slippery.)

"Where about was your brother?"

"In India and in Thailand," she answered, "on the islands. Ku Samoi, something like that?"

"Ko Samui," the soundman quietly corrected her. With the rubber bellows that the sergeant had passed to him before leaving, he blew dust off the recording machine. "Lots of Israelis go there."

The actor asked why the swearing:[7] Didn't they hear the sergeant ask not to corrupt Merav? Outside from the direction of the road the faint sound of footsteps was heard coming closer and getting stronger.

"Ko means island," the soundman blew more dust away.

---

6   Peanut puffs popular with children

7   The name of the island approximates a Hebrew swearing phrase from the Arabic referring to female genitalia

"So is the other thing," said the actor, "I would cross the entire world, believe me – so I might live one hour in her sweet bosom. Richard the Third."

He blew a kiss at Kinneret. She stuck her tongue out at him; the soundman looked at her tongue.

(Perhaps her brother was one of a group of Israelis, all still with army haircuts, who used to roam the beaches together and stare at the girls sunbathing there as God had created them. When he was still going down to the bay – to buy bottles of mineral water or to see human beings – they were there lying on their backs under the equatorial sun, which filled the skies from horizon to horizon and devoured them from front and back. And afterwards – when he was still leaving the hut – they dressed in lungis like the islanders and said namaste at every opportunity, as if that namaste was the password for the entrance to the garden of paradise. But the god of this garden had no temples, no believers who fought each other to the death and the entire island was the manifestation of its name: each one of its palm trees formed one of the letters, each one of its long papaya leaves, each foamy trail that strayed after a fishing boat, each grain from the veil of salt on the shore.)

(A kiss was blown at her and she put her tongue back: saliva can spread it, sweat, nectar of the body. She swallowed her saliva, swallowed salt and grains of sand. Floating on the water, Bamba, a small yellow sesame-like fish, floating around her here and there. From above her she heard the flick-flack of beach bats, flick after flack, but the water trickled noiselessly and the foam rippled and whished. The tiny fish dived and rested on the sea bed, waiting for her to reach out to it. Flick. She lifted her head: the ball passed. Flack. And the rays of light fluttered on the water, fluttered on her hands, on her legs, on the baby-like nipples which she had, fluttered.)

(One of the beach boys, or one from the group of travelers who were squeezed into the old bus on the way from Pokhara to Dunche, a hundred kilometers through the Himalayas in a whole day: the driver's assistant served in place of the missing rear view mirror and the hooter, and on the roof thin

Nepalese men and women huddled together between the sacks of rice and flour, tins of oil and the travelers' rucksacks that were tethered by chains so that they wouldn't be stolen. And in the afternoon, when the monsoon rain suddenly poured from a sky that burst open – a sky very close – they all lowered themselves from the roof to the windows. Nimbly they jumped and pushed through the passageway; women and the elderly too, and one of the Israelis shouted to another in front: "what do you say, Shachar, should we thin out some of the locals?" Perhaps they shouted that way when patrolling the Casbah or searching for a wanted man, dragging snoring old people from their beds, sweaty couples, babies with the whiff of a dream and the smell of pee – he still recalled that smell through the dust – and on the windows the heavy monsoon raindrops flowed, stream after stream, mixed with the tiny bodies of squashed mosquitoes. "Where are you, you little bastard, you're not going to bite my baby, do your hear," the woman who was once his wife continued to say in his head, and her breasts jiggled, full of milk, through the thin material and through the dust and the rain.)

Past the window a group of soldiers came marching left-right with yellow tags in their epaulets. The sergeant leading in front turned his head: "one peep out of you and you can forget about your leave." The lighting man watched them for a moment while they pounded their feet, twisting the roll of masking tape that he wore like a bracelet around his wrist.

"Do me a favor," he said to Na'ama, "move the cable over there a bit, next to your foot."

"Na'ama looked at the floor, at the cable that had become bent there, and shoved it with the tip of her shoe against the wall.

Through the window the staff sergeant stopped, and immediately the column of soldiers behind him stopped, continuing to pound their feet in rhythm. "Did you get what I said Benami?" the sergeant asked. From the end of the column, hidden by the rickshaw that had returned and rattled for a moment longer until it fell silent, a dim voice rose and called out: "Yesss Sirrrr!"

"I can't hear you," said the sergeant.

The door of the room opened. Merav looked at the master sergeant who came in and asked him how the ploy with the rickshaw went.

"I can't hear you," said the sergeant again from the road, "did any of you hear anything?" "Nooo Sirrr!" answered the entire column from one end to the other.

"We'll only know when she arrives," the sergeant slammed the door.

"That's how you enslave people for their whole lives," said the actor. From the corner of the room he looked at the window and half of the dismantled pen was still in his hand. "And then you wonder why everything here looks like this." "Like what?" asked the lighting man who was already preparing himself for a joke. "Like this," answered the actor and lifted his hand, passing it over the room and the entire base. "Go to their graves like beds, fight for a plot whereon the numbers cannot try the cause, which is not tomb enough and continent. King Lear." Through the window high boots pounded left-right, beating the asphalt. "Benami,"[8] said the actor, "you tell me where else in the world there's a name like that, Benami. Have you ever heard of an American called 'People'? Someone called 'America'? You listen to me, America," he spoke through his teeth like an Italian gangster, grabbing an imaginary collar and lifting the one he addressed into the air, "and when thou walkest by the way, when thou liest down, and when thou risest up."

For a moment, from above the microphone, the soundman watched him with bright blue eyes, the colour of the shirt he was wearing, and then all at once bent over again and blew some more dust with the bellows (six hundred thousand grains of dust, sixty thousand grains of dust, and a pillar of fire went before them).

"They only go in for weird cars," said the actor. "Ten meters long, limousines." He moved near to the window through which the soldiers continued to pound their feet. "And my name?" he said. Outside on the road they pounded

8   Literally: son of my people

over and over and the sergeant's rank, fastened by a safety pin, quivered on his sleeve. Above their heads and the treetops the white wisps floated, downy, delicate, whirling.

(And the boy, far from here, beyond the eucalyptuses and the years, felt the pull of the transparent string in his palm pleading with him to lift his feet from the ground, as if the kite was one of Nil's geese or Doolittle's giant moths, but Shechter had never ridden, not on a goose and not on a moth, had never flown a plane, not even a small crop sprayer, and will never fly to America, not to the East and not to Europe, since he had no one to fly to anymore: Dudush, that's what his French girlfriend called her grey Deux Chevaux, and one night he heard how the windscreen wiper struggled to scrape the frost from the windscreen – the young man he was at the time – and when he glanced at her profile he saw the white upright forehead and her nose and her lips, and thought of the funny way she once used to say his name and the words he tried to teach her in his language on the first nights: in the room, on the mattress that almost filled it entirely, Shechter touched her delicate quivering skin and led her hand over his body, while from language to language they translated the different parts: like friendly animals they pushed their snouts forward to open palms and asked to be named.)

"Have you heard one like this?" the actor said.

"Bells and whistles?" asked the stooped soundman, "or the sound and the fury?"

"Michael," answered the actor facing the window. "To you – Who-is-like-God. Ever heard of a girl called Loch Ness? Kinehrrret-" he turned around sounding a thin nasal twang.

(They left her in a pit in the sand, at first waving a packet at her as you would to a puppy: "Bamba? Who wants Bamba? Kinneret wants Bamba!" and skipped and jumped in, the feet disappeared in the water, the belly. She watched. She couldn't see them anymore. And suddenly they appeared again, splashing each other and laughing, she laughed too; laughed from the sand. They drew close to each other splashing more of the scintillating water. Her cousin moved further away, she swam with her boyfriend. First they splashed and now they swam. Only their heads were still seen, floating there, floating until coming to a halt. They stood in the water close to each other, only their heads and shoulders visible. And the sea sparkled. "Nulit," she cried, "Nulit!" They stood clinging, they moved. The water brought with it a multitude of flickering lights and from its depths a tiny fish winked. She stretched her hand out to it. She moved.)

The investigator stretched his legs out in front of him.

"I guarantee you she won't come," said Merav. "What does she need to impress the recruit center for? All right, if it was a film for the officers' course, but new recruits?"

"Give her another chance," said the sergeant, "maybe falling in love's turned her into a better person." He placed the cable next to the wall with his shoe, and straightaway it bent again.

(How's it not going to bend if it was wound up that way? Of course it's going to become bent. That's the problem with reserve soldiers; it's just what they're used to in civilian life: something gets broken, straightaway you buy a new one. Go explain to them what one has to do to get something here, even a bolt. A simple bolt; the most ordinary kind. And the microphone boom? True it was attached to a stick instead of the standard rod, but you show the master sergeant anywhere else in the Israel Defense Forces that's got a microphone like this. Once on corps day they came from the television to film, Benny Lees and his crew, they were just amazed to see a microphone boom like that here. "At the television," said Benny Lees' soundman, "do you know the effort you have to go to get hold of a microphone like this? It's like drawing blood, blood." The sergeant remembered how he said "blood" and how the wind blew a grain of sand into his eye and for a moment it looked as if he winked at the cameraman, and he also remembered Benny Lees' skullcap, which almost flew off into the wind had it not been attached to his hair with a clip. In his eyes the clip was endearing, because not only did it keep the skullcap anchored, but also all of Benny Lees, anchored to the same ground on which he himself stood: real ground, not a filmed one, which is just made up of pixels, like he learned from the course in Tzrifin.)

"Did the new personnel aide," asked the actor from his place, "pump her heart or something else?"

(The sergeant didn't wear a skullcap and didn't even observe the Sabbath, certainly not after he married, though he actually had more faith after he married, yes, each time they traveled to her kibbutz and he would see the orchards and the fish farms and the mountains of the Golan and the clear skies above them, which were made by who, who? And who made her love him that way, yes, more than all the kibbutzniks, and who gave him this child that each time she called him – Didi – he was simply beside himself with joy. Was anyone ever called that, Didi? In America had they ever heard of such a name? In all the world there's no one else who says it like that, Didi, with rosy cheeks like the apples he picked there, standing at the time in the small basket of the mobile crane and stretching out his hand to the tree and picking them carefully two at a time and thinking that life, life is here, this is the life, and if only he could he would resign right away from the army and the base, yes, even though it was relatively nice here, and wear only those blue work overalls that never become dirty from anti-rust spray but only from the earth and the leaves.)

"Falling in love's done nothing for her," said Merav, "besides becoming even worse than she usually is." She tried to place the cable close to the wall from the corner of the room and further along.

"Maybe he didn't pump her enough," the lighting man grinned and rolled the masking tape around his wrist.

"Don't you listen to him, Merav-sweetie," said the actor, "so that we don't completely corrupt you. Then what will we tell your parents?"

She tried to adjust the cable with the heel of her shoe as if she was crushing a cigarette butt under it and the sergeant shouted out: What does she want, to destroy it completely?

"Yes," she replied.

(Merav-sweetie: if it hadn't been for her father's boss she wouldn't have been called Merav at all, they would have called her after her late uncle: Meira, like all her brothers and sisters who were named after the dead, and she wouldn't have let them turn it into Mimi. Her sister Shoshana became Shoshi and then Suzy, and Pnina became Nina, and Smadar became Smadi, but she would have remained Meira. Her father's boss deigned to show his face at the wedding for two minutes and left, at least he didn't see the disgrace: he came in a three piece suit, gave the check and went, still managing to smile at her, a smile not born of happiness but rather the contrary. At least this time he gave something: by then she already knew all the electrical appliances he had at home, one by one they would break down and end up with her father. For a fee, Ya'akov, this time for a fee, you're simply putting me in an unpleasant situation, Ya'akov. He would say her father's name like a radio announcer, and in the holidays, when she went with her father to work, she would lift her head and look at the two of them for a moment, then push the pedal of the tricycle and race down the long passage that had no end and where all the doors looked exactly alike, except for the one from behind which a female announcer's voice said over and over: "Monsieur Legrand est alle au café, il est assis sur une chaise," and afterwards many other voices said: "Monsieur Legrand est alle au café, il est assis une chaise," she would stop opposite it for a while and then immediately race away again like her sisters at the wedding: running all over the marble floor until stopping and sliding, and then she remembered how in summer she took them to the café on the promenade where three Russians were playing, and with what wonder the two of them watched the violins and the cello, and how they removed the miniature paper sunshades from the balls of ice cream into which they were embedded and licked the edges and stuck them in their hair and got up, first Suzy and then Nina, and began to dance with moves they made up themselves on the spot or that were made up by the composer, who two hundred years ago wrote melodies from the place where it's impossible to ever lie.)

"It's just that it's beneath her to come, the madam," said Merav. The road was already emptied of the columns of soldiers and their pounding vanished.

"We'll give her another two minutes," said the sergeant. He opened the leather cap of his watch and glanced at the time.

"Who's she to not want to be filmed with me," said the actor. He nimbly put together the two parts of the pen that he had taken apart and continued to roll it between his fingers as if rolling himself a cigarette.

"Maybe she needs a limousine, that one," the lighting man turned off the lamp so that it would not heat up, "what did you say your driver's name was?"

"Alfredo," answered the actor. "What kind of a life is that, waiting for days on end in the front cabin just to be able to open the door for me when I arrive. Alfredo, I tell him, get out of the car for a bit, man, so what if it's a Cadillac, haven't you ever seen a Cadillac?" He still rolled the pen between his fingers.

"Your Cadillac," said the sergeant, "how many kilometers has it done? Because you better check a car you buy from a rental company very, very carefully. You can't be too thorough, believe me."

The actor put the tip of the pen in the corner of his mouth. "Only the owner's daughter went in it," he answered with the pen stuck to his lip. "All in all from home to work, from work to home. Even the speedometer showed that."

"Sure," said the sergeant, "sure. What's a speedometer, orders from the general staff? Okay so my rickshaw's noisy, but an Autobianchi making a noise like that?"

"Noisy?" Merav pushed some unruly strands of hair behind her ears. "It would be all right if it was just noisy."

The sergeant looked at her from above the second camera. "What's with you today? Did you get out of bed on the wrong side?"

([After they had finished making a complete mess of the editing room and the kitchenette – an electric kettle, which the sergeant bought with points, long before he bought the camera, and a coffee making kit in a light weapons ammunition box, and some salty pretzels left over from a toast given to someone – the actor stuck his head out the Autobianchi window and shouted: "Who's coming with me? There's room for everyone. In any case Merav's going by rickshaw. Right Merav?" She did not answer, but approached the rickshaw. Gidi opened the door from inside and from the rearview mirror his daughter's tiny shoe kicked to and fro. Merav sat down and straightaway shifted herself; she removed two hard plastic dolls from under her. "You didn't break her Simpsons did you?" "I did," she answered. "Did what?" "Broke them," she answered. "Now I'm sitting on what's left." From the seat she caught the smell of his daughter and the other smell, of his wife, and immediately opened the window.]

[They saw Merav getting into the rickshaw and the actor lifted his hand to the inside mirror. A colored peg was attached to the corner and from its jaws he released some calling cards–three–four, thirty-four–as if he, the soundman, still celebrated his son's birthdays. On the last birthday, where was he? He doesn't know where he was, at the time he didn't know the date, not the day, not the hour: the sun set and rose in the windows of the hut like a yellow yoyo or like a bead of glistening sweat from Brahma or Agni, a thousand beads dripped and sprouted there again, thousands; and at nights he lay on the hard mattress after checking that no scorpions or poisonous centipedes were hiding underneath it, he lay and stared at the oil lamp, and between the bursts of spewing soot the flame would sprout and sparkle and lean longingly toward the rim of the glass and the mosquitoes flying above it: a thousand mosquitoes, thousands, thousands upon thousands upon thousands.]

["Take some," said the actor offering the calling cards he had taken out. "Hand them out to friends. Friends will hand them on to friends, and friends to friends, believe me that's how it gets around, like the flu. What do you mean the flu, lice" – or like the other thing, even whose name Kinneret did not want to think of: it gets spread by blood, by saliva, by salty sweat, by honey of the thighs, by semen – the actor watched her from the mirror. "Don't you ever clean the windshield?" she asked. "Windscreen," he corrected her. And does he clean the windscreen? "What for," he answered, "to be able to see the filth outside better?" But he turned the wiper on and sprayed the windscreen with water – tap water, sea water, all fluids spread it: it flowed from the taps, it drizzled with the rain, it fizzed with the foam – and when it was wiped, the tin dummy missile stood out in front of them painted blue and black, on it an engraved inscription: 5.8.92 – another year to go.]

[The missile looked as if it had been taken from an amusement park, like one of the barrels that only took flight in the eyes of the small children who flew them, sitting inside and growling like engines; and a few mothers – five or six, fifty-six – watched him from a distance as if he, the soundman, was some kind of weirdo or dangerous sex pervert, until he removed himself from there and left. A car hooted at him from across the street, a hoot that would have flung the needle from the gauge of the recording machine, but he didn't hurry up. "Dumb idiot," was shouted from it or from within his head, and he nodded and stepped onto the pavement and said quietly: yes yes yes dumb idiot. On one of the previous birthdays, when the sun outlined a yellow-orange rectangle on the wall, he found his son completely engrossed in some book with pictures that his replacement had brought; he only saw the name of the translator, Emmanuel Lotem, and his son's fringe covering his forehead. And when he eventually lifted his eyes he began to explain to him, to his father, that once, everything, the whole universe, was this small: between his thumb and forefinger, whose baby nails she once whittled down delicately so that he wouldn't be hurt by the scissors, his son held a transparent universe as small as a marble. He then hesitated and enlarged it to a tennis ball, hesitated again and joined his left hand to enlarge it to the proportions of the football with which they played together, or the basketball with which he taught him free throws. "Absolutely everything," his son said and his eyes shone behind the round glasses that she bought him, "all the stars, all the galaxies. Everything's expanding, even now. Like this," his son said and widened his hands until they hit the bookcase that they had put together for him – at the time it was summer, the sweat made her T-shirt cling to the nipples that grew and darkened, and on her forehead droplets glistened, six–seven, sixty-seven, sixty thousand and seven droplets, and he licked them all–"but in the end everything will shrink." From the chair, whose seat's padding she had wondrously concealed with patches of leather and suede, his son contracted his hands, whose fine hair had darkened, and in them he held a football, a tennis ball, a marble, a grain of dust.]

["On your left," the actor then said speaking into the car cigarette lighter that he had taken out of the socket, as if it were a microphone in the hand of a tour guide, "you can see the anti-aircraft guns. They don't even down paper planes. I asked you not to stick your heads out the windows. Kinnerehet" – a grey pigeon landed on one of the barrels as if to be photographed for a poster, but promptly lifted its tail, left its droppings and flew away. The actor slowed the car down. "Get in," he shouted from the window, "I can't stand to see you going by foot," – Shechter waved him on with his hand. They drove slowly in front of him, waiting for him to change his mind and get into the car. The jet of water that the actor sprayed on the windscreen reached the roof and imprinted tiny circles in the dust, but in a different country the wiper squeaked on the windscreen covered in thin ice and white flakes fluttered ahead in the light beams.]

["They'll make room for you," the actor called from the window, "no shortage of room in a Cadillac." "Leave him alone," said the soundman, "the guy wants to be by himself a bit." "That's just it," said the actor, "it's not good that man be alone," and still looked into the mirror. "He waits and he's alone, he tarries and he's alone. It's a song I wrote; Mati Caspi put it to music." He brought the lighter close to his mouth again and began to sing softly – microphones moist with saliva spread it, guitar strings moist with sweat, drumsticks with their beating on the tight warm skin: flick, flick-flack – "Aloooone," he sang, and the mirror became empty. Kinneret's father didn't like this one, but did like old Hebrew songs; he once sang one to her mother: he silenced the band with strong, long fingers, waited for all the knives and forks to fall silent, brought the microphone close to his lips around which every morning rough bristles sprouted and said: "I dedicate the next song to the girl in the purple dress." No knife cut, no fork tapped. "A singer is also a show," he once said to Kinneret, "people want him to move a bit, to make eyes at them." And that he did, her father, to contractors and market stall owners and women who pushed banknotes into his shirt pockets and his trouser pockets and his underpants, that's what her mother said: she lay on the couch in the living room in a wide open gown, held a small glass of Cointreau against the light and said: "It's just that they forget to take their hands out."]

["Be by yourself at home," the actor called to Shechter, "believe me there's no shortage of that." The Autobianchi traveled in front of him and he heard perfectly clearly how the wiper struggled to scrape the frost from the windscreen. He laid his hand on the French girl's knee and felt the fineness of the corduroy stripes and the warmth of her knee, when he asked, like someone waiting for a confirmation: "Genou?" And immediately she removed his hand with one shake of her leg on the accelerator. "Giddy up, Dudush", said the Shechter that he was then, unsure if French coachmen and horsemen used to say that, but in front of them there were no coachmen to be seen, no horsemen, not even a motor car: all were swallowed up in the mist or in the space that opened out from the edge of road downwards. "Cuisse?" he asked

and lifted his hand again; and saw it removed immediately
from her thigh as well as the flakes continuing to pile up on
the bonnet as if the Deux Chevaux was a truck carrying the
dead, but as yet he did not see the dead. He lifted his hand
again and slowly felt his way to the place where there was no
more thigh and quietly asked, "Ganedene?"[9] That's what she
once said to him, she tried to pronounce the guttural "ch" of
Chava[10] and led his fingers there and his body after them –
for a moment she was still beneath his hand, until she started
to speed up. In front of them the road was bathed in the light
beams and instantly became dark and was obliterated like the
abyss alongside, and through the squeaking of the wiper he
heard her say, not to him and not to his fingers, but to the
flock of flakes flying in front of her: "Bien, comme tu veux,"
and saw her suddenly let go of the steering wheel and the road
rush toward the wheels. Her hand felt cold when it touched
him, and his voice sounded as if it rose from the growing
distance as he hoarsely said to her, "De toute façon c'est fini,
non?" Over and over and over the wiper rubbed against the
crust of ice until she braked by the roadside beyond which
there was nothing and said: "Moi, je veux vivre, moi," and
for a while they were hidden by the mist, not from any cars
but from the night itself, until it dissolved into the snow and
faded away.]

["It makes the noise of a Vespa," Na'ama followed the
crop sprayer with her eyes as it circled above the eucalyptuses
and turned to the fields. "A farm laborer, this pilot," the
actor strained to make him out in the car mirror, "a farm
laborer but in the heavens." "I can see you really are a poet,"
Na'ama said to him and Kinneret touched her hand and
asked if she still remembered the cadet pilots. On their
left, beyond the treetops, a greenish cloud was discharged
from the plane, perhaps Parathion; it sank, scattered and
evaporated. "They've probably been booted out by now,"
Na'ama said and watched the small plane in the sky. "What's
with you, the second one was already booted out," Kinneret

9   Hebrew for Paradise – literally: the Garden of Eden
10   Hebrew for Eve

answered and Na'ama asked who the first one was and who the second one was: just so that she knows. "The one who was yours in the beginning," Kinneret answered. But he was not hers nor would he ever be, they all just went to a movie and afterwards listened to Dire Straits in the apartment, and right away the neighbor started knocking on the wall. They stuck a candle in an empty beer can, and the wax dripped on the opening, blocking it, and the shadows danced. Na'ama's cadet pilot was shy, not like Kinneret's – he just laid his head on her legs and closed his eyes, he wasn't disturbed by the knocking on the wall and the banging on the door. His head was closely cropped and for a moment she wondered how the bristles would have felt against her skin had she worn a skirt, yes, that's what she was thinking at the time, and how long his eyelashes were in contrast, their edges curling in the candlelight. The weight of his head and its warmth was very, very pleasant until he removed it and got up – the candle caused his shadow to dance on the ceiling – and he went out to the neighbor and very quietly said to her: "listen lady, we keep the skies clean and that's the thanks we get?" For a moment Dire Straits was heard in the stairwell too, echoing between the walls, and suddenly he burped in the neighbor's face. All at once the beer rose to Na'ama's mouth, she didn't want any more music, she didn't want any more of anything, she just wanted to go home at once.]

[The lighting man's Fiat slowed down alongside the rickshaw. "You sure ran over that tin can," the lighting man called out and overtook, the lid of his car boot wobbled. "Not just a tin can," Merav said and the Simpsons pricked her bottom again: he once ran over porcupines. "Less work for the prisoners," the master sergeant called out to the Fiat pulling away and when they reached the office that they had turned into a film studio, it was already parked there. The lid of the boot, which was tied to the bumper with rope, was slightly open, and in the crack an old rolled up carpet could be seen, whose bulges stretched its worn out fibers. "One might think you did someone in," said the actor who also got out of his car. "Looks like a body, the work of the Mafia. Who did you wrong Eran, who?" "There's no one in the whole world that'd do me wrong," answered the lighting man. The rickshaw's motor still rattled for a moment or two until consenting to be silent, and when Merav slammed the door, the baby shoe danced to and fro, Bart Simpson eased himself into the hollow that she left in the seat, and outside too she could smell perfectly clearly the smell of urine and vomit and deodorant.])

The sergeant glanced at his watch. "Have two minutes passed?" asked Shechter. The sergeant nodded. "She's not coming," said Merav, "forget about her," and the phone rang. The actor, with the pen dangling from his lower lip like a cigarette butt, said: "come on girls, who's doing my make up?" The phone rang. "Girrrls," he said to them in a thin nasal voice sounding between the rings, "who's going to make me pretty?" The phone rang, and from the poster the female soldier's smile revealed one blackened tooth and a pimply rash on her cheek, and a voice cried out: "it's for you, pick it up, it's her from before, from your work," and he now turns around, the investigator – the lizard from the ceiling sees his sweaty collar and the sweat stain on his back – and gets up, goes to the table and picks up the telephone receiver.

"Hello?" he says. "No," he answers. He listens for a while, moves the earpiece slightly away and returns his gaze to the monitor. "I don't know," he says, "maybe they filmed it afterwards. There's more than half an hour of footage, apart from the power cuts" (the female medic told the police, the police told him, and the fire then lit up their faces and soared as if trying to dissolve the entire night, but black and vast it sprawled over the fields and the city and the sea: a man was burning in it.)

4

"Girrrls," said the actor with a nasal twang, "who's going to do my makeup?"

Kinneret sized him up from head to toe. "Na'ama," she said, "she'll make you so pretty everyone will be coming onto a guy like you."

"A girl like you," Na'ama corrected her. The soundman, who was fixing the microphone to a rod, lifted his eyes.

"Didn't you read the script?" the sergeant tightened the second tripod's screws. "I didn't get a copy," the soundman answered and wound one more round before putting the masking tape down. "Merav-sweetie," said the sergeant, "I'm really surprised at you. Didn't you give him a copy? Isn't that what you're supposed to do?" "You didn't tell me to," she answered, "am I supposed to guess everything? And also don't call me 'sweetie' anymore, I already asked you." She then moved the masking tape from the table to the window sill on which Shechter was still leaning and gazing outside.

"It's just unbelievable," said the female medic on the phone, "that they call up reservists for such nonsense. They made up some story" – from his chair, sweat-stained not only on the backrest but also on the seat, he recalls how surprised he was by her chattering away – "about some new female soldiers who come to the base, and some wise guy who dresses up as their female officer. I'm not kidding you" – he found her openness pleasing, after all he had never spoken to her before – "and for that there's a permanent force master sergeant, and they brought girls from the corps entertainment group. And if that's not enough, they called up reservists. My father at his age gets sent to the occupied territories and this is what these guys get to do." For a moment the investigator wondered whether she had spoken to him like someone her father's age, and afterwards derived a curious pleasure from her having spoken of her father and not of a boyfriend. And though this was a foolish notion, since what could there be between him and a

twenty or twenty-one year old female soldier, as he drove he wondered
for a while about this girl who had provided him with a lead concerning
the investigation: would she not be impressed by his profession around
which whole television series were centered, or by his maturity and his life
experience, perhaps it would stand out in contrast to the childishness of
the regular army soldiers around her, since it's not going to be his looks
that impress her.

And when he was told to park his Renault outside the base, he saw
the advantage in it: investigators on television had convertible sports cars
or vans with darkened windows from within which it was possible to
eavesdrop on a crucial conversation in a distant room; there was always
someone who had a set of earphones on his head, like this soundman, and
watched women preening in the sealed windowpane, and the other with a
telescopic camera, whose click-click churned out pictures that documented
second by second the switching of identical briefcases full of bank notes
or drugs or confidential papers; and they all belonged to the secret police
or secret service, and their lives were filled with thrilling mysteries, but in
their apartments the fridge yawned like the mouth of an old man and in it
a few moldy tomato halves, milk gone sour and an open can of beer whose
bubbles were flat: well, at least in that respect he resembled them.

"Putting one over them," the actor explained, "scaring
them with the female officer's rank." The chewed plastic pen
stuck to his lip also while he spoke and he inhaled deeply
from it and began to cough as if choking from the smoke.
"Some piece," he said when he calmed down, "next to it
Shakespeare's Marlowe," and straightaway gave another
rasping cough and cleared his throat.

"A fabrication" – he recited to the soundman, forgoing
the Russian accent he had previously used, "a tale told by an
idiot, full of sound and fury, signifying nothing." Once or
twice he tapped the pen with his finger, as if to remove pieces
of ash from its tip.

"And the welfare officer," the sergeant added, ignoring the
ridicule or not discerning any, "catches him red-handed. She
comes in while he's speaking to the girls."

"But what do you care?" the female medic said on the phone at the time.
"The main thing is that what you need they maybe filmed there in the
background. Besides, what difference does it make now, the man's dead."

"And in the end to make it up to them," the sergeant said, "he takes the girls on a tour of the military outposts, in that way we get to show all the corps weaponry. I filmed them with-"

"Don't say 'sweetie'," said Merav as he looked at her. "Just you dare."

The soundman, who was listening to them from his crouched position, kept silent, his face not revealing his thoughts. In the window, between the sill and the frame, white clouds were floating, slow and long like lazy albino lizards.

"Isn't it a good idea?" asked the actor, "That's worthy of an Oscar!" He inhaled one last time from the chewed plastic pen and flared his nostrils to discharge the smoke, but immediately choked again and spluttered and coughed.

(A lengthy self-stimulating spluttering that rasps, draws phlegm up from the depths of the throat and the lungs, pleading for a glass of water, for God's sake, at least give him some kind of attention, do they want to bury him? Don't they have time to wait? Making a living, first thing tomorrow he's going to bring them the fruits of making a living, just as soon as he closes his deal with the Hungarian. They'll replace all the lounge furniture, together with the carpet, just like that. He would have closed it with him ages ago, if it hadn't been for the Hungarian's partner who all of a sudden butted in and started to open his mouth. But tomorrow they're concluding it, first thing; the Hungarian swore on the bible and on his mother, may she rest in peace. Maybe they'll put in a new kitchen, and plus another two or three more plans like that they'll be well off enough to leave the housing project. His father coughed again, rasped, spluttered, choked, waited to be brought a glass of water; but he stayed where he was and looked at his father and wondered how he endured that war and why the crazy woman threw stones at their shutters, and knew that in the next moment his father will sink into the television armchair once more and press the remote control and flip channels: limousines drove there, and in them sat oil magnates and blondes with jewels shining like the drops of spit on his chin.)

"All right, it's not Antonioni," answered the soundman after a moment. "But it'll do for the army."

"Looking down on us?" Kinneret eyed his tanned fingers around the microphone.

"I'm not looking down on anyone," answered the soundman. (Because even someone who seems to be completely lost, the way that Shechter seems to be by the window or the way he himself was before he went away, gets another chance: he had to travel to the East again to get his, to live in a hut on one of the islands in Thailand and to observe the never-ending column of red ants before the storm, thousands upon thousands of red ants that escaped from the thicket and burst through under the reed mat wall leaving a path paved in the dust behind them; for a while afterwards he still imagined hearing their minute ambling legs and thought that were he to die in this storm – which was rushing straight from the horizon toward the cliff on which the hut stood – perhaps they would carry him off on their backs like a cockroach, but he did not intend to die: after all, at the time he had traveled there in order not to die. On previous nights he would stare through the mosquito net at the beam of the thatched roof and at a lizard holding on to it and for some moments he wondered about the sound made by its eyelids opening and shutting, too fast to follow, perhaps they were transparent and fixed in their place; and about the soft crackling of the lit wick reflected in its pupils; and about all the rustling sounds made by skin shed millions upon millions of times, because the lizard seemed primordial as if created during the six days of the creation: "ten billion years ago," his son once said, and between forefinger and thumb he held something minute like the grain from which everything expanded, and asked him if he knew what a black hole and what a quasar were. That's what his son asked him in his room, when he still went there, but he did not know what a black hole or what a quasar were, not opposite the street in which a bus stopped and not opposite the ocean whose waves rushed, at the time he did not think about a black hole but rather about pussy, yes, its friendly warmth and how it held him tightly, at once soft, moist and demanding, and about the drop from which out came that boy and sprouted and grew and expanded, vast as a foreign universe.)

"They're not going to hear one word if he carries on flying around like that," he said as the crop sprayer rattled on again outside.

(Not a syllable, not a letter, not even the foot of a letter – of one mosquito that stood on a puddle; in the morning when he got out from under the torn mosquito net after having lost track of time and opened the door, whose fibers had been unraveled by the storm, the hollows across from him were all filled with still water and in the purified air a mosquito was seen to land and stand on the surface on legs as slender as threads. Vapor rose from the water in which large papaya leaves were reflected without their fruit that the wind had torn off and split open, and at the foot of the cliff the ocean was silken and smooth as on all the previous days.)

"No, it's not Antonioni," Shechter turned to the soundman. "And it's not Tavianni either." His features were limp and seemed as if they had been loosened and undone, "is anyone pretending that it is?" His eyes were weary as before and if a stray spark momentarily flickered in them, it soon turned to ash and vanished. "Who goes to the Cinematheque anymore?"

"Isn't that a pity?" asked the soundman. He passed his fingers through his hair, which was already beginning to grey and which suited his tan as did the deepening lines from both sides of his nostrils to the corners of his mouth. "Sometimes they show good things there." The shade of his blue eyes obscured his virile, confident appearance, not a piercing steel blue, but a soft light blue, like his shirt whose one button dangled from its buttonhole. "Don't ever think that this nonsense is all there is, never ever." He held the microphone again and blew on it, "it's not good for the soul, believe me."

"The soul?" Shechter turned from the window, "we've forgotten all about the soul. You have to make a living, that's what you have to do. Do you know when I was last there?"

(At the time the Cinematheque was still housed in the State Lottery building, and before the film he made for his finals was screened, a few people with worn-out briefcases and worn-out faces left the hall having waited for the big win that would change their lives, just as he, the young Shechter, waited for the applause for his film; and one of them, a thin, unshaven man exuding a bad smell, held a crinkled lottery ticket in his hand as Shechter would later hold the reel of his film. "There's no God," the thin man said to him and squashed a cigarette butt with his shoe until it was torn to shreds. The name Antonioni had a foreign ring to it, as now did the sound of Tavianni, both resounded across the open space of the room like the bell tied to the neck of the crow in the film *Kaos* or *San Lorenzo*, he doesn't remember anymore: ringing in the air, foreign, fading away and falling silent even before they were wiped out by the rhythmic rattling of the crop sprayer; gradually it advanced to the downy white wisps as if intending to spray them as well.)

"Is there enough light?" the lighting man asked. He got down from the chair after attaching a small lamp to the window frame with a clasp. On his right and on his left were the two standing lamps, and on their aluminum tripods streamed murky drops of spray with dissolved rust.

"For the time being there's enough," answered Shechter and returned his gaze to the window.

"No, because if there's not," said the lighting man, "I can fetch the secret weapon from the car."

"Leave it," said the sergeant from above the second camera, cleaning its eyepiece with a piece of flannel.

"I can bring it chop-chop," said the lighting man. "We won't need these small ones at all with the kind of light it makes."

"We can do without it," said the sergeant. He unfolded the piece of flannel and turned it on its clean side.

"A secret weapon," said the lighting man, "and that's what you've got to say about it? Not nice of you, really not nice."

(A large soft-light lamp, heavy and old-fashioned, which he cunningly managed to get hold of from the company that he had begun working for, and which now lay in the boot of the Fiat wrapped in a carpet the way he bundled himself up in a blanket the months following his discharge: he lay in bed at home and did nothing, over and over he repeatedly heard what they said at the grocer the moment he left there – "the higher the tree, the further the apple falls from it. Look at his father and look at him" – again and again he heard it and closed his eyes opposite the phone that he had taken off the hook so that he wouldn't know she wasn't calling: not today, not tomorrow nor any other day.

He was the last to call, during the war, from a public telephone, and when he heard what she said to him, he let the receiver fall and sway to and fro, beneath the obscenities written there. And at nights, in his sleep, he sometimes still heard someone groaning on the other side of the door and begging him to open, but it was just his father with one of his lady friends, and then he would press the pillow over his ears and tighten it; and afterwards, when summer came and made it impossible to remain in bed, he got up and went to find work with one of the large production companies, there wasn't a place he didn't try: he was sure that with his experience, three years in a video unit at an air force training base, he would find work easily. It was just that the look they threw his way made him feel so small, even his father didn't make him feel that small: **let's see if you are a man**. Did you study at university? Camera Obscura Institute? Where did you study, Tzrifin? He made them laugh.)

"What, don't I know how it'll end?" the sergeant said. "When we really need it, it won't work. But of course he has to go. Go on, why not, then we'll be left with nothing."

Opposite him, between the wall and the door that the lighting man opened, a widening strip of sky and foliage and asphalt could already be seen, until it stopped, narrowed and slammed shut.

(For a month the lighting man had been working in the storeroom of a catering company until it became bankrupt, and then he came to this company that supplies sound and lighting equipment for events. But it showed potential for development: you can never tell, not like the others that could only fail. Yes that's how it goes, maybe even his father's could still bomb **let's see let's see**. He told the sergeant that he got on well with the boss, he so wanted to show how he was coping in civilian life, but the truth was that he had to beg the storekeeper; he made his life a misery, that storekeeper, only because he tried to impress him by telling him that he was the manager of the catering company storeroom. A manager. The son of a bitch wanted to see him on all fours, wanted him to lick his ass just for an old lamp that nobody there used anyway: who used it, who? Until in the end he promised to tidy the storeroom with him not when he brings it back, now. First tidy up; then take it.)

"What, don't I know how it'll end?" repeated the sergeant. "There's absolutely no doubt about these things. And there's still light left" – he turned his head to the window – "the sun's hardly reached the eucalyptus tree and he's already putting me under pressure. These kids," he turned to Shechter, "tell me, were we like that?"

Shechter did not answer.

In the window, into which the soundman was also looking, the treetops thrust themselves toward the sphere of the sun like nails into the head of a Fakir.

"The sun is rising in the sky-"

The actor's voice was heard from the inner room and right away Na'ama was heard hushing him from there: "I can't do your makeup like this!" Kinneret looked at the closed door for a moment.

"Mother se-eeeeends her son Yossi-"

(She had her fill of that song; it was coming out of all her orifices, coming out of her straight into the water: in a short, narrow black mini the water rumbled-mumbled and rumbled-murmured pleasing murmurings, slaking starved private parts, salty and soaking.)

"Go and bring-"

(The sun sent flickering rays to her and under her knees the water burrowed, trickled, splashed, pulled. The sun blanched, dazzled, burnt until they blocked it, the two heads. They drifted toward each other, Nulit's sail and the soldier's sail drifted around, drifted until they suddenly bumped into each other: flack. But it was a ping-pong ball that fell in the water and a wave came and another wave. Nulit took her with her soldier boyfriend: he put her on his shoulders, the soldier, she held on to his large head and his hair tickled her nose. She sneezed. Who sneezed? Kinnelet?)

"A bottle of milk,
Go quickly and don't forgeeet-"

"It's enough already," said Na'ama from the other side of the door. "I can't put makeup on you like this."
(Nulit folded everyone's clothes; they were as tall as the sand castle. And who'll put the shells on? Who'll put them on? Kinnelet! Do you promise not to move? They stood above her and a cloud now sat on the soldier's shoulders, pure white. They didn't look at her, they looked at each other. Nulit's bathing suit was orange and the soldier's blue, Nulit's had two parts and the soldier's one. Nulit looked at the soldier's costume and suddenly laughed. What did he have there? He raced to the water, the soldier, splashing with his feet, splashing with his hands, splashing water and sparkles, and Nulit raced too. Don't move! I'll give you a hiding!)

The door opened and the lighting man dragged in a large heavy tripod with four lamps attached to the pole crosswise at the top. "How's this?" he asked and wiped his hands on his trousers.

"You'll roast us with that," said the sergeant. "And in the end, when we really need it – it won't work. I'm talking from experience, believe me. When you need something the most – you can forget about it. Take me, for example, when I needed a car the most, for a furlough, the transport officer decides it's not for use."

"As if he didn't have a reason," Merav said. She moved the roll of masking tape from the sill to the small cupboard, and on the side panel one could see the engravings with which someone had been counting the days remaining until his discharge.

"Reasons?" asked the sergeant. "There's never a shortage of reasons, let him just fix it if there's something wrong with it, not let it stand there for no reason at all."

(What, as if he doesn't know the transport officer. If he had left the rickshaw with him at the time, on the furlough, he could have long forgotten about it. Not that there's nothing to fix, sure there is, it hardly had enough pulling power to fetch his daughter from nursery school. And how much can she weigh, like a bird – he once used to sit her on the palm of his hand when she was really small, and sometimes he would chew a slice of orange for her and pass it straight to her mouth, yes – still, the first day somehow went off okay, but afterwards the children started to laugh at her because of her father's car. They pushed their little faces through the bars of the fence and one of them pointed to the rickshaw and yelled at the top of his voice: "Olls-Oyce! Olls-Oyce!" Obviously their mothers had had something to say about it, because children themselves, well, he's not saying they're angels, he remembers full well what went on in his neighborhood, but who can be mad at children now?)

"But why should he fix it, for all he cares let it stand there for a month."

(Anyway it would have been impossible to travel to the kibbutz with it, besides which, for a whole year his wife didn't tell anyone at all that she had a master sergeant for a boyfriend, let alone in anti-aircraft. He didn't blame her, no, why should he. Not even in the beginning when he still didn't know if he had any hope with her at all. From the shower window he could see her friends sitting on the lawn and talking – green, green lawn, there wasn't a place that the sprinklers didn't reach – all of them were pilots and officers and they looked like that guy who was photographed for the poster of the Techia political party: with a waving forelock, a fearless look and an upright body. At the time he looked at them through the net; in one place it was slightly torn and he was already planning how to fix it, when suddenly the hot water was finished and he realized that he had forgotten the towel. He began to shrivel all over from the cold.)

"Since you've already brought it, you might as well put it together," said Shechter.

The lighting man placed the lamp cable against the wall and patted the back of the plug in order to insert it in its place. He hit it again with the back of his hand to fix the loose connection there, then hit it a third time and only then was the room flooded in light.

"How's that? Who needs the small ones, one like this directed at the ceiling is enough."

He removed the sheets of cellophane from the other lamps and moved them to the globes of the soft-light lamp to compare its shades to the shades of daylight, but when the beams turned blue on the ceiling they seemed slightly cooler than the light of the sun that had begun to take leave of the room. Outside through the window frame, it became more and more refined on the leaves of the eucalyptus trees and also took leave of the two figures standing beneath them.

The prisoner on the right was careful not to make any unnecessary movement with the palm of his hand. "Film me, film me!" he called from the road and the rake stayed balanced on the palm of his hand. The other prisoner stared for a moment at the shadow as it trembled and elongated the prongs on the asphalt.

"Who's filming," said the sergeant from the window, "we haven't even started yet."

The rake leaned, slanted, overturned and Weintraub caught it in his left hand. "Why not? You got problems?" He balanced the rake once again on the palm of his hand. "Is Eran making trouble? Don't be fooled by him busy with his lamps. Eran's a hero, like his father."

The lighting man did not answer.

"As if there weren't enough clowns inside?" The female medic was saying into the phone in an animated voice, "there was also one outside."

Na'ama came out of the inner room, in her right hand an open lipstick and in her left the stub of a black eyeliner. For a moment she looked at the lighting man and then at the prisoner outside, whose rake was wobbling until it stabilized again in his palm. "Ta-tum," she announced like a trumpeter, "here she is!"

From the inner room, in the gap left by the open door, a hand emerged slowly and its red-nailed fingers fluttered in the air. It was followed by a large sole with a calloused ankle slowly extended and a hairy calf thickening to the knee and the rim of the skirt. Only after a while, from above the long tunic and the female officer's rank was the actor's face revealed beneath a brown tattered wig. He was heavily made-up: his lips smeared with glossy lipstick, his cheeks powdered and his eyebrows slanted upwards, thinning at the ends.

"What do you think of him?" Na'ama spun him round in his place as if he was some large mannequin.

(Or like the way she did her sister's makeup on the roof: she didn't stand but sat in front of her on one of the chairs that the neighbors had disposed of on the roof, and when afterwards she combed her out again, she noticed the grey hairs that had begun to appear, another and another and another until she stopped counting, and a flake of dandruff shed from somewhere bringing tears to Na'ama's eyes, and all at once her nose clogged up as well. She picked up a discarded Kleenex and wiped everything away before her sister would notice, because that's all she needed, to think that she's being pitied, moreover by her little sister. The Kleenex was crumpled and in it all the remnants of the lipstick from her sister's blind date – "for a whole hour he didn't say one word, an hour, I swear to you! For an hour he sat and kept quiet like some nutcase. That's my fate, all the nutcases will come my way" – and when she turned her head to Na'ama and saw how her face was smeared with the remnants of the lipstick, she began to laugh a weary laugh, sluggish even before starting. "Sis," she said when it ended, in a voice gravelly from cigarettes, "did you do it for me, to make me laugh?" She hugged her with all her might and Na'ama then smelt her sweat through the perfume that she had previously bought for her.)

She spun the actor around in his place once and once again, over a head shorter than him, holding on to his hips and lifting the tips of her fingers so as not to stain the skirt he was wearing, with lipstick and eyeliner.

The actor blinked, placed five red nails on his hips with a coquettish movement and spun around in his place like a model. "What do you think?" he asked.

(On the street below, when the noise of the cars subsided for a moment, someone said at the top of his voice: "your business is with him, not with me. What did I ever do to you, nothing. You came and asked me for the phone, so what do you want, for me to say no?" Pieces of whitewash fell from the railing, and in the street beneath them they saw a bearded man with a skullcap bending to the window of a delivery van. "I'll tell you what to do." he lowered his voice, "sue him under Jewish law, that's what you should do, to stop other people from being suckers." And the driver said from inside: "what are you talking about, Jewish law. I'll break his balls!" Suddenly her sister began to laugh a hearty laugh, choking, and when Na'ama patted her on the back, through the opening of her dressing gown she saw how her breasts jiggled, heavy and flabby. "It's from the cigarettes," her sister said becoming even hoarser, "I swear I don't know what'll kill me first, them or loneliness." That's how she spoke, Na'ama's sister, on the roof.)

"Na'ama," said the lighting man, "do you mean to tell me that he got dressed in there while you watched?"

"He changed in the toilet," answered Na'ama, "you idiot." She peeked into the lamp and straightaway felt her cheek as if a pimple was already forming there in the light.

"In the toilet," Kinneret repeated what she said. She scrutinized the actor from the soles of his feet to his wig, and when she stood opposite him he seemed like a ridiculous negative of herself: she was almost as tall as him and her lips were fleshy like his, but his jaw was square between his cheeks, and the uniform he had got hold of hung on his body and didn't curve the way her uniform did. She asked him to move a little.

"But I can't move," he twanged. "Everything will get ruined."

She placed her hand on his hip and turned him round slightly. Then she rested the bottom of her palm on his cheek and retouched the line of black makeup around his eye when he began to blink. She held his jaw around the red lips and turned his other cheek toward her; with a pencil she also thickened the line encircling his right eye, elongating and slanting it upwards. All the while he kept still beneath her hand.

"In the end he looked like a sex pervert," said the female medic. "But what difference does it make now."

"Is that what you wanted him to look like?" asked the soundman.

"What difference does it make anyway," answered Shechter. "Let him stay as he is."

The soundman looked at his eyes closely and Shechter turned his head to the window. "Once you wouldn't have spoken that way."

"Once," answered Shechter, "there're lots of things I wouldn't have done once, that's how it is; you grow up."

"When we were students," the soundman turned to the sergeant, who was about their age but appeared younger than both, "he was capable of suddenly insisting on some nonsense, nobody could tell what had gotten into him. It was only in the end that they saw how right he was. Should I remind you?" He turned to Shechter again.

"No," replied Shechter still looking out the window. "I was a different person then. People change. Maybe you're the only one who stayed the same."

"A lot's happened to me," said the soundman. "You yourself know that."

"Yes, but basically?"

For a while the soundman busied himself with the gauge buttons and their quivering dials. "Should I take that as a compliment or an insult?"

"A compliment," answered Shechter. "You think that I wouldn't want to stay as I was?"

"You could still work on yourself," said the soundman. Owing to the heat generated by the lamp, he rolled his shirtsleeves up further. "What I mean is, to do something with yourself – get back into things. It's never too late."

Behind, from the inner room, the actor watched them with his made-up eyes. "Return to the path, lad," he scolded Shechter with his red lips and lifted his hand gesturing in a wide arc to the window: "For across the field – a chasm. Be silent and hear the words of one damned, one whom the land has spewed. It's from the Greeks," he said in his regular voice, "not Shakespeare."

"No, I can't kid myself," said Shechter.

"I didn't mean that you should kid yourself," the soundman watched his back.

"I know just what you meant." In the window frame above Shechter's head, the white clouds were still floating almost at the level of the treetops. "Do you know what your problem is Joe? You've become like those born again believers who think that the whole world has to think the way they do.

Okay if it was just thinking, let them think what they want, but straightaway they try to convince everyone else as well."

"They've seen the light," said the actor. He lifted his hand again and this time gestured to the lamp that cast its bluish beams on the ceiling. "Dark is dark, fair is fair, through the fog and filthy air. Macbeth."

The soundman looked at him for a while above the recording machine. "I actually always saw it," he said. "Long before my trip to the east," he turned to Shechter. "India? The Himalayas? The islands? They just strengthened it for me, but it didn't start there. I also don't remember ever trying to convince you about anything. Not during studies and not during work. Tell me once, just once, when I tried to convince you. I didn't even try to convince my wife. I never even said a word to my son, not a word. I let him think whatever he wants to. Either he'll get there or he won't."

"Okay, forget about what I said," said Shechter.

"One thing I did want was that he wouldn't be like those kids who are glued to their computer games the whole day long and not aware of anything else. That's all that mattered to me, that he keeps his eyes open and looks around. Did I ever force him to do something? Never."

"Okay, let it go," said Shechter. "Forget what I said, it wasn't to the point."

Kinneret, who had returned to the center of the room, touched Na'ama's hand. "The adults are talking," she said. "Like we don't understand."

"Adults?" said Shechter without turning his head to her. "We're not adults at all, just old men." Across from him, between the sill and the frame, the downy wisps continued to intertwine like white loops in the tail of a kite.

"It's no big deal how old you are," said Kinneret. He didn't answer and she looked at the soundman questioningly, but his fingers were already busying themselves again with the recording buttons. On his arm, past the fold of his shirtsleeve, a tattooed spiral with a spiked end was revealed.

"They think we're little girls," said Kinneret. "Isn't that insulting?" She moved through the room between the tripods of the small lamps that were turned off but remained in position, and between the small table with electric extension cables piled on it, and between the seven of them who were standing with her in the room: owing to the equipment that filled it, every movement disturbed the delicate balance sustained there, like between people squeezed together in an elevator.

"Tell them what we've been through in our lives," said Na'ama, "maybe they'll learn something."

The soundman let go of the button he turned, and lifted his head toward her. "You just caught him on a bad day," he said, "he's not always like this." He gestured to Shechter with his eyebrow, and beyond him, between the eucalyptus trees in the window, the road to the base could be seen; grey and empty, and dissected section after section by the painted tree trunks.

"I don't need to be defended yet," said Shechter. "For the time being I can manage by myself."

(In a far off winter before he had begun his studies he was traveling on some mountainous road paved with light beams section after section, in front of him a mass of white flakes piling up on the engine bonnet as if the Deux Chevaux was transformed into a truck carrying the dead, but as yet he did not know about war and not about the dead.)

"What," the actor was reminded and asked from the entrance, "isn't this how you wanted the makeup?"

(Not about the dead and not how their smell permeates the nostrils and ear canals and the body's pores, bearing down on everything in its path: illuminated boulevards thronging with people, paving stones on which pale yellow lamplight shines, a plait loosened on an unblemished breathing back.)

"This way you're gonna have yourself a real star, not just anyone."

(And in a winter even further off, in nineteen hundred and five – a year that was inconceivable, even though Shechter's grandfather had lived through it – out of all the masses who demonstrated outside the winter palace of the czar until they were shot at, it happened to be Rutenberg who saved their leader: he cut off his beard, dressed him in women's clothing and rescued him from being held by the soldiers; that's what his father told him in his room about one January in Petersburg, a city more beautiful than Paris according to him, although he had never visited it. His father was captivated by the spell of Rutenberg, even before he founded the electrical plant at Naharayim, he was captivated by that brave deed and by the action he took against that same priest toward the end, when it became apparent that he had betrayed his people. Overall he admired fearless men, leaders and revolutionaries, explorers and acclaimed inventors, and nightly he would relate their stories to Shechter the boy in his room.)

"The success or failure of a movie rests on its leading lady."

(And years later, when he returned from Paris the day after the war broke out and took his boots down from the storage space, his father looked at him with apprehension, and for one solitary moment with pride too, as if before his eyes his son had become a fearless man. But from above the hotel basin in the Latin Quarter it was not of daring deeds he was thinking, not of his homeland and not of any of the people he knew there, but only of the French girl: that's how he referred to her afterwards and not by her name, because the sound of each syllable was too painful. In the hotel folding mirror he saw his face completely bare not only because of the bohemian beard that was cut off in the basin, but also from that resource from which the previous Shechter had made a movie and the resource from which he had withstood the entire screening and the resource from which he returned to Paris and the resource from which he believed he could do whatever he desired with his life: should he so desire ultimately he'll become a director of full-length features, should he so desire he'll get back the French girl whom he met before his studies: that's what that Shechter thought.)

"Stay the way you are," he said to the actor.

(And before that there had been a different Shechter, one who sat with his father in a boat sailing on the Yarkon, holding the oar with both hands and trying to row with it like Doolittle on his way to rescue the Red Indian researcher who was trapped in the mouth of a volcano; Long Arrow, the son of Golden Arrow was what the researcher was called, the beetle that he sent with a note tied to its foot was called Yabizri, perhaps Jabizri, the way Doolittle was called Johan and his dog Yip in the old books published by Omanut. They sailed to the ends of the earth – once the monkey Chee-Chee dressed up as a woman in a floral dress and a wide-brimmed hat – and they flew to the moon riding on the back of a giant moth and fell to one of its craters, holding on to enormous flowers for parachutes. "Jumping was Extraordinarily Easy," was written on a fine line beneath the illustration and, "We Land upon a New World."

"What difference does it make now?"

(It was meant to be comic relief – the master sergeant learned the term from Shechter – no more, before they start to show the new recruits all the force's artillery and missiles. And now the actor stood before him made-up like some kind of pervert. A genuine pervert, not just some son of a bitch who wouldn't piss your way, no shortage of those. In the movie, *A Gang like Ours*, which he remembered the same way he did the songs from that period, someone dressed up as the company commander and interviewed the new recruits who were being enlisted in a black and white tent, but the scriptwriter said you have to move with the times: doesn't he know what goes on? What, doesn't he ever go out with his wife around town? That's what goes nowadays; nobody makes a fuss of it.)

"Don't do me any favors," said the actor.

(All in all just some comic relief straight after which they move on to a tour of the military outposts. In the middle there's still a flashback to the war, yes, and there's also the theme song that the girls will sing in the background. "What, don't you ever go out with your wife?" the scriptwriter asked him. No, he hardly goes out with her, he answered, they're happy to stay at home. What's wrong with home? After they put the little one to bed and watch a bit of television, their day is over, even though it's still early. They go straight off to the bedroom, but he didn't tell him that. Straight there and whoever was in the mood first turned on the lamp, which the sergeant made from a bottle; his brother-in-law brought it from overseas, it took them almost a year to drink it all. The one who was in the mood first turned the lamp on in the bedroom, so that the other one knew they were in the mood, there wasn't a night that that lamp wasn't turned on.)

"What, don't you think I'm a pretty girl?" the actor asked.

"Take my word for it," said the lighting man, "even your mother wouldn't recognize you now."

"I ask you," the actor pushed aside a strand of hair from his cheek, "not to speak of my mother. My mother was truly beautiful, not like me who turned out like this." Strands of the wig's hair thinned out on to his shoulders and he tried to smooth them down with his fingers.

"Maybe wet them a bit," Kinneret said to him.

"It's enough that my mother's beautiful," he answered her, "was." Again he smoothed down the strands of hair.

"A tiny drop of water."

(An entire ocean advances and withdraws, advances and withdraws, advances and wets the hair and the black dress and the black tights and the black shoes and the black panties.)

"Just so that it doesn't become wild."

(But they weren't there anymore. Where were they? They stayed in the toilet at the pub, after the performance there, and above her, in the grey-blue sky between night and morning, a kingfisher glided, back curved, beak curved. The beak was long, and suddenly it dived to the water, not toward her, but immediately she tightened her legs.)

The actor, who left his wig alone, intertwined his arms with those of Na'ama and Kinneret and led them slowly to the door. "You don't have to be ashamed of me anymore," he said to them wiggling his behind toward one of them and then to the other, "now we can be friends and hug." He shoved the door wide open with his leg, and his hairy calf was lit in the lamplight. "When I was a little boy, a little girl," – from within the lines of makeup defining his eyes he looked alternately to his right and to his left and fluttered his eyelids from one to the other – "the whole time I wondered why my mother didn't come to me anymore at night to hug and kiss me. I really wondered about that, I swear to you. May I drop dead if I'm lying. I waited and waited, I cried and cried and who didn't come? Michael's mother."[14]

Before the door was about to close the two of them released their arms from him and hurried outside; only the female soldier in the poster still watched him smiling her flawed smile. "We can be girlfriends," he also said to her in a trembling high-pitched voice and blew the poster a kiss with his red lips. Outside, above the darkening treetops of the eucalyptuses the crop spraying plane could be heard again, as if the blown kiss had been put into motion by the stubborn rattling engine.

"Are you ready?" asked Shechter.

"We're always ready," said the sergeant. The actor, who sat on the swivel chair behind the table, began to sing softly in a deep voice, drumming with the ends of his lacquered fingernails and blinking in rhythm like a giant doll: "We're aaalllways" – he blinked at the lighting man: "Not so, honey, you and your girlfriend, your fiancée, your future wife, the mother of your children. In the daylight and in the dead of night?" The lighting man began to fiddle with the lamp again.

"Camera ready?" asked Shechter.

"Camera ready," answered the sergeant.

"Soundman ready?" asked Shechter.

"Soundman ready," answered the soundman.

"Camera run," said Shechter.

"I heard them all the way up to the clinic," the female medic said. "But they also filmed before that, they filmed everything with the sergeant's camera." That's what she said on the phone in the morning, before he got into his old car to which the smell of his body clung as to clothing, and all the kilometers traversed with it wore down the tires while at the same time were wrapped around them: in moments of tiredness they seemed to be hanging on the engine's pistons or dragging his body through the floorboard, while at the same time they were rebuffing him and banishing him onwards, onwards, to other places where he only stopped for refueling or drinking or urinating or for a brief stretching of the limbs by the side of

14   Paraphrase of a famous Israeli children's poem, "Michael"

the road, on soft ground that showed him in his shadow the outline of his body, after days of avoiding looking at it in the mirror.

"Camera running!" said the sergeant and a small red light bulb indicated it had begun to film.

(The light bulb was called a tele-light and when anchorman Chaim Yavin would turn to the left or the right he was simply turning to the tele-light that was switched on; the sergeant also learned that at the course in Tzrifin. It was large, not like this light bulb that is only semi-professional, but for their needs it was enough and also for his family it was enough, yes; he's not saying it was legal back then, he's not saying that he didn't know, he's not someone who plays innocent. No, no way. But if let's say he had left it here at the time, on that Saturday, what, would it have been safer? With all those who stay here on a Saturday and with all their friends who come to visit them entering the base freely, without anyone checking them at all. Who broke into the armory, wasn't it one of them? Definitely one of them.)

"Quiet, we're filming!" Merav called from the window to anyone who might be passing on the road.

(Only once during his entire service did he take the camera out with him, only once, and just then the base commander decided on an inspection, and now he's paying for it, the sergeant – with interest: see, he brought his private Panasonic from home, it was only after then that he bought it, with points. Did anyone tell him to bring it? Did anyone say one word? But he brought it to be able to cover everything in long shots as well, if necessary, only because he cares, yes, and so that they'll have a souvenir of all their carryings on. Yes, a souvenir. Because in the end the things you miss most are the silly carryings on. You miss everything, but the very most is the silliness. He learned his lesson very well and he's not sorry. The Saturday when he took the camera, the little one came out so cute that every time he would look at her after that, every time without fail, yes, with all the mess it got him into, there wasn't a time when he didn't laugh all over again at the faces she made, at the tongue she pulled, at the ears that she folded forwards, and the way she blew her cheeks up as if they didn't already look like two apples. And once, when he sat idly at work, not that it happened often but there were times, he even thought of sending it to some production company, to surprise his wife like that: why not, they could use the little one in some commercial or public service broadcast, he wasn't afraid that she might be spoiled by it. She was made of fine stuff, like his wife, a product of love – they called her Keren, but between themselves they called her "the little one"; and never said "your daughter," the way all sorts of couples they knew would say when irritable – yes, let everyone see just how wonderful she is. Perhaps Shechter can put in a word.)

"Action," called Shechter. The door opened.

Kinneret and Na'ama stood in the entrance and saluted. On the other side of the table the actor motioned with disdain, fluttering his red fingernails one after the other. "Come girls," he said to them in a high voice, "please be seated." They drew near to the table and sat opposite him, first Kinneret and then Na'ama.

"What's your name?" he asked Kinneret in the same high-pitched authoritative voice.

"Kinneret," she replied. She pulled her skirt over her thighs and placed her hands in her lap.

"What, did you decide to use real names?" asked Merav. She shifted strands of unruly hair behind her ear, and in her other hand still held the file that earlier she had turned toward the camera with the number of the scene and the shot written on its back.

"Yes sweetie," said the sergeant, "just when your mind was somewhere else." Again he placed his eye to the eyepiece of the second camera and with the zoom button restored the picture to its previous position.

"My mind wasn't in any other place. You must have decided when I wasn't around."

"Sweetie," said the sergeant, "I don't make any decisions when you're not around. We decided that a while ago. You must have been daydreaming."

(But Merav never ever dreams, neither at night nor when she's sick; she just can't lie to herself, she even stopped wearing fancy dress a year before everyone else: she had once been the queen of the night, a butterfly, a ballet dancer, until she decided to stop, and the time she crossed the empty lot in her school uniform she smelt the smell of bits of metal rising from the welding workshop and the smell of sawdust from the carpenters and the smell of pita bread being baked in the small bakery and also the smell of rain, it always rained on Purim. Above the grating of metals and the sawing of wood, the school loudspeakers sounded, and a nondescript voice said, not to her: "one, one-two, one, one-two," from the courtyard where ninjas and beauty queens and Queen Esthers stood, and she no longer envied them.)

"I wasn't daydreaming," she said, inserting behind her ear a pencil stub that had been shut between the pages of the file.

(Her sister sat on the white chair of a queen, seemingly in fancy dress the way everyone appeared to be, all the family relatives and the neighbors who were dressed in festive clothes and wedding garb. The journalists from the local paper where her sister worked also seemed to be in fancy dress, she too was in fancy dress in what Claudine had created for her, as if all the food and drink on the buffet, which Laniado deemed fit to lay on, was a spread of Purim gifts. Her small sisters were still dancing around the marble floor, delicate, light and airy, and from the local paper's table, whose reporters reported only on traffic and sewage problems and on the local football team that was relegated, she heard someone say: "The bride's wearing a Dior dress and the groom an Armani suit," and opposite her Cohen Productions turned on the sun gun and her sister was instantaneously flooded by a dazzling white.)

"I never ever dream."

(There are people who can, but not her. There was hardly anyone in the hall, there had been money for the hall but not for the catering, the main thing is they would say that his daughter's wedding was held in a hall, and above the half empty marble floor all the conversations from the tables could be heard, all those who sat down first were planning to take the flower arrangements home. From the typist's table, behind bottles of family size Fanta in which tiny bubbles slowly rose, someone said: "so what if it's got a stamp saying it's gold, anyone can put a stamp on. Believe me, Esti, it's no problem at all. You can buy them for ten shekels at the Central Bus Station, 'gold' she tells me." It was quiet for a moment and then she said: "what, are you insulted or something, what, have I got gold, Esti? Did you ever see me with gold on?" From the buffet, on which clusters of grapes were piled up and seemed as dusty as the red carpet leading to the bridal chair, some of the neighbors were watching Cohen Productions and a thin girl said: "what, you think Pnina Rosenblum's[15] pretty? Pnina Rosenblum's disgusting. Dis-gus-ting!" Another girl, also a friend of the twins, who below her face had the rounded body of a small woman, said: "yes, but she's so attractive, so what if she isn't pretty if she's so attractive," and from behind her, her grandfather mumbled over and over: "eye of a woman and all those near her – eye of a virgin, eye of a married woman, eye of a widow and all kinds of evil eyes existing in the world that watched and looked and spoke with the evil eye – on Smadar the daughter of Abraham – I decree and swear," and her brother turned his head, because standing in the entrance to the hall was Moshon. "Gucci boots," one of journalists said and fell silent immediately, and from the first table was heard a nose being blown and an appeasing voice: "but what did I say, Esti, what? Gold doesn't mean a thing to me, Esti, believe me. If someone wants us, they'll take us as we are with or without the gold" – Moshon was still watching everyone from the entrance – and from the left the thin girl said: "Sandra, oh yes! Sandra's gorgeous! Wasn't she gorgeous in yesterday's episode? Of course she was gorgeous! But Pnina Rosenblum, no way!" And in the harsh light of the sun gun – Moshon

15   A famous Israeli model

was already beginning to approach from the other end of the hall – her friend asked if she thought Smadi looked a little like the singer Rita? With all that light on her, just like in a performance? In a delicate, hushed voice she began to hum "The Sailor's Love," inserting a word into the humming and then another until she sang them all: she sang with devotion and a singleness of mind against the wall in Laniado's hall, closing her eyes, whose eyelids and short eyelashes were magnified by glasses, and sang: *"heeee never kneeeeeew… that she envieeed the ships"* – "eat something," said Moshon and advanced further, "why not" – and one of the girls quietly explained: "it's because he's at sea most of the time, after all he's a sailor and that's why she envies the ships like that." And for a single moment in the harsh white light, Merav could see them, all those ships sailing with white sails made of wedding dresses, drifting on Laniado's empty floor as if on a sea of marble.)

"Kinneret who?" asked the actor pleasantly after they had begun again. He charmingly brushed some strands of hair aside from his forehead.

"Kinneret Biran," she answered.

"Kinneret Biran what?" he asked, his fingers fluttering on the table and drumming on it silently.

Kinneret stole a glance to her right. Na'ama mouthed a word with her lips and looked straight ahead. "Kinneret Biran, commander," said Kinneret.

"And your name my dear?" the actor turned to Na'ama and his fingers rested on the table.

"Na'ama Kedmi, commander," answered Na'ama.

"Fine," said the actor contentedly, "I see that you are fast learners." With his fingers he smoothed down the strand of hair that had curled and blinked twice. "Do you have a boyfriend, Na'ama Kedmi?" She flinched in her chair with an exaggerated embarrassment, something they perhaps had used in the group's skits. "You needn't be shy with me," he said to her, "I'm forever taking an interest in my soldiers."

Na'ama hesitated and lowered her eyes. "N-no," she mumbled. Across from her the actor took out a piece of paper from the drawer, held a pen, and with much pleasure asked: "so what is your telephone number, Na'ama?"

"Such stupidity," the female medic had said to him in the morning in the earpiece – the pale yellow earpiece of the old-fashioned telephone that he didn't bother replacing with another – "but what do you care? Maybe what you're looking for will be there. I mean from the beginning, what caused it." And for a while during the drive, more than on who got burnt there, he reflected on her, according to the little he knew and largely on what he surmised: a young girl, who possibly had previously taken a course in biology and straight after her discharge will perhaps begin to study medicine, if she doesn't travel first to the Far East or South America; and in another twenty or thirty years' time perhaps she'll be in charge of a department in some large hospital, and in the corridors a trail of interns and nurses will follow and heed her every word, as he himself heeded her on the phone: through the smell of his breath that clung to the mouthpiece he then imagined for a moment the smell of her youthfulness rising toward him from the small holes.

"Okay," said Shechter, "let's say the door opens and the welfare officer appears." He hit the armrest of the chair beside him to signal its opening and the actor rose in a frenzy. The sergeant followed him with the second camera: when he got up, when he looked left and right, when he turned to the window, when put he his leg out over the sill, and when his wig dropped from his head.

"Should I carry on?" he asked in his regular voice and both feet already out the window.

"No," said Shechter, "we'll do it again."

"You've got him all motivated," the actor called out to the soundman, "now we'll never hear the end of it."

"This is nothing compared to what he used to be like." In the corner of the room, sitting and bent over, the soundman watched the recording machine until the fine needle steadied in the middle of the gauge.

"Can we stop with 'This is Your Life'?" Irritability could be discerned in Shechter's voice and as he spoke his posture was no longer slack. "I can also tell a thing or two about you but this just isn't the time."

Outside, from the other side of the back window, the actor spun the wig on the tip of his finger. "Return to the path innocent lad," he recited to Shechter from the yard and the strands of the wig's hair shook from his hand. "A time in which I shall roll down a vast chasm: no bush on which to grasp, not an ounce of water to break the fall." He gestured with his hand to the front window at the strip of darkening sky with its clouds above the treetops. "May the Gods above watch over the way a child watches over a fly whose wings he has plucked. It's also from the Greeks," he explained from outside.

The lighting man, who seemed to be waiting for a humorous punch line, asked if it was one of Giorgio Dalaras's songs that Yehuda Poliker sang in Hebrew.

"Actually, what you said is quite interesting," from the corner the soundman turned his head to the window, "about the Gods."

(But the wings of the mosquito were not plucked, its slender legs stood sturdily on the water in the hollow that the storm had filled; they stood indenting their domains with delicate hollows.)

"It's not me, it's the Greeks," answered the actor. His hands were supported by the sill and he lifted his legs above it. "I just don't understand how you manage with this," he said as he jumped back into the room. He stretched the skirt and when he saw that they were watching him he halted his movements: a grown man, square-jawed, his lips painted, his cheeks powdered and a tattered wig hung from his head. Across from him in the opposite window the crop spraying plane passed slowly, circled above the treetops and again moved away in the direction of the fields.

"Didn't you hear the plane in the earphones?" Merav asked. The soundman shook his head.

(He heard only fingers when the lighting man momentarily rubbed the microphone pole that he was holding for him, and afterwards a breeze could be heard that arrived in the room having caused the eucalyptus leaves to shake outside; their rustling was not heard and neither were the gnats flying there, circling in the air, their wings gilded in the soft light of the setting sun.)

"Are you sure?"

The soundman nodded.

(But even from the highest heaven of all the heavens – the seventh, the seventieth, the seven hundredth and seventieth – there was one who heard them, just as he hears a grain dropped from the grip of an ant, and the flame tightly grasping the wick of an oil lamp, and the lacelike foam forming in the darkness of the deep; but he was a man, Buddha, and not a God, there was only one God; formless yet with all forms: he was the wind that passed through the branches of the palm trees and the thatch, the coconuts that he dropped, the oceans that he disturbed, he was each and every wave storming toward the cliff, he was the entire sky from the window of the hut to the horizon that darkened instantly: he was the storm, he was the silence, he was he himself who endured that night alive.)

"Why would it be heard," said the lighting man, "I directed the microphone toward them."

"You're something," said the actor.

"It's not me, it's the microphone," answered the lighting man. "Quite some tool." And straightaway he glanced at the actor's eyes to check if he had made him laugh.

(Long shlong is what they called the microphone in the regular army, and when his girlfriend used words like that once, when trying to understand why things weren't working out between them, as if it was all his fault, it stunned the lighting man how she could speak that way, this girl whom he knew from elementary school; his total estimation of her completely dropped, that's what he said to himself afterwards, my total estimation of her completely dropped, and for two months he didn't want to leave the house until the night he went down to call her from the public telephone and heard all the noises of the student residence through the receiver. He called from the street, which by six in the evening was already empty the way it emptied on all those days, and after

hearing her answer he let the receiver drop and sway beneath
all the smutty drawings, and her hello-hello sounded faint
from below as if she had fallen in space.)

"Know from whence you came, from a putrid drop," said
the actor. "And to where you are going, to a place of dust,
maggots and worms."

(Through the transparent panels of the booth and the
obscene drawings sketched upon them he saw the empty
street, and in the total silence he identified the sound of an
automatic coffee machine that she was using while talking
to him: perhaps she held the receiver between her ear and
shoulder, put a shekel into the slot and he immediately heard
it being swallowed. Sometimes that coffee machine at the
student residence would eject the coin, sometimes it would
pour the coffee without a cup beneath it, sometimes it would
place the cup alone, but that was the sound of a cup with
coffee, and through the obscene drawings he could almost see
her drinking it with small sips, in the long passageway in which
a door was always being opened or slammed. "I don't think
it's a good idea," that's how she answered his question through
the receiver and drank more coffee, and in the background
– perhaps from the direction of the notice board – someone
asked if by chance she had a spare shekel, first thing tomorrow
morning he'll return it. For a moment there was silence –
perhaps she was going through the small pocket of her jeans –
and afterwards from a distance she said: "Tomorrow morning?
Do you know how long it is till tomorrow morning? We could
all be dead by tomorrow morning.")

"And before whom will you be accountable – this is for
you," the actor turned to the soundman, "before the King of
Kings. You look like someone who takes an interest in God."

(A cat was walking opposite him in the middle of the
road, unconcerned with the cars that were parked or had left
town, and at the time he said into the receiver: "What?" and
heard her say: "I wasn't talking to you, just someone who
passed by," and also heard the new shekel being swallowed
by the machine and the sound of coffee without a cup and
how she then laughed and said: "it's okay, I've got another

one, anyway there's not much point keeping it." She put it in the slot and again her sipping was heard above the obscene drawing, one after another, sips long and low, and he dropped the receiver, letting it sway back and forth in the booth, back and forth, back and forth, back and forth, until he gave her a kick to smash her lips her teeth her tongue her throat **let's see if you are a man**.)

"It's him that's interested in me," answered the soundman in his quiet voice, "in all of us." He had already returned his gaze to the gauge whose dials were quivering.

"Okay, I'm ready for another take," said the actor. Shechter looked at him as he replaced the tatty wig on his head and sat in the chair.

"All your recitations end with death," Kinneret said to him, "I noticed that before."

"Not just mine," the actor answered quietly. "All of ours." He turned around in his chair and placed his hands on the table.

"Yes but you don't have to go on about it all the time," Kinneret said. She left the room with Na'ama and the door creaked after them until slamming shut. In the gilded light in the window the crop spraying plane could be seen for a moment stirring like an irritable wasp.

"Come on," said Shechter.

(From the bowels of the earth the dead reached out their bony hands to pull the others toward them, and below them lay others who had reached out to those same dead while they were alive, and further down in the depths lay their ancestors' ancestors who had already turned to dust. And afterwards, above his grandfather's grave, between his mother and father who grew shorter by the year, Shechter would raise his head to the skies, as if all the sons and grandsons waiting to be born and to grow up could be made out in its lucidity, until he himself will reach his hand out to them from this earth.)

"Let's do another take."

(At least they would appear there in the blue transparency – if he won't have children or grandchildren, not from the

French girl nor from any other woman – the few people he
would yet change into from year to year, until they too will
be buried in this body, which for the time being is standing
here: in his chest on which for a long time no woman's head
rested and no hair from a loosened braid was spread, in his
throat which was already rusted from the silences, in his face
in which the fibers of the sack were enmeshed.)

"Camera ready?"

(He was short-tempered, not firm as was his custom with
the extras that he gathered at the end of his studies, children
and the elderly with whom he packed the film location daily.
Dozens of children were filmed in that short, which was
archived in the depths of the storage space, and a long time ago
he could have been a father of children their age – for instance
he could have placed them atop ponies in the Luxembourg
Gardens, bought them roasted chestnuts, skipped small stones
with them on the frozen waters – and together with them he
filmed the elderly from the old age home next to the university,
greyish like his grandfather in his latter photographs when he
had lost all hope for the country to which he had emigrated
a year before Rutenberg. The line that was etched between
his brows was also slit upon his tombstone, and the grass that
sprouted from it his father would rip out with a sad anger
strengthened by all that bending down year after year beneath
the searing August sun.)

"Camera ready."

(In a voice whose cords did not yet quiver with frailty, he
once told Shechter the boy about the masses who marched
upon the winter palace, all dressed in festive white like the
snow swooping down on everything – the river there was
called the Neva and the avenue was called Nevsky – about their
belief that the Czar would grant them a hearing, about their
singing in unison as one man from the head of the procession
to the tail end, and about the barrage of fire. Detail upon
detail was described then in Shechter's childhood bedroom,
opposite the aquarium and the lone goldfish swimming
in it; for the others that had risen and floated on previous
days, the stirring golden dance had already turned to the

self-same thing that prodded Shechter's grandfather toward the dust. In front of the murky water his father described to him, in order to connect the deaths as well as to differentiate between them, the bodies falling and turning the snow red, thousands of men, women and children, the black robe of a priest waving, rifle bayonets, horses whinnying, hooves trampling; but only years later, opposite a miniature pony in the Luxembourg Gardens, did Shechter perceive the breath rising from the nostrils and becoming thick in the cold January air. The same priest who led the failed mass procession relinquished his cloak and was rescued from the Czar's soldiers thanks to Rutenberg. He then escaped to Europe and unlike Shechter did not feel downtrodden and foreign there, but became a carousing drunkard and in the end betrayed his revolutionary comrades to the secret police. Rutenberg, whose photograph was displayed at his father's workplace alongside the photographs of the president and prime minister, did not hesitate to sentence to death the one he had saved ingeniously with such courage. With his bare hands he hung him from a hook in the ceiling – his father lifted his hand and the mobile caused the little tin fish to hover there as if they were the souls of the dead goldfish – hung him and lost all hope for Russia and the revolution like Shechter's grandfather a year before him.)

"Soundman ready?"

(From his room, through the window on which the leaves of a poplar tree fluttered, Shechter the boy tried to see the mass of white flakes fluttering, falling and covering his fish like the bodies of the demonstrators, masses and masses of flakes, but only until they flew toward her car did Shechter perceive them as they softly struck and accumulated there above the windscreen wipers and gradually turned the entire windowpane white; but at the time he did not have ingenuity or courage other than this: to release the handbrake and cling to those plump thighs as the little car moved, carrying them along further and further to the edge of the road and the black void beyond.)

"Soundman ready."

(A hot spell prevailed on his second trip after the failure of his film, and opposite the fountain in the Luxembourg Gardens the women rolled their dresses up to expose their thighs to the sun. They sunbathed next to him, at a chair's distance, as if he wasn't staring at them with gaping eyes through all the hours in which he didn't go to check at the post restante if the French girl had already answered his letter. "It was fine, really," he answered his father when he asked him how it had been there, "it was really fine," he said and dragged the small ladder to the corner of the room and took down from the storage space, in which the roll of film had grown a thin layer of dust, his boots that hadn't been polished since his discharge from the army; grey socks were tucked inside them and he felt for the identity tags on their sides and still heard the French girl saying in a different room, which has long since been rented out to new tenants: "Raglaime? Regelle?"[16] – before bending over his body. He met her, Shechter the ex-serviceman, on the way out of Rome, a small Fiat stopped there and took them with their rucksacks to Florence, and the driver addressed them as if they were a couple. Two months later, on the wallpaper and its faded ornamentation, shadows were outlined one after another by her bare hands – a rabbit, a dog, a bird – so that from the mattress that filled that room he would say to her: "lapin," "chien," "oiseau"; and then he said, with the same hesitant pronunciation: "toi," because her profile was drawn there, and he said: "ton corp," because he saw her body, rounded soft and friendly, and he said: "vienne," because he desired her and at the time thought – friends suggested by postcard that he join them for a trip to the Amazon – that of all the distances that a man crosses there are only two that have meaning: the distance crossed in the body of a loved woman and the distance he'll cross inside the earth in the end.)

"Camera running?"

"Camera running."

---

16   "Feet" and "foot" in Hebrew

"Quiet, we're filming!" Merav called from the window to anyone who would be passing on the road.

"Action!" called Shechter.

The door opened. In the entrance Kinneret and Na'ama saluted awkwardly. The sergeant lifted his eye from the eyepiece. "Maybe show them how it's done," Merav suggested.

"No, it's actually good," said Shechter, "let them salute like that. They're new recruits, just arrived on the base."

"It's something you already learn to do in basic training," said Merav, "where've you been?"

The sergeant nodded with his eyebrows.

"And on that they wasted the whole day," said the female medic from the depths of the receiver, "a whole day. But for you it'll be enough to see that cassette."

(What, doesn't the sergeant know what's going to happen afterwards? Aren't they going to come and say to him why did they salute this way instead of that way? Aren't they going to tell him afterwards do it again, Gidi, by Sunday? For sure they're going to. What, isn't that what they did to him in the war, after they returned from filming in the south?)

"Let her show them," he said, "just so there won't be any problems."

(From a distance that base in the south looked like a Nachal corps settlement, really, with all its trees and lawns, just like a settlement. And when they stopped alongside the sentry after a four hour journey and one puncture, stopping just like that in the light of the setting sun, even the concertinas[17] there didn't look like concertinas, yes, with all the uprooted bushes caught in the wire. And at night, after they turned off the generator – after all they used generators there –the clicking of sprinklers could be heard in the silence almost like on his wife's kibbutz. But when he told this to Merav, she suddenly began to busy herself with the equipment. She asked him if he didn't have to call home, two hours had passed and he hadn't called home; and he went to call, not home, but the

17   Army slang for coiled barbed wire

kibbutz. The two of them had gone to film the new missiles that had come from America and the sergeant wanted to film them with the secret installation in the background, yes, to show just how important they were: because who will see it, soldiers, only soldiers, but then afterwards what did they go and tell him? After all the work they had put into it and everything? Under no circumstances were they to film the secret installation, what, is he out of his mind? That's what they said to him.)

"What, don't I know what's going to happen afterwards?"

(So in the end he also couldn't show the missiles – not one missile – zilch. Not even the tail end of a missile. Because of the wind there, they filmed everything from inside the sentry booth, once in the evening and once first thing in the morning, and in each one of those windows, narrow as they were, the sky had a different color: if let's say one was night, then the one across was daylight, or the opposite, and all the colors between were in the other windows so that they gradually changed from one to the next; just for that it was worth going there. Not that it doesn't happen here, of course it does; it's just that here, amongst all the buildings, go try taking notice of something like that. Who takes notice here, who? And there, in the small valley below, between the hills, a sort of mist crawled, turning red or blue or something in between according to the color of the sky, just like a chameleon. From inside the sentry booth Merav pointed the microphone toward the radar in order to record its beeping in the wind, and some uprooted bush, perhaps a juniper, rolled fast, skipped and suddenly pressed a leaf close up against the windowpane, the way the little one used to with her nose. As for him, what did he care about saluting? But the others; what, doesn't he know those guys?)

"Show them, Merav."

She showed them, first one and then the other: she approached Na'ama and lifted her elbow and then approached Kinneret, who was a head taller than her, and tilted the palm of her hand.

"Your hands are cold," said Kinneret. She put her hand down slowly and stretched her shirt front.

Opposite her, from the swivel chair, the actor lifted his hand like her and let it fall like her and also stretched his shirt front with fingers whose nails were smeared with red nail polish. "O come ye spirits," he said with feeling and lowered eyes, "O come to my woman's breasts – what are you laughing about," he turned to the lighting man – "and take my milk for gall." He blinked a few times with his made-up eyelids.

"I'm not even going to bother answering you," said Kinneret.

"Lady Macbeth, for anyone who's heard of her," he bowed to her from his chair and removed his wig with a wide movement as if it was a hat and put it back on his head.

"Lady who?" Kinneret asked and stretched her shirt again and began to move through the room between the abundant equipment. In the front window the crop spraying plane was drawing away, but Shechter still leaned his elbows on the window sill and gazed outside.

"Come on," said the sergeant from his place. "Soundman ready?"

The soundman did not answer from his corner, and the two circular gauges shone in the lamp light.

"Yossiii-"

sang Kinneret.

"myyy successful-"

She sang to his bent head as she moved through the room and he lifted his eyes slowly.

"sonnn-"

(For a week and another week and another week he stayed above the holy lake of Pushkar in Rajasthan, India, and day after day he watched the women who bathed in the waters that were infused with the ashes of the dead and continued to watch them also as they stood on the bank and dried their breasts in the wind and examined their faces in fragments of mirror. Every night a pale neon light flickered at the entrance to the temple on the bank opposite him, and every morning a tiny sparrow landed on the stone parapet beyond which stretched the lake whose waters were turbid from the ashes and the filth of the bathers; it landed and puffed up its breast in the wind with ludicrous pride. For a few moments it resembled the sparrows found in Israel and the wind passed through its downy plumage causing it to swell up as if solely for that purpose had that wind been created at the edge of the heavens by the gods or the difference in barometric levels – after Hawking, his son read another book and began to talk about chaos and the butterfly effect, until again he lost hope of his understanding and shifted his eyes from him, with the round glasses that she bought him and the long eyelashes he inherited from her and the color of his eyes that he inherited from him – and beneath the worn away stone parapet, from the bank, more and more human ashes were scattered into the lake. Sack after sack was brought there in Tata trucks from the whole area, unloaded and emptied, and more and more water was sprinkled on erect Shiva Lingas and more and more offerings of rice were made to Ganesh's trunk, they were all idol worshippers there.)

"I was just fixing something," he said.

(From Pushkar he traveled to Delhi, and from Delhi he flew to Kathmandu, and in Kathmandu instead of returning, he bought an air ticket to Bangkok and decided to stop watching television no matter what, even should the world go up in smoke – which was being threatened at the time – gone are the seas, all the fish climbed up the trees, because he no longer had a wife, he no longer had a son, at the time he even had no name: for days on end nobody called him by his name, for weeks and months, not Yossi not Joe not Jojo not Dad, and in the hut on the island only the mosquitoes sticking to the lizard's tongue were heard, and on that night with the firelight in its eyes it looked like a salamander that would never become extinct, not in fire nor in water; in the light of the oil lamp it stared at him from the thatched covering hour after hour the way it stared at the mosquitos it hunted, and did not blink. Perhaps he saw their brother in the puddle that the storm left in its wake – there was no trace of it in the sky, and from all the battalions of waves, only a lapping ripple remained – or their father or their son, who could differentiate between them other than he who created them and placed it like that on the water and indented hollows so minute and delicate in that water beneath its fine legs, my God; there was no need at the time for a magician to part the ocean or to walk on its ripples or to be seated on the petals of a lotus, for him it was enough that one mosquito stood opposite him in a puddle.)

"Soundman ready," he said.

"Actors ready?" Shechter asked and turned his head. Na'ama had already gone out, and for a moment in the gap of the open door a thin line of sky, foliage and asphalt was seen, and straightaway the door shut and muffled the rattling of the plane that was rumbling in the sky.

"No," answered the actor. "Just a minute." He was still looking at his reflection in the window after taking off his wig as if to greet himself. He left the wig in his hand and contemplated it with a thoughtful gaze. "O skull," he said to it dolefully, "you had a tongue, and could sing once, and now you are my Lady Worm's," he put it back on and smoothed down its strands. "Hamlet," he said with his red lips.

"Another recitation about death?" asked Kinneret.

"That's life," answered the actor. To his right the lamp flickered for a moment with all its globes, and the lighting man, who approached the wall, hit the plug with the palm of his hand.

"For that you went to study acting?" Kinneret asked. On her right Na'ama removed the velvet ribbon that tied her hair back and wore it around her wrist as a bracelet.

"I went so I could stand up in front of people and move them," answered the actor. "Make them laugh, make them angry, it doesn't matter what, the main thing is to touch them. But the most fun, really, is transforming into someone else. Do you know what a drag it is to be yourself the whole time? It's enough to make you want to die."

"Again 'to die,'" Kinneret said quietly.

The actor, who again was smoothing down the strands of the wig, asked her why she joined the group: but the real reason, only the truth.

Kinneret hesitated for a moment. "I wanted to be a star," she answered, and the sound of the crop spraying plane that rattled above the eucalyptus treetops sounded derisive. "I'm already over it. It doesn't make a difference anymore." Her eyes followed the plane as it drew away in the depths of the window.

"Just don't let me get you depressed," said the actor and returned to his chair. "It's enough there's that depressed prisoner. What, isn't life beautiful? Sure it's beautiful, if you've got cloudy vision, not so?"

(Have you got the plot number? I've got the plot number: then head straight, all the way to the end, turn left and you'll see it there; at the entrance he saw a sign in marble: "Gravesite of the Holy Rabbi the Divine Cabalist Rabbi Moshe Aharon Cordovaro May the Memory of the Saintly be for Blessing the Righteous shall Flourish like the Palm Tree; He shall Grow like a Cedar in Lebanon," and a tin signpost: "For Public Prostration," and that's what he did afterwards, prostrated himself, but really prostrated himself, until he tasted the ground; have you got the plot number? I've got the plot number; then head straight all the way to the end and turn left and you'll see it there: he saw it there: there were small pebbles on the tombstone, perhaps his father had put them there, they were small, like the stones that hit the dusty shutters every night, but then he bumped into something – an iron hoe or something else – and he prostrated himself. "Know before whom you shall be accountable, before the King of Kings," was written on another signpost, but in the depths of the pit in front of him, between the ants and the ripped out weeds there was nothing, and on the tombstone behind him the hunchbacked man cried: "Won't you get up, Rosa? Won't you come back? Why are you sleeping there alone, why?" And for a moment he tried to visualize his father in place of him, with the frayed edges waving between the shoulder straps of his vest, until he appeared to him in the depths of the pit beneath the stones that he had thrown into it.)

"What?" asked the lighting man, hitting the plug, and again the lamp flickered.

(One after another the small stones hit the shutters and his father would just narrow the slits and say through them in a voice older than the one he should have had: "gey schluffen, bitte, gey schluffen," and give up and go to the living room and sit heavily in the armchair and hold the remote control – what do you mean hold, a drug addict doesn't hold a syringe that way – his eyes glued to the flickering rectangle of the television the way they were glued when he was his age to the glass paving stones on the sidewalk above him: for two and a half years he only saw the soles of the passersby and the paws of the dogs, not each paw, only the fourth one the dog lifted as it urinated against the wall during his walk, as precise as the seasons of the year. "What are you looking at me for?" he said from his chair without turning his gaze to him, "Would you rather I go to the Romanian and then you'll have to drag me from there?" All the other layabouts hung around there, all with one- or two-day stubble and a cigarette stub stuck in their mouths, from a distance you could already hear the checkers of the backgammon and the dice rolling on the wood or being shaken in the leather cup, and sometimes from behind, the Salonikan could be heard talking on the phone: "with kindness, only with kindness. I just say to him: tell me is that nice? Is that the way you treat someone? You don't pay? What, doesn't he have a wife and children to feed, just like you've got? You've got two children, a boy and a girl, no? Just with kindness." Above, a fan turned slowly and on the other side of the refrigerated glass cabinet a few cakes could be seen, what do you mean ancient, Marie-Antoinette broke her teeth on them.)

"What do you mean 'what'?" answered the actor.

(Only the Persian ate from them, and once, when he returned from Tel Aviv after he got stuck there one night and had to sleep in the Meir Public Park with two drunk Russians, everyone asked him if they hadn't tried it on with him, and the Persian said, "those drunks don't know if they're coming or going. You know what they said to me, they said that God was once a man and that he was killed, aren't they crazy?" And his father, before he dragged him home from his table, a seven-year-old boy pulling by the hand a man who looked like his grandfather, gazed at the blades of the fan through the empty glass and said: "no, not crazy, that's what they all believe there." He pulled him along by the hand to their building and as they went up the stairs he pushed him in front of him, and in the apartment he took off his shoes and immediately smelt the smell of his socks and saw the big toenail sticking out from there yellowed and dry like the nails of the dead that continue to grow in the ground: a long one caused him to stumble the time he prostrated himself, and for a moment he imagined smelling the smell of his mother rising toward him through the grains of earth.)

"Should we do it again?" asked the sergeant.

Kinneret went out and joined Na'ama, who was standing at the foot of the eucalyptuses. Their shadows lengthened further and continued to fade, gradually losing their outline in the greyness of the asphalt, which too was darkening.

"They're just screwing around wasting time," said Kinneret. "In the end my parents won't be late at all. Did we use to kill time like that in the group? They would've kicked us out long ago. They wouldn't have heard a sound out of us."

"We're on our way out anyway." Na'ama looked from the pavement to the window. "Don't have any illusions about it, and you say I'm naïve. That's why they sent us to be filmed, it's a kind of compensation, I'm telling you." She gathered her hair again and tied it with the black velvet ribbon.

"I didn't say you were naïve about that. It was about boys."
Kinneret stretched her shirt in front and then smoothed
down her skirt. "If there was only someone half-normal here.
I wouldn't mind having a little fling right now."

"What, you think I didn't see you eyeing the soundman?
At least don't make it so obvious." Na'ama wound the ribbon
around again.

"That's also your sister's advice?"

"She's actually right about that. She's talking from
experience; she's been through it herself. Even by now she's
not over it."

"He's a man," Kinneret said after a short while, glancing
at the front of the shirt that had turned dark, "not a kid."

From the shadows Na'ama turned her head again to
the window.

(Between the folds of the curtain a strand of hair was
curled on a finger, and from time to time the nail appeared
with remnants of chipped polish, until from its sleep, the
dog sensed her, got up and lifted its paws onto the sill and
barked at the roof: a fat schnauzer, who when she brought
him home, her sister said that at last she'll have someone
with a beard with her. Each time Na'ama saw him – lying
down there or standing and barking or howling like a jackal
when the siren of an ambulance or fire engine was heard,
even before the sirens of the war were heard – she said to
herself that she would never ever come to be in a situation
like that, when all you have left in the world to love is a dog.
He also barked at her sister, not only when she returned to
her roof but also each time she wanted to go out, and in a
voice hoarse from cigarettes she would say to Na'ama: "never
mind, let him bark. That's how he talks, it's just from love."
And for a moment that word hovered over the roof, beautiful
and wondrous even above the clotheslines and the whitewash
stained with tar.)

"It's nonsense," said Kinneret. "Believe me, I know all
about leaving groups."

(A mattress coming undone at the seams lay on the floor of the air raid shelter in which they played music – in the drummer's girlfriend's building: flick-flack, he drums on her at night, flick-flack – and when Kinneret sprawled out the springs protruded toward her body, squeaking, itching; and old furniture was strewn there with dusty cobwebs dotted with dead flies: a dismantled cupboard and a trashed armchair in which if she sat – a budding young girl who dreamed of how she'll dazzle them at the pub – she'd be filled with cobwebs; woven on her buttocks, the webs crisscrossed, woven on her concealed private parts, a shady creviced flower craving devouring insects clutching and swallowing.)

(And once in a coffee house, while Na'ama waited for her sister, she saw an elderly couple, each wearing spectacles with lenses as thick as magnifying glasses. They brought them close to the menu almost touching it, and when the bowls of salad arrived the man began to pass the sprouts over to his wife and she the anchovy to him, he the lettuce to her and she the olives to him, he the radishes to her and she the mushrooms to him, he the cucumbers to her and she the onions to him, and all the while their heads were bent over the bowls almost touching them. Despite the thick lenses, their actions were agile and executed in perfect harmony, like a pair of rodents – hamsters or white mice – and how great and wondrous was the beauty of it despite their ridiculous appearance.)

(The elderly neighbors didn't open their mouths, as if taking into consideration the performance in the pub – mouths whose teeth are rotting or false, a palate entirely parched or moist – and from the street the music they played couldn't be heard owing to the brick wall that remained in the entrance from one of the previous wars. On one of the dismantled panels of the cupboard they checked the kind of sound that the stage floorboards would make, they walked on them, pounded, jumped up and down and the wood crackled, creaked, moaned, groaned.)

From the room the lamp flickered again until its light steadied.

(And another time, on the bus on the way to her sister's, Na'ama saw a mother and daughter laughing, the daughter had large dark freckles and the mother a fleshy mole on her temple, her gums exposed with their teeth; the mother stroked her daughter's freckled cheek with a hand completely worn out from housework, from the bottom of the palm to the tip of the fingernails, and the girl lifted her little hand and pressed the mother's mole with her fingertip. She chuckled in a thin voice and said: "pappam-pappam, pappam-pappam," and even there she was – at the time Na'ama saw it perfectly clearly, beautiful and wondrous – in that mole.)

From the room the lamp flickered and died out.

"That connection," the lighting man said from inside and hit the plug again **(let's see if you are a man)** first with his fist and then with the heel of his shoe (gave her a kick to smash her teeth lips tongue throat and left the booth and went up to the apartment and voices could still be heard from his father's bedroom, WD-40 wouldn't silence them. From his father's drawing board he took a red marker, packed an overnight bag and went down to the street, and in the transparent booth the receiver was still swinging back and forth, back and forth, without lips without a tongue without a throat. "I don't think it's a good idea," she said from the student residence, "just someone who passed by," she said, "all of us could be dead here by tomorrow morning," she said. He replaced the receiver to its holder and picked it up straightaway and heard just the dial tone and put it down and wrote above it word by word: "I," he wrote, "am open," "to offers." And opposite the obscene drawing he added: "of all kinds" – WD-40 wouldn't erase it, nothing would erase it – and he began to walk through the empty street in which no car traveled, on which no man walked. Only his steps could be heard as he turned into the avenue and walked to the two telephone booths that were there, no car traveled on the avenue, no man walked on it. Only a cat from the inside of a garbage pail watched him with phosphorescent eyes as he took the cap off the marker and quickly wrote: "Iamopentooffersofallkinds," and above the moist red letters he drew the obscene drawing, detail by detail, and checked it over for a moment and added her name there, moist red letter by moist red letter), "is totally screwed."

"Didn't I know this was gonna happen," said the sergeant. "I was sure this was gonna happen. No two ways about it. Just when you need something the most, it stops working."

"I'll fix it chop-chop," said the lighting man. He hit the plug again, once and once more, and as the ceiling was lit up by the light of the lamp, the tabletop returned a bluish glow.

"That's it," he said.

"Quiet, we're filming!" Merav called from the window and the crop spraying plane, as if obeying her, circled and drew away in the direction of the fields. The silence gradually gathered above its rattling, and the eucalyptus leaves rustled in the wind again.

"Camera ready?"

"Camera ready."

"Soundman ready?

"Soundman ready."

"Camera run."

"Camera running."

"Action," called Shechter.

The door opened. Kinneret and Na'ama stood in the entrance and saluted.

"An entire day," the female medic said.

(Exactly the way Merav had shown them: she lifted this one's elbow, tilted that one's palm; Kinneret's hand was warm. And on the base in the south she almost called out, "quiet we're filming," to some uprooted bush that pressed up against the window of the sentry box and began to rustle. That base was built in the middle of the desert and was almost as desolate as the place in which she lived; there just weren't enough people around to make it really desolate. It was so desolate you knew that even if you were to meet someone now and then the desolation wouldn't be alleviated at all.)

"There's no need for that, no need," said the actor in a high-pitched voice fluttering his fingers to the entrance.

(Reserve soldiers were on guard there so that the regular soldiers could learn how to operate the missiles that arrived for the war, and the captain in charge of them walked around in Adidas gym shorts, a Benetton T-shirt and Reebok sneakers, as if disregarding rank. The way that the editor of the local paper played volleyball with the messenger boy and a half-filled balloon, just to show everyone how he was one of the boys, but he didn't come to Smadi's wedding; as if she hadn't been the queen of the typists, the darling of the proofreaders, the chief referee of nighttime volleyball tournaments.)

"Come on girls,"

(They saw him next to the guard's kitchenette, before they knew he was a captain; looking at the ground and saying to them as they came near: "Seventeen!" Gidi asked: "Seventeen what?" "Wasps," the captain answered and pointed to the trap standing there: family size soft drink bottles cut in two, the bottom half filled with sugar water and the top half turned over in it like a funnel, no wasp entering could get out; each bottle just like the place in which she lived. In order that they manage to film before it got dark, he drove in front of them in a field car that he brought from home, and below them in the middle of the empty plateau on which no one was seen from horizon to horizon – in the place in which she lived Moshon's motorbikes passed twice nightly killing the silence with the din of cut off exhaust pipes – the dome of the secret installation shone, smooth and round. "And here we have the breast of the country, that's what we're guarding," the captain announced and perhaps added a wink beneath his imported Polaroid sunglasses, which like a mirror made the line in her brow visible. "Just don't corrupt the girl," said Gidi, "so that I won't have trouble with her parents afterwards," and she then tightened her grip on the microphone until all her joints whitened to the tip of her fingernails.)

"Take a seat please," the actor offered an invitation with his hand. Kinneret and Na'ama sat down, stretched the front of their skirts and the actor smiled at them fluttering his painted eyelashes. "What's your name?" he asked Kinneret.

"Kinneret," she answered.

"Kinneret what?"

"Kinneret Biran."

"Kinneret Biran what?" asked the actor and his red fingernails drummed on the table.

"Kinneret Biran, commander."

"And what is your name, my dear?" the actor gave a sidelong glance, and the soundman turned the volume button slightly (the needle moved like a slender stalk, like the thread of a mosquito net, like an eyelash: there was someone who moved the stalk, the mosquito net thread, the eyelash, who moved the orbit of the eye and the fire visible in it as if burning in its depths: but the fire was imprisoned in the oil lamp, and when it flickered like this lamp here it still could not cross over the rim.)

"Na'ama Kedmi, commander," answered Na'ama.

"Good," the actor relaxed in his chair, "I see you are quick learners. Do you have a boyfriend, Na'ama Kedmi?" She flinched with embarrassment, which would have worked well in performances on large bases, but in a movie, even a short that the viewers will be compelled to watch, it seemed forced and artificial. Shechter watching from a corner made no comment.

"You needn't be shy with me," the actor smiled at her with lipstick smeared lips, "I'm forever taking an interest in my soldiers."

She hesitated for a moment and lowered her eyes. "N-no," she answered, I don't have one."

"So then what's your phone number?" he asked her pleasantly with a twang in his voice. "Six-four, two-four, five-three-one," she answered after a moment, and the actor wrote it down on the back of a page he had been previously using: "Six-four, two-four-"

Shechter hit the wall with his hand as if fulfilling an obligation and the actor got up. He looked right and left as if the female officer had come in, turned to the window behind him, lifted a leg over the window sill and hurried out. "Cut," called Shechter.

In the other window, facing the road whose shadows intermingled with each other and with the darkening asphalt, a figure moved between the shadows of the trees.

"Are you filming?" Its voice could be heard, loud and invasive. "I thought Eran was still giving you problems." Weintraub's fair head burst forth from patches of leaf and returned to be swallowed up by them as he shifted his stance slightly. "Never mind lamps, I wouldn't give him a match to light up." Behind him, a step away, the other prisoner lagged behind, silent and blank-faced, his rake striking the potholes in the asphalt.

"Is that you again?" the actor looked from the window. "The pilot crop sprayer was just here asking about you, he was wondering where you disappeared to." He lifted a made-up brow toward the sky.

"Weintraub hasn't disappeared," he answered from the road. His voice traveled through the room to the yard at the back where the actor still stood: "Weintraub also doesn't forget. Ask Eran if Weintraub forgets."

Inside the room the lighting man leaned the microphone pole against the wall, turning it around and studying its edge.

"Don't be fooled by Eran, he wanted to be in the naval commando like his father. Right bubbie?" He bent over the trash can and the shadow of the returning crop spraying plane darkened it, as well as the road and the treetops, until it turned and drew away in the direction of the fields. Their furrows could not be seen between the tree trunks, but could be gauged within the empty expanse that contained no buildings to connect it to a sky losing its light.

"Come on," said the sergeant, "let's do another take."

The actor climbed onto the sill from outside: he stood upon it, bent so as not to bump his head on the window frame, looked down at the floor of the room, shuddering (it was so far away, four spans[18] below him) and he blinked and fixed his gaze on all of them with his made-up eyes. "Come what may," he said from the window sill.

18   The depth of a grave according to Jewish custom

"Let's see if you are a man," said the lighting man.

"A lady," the actor corrected him, he held his nose with his fingers and jumped. (When they invited his father over, while still in the entrance the old man asked her if she also wanted to be an actor like his son, a comedienne, to make fun of people. "Musicians I can understand," he said to her as he sat and for a moment watched her placing her long legs together in front of him, "musicians can sometimes still make a living. They can also save their skins even in the hardest of times. That's how it goes my dearie," he said to her as he eased himself heavily into the futon armchair, the chair that she took with her when she left in the second week of the war.)

"That's not what you'd call jumping," said the lighting man. "Go back up and jump again."

("Do you understand," the actor said to her, "we're just like gypsies or pederasts, no better," and his father said: "that's how it is, Miku, believe me, I know what I'm talking about." From the kitchen, whose stove they bought second hand – only the owner's daughter used it, and as for her, how much did she cook, from the kitchen to the dining room, from the dining room to the kitchen – the smell of pasta spread through the passage and reached his open nostrils: when he fell asleep in the television armchair, close-knit hairs could be seen inside them, grey like the curling smoke from the stub that fell onto the pile of stubs. "But she also knows how to cook," the actor said to him," she's been working all evening specially for you," and his father was already looking for the television with his eyes and the remote control with his hand. "My father," he said to her, as if he wasn't there anymore, and indeed he was not there anymore, "just can't do without television, even if it's just snow, he'll watch.")

"That's how you jump?"

(But still, they ate together by candlelight. Spaghetti Bolognese – and what a Bolognese, the Bolognese themselves would have flocked to Tel Aviv for it – afterwards they both went to a play reading rehearsal and when they returned he was still sitting in the darkness opposite the blinking rectangle of light, which one night, when still a boy and watching it from the passage, for a moment he could see in its flickering the masses of soles rushing here and there and the paws of the Gentile dog stopping above four times a day, nine hundred and seven days, until the glass paving stones darkened from its blood and from the blood of its master. Silently and carefully they tilted the armchair backwards and covered him with a checkered blanket and his girlfriend asked: "Aren't you even going to take his shoes off?" She looked at him for a moment until he said, "Leave it, believe me I know what I'm talking about," and then he said: "I told you there's no need, why did you start," because already his big toenail appeared, poking through the sock, yellow and growing and at the tip a crescent of dirt. Do you have the plot number? I've got the plot number. Then head straight to the end and turn left and you'll see it there. He then saw it: small stones were strewn on the marble like beads from an unraveled necklace that she left behind; just as her clothes had been left and all her odors and on the first summer some of her body heat as well.)

"Isn't that how you jump?" He stood up straight in the room, stretched his skirt and put the wig back in place: tightening it on the forehead and smoothing it down gently. "Isn't that how they wobble?" he winked at the lighting man, who drew close to the plug in the wall. "Not only ours," Kinneret said quietly.

"You hear that?" he turned to Shechter and spread out his palms. "When I was her age-"

"It's no big deal how old you are," Kinneret answered. There was a defiance in her voice, which perhaps she would not have permitted herself had the actor not been dressed up as a woman and his appearance not been so ludicrous. Without the costume perhaps she would not have said things like that, and now that she had said them, she promptly turned her gaze from him to the female soldier in the poster: to the tooth that had been made to disappear from her mouth and to her lips that had also been gnawed at by the black marker pen.

On her right the lighting man began to pull the lamp's plug from the socket so that it might cool down a bit and he moved his fingers forward to improve his grip on it.

"Are you crazy?" the sergeant shouted out from the corner of the room, "what are you sticking your fingers in there for? Do you want to get electrocuted or something?" The lamp flickered once and once again, its oscillations becoming more noticeable as the sunlight lessened.

"You don't get electrocuted so quickly," said the lighting man, "the prongs are already half way out." The lamp flickered again.

"Yes?" said the sergeant and the lamp flickered again. "So where's the electricity coming from in the meantime, from the air?" The light flickered again and again on the walls and on everyone who stood within them. "You got some kind of special method?" The light flickered, paused and was extinguished.

And in the dusk, until it will be measured by the light meter and the camera adjusted accordingly, in the small screen of the monitor emptied of its picture, once more was the reflection of an extended forehead to a sparse hair line, a nose ruddy from having caught cold, dark bags beneath the eyes (at two in the morning the secretary had phoned, and in a bedroom voice told him he'd have to investigate, and this time to get to the bottom of it immediately; she herself managed to get this investigation for him, had it not been for her he would never have been given it, yes, he should thank her; he can invite her to a restaurant if he wants, why not, or to a movie, it's surely preferable to the way he kills time; the point is nobody's getting any younger, not him either, despite his insistence on clinging to the past; he knows full well what she's talking about. She sleeps by herself, how else, and what about him? He will write his report by hand, which should be short and to the point this time, and should tell exactly what happened: not approximately, exactly, be precise for a change. From the small holes of the receiver her voice rose to his ear, familiar and strange, and as she spoke the fire was still burning in the empty fields, causing its flames to dance in all directions, biting into the darkness with long yellow fangs, caressing the dark with delicate fingers, chafing against it, scratching with claws, mischievously misbehaving and casting glowing pebbles into the night's jaws, too tiny to reach the depths of it and be released from the heat: a man was burning inside.

5

(At the table with the reporters from the local paper –
the wedding hall was actually in the same building as the
newspaper bureau: it was occupied mostly by offices, but
on the first floor above the small steakhouse and the shop
that sold aluminum profiles for windows, the walls had been
broken down and the space turned into a hall for functions
and social events; and at night, when all the floors were dark
except the top two, which were used by the local paper,
dancing shadows would appear in and depart from the
windows at the bottom, a waiter with a tray, a man balancing
a bottle on his forehead; in the winter all the gutters spat
murky water from their mouths, and in the summer the air
conditioners would drip on everyone passing beneath them,
but the hall windows were wide open and sometimes a stray
balloon would float through them, an ordinary balloon,
not made of aluminum paper and with no decorations or
drawings, a balloon that would never rise above the typists'
floor; and at each wedding-with-a-band the musicians would
park their old Plymouth in the alley across from the shop
with the profiles and stand in a row facing the wall and
urinate there, once before the wedding and once afterwards,
and the typists would watch them from their windows:
placing on the sill a cup with red hearts drawn on it or
Pisces or Aquarius, according to the sign, and if one of the
musicians spotted them he would call out from below, "just
be careful not to spill on it sweetie," and they would blush
and withdraw to the room – at the table with the reporters
from the local paper, around the floral arrangement and the
family size bottle, whose bubbles were becoming smaller,
the music reporter was also seated, a tall bespectacled guy

who drove Merav's sister up the wall with the pompous words he stuck into every little item; even for just a demo of one song he was capable of writing how they attempted to encapsulate the morbid depressing schizophrenia of the notorious seventies with its universal decadent hedonism and the portentous waning of the century's end, and on his left was the crime reporter, a thin guy with sad eyes, who took great pride in having connections in the right places and never tired of relating a human interest story he once did on the prostitution area of the Tel Baruch beach and how half the people there thought he was a pimp and half an undercover cop, and on his left was the gossip columnist whose items she received from the spokesperson of the local council and from some women working in public relations from home and whose children could always be heard in the background, and on her left sat the proofreader, who came to the local paper from a nearby communal settlement because she was afraid to stay there by herself with the Arab workers, and for the whole month prior to Smadi's wedding, when everyone was still busy arguing with Laniado about what's included in the price and what's not, buffet or no buffet, free drinks or not, beauty treatments and manicure and pedicure or not, for the whole month she would tell Smadi to not get herself so excited, really, and to stop making such a big deal of the wedding: look at her, on her wedding day she went with her husband to the beach, just like that. All that was during the six months before Merav enlisted, when she earned some money doing cleaning: sweeping two floors of defective bromide paper, crumpled computer sheets, cigarettes butts that were smoked there in quantities as in one of the nationwide newspapers, and cheap filthy napkins of pita bread from the late night suppers that came from the gas station canteen: everything was dismal; dismal dismal dismal. Only alongside the junction, illuminated by light cones from tall lamps placed there after the last accident, only there in the new transparent bus stop some advertisements turn white and their fragments flapping in the wind at times seemed like small wings.

But the typists, whom Merav saw from behind, were almost as excited as her sister: Aliza, married for just three months, on Thursday mornings having typed all night, would phone her husband to wake him with a kiss and ask him to try and guess from the taste what they had been brought for supper; and Phyllis, an older woman and mother of four children, whom she would instruct over the phone the moment they returned from school, the receiver between her ear and shoulder, when to turn the boiler on and when to defrost from the freezer and when to put in the oven and when to take out and absolutely not to open the door to anyone, recalled her own wedding in a city whose mosques were the whitest white and the sea the bluest blue, and each time they asked her about her wedding night a deep blush would rise on her face and she would quickly reply: "you don't talk of things like that." During that vacation, before Merav enlisted – the two years of army service seemed to her then both fascinating and frightening, lending hope and despair, presenting an opening but right away blocking it – Merav already knew exactly what her sister was doing on her floor. Almost always, when from each supper there remained only oily napkins, pieces of flaky pastry and the drippings of diluted tehina, the editor would come down from the reporters' floor and play volleyball with the messenger boy using a stray balloon from the wedding hall – a computer sheet stuck from one wall to another served as a net – and at that late hour they would appoint her sister Smadi as referee: they seat her on the table and together ask her if she's comfortable, maybe this position is more comfortable. Together they cross her legs to a seated squat and tell her to whistle when necessary, using two fingers; like this, maybe it will work with their fingers. And Merav, who watched them, realized then that perhaps the stories that circulated round the neighborhood about her sister were true.

One day, to everyone's surprise, she decided to get married to a short, quiet boy from a traditional background, who at the end of elementary school began working in a book bindery

in town and was already made shift supervisor – Merav once
asked him just what they bound and he said: "there's nothing
we don't do; the phone book –that's ours, the yellow pages
also, receipt and payments books as well, diaries, you name
it, everything"; everything was dismal; dismal dismal dismal,
and in the reddish light of the cones at the junction nothing
appeared: not a car, not a truck, not a convoy of motorbikes
– and at his wedding he looked like a shy guest waiting to
be invited to join one of the tables: he passed the buffet,
rearranged a fallen cluster of grapes, glanced in the mirror at
the entrance and tried to straighten his shoulders in the suit,
looked at the twins sliding on the marble floor and wanted
to warn them about getting hurt but still didn't know who
was who, and greeted the reporters of the local paper meekly,
went slowly by her grandfather so as not to disturb him in
his mumblings, and when the sun gun was lit up opposite
him – he was instantly flooded by blinding light – startled
like the porcupine on the road in the south: he stopped and
froze opposite Cohen Productions' video camera, as if it were
a stills camera in front of which one had to stand and smile
until the click, and did not stop smiling in the harsh white
light when the convoy of motorbikes was heard nor when
they at once became silent.)

(The sea – the last vestiges of light flickered on it like
minute blood vessels exposed when the skin above is flayed,
the skin of a living breathing giant, but when the boat's rope
was stuck out, stretched and slackened, the sea looked like a
drowsy giant allowing the boat to test its alertness, feeling the
anchor rope in its ripples as if testing a muscle displayed by
a child. And on a round table in a restaurant on the beach,
beer in a glass turned amber, wine sparkled on a slender glass
stem and two female tourists got up and photographed each
other against its background who will photograph the two
of them, who? On the damp sand a bicycle outlined a long
furrow, as fine as a scratch, and one of them pulled her shirt
over her head, and wriggling her pelvis, removed her cut-
off jeans until they reached her knees and fell to the sand,
and on her tanned body a tiny bathing suit, golden-hued

in the remaining light. The sand was a mass of indented hollows, all of it footprints and the imprints of limbs. The other tourist undressed as well: through the material of her dress she pinched her panties and slid them down the slope of her thighs to the sand, they were tiny and looked like a mouth, and the bicycle rider pedaled. She raised the bathing suit bottom over her calves, pulled them toward her thighs, grasped them through the material of the dress and lifted them until they covered her buttocks and held them tight, and the bicycle rider pedaled. The spokes spun around and the light was cut and spliced together, cut and spliced together, when she tied the top on her stomach and turned a quivering string butterfly to her back: through the thin material of the dress her breasts pointed to the fabric and presented them with their barbs as it mounted and covered them like the palms of hands, and the bicycle rider pedaled: the light was cut, spliced together and dimmed. She lifted the dress further above her head and took it off, and on her tanned velvet-like skin, both parts of her scanty bathing costume were golden-hued and in the fullness of her thighs were two small dimples, which her girlfriend bent over and kissed one after the other – breathed heavily and became dark.)

"Great," said the sergeant, "now put it back in."

(Because right after that, at the very most one more take, they're moving to a flashback. Shechter wanted a flashback, so let them have a flashback, only for a flashback it's a very poor lamp, and it's a very poor training base if you have to bring defective equipment here from civilian life. But just where else would he go if he didn't have this base? To the main Tel Aviv army compound? He would feel stifled in a second there, and here at least there's some air to breathe, not all that poison they breathe in the city. All in all he could get used to the commanders, over time, anyway in the end they'll leave, and he, the master sergeant, will stay. Yes. Only once did he try to leave for civilian life and really fouled up, big time, actually twice, if you count the second time, which lasted half an hour. What do you mean big time? He fouled up so badly that he was ashamed to go home, sure he was ashamed, after all the plans he had made for his wife.

After all, she didn't want to hear about living on her kibbutz, she was completely taken by the city, it's just that he was so out of touch at the time that all of a sudden he started talking about opening his own business. And in the end? In the end he went to work for the Renault garage, after all not only did he know how to take apart his rickshaw with his eyes closed when there was no option, if he could just get hold of spare parts from somewhere, but also the section commander's Renault. But after just one month there, less than a month, barely three weeks, he quarreled with everyone. "Don't be a saint here," they told him at the Renault garage, "this isn't the army. This is business. We have to make a profit not a loss, they've got plenty. Have you got a car like this?" In the end he went back to the base on all fours, no mention about getting a Peugeot for Saturday, no asking for more courses; nothing at all. He crawled back.

And the second time, on his last furlough, he went to some photo shop in Bat Yam from a notice in the paper. It was on the main street, just when palm trees were being planted on a traffic island; they were pint-sized and wrapped in jute material. They looked like babies in diapers, those palms, not like trees. In the shop window there was an empty aquarium, not quite empty so to speak, in it was just dirty water and some algae. The shop owner took him to a room at the back and all over the wall there were huge scenic photographs of the Alps or something similar: maybe firs with some winding stream and a waterfall, and between the trees, far, far away, a valley and a small village and cows could be seen. He put a camera in his hand, the shop owner, you should have seen what shape it was in, it didn't even have an eyepiece, and said to him: "never mind, watch what you're photographing in the television set." The camera was then attached to a defective television with some cable whose casing had come loose, and the owner said: "what I want is for you to travel through the forest with the camera, just so I can see what kind of a hand you've got." He had a good hand, the sergeant, he knew he had a good hand, everyone told him he had good hands, he didn't only fix things but also knew how to build furniture – who built the cassette cupboard if not him, and the wall cupboard at home and the chest of drawers and the lamp made of bamboo? – It's just that the camera was barely attached to the tripod and it swayed, a ship doesn't sway half as much. He shook like someone on drugs. "It's all very well that you're a master sergeant in the army," said the owner, "I've got respect for master sergeants, really." But already he only saw his back as he took from the sink in the corner a cracked white cup with "To Dear Mother" written on it and washed it. There was a blockage in the sink and as the water rose an inflated cigarette butt floated on it, half of it disintegrating. And on the photograph of the Alps, leaning against the wall beneath the umbrella of the portrait lamp, the sergeant saw a bicycle with a plastic box for vegetables on the seat post, and at the time it seemed to him that whoever rode it and placed it here in the back room of the photo shop in Bat Yam got off it to wander in the woods amongst those high firs, around and around until getting lost or deciding never to come back here.)

"I told you not to disconnect it."

"I can easily put it back in," said the lighting man.

(Moist red letter after moist red letter, and he turned to the phone behind him and drew the obscene drawing above it as well, and from inside a trash can a cat peeped at him with phosphorescent eyes like someone peeping into a shower: the avenue was completely deserted, no one walked along it, no car drove down it, and the patrol car wandered through some side street in the meantime and between the trees its flashing blue light could not yet be seen.)

The soundman was still crouched down on his heels. "As long as you don't make a short circuit," he said (he was crouched down like the Bedouin and the Nepalese and the Indians and the Tibetans and all those who go through their lives wandering, never having the money even for a stool) "and put us all in the dark."

(Only when the sun went down did they bundle themselves in their sacks on the ground, the emaciated elderly and nursing mothers whose milk was murky from the dust, and from the entrance of the houses and behind the rickshaws and roving cows all the hustlers of Kathmandu suddenly appeared and called silently with sealed lips, as if ventriloquists: "Change? Dope? Change?" And by ten in the evening, when the lights of the small one dollar hotels went out, the entire city was swallowed up by the dark; there was only one who could still see it from his heaven the way he saw the blaze of the primordial fire in the depths of the earth and inside the hut on the island, but at the time he didn't know he would reach the island.

On his first journey he didn't meet Israelis in Kathmandu, there were only aging hippies from Lennon's generation and the street in which they lived wasn't yet called Freak Street on the stenciled maps whose copies were made by the Ministry of Tourism, a dim alcove in which a weary fan rotated from the ceiling, shaking the thick cobwebs that were covered with frost in winter. Every night small bonfires were lit in front of the shop entrances, illuminating sacks of spices and rice and the filthy palms of the hands that were warmed above them, the palms of his hands too, as he stood there in front of the crackling bits of wood or the burning animal droppings. Twelve years later he traveled to Kathmandu again, leaving behind him an apartment and a wife and a son and even his name, traveled and found a new city almost completely lit up, and in the Thamel quarter dozens of restaurants and small thin shoeshine boys buffing the hiking shoes of the Israelis. In the restaurants menus were already prepared for them in Hebrew and there were signposts and cassettes in Hebrew in the lodges in the Himalayas, and after they moved on, those children, the age of his son, would leave their brushes and return to play checkers with cigarette stubs smoked to the filter, moving them here and there above the lines drawn in the dust. Sewage flowed through the open ditches and through which pigs rummaged; other small children would kneel there and watch the droppings floating by like a fleet of dinghies. But when it became dark and above the curving gables of the temples the night opened wide, deep and translucent, its stars large and shining, the garbage and the mire were then swallowed up by the darkness as if they had never existed, and from immeasurable heights, from one of the sparkling stars up there, perhaps the filth of the city was purified and shone back at them from the depths of the night.)

"That's all we need, to work in the dark."

(All the shoeshine boys gathered at the corner of the street, huddled together like puppies and wrapped themselves in tattered sacks with their brushes and polish. Each night he would pass there, freed of everything linked to home – in the first apartment that they rented the window was broken and the shutter stuck, the landlord didn't bother fixing them, and the leaves that fell from the ficus tree outside reached the room and rustled on the floor; she tried to stop up the opening with a piece of carton, and he said: "leave it," and pulled her to the floor on a bed of dry leaves and small sticky fruit, which they later scrubbed from their bodies with cold water, the boiler also being out of order; a small sparrow stood on the windowsill and watched them, puffed up his chest and whistled like some young upstart and the universe did not expand nor did it contract, it was precisely the right size – and amongst them all, he spotted the head of the boy, even filthier than the rough fabric in which he was wrapped: his lice enveloped by the dust, his eyebrows obliterated by the dust, his eyelashes knitted together by the dust, even the dreams he dreamed were dusty.)

"It's not a short circuit," said the lighting man, "just a loose connection." He gave the plug a pat: "here you are," and the light flashed and turned on (flashed and spun round, flashed and turned blue and grew between the trees on the avenue).

(Even on the first day in Kathmandu the boy stuck to him, caught his shirt and called out: "Shoe shining? Shoe shining?" At times they were so annoying that you just wanted to shake them off and hit them, to get rid of them and their poverty, to hell and gone, until the little old urchin appeared through the filth in which he was covered.)

"Camera ready?" asked Shechter.

"Camera ready," answered the sergeant.

"Soundman ready?" asked Shechter.

"Soundman ready," answered the soundman.

("Only one shoe," he said to the boy on the first day, after he put up three filthy fingers to show him how much he would have to add for the second shoe. Opposite them, in the alcove of a shop entrance, the money changer chuckled as if that boy did not repeat his trick all the days he knelt there in the dust, all the months, all the generations: the boy seemed so old to him. They had ascetics with mounds of ants heaped around them up to their necks, and others who stood on one leg from their births to their deaths, and gods who between two blinks of an eye created worlds and destroyed them, but all that boy wanted was another three rupees.)

"Camera run," said Shechter.

"Camera running," the sergeant confirmed.

"Action," cried Shechter.

The door opened. Kinneret and Na'ama stood in the entrance and saluted. "Come on girls," said the actor, "take a seat please." They drew near the table and sat down.

"What is your name," he asked Kinneret.

"Kinneret," she answered and stretched her skirt over her thighs.

(The sea breathed and became dark, and the light no longer flickered on the sides of the boat. It flickered only on the table, between the salt and the perforated lid, there the last light was stored and gleamed, until the salt darkened too and became peppery, charcoal-like, and a cigarette glowed. Her father said: "those types don't give a damn about anything," and her mother said: "I saw how your eyes were devouring them." She inserted a small teaspoon into the Bavarian cream, went deeper, made a quivering, whitish breathing hollow in it and lifted it to his lips: "have some in the meantime.")

"Kinneret what?"

"Kinneret Biran," she answered.

(On a beach exactly like that: not in a hotel, but on the sand full of footprints and the imprints of limbs. "Is it my fault that they got undressed right in front of me?" said her father having already swallowed a mouthful of the cream: it slid down his throat, his chest, his stomach, moving to the belt of his trousers. The two tourists were in front of them, only their splashing was still heard and the water breathed and rumbled, curving like muscles. "They didn't know you were looking at them like that," her mother said, and at the foot of the table, the restaurant cat got up and stretched. When there had still been light – blinding, sparkling until gradually turning to a golden honey – it dozed, letting the rays of the sun grasp the edges of its fur, and her mother sketched it on a table napkin. "What do you think?" she asked. "Nice, really," her father answered, but didn't look for long. "Thank you, really," said her mother and crumpled the napkin, letting the wind blow it onto the sand: it was all hollows and jags. They were on it then, the two of them, on the sand in the dark – the honeyed light poured out and was all used up – at the water's edge, in summer, in July, while still on honeymoon: the fishermen were busy with the fish, and the airplane was after all too far away in the sky. Her mother told her; she waited for him on the couch in the living room for half the night in an open dressing gown with a glass of Cointreau.)

"Kinneret Biran what?" asked the actor. His nasal voice became slightly firm, his fingers drummed on the table and his nails sparkled.

Kinneret looked at Na'ama and Na'ama whispered to her.

"Kinneret Biran, commander!" Kinneret said causing the recording needle to quiver.

(The following day he returned to the waste-water ditch and to the dust and to the boy, as if they were old acquaintances. He bent toward him and put out his hand, until the small hand was cautiously set down in it, like a lizard prepared to shed its tail. "Me – Joe," he said to him, "and you?" The boy eyed him with suspicion and took a sidelong glance at his shoeshine box, all his worldly possessions, the way his son looked at Hawking's book, in his room, in their town, in a far off country moving in expanding space: moving on and on, by then he saw it as being small, it and its peoples and its wars, like a whirling grain of dust.)

"And what is your name, my dear?" asked the actor, tempering his voice again.

"Na'ama Kedmi, commander."

"Good," he said shifting a strand of hair on his forehead, "I see that you are quick learners." He smiled and fluttered his eyelids at her, his wig moving with each flutter. "Do you have a boyfriend, Na'ama Kedmi?"

Na'ama hesitated and flinched in her chair, she almost blushed.

(And once on the bus, going to her sister – it was before the war and there was no need to think twice before each journey – she heard a girl who was all flushed say: "I don't know why I always talk such nonsense when I'm with you, do you believe me Natan? I just see you and that's what comes out." And the boy she sat down next to, tall with curly hair – at the time Na'ama liked curly hair – answered: "What, and I'm not like that? I also talk nonsense." "Not you," the girl said, "Just me. How's my jacket? Does it make me look fat?" "N-no," answered the boy after a moment, "what makes you think so, it actually looks good on you." "That's because I'm filled out in all the right places," the girl giggled, and Na'ama liked her voice, as well as her giggle of embarrassment. "I told you Natan, whenever I'm with you I talk nonsense. You see over here, Natan? Right there? Just where we passed? That's where my boyfriend used to work. Just two days ago I walked past there and I felt nothing anymore, nothing. Not a thing. Finito; it's over." "So are you on your own now?" the boy asked politely. In the girl's window a man wearing the orange cloak of the road works company could be seen dragging a jackhammer on the road. "What can I do," she answered quietly, "that's what there is. But in the end I'll find the love of my life, Natan, you don't give up on something like that." In the passageway between the seats a black Seeing Eye dog led its owner to an empty seat and waited there patiently, not like her sister's wild schnauzer. "Those dogs are really something," said the boy. "I swear they're a man's eyes." "But you already found yours Natan," the girl said. "How many years has it been, three already?" The bus slowed down further and the boy lifted his gaze from the dog. "Three and one week," he answered and beat three times on the back of the seat in front of him, and the old woman who was sitting there, a religious woman with a wig, turned her head and shouted: "What are you hitting me for? Hitting me!" The girl burst out laughing, a hearty laugh, which shook her shoulders until she wiped her eyes with her fists. "Sorry lady," said the girl, "Really, please excuse me, I didn't mean to." In the window two workers in orange cloaks moved the barrier that had been placed in the left lane, and then the boy opened the small rucksack on his lap and rummaged through it. He took out a book with a shiny cover, and from her seat Na'ama could make out a few of the large letters of its title: "How to Change Your Life-" "Do you really believe in these things?" the girl asked still emitting small peals of laughter. "No," the boy answered, "it's just that sometimes I think about something and I don't know exactly how to put it into words, so it's for that. I got it as a present, not that long ago." He opened the book, leafed through it and began to read slowly, between the rocking of the bus: "Every-person-needs-love-love-is-the-longing-for-human-contact, those who do not-" – the rattling overshadowed his voice – "are doomed to become destructive and impossible to live with. There are those who try to find substitutes-" the jackhammer drowned out his words again, rattling like a crop spraying plane – "in other areas as well, but a person with no love, ultimately becomes angry and narotic-" "Neurotic," the girl corrected him politely. "Neurotic," the boy repeated after her. "I told you Natan, I've got brains, don't get me wrong, I only talk nonsense when I'm with you." The bus's brakes screeched and the Seeing Eye dog pricked up its ears. The bus stop appeared in the window. "This is it, no? Isn't your apartment here Natan? Over there?" The boy nodded and the Seeing Eye dog looked at him as he got up. "Bye Natan," said the girl, "I wish you both all the best, really, believe me, all the best." And right away she turned her head to the other window, and then Na'ama, like her, lifted the tip of her finger to her eye.)

"You don't have to be shy with me," said the actor to her.

"N-no," answered Na'ama quietly and lowered her eyes.

(Even her mother blushes: "Believe me sweetie pie," she said about her sister, those who don't try, wait for a long, long time. What do you think, your father would have made a move if I hadn't given him a hint? I'm telling you, the men who seem the roughest are the shyest of them all. So I gave him a hint." – And suddenly her mother blushed, becoming very lovely beneath all the doughy skin. For two months Na'ama tried to convince her to go to the cosmetician, the one who's been treating her pimples since the seventh grade and promises her that by the time she's twenty it will pass and she'll have the skin of a baby; but she didn't want the red skin of a baby, she wanted skin like Kinneret's, fine and delicate: it could be seen in the opening of her shirt, and between the buttons, fine and delicate. In the end Na'ama's mother came back from the cosmetician looking like a beauty queen but her father hardly noticed her. With the paunch he had acquired, with the black bags under his eyes and with the rumors that for six months have been trailing him, he made no sign that he noticed anything. "I swear to you," her sister said lying on her back, across from the waving sheets, "if I don't get married it'll be just because of that. A marriage begins and love ends." She pressed a glass against her forehead to cool it and then moved it in her hand, a square glass tumbler, she never had two of a kind. Ice cubes floated in it and clinked. "You have to love," she said and the cubes hit each other and above them a brown stain of chocolate powder that had not dissolved, floated. "If you don't love, you die. Simple as that. There's nothing simpler.")

"And so, what's your phone number?"

"Six-four, two-four, five-three-one."

"Six-four," the actor wrote down the numbers on one of the sheets of paper he took from the drawer, "two-four-"

Shechter gave a weary pat on the wall and the actor rose from his chair in a panic. He turned to the window, gave a last look back as if the female officer was standing there, lifted his leg over the sill and hurried out to the yard. He was skilled in his movements, not only from the previous times, but perhaps from the regimen of rehearsal he was used to from his studies and from the recurring takes of the few student films in which he had taken part. "Cut," said Shechter, again as if fulfilling an obligation.

"Is that really your phone number?" the sergeant lifted his eye from the eyepiece and its print appeared above his eyebrow like an extra brow.

"Yes," answered Na'ama. "Why?" Her hand was already lifted to her cheek, touching her skin back and forth.

"Cookie," said the sergeant, "all sorts of types will start calling you. You don't need that; never mind giving your name, but why your phone number?"

The actor, who watched them from the yard, scratched his forehead through the wig. "What, don't we know those guys?" He spun a strand around his finger as if it were the chain of an army identity tag. "We've got a doctorate on those guys. Right, Gidi?"

The sergeant gave him a quick glance and said nothing.

"Come on, who's going to see this," said the actor from outside, "a few poor new recruits at the center? Tell him Shechter." He lifted his right leg from the yard to the sill and put it down on the floor of the room and pulled his left leg inside. Shechter watched him for a moment and kept silent.

"Yes, you never know what can get into their heads," the sergeant fixed the handle of the second camera into position.

"A few poor new recruits," said the actor from inside the room, "do you think they've got girls on the brain at the recruitment center?" He smoothed down the skirt over his thighs. "When I was there is that what I had on the brain?"

"You just looked out for your own ass there," the sergeant was suddenly angered by his provocation, and like Kinneret previously, perhaps would not have answered the actor had it not been for his ludicrous getup. He curbed himself immediately and began to tighten the side screws of the tripod; tightening them more and more, and Merav watched them or the knuckles of his fingers that whitened.

"It doesn't matter," said the actor. "Let's just say a plane passed over and I didn't hear a thing. Me, sweetie?" – He returned his gaze to the window – "I had one thing on the brain in the recruitment center and that's where they were going to shove me, to the occupied territories or to Lebanon, if I was going to beat up Arabs or get beaten up myself. Right, skull?" With one sharp move he removed his wig and held it again in the palm of his hand like Yorick's skull. "That skull had a tongue in it," he said to it as if practicing a part he had played or dreamed of playing, "and could sing once. We fat all creatures else to fat us, and we fat ourselves for maggots." He looked at the wig for a moment longer and then transferred it to his left hand.

"We've heard that already," the sergeant tightened the elevating screws as well. "Generations have heard that," the actor put the wig back on, "and generations are yet to hear that. Explain to him, Shechter, about the classics."

Shechter was still leaning against the wall and the whitewash around him turned slightly blue in the lamplight. His eyes turned to the window, to the streak of sky deepening above the treetops.

"Okay, so where do we go on from?" the actor asked him. "I mean, from before or after the catharsis?" He stood in the female soldier's uniform, tall and cumbersome and ludicrous, his mocking lips smeared red and his eyes made-up.

In the window the streak of sky darkened further and the treetops below darkened as well. "From the phone number," Shechter answered after a moment. The soundman, who was crouched in the corner of the room, heard him in the earphones, lifted his head and looked at him.

"Ah," said the actor, "to what base end we are condemned." He tightened the wig on his forehead and his red fingernails shone in the lamplight. "So what have you decided about the phone number Na'ama?" He curled a strand of hair around his finger over and over like someone falling into a state of complete self-absorption.

Na'ama took a small mirror out from her purse. She gazed at one cheek and then at the other, and for a moment Shechter, leaning against the wall, saw a large eye held between her fingers, a lovely brown eye, sparkling in the lamplight: the eye met his.

"With all their talk," said the actor, "in the end they make a big fuss about giving out a phone number. In the end they're just little girls." Na'ama peeked at him in the mirror, and between her fingers Shechter saw a bit of rounded cheek and a small pug nose.

"Women, not girls," Kinneret said and turned her head away.

(She was no longer crawling on the sand nor flooding damp hollows at the water's edge; the water did not tickle, did not make her laugh, did not lick, did not lap, did not kiss: she saw nothing, no Bamba, no ping-pong, no tiny fish, no sea-leed, she saw nothing: glug, she sank in the water, it was cold, biting and pulling, glug-glug; she sank more, surrendered, swallowed, and bubbles rose from her mouth, bloob; until no bubbles remained, just water, attacking, devouring, in the mouth and in the nose and in the stomach, in the stomach devouring her from the inside; she was in its belly, swallowed, imprisoned, and suddenly she was pulled out and hugged, she felt two scales pricking her stomach, cold, burning; "Kinneret," a mermaid said to her, "Kinneret," she had sea-leed below, and she spoke in her cousin Nulit's voice and cried in her cousin Nulit's voice, and where was the soldier? He was far off in the sea and the bulge touched the waves, the foam, the wind: everything spreads it.)

"How old are you," she asked Merav.

"Nineteen," Merav answered and erased the number of the take from the binder with a piece of flannel.

"What's your sign? What's your sign?" the actor twanged nasally at her in a thin voice. "Isn't it true that you're sincere sensitive shy delicate wise attentive to others?" Merav did not answer. "I knew immediately," he said to her. "It's all written in the stars."

(Michael on Saturn, Barkiel on Jupiter, Gabriel on Mars, Raphael on the Sun, Chasdiel on Venus, and Nuriel and Kadumiel, where are they? But above the marble floor only the twins flew around in the whitest of white dresses, and their once angelic faces were already beginning to become spoiled: Shoshi called herself Suzy, Pnina called herself Nina, and both already wanted to wear makeup like their big sister Smadi. You could already see how they'll type like her at the local newspaper bureau, the receiver between the ear and the shoulder, and how at some late night hour they'll sit on the laps of the music reporter and the crime reporter, or make signs for the pot plants: "I am not an ashtray!" or "I am not a trash can!" – so that the music reporter and the crime reporter or the editor or all of them together will ask her: "So then what are you honey? No, just so I know. Can you be a volleyball referee? Then sit here, isn't that more comfortable? Now whistle; not like that, with your fingers. What, can't you get them in, there's no such thing as not getting them in." They'll sit and whistle at droopy balloons floating over an improvised net made by a computer sheet or by the kettle extension cord: it was all so dismal; dismal-dismal-dismal. Smadi's face turned white under Cohen Productions' harsh light as if under an interrogation lamp, as if all her secrets were unknown to everyone, and her brother Eli looked at their grandfather: from his wheelchair he mumbled to all the angels in all their heavens and to the devils in all their hells, because as the ant has no bones and the sea no passage and the fish no kidney, so the evil eye will not rule over Semadar-daughter-of-Abraham forever and for all eternity. "Do they still come to him to get a blessing?" her brother asked at the time. "Yes, but not as much," she answered and from a distance she heard the motorbikes, still buzzing, dull and harmless. "And does he still light up smoke from below for them?" her brother asked. "Yes," she answered and remembered what he once said opposite the tree they saw at the university, from their father's repair room – the tree that each Passover would

become filled with yellow flowers and over whose pollen a
mass of bees would be bent – "look how the bees are fucking
the flowers," and how her father said to him: "Don't talk like
that, d'you hear? Don't put me to shame." "Grandpa worships
stars and signs," her brother said and above the Fanta, whose
bubbles rose slowly and burst, he quoted to her: "there shall
not be found among you any one that maketh his son or his
daughter to pass through the fire, one that useth divination, a
soothsayer, or an enchanter, or a sorcerer," and she asked if he
also learned that from his friends on the religious settlement
and heard the motorbikes stopping in the almost empty car
park, rattling and thundering like a fleet of airplanes.)

"Are you sure it didn't get recorded?"

"Definitely," the soundman answered her from the corner
in which he was crouched down. "Don't be so worried."

"It's her star sign," the actor explained. "They're always
worried and anxious and sensitive and delicate and attentive
to pilots. So what have you decided Na'ama?"

Na'ama looked out the window.

(She always had difficulty deciding, ever since she can
remember it's been a difficulty, and when she finally does
decide it's almost always already too late. Once she even
lost someone like that over the phone when by accident
he got a crossed line on her conversation with her sister
– actually it was only the answering machine with one of
those messages her sister recorded, and suddenly he started
talking – he was kind of nice, so that Na'ama almost agreed
to meet him, why not, but in the end she changed her mind
and put down the phone. Later she was sorry and waited
for him to call again, but how could he call again? After all
he didn't have her number, it was just by accident that he
cut into her conversation. And now, in this short film for
which they were brought from the group to act in, it could
be like those personal ads in the paper that she reads every
Friday: good looking academic seeks tall and wealthy man,
successful engineer looking for you, shapely and attractive
lady, domineering man seeks submissive woman for wild

pleasure in the morning hours, widow seeks lonely woman for serious relationship. Her sister said that everyone was looking for the same thing, but she tried once, yes, what's she got to lose? "Life's short, sweetie," she said to her on the roof, across from the sheets hanging there, "you don't know yet how short it is, you have to grow up to grasp just how short is. So you meet, why not. At first each one tries to show how smart they are, afterwards let's say you go to a movie and he lets his hand slip here and there by mistake, then you go to drink something, and then you ask your place or mine and go up to your apartment unintentionally bumping into each other on the stairs, and after that, from all the smart remarks at the beginning, should I tell you what's left? Stains on a sheet, that's what left." But Na'ama didn't want to hear that; she'd prefer to hear the dog barking. Because sometimes, amongst all those personal ads there were some really lovely messages: "to the girl who sat in front of me at the movie *Dances with Wolves* on Saturday night, second show: I couldn't stop looking at you. Would you like to dance with me? Please contact me through this column. Or: "to the girl with the green eyes and the black polo neck sweater. I'm the curly-headed guy in the grey sweatshirt: our eyes met on the escalator in Dizengoff Center, please contact me through this column." Or: "bus number sixty-four, opposite the square, you went up to the driver to get your change and stole my heart." Any place turned into a place of possibilities: someone was looking at her and she didn't know, someone had already written to her and sent it to the paper and she didn't know yet, and it was possible to just walk in the street and think: right now, Frishman Street in the afternoon, across from the Cameri Theater – there was a Chinese restaurant that she was dying to try out but didn't have anyone with whom – you with the dark brown ponytail and the black ribbon; or right now, at the kiosk in front of the Atarim Square, you stood and drank Coke with a straw – Diet, she drinks no other; she doesn't want to end up like her sister, she'd rather die than be like her sister – so right now, at the pedestrian crossing opposite the Faraj photo shop, you in the black mini almost

caused me to have an accident; or at the corner of Arlozoroff
Street, you in the red Bianchi, even the traffic light changed
color as you went by: please contact me through this column.
But she didn't wear a mini and didn't have a red Bianchi. She
was herself, Na'ama.)

"It's her karma," the soundman said from his corner,
perhaps to the actor perhaps to himself.

"Her car what?" asked the actor.

"It doesn't matter," answered the soundman. Due to the
heat that the lamp emitted he rolled up his sleeves further,
and on his right arm another tattoo spiral was revealed.

"It's all written in the stars," said the actor, "everything
that'll happen to us because we're sensitive and attentive.
Your warrant officer Gidi, Shechter's, and my Oscar. Look"
– but only the crop spraying plane passed over there again
above the tops of the eucalyptus trees, turning yellower in the
refined light – "and our Golden Globe and the Silver Bear.
And my girlfriend having left and Kinneret replacing her."

"You're not for me," she said to him.

"But why?" Hair ends sprouted from the T-shirt he wore
beneath the tunic and his Adam's apple moved up and down.

"Look what you look like," she answered him and crossed
her legs.

He drew near the levered window and looked at his
reflection: he smoothed down the wig, stretched the skirt and
blinked at Kinneret from the pane with his made-up eyes.
"It's actually good that you tell me the truth," he said to her
from there, "I always prefer to be told the truth. Even if I go
to pieces because of it, I prefer to be told the truth. What, do
I need to be lied to? To be told I'm a beautiful girl? Really,
just the truth. Didn't my girlfriend tell me the truth in the
war? She sure did. What, do I need to be told that I'm brave?
That I'm generous? That I'm any better than my father?" His
Adam's apple moved again, round as a ball, also as he sat
down in the chair again.

"Maybe leave her alone already," said the sergeant, "in the
end she's not going to want to act in the movie."

"Of course she'll want to," said the actor. "Those girls have been bitten by the acting bug. I can already see them at the end of an audition line, starting from here to eternity, standing like that on the stairs biting their nails," – he moved his nails over his lip, his teeth chattering in the air – "chain smoking and forgetting their lines and becoming hysterical: God, what am I going to do now?" – he sobbed – "But right away they're willing to be satisfied with a supporting role, that's good too, why not. And if not that, then a smaller part; in fact why not, doesn't everyone start out that way? And if not that, then a walk-on role, because there aren't any small parts only small actors, and if not that, then the third soldier or the seventh servant who weren't even given names, what for. And if not that then Miki-Le-Mic-happy-occasions-and-special-events-for-the-whole-family from age zero to a hundred and twenty. He spun round in the swivel chair like a ballerina doing a pirouette until his feet hit the table. "I'm always asked what the events are and why I'm not specific, so I say: events are everything. Because just what are events? Events are circumcisions, events are Bar-Mitzvahs, events are weddings, events are divorces, a stroke is also an event – heaven forbid – and even funerals, yes why not? And all our yesterdays have lighted fools the way to dusty death."

(Gravesite of the Holy Rabbi May the Memory of the Saintly be for Blessing for the prostrating public: head straight, all the way to the end and turn left, and right away you'll see: right away he saw. The Romanian had not yet turned on the fluorescent lighting in the café; only the beauty salon was lit up, half its height was below ground. The one who had replaced her, sat on her chair and opposite her a fat lady with the appearance of a Polish woman. With a small brush she slowly painted the lady's nails, nail after nail, and afterwards moved her head and looked at the nails through half-shut eyes, like an artist looking at the masterpiece he painted: nails. He hid behind Dadon's tow truck as the Polish woman paid and left, hearing her heels beating on the pavement like his little heart, and peeked again from behind the tow truck: now she was painting her own, the manicurist who had replaced her, nail after nail, gently, gently, and finally she moved her head back and stretched out all her fingers in front as if in a moment she'll begin to play something, Concerto number five for nails and polish, and Dadon shouted from the balcony: "What are you looking for here, boy," and he kicked the bumper and found a tin can and kicked that too and under his breath said to it, before shooting it into the street with a tremendous toe kick: for my mother, and ran after it and dribbled and stepped on it and squashed it until it looked like it had been run over by the tow truck, the double cab, the Bulgarian's truck, the train that they watched from the hill, waving to the passengers who never waved back. Toot-toot, he ran from there and hooted, he panted, he choo-chooed, he pushed the passersby like a train engine in a western pushing cattle; he drew and shot them all. Afterwards he went up the stairs and opened the door with the key that hung around his neck with an elastic band from underpants and saw his father in the television armchair changing channels and again he drew and shot him from the door, with a silencer, but his father just coughed from the television armchair and said: "won't Miku bring his father a glass of water?")

"Once a Hungarian woman came to me asking to cheer up her grandson who was in hospital with a broken leg. I came to the ward dressed up as a clown and he hardly took any notice, you'd think he was used to seeing clowns from morning to night. I said to him, 'tell me little Igan Migan[19] don't you know how to say thanks in your grandma's language?' 'Köszönöm' the little midget tells me. 'Nice,' I say to him, 'manners never did anyone any harm. And how do you say grandma in her language?' 'Nagymama,' he says to me from the bed, but looks at the nurse. Small as he is, he's looking at the nurse like that. 'What would you call someone like that in your grandma's language?' She was young and really sweet, not like the two of you. 'Ishterem samla'[20] he

---

19   Derisive name for people of Hungarian extraction

20   The Hungarian sounding phrase literally means "nobody has put it to her yet," originating as the retort to the joke: "How do you say virgin in Hungarian?"

says to me straightaway, with the foot and its cast filled with drawings, dangling like that in the air, and then swinging the foot in a way as if to show grandma she wasted her money, let her bring chocolate instead."

(And the Persian, ever since he slept in the park with the Russians, they'd ask him every night: "come on, if his mother was like that, where did he get into her pizda from? Just tell us, we want to understand." And his father, sitting at a corner table, beneath the cobwebs that the fan made quiver, said to his glass, as silent as the glass, at the level of the glass: "but that's what they believe over there," and as he was led by the hand he said, "not just the Russians, everyone," and as he was guided between the chairs and the tables he mumbled: "the Ukrainians, the Poles, the Germans, everyone there," and when they reached the display cabinet he said to the ancient cakes and salads: "that he was born like that, and to them we killed him," and when he pushed him up the stairs to the apartment – in front of all the doors there were trash bags smelling of garbage and drippings, and all the walls were full of bicycle tire marks, nobody left them downstairs – he said: "and for that they killed us in the war, Miku, just for that," and he thought that if he takes his hands off him now in the middle of the stairs he'll really die.)

Shechter let go of the wall.

"I'm through," said the actor. "Don't get mad."

Shechter looked at Na'ama. "So what have you decided?"

"To let it be with my phone number," she answered. "Let them call, I don't care."

"Just give me the number afterwards," the lighting man again fixed the lamp cable to the wall with his foot.

The actor folded the page once and then again and returned it to the drawer. "That depends," he said. "Depends on your intentions. Are they honorable? Are they pure? Will Na'ama in fact find happiness with you?"

"Don't do me any favors," said the lighting man. He bent over the lamp plug, sniffed around and repeated the number by heart. "Did I remember right, Na'ama?"

"Yes," she replied and returned the small mirror to her purse.

(First he enlarged the picture of her, striped her with stripes; and on the pavement of the editing room he rummaged through her purse, but what she had hidden there, what she had bought because the time had come, because she's not a girl anymore, that – he didn't find, also when she thought to herself, in place of him: "right now, you with the dark brown hair and black purse, we were both sitting opposite the master sergeant's geraniums, and the most beautiful flower-" but he didn't say anything.)

"It's just that I don't get involved with married men."

"I'm not one yet," he said, "only next month."

She moved her eyes from the bristles of his head and looked out the window: between the growing stripes of shadow outside, the rake was being dragged and struck the ground, rattling like the crop spraying plane. One of the prisoners was dragging it and the other prisoner pushed the trash can and above them the eucalyptuses shed the last specks of light.

"Let's do another take," said Shechter (in the voice of a director, for a moment shaking off the dust and cobwebs and the sack-like covering woven above him, which hardened like a calloused skin, thickening more and more into the flesh, until the heart reduces its beating like someone stuck in an elevator filled with strangers: a plump grinning baby, a young boy in a khaki shirt, a long-haired boy, a young man whose beard is downy on his cheeks, a bald man whose eyes are extinguished, an old man held up by a stick, all the other Shechters he carries around inside himself and all of whom are huddled together there, and where one moves an elbow the other pulls in his ribs, and where one turns a shoulder the other hollows his upper back, and where one rejoices the other becomes silently sad), "one last one, for safety's sake" (and they're already being joined one to another the way King Mezentius's captives were to corpses in the mythological stories his father used to read to him, years before he told him about Thomas Alva or Rutenberg; and that room in which he heard the stories sometimes still appears in his dreams with its toys and illustrated books and playpen bed, in which he continued to sleep with his growing, swelling body and the bars slit into him and are swallowed in his flesh with the rattling balls hung between them. The grinning baby; it's been a long while since his grins have been wiped off, and the young boy in the khaki shirt who marched at the head of the column of children and called out: "To the spr-ing!" And they answered him, and he called out again: "a goat came, came a white goat," and they answered him, and he embellished the call in full voice: "tooo the spr-ing came a white – goat," and they all answered him, also embellishing the call in full voice: "toooo the spr-ing, came a white – goat," that boy has already been strangled with the white string cord, and the long-haired boy was dead too, as were the bearded young man who tried to look like a Frenchman and the student who dreamed of changing the face of cinema and all the others.) "Anyway it's still not possible to start the flashback" (he heard himself from a distance, from where each word of his became dismantled one after another like coaches of a train on a bridge in some war, not the one in which he took part, after which he ceased to be a combat soldier; but a different one, an old one that was shown in yellowing black and white on a sheet at the scout den: hunchbacked tanks like beetles became wrinkled there, Stuka planes buzzing like wasps skipped from one fold of the sheet to another, and in the projector's spotlight the thigh of the girl who sat next to him shone all the way to the shrunken edge of her gym shorts. The speaker was wrapped in a blanket to stifle its grating noise, but the reels of the film also rattled and clanged, and if the picture moved from its place and the sky suddenly opened up beneath the battlefield, everyone would burst out and shout back to the counselor in charge of the screening: "projectionist projectionist!"). "There's still too much light" (and on the banks of the Yarkon, which they called a river since they had never yet seen a real river with ducks drifting on it or floating sheets of ice or the remains of the clochards' vomit, on that ground that concealed nothing besides the small stones that tickled their backs through the sleeping bag, he and the girl looked at the bank across from them, and at the eucalyptuses that rose from it, eucalyptuses higher and denser than these, which in the dark resembled giants wearing cloaks, until a group of sleepwalking clouds appeared to be moving forwards in the sky, and beneath them they seemed as if to be gradually falling backwards in delayed motion, like the motion of his hand on her thigh inside the sleeping bag), "and not everyone's here" (within the small night waiting there, the concealed kernel of the night outside, a hidden fruit was unfolding not in his small trembling fingers inside there, but as though in the beating of his heart alone). "Come on girls, let's do it one more time."

Kinneret opened the door and its hinges creaked. In the widening gap of the opening a section of the road could be seen, its edges turning honey-colored by the light, and the shadow of the rickshaw that passed the fire hydrant and covered it. The door creaked, its hinges shrieked.

"I can oil that," said the sergeant and looked at the soundman who was crouched in his corner on his heels.

"Leave it," he said from there, "what difference will it make."

"That's your attitude to the film?" asked the sergeant already turning to the door.

(Because why should it make a noise? All right if it had been a pleasant noise, but just creaking? Once at home he was awakened by the little one's screaming, he almost had a heart attack: he thought there was a snake or a scorpion inside, until he heard the chirping of a cricket. For maybe an hour he searched for it, the little bastard, going through all her toys twice, the teddies and the Snoopys, the slippers with the pompoms, the rubber ducks, until he finally found it, small, the size of a bug, but likeable.)

The soundman lifted his head from the recording dial. "It's a one-way microphone," he explained quietly, "it'll hardly be heard."

"Are you trying to make me feel better?" asked the sergeant.

(At the time he just wanted to catch it in his hand, that cricket, and throw it out the window, to set it free, but it became slightly squashed in his hand: not actually squashed, but perhaps by accident he pressed it just a tiny bit. It was a small one. Afterwards he felt sorry for it, as if they had known one another, he even missed the chirping; it sounded just like on the kibbutz.)

"No," replied the soundman. "It's just that it's a professional microphone, even if the rod isn't standard."

(Before the filming it had been a broomstick and in some distant time a branch, until its leaves were plucked and it was dried and planed: but it was not dry in the mountains and when he walked there his hand felt the moisture of the sap even after it had been cut down: at the time he made a walking stick for himself from the branch of a tree with which he wasn't familiar, though the entire view was astonishingly familiar.)

"My compliments to the microphone."

(Below an altitude of three thousand meters the Himalayas looked like the Jerusalem hills or the Carmel, but there were no forest arsonists and no settlers with skull caps fixed to their heads as if they were the fingerprints of God: and on the pathways, instead of hungry lively goats, mild-tempered yaks walked leisurely, their eyes so human-like that he almost expected them to put their hairy hooves together and greet him like their owners with "namaste." Then the undergrowth became sparse and the ground so arid that the Himalayas resembled the mountains of Sinai, for a few moments he waited to see on the horizon a desert whirlwind of uprooted shrubs and grains of dunes, until the ground became rockier and patched with snow and his breath became short. When he returned to Kathmandu – at the time he didn't yet know he would travel to the island, he was not as yet aware such an island existed at all – he found the boy in his corner, crouched down in the dust with his skimpy brushes and his rags, and placed his shoe on the polishing box and said to him: "Only one shoe," and smiled. The boy cast him a cautious and suspicious glance and became startled when he reached out his hand to his small head, but he stroked the hair with its lice and the dust that stuck the hairs together, until he became reconciled to it and was captivated by the stroking like a puppy. Every morning he returned to him to have his shoes shined, adding another rupee for each sole so that he would brush the high sides and another rupee for each lace just so that they wouldn't be smeared with polish, until one morning the boy said to him: "Today, me present," and smiled at him through the dust. "Magician, magician," he replied to his raised eyebrows, and wondered then what magic could be made in a place like that in which idols spew out the rice offerings presented to them, and on the steps of its temples sit barbers cutting clients' hair; the chickens pecking and picking at the lice in the shorn locks.)

"It'll take a minute to oil it," said the sergeant. "Last take – let it be a good one. Anyway it'll take time until the flashback. Her parents are nowhere to be seen at all." He went out and the door creaked after him.

("Shaman," he tried to explain to him and packed up his brushes, pushing the polishing box into the corner of the alcove in which the money changer would list for one of the Israelis: "grass, coke, opium, you name it brother," and he held his hand and from there pulled him through one alley and another and a third and a fourth to a small room whose floor was covered with filth and the legs of the table stuck into it like stakes, and the thermos was lodged in the filth of the table and the tea that had been poured was lodged in the filth of his stomach. "So you want to see the magician?" the father of the boy or his uncle or his boss asked him and refilled his glass, but when he took a bill from his belt he refused it and said: "Be my guest, please. Ram" – that was the boy's name, like the name of one of the Gods – "told me about you." Flocks of crows circled in the sky when they went out, all crazed by the smell of the burnt dead on the other bank, and they continued to soar above them as they led him through inner courtyards and shady lanes and alleys whose entire width was the size of a chicken, and staircases in whose cracks lizards darted, and passageways up against whose walls pigs rubbed, shedding scabs of sludge and silt to the ground. One after the other dingy rooms full of sighs and others full of groans opened to them, for the entire length of their walls gaunt and wrinkled old men and women were bent as if in a clinic in which no one is cured, but instead metamorphoses into an agamid lizard, year after year they metamorphose and meanwhile allow him to bypass them without becoming at all irritable. From a distance he imagined hearing faint bells and drums, and the fragrance of incense thickened and mixed with the smell of the elderly, until at the end a door opened and he was drawn into a dense dusk pervaded with smoke. A ray of light beamed diagonally from a small window and soaring incense swirls caused it to waver and immediately spiraled and twirled in the air like a den of cobras, as if the shaman created the dance with her bangles and bracelets for the scores of the old people who bent down along the length of the walls there, in the depths of the dark, and waited.)

The door creaked further until it came to a halt. "My parents?" Kinneret said from outside. "You really found someone to depend on." In the small covered area, she stood with Na'ama opposite the cork notice board that was hung on the wall and they both read a pink notice announcing a blast of a party on Cliff Beach offering a special discount for soldiers. Behind them in the shadows of the eucalyptuses, the upraised rake became tiger-like with stripes of a soft light, and from there Weintraub said: "I'll count to three for it to fall, one two-" the rake tilted diagonally and collapsed to the asphalt. "Why did you have to talk," said the other prisoner.

From deep in the room the actor called out: "Is that you there Weintraub? How you doing buddy? How's the garbage?" "Garbage" he vocalized in a Hungarian accent.

"Why, you wanna ride?" Weintraub asked him. Alongside him the rake was balanced again, shining its teeth toward the treetops as if yearning to rake their leaves.

"Believe me," said the actor from inside, "I've got enough troubles of my own. I could even lend you some."

In the door's remaining gap the rake swayed like a dial leading the other prisoner on from there. "Did you hear me, Gidi?" Weintraub turned to the sergeant. "You ask Gidi whose life on this base is in shit the most – Weintraub's."

The sergeant turned from the rickshaw holding a dipstick dripping oil in his hand. "It's your own fault," he said to him, "you get yourself into it." He went to the door and lifted the dipstick to the upper hinge and let the oil drip into it and lowered it to the bottom hinge and tapped it to shake the last drop from it, and with his left hand he moved the door back and forth a few times. "How's that?" he asked the soundman.

"Like butter," Weintraub said from behind, "well done, Gidi, you and your special methods."

The sergeant was still looking at the soundman. "Do they also do that in your East?" And straightaway he returned to the rickshaw, keeping the dipstick at a distance from his trousers.

(What, doesn't he know what'll happen in the end? At the last moment it'll drip onto his trousers and when he gets home and the little one comes to hug his leg, running in her funny way, he'll have to tell her: wait sweet pea, wait. Isn't that how he returned from filming in the south?)

The dipstick dripped on the road.

(One would have thought he had fought there or something, after all he just went to film. Squeezed together with the tripod and Merav in the sentry box, the Manfotto actually worked well there as if it were a tripod for a machine gun, and when he turned the camera to the missiles he saw Merav opposite suddenly blush at what was carved on the side panel there and straight away said to her: "you don't have to look at that, sweetie. Are you giving me sound?" He waited for her to point the microphone to the radar that rotated across from them and beeped, but Merav was still looking at him and said: "don't call me 'sweetie', haven't I asked you a thousand times?" The color of the sky was gradually changing and on the way down to the living quarters, no matter where he turned his head, there was nothing that disturbed him, not the buildings, not the sun heaters, not the antennas, nothing. The headquarters company commander had just then left on some errands, so they still didn't know where everyone would be sleeping, and the captain, after he finished counting the wasps in the soft drink bottles again, winked at him and said: "listen, there's a room here belonging to those who've gone home, for my part you can get organized there," and he answered him immediately: "it's okay, we'll wait here in the meantime. It's not really cold yet." Across from them, in the square between the headquarters living area and the girls' quarters, a water sprinkler revolved; revolving there in the middle of the desert and scattering them with sprays of water in the wind, clicking like the sprinklers on his wife's kibbutz, and Merav said: "maybe you're not cold, but I am." Opposite, the grass patches glistened with drops that covered its blades, and the rockery, which they made there from all sorts of colored stones that they must have brought from the nearby crater, glistened too. "So what do you say?" the captain asked. "It's all right," Merav answered, "he'll fetch an anorak from the car for the little girl." And the sergeant was still just thinking about that headquarters company commander; he really deserves credit for succeeding in making his base look like a kind of Nachal settlement, despite all the missiles and the radar and the secret installation, from which in the darkness only three tiny lights could be seen down below, as if it was nothing at all: it could have been concealed by a raised fingernail. "The little girl wants an anorak," said Merav again and he walked to the Peugeot truck that he had been given – really something special, that Peugeot – and pulled out the anorak, which she had previously made into a cushion for her head, and from the compartment used for documents he took out a small bag of telephone tokens that he had prepared. Because is he going to depend on favors from the war room? Doesn't he know the guys who sit in the war room? It's just that maybe they really would need the line, after all there was a war on. That Peugeot was some vehicle; it really was the lion of the fleet like they said in the advertisement: not some rickshaw whose dipstick was bigger than the engine.)

   "It's not mine," the soundman answered from the entrance. From there he watched the sergeant who was replacing the dipstick. "The East is not anyone's, except those who live there."

"You were there for a year, weren't you?" the sergeant wiped his hands on the rickshaw's canvas and turned them over and looked at them.

"What's a year in the East."

(In the alleys and in the courtyards and in the lanes and in the passageways and in the rooms full of sighs and groans and wheezing and in the room itself, in the dense dusk in which mutterings beat rhythmically again and again, syllable by syllable, as if the walls were built from them and would collapse should they cease, and at the end of the light beam coming from the small window and obstructed by the smoke and outfoxing it and continuing on its way, was a glittering copper bowl and an old man lying there on a small carpet. And the Shaman crouches over him and tosses her black hair to the sounds of the drums the bells the bangles the bracelets here and there, up and down, casting out strands and retrieving them with a motion of the neck, casting out and retrieving and bending toward the shriveled chest and placing her lips on his ribs and gradually suckling from them with gentle lingering movements, until the wheezing imprisoned in them diminishes and is drawn into her mouth and spat out into the bowl in a thick murky globule. All around the dusk beats rhythmically again with drumming pealing rattling, and the boy and his father or his uncle or his boss prod him with their elbows from both sides and say to him: "now you, now you," but still he hesitates. A small old woman advances into the beam and stands in the illusory light, wrinkled and crushed, and she takes off garment after garment after garment, all filthy, and takes off undergarment after undergarment, all grimy, until all the limp skin is completely undressed and her lean bones stick out from it and the curls of her privates are lusterless and withered and the light cuts off and rejoins above her as she slowly spreads herself on the carpet to the sound of the drums the bells the bangles the bracelets and turns slowly on her side, directing a sagging breast to the light beam and through cracked lips she emits quiet dry sobs that have already used up their tears: more and more inconsolable

exhausted sobs, until the shaman bends down and listens to
the lips the throat the lungs, passing her black strands across
there and tossing them again here and there, sliding and
gathering them and casting and scattering and hovering and
whipping and caressing with them, until the teat stands out
like a kind of bony, demanding finger and she places her lips
on it and suckles, suckles, suckles, and they prod him with
their elbows from both sides saying to him: "now you, my
friend, now you.")

"Me? If I'm not at home for even one day I start to miss
it," said the sergeant.

(He made the call unconcerned about the telephone
tokens, and when calling from the south every second a
token dropped, half a packet went on one phone call. Both
of them were on his wife's kibbutz, at the very start of the
war he sent them, he wouldn't hear any arguments on the
subject: what, did they all have to be killed together? As
for that city mayor, the sergeant was certain that if he had
small children he never would have spoken the way he did:
he would have liked to have seen him standing in front of
the little one and telling her straight to her face that she had
to take a missile on the head. Why? For what? For his ugly
city? That the few avenues it had he was planning to turn
into parking lots or skyscrapers, God knows. He phoned
them from the army canteen, and two men, who from their
low-rise pants looked like drivers to him, were playing ping-
pong the way the Chinese play, holding the bats between two
fingers – it's just that they were swearing like troopers. The
canteen worker who was watching them from his window
said: "for God's sake let the guy speak on the phone in peace,
an army photographer, what will he think of us" – at the time
he had that tag on his epaulets, and anyone who saw him like
that would have thought that he worked for the television
or something, at the very least Benny Lees' deputy – and
when they were finally silent, suddenly he could be heard
throughout the canteen: "Precious! Did Mommy give you
the lelephone?" That's what she used to say then, lelephone,
and Merav came in. "Are you also an army photographer?"

the canteen worker asked. "No I'm just his big girl," Merav answered, "give me a chocolate bar and something to drink. It doesn't matter what, as long as it's not fizzy." The guard's jeep stopped outside and through the rattling of the engine he heard his wife saying into the receiver: "She's nodding 'Yes' with her head, Gidi," and in the middle of the canteen he shouted: "Poppet? Are you making yes with your head?" And in the far distance, beyond all that desert and the missiles and the radar and the secret installation, he heard her suddenly say a thin, tiny and sweet "yeth," just like that, in the middle of hell-and-gone; whoever invented the phone was a genius. The red light of the security jeep flashed on the wall and when he asked Merav if maybe she also wanted to phone, she peeled the chocolate bar from both sides like a banana and said: "what for, after all I know what they're doing now."

["I deliver him to you, angels of wrath and ire, that you may strangulate him and his form and cast him to his bed and deplete his bounty and carry off the very notion of him that he may dwindle to death" – her grandfather's surely still mumbling in front of the video, "look look," Nina said to Suzy. "He made you into a queen," her father said to Smadi, "every cent we paid him was worth it, if only Laniado was more like him," like Cohen, who wandered around the tables with his half-inch camera and filmed everything except what was really important, and then afterwards went and planted Clayderman piano melodies in the background from the beginning of the cassette until the end: as if all the talking at the tables was just some humming of the piano melodies, and all the burekas were eaten to the piano melodies, and all the aluminum balloons were flying to the piano melodies, and all the Fanta bubbles in the bottles slowed down to the piano melodies, as if six motorbikes with cut off exhaust pipes did not stop in the half-empty parking lot and were all turned off at once and the silence more frightening than the noise.])

"And I didn't miss home?" said the soundman.

(He lay there on the small tattered carpet, putting his head down on the jumping fleas and on the hatching lice eggs and on the worn out threads of the woven material and on the ground that extended from the place upon which his head was laid down to the other side of the world. "Now you, my friend, now you," they said to him, and he still didn't know which of his pains he'd present to her lips until he rolled up his right trouser leg above the knee, as if they were all reduced to one bruise that developed there from when he stumbled on one of the paths with his rucksack, an old-fashioned backpack with a cumbersome frame of aluminum rods, and straightaway she bent forward to him in the light, which cut off and rejoined, tinkling her bells and rattling her bracelets and fastened moist warm lips to the bruise on his kneecap and his skin was drawn to them when sucked gently, him and his redness and the pain inflating it, and for a moment he considered the woman bending over him and stopped. At the time he had no desire for women, he wanted nothing that connects a man to a place: his home was his rucksack, or walls made of mud, and in cities his home was a hotel room reeking of the monsoons, in which a weary fan rattled on the ceiling and next to the door was a peeling mirror spotted with the tikkas of Indian women who stripped themselves even of those spots on their foreheads. In the heat of the night, which was stirred slowly by the blades of the fan, he sometimes saw them sweaty like himself and their privates dewy with salty droplets, until he would awake from his sleep and see above him the damp stains on the ceiling like a map of the world that only its damp peeling continents would still accept him. In the small hotel next to the railway station in which he stayed on his first trip, thin girls swung their bony hips and called out to him: "hey mister, you want fucky-fucky?" Till he said to them from the hard, stained mattress: "leave me alone, girls, please. I'm going to get married when I go back," and giant bugs, whose feelers quivered, poured out from the toilet hole that wasn't concealed, not even by a plastic curtain. Later he returned to his country and got married and fathered a son, he fathered him on the floor, on a bed of ficus leaves that flew inside, and on the windowsill a small sparrow stood and puffed up its plumage and whistled.)

"Sure I missed home."

(Through the worn out fibers of the carpet and through the unpaved ground and through the rocks in its depths and the lava he still heard that sparrow whistling when he took off the money belt and opened the buttons of his shirt. He showed her his chest, where she had bent over before moving down to his navel and further on from there, and said to her: "here, please. Big, big pain, unbearable pain." And on his chest he felt the black strands sliding and the moist, warm lips hovering and being placed there and suckling him gradually with gentle lingering movements, suckle after suckle after suckle until he was diminished and shrunken and all of him drawn though the hole of his teat, his entire miniature heart like the kernel of a kernel, sucked and spat out into a copper bowl in a murky globule in which his entire life was reflected. Above him, from the small window, the beam wavered in the swirl of incense, and the dust twirled in it like an expanding universe or like the whirlwind in the desert that he saw years before.)

"How could I not."

(At the time uprooted bushes were caught up in a whirlwind with grains of sand, and from the ends of the vast expanse they were directed toward the small soot stain, which remained from the night; in the night a jerry can of benzene was in his hands; he had filled tin cans containing sand and cloth material in order to light up the dummy targets for the shooters who were not at all visible in the depths of the dark; and suddenly it caught alight. A stray spark touched the vapor of the benzene: he then saw a white light around him and for a moment was blinded and spellbound and did not move, until he was thrown to the sand and rolled in it from his boots to his hair and was extinguished, but no one was there; when he returned the following day he only saw his footprints and the soot stain; and all around the desert spread out as before from horizon to horizon, completely empty except for the whirlwind: like a giant translucent finger stirred into the sky itself it grew and advanced from the empty horizon on the vast plane, directed precisely at the black ring of the soot and wiping it from his eyes since it had already been etched into his guts.)

"So what did you do about it?" the sergeant examined his elbow.

(The flecks whirled, twirled and danced, the drums banged and the bangles and bracelets rattled, and he sat up on the carpet and fastened his shirt buttons, and in the depth of the dusk did not see the boy anymore nor his father or the money belt he took off, and beyond the small window and the dust, the crows circled and shrieked as if maliciously rejoicing in his predicament. Incense spirals continued to swirl and he separated them with his hands as beads of a curtain in some alcove in Bangkok in which women copulate with their mouths and smoke with their privates, and again passed through the damp passageways in which frogs hopped and through inner courtyards at whose garbage scrawny chickens pecked and through lanes and alleys until coming out onto the square in which the rickshaws parked. He didn't even have one rupee on him, and beneath the shrieks of the crows he walked to his hotel and locked the door of his room and from the aluminum rods of the rucksack he took out the banknotes that he rolled up there for an hour of need such as this.)

"For me, the longing really gets me down," said the sergeant and also checked his trousers (at the last second it dripped, why wouldn't it drip if it could drip? It dripped right onto his trousers; it almost didn't drip, but just then that plane passed and shook the dipstick and it dripped.)

"It also got me down," said the soundman.

(But from the hotel he went down to the street and stopped a rickshaw and went to the offices of the Royal Airways, that's what they called themselves, as if the airport didn't look like a remote parking lot in a suburb of a suburb, and bought a ticket to Bangkok. For a while he wondered if in that hotel next to the railway station the girls still wiggled their behinds on the other side of the flyscreen door and if they had put some flesh on their hips, but he did not stay there, rather on

Khao San Road, so that he could check where to find himself
an island: he didn't want fucky-fucky, he didn't want to see
people around him, hc didn't want to be called friend, mister,
Joe or Dad – how his son hurried to the phone, a new phone
with a digital ring, ran to the living room and listened to the
receiver for a moment and immediately called out: "Mom!
It's him!" She came out of the shower wrapped in a towel
gown and a towel turban, spread out on the couch and said:
"no-no, you're not disturbing at all," and the flap of the gown
rolled back revealing the purity of the inner thigh; "I was
just showering," she explained, as if he wasn't standing in the
passage and watching her, "I also washed my hair, yes, do you
want to smell?" And she loosened the towel from her hair
and stuck a cushion unfamiliar to him behind her back and
asked the mouthpiece: "Do you want to hear him?" and she
placed the receiver on her belly between the flaps of the gown
and for a moment he saw a pure white curved area and rims
of dark rings and recalled how she once stalked a mosquito
above the boy's bed and how at the time they jiggled through
the T-shirt, brimful of milk – nor any other name.)

(He passed by stalls with fake Levis and fake Lacoste
and fake Benetton shirts and passed by smoked crustaceans,
cuttlefish and crabs, and all sorts of dumplings bubbling in
black oil beneath posters of Thai boxing stars, as murderous
as himself, when he headed south from Khao San Road to
Surat Thani, and from Surat Thani sailed to Thong Sala,
and from Thong Sala to Haad Rin, and from Haad Rin
with his rucksack he climbed to the top of a small mountain
from which point onwards the loudspeakers of the beach
restaurants were no longer heard, and went down the path of
a slope on both sides of which the thicket had placed all its
trunks, roots and shoots and branches and tendrils. Further
and further he went, and further still, until he came to a
village of abandoned huts whose thatched roofs had become
unraveled, and turned to one that stood on a cliff, one whose
reeds are sparse and whose door has long fallen from its single
hinge, the wooden window swinging and slamming in the

wind, and from the thatched roof inside, the lizard watched him as he entered, as if it had waited for him there from the beginning of time.)

"He does exactly what he likes," from the shadows of the eucalyptuses Weintraub lifted his eyes to the sky, "come on, Gidi, aren't you going to issue a warrant? Don't let that pilot ruin your filming." On his left the second prisoner was still balancing the rake on the palm of his hand and a few bleeding freckles of light were bitten by its teeth.

"You'll forgive us now, Weintraub," the sergeant passed between him and the fire hydrant.

"Ask Eran if Weintraub forgives," answered Weintraub. Inside, the lighting man was busy again with the lamp: he was narrowing the opening of its shutters and reattached blue cellophane to them with clothes pegs. "Weintraub Never Forgives, there's a movie like that, haven't you heard?"

"No," answered the sergeant. He turned to the small covered area where Kinneret and Na'ama were still standing and reading the notices on the cork board.

"Come on, Gidi," said Weintraub, "I swear, you're all freaked out. He wasn't always this way," he addressed the window from the shadows. "It's just that being made master sergeant's gone to his head."

"Honey," the sergeant said to him and waited a moment for the rattling of the crop spraying plane to quiet down a bit, "I was a master sergeant when you were still in your pram shouting – look mommy, soldiers!" Above him the rattling had already become distant and swallowed up by the rustling of the treetops.

(All at once the half empty parking lot became silent – no one had taken the trouble to tar it, and every winter it turned into a giant puddle – and all at once a voice was heard from there saying: "let's go guys," and their steps were heard. "And the mouth of injustice shall be sealed tight," her grandfather mumbled about him or about other unjust characters, because from the edge of the red carpet that led to the bridal chair – a throne which all in all was a fauteuil draped by a sheet with a few wild flowers wound around the armrests – he was already standing with the other motorcyclists, all in black leather jackets and black helmets except for himself who had removed his helmet. Across from Cohen Productions' monitors he bent down and examined Merav's sister Smadi, close-up in the right and long shot in the left, and gradually he placed the long nail of his little finger close to Smadi's filmed lips and parted them, and with great delicacy he extended the fingers of his left hand to the left monitor and on it spread them in all their darkness on Smadi's white dress and Smadi's breathing body, and his deputy, Ovad, grinned.)

"Sometimes it just takes time until it goes to your head," Weintraub explained from the road, "everyone in his own time. Take Ezra, give him a life sentence and it means nothing to him, as long as you give him a rake to play with. Right, Ezra?"

"Weintraub," the sergeant said to him, "get going already."

(Short and stocky, the studs on his jacket sparkled in the light of the sun guns and the dazzle of the marble when he left the monitors, silent and lithe and springlike he passed the first table – "she had a home, Esther, what do you mean a home, a villa, right across from the synagogue. With a living room, Esther, that you could drive a car into" – and the second table – "because Claudia Schiffer's beautiful and Pnina Rosenblum's not! Take Richard Gere, would he go out with someone like Pnina Rosenblum? He'd never ever go out with someone like Pnina Rosenblum" – and the third table – "Man, after all I done for him, he tells me lies, how can I say nothing, how?" – and the fourth table – "just health, believe me. What do I pray to him for, for money? That he should give me money? How could I say such a thing to him, I'll thank him for whatever he gives me" – and the fifth table – "he'll come back with an accent, they'll make his life a misery. I once had an 'r' like that, I couldn't say 'rah', I'd say 'wah'" – and her sisters racing on the white marble and suddenly stopping and sliding on it, and her grandfather with his mumblings from the Psalms and from the Zohar, until he reached the buffet covered with a white tablecloth and bowls

of fruit and plates of snacks and round trays with glasses of
Fanta, only Fanta, and pinched a grape from a bunch of the
black ones and looked at her sister Smadi and raised the grape
to his lips thin as a knife scar and sucked it slowly and with
great delicacy.)

"Are we gone?" Weintraub asked the other prisoner and
straightaway turned to the sergeant. "Until the rake falls,
Ezra's not moving. He's decided to break the record today.
Come on, Gidi, his world record will be on your conscience."

(He pinched another grape from the bunch and moved
forward to the fauteuil, which they tried to make grand like
a queen's throne, because for one single solitary day in their
lives they could be like queens in a rented palace on a rented
throne and sometimes in a rented dress, and stood opposite
Smadi and brought the grape close to her made-up terrified
eyes and to her flared breathing nostrils and to her red lips
parting hastily in order to swallow the shame before someone
sees it, and even before it was swallowed he bent down and
kissed her on the mouth, a sucking kiss. Only the deaf didn't
hear it: her grandfather, since his attack – "in the middle of
Allenby Street," that's what they said, as if it happened there –
you couldn't know what he heard and what he didn't, and her
father, who was still shining his boss's soles with his tongue,
and her brother, Eli, who was surrounded by all his old
friends, who patted him on the back and thumped him and
asked: "so what's it like to become religious, come on, Eli,
tell us what it's like, maybe we'll also become religious, hey,
Eli? Wouldn't it be something if we all turned religious? And
football on Saturdays, do you still go anymore? And movies,
buddy, movies with sex? Also not?" And she remembered
the *Playboy* that he hid under the mattress and the creaking
that was heard from there at night. "Adon madon nadon
nachdan nashtan nashkat," her grandfather mumbled and
in the harsh white light Moshon shoved her sister, Pnina-
Nina, shoved her as if she was a box of vegetables and not a
Russian dancer skating on the ice, and returned to the buffet
and pinched another grape from there and again passed the
tables – "there was that neighbor's dog, used to follow me and

because of it the whole time they shouted after me 'Wover! Wover!' Believe me, I wouldn't wish it on anyone, certainly not on my child," "Let's say I leave now and find something? Let's say even five shekels? Then I'll say thank you to him, of course I'll thank him, even for one shekel," "Would you have said something to him? Sure, we've heard all about you, like hell you wouldn't have said something to him," "He wouldn't even keep her as a housemaid! Don't make me laugh, Richard Gere with Pnina Rosenblum," "She gave up everything, didn't even want the car from him and told him: 'I don't need your money sweetheart,' and went off with his cousin who had nothing, nothing, all for love" – and went back to Cohen Productions and reached his hand out to the left monitor and squashed the juice of the grape on Smadi's white dress and on Smadi's heavy breasts and on the narrow hips and on the belly and on the place that her hands hid and winked at Cohen's assistant who was working the editing machine and a second wink to Merav, because she too was filming and recording and editing: with the two cameras of her eyes she filmed, with her two ears she recorded, and edited everything with the editing machine of the heart.)

"To hell with his world record," said the sergeant. "Get out of here already." In the shadows of the eucalyptuses Weintraub slowly bent forward over the trash can. "Did the plane wake you up, honey bunny?" He lifted his head, shaking off flecks of light and being dotted by others; he began to sing in a loud and out of tune voice:

"E-den – my successful sonnnn-"

"Is your name Eden?" the actor shouted from the depths of the room, "köszönöm for your performance, Eden."

"You can take the performance and shove it up your ass," Weintraub answered from the road.

"E-den's strolling down the a-ven-uuueee-"

He began to move slowly into the distance and the other prisoner behind him, carrying the rake on his shoulder.

"What do you think about that performance?" the actor asked Kinneret. She did not reply. Across from her, on the cork board, a notice proclaimed: "blast of a party on Cliff Beach with a special discount for soldiers, from midnight to the morning light."

(The wind thinned the sand, purified it, made it sparkle with glimmerings, brushed the shells to a shine. It gave goosebumps to the breathing skin of the giant animal lying down opposite them, the female tourists on its back, reclining or riding above. It inflamed the ash of the cigarette, glowing in her father's eyes. "You can also go for a swim," her mother said to him, "don't you feel like swimming a bit?" At the foot of the table the black cat got up and stretched; reached its front legs forward close to the floor and lifted its backside into the air. All at once its fur was blackened on the table napkin too, and her mother said: "Watch how he'll say to me now 'it's actually nice.' Actually. Go and swim with the little one, go and swim," she said, "They won't be frightened if you go with the little one." And Kinneret – in a new bikini and a T-shirt with two damp circles on it – said: "I'm not a little one." Only the waiter looked at her, she felt his black eyes there, two black circles on two damp circles, but he was an Arab: each time the radio became silent his throaty conversation with a co-worker, a dishwasher, could be heard. "One day they'll frame it," her father said, "sell it for millions," and framed the napkin: he pinned its edges down with the salt and pepper cellars so that it wouldn't blow away in the wind. "Now he's being flattering," said her mother. "See that? Now he's being flattering. He measures everything in terms of money. The great artists didn't have a cent to their names, not a cent. Van Gogh?" But she wasn't Van Gogh, her mother: she studied at the Avni Institute for one summer and ever since has been dreaming of a house in the Ein Hod artist colony: because in the atmosphere there, without contractors and stall owners, she can bring out all that she knows is hidden inside her and simply begging to be released; that's what she said to Kinneret one night in the living room, while she waited for him on the sofa. She then lifted the glass to the light, placed it on her belly and the glass moved up and down. "Do I have a belly, Kinneret?" "No," she replied. "I don't have, right?" "You don't," she replied. She came out of there: from that belly, which the dressing gown did not hide, from between those legs with their blue veins, once beautiful like hers: they were lifted, bent, opened, the heels to the thighs, or wrapped around his hairy back.)

The sergeant looked at his palms and mumbled something to himself.

Merav looked at him from the window. "Don't swear," she said to him, "you might corrupt the little girl."

The sergeant turned back. He bent down next to the fire hydrant and began to turn the valve forcefully (if there'd be a fire here, with the greatest of ease there could be a fire here, not just in summer, anytime, if there'd be one they'd have to search for a crowbar to open it, and after that, after that then what? After that, a commission of inquiry), and a stream of water burst out. "Shit," he said to the water and turned the valve in the opposite direction until it drizzled. From the edge of the asphalt he gathered some sand and scrubbed his hands with it and washed them again.

"Do you want some cologne as well?" Merav asked him from the window. "Ask them, they've got some for sure."

"Are you talking about me?" Kinneret asked from behind.

("Be at ease," her mother said, "just don't start moving in the middle." She dressed her in her purple dress with a purple scarf and a purple hat with an enormous brim that turned heads when she wore it in the street. She herself wore a white djellaba, not a dressing gown; she wanted to feel festive when she painted: like a priestess. She brought the paint brush close to the palette, which they had told her to buy at the course, touched it here, touched it there and mixed the colors. Her father, peeking from the passage, saw the dress and the scarf and the hat on her – she was all in purple right down to the shoes – and he said: "a real little lady," and returned to the kitchen straightaway and continued speaking to his friend, the contractor; and the kettle whistled: it put two fingers into the mouthpiece and whistled. "Don't move!" her mother said, "Kinneret, what did I ask you?" The whistle was silenced; two fingers were removed and glistened. From the kitchen, through the clinking of the spoons, the contractor, who had renovated their apartment and now wanted to open a modeling agency, spoke: "Models are the best thing," he said to her father – they heard him from the room, which once was called the workroom and which now her mother called an *Atelieu* – "they pay you to publicize them, believe me they're willing to do anything for it." "A bit more," said her mother. "What, are you shy in front of your mother?" But she was not shy, she opened another button: and already she saw them inside there, moving around like puppies. "Bring something strong to drink, to celebrate the deal," said the contractor, "he brings me coffee." And her father said: "I'm doing fine with the old stuff, it's started doing well again." "I can see you're becoming optimistic again," the contractor said and stirred the spoon. "What have you got to lose, what? Ten grand?" The paint brush stopped in mid-air. "Purple suits you," her mother said. And from the kitchen, which opened out to the living room, her father asked where they would get models from. "Models are no problem, believe me," said the contractor. "You put a notice in the paper and afterwards you don't know where they're coming from. Every girl wants to be a model today. Take my word; they'll do anything for you to start them off." "Think of something beautiful," her mother said – the brush's edge had already become curved like the beak of a kingfisher over water full of light gleams; but it was purple, and so was the water – "about someone; the prince of your dreams." And her father now asked who would pay for the notice. "The notice is small fry," said the contractor. "What, you worried about who's gonna pay for the notice? You worrying about something like that?" "Think how he's the handsomest of them all," said her mother, "that he's the most elegant of them all. That he's got the most beautiful voice that you've ever heard. And when he sings you want to cry, even though everyone around is concerned only with eating." "So do we have a deal or not," asked the contractor. "And he sings for you," said her mother, "takes the microphone in his hand and puts it so close to his mouth as if he wants to kiss it, and sings to you."

The sun is rising in the sky

But that's not what he sang.

And suddenly he sees

And not that either.

The purrrrple dresssss

He sang.)

The lighting man stood next to Merav and with her watched the sergeant through the window as he still bent over the fire hydrant outside. "Just don't touch my electrical stuff with wet hands," he said to the sergeant. "After that what would I say to the wife?"

The sergeant scrubbed his hands again. "Don't you worry," he answered and washed his hands in the drizzle. "Believe me I'm not planning on dying yet." He swept up another fistful of sand with his fingers and rubbed the bottom of the palms of his hands with it.

"What did you start with the oil for anyway?" The lighting man leaned his elbows on the window sill. "WD-40's not good enough for you?" Above his head the ceiling turned blue from the lamplight.

"If we start oiling doors with WD-40," the sergeant answered from the shadows of the eucalyptuses, "later when we really need it, where we will get it from, the army canteen?"

"Two Bamba and a WD-40," the actor called from the depths of the room. Outside the treetops rustled and the actor asked if anyone knew how to say a small forest of eucalyptuses in Hungarrrrian. Nobody answered, and the actor vocalized: "A Pah-rrrk." And how to say an electric current? A Spahrrrk. Maybe at least the girls are laughing there? Hey, girls?"

Kinneret turned to the door of the clinic and Na'ama was still looking at the cork notice board: "blast of a party on Cliff Beach with a special discount for soldiers from midnight to the morning light first drink free with the top hits-"

(From midnight to the morning light I gazed at you, you the girl with the light brown hair: down below, the waves crashed against the cliff like my heart against your heart. Monday toward evening, I was walking on the road while you were reading the notice board: come and read my heart like that. But only Weintraub and the other prisoner were walking there, becoming spotted by the shadows of the leaves. I sat on a branch of a eucalyptus and watched you; but nothing could be seen amongst the leaves, not even a bird; right now, Monday toward evening, I peeked out at you from behind a reddish cloud, you the girl with your light brown hair let down and a velvet ribbon on the wrist: wrap it like that around – but the crop spraying plane was already obstructing the cloud, rattling, moving forward.)

"With-the-top-hits-on-the-most-advanced-sound-system-in-the-middle-east."

(During the war, while traveling once by bus from her sister's with a gas mask in its cardboard container, she heard a conversation in front of her between an elderly woman and an old man, and at the time Na'ama was amazed that women of that age still had dreams just like her own. It seemed somewhat funny to her, and sad as well, and so lovely that those dreams never end. The woman, only whose rounded shoulders and black hair, which perhaps was dyed but still thick and shiny, were visible to Na'ama, said: "Of course that's what I need, what do you mean, who doesn't? Someone to do things with, to do everything with. What do you mean? To go out with, to talk with. I want him to look after me, to care for me, yes, but not only. To pamper me, why not, but not only. That's not what it's like with my boss at work. There is an attraction, there is, I'm not saying there isn't. But first of all his wife works with us, and anyway I'm definitely not looking for relationships with married men. What do I need it for? I need someone steady. Even if there is an attraction, and there is, I'm not saying there isn't. But what's attraction, attraction's not enough. Only today I went out to buy something in the afternoon, just some cake, something to have with coffee. I asked for a packet to take it with me, for when I have something to drink, and the shop owner says to me: 'sit, sit, have something to drink here, on me. Is that okay?' And then he says: 'you've got a quiet, gentle voice.' There were two of them, his partner was also there, he had just come out of the kitchen having said something to the Arab, and then his partner also says to me: 'sit, sit, you must be exhausted from working on your feet all day.' And he looked at my legs, from top to bottom. Does it embarrass you that I'm telling you this?" "No," the old man said, and Na'ama saw only his neck and the shirt collar whose edges had become worn out. "You see what I mean, things like that. But that's not what I'm looking for, there's no problem finding things like that. If that's what I wanted, it wouldn't be a problem at all, but what is that, nothing. Today comes, tomorrow goes. Don't get me wrong, of course I want to be hugged, who doesn't want to be hugged? But not by just anybody. Look, I'm used to very high standards and after that you only want even higher. Isn't that how it is in life? You must know that. As for young men, they don't interest me at all. There's no way I could reach some boy. Just maybe he'll understand you, just maybe. But older men are different, they've been through things, they understand you. Forty-five, fifty, I'm looking for someone like that. It's hard. It's hard. A successful man, one who succeeds in everything he does, who's already well established and everything isn't going to make compromises. Someone like that, who can get any girl and live with her in style isn't going to make any compromises. And me, I also don't make compromises, d'you understand me? It's not that I'm naïve, believe me I'm not, it's been a long, long time since I was naïve. In the end life will bring someone who's naïve down to here, like this," and Na'ama then heard her rubbing her shoe on the floor of the bus like she was putting out a cigarette, and then right away the little laugh she laughed. "Don't get me wrong, sure I look young to you, you might think – what does she know? Believe me I've been through things in my life that I wouldn't wish on anyone. I didn't have a mommy or daddy to tell me the whole time tatam-tatam, do this, don't do that. So I tried everything. Believe me there's nothing I didn't try. Now what's love anyway, really what's love? Sometimes I tell myself there isn't any love Rina, none, it's just all in your head. I stand in front of the mirror – does it embarrass you that I'm talking like this?" The old man shifted his neck slightly and moved the cardboard carton on his lap. "I look and say to myself: there isn't any love, none, that's it. All in all what there is is neediness. Neediness, yes. It's just one person needing another, and neediness isn't love. Neediness isn't love, neediness is neediness. So what's all that talk about in the movies, it's only like that in the movies, not in life. When do things like that happen in life? But right away I catch myself and say: who are you telling stories to Rina, what's neediness, what are you going on about? Neediness is neediness and love is love." And Na'ama, who leaned forward a bit to listen to her, thought then about her sister who was left alone on the roof at night in the sealed room that made up her entire apartment, and about her parents, who in their wedding pictures still smiled, upright and good looking like movie stars, and about herself, Na'ama: Monday toward evening, you, the girl with the light brown hair and the black velvet band, from the inside of the plane I sat and looked at you from under the cockpit canopy, by myself in the meantime: I waved hello with my hand, and you didn't see, I blew you a kiss in the air, and you didn't feel it: right now.)

The eucalyptus leaves were silent and she turned her head to Kinneret who was still looking at the door of the clinic. "Weren't your parents supposed to arrive already?" she asked her.

The sergeant lifted his head from the fire hydrant, still struggling to stop the drizzling from its mouthpiece. "Yes, what about them? In a moment there won't be any sun."

The lighting man watched them from the window and his elbows leaned on the sill. "Do you know why he's fiddling around with it such a lot," said Merav from behind, "with the water? God forbid he comes home dirty, it'll be a disaster if he comes home dirty, a disaster."

"You better pray that they're on the way," Kinneret answered, "it'll be a miracle if they arrive on time." From the door of the clinic the naked girl drawn on the poster looked straight at her, large letters turned red above her and a line that someone had added by pen turned blue.

"What do want of him?" the lighting man said to Merav, "when I get married I'll also-" he didn't finish the sentence. Opposite him, on the side of the road, the fire hydrant continued to drizzle.

The upper body of the girl exposed in the poster was outlined like an illustration in a textbook: two small arcs indicated her breasts and her hand placed close to one of them: "early detection will save your life!" proclaimed the title above her head, and on her stomach in diagonal blue letters was written: "could I examine them for you honey?" The drawing pins in the corners were rusted and remnants of paper from some old poster were stuck to the two bottom ones.

"An electrical cord," said the actor from within the room, "how do you say that in Hungarrrrian?" Straightaway he told the lighting man by vocalizing: "a virrre." And also told him how you say a harp: "a lyrrre." "And where's this movie about new recruits?" he asked. "In the mirrrre," he answered himself after a moment. "Don't take it personally," he turned to Shechter, "I include myself in it." Shechter was still leaning with his back to the wall.

On the table, between the telephone and the incoming post tray, the actor held a page on which he had written

down Na'ama's telephone number and was now folding two
of its corners to the center, aligning the folds diagonally to
each other.

"Keep her number for me, okay?" the lighting man asked,
removing his elbows from the windowsill.

The actor folded the two paper diagonals to the side.
"Aren't you getting married in a month?" From both sides
of the spine of the page he made two white, diagonal, delta-
shaped wings, striped with lines. "And how do you say a crop
spraying plane?" A number stuck out from under one of
the folds. "A sprrray cruiser," he said and promptly held the
paper plane by its underbelly and tossed it over the table in
the direction of the window. "And how do you say Miki-Le-
Mic-Special-Events-and-Happy-Occasions, the greatest? Big
looo-zer," he answered himself, and for a moment the plane
rose in the air, glided, slowed down, spun and fell sticking its
nose into the floor. "What did I tell you?" he said.

Across from him, between the window frame and the
still darkening shadows of the eucalyptuses, a sky whose
redness lingered in a few clouds could be seen, and when
he got up from his chair he appeared to the sergeant in his
tattered wig, his made-up face and the female soldier's tunic
he was wearing, lit up by the bluish light of the lamp. "And
how do you say cloud?" he asked. "Sheeeep," he bleated
the reply with smeared red lips, and from the fire hydrant,
which was still dripping, the sergeant saw him lifting his arm
to his breast, clasping five red fingernails to it and reciting
with great intent to the open window and the setting sun:
"tomorrow and tomorrow pass like sheep before down to lie,
and all our yesterdays have lighted fools the way to die," as
the bluish light flashed around him over and over whitened
and dazzled and blinded.

On the right, from the entrance whose door was pressed close to the wall,
a voice said: "now they definitely won't be able to see a thing in the dark,"
and the investigator – balding, shoulders hunched, the top button of his
trousers unbuttoned so as not to put pressure on his stomach, and his two
eyes with the dark bags beneath them reflected in the dimmed monitor –
turns his head to the female medic who is standing there again, the palm of

her hand on the door handle (she who told the police; the police told him). Her coat whitens on her khaki uniform and her chestnut ponytail dances for a moment while she nods her head opposite the darkened monitor, and right away she hastens to soothe in a firm voice, too big for her size (as if he might really be shocked by the death of a man whose existence in the world he was not aware of the day before, as if he might be glad about the saving of the others, complete strangers too. In the middle of the night the boss's secretary phoned and said he would have to investigate, what's he getting so annoyed about, surely she's not disturbing anything. He should thank her for the investigation, if it wasn't for her they wouldn't be giving him another chance: as far as they're concerned, just so he knows, he's already a lost cause and honestly it's hard to blame them, no? And besides that, if he'll just open his shutters a bit now, he'll even find that there's a full moon tonight, when was the last time he looked at a full moon? When she had a dog – does he still remember the dog? – He would howl just like a siren on nights like these, looking at the moon and howling like a lunatic; with him he actually got on well, with the dog. Or has he wiped out everything from his memory? In other words, since his mind became messed up, never mind his mind, his life itself. Maybe he doesn't see it, but everyone around him does, especially those who care about him. Now he should get some sleep for tomorrow, if he's cold then he should put his hands where she put hers. And tomorrow, first of all he should come by the office, first thing in the morning and get all the details. And he should set up a meeting at the police station there. No, she didn't set one up for him, why should she arrange his meetings? She's not his secretary. She's not his anything. He should also take into account the time the journey will take and the state of his Cadillac, which no doubt is also a wreck: what does he think; they'll wait for him forever? Does everyone have to wait for him forever?), that perhaps they'll notice afterwards. With her finger she raises her round glasses, which had shifted, and leaves hastily. The door that slammed behind her shakes the monitor and the window that was sealed and the lizard grasping the whitewash in the corner of the ceiling, a little lizard that perhaps saw everything on the previous night as well, if in fact everything was seen: the growing fire, the billowing fire, the fire that sprouts and blossoms and sheds leaves and yellow flowers into the dark heights and in whose roots a man is trapped.

6

(In the factory, out the front of which a tiny garden survived from the days when his uncle had still hoped to build an exemplary plant in Israel in the European style until he became indebted to the banks, and around the blocks, scrap perforated steel began to pile up with metal remnants and hand-cut twisted slivers, in the unplastered small hall, locks for post boxes and wall cupboards were manufactured and different sorts of simple locks whose sole purpose was not to permit "the opening that beckons a thief" – that's how his grandfather, who in his old age also worked as one of the ordinary laborers, explained it to him – and from all its machinery that engraved, stamped, attached, and from all its corners that were heaped with large and small cardboard boxes and oily rags stained with yellow and black grease, and from all the sounds, the noise of the engraving, the cutting, the attaching, the throaty flourish of the lathes operating and the gentle humming of the women packers, he remembered the place in which the worker Yom-Tov, who in his eyes at that time seemed as giant and black as an African and who even his uncle treated with respect, used to open a small thick steel door from which the heat emanated before it was opened, and when it was opened – slowly and carefully – the fire confined behind it was revealed, moving gloriously and wildly like the leopard he himself saw that summer quivering its yellow stripes and baring fangs and growling around its cage. That summer his parents traveled to Europe and every week postcards turned up at his grandfather's apartment; on them were Andalusian castles or bulls charging at red capes or a crumbling ancient stadium or the Eiffel tower with a setting sun, and on the back they wrote to him: "Kisses – Mom and Dad," and added an explanatory line: "the man fighting the bull is called a toreador, kisses Mom and Dad," or "here only Dad went up by foot and I went up in the elevator," or "this is the river that we'll be sailing on now, kisses Mom and Dad," and his grandfather would hold the corner of the postcard over the mouthpiece of the kettle in order to remove the stamp with steam. His grandfather's palms were large and rough and their lines were always dark from the oil of the machines, and he liked to see how he held the tweezers in his strong fingers, handling the stamps delicately. Sometimes his grandmother watched them from her corner and once in a while she would say: "you'll see what lovely things they'll bring you," or "they'll bring you things you didn't even ask for," or "such things from overseas, you can't imagine," or "you'll see how happy they'll be, we'll take a taxi to the airport and wait for them," and his grandfather would continue to arrange the stamps in silence. Before that summer, every time his grandfather and grandmother would arrive on a visit from Bnei-Brak to the project of terraced apartments that was separated from an Arab village only by a wadi, arriving and descending the stairs that led to their apartment, the neighbors' son would right away call out to him from his balcony in a deep voice and ask how his grandfather sleeps at night, with his beard above the blanket or below it, and if he ties up his sidelocks so that they don't get in his way and if he does it with his grandmother through a hole in the sheet. And although he more or less knew what he meant, in his eyes the very idea seemed so strange, enough that he never became angry: for a moment they were still hidden by the ugly awning that the neighbors installed over their kitchen balcony – his father said that they were turning the neighborhood into slums and that he wouldn't be surprised – and straightaway they would go inside with their bags and their baskets and their packages, and his grandmother would take out large and small plastic containers from them with cooked food that she brought with her and peek into the fancy kitchen cupboards and the huge two-door American fridge, and the window in which the mosque always stood out.

He caused his grandmother much sorrow all that summer, because he wouldn't taste her dishes and insisted on eating only steak and fries like his father, but in her small kitchen in which the smell of cooking thickened she was not at all annoyed when they entered with the postcards to remove the stamps with steam – WD-40 didn't remove them, only steam – "this dance is called flamenco," was written on the back, "kisses Mom and Dad," or "this fountain was made by a man called Bernini, kisses Mom and Dad," or "on this bridge a man stood and sang with a guitar, kisses Mom and Dad." And at nights, when he slept in the guest room on a couch next to which his grandfather placed two chairs so that he wouldn't fall to the floor, God forbid, he wasn't able to visualize his parents, hard as he tried, traveling there in all those places – on the bridge, around the fountain, in the ancient stadium – without him, without holding his hands from both sides and saying: "one, two-ooo and thr-" and lifting him up, even though that memory is already very distant and for many Saturdays they haven't been out walking, not on the paths of the Ben Shemen forest, not on the promenade of Tel Aviv and no other place.

The neighbors' son, who would watch the next door apartments from his balcony and the Arab village where in the darkness of its garages welding sparks were always flying, also asked if his grandmother takes off her wig every night, like all the religious women, and if he had ever seen her bald head, but that summer every evening he would see her loosening the bun of white hair and combing it and was amazed by its length and beauty, as if only girls and young women were allowed to have their hair so long and to comb it like that in front of the mirror. At the end of that summer his parents returned and brought him all that he had asked for and other things as well: castanets from Spain, small leather boots from Italy and a jacket from France, but in the winter, after a month in which Saturday mornings remained quiet, already the hushed voices and the voices bursting out returned and rose from their bedroom, and when they cease his mother says: "it's enough, the boy hears everything," but now his father's voice adds to that saying: "so what, let him hear. In the end everything will blow up anyway."

And in the middle of winter, which ever since its first rains he's been proudly showing off the flaps of the pockets of his French jacket and the hood tied to it, his father moved to Tel Aviv, and since then would call and talk to him on the telephone once a week. He fixed a time in which he could speak to him directly without them having to disturb his mother, and then his father would tell him about the sea in Tel Aviv and about the promenade and about the building for which special care has to be taken so that it wouldn't be spoiled by the wind and by the salt. And another time in the week he waited for his father who would maybe pay a visit, and afterwards, he was already in a different class, he started to tell his friends that his father received offers not only in Tel Aviv but also in Haifa and in Nahariya and in Ashkelon and in Eilat and all over the country, and even overseas they've heard about him and want him to build buildings there, fountains and bullfighting stadiums. But one afternoon the neighbors' son called out to him from the balcony as he watched a small truck through binoculars drawing away from the Arab village, and in it an old fridge and two straw armchairs and three sheep who stood between them bleating, and said to him: "you little idiot, ask your mother who your father's fucking now," and for a long time after that he didn't go out onto the balcony for fear he'd call out to him again.

Since then he looks out on the Arab village only from the kitchen, and five times a day the loudspeaker at the top of the mosque would sound throaty flourishes, and from the garages, even after the wavy tin shutters have been closed, sharp sounds of metal being cut still erupted. And one evening he heard his mother talking to his aunt on the phone in a voice he wasn't familiar with and telling her about that trip to Europe: she was speaking from the bedroom and didn't know that he hadn't gone outside to play, and from the kitchen he heard how after they were finished with all the museums and the churches they didn't even have a word to say to each other, and how in Italy when an Italian once said to her "bella donna" she had to remind herself the last time she had heard a compliment about her appearance, and how in one hotel they had adjoining beds, but each one was made up separately with the sheets and blankets tucked under the mattress the way they do in hotels, they didn't even bother to pull them out at night, and how she almost got lost twice and he hardly noticed, once in the bullfighting stadium, to which he dragged her almost by force, she didn't want to watch at all, and the second time in the Metro tunnels after she saw him unashamedly making eyes at some French bimbo, and she then said to herself, to hell with it all, and if it wasn't for the boy she would have turned over a new leaf a long time ago. And worst of all, even more than those nights in the hotel, were those damn postcards that she had to send to her parents, as if everything was just fine with them, and how the "kisses Mom and Dad" that she forced herself to write on each one simply broke her heart.

Beyond the wadi, in the darkness of the garages in which sparks flew, they continued to solder knives and axes with which to slaughter them all one night in their sleep, and when he took down the stamp album from the shelf he still hesitated, as if all the rough fingerprints of his grandfather and all the steam vapor were there between the pages – WD-40 wouldn't remove them, only steam, but nothing would remove what he wrote in the booth – and with them as well all the smells of the dishes, whose names he never learnt and all the abundance of his grandmother's white hair. But right away he put the album in a nylon packet and walked to the dumpster that stood on the way to the supermarket, large and rusted like one of the armored vehicles at Shaar Haguy on the road to Jerusalem, and threw it in, and after it the matches. One by one he threw them in, burning match after burning match, until someone shouted at him: "do you want to cause a disaster here, boy? Isn't it enough we've got them to fear?" Across from them, on the slope behind which begin the desert hills at whose end the Dead Sea sometimes gleamed, black goats slid like pieces of the shedding soot or public telephone receivers thrown from the hand, thrown and spewing coffee-without-a-cup or a cup-without-coffee or coffee-with-a-cup, when shekel after shekel is swallowed in the slot: tomorrow-first-thing-in-the-morning they'll pay her back, pay her back right into the slot.

"I don't think it's a good idea," that's what she said to him, his girlfriend, and the sound of her voice echoed from the receiver through the entire street, which had already emptied in those first days, and for a moment he thought of dialing his grandfather and grandmother or going there without phoning – going up the stairs whose walls were painted with oil paint to the height of children's heads, ringing the sonorous bell, hearing them say to him: "Ran-Ran, what a surprise, welcome, come inside," and not telling them anything but lying down right away in the guest room on the couch, which is clearly already too small for his size, and waiting for his grandfather to place next to it two chairs from the small table, which was covered by an embroidered cloth and on which a vase of flowers always stood – until his leg rose and gave a kick to the receiver as if he kicked her in the mouth the lips the teeth the throat. With a moist red felt-tipped pen he wrote her name and her telephone number next to cockintocunt, and above the telephone next to it – the blue light of the police car was already flashing at the end of the avenue – next to cockintomouth he wrote "blowjob for a shekel, Anat, 645321," and he bent down between the trash cans that had been brought out onto the pavement, and opposite him the blue light was cast on the tree trunks and on the tree tops and on the twisted aerial roots, until it stopped a meter away from him and the white lights were turned on there, large and blinding and then were extinguished.)

("Foul is foul and fair is fair, hover through the fog and filthy air.")

(What, didn't he know it would happen? He could have sworn to them that it would happen.)

("On the 20 April, the sun set for the last time for four
months. Each one of them would go out to clear the snow
carrying his lamplight with him.)

(Just when they were about to finish this take at last and
move on to the flashback, that's if Kinneret's parents don't let
them down, the lamp chooses to turn off. It was the General
Staff's bad luck orders and nobody messes with them.)

Above the fire hydrant, which continued to drip, the
sergeant looked at the window that darkened all at once. The
drizzle of water was already floating a few eucalyptus leaves
down the slope of the asphalt and Merav called out to him
from the room: "stay there with your wet hands, we'll manage
without you," and inside a chair fell and someone bumped
into it and swore.

("Foul is foul and fair is fair, hover through the fog and
filthy air," the actor could be heard.)

"Are you all right?" Shechter asked.

(From Dan in the north to Eilat in the south the General
Staff bad luck orders were upheld: during all his service, on
one Saturday alone, the sergeant took the Sony to film his
daughter and just then the commander of the base chose to
inspect the section: on a Saturday. Didn't he have anything
else to do on a Saturday except make an inspection of the
section? He phoned them immediately at home, leaving a
message on the answering machine as if talking into a two-
way receiver, you would have thought a war had started or
something, and that was way before the war, who thought
about war at all then; immediately a phone call to his wife's
kibbutz as well; suddenly from her parents' room she called
him, from behind the mosquito net that he himself replaced
for them. "There's a call for you from the army, Gidi," she
said, and he even felt important at first as if he was a pilot or
in a commando unit, as if receiving a sudden call like those
kibbuztniks, about some daring mission at the enemy's rear:
how could he have known the commander of the base would
make an inspection on a Saturday? But as for him, he's not
sorry about anything. Every time the sergeant watched the
cassette that he filmed he wasn't sorry all over again. Especially

during the war he wasn't sorry because if it hadn't been for that, if he didn't have all that film that he shot at the time, how could he have been able to stay at home alone at all?)

"The globe's gone," the lighting man said from the dark rectangle of the window, "but I'll replace it chop-chop."

The door was pushed and he left the room, passing Kinneret and Na'ama, one of whom was back looking at the poster on the clinic door and the other at the notice board (from inside the dark room I went out to you, you the girl with the light brown ponytail and the black velvet ribbon.) He opened the electricity box (I put my life in danger to light up your face, you the girl with the light brown ponytail and the black velvet ribbon), behind whose doors were the fuses of the office and the clinic.

The crop spraying plane, whose rattling was heard above the entrance hall, passed the eucalyptus treetops and drew away into the darkening sky.

("The navigation bridge and the map room of the ship buzzed with activity. Ralph Lenton worked the radio signals, and in the map room Gordon would write down the state of the airplane and the state of the ice. During the patrol, which lasted an hour, a row of open lakes appeared, stretching to the southeast and looked as if continuing for fifty kilometers to the open sea.")

(The General Staff bad luck orders trailed him even to the kibbutz, why wouldn't they trail if they could? The first time he went there, just as they were sitting in the dining room and he was about to put some salt on the salad, the salt cellar opened and all the salt was spilt, just when it was in his hands, those hands that everyone said were golden; he wanted to pour for all of them at the table, the way it's done in the army dining room, so after pouring coffee for them, what do the two clowns sitting opposite say: "But we actually wanted a cup of tea"; they called it a cup of tea, not just tea, and behind their backs they called the blonde volunteers who served the meals geishas. And finally, at the hitchhiker station, just after having put on his uniform, because otherwise he doesn't stand a chance of someone stopping for him, just at that moment a car leaves the kibbutz, when he's already in his smartest air force uniform with the master sergeant band around his wrist – at that time it hadn't been moved to the collar – and he just didn't know where to hide himself. Straightaway he stood behind the concrete barricade again and pretended he was pissing there so that they wouldn't stop for him, and a bird he wasn't familiar with whistled above him as if to say: maybe they didn't see, but I did. It disappeared immediately into the sky above the mountains, a deep blue sky with white white clouds in which you could see all sorts of forms taking shape, absolutely everything. And afterwards, when the little one was already born, he would lie with her on the lawn and lift her teeny finger up to the sky and show her: here's a lamb, and she would say from her little mouth, which barely found room between her cheeks: "am!" and here's a mushroom – "ushroom!" and here's a palace – "allis!" Wherever they looked, the entire sky was filled with ams and ushrooms and allises.)

("On the afternoon of the 22nd of the month, we entered an area of graveled ice and smooth-stoned ice strewn on the water as far as the eye could see. Captain Mara now stood on the lookout post of the mast," – Shechter's father read to him – "and by the light of the lamps he steered the ship along a route that extended the length of the vacant water ways. At first the ice was between one and two meters thick, but as we progressed the following days the ice became firmer and thicker and its fields grew and grew, narrowing our path.")

Amongst the eucalyptus leaves, which in the drizzle sailed to the edge of the asphalt, a cigarette butt floated, swelled up and slowed down.

(It's just that his wife was completely taken by the city. All the grassy areas in front of the dining room meant nothing to her, and how he would pounce on the sprinkler like a lion tamer in a circus while the ill-tempered lions were still growling at him: pouncing and taking control of it, just so that the little one, together with him, could spray Mom with water. The stalks had no need; all the drops already sparkled on them just like pearls, until she would draw close to them, the little one, and blow up those cheeks of hers and go: foo. "What do you think," his wife said, "there're good people and bad people everywhere, and because it's small there, everyone watches everyone else's ass" – he had already got used to her speaking that way, and at night he even liked it, but at first he was afraid that maybe she was ashamed of him: yes, because how's she going to tell them on the kibbutz that she has a master sergeant for a boyfriend and in anti-aircraft too? Even when they were living together and everything, from time to time the thought would arise, even though every night the light was turned on in their bedroom. At times she would turn on the bamboo lamp and at times he would, and one night she even etched lines with her nail on the label to see when they would break the record. And despite all this he sometimes still feared that she was ashamed of him, until one Saturday morning, he'll never forget it, never ever, even when he's old and doesn't know anything, he won't forget how she sat up in bed and very quietly asked, even though the neighbors' radio was blaring, if right now he would make a child for her: just like that, the way she asked him to make a chest of drawers or a bookcase or a television table or all the other things that he knows how to make with those hands of his.)

The fire hydrant, which the sergeant first struck with a stone and afterwards turned off with the help of a broken eucalyptus branch, trickled its last drops. At the edge of the asphalt the leaves floating on the subsiding water slowed down and stuck to the cigarette butt that had swollen up there.

("From both sides of the vacant waterway an unbroken continuity of ice was visible, and as far as the eye could see, crushed, overturned blocks were spread out, their sharp corners pointing upwards. The route narrowed more and more, until by midnight it was a kilometer wide and as time passed – just a hundred meters; and the water, which was as smooth as glass, rose in small waves passing the ship.")

The drizzle, which the tap traced, came up against a small stone and skirted it wearily.

("From that moment on, hope and disappointment alternately accompanied our progress – the ice momentarily opens, we advance for fifty meters and again are trapped motionless. It was only seven or eight kilometers from the place in which Shackleton's ship had been trapped and crushed between the enormous blocks that cleaved it.")

The lighting man's head was still hidden in the electricity cupboard and beyond him a part of the poster on the clinic door could be seen, in it a shoulder and the thin crescent of a breast and the end of the heading in red: "ave your life!" From deep in the room the actor nasally inflected: "Kinneheret? What are you looking at?"

Kinneret did not answer. On her right, from within the electricity cupboard, muffled cursing was heard, but she did not turn her head and continued to look at the poster (will an early examination save you? Nothing will save you.) On the edge of the asphalt the drizzle of water slowed down, still with the cigarette butt and the floating leaves in it, until it stopped for a moment by one of the wheels of the trash can.

From the gap in the open door of the room, the actor looked at the lighting man and blinked his eyelids.

"Out, out light," he called in a loud voice toward his shorn neck, also waving his arm in the air in a wide movement, "life's just a shadow in flight. How's that for a rhyme? It is a tale told by an idiot full of sound and fury, signifying nothing." He removed his gaze from the neck of the lighting man who continued to busy himself with the fuses. "Nah-thing," the actor intoned the syllables in a Hungarian accent. "And how do you say a tale?" He posed the question to Shechter, who was leaning against the wall and still looking out motionless even when the lamp went off. "Bluh-ffing," he immediately replied in the same intonation, and what do Hungarians get electrocuted by?"

("It was one of those situations in which the fate of the expedition completely hung in the balance, for we had no option before us other than to try and move forward between the two fields of expanding ice, with the slim hope that we could escape their pressure before the freezing stage.")

Shechter separated himself from the wall. "Maybe calm down a bit?"

"But I am calm," said the actor, "I'm the calmest girl here!" again blinking his eyelids with their made-up lashes. "Have I got dreams other than making movies for new recruits?" he spread his palms to the sides to show them being empty and when he returned them to the table the polish on his nails sparkled.

"I don't have any either," Shechter answered and moved forward to the entrance.

Opposite him, in the window frame, the rake swayed for a moment like a large dial. Weintraub balanced it on the palm of his hand and behind him the other prisoner steered the trash can; one of its wheels widened the damp line that the drizzle had drawn.

The soundman, who had first emptied his pockets, began to roll himself a cigarette. "You've changed, no question about it," he said to Shechter quietly, and inside the thin paper that he held for a moment, brown tobacco stalks could be seen before being enveloped. "What, don't I remember how you dreamed about making a full-length feature one day?" He licked the edges of the paper all the way with the tip of his tongue and Kinneret watched him until he finished. "Already during first year you started looking for actors, a cameraman, budgets, what not. And you know what? I was sure you would do it. Out of all that year there were only two I would have bet on; on you and on Calderon."

"Calderon?" said Shechter.

With his fingers, the soundman joined the edges of the paper he rolled and smoothed them down. "Maybe it's not too late."

"There were many things I wanted," replied Shechter. "Who doesn't?" His voice did not have the irritable edge that previously erupted from it, just weariness from the filming or from something else that had nothing to do with it. "We were young then," he said.

("Day and night we would go down with axes, picks and hooks in order to clear away the ice from the sides of the ship," his father read to the boy he once was, and one evening, the young man he afterwards became went with the soundman and his wife to see some amateur play on a kibbutz near Netanya – at the time he was looking for an actress for one of the films he was meaning to make – and on the dirt road on which they got lost with the car, low bushes chafed against the underbelly. The soundman's wife, whose name slipped his mind but the way her face glowed throughout her pregnancy he still remembered, said: "It's like the noise of the waves at the bottom of the ferry, do you remember that Jojo? The noise of the waves in the ferry?" And in the weak light of the dashboard Shechter saw her stomach rounded within the denim dungarees, blue as the Aegean Sea in mythological stories, or like the Weddell Sea before it froze over, or like amniotic fluid, which he didn't exactly know about. "Jojo," she called the soundman, who at the time was already planning to buy a Nagra tape recorder with which to support his family, and Shechter they still called Noam, the name he gave back to himself after the army, that's what they called him while believing in all his grand plans.)

"Besides you, who didn't want to be a Fellini or a Bergman then?"

(He himself floated on water like this, a survivor from the ship that his parents set sailing when his father was still as upright as Captain Mara and his mother a beauty like the lady on the bow slicing the waves: they had not yet become cumbersome and shriveled, treading to the kitchen in slippers whose backs were trampled by their heels until they turned into flat clogs, sitting wearily at the table, which was dotted with dry crumbs, and eating wearily and drinking wearily; why even there, within the warm cradling water – water that can never freeze – he heard dim voices nearing and retreating and could not understand the words, swaying back and forth there for months on end, until he was released and allowed to go, but on being born he was so exhausted that he only ventured as far as the other sack.)

"It's what I wanted then. It's not the only thing I wanted that didn't turn out."

The lighting man's shorn head stuck out from the electricity cupboard and was concealed again, and Na'ama turned her eyes from him to Shechter. "Like what?" she asked. She curled a strand of light brown hair on the tip of her finger for a moment then let it go.

"It's a long list, all the things I wanted." From beneath the shadows of the eucalyptuses, whose last specks were waning, the rake plunged to the side of the asphalt, spraying water from there.

"Actually for me one thing's enough," said Na'ama. In the dwindling twilight Shechter saw the shy gaze sparkling in her eyes; her light hair darkened, but under it her features could still be made out; they were not beautiful but had a certain charm about them and in the darkness the pimple on her cheek was eradicated and no longer bothered her. Across from them Weintraub lifted up the rake and its prongs trickled drops of water.

"What thing?" asked Shechter.

"You tell me first," she said to him.

A small flame was released from the soundman's lighter and when brought close to the cigarette it began to lick the tobacco stalks sticking out the edge. "Mine's a complicated story," said Shechter, "maybe some other time."

Na'ama lifted her hands to her neck. "After the filming?" she asked and loosened her hair. She glanced sideways at the electricity cupboard whose fuses the lighting man was still busy with.

"If we ever finish it," answered Shechter.

(The Shechter here, whose eyelids are heavy, whose body is limp, whose whole being doubts not only the filming of this short and the shorts he has to make for a living, but all the coming years as well, which at times seemed to him like a long empty passage in which nobody walks other than him, and through locked doors come the muffled sounds of laughter and groans and sobs and other sorts of vague sounds, whose meaning he's already forgotten, and at whose end – which isn't that far off – there's nothing but a blank white wall against which he, Shechter, will be squashed though he is not running at all; squashed in his slow gait and imprinted in it like one of the cartoon characters that he saw as a child with these very same eyes; their lids were not heavy then, being wide open throughout the day so as not to miss a single sight of the world, and at night they hung on to his father who told him about Hilary who sailed to the Antarctic after having conquered Everest; sailing the same year in which Shechter was born.)

"Of course we're going to finish," said the sergeant and went toward the electricity cupboard. "What's up, you taking a nap?"

(His father also told him about Amundsen and Nansen, and for a time he believed that one day he would reach places where no man had trod and do daring deeds that no man had done before, and if not there, he would at least get to Europe, which was waiting for him with its giant cosmopolitan cities on whose avenues and station platforms anything could happen, because as yet he did not sense the sack's fibers. After returning from Europe he rented an old house in Kfar Azar. On Saturdays from an armchair, he would look at the loquat tree, which would darken slightly in the window like the treetops of these eucalyptuses: its leaves gathered together into foliage, and the foliage covered up the few spots of yellow fruit that the children left, and eventually the black silhouette was swallowed up entirely by the night. To the sight of it and the sight of the small windows of the neighbor's house he no longer missed the window of the Deux Chevaux and its view – low hills on which cows grazed the rain-soaked grass, a grey sky through which the light would suddenly burst in a giant beam until it became rejoined again – nor the window of their room. That room had no curtains and no shutters, and at the time they said, he and the French girl – that's what he called her after returning, so as not to recall the ring that

her name still sounded and in order to delimit her whole
being, her face her voice her body, to a faraway land across
the sea – anyone who wants to can peek in. They were not
ashamed, not concerning their neighbor on the other side
of the wall either who must have heard them as they heard
him: he coughed, they moaned, he cleared his throat, they
groaned; they were young. That Shechter, after returning
from France the first time, didn't at all shout at the children
who picked loquats, and at the age of twenty-two he felt like
someone who'd experienced a lot and would now lead his
life or spur it along the path of his own choice and nothing
would divert him: he'll study film and make movies that will
speak to nameless people who would listen to him, as if those
things happened to them in a room in which they're now
sitting opposite a darkening window such as his window; you
out there, beyond the darkness, he almost called out to them
from his room and drank more and believed that through
the voices of his actors his voice would be heard and through
their storylines his life would be seen like a picture formed
by fragments of a kaleidoscope – that's how he saw his life
at the time, colorful and vibrant, a life with which anything
could be done: should he so desire, he'll complete his studies
here; should he so desire, he'll go back to Paris and study at
IDEC, he had no doubt he'd be accepted at IDEC, and in
Paris he would rent a studio apartment and invite her over,
the French girl.)

"The whole problem is the plug," said the lighting man.
His head stuck out again from the electricity cupboard:
yes, it's the plug that's shorting, all along he knew; it's that
missing screw.

From within the room the actor asked if he noticed that
he had begun to speak in rhyme: "all along I knew, it's that
missing screw."

(You out there beyond the darkness, said that Shechter
and then drank more white wine from a cup whose handle
was stuck on to it and thought about the Chablis that
Gielgud drank in "Providence" and about the Beaujolais he

bought for their room and the Chianti that they drank on
their first meeting in Italy; that Shechter, the young man, did
not yet look at his member as a surplus of flesh which had
no use other than for pissing, and of which every morning
he was shamed by the dream that awoke him: the memory
of her soft breasts and their warmth, or the line of delicate
hair, which descended from her navel, or her body's grasping,
which he would decipher like Morse code, short-long-short:
he was then a radio operator on a soft and warm ship, and
she transferred dispatches to him with her body. On night
field exercises long ago on the banks of the Yarkon, to each
letter with which they signaled they would add the syllables
eee and ah to mark dots and dashes – E became each, dot,
N was naïve, dash dot, M was madame, dash dash. G was
guarantees, dash dash dot, R was rivalry, dash dot dot – Each
naïve madame guarantees rivalry, they signaled from the bank
of the murky river. But she had a different name, and now
she had no name: she was the French girl, and she shifted his
hand from her thigh; in front of them were masses of flakes
flying toward the windscreen, crowding and joining together,
fastening on to the small Deux Chevaux as if it were Hilary's
ship. "Moi, je veux vivre, moi," she said when she stopped at
the edge, which was obliterated by the mist, and put his hand
back and for a while their breath struck the windscreen like
axes, picks and hooks.)

"Rhymes," the actor said. "Like, at the foot of the peak, to
the shore of the creek?"[21] From the gap left by the open door
he turned aside toward Kinneret.

"Then the sound of the Jordan River daddee daddah-"

"Then the sound of the Jordan River was heard in the air,"
the sergeant called out to the room. "At least learn the song. I
noticed that you were good at learning by heart."

"Yes commander," said the actor. He came out of the
entrance, wearing the skirt and tunic, his lips still red and

---

21   Opening lines of the song, "A Girl Whose Name is Kinneret"

his eyes still made-up and on his head the tattered wig. Weintraub whistled with two fingers at the sight.

The investigator fast-forwards, the actors bow and his question (why is he still "going around like a putana"), the saying that the one prisoner said to the other ("everyone's got his own fate, right Ezra?"), and also the actors appeal to the sergeant (after all they're not going back to the last scene, they're moving on to the flashback, aren't they? And maybe they'll eventually find a role for him there), because all of that doesn't seem of any importance to the matter for which he came here.

"No, it's really not okay," the actor turned to Shechter, "a flashback at last, like in a real movie? It doesn't matter that it's just for new recruits. One would think this corps actually did something in the war other than fouling up. Anyway it's a flashback, and who's not going to be in it? Michael. I was a war hero," he said to everyone, "don't get me wrong. Boy did I shrink against the wall, let's say a thumbtack was missing here," he pointed to the poster that was on the door of the clinic. "On the spot I would have been stuck here. I just stuck to the wall and stank from the sweat of fear."

(He then tried to think of a joke, a Persian and a Georgian and an Iraqi are stuck together in a room, so the Georgian says, so the Persian goes, but at night, when he finally managed to fall asleep, he saw himself appearing at some birthday with a mask stuck to his face as if it had already become a part of it, and all the children he didn't manage to make laugh are throwing candy for him to lick up from the floor with the filter like an anteater: they threw candy at him and wafers and pretzels and soda bottles and plants and clumps of earth full of ants like those that the twins fed him in the neighborhood, when he was still so small he barely reached the table of the café when he had to drag his father from there. They rode him on the empty lot, one twin on the back and the other on his legs, and they pushed his head into the ground and lifted him by the ear and shrieked into it one after the other with their skullcaps waving on the side, fastened only by black hairpins: "let's hear you say it now, let's hear it, you midget, say that there's no God," and with a mouth full of earth and ants and small stones he still tried to say that there wasn't any, that he's dead, that his mother was a virgin and that people killed him.)

"No I didn't find a part for you," answered Shechter. "Only Kinneret and her parents will be in the flashback."

(He himself – the one he was that year – was then sitting in an empty bath with his clothes and his shoes on; on his left a bottle of anti-dandruff shampoo and on his right a bottle of white wine; he sat there and sang: "Stand up, damned of the Earth!" but nothing stood up, not in his chest and not in his pants; and years before in a different war, he lay inside a sleeping bag in his uniform and boots in the regiment's rear camp, a few kilometers south of Tyre, and heard how one of the patrol guards threw up after the assistant battalion commander explained to him what will happen if he falls asleep: the commander made a slaughtering motion across his neck and just in case the guard missed his meaning he added: "and in the morning they'll find all of us with our dicks in our mouths." When he was even younger, a month after his release from the army, he saw how the French girl spreads a sleeping bag on the banks of the Arno and lets her hair loose and covers herself with the darkness and comes into being again below it, lying on her back and giving birth to it; and years before that he lay in a sleeping bag on the banks of the Yarkon and saw somnolent clouds above the eucalyptus treetops and with his small fingers touched the warm darkness next to him and touched it once more, and between its lips, the sight of which he didn't know at the time, the tiny heart of the night sprouted, concealed between them like a black pearl in a shell: he touched it, the pearl, it was moist and throbbing; for a moment all those Shechters assembled one alongside the other like the folds of a compressed accordion, and for a moment they separated and drew away from each other and a melody played, rose up and retreated, shrank, emptied out the air and was silent.)

From inside the clinic a dim voice said – perhaps the voice of the female medic – "I won't have anything to do with actors, forget about it." A chair was moved inside and a moment later the door with the poster on it was opened and the freckled face of the medic shook a red ponytail behind it. One by one she surveyed them all through round glasses, until in a voice too deep for her size she said: "clowns inside, clowns outside, it's enough to make you crazy," and turned around right away and went back inside.

The investigator fasts-forward the sergeant addressing Kinneret ("they're still nowhere to be seen, your parents"), and her silence as she continues looking at the poster on the clinic door ("an early examination will save your life"), and the actor singing softly ("Kinneret, Kinn-ne-ret, Kinne-re-het, whispered the wind, whispered the wind"), because these also seemed of no importance to the matter for which he transported his weariness from last night and from all the previous nights all the way here by car.

"Sang the wind," the sergeant corrected and from within the shadows of the eucalyptuses one of the prisoners sank a stone into the trash can.

"Haven't you had enough of those songs already?" Kinneret said still looking at the poster.

"Gil Aldema[22] wrote it," the sergeant handed the lighting man a piece of flannel with which to wipe the screwdriver before using it.

"Gil-Al-dema," the actor said slowly, separating each syllable. "Tell me, what were his parents thinking, that if they called him that he would never cry?" He looked at the sergeant. "No really, each time he uttered the smallest cry other children must have hassled him. Children are a cruel breed. Their beatings can kill you. Cry Aldema! Cry Aldema!" – he wiped his eyes with his hand in a childish manner – "And in basic training they must have made his life a misery. There are grains of sand in the barrel of your rifle Aldema, but not to worry, you've got all of Saturday to clean them. No tears – Aldema."

"You don't think that far off when you name a child," the sergeant said after a moment. "You give it from the love you

---

22   Songwriter whose surname, Aldema, translates literally as "no tears"

have for it, as if you were thinking what you'd want it to have most in life. Just like that. When you're married you'll see for yourself. Take him," the sergeant motioned with his head to the lighting man who was wiping the screwdriver with a moistened flannel. "In a month's time he'll understand. He's a kid now, full of nonsense, carefree, but in a month's time? Believe me he'll start behaving otherwise."

"The Jordan sun will shine on you,
setting in the mountain, the mountain."

The actor sang and another stone was thrown at the trash can.

(But in the café they didn't listen to songs like that, they only listened to Greek or Middle Eastern songs, and every night they'd ask the Persian: "so, did they kill him, did they kill him?" And every time his father would mumble from the corner table into a glass or a bottle: "but that's what they all believe there, that it was us who killed him." To the sound of the dice and the checkers – which was not rhythmic like the rattling of this plane, but disorderly like the stones hitting the tin or the shutters – he dragged his father home by his dangling hand. There he would sit him in the television armchair, almost dropping him in it, so that he could stare at the flashing rectangle the way for two years he stared at the glass paving stones of the pavement above him – at the glass paving stones and at all the soles that continued to pass there, as if there was no war in the world; at masses of soles and the paws of the Gentile dog who would stop to urinate above him four times a day, as precise as the seasons of the year: nine hundred and seven days, until it soiled the paving stones with urine and with blood and a moment later the man leading it fell too.)

"No tears – Aldema, Kinneret," he said to her, because he saw her face as she looked at the poster.

(First the cane he was holding rolled – what do you mean rolled, bottles in the Majestic Cinema don't roll like that – and after it a heavy body rolled in a raincoat whose collar alone was enough to live on for a year. "Believe me Miku," his father said, "that's what it was like then," and retold it all even though he didn't want to hear it, not even once. That's how the body rolled and darkened the corner of the cellar for them, the alcove they made for themselves there: an alcove the width of two thick glass paving stones that reflect the daylight outside or the street lamps, and in the depth of the dimness below, two people sit squashed, one across from the other, knees touching knees, and under the chair of each a bucket with their excretions, so that it would always be clear which of them was responsible for the stench. Only at night could they leave there: moving the false wall partition and the mirror that reflected the room back, pushing aside the rolls of material that were stored at the back, passing by the cutting table with the colorful cuttings and the sparkling buttons made from shells, passing the sewing machine whose ornamentations still convolute as if there was no war going on in the world, and going up the acrobatic staircase gradually and heavily, because hunger has its weight too.)

Kinneret did not answer.

(Going up with bony stiff legs to the shop itself, which now looks as if a great wind had raged in it: not only did it try on what had been folded on the shelves, but also the clothes of the mannequins in the shop window, a window that at night was shut by a wavy tin shutter and now had no shutter no glass and no mannequins, they lay fragmented, amputated and naked and it was not at all clear to whom a leg in a fishnet stocking with the seam at the back belonged: to that one or to that one or to that one, or perhaps to the shop girl lying next to them, who once used to flirt with both of them, each one in turn – "she was a whore Miku, as blonde as she was so black was her soul" – until she transferred her affections to the one they sold the shop to in return for his keeping silent and the leftovers he threw to them like pigs. One evening before closing up shop they heard her voice just slightly muffled: "they say that's where the Zhids are now," and they shrank in the alcove because they did not know where she was pointing at, until they went out at night and saw the cigarette butt in the ashtray stained with dark red lipstick, which they both recognized, they could still smell the smoke.)

Again one of the prisoners threw a stone that struck a beat as it hit the garbage pail. For a moment Kinneret looked out there, but right away returned her gaze to the clinic door and the poster on it: an early examination will save you.

"Just what do you think," a voice was heard on the other side of the door, "you found yourself a sucker? Go on, get out of here before Abudi comes looking for you." Once again a chair was moved inside and the poster drew further away from her gaze as Weintraub left, limping on his right leg and groaning.

(They pass that leg with the fishnet stocking and go outside to the street without looking; not at the sky, which they had not seen for more than two years, and not at some of the cornices of buildings that still survived, and not at sandbags piled up on the window sills, and not at the treetops from which it was impossible to tell who had picked their leaves, the season of the year or the bombs, and not at the statue of the horse: every New Year's Eve the rowdies would put a dotted tie on it, but now it no longer had a neck. Its white head lay on the ground exactly like the real horse, the bleeding brown one whose belly burst open spilling its guts, and its wagon overturned with the wheels still spinning in the air. And they don't look, his father and his uncle – what do you mean uncle, he's never ever seen him – not at that crushed coachman there who still holds the whip as if with one flick everything will start to move, and not at the lady he was driving who was thrown from the impact and whose plump curves were revealed as if there was no war going on in the world; not at them and not at the dog whose tongue sticks out between bubbles of froth, but at his master, the man in the coat: from the depths of the alcove they had already learned the times he went for his stroll with the dog and his whistle for the dog and how many times he knocked his pipe against the wall to empty it, and now he's laid out there on the pavement with eyes wide open – what do you mean open – a baby doesn't open them that way – as if he didn't believe that human beings could be so pale and thin, with such skeletal fingers, fingers that crawl over his body, rummaging through his breast pockets and pants pockets: one on the right and one on the left, with the same hostile co-ordination in which they sat in the darkness of the alcove above buckets of excrement, knees opposite knees.)

"What a world," said Weintraub, "people don't have any trust."

He went past Kinneret and carried on limping to the eucalyptus tree in whose shade he had parked the trash can and carefully lowered it on to the road. "Did you miss me honey?" he said to it and pushed it in the direction of the rickshaw. "They think I'm the biggest sucker on the base," he called out turning his head, "but Weintraub's nobody's sucker. You think I don't know there's a commissioner for soldiers' complaints?"

The other prisoner got up, dropped the stone he was holding in his hand and patted his trousers to shake off the grains of dust that had stuck to them. He bent down and lifted the rake from the asphalt and began to drag it again, Weintraub watched him closely.

"You don't care about anything," he said to him, "you've gotten used to being treated that way Ezra," and he bent his head over the wagon: "What honey, what? Your life will be different."

"the Jordan sun shiiiiines on you,"

The actor was singing again and Kinneret turned to look at him. "No tears, Kinneret," he said to her, "you can go to pieces inside, but no tears on the outside," and from the collar of the tunic his Adam's apple moved up and down, large and round like a ping-pong ball.

"Her father's coming," said the lighting man, "he'll make mincemeat out of you if you annoy her," and right away put his head back into the electricity cupboard.

"settinnnng over the mountain,"

("That's how it is Miku," his father said, "how can you share an identity card? Half for me and half for him?" In the ravaged street they flipped a coin, his father flipped it and his uncle bet on the side with the number: his father shook the zloty once next to his heart and then once next to his lips to kiss it well on its way – what do you mean kiss, he never kissed him that way, if only to prepare him for life – and flipped it in the air. He flipped it high up in the air to the searchlight beams that still tracked the skies for planes, intersecting and separating and intersecting. And from the pavement the dead man looked at him still holding the dog's leash, as if any moment they'll get up and return to their walk: he looked at wormy fingers whose agility had returned to them and at the coin that flew high up between the grains of soot and the dust of the debris and smoke, until it slowed down and stopped and fell heads up – what do you mean heads up, anyway it would have fallen, the coin would have been heads up – "that's what it's like Miku when you want to live, from all that hunger a man would steal a piece of bread from his own brother, and me, all I did was to throw a coin. I left him the whole wallet, let him have it, why not, let him have everything; and wouldn't I have won anyway, with his zloty?"

Right away he rummaged through his pocket and not finding anything asked him for half a shekel from the money put away for groceries and shook it in his palms, once next to the heart and once next to the lips, and he kissed it and flipped it into the air so that it would fly and slow down and drop, and with an all too agile movement he turned his hand over and said: "here, Miku, didn't I win, I won.")

"the mountain."

(He felt then like the uncle who attacked his father in the middle of the ravaged street and rolled with him between tatters of skirts and dresses and shirts from the shop and amputated limbs of mannequins and fragments of glass from the shop window and decapitated horse heads, one bleeding and one marbled and cracked, and tried to take the identity card of one, Vladislav Makoshinsky, engineer, from his hand. With the very same desperate and hostile coordination with which they had sat in the alcove, they rolled together on the pavement and in the road, wrestling with each other not like two young men of twenty-five or six, but like women in the market or children on an empty plot: no fist struck, no head butted; just wormy fingers trying to clutch and long fingernails scratching and bites from mouths exuding the smell of hunger. And afterwards there were fistfuls of rubble dust lifted up in order to choke and blind, followed by strangled, blind groping on the pavement and in the road, toward some marble block marble shard marble fragment, which had previously been a horse ear or lock of hair from a horse mane or horse tail and now would become an instrument of manslaughter.)

"Aren't you through with that song already?" asked Kinneret, and his Adam's apple moved again.

(Flick-flack: like beach bats by the sea or like a billiard ball in a pub. The long sticks drummed flick-flack on the felt, and the beer taps dripped in a line flick-flack like men's urinals; and the drummer wasn't drumming anymore, he leaned the stick on his left hand and made a circle with his thumb and forefinger and put it in and took it out, put it in and took it out, in and out, and he passed the stick to her and bent over together with her; and within the aquarium, a silent tiny shining sea, the fish stared at them without blinking; stared at them above the seaweed, stared at them above the gin and tonic he had poured in, all floating there and their bellies gleaming; he moved her hand that held the stick, moved her body with his, and she hit the ball: flack. Flick-flack.)

"I'm through," answered the actor. "The bit about your father scared me." The lighting man's head was still hidden by the small door of the electricity cupboard.

"First, let them just get here."

"That's how you rely on your father?" the actor asked.

(A horse, a horse, my very life for a horse, its ear or a lock of its mane, and above, searchlight beams were still roaming: intersecting and separating and intersecting, until trapping a small plane like this one in them, and immediately from below tracer ammunition was trained on it and his father disappeared. From now on he became Vladislav Makoshinsky, engineer – what do you mean engineer, in the village he even advised farmers how to reinforce the roof of the church, yes, so as not to fall on God and kill him once again – "what else did they feed you, Parsi? Come on, Parsi, tell us. Tell us once more what they call the Russian's river, hey Parsi? Don't they call it Vodka?" "Volga," the Persian replied.)

"I actually do rely on him," Kinneret replied after a moment, "the problem's not with him."

She turned to the soundman and asked him to roll her a cigarette, and he passed her his and began to roll another one for himself. She inhaled deeply and rounded her lips and blew out two smoke rings and followed them with her eyes (smoke spreads it, the flame, the tobacco, the spit: She could kill the crop spraying pilot with a smoke ring.)

"My mother," she said, "gets out of doing things just like the welfare officer, and then you can forget about the both of them." She tapped the cigarette with her finger shedding bits of ash from the tip.

"You're just saying that, they're probably a bit late," said Na'ama. She too looked at the empty road, but no car was to be seen in it, not a long American car nor any other.

"I'm not just saying it," Kinneret answered, "I just know them. They're my parents, no?" (On the trampled, dimpled sand, and the water lapping their bodies, then biting, trickling, licking, kissing.)

The soundman compressed the tobacco with his fingers, wrapped the paper around, fastened and licked the edges. "Are we back to the system of bringing extras from home?" he turned to Shechter. There was no sarcasm in his voice but rather a slight bewilderment.

"Didn't you want me to be like I was in the good old days?"

The sergeant came to Shechter's aid and explained that they needed older people for the flashback: "Where would we get older people from? So we asked her to bring her parents along, their daughter's acting in it, why shouldn't they help out? Anyway they're also artists. Her father's a singer and her mother is also someth-"

"A painter," Kinneret said. "At least that's how she sees herself."

A small flame was drawn from the lighter again and the soundman drew it close to the tobacco stalks. "Who didn't we use to bring along then" – he inhaled the cigarette and for a moment his cheeks were sucked into his palate – "not only parents. Aunts, grandmothers, cousins, not to mention the girlfriend. If she wasn't acting in it, then at the very least she was the production assistant. She drove people, helped with the equipment, made sandwiches for everyone, not just one or two, a whole lot."

"She used to make great sandwiches," said Shechter. He was still staring at the sections of the road seen between the trunks of the eucalyptuses, vacant as they had been but darker.

"At school?" the soundman expelled a smoke ring and opposite him Kinneret blew one, more precise than his. "The kids used to argue about who'll get a bite. In the end she prepared two for him, so that they wouldn't finish all of his."

Shechter turned his head to him from the window.

"Maybe it's also like that now," the soundman said to him. Across from him Kinneret blew another smoke ring.

The investigator fast forwards her speech ("In the end you'll have to call your parents"), Na'ama's astonishment and the lighting man's response from within the electricity cupboard ("why not, if they're as nice as their daughter").

The lighting man became silent, even before the mounting sound of the rattling plane.

"Have you ever seen anything like it?" said the sergeant. "Getting married next month and no shame. Grow up already little boy."

"A month's a long time," the lighting man answered still busy with one of the fuses in the electricity cupboard.

(But when the blue flashing light stopped opposite him he didn't speak, he didn't breathe, only his heart pounded: the two doors opened at once like in an American television series and were slammed shut, and from between the trash cans he saw the two policemen getting out and crossing the road chop-chop toward the avenue chop-chop to the telephone he had vandalized there **let's see if you are a man.**)

"At any rate, they've got more important things in mind," said Na'ama. On her finger, over and over she curled a strand of hair whose shade of light brown had become dark in the dusk.

(On the roof, which the neighbors accused her of taking over, and in opposition a tenant's meeting was called until they gave up on her and took to whispering behind her back, on the roof her sister said: "Men? Men think that they should never be seen to be weak, as if it's not masculine. We're the only ones who are allowed to be weak and sometimes want to jump off the roof. What are you looking at me like that for, I was kidding." But Na'ama actually thought she was speaking seriously, and at home she saw how her father would go down to the grocery store to buy a newspaper and read all of it while still on the way, as if on one of the pages he would finally find some news item that would fundamentally change everything and give him back his job and his respect. From the living room balcony, five floors above him, she would see a small man reading a large newspaper – he seemed so small to her, as if he would fit within the lines he marked on the door frame in her room when he still measured her height

– reading it also while crossing the road, and once someone shouted at him from inside a battered Subaru that came to a halt a centimeter away from him: "watch where you're going, asshole," and her father then became smaller still.)

"More important than me?"

(From between the trash cans he saw the policemen nearing the telephone booth, whose receiver he had not kicked; on the contrary, he wanted it to remain whole, so that everyone could call the number that he wrote there with a moist red felt-tipped pen, the name that he wrote there with a moist red felt-tipped pen, above the drawing of cockintocunt and cockintomouth. Between overflowing fetid cans he saw them reaching the booth, peeking in and reading what was written and looking left and right, each one turning toward a tree trunk and hiding beneath the twisted snake-like aerial roots and for a moment there was total silence in which only his heart could be heard, until one of them said: "Lucky the street's empty, if there wasn't a war on, my bladder would have burst.")

"Of course more."

(And another time, in the middle of the night – they almost haven't slept since his being fired, every minute someone else would get up and she would block her ears in bed so as not to hear the drizzle or the trickle and the raging of the water and the noise with which the tank was filled afterwards – she got up and saw her mother looking at him from the kitchen balcony while he sat at the dining table smoking cigarette after cigarette, filling ashtrays until the morning, head sunk in his shoulders as if he had no neck anymore; Na'ama's mother was dressed in her old nightgown – Na'ama tried to persuade her a million times to buy a new one – and stood there peering at him from between the cartons of toilet paper and empty jars, exactly as Na'ama would have peered into this room if she only had someone at home to peer at like that. As if her mother was silently saying: two-thirty in the morning, I'm the plump woman in the worn out nightgown;

I stood on the kitchen balcony and watched you while you smoked, you, the boy I fell in love with thirty years ago.)

("We chose a lousy job, believe me, lousy," the one policeman said to the other. "Sasportas? Take it from me Sasportas did the smart thing, he left in time." And the first one, who concentrated for a moment said: "Don't use Sasportas as an example, Sasportas is loaded, he could afford to leave." The other one had already gone down to the road and said from there: "What do you mean loaded, where do you get loaded from, he got loaded afterwards when he started buying and selling, believe me before that he didn't have a cent to his name." The first policeman, who had also crossed the road, said: "What, don't you need money to buy? What did he buy with? Matches?" And all at once the two doors of the police van opened and were slammed shut, and all at once the white lights were turned on and the blue flashing light, and all at once they sped off into the distance. He came out from behind the trash cans, the moist red felt-tipped pen still in his hand, and went back to the telephone booth and for a moment thought of speaking to her through a handkerchief like he had seen on television and to say to her in a distorted voice: "it's written here that you-" just to ruin her night, but he let the receiver drop and kicked it as if kicking the mouth itself to smash the lips that kiss the teeth that bite the tongue that licks the throat that swallows, and he already knew where to go from there: not to his grandfather and grandmother – the couch on which they had put him to sleep was already too small for his size, by now the weight of the chairs that they moved next to it so that he wouldn't fall off had exhausted them, and in the vase on the table there were only dusty plastic flowers – not to them and not to the base, he still had energy to expend in the empty town before going back to the base.)

"And what if we really need them?" Shechter turned from the window. In its depths, between the eucalyptus trunks, the sections of asphalt that could be seen were darkening further.

"Then the director will have himself a problem," answered Na'ama.

"The director," said Shechter slowly. Behind him the white of the whitewashed trunks darkened to grey.

"So what should we call you?"

"Shechter," replied Shechter.

"the sound of the weeping of a boy whose name issss-"

The actor sang. Shechter removed himself from the wall and suggested they start putting the room in order.

(Verse by verse those songs were projected onto a wrinkled sheet at scout meetings, and sometimes just an empty shining white appeared, which in the dark lit up their faces, small and rounded, and all the scores of years that will be woven above them and be joined together in their flesh are still as airy and transparent as the beam that emerges from the blind eye of the projector. Weary coils of smoke had not yet woven themselves into it, nor murmurings, nor hushing, nor the creaking of seats being vacated, and at its tail end, not yet visible on the screen of the old Cinematheque, the credits of the film he made at the end of his studies; at the time a great silence prevailed and the credits hurried to be drawn up into the ceiling in order never to be seen again. Late at night from the window of his room he again saw the banks of the Arno or the Po, already he didn't remember which river flowed there in the darkness, and on the banks were the sleeping bags, he could still imagine hearing the sound of their zips and recalled how she saw him in all his awkwardness and guided him and quietly said to him "ici" and then said to him "viens" and then turned over and moved beneath the nighttime clouds and her breasts fell back gradually in a delayed motion that he thought would never end. After the screening he drank "Carmel Mizrachi" wine and didn't think about Gielgud's Chablis anymore but rather of clochard wine made from leftover grapes and packaged in plastic bottles, wine on which he would get drunk in Paris if she didn't invite him over, the French girl: he would lie down on hard Metro benches, on the Metro air vent coverings, on the Metro platforms, on the gravel between the Metro tracks, where nimble lively mice scurry like Shechter-the-director.)

"Shechter what?" asked Na'ama looking into his eyes again.

"Schechter commander," he replied to her after a moment, but with just a very faint smile on his lips.

(From the opposite end of the convoy buried in his body he ridiculed that Shechter in all his upheavals, while at the same time envied him for those upheavals; and in the depths of the sky the last ones who had not yet taken form in the convoy could also be made out for a few moments; none of them can yet see, as the first ones could, the sights around him as an extended prologue – as if all of the sights are parts of a trailer shown before the film itself, just lively bits and pieces meant to arouse curiosity and during which one could still chatter and eat popcorn and open a can of coke and drink from it, until at last the real thing, taking its time, will begin: then the doors of the theater will close, the din from outside will vanish, the last lights will dim, the small torch that the usher shines on the tickets of latecomers will be extinguished too, and all at once, at the far extremity of the darkness, a foreign and exquisite vast expanse will glow and spread to here – none of them will think that anymore, because they all already know that there is nothing other than these sights around them and that there will be no others.)

At the end of the road Weintraub and the other prisoner wandered around and turned back again.

"Tell me, on all your rounds did you see the welfare officer?" Merav asked when they drew near.

"I only saw the medic," Weintraub shouted to her from the road, "and that was enough, believe me. Small as she is, she's so stuck up."

The clinic door opened slightly and the freckled face peeked out without saying anything. The door closed and on the other side the sound of sniffling could be heard and all of a sudden the office was lit up by a bright light flashing and stabilizing.

"Yes!" the lighting man called out and the rattling of the plane rose above his voice.

"And in the midst of night" – the actor gestured with his hand and all its red nails to a sky devoid of light – "day is created. And its sun shines upon all: comrades and outcasts, the honored and the ostracized."

"I fixed it," the lighting man said and the crop spraying plane circled and drew away.

("I decreed and swore an oath that all kinds of the evil eye will be removed and expelled and distanced and shunned from Smadar the daughter of Abraham," her grandfather mumbled until the rattling of the motorbikes rose above his voice, and in the harsh white light, on a wheelchair that was polished and shined in honor of the wedding, with the combed beard and the three-piece suit and the braided shoes and the vacant marble floor around him, he looked like the deposed ruler of some miniature state: after all, wasn't their neighborhood like some state within a state? It was third world, her brother Eli said, and at the wedding, in the din of conversation coming from neighboring tables, he asked if they still came to him, all those stupid women from the neighborhood, to receive his blessing. "They come, but not so much," Merav replied, after all they were scared of tiring him out ever since his attack on Allenby Street – that's what they called it, "his attack on Allenby Street," and even added: "lucky he wasn't hit by a car, God forbid," as if he had fallen in the middle of the road or from the pavement – and in the jumble of conversation her brother muttered angrily: "stargazer, soothsayer, sorcerer," and reminded her how they both peeked at him when he felt the bellies of pregnant women and foretold what it would be, a boy or a girl, or rested his hand there in order to ensure that the birth would not be difficult, and whisper together with them, "which is as a bridegroom coming out of his chamber, and rejoiceth as a strong man to run a race," or get rid of spells with branches of rosemary and cockscombs, whose smoke rose between their thighs – a remedy for opening the wombs of barren women – and how he would suddenly become hoarse from the smoke. That's what she thought then, Merav, and her brother said

that she didn't understand anything about life: this screwed
up, miserable, ridiculous, funny, ugly, beautiful life, and that
maybe there'll come a time when she'll be able to show it as
it is to all the people from the first and second worlds and
maybe even to them themselves.)

The plane flew low over the fields, and the darkness that
fell and filled them concealed the horizon line and for a
few moments the wings of the plane as well, as if they were
gnawed by its mouth to the sound of the rhythmic rattling.
When it drew away, the footfall of the two prisoners retracing
their steps rose from the empty road.

"That medic," Weintraub shouted from there, "hasn't ever
heard about the Hippocratic Oath, but never mind. Every
dog has its day. Right, Eran? Tell them what Weintraub does
to someone who screws with him."

"What's he going on at you for?" asked the actor.

"Nothing," answered the lighting man and busied himself
with the door of the lamp to direct its light.

The clinic door opened again and the female medic's red
head stuck out from the widening gap. "Have you also got
some issues with him?" she asked.

"I haven't got anything with him," said the lighting man.
"Why should I have any issues with him? Didn't I get along
with him well in my army service, Merav?"

Merav did not answer and her eyes followed the sergeant
who turned toward the rickshaw.

("And thou shalt not have dominion over her not by day
nor by night not awake nor in a dream not over any organ
of her 248 organs nor tendon of her 385 tendons and not
over her hair and nails, from now to eternity everlasting
Amen Sela," her grandfather mumbled seven times beneath
the saccharine melody that had been planted in the cassette.
And when she left the photography shop, Cohen still called
out after her: "send regards to Eli, I hardly managed to talk
to him," and she said: "yes, sure, thanks," as if she would be
seeing him before the next wedding or circumcision or bar
mitzvah or funeral. On the way to the base in the south she
suggested to the sergeant they pay a visit to her brother, if

they'd travel on the Jerusalem-Jericho road, but Gidi opposed
the idea. "That's all they need," he said, "more dealings with
the commander of the base: after all, until he got the Peugeot
– the rickshaw wouldn't have even made it a seventh of the
way – they put him through the wringer, and now to leave
the main road by a centimeter? They'll get a puncture for
sure, not to mention a block in the windscreen or a Molotov
cocktail." [He never forgot, the sergeant, the one who once
said on television: "walk all over us, but in the end we'll
bite you like snakes," and his hands, the hands of someone
intelligent, were cut by the stones that the soldiers forced him
to remove, and how he showed them to the camera and said:
"until now I didn't know what a homeland was, now I know.
This is a homeland, this, these stones," and how he walked
up to the large heap of stones that he had removed and kissed
the stones one by one: behind him tires were still burning
and on the side a little girl wiped her nose with her sleeve,
and for a moment then the sergeant didn't know whose side
he was on, with the soldiers who were the cause of the stones
being thrown or with the Arab man and the girl, who all of
a sudden became so shy of the camera that she hid her face
with two tiny hands, but it's just that he saw her eyes peeking
like that between fingers.] In the end they actually did have a
puncture past Beersheba: he cursed and stopped the Peugeot,
which did not exude any smells of pee or vomit or milk, had
no Simpsons that were stuck in the rear and no baby shoe
swaying to and fro from the mirror, but one of its tires was
worn out exactly like the rickshaw's tires. "That transport
officer," Gidi said, "a parasite. I always said so." She insisted
on changing the tire with him, after all she didn't agree to
them making allowances for her sex, nor her age and also
not for what they called her background, meaning that she
would never escape from it – as if the entire neighborhood
was a spell that could not be broken, not by whisperings
and talismans, not by coals and cockscombs and not even
by studies and university – and he, Gidi, continued looking
around for more porcupine quills. Not so that they wouldn't

get stuck in the wheels and delay them again, but to bring for his daughter, it was the only thing he hadn't brought for her or bought for her or made for her, porcupine quills: he wasn't at all afraid, not for a moment, that she would hurt herself with them, stick them in her nose like little children do, the twins did, or poke her eye or insert them deep down into her mouth and choke. But late at night, after ringing his wife's kibbutz – to where he had sent them both for the duration of the war – they left the canteen and began to walk the length of the barbed wire fence and the old newspapers caught in it and the uprooted bushes, and at their feet was a slope lit up by the searchlights from the guard posts in the wadi, beyond which nothing was seen: all was black like the open space around the junction that led to her home. They passed a guard post, entirely darkened, and turned left with the fence and advanced further into the darkness, until suddenly in the distance opposite them the lights of Dimona were visible, small and sparkling. "They look like pearls, don't they?" that's what he said to her then, that Gidi, as if he and she, with their backgrounds, had ever seen their mothers in pearls, and as if there was anything in Dimona that sparkled except for a few street lamps, which only by chance weren't bashed in, and some kiosk with cigarettes and above a soda fountain magazines of girls spreading their legs and a pita bread bakery working the night shift and some wedding hall. "Yes," she answered suddenly, using a phrase from school, "like a garland of pearls." Because for a solitary moment, when the wind blew in the dark, the entire Arava was like a black woman from the magazines that her brother bought at the kiosk, lying there beneath the sky wearing only that necklace and breathing heavily.)

"Will it stay like that now?" the sergeant asked outside. He didn't wait for the lighting man to answer him, but stuck his head into the back of the rickshaw, concealing it inside. The glossy end of a roll of plastic nylon stuck out from there and was lowered to the asphalt. "Why not," said the sergeant from within, "leave me to do everything by myself, why not."

"He waits and he's alone," said the actor. "He tarries and he's alone-"

"Merav-sweetie," the dim voice was heard from the depths of the rickshaw. "Tell them which list is for the flashback, if you haven't forgotten."

"Merav-sweetie hasn't forgotten," she answered him still leaning on the window sill. "I'm just like Weintraub, I don't forget."

Against the consolidating darkness that gathered the separate eucalyptus leaves together into clustered foliage as well as joining one cluster to another, she opened the screenplay folder, to whose binding the list was attached. "One bed," she began to read, "one mattress, one sheet, one blanket, one bedcover" – she paused for a moment – "two civilian posters, five cushions, two teddy bears, one mop, one roll of plastic nylon, one green masking tape, one utility knife. Merav-sweetie also knows how to read in the dark," she said and shifted a strand of black hair behind her ear so that it wouldn't fall forwards.

In the distance, on the road outside the base, car lights were moving, and after a short while only the orange backlights were visible until they dwindled and disappeared.

"Let me break my back," the sergeant said from inside the rickshaw, "why not."

"If you prick me, do I not bleed?" the actor recited from the room. "If you poison me, do I not die? If you break me do I not collapse?"

"If Kinneret forgets the clothes now," the dim voice of the sergeant was heard again. "That's all we need now. It's not enough that that one didn't come, that snake, and it's not enough with the others coming late. Didn't I know it would happen, I could have sworn to it. At least let's just start getting the room in order already."

"What were they thinking," that's what the female medic said on the phone, "making a film studio here, no less. Turning some miserable office in the army into the room of a house, and what was it all for, for some instructional film for new recruits. But why should you care, maybe they

filmed something you need. I don't mean only the end, but also how it
began." That's what she said to him in the morning, and while traveling, for
a few moments he wondered what she looked like, inside the old car, that
all the distances it had crossed were registered not only on the speedometer
but also on the tires and the brakes and the bodywork and the noise of the
engine and even in the grumbling of the asphalt in front of him, a grey
never-ending dragon, which will yet swallow him one day into its guts. At
the time he tried to picture her not only on the base where she served but
also at the high school in which she studied before enlisting, classifying
petals and loose pollen or examining germ cultures in a microscope or
watching the dissection of a frog without batting an eyelid: and later in
the corridors of a large hospital, in which in thirty years' time she'll head
a department with that same vigorous voice of hers, he'll be lying in one
of the rooms at the end with pupils fixed on the wavering lifeline on the
monitor, if he won't have been felled down before then.

"I actually didn't forget," Kinneret said. She sat on the
edge of the step at the entrance to the office, her hands
hugging her legs and in her mouth the cigarette, which was
becoming shorter.

(Fire spreads it, soot, charcoal and smoke: she's already
killed the crop spraying pilot with a smoke ring and the
others she'll kill with bits of spit she'll spray from her mouth,
with sweat she'll excrete from her body, with exhalations still
left for her to exhale.)

The soundman, who was leaning against the cork board
hanging in the entrance hall, saw the chunks of ash that she
shed fall to the road and disintegrate.

(And there was one who watched from the heights through
all his eons – thousands and thousands of thousands whose
each moment was like a thousand years – cliffs crumbling
into sand, ridges curving from the earth like waves of the
ocean and waves becoming cloudy in the sky, impregnated,
growing bellies and giving birth to rain that still exudes the
smell of seaweed and crustaceans.)

The actor still wearing the skirt and tunic came out from
behind one of the eucalyptuses. "Lucky I didn't get changed
yet," he called out to them, "easy as anything to do it that
way." He shook his leg and on seeing Kinneret stopped and

placed his hand on his chest and began to sing with great intent:

"She was sitting alone –
Will you ever know her secret?"

He paused for a moment, no one answered him.

"Then the Jordan na-na-na,
Mount Hermon na-na-na,"

"Then the Jordan chuckled," said the sergeant and his head was again swallowed up inside the rickshaw, "Mount Hermon laughed once more. At least learn the words already."

"Then the Jordan chuckled,
Mount Hermon laughed once more,"

"Only the silence told," the faint voice of the sergeant rose from under the canvas covering, "how she waited for him." "Yeah!" said the actor.

"Only the silence tooooold
How she waiiited for himmmm –
Then the sound of the Jordan ti-na-na was heard
And the sound of the weeping of a girl whose naaaame – "

Kinneret dropped the cigarette butt and squashed it with the sole of her shoe.

(One was stuck between the floorboards, as if feet were pressed on it, and the drummer drummed: flack, flick-flack. Previously she had stood opposite the actor, skirt opposite skirt, and applied his make-up, and his eyelashes fluttered, quivered. She'll make him pretty the way her mother used to make her pretty before they entered the *Atelieu.* "Aren't you my size by now?" They stood in front of each other. She dressed her in a purple dress and a purple hat. "Wait and see

what Daddy will say," she said, but her father, above a large
emptied beer glass – white lines of foam were outlined on
it like on sand – was only interested in the female tourists.
As they were putting on tiny golden bathing suits over
their dark skin her mother was blackening the table napkin
further. "Just be careful that the table doesn't start rising,"
she said while blackening. Her father's cigarette glowed and a
smoke ring was emitted. "Don't you go ruining her," he said
quietly, and her mother said: "just who's doing the ruining,
who?" And at their feet the cat opened its eyes, its pupils
as narrow as a blade. The drummer couldn't care less about
anyone, he's drumming. Flack, flick-flack. There was just old
furniture in the hairdresser's air raid shelter, still the noise
echoed throughout the building; a sofa a cupboard a mattress
and stubs of candles from some old war, and they too were
covered in cobwebs. Cobwebs woven on her buttocks, woven
on her lustful craving concealed private parts. And what will
she hold on to when he seats her on his motorbike, she'll
encircle him with her thighs, keeping close, what will she
hold on to, Kinellet? But it's not her that he'll seat, but rather
the hairdresser. She went twice to have her hair cut there,
Kinnerehet: a small hairdressing salon on Ibn Gvirol Street,
not even in the fashionable Ministore, and the hairdresser
wasn't even a hairdresser, just a hair washer and sweeper.
For an hour she futzed around with her head in the basin –
foam bubbles fizzed and popped: puk-puk – and with ears
blocked by L'Oréal-Paris-Ma-Cherie she heard the owner
saying to a customer: "only disposables, nowadays no one
takes any chances." And from the corner of her eye she saw
the sparkling razor flung to the bin: the blade spreads it, the
bin spreads it, the floor.)

"At least I didn't forget that," Kinneret said to the sergeant.

"And what did you forget?" From where he stood next
to the cork board the soundman looked at the trodden butt
from which tobacco stalks had been displaced.

(And there was one who from his height, without
questioning at all, knew all deeds even before they were
done, knew them from his skies the moment they arose in

a mind on earth and also punished for that very thought, that it should never be repeated: once He saved him from a fire that seized him in the desert – at his sides were dummy targets and it was as if he had become one of the them – with an enormous transparent finger He pushed him to the sand and extinguished the flames, and years later He almost set fire to him on a Thai island because of the evil that rose within him. But first across from him He caused the waves to rise steep as ridges and flung the wind like thousands of spears and shook his hut like the hut of Manu the fisherman when the flood began.)

"It doesn't matter," Kinneret said, "will you roll me another one?"

("It's just to have a place for rehearsing," he said when he moved to the hairdresser's, but bites were bitten on his neck, scratches were scratched on his back. She saw them all when he took off his undershirt in the shelter, dark with sweat, saturated. He threw it her way, heavy wet dirty, and at once it moistened her with his smell.)

"If you're asking," said the soundman.

(Soldiers from the central Tel Aviv army base came to have their hair washed by her in the basin, and in the afternoon, at least the times when she had her hair cut – bubbles of L'Oréal Paris popped in her ears – a beggar came rattling a tin can: "Charity will save you from death! Charity will save you from death!" As if there was something for him to save: he received a shekel from the hair washer, received a shekel from the apprentice and the tin can clattered: flack – flick-flack. No examination will save you.)

(The foam soared high up becoming gloomy clouds, and through the barrage and the lightning Manu saw the giant fish that he had reared, squirting jet streams from his blowhole and extinguishing the stars one by one, because the era of the sinners had ended. And with the point of its horn the fish sliced clouds in whose interior there was still an entire ocean with all its seaweed and monsters, and in the spray of the water each one could be seen germinating in a drop.)

"Why not."

(The island was seven degrees from the equator and at the tip where he stayed, an entrepreneur from a small coastal town had once tried to raise a village of bungalows for tourists who wish to seclude themselves, but they all chose to crowd together in the bay: in its restaurants and in its shops and on the white sands that on moonlit nights were filled with drugged shadows dancing to breaking point to the sounds of Techno, which sometimes, when the direction of the wind changed, would reach him. He was years older than them and in their eyes clearly must have seemed a complete weirdo, and when one of the Israelis once tried to make conversation – "tell me, don't I know you from somewhere?" – he didn't answer. From time to time, when he still went down to the bay, one of the girls stretched out on the sand would cast him a brazen or sun-soaked gaze until he almost stopped, and immediately his legs would lead him further along the slope of the small mountain, on a path that the thicket had invaded and climbed and slid along and thickened up to the huts that were demolished by the winds and the monsoon. All around, the thicket gathered and crowded together with all its insects and bugs and hidden troops of monkeys, which every day came closer and were already identifiable here and there, besides by their screams, by their darting leaps as well as the movement of branches in their wake. Not only was his job forgotten there – recording for filmed commercials that glorified banks and soft drinks and the Rolls Royce of air conditioners and refrigerators, as if the world was founded on them – but also his son and the mother of his son; that's what he told himself every morning on opening his eyes under the mosquito net, and in the window across from him was the smooth and pellucid ocean leaving the fishermen's boats to momentarily carve trails of foam in it. Beneath the equatorial sun that was already luminous in its rising –and the entire sky with it, the summer in which he taught his son to swim was forgotten, and the previous summer in which together they crawled on the sand toward her – the winner's prize an ice cream bar whose chocolate covering, which he didn't like, she peeled off with her teeth – her giant belly, which contained him and which was arched in the water like a mountainous island, was not seen in the window, nor were the times that preceded the belly. After a row one evening at the end of September they went out, which only served to provoke her once more about his temporary jobs, about the delayed payments, about his weird friends and about his idleness around the house, "you don't do anything, not a thing, and you know when I first noticed it? From the very start, from day one. Those shutters, when we moved in, it took you maybe a year to fix, a year." When they walked along the promenade across from the Dan Hotel and in front of them there were Japanese tourists being photographed against its background, he leapt onto the dark sand and called to her from there to join him. They were twenty-eight years old at the time and he reminded her how she used to once jump from dusty armored vehicles when delivering the company soldiers' post to them; and when she stayed angry, with skin whose freshness had already faded and with curves that had already lost their suppleness, he turned his back to the wall and offered his shoulders to her. The smell of urine rose from the wall and for a long while only the sound of the sea in front of him was heard, very dimly despite its proximity, until suddenly he sensed her warmth on his shoulders and on his neck through the material and ran with her on the sand till the water to the water in the water.)

"I am asking," Kinneret said.

(He did not think about them nor about an Indian train whose numerous carriages were invaded by dust that was heaped on the thousands of passengers, on the masses, on the millions: day and night he breathed the dust on his first journey after his army discharge. He sweated dust and coughed dust and dripped dust from his nose and shed dust tears from his eyes and urinated dust and touched the dust when he still reminisced about her in the sleeping bag at night on the jiggling bunk; at the time he traveled for weeks on trains and from their windows watched so many sunsets and sunrises that he sometimes wondered if he hadn't been born on a train on one of those dusty bunks amongst sacks of rice and chickens and bare-bottomed infants and the filthy hands of peddlers proffering from all sides small clay cups of sweet chai and fried samosas wrapped in leaves, and for a time, days and weeks and months, it was possible to believe that he was born in a carriage and that he'll die in a carriage – time was measured then only in kilometers and stations, in cities and towns – and that he never saw other than those views retreating through the windowpane. Until finally he alighted from the carriage in a small town whose name he didn't know, and from his hotel window watched how the night fell slowly over the rooftops like black dust. A window in the building opposite, a building crumbling while still being built, was lit by the fluttering light of a kerosene burner, and on a table a white shirt was spread out and the dark hand of a woman led a charcoal iron over it back and forth, back and forth, back and forth, back and forth, until he realized the time had come to go back. Years ago he had seen that hand – a thousand years, thousands – and after he went back and married and had a son and divorced and flew off again, he settled into the deserted hut and from its entrance saw the ocean encircling the island and streaks of light turning it silver and its horizon blurred by mist and a fishing boat rattling like this plane drawing a white evaporating trail behind it.)

Kinneret lifted her sole onto the cigarette butt and squashed it again.

("Someone comes and asks you how many more years he's got" – the apprentice swept and kept silent – "what you gonna tell him, that in a year's time he'll be like an egg? So you say to him, no no, no way, thinning is thinning and bald is bald, and never ever tell them they've got dandruff. That's something you don't say. A person who wants his hair washed gets his hair washed. He wants L'Oréal anti-dandruff, he gets L'Oréal anti-dandruff. At the very most, if he asks you, but believe me the majority don't ask, at the very most tell him: you can already see the results sir, you can definitely see.")

(In all the world there was no one except him and the lizard that clung to the beam of the thatched roof above him, and opposite him the blue green grey expanse, and in his mouth Mentos candy, which he sucked from morning to night to remove the foul taste of hunger. The city in which he once lived had already become so distant, that he no longer remembered how he taught him to ride his bike down the avenue, nor the day when he dismantled the fairy wheels, nor how she would lick the wounds on his elbows and knees like an animal its pups, and how he too would extend his elbows and knees to her, and his son would then giggle.)

The soundman moistened the edges of the new paper he rolled and joined them together with his finger.

(The sun set into the ocean, not over the mountain, and there was one who heard it not only when it was swallowed by those fathomless waters, but while its rays were still being gathered from the unraveled thatch roofs and from the thicket in whose depths monkeys shrieked and from the naked cliffs and from the outspread domed branches of the palm trees. At the time, when he still ventured out from the hut, he was careful to avoid their shade so that his head wouldn't be split open by a falling coconut: there he was scared of coconuts, not of missiles. Afterwards he no longer left the hut, and beyond the fibers of the mosquito net, whose tatters he no longer tried to mend with stalks, he saw all the apartments in which they had lived, her and him, and afterwards their son, rented apartments, which they painted and decorated until they became home to them; he saw them like magic palaces from the Vedas that were skewered one after another on a single arrow, Shiva the god of destruction skewered them in his wrath. Above him, from the beam of the thatched roof, the giant lizard, the likes of whom he had never ever seen, watched him as it had perhaps watched dinosaurs and ichthyosaurs of which his son knew all the types, it also watched the expanding universe from the point where it began and Manu and the little fish that he kept in a jar and in a barrel and in a lake, until he filled the entire ocean and came to the rescue in the flood. It watched the mosquito net too, his sweat pouring beneath it, his staring at the unraveled thatched roof, beyond which was an abundance of white hot light or the darkness of an equatorial night, whose tenants were crickets and cicadas and bullfrogs and fireflies. Over and over he repeated to himself there that he doesn't envy and doesn't hate and that he's forgotten everything – forgotten the puppy who would curl up in a slipper, forgotten the rearing of it and its roundness that vanished and how his son pulled its tail and how the dog would accept it, forgotten when they began to neglect it and let it roam at night and get injured in dog and cat fights and to get old without care and cough for hours in the corner of the balcony, not like a dog but rather like an old man; "he's like our marriage," she said to him one night, and at the time he still remembered how they discussed it when it was still just a thought, after a hot and dry Yom Kippur in which she had been careful not to eat next to him and the whole time worried that he should drink: in the bed, which the previous tenant left them, to the sounds of their full stomachs, each one dug up a shameful secret from preceding years that they had kept from each other, and after it another secret, deeper and darker still, a secret they feared that on hearing the other would get out of bed and leave, but it was listened to and so to the one after it – he forgot everything and went traveling just to clarify to himself the way lying ahead of him. He distanced himself from them and his life with and without them and from the country in which he lived, a country in which war was like lava that erupts once every decade, and its inhabitants like those children at the foot of Mount Pinatubo, who know nothing other than the basalt landscape. Across from him the ocean sparkled with its thousands upon thousands of scales, and in the window of the hut the horizon dissolved into vapor and evaporated, until he heard himself say in a voice rusted from silence: let them evaporate into air, let them die there let them die. For a moment, through the threads of the mosquito net, he saw Shiva's arrow stringing together shutters and curtains, a living room couch with its new cushions, the boy's room with the bookcase that he assembled for him and with books received from his replacement, and a mountain of ashes grew within his chest and stretched his skin like the skin of a yak upon which a thousand crazed shamans drummed from inside, let them all die let them all die lethemalldielethemalldie.)

("Now I'm not telling you not to give him a shekel. If you feel like it – give him a shekel. It's just that you don't have to every day because if people like them get used to it, you never get rid of them. Ask him what he does for a living and he'll say to you 'I'm a beggar.' Now work it out, say you give him a shekel every day, six shekels a week. Say you work every day" – and the hair washer stays at home and washes him in her own personal basin between the legs – "twenty five a month, round about, a hundred each season, three hundred a year. Now think what you'd buy with that three hundred shekels. Wouldn't you buy yourself some nice jeans? Sure you would, I can tell you'd buy some. Now go and remove the suds from her.")

(That's what he said in the hut in his weakened voice, but there was one who heard him from his heights and released the storm from the horizon toward him: spurred it over the ocean whose scales overturned, urged it on to gallop on the blackening waters through the thick air that was stirred by a giant transparent finger in the heaven of the heavens.)

The soundman offered Kinneret the cigarette that he had prepared, and in the room, against the wall, the sergeant leaned a roll of nylon that he took from the rickshaw. "She asked for one roll of nylon," he said.

(But they didn't use it, flick-flack: the cigarette butt had previously been long.)

(And from within the hut the screaming monkeys in the thicket were heard and the birds and the cicadas whistling and the branches of the palm trees being beaten in the wind and the coconuts striking the ground – thousands of years before, he had seen how the skies reacted to a different prayer; "Of the Peoples of Zaglembia and Sosnowiec" was written on the entrance to the synagogue, and in his eyes those names then seemed like the names of exotic countries

across the seas; but the building was covered by dirty rough
stucco and the entrance concealed in a brick wall and the
columns painted with murky oil paint up to head height
and the worshipers were elderly and sweaty in old-fashioned
brimmed hats and the holy ark in its alcove had an ugly
iron gate like the gate of a courtyard, but when he peeked
his little head out, the dry voices were heard fortifying each
other, and high on up, above the solar water heaters and
antennas, the evening clouds suddenly moved revealing a
moon as round as the pupil of an eye, golden and glowing –
and the pawpaw are squashed and their leaves ripped off and
the thatch rustles and the threads of the mosquito net quiver
when he extricates himself from it and closes the door, which
is nothing but a reed mat stretched over wooden molding.
With effort he placed the curved latch over the bent nails
and immediately it shook back and forth as if at any moment
the hut will be uprooted from its place: will be washed away
and swept in the water that covers the beach from the bay
and its restaurants that were instantly emptied, to the cliff
blurred by the barrage of the rain. The lizard remained with
him in the hut and its wrinkled throat gargled as it gazed at
him. And then the column of red ants invaded from beneath
the door and crossed the hut in a never-ending straight line,
and in the window the sky darkened further as if the night
had been severed from its place, a vast black sheet torn in the
wind. Lethemalldiethereletthemalldie, his curse echoed as he
kindled a fire with trembling hands and right away the moths
flew toward the glass and were shattered and scorched, and
the mosquitoes swooped and buzzed with a thousand drills
aimed at his brain.)

"Does anyone know why it's called nylon?" asked the actor.

(It's called Latex, latex: fine and thin, clings to the body:
store in a cool place. Note the expiry date. Take care not to
tear with nails.)

"I don't know either, how should I know?" he looked
away from Kinneret and went into the inner room to change
his clothes.

"And why'm I called Miki Le-Mic?" he asked from there. For a moment he waited for an answer and then replied himself: "It's from the family, what do you think? An aristocratic family, don't get me wrong. What, can't you tell I was born with a silver spoon in my mouth?" And after a while, since nobody answered, he coughed and spluttered and rasped, as if that same spoon was stuck in his throat.

"One thing I do know" – the door slammed after him – "if there's ever a need to seal rooms again it's not going to be with nylon. At the very least with blocks. What d'you mean how will I live?" – From the other side of the inner room a shoe dropped to the floor – "I'll hoard, not a month's worth, a year's, and when that's finished" – another shoe fell to the floor – "I'll live on leftovers thrown to me, what d'you mean leftovers, garbage that even dogs wouldn't bother to smell."

The soundman still leaned against the wall and smoked (and slipped his stung body back into the mosquito net as if it was a womb made of webbing, and through its threads and the reed mat panels he heard the storm unraveling the ocean into waves and the thicket into leaves and the air into lashings of rain. And opposite him, inside the lantern in whose base the oil bubbled, the flame licked the glass, tongued like the lizard, turned yellow and then blue, shortened and lengthened and spread.)

Opposite, inside the rickshaw, a heavy metal object was being dragged and scraped against the floor. The head of the sergeant stuck out from the rear: "you could give me a hand, believe me it wouldn't do you any harm," he said to the actor who came out to the entrance dressed in his trousers and shirt, his facial features blurred in the dusk.

"Of course it wouldn't do any harm," the actor answered. "Yeah, I do so prefer," he proclaimed, "since every kind of thing is inasmuch a jester fool." He flung his wig toward the entrance; the wig floated and landed on the floor. "You" – he turned to Kinneret who was still sitting on the edge of the sidewalk and to the soundman who was leaning against the wall – "who pale in horror at this my fate" – and to Na'ama and to Shechter who were also waiting in the entrance – "if time be afforded me, and if the bitterness of death not oppress bitterly and briskly" – and to Merav and the lighting man who remained in the room – "but alas, my time is all past and gone."

From inside the rickshaw the head of the sergeant stuck out again and his features darkened further still, as if the dusk of the interior had been added to them: "so many words without saying anything." His head disappeared again.

"That's also what my girlfriend used to say to me," answered the actor, "Did you know my girlfriend?" he drew close to the clinic door and looked at the poster stuck on it.

"Also an actress?" the sergeant asked, his head still hidden.

"An actress, yes."

"For birthdays?" the sergeant was speaking from the depths of the rickshaw.

"Dubbing," answered the actor. "I don't know what she's doing now and don't really care. Why should I care?" He stretched out the palm of his hands. "What, did I once love her? What, were we together for a year? What, did we plan to put on a show together, till I screwed everything up because I behaved like a son of a bitch? Me? Son of a bitch? What do you mean son of a bitch, next to me the worst soccer referee's the son of a virgin."

The sergeant took out a metal army bed from the rickshaw and opened its folded legs on the road. He kicked the edge to steady it, and in the light coming from the room the corners shone and the scratches that were etched in the metal could be seen. Na'ama, who watched him from the entrance, turned to the actor. "What did you do to her?" she asked and twirled a strand of hair around her finger.

"What did I do she asks," said the actor. "Pay heed to the wicked malicious deeds and a conspiracy; but removed, it fell back on the head of the conspirator. I behaved like a son of a bitch, that's what I did." He turned around to the cork notice board and punched it and right away blew on his fist; and a corner of the notice came loose from one of the drawing pins that had been stuck into it.

"Can't it be put right?"

"Things like that you can't put right," answered the actor.

Opposite them, on the bed that was lowered to the road, a green army mattress was spread out and on it the sergeant laid a large packet in which were a sheet, a blanket and a bedspread (brought from home, he promised he'd return them clean), five cushions tied up and wrapped in nylon (also from home), two rolled up posters (from his brother-in-law's advertising agency, there's nothing that they wouldn't advertise, just pay them enough they'd even advertise the rickshaw), two tattered teddy bears (from his brother-in-law's children, who haven't been children for a long long time: they were almost his height by now, and once, wanting to do him a favor, they lifted the rickshaw onto the pavement for him when he couldn't find parking; only after that there was such unpleasantness from the neighbors, you've got no idea), one Snoopy (which he went and bought with his own money and which would be for the little one afterwards: she was just crazy about furry animals like that, only it was after she had chewed the ear a bit that they really belonged to her), an empty box of batteries with green masking tape in it, regular masking tape and a box cutter.

"Do you need help?" Shechter asked him.

The sergeant's head and arms were again swallowed up inside the rickshaw, and above the eucalyptuses rustled in a light breeze, which passed and faded. A heavy object was dragged inside and a moment later the sergeant took out a large knapsack and placed it on the bed (one haversack with all Kinneret's clothing and the spikes of all her high heeled shoes, as well as one ant that climbed up one of the bulges in the) canvas.

Shechter approached him, knelt down and gripped the edge of the bed. He was the sergeant's age but looked older than him in his carriage, his gait and his movement, and even the friendly gesture of sharing the burden seemed bound to lead to mishap.

"Heave," said the sergeant and gripped the other end
(could her parents still do a vanishing act? Sure they could. It
took a whole day to convince her to mention it to them, why
not, is it only a movie for the army? It's also their daughter's,
besides which they're also artists) and lifted the bed with
Shechter. In the light entering the room from the window,
for a moment the packet and the wrapped cushions shone.

(He even tried talking to them himself, the sergeant; it's
just that after a second the switchboard operator cut in on
the line and asked him why he's making private calls: his
explanations had no effect on her, his rank had no effect;
nothing had any effect on her. It's just that ever since that
Saturday when he took the camera they've been making his
life a misery, a misery; and she disconnected him even before
he managed to determine what kind of people they are. With
a daughter like that he wouldn't be at all surprised if they did
a vanishing act, not at all. Yes, the tree's also not far from the
apple, that's just the way it is. Let's say if someone saw his
daughter for only a minute, how she chews the teddy bear's
ear let's say, or that laugh of hers when she sees him looking;
those little dimples that suddenly appear in her cheeks and
those eyes that look at him through fingers, straight to the
heart. Right away they'd know what kind of a mother she has,
and that she was born from love, yes: on a Saturday morning,
with the neighbors' radio blaring – those types, you'd think
they were alone in the building – with the lamp that he made
from bamboo and the lampshade that his wife made from
macramé still turned on from the night, even though you
could barely see it's light on that morning.)

"Do you need help?" asked the actor.

"In setting the rhythm," he explained after a moment,
"why not, like a stretcher-bearing march," and did not budge
from his place. And why, he said, why shouldn't he lie on
the bed to help get them into shape a little? "Go figure when
you might need to haul a stretcher." With his hand, whose
nail polish hadn't been removed, he invited Kinneret to join
in: "Kinneheret? Why's your head in the ground?" And right
away with the same ceremonious gesture, he invited Eran

the lighting man too, "a reward for the champ of the lamp,"
and the soundman – "this one's used to being hauled around
in the East, they call them coolies, coolies?" – and Merav
with her folder, and Na'ama – "looks as if your head's in the
clouds" – and also the crop spraying pilot: "That one? If he
carries on flying like that at night, only God will be able to
lift him up."

"Better you keep those ideas to yourself," the sergeant
progressed with the bed, keeping in step with Shechter's pace
and the tossing of the belongings. "How come you're not
wearing the skirt? Tired of being a female?"

The actor watched the two of them from the entrance;
ten years younger than them, but from his stance already
showing signs of the beginnings of someone conceding that
he may never get to act roles greater than this one: "I just
wanted to check how the girls take a leak with it."

The sergeant progressed further and the exertion was
evident in his steps, "don't you want to check where a
fish pisses from?"[23] Because if so; he's willing to volunteer
showing him.

"Show me," said the actor. He came out of the entrance,
gangling and ungainly in his own clothes as well, and stepped
in the water from the fire hydrant that lined the side of the
road. The spray stained his pants and he tried to wipe them
with his hand before it would be absorbed into the material.
"Through fire and water," he proclaimed silently to himself,
"through blood and sweat a new breed will rise, noble, fierce,
and wise."[24]

The shadows of the eucalyptuses were already merged
into the dusk of the asphalt; his wet shoes merged with it
too as he advanced toward Shechter and the sergeant. "Lef-
right-lef!" he gave the order to himself, "lef-right-lef!" With
his rhythmic steps he accompanied the bed carrying the
equipment on it until it reached the beam of the lamp that
bore down through the gap in the door. "Halt!" he ordered

---

23   A colloquial saying that contains an inherent threat

24   Lyrics from the anthem of the Betar, a right-wing youth movement

himself and pounded his feet on the spot and looked at the rucksack being conveyed. He bent down to it, nearing his eyes, whose makeup had still not been removed from them, and inspected the bulges where the high heels had stretched the canvas. "Kinnerehet?"

On the right of the clinic door, in the corner of the entrance, she still sat hugging her knees (no examination will save you). In front of her was the butt of the cigarette that the soundman had prepared for her, trampled, its stalks disintegrated.

(Into a chunk of ash, into a mound of ash, into a mountain of ash whose summit is in the sky and once in a thousand years a blind dwarf ascends and severs a grain from it with which to fill the gaping abyss of eternity.)

"Did you bring that from home as well?" the actor asked in a congenial voice, "the ant?"

"Maybe you've got ants at home," Kinneret answered, "I haven't."

(They had Sano[25]-against-ants, Sano-against-cockroaches; everything at home shone and sparkled: the marble, the basins, the tiling, everything shone and sparkled. The housemaid cleaned the shutters with a special brush, wearing rubber gloves; cleaned the windows with a magnetic brush, wearing rubber gloves, cleaned the pots with Scotch-Brite, wearing rubber gloves.)

"With us there's not a single ant," (and she buffed the enamel of the bath and the surface of the oven with a cloth, and cleaned the oven from the inside with oven spray, wearing rubber gloves) "and there never will be."

(They had Sano-for-ovens, Sano-for-mosquitoes, Sano-for-mole-crickets, Sano-for-lice, they only didn't have Sano-for-sperm and what's inside them: a baby boy or baby girl or your own death.)

"I've definitely got them," said the actor. He opened the door of the room that was closed and pushed it with his hand before the bed being carried; his fingers left a wet imprint on the handle. "Only yesterday my maid resigned and boy did

---

25   Brand of household cleaning and disinfecting agents

I beg her to stay. She said she just has to stand still for one moment and right away they start climbing up her leg."

(Leg after leg, arm after arm, breast after breast, they'll gnaw her nipples, her lips, her nostrils, her eyelids, the whites of her eyes: no examination will save you.)

In the entrance the actor made a trumpet sound with his hands in front of his mouth as if announcing the arriving cavalry: a bed laden with belongings. High above him in the darkening sky, the crop spraying plane circumscribed a large circle and drew away in the direction of the fields again, buzzing and diminishing.

"What a racket you make," Merav said from inside, "it's worse than the plane. Don't you get tired?" On the table she put down the folder in which a pencil was inserted as a bookmark.

"Leave him alone," said the sergeant and progressed further. "Let's film it already and go home." He entered the room walking backwards, watching out for the corners of the bed and one of the rucksack straps that curved toward the wet door handle and almost wrapped around it.

"Just don't step on the cables," the lighting man cried out from his corner, "never mind getting electrocuted, just don't let there be another short."

The sergeant progressed further, and Shechter behind him. "All this time you could have stuck them to the floor," said the sergeant, "isn't that what the professionals do?" He turned his gaze to the soundman and continued moving backwards with the laden bed. The soundman nodded his head. "Isn't that what I sent you out to civilian life for?" the sergeant asked and moved further back, until the other rucksack strap wrapped round the door handle and stopped him. "Wait a second," the soundman came toward him and released the strap, "where do you intend to put it?"

(In a hut, inside a mosquito net into which mosquitoes penetrate and split open the brain and its thoughts, and the thatch rustles and murmurs and the reed mat panels are torn and arched and the dangling latch tosses to and fro on the door letthemdieletthemdie.)

"At the opposite wall," Shechter advanced further forward, "that way the window will be seen." The door slammed behind him and Na'ama opened it and came inside as well, the black velvet ribbon on her wrist. "Aren't you coming, Kinneret? They're filming," she called to the entrance; in the gap that the door left, Kinneret's bent back could soon be seen and her shadow cast by the lamp on the road, far beyond the trampled cigarette butt.

"Just be careful of the cables," the lighting man shifted the lamp cable to the wall with his shoe. "This one doesn't mind if you get electrocuted," the actor said, "just as long as he doesn't have another short." The soundman lifted up the recording machine in front of the sergeant's legs that were stepping backwards and bent down to also pick up the spray canister (and his clothes so that ants won't swarm over them, and his shoes so that centipedes and scorpions won't snuggle up inside them, but then he left them all and lay down, and through the round sooty glass of the lantern all the bonfires of the dead could be seen burning as if the wick caused them to flicker in the wind, the bonfires of Pashupatinath and Benares and Pushkar and Delhi, and at the time he clearly smelt scorched shrouds and burnt hair and human flesh.) "All you care about is a short," said the actor. "And also the leg of the lamp-" the lighting man began to say, because one of the metal legs of the tripod slanted toward the inside of the room to trip them up, and the telephone rang.

"No no," the investigator repeated into the mouthpiece, "not for the meantime at least."

"Maybe now," he said after a moment, "or in a short while. If you let me carry on."

"No, you're not disturbing me," he said. "It's not going to make any difference anyway by now, is it? Whoever died, (in the middle of the night she rang and said to him that he had to investigate and that he should thank her for the opportunity instead of becoming annoyed. Yes, it's really lucky she caught him at home; one would wonder where else could he be, either on one of his trips or at home. And what's she disturbing now, his sweet dreams? He probably tossed and turned half the night like someone at odds with himself, someone incapable of deciding what to do with his screwed up life. So the time has come; it's really come. Let him take a look in the mirror if he's suddenly forgotten how old he is, he's still got a mirror there, no? Or does he now comb his hair only in the car mirror between trips, on his investigations, naturally on his investigations. He only travels on investigations; he never travels for no particular reason, just to kill time. Maybe he also feels like traveling abroad? Why not, let him travel there too, let him try everything. Some do it at twenty and there are those who only do it later. What do you mean how's he going to make a living there; he'll investigate. No lack of things to investigate. Surely he'll find himself something to investigate there. Besides which, Interpol simply can't manage without him; someone with as illustrious a career as his. After all he barely even completes his investigations here, and considering all the time he wasted on them, does he have any idea what he's like, no, really, does he have any idea what he's like? Like those athletes, the ones who waste years of their lives just to take a few stupid seconds off some sprint of a few meters; it's just not worth it. Let him look outside for a moment, let him get out of bed and open his window and take a look out, after all even when he's traveling in his car he doesn't look: there's a full moon. When was the last time he looked at a full moon? A moon, does he still remember at all what a moon is? That sphere in the sky that the mice gnaw at. Is his window closed? The smell of sex when you're having it is very pleasant, but when was the last time he had any, she knows when. And afterwards what remains? He knows full well what remains; only the smell of the sweat and the mouth and that fucking son of a bitch, loneliness. It's only because of the time of day that she's talking this way. But let him go traveling, why not. Better he should travel than bury himself here. Let him travel a bit and see the world, let's say she's getting this investigation for him as a going away gift. With the money he'll earn, the millions, what do you mean, as soon as he gets there he can rent a decent car for a change. At least he can kill time there decently. Or buy some perfume for the love of his life who'll surely be waiting there for him, what do you mean, everyone waits for him. For that, at least, it'll do. At the duty free, yes, she can also advise him which one. And every time he smells the perfume he'll also wonder what kind of a life he could be living here, yes, despite everything, exactly the way she does, despite everything. She's no Claudia Schiffer, but that's what there is, he's also no Richard Gere, as far as she can remember he's not even Colombo. For each bad day maybe they'll have two or three good ones, but sometimes you just have to be thankful for what there is, there's no other life honey) died."

7

(You, the girl with the light brown hair spread over your shoulders and a black velvet band worn around your arm, from inside the room I watched you as you entered: the lamp lit up your face, its light glowed in your hair. Monday toward evening, you, who with all your meager strength tried to help the two of them who were carrying the laden bed; my heart went out to you and it still hasn't returned, please contact me through this column. But only the Bristol board with its singed edges appeared before her eyes as she entered and its black lettering, like the cats that were described in it, said to Na'ama: "you have to envy them, my boyfriend said, because they don't howl with pain."

During the summer before enlisting, which in her eyes now seems so very long ago, she went once to meet her sister in the Dizengoff Center and in the entrance she stopped for a while next to the beggar who almost always sat there, before him an empty yoghurt carton with a few coins. On his right stood an old pram laden with empty vegetable boxes on which he would write long sentences in curly lettering with no punctuation and no spaces between the words, for example: "Attheoutsetandinconclusiononewhichspeedilyapp-roachesfrommanygenerationsinourtimeAmenandAmen." The pram had Formica side panels, and a defective transistor radio with a large battery stuck to its back was tied to its handle, and opposite them, next to the Hard Rock Café, a group of high school students gathered and one of them said, "what you talking about, it's the Rolls Royce of motorbikes, not a Honda or a Kawasaki or a BMW, they're Vespas compared to it." The beggar did not lift his gaze from his box, which was filling up with more and more curly letters, and Na'ama then smelt the sour stench that rose from his clothing.

"Shometimes people shtop," he said to her suddenly and she smelt his breath too, "they shay he's crazy, they shay what he's shcribbling there, old age doesn't make you happy and death is no wedding. No one gets a divorce from death. Am I shcaring you?" "No," answered Na'ama, "not at all," and his Adam's apple moved slowly beneath the wrinkles of his neck from which white stubble sprouted. He was bent over there at her feet like some kind of small animal who's already matched its size and color to the slates of the sidewalk, and at the time Na'ama tried to think about the young man he had once been, when he was still upright and worked and didn't beg for charity – because maybe he was fired when he got old or maybe before that, because of his speech impediment? Or maybe for some other reason, like they did to her father. But his eyes were still fixed on her and she noticed the sleep lodged in the corners. He asked if she was in a hurry and Na'ama answered: "no, not at all," not only because her sister was always late, but because she never wanted to hurt people, and certainly not a miserable beggar who has no one to listen to him in all the world. At times, at night before falling asleep or in front of the mirror when putting on her loveliest facial expression, Na'ama would think to herself that if only everyone would behave the way she does the world would be a much better place; and right away she would swear to herself that even if everyone hurt her, absolutely everyone, she wouldn't allow anybody to spoil the good inside her – sometimes she could actually feel it, that goodness, like some kind of small baby, in spite of not knowing at all how a pregnant woman feels, or how she feels before that, in those moments when she becomes a woman – nobody, she would always, always remain herself: Na'ama. Passersby spilled over onto the sidewalk and were replaced by others, and the beggar, after turning his head toward the pram and making sure it stood in its place, continued to talk to her, not as to a girl who could be his great granddaughter but like to an adult: that's how he spoke to Na'ama. He told her how every night he sleeps on a vacant lot, "fallow land with nothing but a demolished building, but it will be built, as they shay: they shall build the old washtes, they shall raise up the former desholations, ruins will be redeemed. I don't need people's pity. Two days ago, on Shunday," "Monday," Na'ama corrected him and instantly regretted it, and from the entrance of the Mashbir department store a few women came out carrying large packets and their children after them. "Monday," said the beggar and was silent for a moment. "Monday, the shun alsho ariseth and the shun goeth down and hashteth to his plashe where he ariseth until the day breathe and the shadows flee away. Monday." For a moment Na'ama hesitated whether to stay, but the beggar, in the same cracked voice that struggled to pass between his drawn in lips, carried on talking to her and told her how on the previous Monday he slept on his lot, and how they appeared there suddenly and woke him up, "three thin catsh, without a home, without a name, not old but shtill being weaned and crying out for shomething over and over, as they shay: O Lord, shall I cry and thou will not hear! Even cry out unto thee of violenshe and Thou wilt not hear!" "Perhaps they wanted milk," Na'ama was about to say but didn't say, and to their right a car hooted at a boy and girl who crossed the road at a red light. The beggar, bent as before, pointed to the empty yoghurt carton in front of him, and for a moment she thought he was waiting for her to put a coin there, but straightaway he returned his finger to the cardboard box and the words written there. In the same quivering voice he told her how he led the cats to the box with this yoghurt, and from there to his pram, and how he transferred them like that to the seashore, "as they shay: sheparate thyshelf, I pray thee, from me" so that they wouldn't disturb his sleep anymore: "for they turned night into day." She did not ask what he did to them, fearing that he perhaps had drowned them, even though he looked like he wasn't capable of doing any harm, not only because of his impediment but also because of his smallness and his dirty trousers, whose edges were rolled up like children's trousers. On their left, next to the Hard Rock Café, one of the high school students shielded his eyes and peered inside the window, and from the group someone else said: "get it into your head; Harley Davidson is the national league, the top, it's the NBA. Next to it Kawasaki's the high school team," and from the entrance of the Mashbir more women came out and in their hands bulging packets; they passed them by and did not stop. "Bashan cows on Mount Shamaria," the beggar mumbled quietly, "behold, the days are coming upon you when they will take you away with hooksh, and the last of you with fish hooksh." He watched them for a moment and was silent, until turning to Na'ama again: on that night, after he got rid of the three cats, he returned to the vacant lot with his pram and spread his jacket and tried to fall asleep once more, "as they shay: and not at night do men shee shleep with their eyes. Monday night, out of the mouth of babes and shucklings. I laid down my head and closed my eyes and shaid to myshelf, now dreams may come bringing balm for my shoul, as they shay: lighten mine eyes, lesht I shleep the shleep of death," but right away his sleep was disturbed. "Thish time I was frightened almosht to death, eighty-shix years have inhabited thish body in front of you, and thish time it almosht passhed away. I opened my eyes to shee in the darknessh, three thin layaboutsh dresshed in black from head to toe, coming up from the corner of the lot and moving toward my pram as if I wasn't ashleep at the foot of it. They came closhe shilently and bent over my head and took off all the wheels one after another and put them inshide their coatsh, until my pram shtood on its shtumpsh like a shtunned pershon. They left the transishtor, but it had no voishe, as they shay: but the Lord was not in the noise. Shleep fled from my eyes, and in the field and in all the alleys of the buildings thin layaboutsh dresshed in black lurk in the dark until I'll fall ashleep and understand that those three kittens were turned into human beings for their honor to be reshtored by me. As they shay: now a word was shecretly brought to me, in thoughtsh from the visions of the night, when deep shleep falleth on men, then a shpirit passhed before my fashe, that made the hair of my flesh to shtand up,

it shtood shtill, but I could not dishcern the appearanshe
thereof." He let go the chewed pen and lifted his hand from
his box to the corner of his eye and wiped it with a childish
motion, and Na'ama noticed the age spots that blemished it
and how the tip of his finger glistened as he held the pen
again. Afterwards he didn't fall asleep, he told her. "The third
part of the night passhed and I roused myshelf from the
ground as if to shay to my body: O ye dry bones, hear the
word of the Lord, and again my legs plodded to the shea with
my pram, unto the plashe whither the rivers go, thither they
go again. All three catsh were shnuggled up there in the
shand, and tempting them with the leftovers of the yoghurt
at the bottom of the carton I lifted them into the pram onshe
more and returned them to the field. As they shay: to you I
have thish as a possession, be fruitful, and multiply, and fill
the land. They meowed and shtared at me with large eyes as
if to shay: woe to him that buildeth a town with blood, and
eshtablisheth a city by iniquity, your transhgressions are
forgiven." For a moment he looked at Na'ama from the
pavement with moist dull pupils, until she nodded her head
to him, and across from them more women passed with
Mashbir bags and did not stop. "And to my ears their
meowing around me will be like a musician playing," he said
to her and she saw how the wrinkles of his throat quivered,
"And blesshings for my shalvation. For the Lord of hoshts
hath a day upon all that is proud and lofty" – above his box
he looked at the women passing and their overflowing
packages – "And upon every lofty tower, and upon every
fortified wall" – from within his small shrunken body he
raised his cracked voice to drown out the din of the street,
and his eyes, which were lined with fine blood vessels, he
lifted up above Dizengoff Center and the luxurious high-rise
apartments that were built there, up and up he lifted them
from the pavement to the dark skies, as if for one moment
the Lord of hosts flickered there like the passing plane – "shall
not the day of the Lord be darknessh and not light? Even very
dark, and no brightnessh in it?")

   "And also on the foot of the lamp," said the lighting man.

The sergeant shifted its leg and advanced further with Shechter, both putting the bed down on the floor and placing it close to the wall.

("On that day a man shall casht away his idols of shilver and gold and all his valuables," for a moment he was silent in order to inhale air and uttered a strangled sound with his wrinkled throat across from the passersby, and behind her suddenly her sister said: "why are you letting him bother you, have you lost your marbles as well?" But Na'ama took three shekels out of her purse and one more and another half, and placed them in the empty carton and didn't think about the prophets and high school bible class, but rather of the boy the beggar once had been: after all he too had parents who must surely have loved him and hugged him, and brothers and sisters, and uncles and aunts, and games and toys. And maybe he lay in that very pram then, which is now full of rags and boxes, and women like those who passed them by and didn't stop, would bend over him then and pinch his cheeks.)

"Kinneret," the sergeant called out from the entrance, "maybe show us how yours is arranged?"

(Because how could he know how a room of someone like that is, how? Had he been told to construct a child's room, straightaway he would have known what to do, but someone like that? Straightaway he would have built a bookcase by himself, a table, a chair, a bed, what not, even a cupboard, yes why not, but first of all they would have painted it together, he and his wife, his wife the walls and he the ceiling: he would have stood on the ladder and moved it with his legs, walking with it like some professional painter or circus clown, until his wife would split her sides with laughter and say to him from below, "stop it, Didi, stop it." For a while she's been calling him that, Didi, like the little one, and at night – in the apartment in Holon that they bought with a mortgage and have already fixed up with everything – she would sometimes ask in her special voice: "Didi are you sleeping?" And he would immediately answer: "no," and turn over toward her and see her eyes shining in the dark, until he would turn on the light.)

(But Na'ama could also have showed them: after all she slept over at Kinneret's one night, a night that she'll never forget; as long as she lives she won't forget it, even if she's eighty-six and writing letters to the Lord of hosts on vegetable boxes in the street. Her cadet pilot, who until that moment seemed to her quiet and shy, suddenly got up and went out to the stairwell to the neighbor who had knocked on their wall. Until then he seemed like a goody-goody air force boy, as he still rested his shorn head on her thighs and shut his eyes and listened to music, and she looked at his high forehead and his long lashes and his lips, which looked as if they'd open to her any moment, any moment, in a second, now, now: that's what she said to herself, Na'ama, when he got up and went out to the stairwell. "Tell me lady," he shouted at the neighbor, "that's the thanks we get for keeping your skies clean?")

In the window, above the shadows of the eucalyptuses the crop spraying plane drew away, perhaps still blowing clouds of poison in the dark.

(She was old, the neighbor, even older than her grandmother, and in the lit up entrance the cadet pilot could be seen moving closer to her, until he stood opposite her and suddenly burped from the beer, the sort of burp after which Na'ama couldn't stay there for even a moment longer. Right away she dragged Kinneret outside – after all she had asked her before not to let her do anything stupid – and throughout the stairwell, on whose doors were small ceramic signs with the names of couples or signs in bronze or even just scraps of paper with their names, the Dire Straits song echoed. It echoed from the third floor to the post boxes and they both stood on the street corner trying to stop a taxi. For half an hour they stood there until one stopped for them; he looked at them askance but agreed to take them anyway and only inside the taxi did Na'ama realize just how much they both stank of beer. For the whole journey, which seemed to her would never end, the driver looked at them in the mirror watching out that they don't vomit over the upholstery, and suddenly, in front of his sparkling eyes right there, she also burped: she, Na'ama. She was so disgusted with herself that she almost burst out crying and when they arrived at Kinneret's and went up in the elevator and into the apartment, she ran to the bathroom and vomited everything up. She vomited her guts out, and when she thought she had finished and that there was nothing left, she was reminded of the cadet pilot's bathroom and how she came out and said – yes she, Na'ama – "maybe you should leave it down already? What, don't you know how to aim?" And right away she vomited all that remained. Afterwards she washed her face and looked at herself in the mirror above the basin, a large mirror lit up all around and didn't like what she saw in it, didn't at all like who she saw there: You, the girl with the wild hair and bloated face, that's what Na'ama said to herself, you, who made a fool of yourself. You, don't ever get drunk anymore and don't ever fall in love with a cadet pilot, nor a pilot nor with anyone else, never ever ever; and not right now as well, Monday night, an army instruction base somewhere, you there beyond the dark.)

"I don't feel like it," Kinneret entered and slammed the door. "Ask her, she also knows my room." She moved slowly to the interior of the room with all her height, transporting her curves between the tripods of the small lamps and the tripod of the large lamp and the tripod of the second camera on her way to the bed and the equipment on it.

"Anyway" – she placed her finger near the rucksack that was on the bed, squashed the ant that was walking over it and lifted her head toward the sergeant – "first of all, show me the posters. That's the first thing. What does it matter how my room's arranged if the posters are all wrong?"

(LL Cool J, Slick Rick, Notorious B.I.G., Craig Mack, Snoop Dogg: rappers and rockers and blues players [all sorts of singers and groups whom Na'ama didn't know, and clothes were strewn everywhere: on the bed, on the chair, on the pouffe, even on the table. All Kinneret's shoes were arranged in a row under her bed, and on the window, in the transparent squares between the remnants of the masking tape glue from the war, the entire city could be seen, minute, the way pilots and angels see it, and just one distant traffic light flashed: at the time Na'ama saw her building from there, and her sister's roof, and the cadet pilots' apartment and the old age home in which her grandmother lived and other buildings, masses of dark buildings in which tenants are sleeping, but perhaps in one of the their windows a man stood in the dark looking out like her, pressing his face to the pane like her,] who didn't sing oom-pah oom-pah, they sang from deep down in the throat, from the lungs, from the stomach, from the guts: all body fluids spread it.)

"How's this?" asked the sergeant.

He removed the elastic band from the roll of Bristol and in front of Kinneret he spread out the posters that had been rolled up in it. "Does this pass inspection?"

Right away he had to straighten the edges again because they rolled back like the tongues of whistles (you should have seen his little girl on Purim) or like a lizard tongue (whose throat gargles thousands of mosquitoes and its eyes that never shut see the ocean flooding and foaming, perforated by arrows of rain and spears of lightning) or like the ribbon from gifts (which they bring instead of checks, so that no one will know the small amount of money they've spent; they bring them and shoot a glance at the wheelchair parked in the corner of the hall on the snow white marble; her grandfather looked like a deposed king after the attack, that's what everyone called it, the attack, and still added: "lucky a car didn't run him over," as if he had been brought over from the road or the pavement and not from the red-cushioned sofa of the bar, reeking of eau de cologne and ruddy from alcohol and from lipstick and from exertion) or like the skin of an apple (peeled in one go, around and around, from top to bottom, and curling from the large palm of the hand to little Na'ama's mouth, or he would put her, Na'ama's father, on his shoulders, which at the time were still upright and strong, and gallop with her throughout the house from room to room shouting "horsey-horsey, horsey-horsey," or stand her on them to reach the tassels of the lampshade and wink at the firefly confined there) or like a telephone cord (with a shattered mouthpiece with bleeding lips with smashed tcethtonguethroatneck, and above it a moist red felt-tipped inscription turning blue in the flashing light) or like the tongue of a drummer (tonguing and rolling in and out, in and out, pinkish thick fleshy warm, to demonstrate what he could do with it to her there) or like a radio communication cord in a command car (which swings back and forth with the small mouthpiece at its end, shrinking and stretching, shrinking and stretching, and from the tiny holes of the earpiece and the tiny holes of the speakers you could no longer hear someone who called over and over: "Juicy dachvan, your location – over, Juicy dachvan, your location – over"; that's what Shechter's code was in the war, Juicy dachvan, and he didn't give his location because he was nowhere to be found in the world: it was a suburb of a coastal town, whose buildings were destroyed and burnt, and the skies above him were bright and clear and very blue after the smoke had been swallowed up by them. "Juicy dachvan, Juicy dachvan, your location – over," that's what they called him at the time, and on those first days he still tried to imagine how the French girl would pronounce it, and how she would certainly have had difficulty, like the time he taught her to count and she said to him, "ahat, shetaime," and put up one finger and then another and pointed here and there on her body, and folded one and pointed again, and afterwards on the wallpaper his silhouette moved on top of hers. Nothing was heard anymore through the tiny holes of the mouthpiece, because the smell that seeped through them had already split over the cord and filled the whole communication device, the way it filled Shechter's body: it rose from beneath the ruins, and without it you couldn't tell when it had collapsed, but those who lay there, Lebanese covered by ceilings and floors, gradually rose in that smell, body particle after body particle, not to the heights of the heavens, but into Shechter's body: seeping in and filling him from the soles of his feet to his scalp and setting him in motion in all directions at their will, after getting rid of the remnants of the smell that preceded it – a smell that could not be washed away, not in the hotel shower, not at the airport, not on the plane, not in his parents' apartment, and not at the base in the Golan Heights – the smell of the French girl, from the single night on which she agreed to meet with him again. She no longer had a name, the French girl, she had no characteristics, she had no voice nor facial features, she only had a place and Shechter was not in it: the room, whose entire floor the mattress almost filled, he no longer was in; the small bathtub, which almost touched the basin, he no longer sat in; the window, which turned into a mirror when the dark covered it like a curtain, he no longer was reflected in; the door on whose handle they hung their clothes, since she had no cupboard, he did not lock; and her soft warm breathing body with her breasts flattened beneath him like two faces, he did not touch. His fingers now touched the seat of the command car: the dead caused them to move over the torn fabric, the dead touched the protruding sponge with them, smoothed over the hollow that he indented before the driver left him there alone and then still shouted at him from a distance that they could all lodge a complaint of desertion against him – Shechter, the regiment commander and the chief of staff together: he's got a wife and small children to feed, it's not his fault that Shechter returned from abroad just to get killed in the war.)

"Not bad," Kinneret said, "considering."

The sergeant turned the posters around and showed them to the others.

(Ratzabi was the driver's name, and to every reserve duty he brought along with him packets of mint leaves and packets of sunflower seeds, and sometimes he brought notes of exemption from guard duty and from wearing military boots and from lifting loads, but he didn't make use of them. He came to the war two days after the regiment had already been sent to Lebanon, and Shechter found him in the mess hall on the base in the Golan Heights playing backgammon with the cook, as if they were on one of their regular reserve duties, during which he would always ask when's he finally getting married and when will he see his movies on television, and then he would still imagine to himself how he would say to Ratzabi on one of the trips in the command car: "next week, on Sunday night," or "on Tuesday, right after the news," while together with the quartermaster they loaded a barrel of spirit, or a giant pot of cracked hard-boiled eggs with trails of egg white that dragged behind in the water like clumps of sperm that never reached their destination and on way grew old and died: they died under the blanket, died under the hotel ceiling. And above, the sky was heavy, brushing against the slate roof and not drowning out the chimes of the Sorbonne clock that rang out every quarter hour across the alley: one chime on the first quarter, two on the second, three on the third and four on the fourth, and after them all the chimes of the hour that struck and struck until one's head would burst, had it not been filled with wine. For two months he stayed at that hotel and waited, and on the other side of the thin walls, on his left and on his right and below him, were Italian, German and American tourist couples as well as French from small country towns causing their beds to shake in one language and breathing heavily in one language and moaning and groaning in one language, and sometimes he imagined hearing a woman shouting out from there "amore mio" or "meine liebe" or "ouvre tes yeux, je veux voir tes yeux," but it was the wine shouting in his ears, cheap clochard wine made of grape remnants.)

"How's that?" the sergeant asked the others.

(Every quarter of an hour the clock struck, and from the hotel room he heard it cutting and slicing the time, all the days in which he waited for her to invite him again – to a small town that no tourist other than he had visited and no Parisian had ever heard of – cutting and slicing the mass of minutes that had passed since the showing of his film at the Cinematheque. At the end of that night he wrote her a letter, completely drunk at the time, but sober to all the dreams of grandeur: she was a nursing sister in a small hospital in

the town of Bourg and loved Hollywood movies and had
never heard of Alan Resnais or Truffaut or the New Wave;
and she spoke much about her family, as if the world ended
in that small town in which she lived, and only by mistake
she traveled one summer to Italy and by mistake they spread
their sleeping bags together on the banks of the Arno or the
Po; her face was transparent, changing from moment to
moment, you could tell immediately if she was happy or sad,
when he made her angry and when he put her off and when
her desire was aroused. Then it could be seen in the depth
of her eyes and in the slight movement of her thigh, first
through the corduroy and then naked, when she tilted it, the
pure pudgy thigh, and lifted her pelvis to him and said, as if
inviting him on a journey: "Viens".)

But one of the posters rolled up again and when the
sergeant hastened to hold it open another rolled up.

"Refusing to obey a command," said the actor. "Aren't you
going issue them a warrant, Gidi?"

The sergeant spread them again.

(And this is how the film was shown at the Cinematheque:
it was laid out in the flickering beam into which cigarette
smoke intertwines and into which mumblings disintegrate,
and grains of dust that rose from those who left make it
fuzzier, and each time the door was opened the man standing
outside appeared, holding a tattered lottery ticket in his hand
and saying to those leaving: "a difference of just one number,
one number! There's no God, believe me, none!" Throughout
the showing Shechter sat at the rear of the hall, shrunken and
fearing that someone in front will shout out: "Projectionist!
Projectionist!" the way they'd shout out in the scout den
when the picture moved and the sky suddenly opened up at
the bottom of the sheet: or that those at the back would turn
their heads around – the way they used to do in the scout den
during boring films – to check how much celluloid was still
left on the reel. He now looked at his life that way, checking
how much celluloid was still left: a day or a decade or a
generation ago, he wore a blue scout's shirt and watched fiery
burning letters in the night sky and together with everyone

cried out: "fear not, be strong!" – though it was no more than jute sacks wrapped around iron wire; a day or a decade or a generation ago he lay on the bank of the Yarkon and somnolent clouds passed above eucalyptus silhouettes, dark as these eucalyptuses; and lay on the bank of the Arno and heard a sleeping bag zip buzz and open; and saw buildings whose floors condensed like the folds of an accordion and choked from the stench of the dead; a day or a decade or a generation ago he sat in the bathtub in his apartment in his clothes, and beyond the sheets of nylon that seal the windows was a sheet of jute enveloping the entire world, and beyond it there was nothing.)

"Isn't my okay enough?" Kinneret asked. "After all it's gonna be my room."

The sergeant had already unfurled the two posters again and showed them to the others as well: in one, a group of well-built sweaty young men in a large hangar tilted "Maccabi" beer cans to their mouths, and in the other, beneath a roaring waterfall, a man and a woman embraced and "Eden Water - Your Mineral Water" was written on it.

The actor struck the wig against his thigh and dust rose from it. He then placed it on the table next to the spray can and in a nasal twang, which he had used in the filming, informed them that he doesn't drink "Maccabi" at all – has he got the muscles for drinking "Maccabi"? – And neither does he drink "Eden Water" he said in his regular voice, because he doesn't have anyone to embrace like that beneath waterfalls, no one. "Me?" he said, "I only drink water from the national water carrier from the –"

"Kinneret Kin-erehet Kineeereehet-"

He sang.

"I swear to God she blushed," he stopped and said.

But she had already turned her head to the window, and from its darkness the sound of stones that the two prisoners sank into the trash can was again heard: (trash cans spread it, garbage trucks, roads and pavements and buildings: the entire city spread it): their sound when they hit the plastic and their sound when they hit the iron and their sound when they missed and fell on the asphalt.

"A Jordan rebound," Weintraub said from there, his body merging with the shadows of the trees, "forty-two eighteen."

"Twenty" said the other prisoner.

"Eighteen," said Weintraub, "but who's counting. Jordan's got a big heart, make it twenty." And right away the hits were swallowed by the rattling of the crop spraying plane.

"Kinneret honey," said the actor – he lifted the canister of anti-rust spray from the table and tossed and shook it – "ever since Miki Le-Mic's girlfriend left him in the war he's become such a monk, he only thinks about holy water. I heard that the water that Jesus walked on" – he took some hovering pantomime steps on the spot – "they're selling in Tiberius with his footprints, a hundred shekels a bottle."

Kinneret was still watching the two prisoners from the window. A stone hit the iron and after it another stone hit the plastic. "Forty-four twenty," Weintraub said. "You're not much of an opponent Ezra. You can tell right away that it's your first time in detention." In the distance, beyond the shadows of the eucalyptuses, the rhythmic rattling of the plane dimmed and dwindled, as if the darkness bit into it with its teeth, bite after bite.

"Is that you again Weintraub?" the sergeant called out. He drew near to the window and stood there next to Kinneret.

"What, do you mean to say you're still waiting for the welfare officer?" Weintraub asked from the road. "Tell them Ezra. Didn't we see her earlier with the personnel aide? Having a real good time, she didn't stop laughing with him."

Together with him she passed the limp white rope that was dropped in front of them, after they woke the sentry up with a long and adamant hoot, and together with him she drew into the distance when the sentry tied up his slipknot again and sat

back in his chair, his head falling to his chest
again. On the exit road from the base, on
all its potholes and on the black stripes that
the base drivers left when trying out their
brakes, was where she was now traveling,
the welfare officer, in the personnel aide's
Renault 4. On her left the fields could be
seen, which after the plowing season were
speckled with white heron, and on her right
the duplexes that were built this last year,
and at the hub a small shopping center that
in giant neon letters called itself a "mall."
Here and there a few windows were lit,
curtained or covered with slats or exposed,
and in one of them a boy waved at them
with his hand –perhaps not at them. Rather
at the old American sedan parked at the
side of the road, its engine bonnet lifted.
A man and a woman stood there in front
of it and waved their hands – but she and
the personnel aide were hurrying off to the
first show. That's all they needed now, to
stop, after she slipped away like that from
the sergeant's film. Who at all would want
to take part in his films, and what's more,
about the war? They didn't have battery
cables anyway, so what was there to stop
for, just to say that they didn't have any? In
the rearview mirror of the car she saw how
the couple turned around and watched the
Renault drawing away, two small darkening
figures, becoming further dwarfed by the
side of the road, until they vanished from
her eyes.

"Corpus Domini Nostri," said the actor. He moved
forward from the table swinging the spray canister in his hand

from side to side and spraying here and there as if scattering holy water or dispersing incense smoke.

"Have you gone crazy or something?" the sergeant shouted, "where will we get some when we really need it?"

Na'ama, who had gathered up her hair again, gently took the posters from the sergeant's hands. She spread one out and looked at it, and then spread the other one out too, her gaze lingering on it: a boy and a girl embracing opposite her beneath a waterfall whose water covered them both.

"Should I put them here or here?" the sergeant asked. He had already cut small pieces of tape with which to stick the posters up and meanwhile placed them on his watch strap, a brown worn out leather band, which had perhaps also been used for the same purpose in the past.

"Here," answered Na'ama, pointing to a part of the wall above the bed.

The sergeant spread the first poster there and smoothed it over with his right hand until it was stretched out, moving the side of his palm over the muscular boys photographed there (they looked like Kibbutzniks after a day's work, or like guys from the elite corps after a daring incursion in the enemy rear: sweating, two-day stubble, and each one giving the other a friendly slap on the shoulder; the curly-headed one even poured beer freely over the head and muscular shoulders of the one next to him).

Na'ama, who drew close to the sergeant again, removed a few pieces of tape from his watch strap.

"Not all of them," he said to her, because he saw that one was needed for sticking down the legs of the boy who was wet from the beer (you couldn't tell what all those muscles of his glistened from, from sweat or from beer), "leave some for him. He also deserves some."

(The month he tried out civilian life? On the corrugated tin wall of the garage, between all the pictures from *Playboy* of girls with breasts the size of watermelons, there were also two pictures of Schwarzenegger; the panel beater had stuck them there, and every small break, for even five minutes let's say, he would practice lifting weights there. Not real weights, axles and differentials which he turned into weights, what does it matter, the main thing is that they were weights. And one time, when the sergeant passed him on his way out, not on purpose, he just happened to be on his way out, he noticed how his muscles bulged and suddenly had the urge to touch them, just for a moment, just to see how firm they were, that's all, for one second, no more. But right away he increased his stride and speeded up. He soon entered the office – they had a hot water machine even more defective than the one in the army and just one teaspoon tied to a nail by a string – and rang his wife from there. Yes, despite that he was on his way home, after all that's only why he passed by there, because he was on his way home. But he called just to hear her voice again, and her laugh too, that laugh, which rolled like a mass of marbles and made her tits jiggle even when she wasn't naked, and also to ask her if she minded turning on the lamp now: yes, even though it was still daytime.)

Na'ama lifted her hand to stick up the other poster. Her shirt was pulled back by the weight of the beret in her epaulet, revealing a section of rounded shoulder, and for a moment Shechter looked at its pureness. She let her eyes rest on the couple in the photograph embracing beneath the waterfall covering them both like a transparent sheet adorned with sparkles, but through the water their beautiful bodies could be seen close to each other and their glowing faces kissing (Monday night, you, the girl whose hair was wet by the waterfall: I gazed into the depths of your eyes and what I saw there I'll never forget).

Shechter, who pulled at the corners with his hand, looked again at the revealed shoulder and the darkening bra strap there, and when it was concealed he looked at her neck from where her hair was gathered up in the black velvet ribbon. The neck too was clear skinned and the soft down turned gold in the lamplight, and he rested his eyes there for a moment.

"What?" asked Na'ama and turned around.

"Nothing," answered Shechter. He turned his gaze to the room: "who's good at making beds?" And right away he lifted up a package of bedding and opened it, a large package from the army store with blue felt-tipped scribbling that could briefly be seen on its side.

"He was looking at your neck," the actor said from his chair.

"What's wrong with it?" Na'ama lifted her hand and began to touch her neck slowly with the tips of her fingers, the way she would feel for pimples on her cheeks.

"I didn't say there was anything wrong," Shechter answered quietly and took out a sheet from the package and began to unfold it: a sheet of reddish orange shades, which you could see had been chosen with care when bought.

"What he wanted to say" – the actor turned around with the chair – "it may shine no less than the radiance of your face in a lover's eye, as you part from him never to return."

Shechter continued unfolding the sheet and Merav asked if he didn't prefer that she did it: "Maybe let me do it?"

He opened another fold in the sheet with a tug.

"Gently for God's sake," the sergeant called out. "It's my sheet from home and brand new. Maybe first clean there a bit just so that there won't be any problems afterwards. Besides which, first of all you have to remove all the stuff, no? What, you gonna put it on like that on top of everything?" (On top of that entire list that they loaded, he and Shechter, and brought here from the rickshaw: 1 pouffe, 5 cushions, 2 teddy bears, 1 Snoopy, 1 cardboard box with 1 green masking tape, 1 regular masking tape and 1 haversack of Kinneret's with 1 ant.)

Shechter removed Kinneret's rucksack from the bed, his shoulder pulled by its weight as he carried it to the foot of the table. His shadow cast by the lamp swayed on the floor tiles until ceasing.

"Corpus Domini Nostri," the actor gave his blessing again as he bent down at his feet and laid the rucksack on the floor. The actor's eyes were still made-up, and with a ceremonial gesture, in which his red nails shone, he proffered Shechter a page folded up the size of a stamp as if presenting him with holy bread. "Costodius animam tuam," he made the sign of the cross over him with his left hand, with a proficiency acquired from some play in which he had acted or from watching movies or from somewhere else.

"Isn't that Na'ama's telephone number?" asked the lighting man from his place next to the lamp. He was still trying to open the butterfly screw of one of the parts.

"It is," answered the actor. "But just you wait, in a month's time I'll blab about you to the Rabbinate. Domini Nostri Jesu Christi," he blessed Shechter for the third time, holding the paper opposite him between thumb and forefinger and his little finger gracefully lifted in the air. "No, really," he said in the voice of someone trying to prove a point, "what's eating paper when it's for Na'ama's phone number?" The little finger that lingered for a while was put down with its shiny red nail. "Shechter doesn't love you enough Na'ama."

On the wall above the bed the loving couple was stuck by the bottom corners as well and the water that gushed above their knees turned white around them like a lace hem. Na'ama turned her head from them when the note fell to the floor and Shechter bent toward it, supporting himself with his left hand on the table.

"Shechter's repenting," the actor declared from the other side, "he does love you Na'ama."

The note was placed on the table next to the spray canister, just as it had been folded.

"He's not repenting," the actor announced to everyone and turned with his chair, "Shechter's not one to eat paper for love. He wouldn't do a thing for it, Shechter."

On their left Na'ama removed the pouffe, which was piled on the mattress, hugging it to her body. "Doesn't anybody love me?" she asked in a childish pampered voice and patted the pouffe again and again to puff it up as she lowered it to the floor.

"Shechter's just shy," the actor said from the floor. He peered at him as he bent down again to the rucksack and with his middle finger tried to flick the ant that was walking there. "Shechter's just not one to show his feelings, what him? As a director? The pitch-dark depths of his passions no man shall behold, and no light endeavor to encroach upon the fathoms of his heart. Not so?"

Na'ama lifted two teddy bears from the mattress, hugging them to her small breasts, and Shechter, who did not open his mouth all the while, lowered the cardboard box to the floor. The actor turned around in his chair and peered at him again.

"You've got something on your neck," he informed him, and right away swore that this time he's speaking seriously: yes, for a change. Sometimes he's so very serious he announced placing his hand on his chest, even his mirror at home doesn't recognize him. At the time it simply said to him: "listen, this is no place for one of us." Just like that, the exact words his girlfriend said to him in the war: straight to his face, without mercy, not that he deserved mercy.

"You really do have something there," said Na'ama. "Don't you believe me as well?" And since he was resolute in his silence, after a moment she reached out her small hand to Shechter's neck to remove the small piece of tape that was stuck to his thinning strands. She peeled it off slowly, carefully, so as not to pull the hair out and hurt him; crumpled it into a little ball and dropped it to the floor. "There we are," she said and smiled, like a nurse who had removed a plaster from an apprehensive patient.

Shechter (for a moment he still felt the warmth of her fingers, he didn't only feel it on his neck but all over his body, until he reminded himself that this girl, had he married at twenty – but he didn't marry at twenty and not at thirty, and his bedding, which he seldom changes, he brings to the neighborhood laundry, and each time he hastened to leave before the Russian woman who worked there would sniff them, taking consolation from old widowers whose bedding gave off smells of must and intestinal gas; those he did not yet emit from his own body, which wasn't wounded in the war, not even by shrapnel – she could have been his daughter, and the uneasiness he now feels has something indecent about it, something that sometimes reaches newspaper crime columns. At the same time all sorts of famous singers who live with girls they met backstage came to mind, and respected professors who even married their students: people he's not the lesser of in his youth, but rather in his talents in which he no longer believes) still looked at the small palm that touched him and its nails chewed like the nails of a child, when she turned and moved the Snoopy from the bed to the table, seating it there next to the two teddy bears.

(And next to the candy boxes, and beach balls, and packs of cigarettes, and a plundered gold necklace that the soldiers vied for, as if the dead man outside was not becoming bloated, its owner, whose face is concealed by jute except for the hole of his open mouth in the place where he managed to gnaw the sack with his teeth.)

"At this rate," Merav said, "by the time you finish all this arranging, at home they'll be marking him down for going AWOL. Won't they mark you down for going AWOL?" She glanced at the sergeant and approached the bed, grasped the sheet and spread it with one skillful move: she whipped it in the air, floated it above the entire mattress until it landed on it and right away she tucked the edges beneath it. In the space of the room, which the bed reduced even more, a breeze still stirred strands of hair that it touched here and there.

(God knows what they were doing there, but she also knows: after all, at the time throughout the whole Negev Desert they heard him shouting to his wife's kibbutz in the north: "Poppet, are you making yeth with your head?")

Merav grasped the edge of the blanket, whipped it as well, floated it, landed it and tucked the edges beneath the mattress too.

(But afterwards they left the canteen and both walked the length of the barbed wire passing a guard post and another and climbed the hill on whose top was a machine-gun post. The guard there didn't shout out "halt, what's the password" as they drew near nor "stop or I'll shoot," but just said: "what a surprise, come in come in." And right away he asked them if they wouldn't mind remaining there for a while, since they're already there, just so that he can hop out to fetch something from the kitchenette, nothing big, just a few apples or pears for some refreshment, that's all, one second and he'll be back. "Sure, why not," said Gidi. "Just don't stay away for too long, okay?" he called out after a moment to the shadow retreating into the darkness. The guard post, which was identical to the post in which they filmed the missiles, became even smaller at night. In the faint light that came from the gate, writings that were engraved in curved rusty letters could be made out – "Life is not a … it's always hard" – with a drawing in the middle, and they both were careful not to look at it, as if that way it would be erased from their eyes and vanish. In the complete silence the rustling of sunflower seed shells that were piled up in a thick layer beneath their shoes could be heard, their breathing could be heard as well, very clearly, and from time to time some sounds of oriental music warbled toward them from the sentry's post. In the opening of the small booth at the foot of the hill a black shoe could be seen drumming to the rhythm of the song, in the entire vast dark expanse, only the small illuminated white rectangle of the opening with the shoe drumming to the rhythm of the song could be seen. "They're so laid back," Gidi said, "if they guarded like that with us they would have landed up in jail long ago." In the compressed darkness in the post she then saw his eyes turning to the field telephone, whose mouthpiece dangled from its canvas covering, and wondered if in a moment he's going to try to get a civilian line and talk to his wife and child again, whom he had sent to the kibbutz until the war ends. On their left, through the narrow window on which someone scratched the days left until their discharge, steps were suddenly heard, though not advancing from the path but rather from the road at the foot of the hill: one of the female soldiers, whom they had seen earlier in the canteen, was walking there and in her hands two bottles of juice and a large packet of wafers. Due to the wind that permeated the post – a cold whistling wind almost like in the place where she lived – they couldn't hear what she said to the sentry and what he answered her, and when the direction of the wind changed only the transistor could be heard from there. Popular announcer Yossi Sayass was calling all listeners with a willing heart to donate toward a liver transplant operation that had to be performed abroad – that's what he said in a voice familiar to her ad nauseam – and from the illuminated opening an empty bottle was suddenly hurled, gleamed and burst in the darkness. A slow song began to be played and was cradled in the cold desert wind; and on the sentry's thigh, which swung to and fro, the female soldier sat and moved with it; they saw her from the back and didn't say anything. Afterwards from the opening the sentry's hand was seen rising and pulling the shirt from her trousers, it pulled slowly and disappeared beneath the material, and the wind slowly rolled a tin can on the road: firmly but with great gentleness, the way her grandfather rolled mandrake stalks on barren stomachs. It rolled it further and further, rolled and rolled, and in the dense darkness a voice suddenly called out: "you can go now, there's a phone call for you. By luck I just happened to be in the kitchenette.")

Merav looked over the made-up bed and with one flick spread the covering on it as well.

(The way she had learned in the hotel in which she worked all summer, and the way she used to make her own bed and her sisters' and her grandfather's, replacing afterwards all the notes he would hide beneath the pillow: "I decree and swear to you on that supreme eye" or "in the holy name spreading from the light of the lower chariot Alad enclosed in its source Ahahalida, who with your manifold mercy and your loving kindness spread above us and above all our house, will abolish all decrees slight and evil and restrain all who prosecute and bedevil us," as if they didn't have anything else to prosecute or bedevil: and after all with her own eyes – those eyes that see everything and that love and hate sometimes in the very same moment – she once saw him with a girl from her class when the two of them went to look at shoe shops at the end of Allenby Street, as if they could afford to buy even just the laces for themselves. As they went down in the direction of the sea and passed a café full of Romanian workers, who were watching a karate film over the bottles crammed on the tables, her friend said: "take a look at him there, on the prowl." "Who?" Merav asked. "The old man there," her friend answered, "the one with eyes in all directions." She then looked right and left thinking to see some old Romanian – after all they didn't only bring young people from abroad to work in place of them or in place of Arabs – and when she recognized him in front of her she said nothing. Quietly she watched him as he walked on the pavement, looking here and there and not sure of himself as he was in the neighborhood, with all the stupid women who came to him to receive a blessing: as if that blessing would stop their husbands' blows or prevent the boy from becoming a criminal like his brother Ezra or Pinchas or Yakov – those were the names given to boys, each one with biblical names as if they received the Torah straight from Moses' hands; as if they wouldn't start to sing, not waiting a moment, putting bottles on their foreheads, getting drunk on the remains of the Cognac that some Laniado mixed, since what else did they have left but to dance like that in the juice of the garbage – or he'd feel their bellies and tell them what they'll spawn, boyorgirl, or he'd open their wombs with stalks or with the smoke of cockscombs that he would light beneath the dress between the legs and suddenly become hoarse and run to the bathroom and lock himself in there. "Can't you see that he's on the prowl?" her friend said, and she asked: "What?" "What do you mean what," her friend said, "so old and so horny. Can't you see? Look-look," and she pointed to a dim entrance where a row of bottles gleamed above the bar, and a bleached blonde shouted out to him from inside: "how you doing honey, are you coming in," that's what she called him, her grandfather, and honey slowed down.)

"Bravo on your professionalism," the actor said to her and swiveled around in his chair.

(Eyes made-up even more than his were, and eyebrows almost completely plucked, and her friend said: "those types pluck out almost everything, just hope he doesn't have a stroke right in the middle with her." Inside, in the reddish dimness, someone sat and cleaned his nails with a large penknife, and from behind them on the pavement someone said: "I could buy a shoe like that for a hundred shekels in Italy, believe me for a hundred shekels and still get change," when Merav stopped in her tracks. "The action's just starting," said her friend, "what's got into you." But he already turned his head and mumbled to himself quietly when the bleached blonde shouted out to him from the depths of the bar: "just don't go to the Russians, old buddy. Who knows what they've brought with them from Russia." And at the end of the road, where he looked right away, the sea was smooth as silk and blinding in its whiteness and a small sailboat slid slowly over it like a dancer on the ice.)

Merav moved the bed close to the wall.

"You could at least maybe take your clothes out by yourself," the sergeant said to Kinneret, "she's already made your bed for you."

Kinneret looked at him from the space that remained between the bed and the corner of the room. Afterwards she glanced at the soundman crouched in the opposite corner, turned to the table and leaned down toward the rucksack that lay at her feet. With a long fingernail, she flicked the ant that walked on it (convoy after convoy advanced in the burrows of her body, bent by their loads: dry seeds on their backs) and bent down further and grasped the ring of the zipper (the tiny iron teeth clenched tightly; she struggled, they giggled) and pulled it. Again and again she pulled it, bent over in her heels and turning a wide pear-shaped pelvis to the narrowed breadth of the room.

"Can I help?" asked the soundman.

"No," Kinneret answered, "I'm not dying yet or something," and again grasped the ring of the zipper and pulled it forcibly (until the teeth separate one from another, one from another, onefromanother).

"Who says you're dying," said the soundman.

In the window, above the eucalyptuses the rhythmic rattling was heard again, and in the sky that darkened and deepened a small reddish globe moved slowly, tiny as a firefly.

"That crop-spraying pilot," the sergeant said, "doesn't his workday ever end?"

"That one," answered the actor, "if he falls even God won't catch him, that God's got holes in his hands. Sorry if I offended you," he turned to the soundman.

"You didn't offend me," answered the soundman from his corner. "And not him either. You can be sure."

The ant, which was flicked off the rucksack, landed next to the lamp cable and continued walking along its length.

(In an infinitely long column that crossed the hut; and apart from them there were the mosquitoes and the moths and the gnats crashing against the sooty glass and the lizard lying in wait for them on the beam of the thatch; the island was called Ko Phangan, and all around, in the never-ending waters, Ko Samui and Ko Phi Phi and Ko Tao were scattered, but at the time the entire world ended with the reed mat panels that the storm arched outwards and curved inwards and unraveled fiber after fiber. Previously he cursed to himself – inside the mosquito net, which by then, for all those months, had already become like a garment or a skin to him – but there was one who heard him from his heavens the way He heard ants in their burrows and the primordial fire blazing in the bowels of the earth, and immediately He caused darkness to fall from his sky and released the storm from the edge of the ocean to annihilate him. Somewhere above the beam, far above the unraveled thatch and the clouds that the lightning pierces with a thrust, all his deeds were observed, all his thoughts heard; and He who watched and paid heed had already decreed judgment from the farthest heaven where He sat on a throne or on lotus stamens or flew around with his thousand arms or was grasped tightly below it like a lizard on a beam.)

Merav lifted the cushions from the table and carried them to the bed like a small tower clasped to her chin.

Na'ama, who was hugging the teddy bears and the Snoopy like baby triplets, seated them on the bed and leaned their backs against the wall. One woolly ear was raised and she returned it to its place and stroked the fluffy head again and again. "Isn't he a sweetie pie?" she asked.

The lighting man brought the doors of the lamp close to each other reducing the light beam. "In one second," he said, "his eyes will really shine like a cat's eyes in the dark." Right away he reduced the beam even further, and its light sparkled in the button eyes and the snouts.

"Let him stay just as sweet as the way he was born," said Na'ama. "Right Snoopy?" she bent over him and rubbed her nose on his button nose and her light brown ponytail tossed back and forth on her neck, covering and revealing its pureness. When she sensed that Shechter was looking at her she waited a moment and slowly turned her head to him.

"Aren't I right?" she asked him, "you tell him, you're the director aren't you?" She brought the teddy bears close to each other and rubbed her small nose on their snouts too, perhaps recreating some Eskimo game from her childhood.

In the window on her right the darkness became denser, devouring the treetops in it, covering them and the road like a vast sheet that fell from the sky or like an eiderdown for huddling in or a sack. "Yes," answered Shechter quietly, "I'm the director." From the roll that he moved from the wall he extracted transparent nylon the size of a window and stretched it. The sergeant checked the size with the spread of his fingers, pulled it further and placed the box cutter close to the edge of the nylon.

From the rucksack (the teeth separated onefromanotheronefromanother) Kinneret took out faded jeans with torn knees and threw them on the bed.

"Just don't mess up the bed," the actor said from his chair. "Isn't it enough you didn't lift a finger to help?"

"Look who's talking about helping," she answered and from the rucksack she pulled out two pairs of black jeans and threw them onto the bed as well.

"It's just that there are those" – Merav wiped the back of the folder with a piece of flannel – "who are used to it from home. With them it's always like that."

From the rucksack Kinneret took out black stretch jeans and threw them onto the bed and after them a purple cotton dress, a purple belt and a purple scarf and threw them as well.

"Maybe be a bit more careful?" Na'ama asked, "think what it would be like if someone threw a belt in your face like that?" She gently put Snoopy's ear back in place and pacified him again by stroking him.

"Let them throw," Kinneret hurled a denim jacket on the bed, "I couldn't care." The soundman, who was bent over his dials, looked at her for a moment as she put her hand in deeply and extracted from the rucksack a pair of green slacks, black bell-bottoms, two orange belly shirts, a beige sweatshirt and shiny black leather pants.

"Nice wardrobe," the actor said, "are you going do a fashion show for us?" He leaned his chair against the wall and lifted his feet onto the table, and in the window behind him the low buildings of the base sank further and further into the darkness. "Kinneret the supermodel."

"Supermodel?" Kinneret stuck her hand into the bottom of the rucksack and rummaged around. "Soon I won't even be a singer," and with the same ardent searching movement she pulled out a dark purple stocking and right away fished another one out.

The actor placed his hand on his chest and his red fingernails glistened in the light of the lamp.

"Top model, top mohodel, top moho-ho-del-"

Again he crooned and closed his eyes from which the make-up was still not removed and his Adam's apple moved up and down, while taunting Kinneret or himself for having to be involved in such nonsense.

"That's just the way clothes are thrown on my bed," Kinneret was still burrowing in the rucksack. "Tell them Na'ama. Even worse. What's the point of putting them in place?"

"Se-tting over the mountain, over the mountain."

For a moment the actor kept his eyes shut and then opened them again.

"I actually don't mind the dark," the lighting man looked in the front window: no buildings could be seen and on the road leading to the base no car lights moved between the shadows of the eucalyptuses. "It's really good for the flashback, that way it'll look as if that battered window's got shutters."

"Why would it have shutters," said the sergeant. "What, are we a flight squadron?" He returned his gaze from the dark expanse outside to the room. "In the elite corps it's the same; air conditioning and a television in every room, like permanent force conditions, believe me nothing is spared. After a military operation it's straight to a five-star hotel in Eilat; the army resort at Givat Olga's not good enough for them. You can even ask your father."

"What's the elite corps got to do with it," the lighting man answered, "I'm talking about shutters. Have you ever seen a sealed room without shutters?" – "and on that," the female medic said the morning after from within a telephone earpiece and a twisted wire and the wall; and from within cables stretched tautly in the sky, hosting weary birds on them, "on that they wasted hours just to show all the corps' missiles afterwards. But what do you care?" And in his car, in moments when the investigator wondered about her appearance to distract himself a bit, he also tried to imagine the small child she had been in earlier years, before her voice deepened that way, when perhaps she played with the boys as an equal and together with them took apart the legs of ants or the wings of flies or tied a thread to their bodies and watched as they joggled along like his car, which all the kilometers it traversed, by necessity or not, seemed to be wrapped around it to exhaust the engine until it's muted – "The biggest loonies didn't sit in a sealed room without shutters."

(They just walked kilometers in the middle of the night in streets where there were only alley cats with eyes without eyes with tails without tails, and alley cats that yowled and lifted their backsides to them, and a police car that drew away with the blue flashing light, and he no longer had to fear **let's see if you are a man.**)

The sergeant went forward to the window with the nylon sheet that he had cut.

"Spot on," he stretched the nylon on the window frame. "My fingers are more precise than a ruler."

"As long as nobody drives here," the lighting man lifted the canister of WD-40. "Because with their lights on you'll be able to see that there aren't any shutters. Maybe use your rickshaw as a barrier opposite." He sprinkled more of the spray on the butterfly screw of the lamp's tripod and the rusty drop lengthened beneath it.

"Who's driving," the sergeant answered, "everyone's at home with their wives and children long ago. And her parents?" – He looked at Kinneret – "First let them get here at all."

(Because, as for them, according to the general staff bad luck orders, something's definitely gone wrong. They got the time confused or just didn't feel like coming, what do they need his movie for? Go figure where they are right now.)

> Beyond the eucalyptuses, between the fields in the distance that after the plowing season were sometimes dotted with white herons and now their furrows were filled with darkness; between them and the suburb of duplexes, which had been built in the past year, the two of them stood on an empty road, next to the lifted bonnet of their car, a long American model, old but well looked after: the silhouette of a man and the silhouette of a woman, small and diminishing and swallowed by the night.

"In the meantime they're nowhere to be seen at all."

On the back of the folder Merav wrote down the number of the next scene with a red felt-tipped pen and the sergeant sniffed the air and turned his head to the lighting man. The number of the shot was written as well, red and moist and shining in the light of the lamp. For a moment Merav widened her nostrils and right away added the number of the takc. She too turned to the lighting man with the felt-tipped pen in her hand.

(Red moist **let's see if you are a man** before throwing it at the pail with all his might, at the cat to gouge out its eye, and starting to walk in the street, in which no car travels and no man walks, empty and completely silent except for the tuk-tuk of his footsteps all the way all the way all the way from the public telephone to the base. But in the middle he still stopped at the building that his father had begun to build opposite the sea: a regular apartment building, which won't be photographed for any postcard, without curved cornices and without couples who'll be photographed at the top of it and write on the back below the multicolored beautiful stamps, "Kisses Mom and Dad." The red felt-tipped pen remained with the cat, stuck in the eyehole or lodged deep in the throat, and he looked for some board from the guard's bonfire just to write on the fence – ordinary tin sheeting on boards with no arenas for bullfighting or gladiators on the other side, no Gothic church and no Eiffel Tower, just the building being built and a whitewashed pit – "open to offers" or "wild pleasures Yael" or "blowjobs for a shekel Yael Belkind 425381." But the guard had promptly vanished with the start of the war and some beggar lay like vermin on the concrete there, even filthier than the rags that filled his pram. He was maybe a hundred, that beggar, even older than his grandfather, and slept on the concrete like a baby – his grandfather no longer collected stamps from postcards for him, no longer removed them gently with steam from the kettle; the entire collection was thrown away and burnt, and across from the desert hills and the mosque, a swarm of sooty pieces that had previously been miniature portraits and landscapes from Spain and Italy flew around, and surrounded by white edges of which even one perforation must not be damaged. Sometimes his grandfather would doze off in the armchair in the middle of a conversation and his grandmother would get up and cover him with a

checkered blanket with tassels, as if he too had become her
grandson, a grandson whose beard had become yellow and
unkempt; and from her chin white bristles sprouted, and the
silver candlesticks darkened, the kitchen sink yellowed, and
from all the mezuzahs a rank smell of gastric juices and false
teeth was emitted – and even content, the idiot, smiling in
his sleep as if the building was being built for him. Or for
his boxes in which there wasn't even one rotten tomato, just
scribbling. Or for his defective transistor that was attached to
the handle of the pram as if it was a car radio or something.
Around him were piles of blocks, and protruding from the
sand were used condoms and broken bottles and torn pieces
of newspaper stained with feces. Above them was a lamp,
which the Arab fixed for himself before he fled, spreading a
yellowish light and swinging to and fro in the wind just like
on television when extracting from the suspect something
he's trying to conceal – where did you hide the money, eh?
Don't tell me stories, eh? Every beggar's sitting on some pile,
eh? So where did you hide it eh, where where where – and
beyond the blocks and the cement the sea could be heard.
All the cafés opposite were closed in the early afternoon
and were also empty in the morning; at the time the city
was completely empty. He could have swiped his transistor
effortlessly without him knowing, with the greatest of ease,
it's just that it didn't work anyway. He could have swiped
his coat effortlessly, just for the fun of it, waving it at him
like some wounded bull full of knives, kisses Mom and Dad.
He could have overturned his pram effortlessly with all the
rags and boxes, or electrify it with all the abundant electric
wires, or set alight the rags together with the whole of his
father's building, but suddenly he became merciful: he just
removed the wheels, taking them apart effortlessly, one by
one, the nuts were halfway out anyway, until the pram lay
on its rims. Before, its shadow could be seen below, swinging
from the globe, faint but visible, and afterwards nothing. The
beggar didn't even wake up: he continued to sleep and smile
to himself in all his filth as if he held God by the balls. He
also didn't wake up when the wheels were flung right into the

whitewash and drowned one by one like alley cats: no sign of them remained.)

"What you looking at me for, the smell's not from the lamp."

Na'ama lifted the chubby fluffy hands of the teddy bears placing them one on the rounded shoulder of the other. "Isn't it nicer that way," she asked, "so it looks like they're embracing each other?"

"Believe me," said the actor from his chair, "their character acting is what'll save us. Did they study the Stanislavski method?" He narrowed his blackened eyes and peered at them.

"Who's asking you," her hair tossed behind her, "I was asking the director," she said and her neck was revealed again, pure with golden down on it. "Isn't it nicer this way?" She turned her head around.

"Yes," answered Shechter quietly.

(There they were, placed together, teddy bears and candy boxes, as if the burnt big wheel skewed on its side couldn't be seen through the gaping hole in the wall; teddy bears and bunnies and little monkeys and all the other prizes were placed one alongside the other, as in all amusement park stalls in which rings are thrown onto wooden pegs. The father of Shechter the boy once carried him to a stall like that and closed his fingers on a ring and together said with him: "o-ne-t-wo-and-thr-" and lifted up his little hand, which was buried in the depths of this hand that is now lifting a roll of masking tape from the table, and in less than a generation, less than a decade, will begin to wrinkle and become blemished with murky freckles like the hands of his parents, which were not freckled by the sun but rather by the gloom toward which they advanced year by year, dragging Shechter behind them by a transparent umbilical cord as strong as a fisherman's line.)

"It really is nicer like that."

(They were placed together, teddy bears, bunnies, furry monkeys, candy boxes and a necklace, the loot that was the first prize for which they competed not with rings, but with helmets, which they tried to place on poles by throwing them. In the morning someone rolled the dead body outside

with the sack on its head and they were still waiting for the
medic to bring lime or Lysol or benzene, and on the spot
where it previously lay they emptied out a bottle of aftershave
in order to mask the stench. They found him next to one of
the bumper cars that was cut off from the electricity line as
was the entire small amusement park in which only the big
wheel still moved its burned carriages, slowly in the wind. All
the bumper cars were pushed into a corner of the hall, strips
of dark cement sprouted between the blocks of its walls,
and in another corner they brought in a large burning gas
balloon and a burner for cooking. A soldier in an undershirt
was preparing shakshouka and another shouted to him: "you
just better be careful to wait till they turn brown. If you don't
keep an eye on this one he makes the onions soggy." They
threw the eggshells into empty field ration boxes and from
time to time someone would start to sing with feeling one
of the songs from last night's performance, placing his hand
on his chest, closing his eyes like the singer, he sang: "give
me, give me your he-aaart, the pain, is tearing me ap-aaart."
And Shechter, who already realized that such rhyme would
exist in French – a rhyme that he never managed to say, not
one better nor worse than that, on the single night on which
she agreed to meet – watched the small cars that huddled
together in the corner of the hall and remembered others that
used to shower sparks each time their rods hit the net above
them. They went everywhere in the Exhibition Gardens, and
his father, colossal as Captain Mara at the time, omnipotent
as Edison and Rutenberg put together, closed his tiny fingers
around the steering wheel and turned it with them here and
there, more joyful than even Shechter the boy: he was called
Noam then, and real freckles dotted his cheeks, and with a
delightful fear he waited for them to bump into other cars.)

　　"You're just saying it," Na'ama said, "your head's not here
at all."

　　"My head?" Shechter said.

　　(The previous day the dead man still sat in the car seat in
which he had been interrogated by whoever was interrogating
– "those types have got no God, they kill each other for

nothing" – until he began to reek. Then he was heaved onto
the floor and afterwards rolled outside, and the cars were
moved in order to make place for the performers that the
division promised to send: an entertainment group or a
magician, whoever comes will be welcome, and for the time
being they were competing for the prizes. In the center of the
concrete floor they marked a line with a belt, and according
to the queue threw the helmet with a circular motion, like
throwing a Frisbee on the beach, but on the beach that they
passed nobody threw Frisbees or sunbathed; there were only
dead fish glistening in their hundreds ever since a stray bomb
drew them out. "Who knows if those bastards didn't booby-
trap the candy boxes," they said, but anyway they weren't
competing for them and neither for the dolls, but for Lauda's
golden chain: that's what they all called the man who died
at the wheel; after the racing driver. They wrapped it around
one of the poles and the small gold cross tossed each time
the helmet hit the pole and continued on its way, and it still
swung as the quartermaster flung the helmet back: after all,
they said, whose job is it to hand out helmets and teddy
bears and bunnies if the not the quartermaster's? So what's he
complaining about. "But aren't these Christians on our side?"
said the soldier who missed, and another, around whose head
flannel was wrapped like a tennis player's bandana answered,
"take it from me, they're all the same trash, Christians,
Moslems, Druze. They all smell the same," and grasped the
helmet, narrowed one eye, aimed and hurled the helmet
again. On their left flies swooped down upon the remains
of the field rations that lay on an empty ammunitions box
and the tall soldier said: "what's their problem, they should
go outside, there's a whole human being for them there," and
from the hole gaping in the wall the big wheel turned black
and around it the sky clear and high, silent and majestic.)
    "I was actually thinking about them."
    (Not like the grey heavy skies of Paris that were filled
with chimes until your head burst, had it not been blurred
previously by wine from ear to ear: cheap clochard wine made

from grape remnants. At the time Shechter waited fifty-four days until she would invite him over again or would come to him in Paris, and every day he went to the Poste Restante on the Champs-Élysées and every day the female clerk told him: "Je suis désolée, monsieur," till he began to buy the wine, and on the one and only evening she met with him the smell of it surely exuded from him like the clochards who stared at them from the bench afterwards. Empty bottles rolled between their feet and on the gravel between the tracks mice scurried, and the French girl said: "Eh bien, c'est comme ça, c'est comme dans les films que tu voulais faire, non? Pas de violons, pas de trompettes," but allowed him to cling to her body for a moment – all through the years of his studies he recalled its softness and its warmth – until the lights of the Metro burst from the darkness of the tunnel, followed by a multitude of illuminated windows linked to each other. "C'est pas ça que tu m'avais dit? Chacun a sa vie, ses projets, son pays?" She reminded him of things he had said years before and removed his hand from her waist, her gaze evading the ridiculous stiffening occurring in his trousers. She hastened to get into the coach as if another would not be arriving in a moment, and from it she said to him: "Mais tu peux pas partir quand tu veux et revenir quand tu veux, tu peux pas, c'est fini, tu comprends? Fi-ni," and suddenly lifted a hand to her eye and wiped it, and across from them a clochard crossed himself and burped.)

"For my part, let them embrace each other, why not?"

Na'ama affected the pampered voice of a child: "Then tell them it's nicer that way-"

"I'm telling you," said Shechter.

She glanced at him for a moment and went back to stroking the teddy bear's head. "Nobody loves us," she whispered in his ear, "nobody."

(And once, while she waited for her sister in the Kapulsky Café at the Dizengoff Center, someone who was deaf and dumb passed by and on the tables placed little dolls and leaflets with the sign language alphabet. He left a small teddy bear on her table and a little monkey on the table in front of

her, and the man sitting there said to the woman opposite
him – Na'ama was eavesdropping on them, the way she always
eavesdropped on conversations – "Do you want it?" and the
woman shook her head and said: "No." She also didn't want
cake when he offered her cake, she only wanted coffee, and
from this meeting of theirs, which sounded like a blind date,
or perhaps even set up by a matchmaker, according to their
ages and the questions they were asking, at the time it didn't
seem to Na'ama that a love affair would emerge; that's what
she thought in the beginning.)

(They were placed together there, the teddy bears the
bunnies the monkeys and Lauda's gold chain, and the tall
soldier missed again and said: "Some job this Lauda found
for himself, bumper cars and prizes in an amusement park,
what's wrong with that. Wouldn't you like to swap him with
Chaimon? I mean before they did him in.")

(They didn't succeed in finding a topic of conversation;
they just spoke a bit about the coffee, a bit about the waitress,
a bit about the weather and were alarmed by every silence
that lengthened between them as if they were Na'ama's age
and not two adults. The man was short and the sweater he
was wearing, with a zigzag pattern woven into it, was by now
stretched from all its washings, the way his face seemed to
Na'ama, stretched and quivering. The woman, who had thin
brown hair that fell straight to her shoulders, wore glasses
with a thin frame and her two faded eyes were enlarged in
them when not lowered to the table. That's how they both
drank their coffee, slowly almost without speaking, when
the deaf and dumb man placed the little monkey and his
sign language alphabet on the table. "What can you do," the
man said when the deaf and dumb man departed for other
tables, "to each his own livelihood. Lucky I wasn't born like
that, one should thank God every day," and he took out five
shekels and placed them on the table. He and the woman
were no better looking than their monkey, that's what
Na'ama thought at the time as she watched them from her
table; and also that if those two find love then everyone in the

world without exception has a chance of finding love, like her sister says: "every pot has a lid and every lock a key and every garden a gardener." But her sister hadn't arrived yet; late as usual. At a table in front of them someone lit a cigarette and the short man tried to dispel the smoke with his hand, but only attracted the swirls even more. "Leave it, it's okay," the woman suddenly said, "I'm used to it from work. Everyone smokes there from all the stress." "There are habits and there are habits," the man said and waved the menu to dispel the smoke with it, "you don't have to agree to everything. Not everything. Believe me, it's just that my mother passed away from it." The woman, who was then drinking the coffee with small bird-like sips, put the cup down on the table and looked at the man. "Almost a year," the man said, "and like yesterday. Just because of that I'm careful, if it wasn't for that what would I care?" For a moment the woman peered at the remnants of the coffee in her cup, until lifting her eyes again. "All the treatments," the man said, "the chemotherapy and all that, whatever they did for her, nothing helped, nothing. On the contrary, all the months they were giving it to her, for six months it just-" he couldn't find the word he was looking for, not on the table and not in the menu, whose pages he suddenly began to turn, and when he let it close the woman turned her gaze from it and looked at the man, "prolonged her suffering?" she asked him quietly. "Yes, her suffering," the man said and looked at the woman, and something unnamed, larger than the entire table that stood between them, suddenly softened.)

("That asshole of a medic," said the tall soldier, "that parasite. If he doesn't get rid of it from here, he'll poison us all, believe me." A breeze carried the smell of the dead man inside and the soldier threw the helmet at the pole again, missed again and said: "Fucking hell, there's no God." From the base of the pole the golden chain swung to and fro with the small cross at its end, and from the back of the hall Shechter recalled the filthy hand making its sign and with absolute clarity heard the burp again from the other side of the window, which was replaced by another which was replaced by another which was replaced by another, until the Metro platform was again revealed with the bench and the clochards sitting on it there, and the bearded one reaching the bottle out to him as if he'd already become one of them. "L'amour est mort!" he had called out to him before that, when she entered the coach, and afterwards when the coaches had been swallowed by the tunnel and many others after them, Shechter hoisted himself up to the street, step by step, exuding the smell of cheap wine around him. Next to the café the juggler stood as before, swallowing and spitting fire, but she wasn't there; and the flame spread again and again until the bottle was emptied and the juggler smashed it on the stone floor. Beyond the square was the street that they had crossed together and a mass of floating yellow lamps, and above the pieces of broken bottle and the moving tin roofs he already saw the barrels of spirit and benzene and the canvas roofing of the command cars and the protective covering of the armored personnel carriers: he saw them with absolute clarity when the juggler crushed the broken bits and made a pile of their fragments with pieces of razor blades and began to swallow them. One by one they were swallowed with lip smacking and a gurgling delight, and with each swallow Shechter sensed how they turned over in his stomach and cut his intestines. He already knew that he would not remain in this city and that on his return would sell his backpack – perhaps even to a film student destined to fail with his film as he had done – or he would banish the backpack to the storage space in his parents' apartment; and first of all he'll get on a plane at Orly and land at Ben Gurion and travel by taxi to Tel Aviv and take out his army boots from that storage space and hitchhike to the Golan Heights and from there to the war.)

("Take, my friend, take," the man said to the deaf and dumb man who passed by again from table to table and gathered up the shekels or the dolls that were returned to him, "to your good health," and the woman gazed at the bottom of the cup again as if trying to read the coffee. "I'll never ever forget it," the man said to her, "my whole life. Even in a million years I'll never forget it. I heard a noise in the apartment, at first I thought it was a burglar, that whole month there were break-ins in the neighborhood, except for us, until I heard her voice and calmed down. I calmed down, you understand? Because suddenly she began to sing in her language from home, so I calmed down, how was I to know? Only afterwards I went into her room. I saw her on the floor with her head on the tiles like that, her face flat on the tiles. Something like that you never forget your whole life, believe me, even when I'm-" For a moment he was silent and the woman hesitated, and the waitress, who saw her eyes enlarged in the glasses opposite her, asked if she wanted to order something else, and the woman said: "no-no-" and then said: "you know what, actually I do. Cake, cheesecake. Do you also want some?" And after a moment the man said: "Okay." People coming out of the first show from the "Heart" cinema passed through the passageway – and afterwards the name seemed so symbolic to Na'ama – and someone wearing a blue anorak stopped and called out: "Gershon! Well I never!" And from the table the short man said with scant delight: "Hi, Gera, what's up?" The fellow called Gera came close to the table and right away asked how things are going and if the course helped anything; meaning not only if he's working in the profession, that's easy enough, the Ministry of Labor wouldn't hold a course like that if people weren't needed, but if he manages to bring home enough money from it – for a moment he glanced at the woman – because he himself, Gera, is after all an employee, and would gladly become self-employed if only he could find a partner. Gladly. It's just that after the course, straightaway everyone got up and vanished, go find a partner after that. Where would he find a partner, in the street? And if he only had a partner, straightaway he would become self-employed and boy would he make a killing now that he knows just what's what and everything; he'd build up an empire, an empire, if only he had a partner. The woman continued to gaze at her coffee sediment and the man said to the fellow in the anorak: "Being employed you really can't make a lot of money, but on the other hand, you don't make losses. I know that every month my salary's in the bank. A lot, a little, it goes in. So you make do with it, that's if you don't waste money." The woman watched him as he spoke and Na'ama saw her eyes, which the glasses enlarged, scouring his face and his sleeves that were stretched and the strands of their thinning wool. The fellow called Gera took out a fresh packet of "Parliament" from his anorak pocket, peeled the cellophane from it and proffered it, and the woman shook her head and right away lifted her glasses onto the bridge of her nose. "As for you," said Gera, "I remember how you smoked, what, don't I remember Gershon? Take one take one, don't be shy. He smoked a packet and a half a day during the course, what, don't I remember? I remember everything from the course, believe me. Yaki? The one from Tiberius? And Davidov? The jokes he'd tell first thing in the morning, eh? And Kashtan? D'you remember Kashtan?" The woman, who lifted her small head to him, took off her glasses. "He hasn't smoked for a long time," she said to him folding her glasses, "for a year maybe." She put the glasses in a case and the fellow called Gera put the packet back in his pocket. "It's just that his mother died from it," the woman said, "from cigarettes. The cigarettes ruined her completely. No matter the amount of treatment she was given, whatever they did, chemotherapy and everything, it just prolonged her suffering." With her short fingers, whose nails were chewed, she fondled the little monkey whose woolen threads curled out. "That's how it goes Gera," the man said, "what can you do, that's life. One has to be strong." He looked at the small monkey when the woman gently removed her hand from its threads and said: "Yes, why not. Take it, Gera, take it take it. It'll be a lucky charm for the business, why not. It'll bring you good luck." And Na'ama then thought that everyone in the world, even the most miserable and despondent, who've given up on everything, gets some chance of happiness in the end: not only these people here, but everyone in the world, it's given to all, this chance, to the ugly and the poor, to the old and the loners and the solitary, to her sister looking for a groom on her roof, and to her herself who still hasn't loved completely not even once, and to their parents whose love has eroded like the wedding photos in an album; and that sometimes, in all sorts of unexpected places and in moments absolutely impossible to imagine, a mere touch is enough, not the Lord of Hosts but rather that thing they call life; and that life isn't at all what was explained to them in biology lessons, when they examined tissue under a microscope and defined plants and amoebas and coral, it was just made up of everything around, everything seen or heard or smelt or touched or tasted: the two cheesecakes that the waitress placed on the table, the ring of the cash register, the voices of people in the passageway, the woolen strands of the sweater, the furry little head now sticking out of the anorak pocket, cigarette smoke still swirling from the other table.)

"The smell's not from the lamp," the lighting man said, "it's from the plug."

("He could kill us like that," the tall soldier said, "what a nice way to kill people." A breeze carried the stench inside and for a moment it seemed as if the dead man had been reconstituted and floated above the bumper cars, a ghostly figure with a ghostly sack worn on his head, and beneath the sack were none of his facial features except for the gaping mouth hole in the place where the cloth had been gnawed. "That medic thinks he's a somebody," said the tall soldier, "you'd think at the very least he was chief medical officer," and his friend, on whose neck the corners of the flannel dangled like a Tartar braid, threw the helmet again. The gold chain still swung from the last throw and on its end the cross, but there was no more the Metro, no more the tunnel, no more the square and the juggler: just a burnt amusement park at the end of a bombed suburb, and a different Shechter stood there. His body was in uniform, stained with oil that the rifle exuded, and on his face there no longer was the beard that he grew during his studies, since that had been left in its entirety in the basin of the hotel in Paris: he hastily sheared it and shaved what was left before he would sober up and regret it, and hastily washed down the hairs, and right away the basin became blocked the way it became blocked with the remnants of the tin cans that he cooked there. All the fifty-four days in which he waited for her to come from her village or to invite him over, the pockmarked mirror would show him his eyes and the bags darkening beneath them and his beard ruffled and wild, and sometimes the gleam of her thighs was visible as she guided his head and held his neck and after a moment said: "Tu me chatouilles avec ta barbe" – that's what she said to him once, the French girl – and when she lifted his face from there said: "Mais non, n'arrete pas, continue," and he glanced at her from there and saw her face pleasured with the gentlest and most wanton pleasure on which all of her was focused and to which all of her flowed, and afterwards their shadows moved on the floral wallpaper.)

"Is that supposed to cheer us up?" asked Shechter.

(They were placed together there, the teddy bears, the bunnies, the little monkeys, and in the gaping hole in the wall the burnt big wheel turns black in the pale blue like a dead pupil. And Rastabi – they both came to find out if the artists could come and perform afterwards at the anti-aircraft battery – said: "They think they've come to a picnic, just as well they didn't bring hampers with them." "Did you say something, Anti-aircraft?" asked the soldier around whose head the flannel was wound. "Go for it buddy," Rastabi answered from the back of the hall, "I've got a feeling this time you're gonna get it." A fly landed on the open tin can of corn taken from the field rations and the soldier said: "from your mouth anti-aircraft to God's ear," and as he threw the helmet Rastabi held the sunflower seed shell between his teeth. He ate only sunflower seeds during that war, and when Shechter tried to cheer him up and asked to see photos of his children, he rebuffed him saying: "You, what do you know, you don't know anything, not a thing. To you this is all playacting. You left, you came back, took a trip." Across from them the helmet passed high above the pole and hit the shelf on which the teddy bears sat. "God didn't hear you,

anti-aircraft," said the tall soldier, "How's he gonna hear if
you shoot at his skies." From the helmet being struck, one of
the teddy bears fell to the floor and the quartermaster bent
down to pick it up. "Them?" he said from his bent forward
position. "They only shoot at Skyhawks. When a MiG comes
their way they don't shoot. When at long last one comes their
way, from the shock they forget to shoot." The quartermaster
got up from behind the counter and returned to the shelf
the teddy bear that had fallen from it. "But they came to the
show like big shots," said the tall soldier, "you'd think they'd
done something to deserve a show." The frying pan sizzled
on the burner and for a moment the three of them looked
there. "What," said the tall one, "don't they deserve to do
some work? Don't they?" For all his height his face was boyish
and even childlike, and he tried to conceal his gaunt slimness
with upright shoulders and also with his thumbs stuck in his
belt in the stance of a commander. On his left, from the table
improvised from an empty ammunitions box, the buzzing of
the fly was heard, stirring around and irritable, until it flew
away from the tin of corn that stood there. "Of course they
deserve to," the other soldier answered, and when he winked
the flannel slid down to his eyebrow: "Justice is justice, not so
buddy?" His nostrils sniffed, "otherwise this one's just gonna
kill us with his smell." The fly, which flew above the leftover
slice of bread, propelled its shadow between the cracks
made in the chocolate spread until landing between them.
Beyond the ammunitions box and the tin cans on which the
bumper cars reflected back a faint glow, except for places
where "Golani Corps was here" had been engraved and "the
parachutists were here before," and on the covering stretched
above them waved a piece of yellowed newspaper, which the
wind blew in: no sparks were showered, not even one; and
Shechter's father seldom drove his car and no longer asked
when he'll have grandchildren to take to the amusement
park, because he already saw, through the cataract that had
begun to form in his eye, the last Shechter.)

     "Just so that I understand."

(Behind the counter the quartermaster twirled the helmet on the tip of his finger, "whose turn is it now?" He grasped the rim and lifted it back and forth, back and forth, like a toy car driven on the spot to tune its miniature engine. "Give it to anti-aircraft buddy," said the tall soldier, "let's see if they can hit anything, maybe they'll win back some respect." With a movement of the eyebrow he indicated to Shechter, who was standing at the back of the hall with Rastabi, and on their right the onion rings in the pan turned brown in black bubbling oil; their smell did not clear the smell of the dead man, as the puddle of the evaporating aftershave had not cleared it. "I'm not good at it," Shechter said quietly. "Did anyone say you were good, anti-aircraft?" asked the soldier with the flannel and shot a glance at the frying pan. "We just want to give you a chance to lose with honor." "I'll pass on the chance," answered Shechter. The fly took off from the slice of bread and for a moment hovered above the frying pan, buzzed and turned away from there as well. "Whoa," said the tall soldier. "Did you hear him, buddy? They've become so sure of themselves, they shot at a Skyhawk and some buildings and think they're Rambo. Ever killed a human being, anti-aircraft? One-on-one? "No," answered Shechter after a moment from the back of the hall. "One-on-one," said the tall soldier, "so that you first see the whites of his eyes? So that you smell his sweat, smell his breath? So that you know what he had for lunch and if he brushed his teeth or not?" For a moment the sound of the onion rings in the pan was heard, and then the buzzing of the fly again, and after that Shechter heard the cocking of the gun before a shot, and the shot and the sound the bullet made as it was sprayed from the concrete floor to the car: a drawn out grating sound fragmenting in the air. "Like that," said the tall soldier, "like this," and another bullet was sprayed from the concrete in front of Shechter's boots. "Like that," he said again, and Shechter withdrew from the hall step by step until he moved out to the place from which the smell rose to the pale blue sky filling it all around, from the banana and cherry orchards to the bombed buildings of the suburb. "Go for it, Anti-aircraft," the soldier with the flannel said from the entrance, "I've got a feeling this time you'll get it. Right buddy?" He turned to the tall one who nodded with the rifle barrel. And below the rim of the sack – a new sack, which wasn't unraveled except in one place; only the mouth hole could be seen in it – the swollen neck of the dead man was indented by the chain that had been torn from it and black stubble sprouted there, and his smell rose and wafted toward Shechter, nauseating and congesting the nostrils and the mouth and the throat and the lungs. From the sharp points of his shoes to the jute hood on his head the dead man seeped toward him, not in order for him to roll him out from there as they wanted, but rather that he should lie there in place of the dead man and cross his hands on his chest and shut his eyes, and under the fabric of his eyelids bury all that high pale-blue majestic sky arching above his head like the ceiling of a tunnel.)

"It's just the plug causing problems," said the lighting man, "must be something to do with the contacts."

("Something else to drink?" the waitress asked and the woman answered: "yes, another coffee for me," and put her glasses in the purse. "For me too," the man said and Na'ama saw with what gentleness he stuck the small teaspoon into the cake's quivering jelly and with what care he lifted it to his mouth and tasted it. "Once I didn't know how to make these, I only learned later. There was a time when if someone's mother didn't teach her she could forget about it, her husband and her children would be miserable. Today it's not like that, today everything's changed. It's all in the books, all the recipes. Cakes, Chinese, French, everything. There's Benny Saida's cakes and Aharoni's Chinese and all sorts of Nira Russo, everything. I learned all of it from books, don't see me as someone who sits in cafes." "No," said the man, "not at all, one can see that you're not someone like that. I saw that immediately, soon as I arrived." Beyond them the passageway was already emptied and Na'ama's sister still nowhere to be seen, maybe she met someone in the street or

on the bus or in the Center on the way to the café, the way
she too, Na'ama, would meet her soulmate in the street or on
the bus or in a café, the one coming toward her day by day
hour by hour – even now – from some faraway place that
Na'ama's never seen, or maybe from some place near in which
she's already been a thousand and one times and a thousand
and one times missed him, but there'll be others.)

"That's really encouraging," said Shechter and the
soundman looked at him over his gauges.

(From above their needles quivering to and fro like stalks
in the wind or like singed wicks whose flames are imprisoned
in the lantern or like enormous balance scales still hesitant in
the skies above the flashing lightning and the barrage of rain.)

(Another thousand, which in one of them they'll meet –
Na'ama and her soul mate, just as her parents would also be
given another opportunity of finding the thing that made
them so good looking and content in the photographs: after
all it would be enough if her father stopped sitting at the
kitchen table all night and poisoning himself with cigarettes,
because after all they loved him, all of them, yes, even if what
they said happened at work did happen: he would finish off
a whole packet by morning and stare at the smoke as if all
that was never printed in the newspaper was written in its
swirls: how it wasn't his fault at all, not even one bit, and
how anyone else in his place would have behaved the same
way, but everyone without exception –speaking up now is
easy, nothing smart about that – all those righteous ones who
suddenly remembered to open their mouths, those thirty-six
righteous ones;[26] but they're all far from being paragons of
virtue, oh oh, so very far. That's what he would say, Na'ama's
father, to acquaintances who still had the patience to listen,
and sometimes just to the empty table in the kitchen in the
middle of the night, moving some flakes of ash here and
some flakes of ash there to show it all again, detail after detail:
let's say this is the section, this is Bloom's department, this is
Amrami's department and this is him with what he's in charge

---

26   Concept from Jewish mystic teachings stating that there are at least thirty-six
especially righteous Jews in the world who are themselves unaware of their status

of. So then how can you come and tell him that he's got some connection to it, he didn't have the slightest connection to it. Just like that you shove the responsibility on a person who before that wasn't given any at all. Not that he didn't ask for more responsibility; he asked, he's not saying he didn't, but did anyone give any to him then when he asked for it? After all nothing was finalized then, nothing, everything hung in the air. And let all those wiseguys tell him what they would have done in his place; please tell him; and afterwards, in the empty kitchen in the middle of the night, his shoulders would sink even more, the shoulders of the farmer he once was, the shoulders decorated with ranks when he met her mother, and on which he would carry the little Na'ama and run with her through the whole house from room to room and together with her shout: "horsey-horsey, horsey-horsey," or stand her on them so that she'd reach the tassels of the lightshade: on the other side of which was the firefly in its glass cage, not like the one that now circled in the dark above the shadows of the trees and rattled and drew away.)

"All the wiring must be fucked here," the lighting man was still bent over the plug.

"Don't say 'fucked'," Merav said to him, "in a moment he's gonna say that you're corrupting me." She glanced briefly at the sergeant and closed the screenplay folder, replacing the pencil stub behind her ear.

"What's up with you today?" the sergeant looked at her from the other corner, raising the tripod of the second camera.

"Nothing," she answered, "what should be up with me?" and moved near the window and looked out with Na'ama.

"That pilot," the sergeant said, "hasn't he got supper waiting for him at home?" He tightened the screws of the tripod one after another and fixed its height.

"Maybe God gives him food," said the actor from his chair, "Who knows. Right from the hand, like to a bird. Corpus Domini Nostri." In the window the crop spraying plane circled and became smaller in the sky until swallowed up by the dark, its rhythmic rattling no longer heard.

"Those stuffed animals of yours," the actor turned his chair to Na'ama, "will steal the show from us. In the end they'll only write about them: 'A beautiful friendship formed between two teddy bears and a dog, a story for ages seven to seventy that will move you to tears, starring-' – forget about your names girls, what comes in darkness departeth in darkness." He lifted his hand and outlined vertical, horizontal and diagonal lines in the air, perhaps the letters of his name, dazzling them with his nails from which the polish had not yet been removed. "Another film created by-"

Opposite him Shechter struggled to peel the edge of the masking tape with his nails. "Give it to me," said the sergeant, "what are you fiddling with it for. Don't you want to rehearse them in the meantime?"

"Rehearse what?" answered Shechter battling with the sticky tape. "All in all they sit on the bed and watch television. There's already a soundtrack, you yourself recorded it."

"Yes," said the sergeant, "I didn't have that much to do then." For a moment he lingered in his place, and Merav, who turned from the window, began to leaf through the pages of the screenplay. On the back of her hand two words that she had written there in pen could be seen, perhaps items from the list of the equipment; and below them another word crossed out with a line.

"It's just that Shechter believes in spontaneity," the actor explained from his chair, "only improvisation. Pirandello and Shechter ate from the same bowl" – he scratched the nail of his thumb with the nail of his middle finger in order to scrape the polish from it – "they were stretcher bearers together, Pirandello and Shechter, what do you think. As for Cassavetes, next to Shechter he's a master sergeant in charge of discipline, a real master sergeant, not like you" –he glanced at the sergeant still scratching his nails – "Na'ama honey" – he swiveled his chair around to her – "in this movie you'll yet be like Gena Rowlands. Gena Rowlands at the very least."

A furry hand slumped and Na'ama gently lifted it up onto the other teddy bear's shoulder and soothed them both with a stroke. "She doesn't know who Gena Rowlands is," the actor blinked to his right and to his left with his blackened eyelashes, "she wants to be an actress and doesn't know who Gena Rowlands is. Cassavetes' star, Gena, his inspiration, his wife. Just like me and my girlfriend could have been, if it wasn't for the war and the screwed up nature I got from my genes."

Merav shut the screenplay and crossed another line through one of the words written on the back of her hand.

"I knew you'd ask what happened between us," said the actor, "what, didn't I know you'd ask and that soon you'll be taking an interest and show some empathy?"

"It's because you're getting on everyone's nerves with your remarks," Merav answered. She tried to erase the word from her hand with a finger moistened with saliva, rubbing it until she gave up. "You make fun of everything. Soon you'll be making fun of this too. It's the easiest thing to make fun of something."

"I also make fun of myself," he answered her and again scraped his fingernail, one with the other, to remove the polish from them. "That's my way in life, what can you do? My way of dealing with my despair – my mirth. If I said what I really thought – to dust shall you be crushed."

"Even now you're making fun." She took a felt-tipped pen from her pocket and retouched one of the numbers that she had written on the back of the folder, and after it retouched the others as well with a vigorous motion. On her left, at the foot of the table, Kinneret took out white Reebok running shoes from the rucksack, yellow All Star sneakers, black platform shoes, and reached her hand further in and pulled out purple canvas espadrilles with rope soles.

In the front window the rattling of the plane waned, but after a moment or two returned slowly from the darkness.

(Like exhausted steps rising from the depths of a cellar.)

(Like a fly from within a tin can.)

(Like the detached wheels of a pram from a whitewashed pit.)

(Like a corpse from the ocean.)

Beyond the shuttered pane, in which the reflection of the room was drawn, two silhouettes leisurely pushed the

silhouette of the trash can. "Need my help?" Weintraub
called out from there. "Seems you can't do without me."

Shechter began to stick strips of masking tape on the
windowpane, one after the other vertically and horizontally,
cutting them with a box cutter and slicing the reflection of
the room and the road beyond it, with its trees and potholes,
into equal squares. The shadow of the sergeant's rickshaw
was seen in one square, and further on the trash can could
be made out, and one square away the other prisoner stood
raising his hand and a strike was heard.

"It's not gonna help you, Ezra, take it from me," said
Weintraub and moved forward to the window. "You can't
close a gap like that in one half, even if Jordan's having an
off day."

"Eighty sixty-two," the other prisoner answered quietly.

Inside the room the actor took his feet off the table and
held the spray canister again. "Weintraub, I heard you were
thinking of retiring, what happened, you got old?"

"Take it from me," Weintraub moved further forward to
the window and was pierced by its strips, "with Abudi's jobs
each day's like a year. But never you mind. Weintraub doesn't
forget. You ask Eran if Weintraub forgets."

The lighting man, who once more tightened the cellophane
to the lamp and sniffed it, hit the plug with his fist.

"Pretends he doesn't hear," said Weintraub from the other
side of the windowpane, "yeah right, the light's gone into his
ear, hey Eran?" A green strip cut across his chest and another
his ankles. "Some water from the naval commando got into
it, that's why he doesn't hear. There he was, like his father,
don't take him for what you see."

In the square next to him the other prisoner moved, his
hand was raised again and a strike was heard. "Eighty sixty-
four," he said quietly.

"You know what Ezra," Weintraub said to him, "call
me when you reach eighty. How's that? Go collect stones,
why not." His face was pressed up against the pane and the
sergeant asked if he didn't mind getting lost: just what they

need, his face in their frame. "You've lost it, Gidi," Weintraub answered. "This morning when you arrived straightaway I could see you'd lost it. He did me a favor by saying hello. I'm talking about 'hello,' not returning a salute. Just to say hello to a person, to start the day off, was that asking too much? Something happen? Your wife not giving you any?"

"You leave my wife out of it," said the sergeant, "buzz off." Weintraub turned around on the spot and the green strip cut across his waist. "Did you hear him?" he asked the other prisoner and right away turned around again. "Don't take Ezra for what you see, Ezra also doesn't forget. Hey Ezra? Real quiet, until he flips out. He'll make you an Intifada, Ezra. Should I tell them what they put you in for? Not for a week like me, he'd die for it to be a week."

"Come on," said the sergeant. "You still here?"

Weintraub spread his arms out to his sides and lifted and lowered them as if flying until he reached the trash can. "Come on garbage," he said and bent over, "how you doin' my honey." Right away he turned to the window again: "You just ask Eran what he was like in the war, eh Eran? What a hero you were?"

"That clown," the female medic says from the opening and with her round glasses shining, "sorry if I disturbed you." "No-no," the investigator hurries to refute in his weary voice, "a moment more, a moment less" – on the phone as well, from within the earpiece in which for a long time a new female voice hasn't been heard, she gave them all sorts of titles, as if she had found an ally in him, in the stranger who'll be coming to investigate the death, and anyway her opinion of them wasn't asked for at all, even if it was accurate and impartial –but he's already turning his head and restoring his gaze to the monitor.

"So many shoes," said the actor.

In a row at the foot of the bed Kinneret arranged the clogs, the Reebok running shoes, the All Star sneakers, the platform shoes, the sandals with the long straps and the purple canvas espadrilles.

"Aren't you worried about them here?" he sprayed his nails with anti-rust spray and tried to scrape the polish from them again.

"I couldn't give a damn," Kinneret said. She placed the heels close together and as she swiveled around kneeling down, the lamp turned the delicate skin in the cleavage of her shirt blue and the shadow deepened in the center. "Not just about the shoes, about everything."

("That one?" her mother said. She arranged her drawings from the course in the *Atelieu*, rough paper blackened by charcoal. She went to the kitchen and returned to the living room with a transparent gleaming glass and lay down on the sofa in an open silk dressing gown: she looked at her flabby belly, at her legs, which she shaved before. "That one hasn't got a drop of shame about becoming a model, just look at what people are capable of doing for money today." She stood the glass on her belly. "If someone like that came to your father completely naked he'd turn his head away. He wouldn't so much as glance in her direction" – she lifted the bottle, tilted it, poured out transparent sweetish liqueur: glug, glug-glug – "don't take him for someone whom they all come on to." She looked at the glass of Cointreau opposite the light, as if it were a crystal ball that would foretell the future, placed it on her belly and moved it from there to the table. She'll wash the glass with Sano-for-dishes, the rings on the table with Sano-for-furniture, the drops on the sofa with Sano-for-fabrics, the drops on her belly and on her legs with Sano-for-drops. "Let's say even if he was alone with her in the middle of the night on a beach with no one around, he'd turn his head away, your father. Believe me he'd turn his head away even if everyone had already gone to sleep, the whole hotel. Up and down there wasn't one window lit up, and those fishermen weren't interested in anything. People from Tiberius, they only have mullet fish on the brain. And anyway your father's fastidious, believe me, he'd never say such a thing to some bimbo, never. 'Close your eyes, close them honey, can you hear the crickets? Who are they singing for?' He'd never say something like that to her. 'What do you need a five-star hotel for, it's better outside in the dark,' would he say something like that to her? 'Your dress is so flimsy, so purple and so flimsy. Now close your eyes, love, close them, what, don't you trust me?'")

"Everything," Kinneret straightened up. "I couldn't care less if it all went up in smoke."

(But all the smoke just swirled from the smoke machine, it coiled around the stage, bent around her calves, thrust her knees apart, one from the other onefromtheotherfromtheother. It hovered over her thighs, lapped, caressed, trickled between them. That's how everyone saw her there, in the depths of their eyes she saw how they saw her while she accompanied the song with her body and with the voice of a bedroom a carpet a floor a table, wherever it's done, in the sea as well: belly to belly, flack, flack-flack. But they didn't appear at the Roxanne Club, nobody at the Roxanne gave a piss about them. "He'll call us, yeah right," the drummer said leaving there, "when hair grows on the tip of my dick." He loaded his bass drum onto the taxi again, the floor tom, the toms, the snare, the hi-hat, the cymbals that clanged in the boot. She carried the shekeres, the cabasas, the maracas and the tambourine in a packet, and the taxi driver looked at her; assessing her from the soles of her feet up to her breasts – and asked if they were sure that they had enough money on them. "Not that I've got anything against music, on the contrary," he said while assessing, "it's just that I've had bad experiences with people coming out of here. Don't take it personally." "Relax," the drummer said, "you'll get your money. There's never been anyone who Bungee owes something to. He got on the motor bike and gripped a shiny round tank between his legs and started it again and again: flack, flack-flack.)

The soundman looked at her from above the recording gauge and the needles that quivered in them.

(Like balance scales still hesitant in the skies above the thatch and the spray of water and the threads of the mosquito net and his pouring sweat – not from heat, but because at the time he was waiting for his end on the island – he heard palm branches through the rustling of the smoke and through the beating of moth wings and the buzzing of mosquitoes and the claws of the fire beating against the glass and drawing close to him with it. At the time the entire hut was being tossed from its stilts up to its roof, and across from him the oil lamp moved further and further forward: to the edge of the shelf, to the mosquito net, to the mattress, to his body, to devour him.)

On the asphalt outside pounding steps were heard, a rhythmic pounding growing stronger. Into the corner of the window, between the green strips, a column of silhouettes entered advancing from left to right. A tinny sound was heard between the pounding, and the sergeant who marched at the head called out to the back: "Ackerman, do you want detention as well?"

"No commander!" the silhouette shouted out from the end and moved with the column from square to square.

(They decided to start out small: if they're not wanted at Roxanne then they'd give Roxanne a run for its money. They found a pub at the end of Dizengoff, not far from the old port – at night you could hear the sea there, rumbling growling threatening – and they convinced the owners to give them a chance. What have they got to lose? Only UN officials and prostitutes and semi-prostitutes came there at the time, but there was enough space, and with some public relations, the drummer said, half the city will be waiting outside to get in: doormen and selectors and what not. Because they're not going to be like their parents, clerks or wedding singers, housewives or painters taking class – did van Gogh paint in classes? Did someone teach him to paint sunflowers or cypresses and fields with crows? And to cut off his ear and the other ear and the nose and the nose below – there was a billiard table at the back and above the bar an aquarium in which goldfish floated and darted and glistened. The bottles that were hung upside down like a row of udders also sparkled, and from within the dusk the protruding beer tap shone and a drop fell. On the beach – for hours she thought that the sun wouldn't rise, like in the place that the UN officials spoke of, but in the end it rose: it gradually rose up behind her, swelled and rose, it cast the cliff's shadow on small wrinkled waves, on her ravaged legs, and rose – a scorched, chewed corn cob could be made out, and opposite her a fish was being tossed: approaching-retreating, approaching-retreating as if it too had drunk all that was left in the glasses or as if she had put it to death between her legs. And where are Kinnelet's shoes, weh de shoedees? On the way she kicked-took them off, but even if she had had high boots on or leather trousers or denim dungarees she would have felt naked; she was bare to the bone: the bone back and forth, back and forth; flack, flack-flack.)

"I didn't hear you," said the sergeant.

"Noooo Commaaaander!" the silhouette shouted out again.

("The drinks are on me, how's that?" the owner said. Toothpicks were strewn on the bar like pickup sticks: stick on stick, stick with stick, a stick here a stick there. "Sure you'll bring the whole of Tel Aviv here, sure. But first of all I care what the regulars will say. Haven't I heard about those places that last a week and then fade? Isn't that right, Sima? They've come to teach me how to do business. Didn't it work out with him? Never mind. There'll be another. They're all the same anyway. And besides which, who knows what they've brought with them from their countries? As cultured as they are, they're full of diseases." A UN official went out to the street; another stood next to the toilet door and washed his hands in the toilet basin, looking in the toilet mirror above which hanging on a burnt out globe were the black panties of someone who'd already done it there, in the toilet.

Shechter stuck another green strip on the window and cut its end with a box cutter.

(When they performed – she remembers nothing of the performance, not what they sang, not what they played, not what she drank, all the faces were swallowed up in the dusk and the smoke; "a real branch of hell," the drummer said and drummed, "like the devil's rectum" – the girl was already occupying herself with a different UN official. They all had clear blue eyes and cropped blonde hair, and the television set that stayed on without sound flickered on their scalps: instead of spotlights there was a television set, instead of a smoke machine there was cigarette smoke. Carlsberg in neon lettering, the bottoms of Guinness and Tuborg, shining glasses and bottles, dripping taps. And at the feet of the tables made of rough, coarse wood were the gas masks of the Israeli girls, a box spotted with beer spray. And one of them asked her UN official: "Vot vill you do den? I mean, if it falls hir? I vill not give you mine. Vy should I? You gave me somesing?" And his answer was swallowed up in the noise coming from the street.)

The crop spraying plane moved between the strips, advancing and rattling, making a wide circle and retreating, opening an eye as minute as an ember in the dark.

(Like the seed of an ember: Agni the god of fire sought refuge in the clouds and the clouds rebuffed him, sought refuge in the rivers and the rivers rebuffed him, sought refuge on the cliffs and the cliffs rebuffed him, and he roamed and rambled finding no rest, until the trees accepted him because he promised they would not crumble like stone, and not flow like water and not unravel like clouds; and leaves and flowers shall bud and birds shall be hosted to warble for them year after year until he emerges from within and prances from branch to branch and dies.)

(A car hooted: pahpim-pahpim, paphim-pahpim. Who's got a whistle in her tummy? She had cabasas and maracas and a space in which to move around; in place of the billiard table that had been moved to the wall as all its balls clacked. "Afterwards put everything back the way it was, eh? It should look like you were never here at all." But moist stains remained on the felt, the dark green of wet grass: dew spread it, dew from the sky and dew from the body. She didn't remember what they sang and what she drank, she only remembered her tiny solo and the girl saying at the top of her voice: "You mean never? Never-never?" And the UN official answering: "Well yes, nothing but darkness in Trondheim. But then comes summer and it never goes down." And Kinneret sang.

"You're kidding me, right?" the girl said. "No, I am not," the UN official replied, and Kinneret sang. "It's eemposibell, hah Sarit? He's bluffing me, no?" And Kinneret sang. "Tell him you want proof, let him bring you a ticket for Trontheim, so you can see it with your own eyes. What, the same sun's in all places," and Kinneret sang.)

Shechter pulled another strip the width of the dark window and cut it with the box cutter.

(But the sun rose from behind, and the fish grew large as well, retreated and advanced and grew large: the sun flickered, shimmered, honeyed bubbles of foam and floating seaweed and her legs spread out in front, to the sides, in the water, the water, from the purple toenails to the thighs. The fish was being tossed there, shining, opening mouth to mouth, turning over to the wide open throbbing bleeding sky. And she sang: "Yooou," she sang, "will wearrrrrr-" she sang. That's not what she sang, that's not what she wore, and hers was rolled up too, up to the neck.)

The rhythmic pounding steps on the asphalt were heard again outside, and in the squares of the window between the green strips, another column of silhouettes advanced from right to left. Another stone struck the bin, and the sergeant who marched at the head called out: "Ackerman, now you've had it."

"It's not me commander!" a blurred silhouette answered from the column. "It's that prisoner over there!"

"If not him then who," the female medic said from the entrance. "A room full of clowns and the biggest one is outside. Did I disturb your concentration?" "No-no," the investigator answers again. His finger, whose nail was chewed to the flesh, touches the button, and the picture on the screen stops. "It can wait a bit. Besides, without you" (she told the police, the police told him: in the middle of the night the boss's secretary phoned him, and in the morning the boss himself spoke to him: not that it was his idea to hand the investigation over to him, it's worth him knowing that, but anyway, she woke him up in the middle of the night and so at least for that alone he'll be compensated. It's just that he should know: there was no special reason for giving it to him, because there's no need to mention what had happened on all the previous investigations. Never-ending probing, that's what he did, yes, but results on the ground? Results, without them you might as well fold the business. So if it was she who gave him the investigation, he should at least earn it, for a change. Earn it or make a career change. There comes an age when a person has to start asking himself questions, everyone, what they had planned on doing with their lives and how it turned out. How did it turn out? Someone who only by chance still gets an investigation and not even a big one, just an ordinary investigation. A man got burnt, with all due respect, there are more complicated matters than a man getting burnt. So this time there really is no reason for him to delay the report and then to blow it up without saying anything explicit in the end: bottom line, yes, that's what's important, to hell with all the rest. So this time it's worth his while succeeding, they are even willing to make a deal with him: to make the most of this opportunity and get things moving one way or another: maybe he won't be given a new car, but at least they'll contribute substantially, how's that? Only toward for what he does for work, of course only toward for what he does for work. The mileage he does outside of that in his free time, he's already heard stories about that, not that he needed to hear: what, doesn't he remember? He remembers perfectly well, despite all the time that's passed. Suddenly he goes crazy after some week in which he didn't put his nose outside, and after all, amongst their friends there were those who really did travel far; Tierra del Fuego, Alaska, North Sea drilling, what not. As for him? He only covers these roads from top to bottom, to kill time or to kill something else: yes, that's what his wife says about him and she's someone who once knew him closely. Sometimes when they speak about him, the boss and his wife, they say: if something would have come out of it at least, if he would finally have found himself in all those wanderings. It's not funny. His situation is not at all funny, and that's the truth: not advancing at work, living alone in a one-room apartment, driving the same jalopy. After all, that's what this conversation is for, for him to finally take himself in hand: for old time's sake. Between us, things are actually much better now, and from his manager's chair he's got no qualms saying so: one should take a look where one also could have got to, after all they both started out together, didn't they? Who would have believed that this is how he turned out: someone who gets woken in the middle of the night and an interim report demanded by tonight already, yes, he shouldn't waste everyone's time again or his own as well, because he won't be getting another opportunity) "I wouldn't even have had the slightest clue."

8

For a moment the silhouettes were still advancing in the window until it was emptied of them, the last square as well. Only the pounding was still heard on the asphalt, rhythmic, dwindling and fading away.

"Step by step," the actor said from his chair, "to the last letter of recorded time." Shechter stretched another green strip onto the window and the lighting man sniffed the cellophane that was on the lamp, and after it the plug. "Fade, fade, oh light," said the actor, "life is but a shadow in flight."

Merav grasped the bedspread. "Haven't you finished yet?"

"Not as yet," the actor answered in the same sneering tone that he used to mock others as well as himself.

She pulled the bedspread taut beneath the stuffed animals and Kinneret's strewn clothing, and a pair of black pants fell to the floor. "At least if you had something of your own to say, but you aren't capable of saying anything that's your own, you just joke the whole time. Mimicking and mocking everyone like a parrot." Bending down she swiftly picked the pants up from the floor and shook them briskly, raising bright illuminated grains of dust from the fabric. "There's no shortage of things to mock, you can mock anyone. Nobody's perfect, only when you're little you think about grownups that way." For a moment she glanced at the label on the pants and right away dropped them onto the bed.

"What can I do," answered the actor, not changing his voice. "I've got no personality. I'm a chameleon." – He swiveled in his chair to the right – "Laid on grass I'll be green, on stone I'll turn to stone" –and swiveled again to his left – "on sadness I'll sadden, on joy be joyous" – and stopped opposite her – "my concealments no one shall perceive, not even I, in times of sleep I too will be colored by my dreams."

Beneath the column lock of the fixed tripod a murky droplet flowed out twisting and lengthening. "Is that also Shakespeare?" The lighting man was trying to open the butterfly screw.

"Who else, me?" The actor stretched his fingers on the table and remnants of polish sparkled at their tips." "Every pen I break, my heart unable to ache. A screwed up person. Like my girlfriend used to say – can't love anyone, dead inside." He angled his fingers in the air, spread them, rejoined them and placed them on the table.

"And what, wasn't she right? Of course she was right. Struck to death by the hands of a hangman to fear, familiar yet queer, neither god nor seraph" – on his right he grabbed the spray canister with a vigorous movement as if it were the handle of an axe – "returned from the looking glass, passed sentence and lopped off my heart. This WD-40?" – he sprayed the nails of his left hand in an arc – "if only it removed rust like it removes nail polish" – and sprayed the nails of his right hand as well, one after another – "your butterfly would never get opened" – and sprayed another long wasteful arc in the air until the sergeant shot him a look.

Outside, beyond the windowpane a stone was heard striking plastic and right away another striking tin. Between the strips stuck on the window a voice said: "Whatever you try Ezra I'll still beat you. It's written in the stars, 'Weintraub wins, Ezra loses.' What, didn't I tell you? Look what's written there: eighty-six seventy. Eighty-eight. Let's use him as a referee, hey Ezra? That pilot – I think he can see everything. Ninety seventy. Ninety-two." Another stone struck the plastic and another missed, making a metallic sound.

(If only he had done something to the rickshaw, not something small, but something big, something really big, not just some small stone, let's say he threw a brick at it, yes, say a block, even a rock, even that would make no difference: because does the rickshaw belong to the master sergeant? Anyway the little one's ashamed to ride with him in it ever since the children made fun of her at kindergarten, but he's not angry, no, why should he be, how could anyone at all be angry with them.)

Another stone struck: "Ninety-four seventy."

(And as for her, of course he's not at all angry with her. Even this morning, when no one was looking, he searched the lawn of his section for beetles, to bring her one in an empty matchbox so that she could put it on her teeny hand: a red one with shiny black spots, she'd put it in the middle of her hand and say to it softly-softly, putting her head close to it: "Baydybug. Badybug." It just killed him, the sergeant, when she spoke to it like that, badybug, and how she looked at them when they suddenly flew from her hand. One moment they're standing there and suddenly nothing, only her eyes filled with amazement.)

"Ninety-six seventy."

(Or how she stands opposite him and says: "Squito! Squito!" And waits for him to kill it for her right away with his hands or with a pillow, as a knight would for his princess; or at the very least to wag his finger at it and say: "Bad squito! Bad bad bad!")

"Ninety-eight seventy."

(First thing in the morning he searched the lawn of the section for beetles until the commander of the base saw him, how could he not have? Right away he asked what he was looking for there on the lawn. "A key," he replied on the spot, "I dropped it," so quickly had he learned to lie to them. But still he actually did care about this movie, yes: it's not for no reason that he brought from home the camera he had bought, not only to partly make amends for that Saturday: he just can't go home at peace with himself if all he did the whole day is scratching his balls. That's the way he is. Every person simply has to do something with himself, that's what he thinks, and to do it the best way he can. So at home it's the carpentry he does on Saturdays, and here it's these instructional films; but he's not the only one like that, it's everyone. For example once, when he arranged to meet his wife and the little one at an ice cream parlor opposite the Center, some Arab was sweeping the pavement in front of them. It was a lovely day;

even Tel Aviv looked less ugly than it usually does: somehow the sunbeams fell in a way that the soot on the ficus trees couldn't be seen and all their leaves were the color of honey – and that Arab actually was making an effort to sweep the pavement without cutting corners. All-out like that, as if each sweep wouldn't be wiped out in a moment and as if he didn't sometimes feel like smashing everything. The sergeant looked at his knotty hands, the hands of someone who works with them; they too were the color of honey, even with the swept up dirt. And he then thought to himself: you also aren't capable of letting the day finish just with scratching your balls. He was already thinking of throwing him a coin, why not, which he would sweep up and find and be glad, to his health, what, aren't Arabs human beings? But when the Arab saw his uniform, he lowered his head to the pavement and began to sweep even harder than before. He swept so hard that watching him became unpleasant and even eating ice cream became unpleasant.)

Shechter stuck another green strip on the window. He cut the end with the box cutter and when he lifted up his hand, a sweat stain perhaps caused by the heat of the lamp was revealed in his armpit. On the arm of the soundman, who was looking at him from his corner, the tattooed spiral glowed and was swallowed into the fold of the sleeve.

(So he cared about the movie as well: let others rack their brains whether it's a masterpiece or not, he just wants it to work. Yes, against all the general staff bad luck orders: against those welfare officers who don't show up, against those parents of Kinneret's who are also late, against all the power outages and against all their defective equipment. Just that the movie should come out okay and that they won't have to replace it for the next intake. Because a film like this about artillery and missiles could be good for years. That's the way it is, he's not under any illusions – he's got a doctorate on people. Of course there are good Arabs, just as there are good Jews and shitty Jews; it's just that people on the whole, all in all, have it in their nature to fight over nonsense. So maybe there are

more good people than bad, he's not saying there aren't, even
in the worst of the worst you can still find something good.
But what happens, most of the time everyone's busy fighting
over nonsense. Everyone, it doesn't matter who. Even that
captain, someone who was a senior systems analyst in civilian
life, something like that, what was he doing on the base in
the south? Wiping out wasps. In the middle of all that desert,
on that base that looked like some Nahal settlement with
the ready lawn they put there and the sprinklers, and with
that strong yellow of the wasps that doesn't resemble at all
the yellow belly of a bulbul or the yellow of acacia – in the
middle of all that the captain was wiping out wasps: all those
brains of his just for that. So even if those missiles that they
filmed there are going to be replaced, as some people say,
there'll always be missiles, yes, there'll always be wars. And
many many they'll sit in a room like this and softly softly
pray for everything dear to them, yes, not possessions, to hell
with possessions, for the few people they can't live without
not even for one moment.)

"Should we put the nylon on now?" asked Shechter.
The window was already entirely cut by the crisscrossing of
green strips.

"Yes," replied the sergeant and brought the sheets of nylon
from the table and opened their folds in the air.

(As for him, he'd give up everything for what's really
important to him: everything. Because what wouldn't he do
for her? He'd sell up everything, even the furniture, which he
himself made at home on some hundred Saturdays to furnish
their nest – that's what his wife said at the time, when they
were still just the two of them – the chest of drawers and the
bookcase and the living room table and the armchairs and
the wall cupboard, which was the most cherished in terms of
materials and workmanship, and the night lamp table, which
was the most cherished in terms of the heart: he'd sell them
one by one, yes, for the little one. Without giving a damn.
Even take them apart if necessary and sell the timber, yes, and
even burn them with his own hands if necessary: if she was
cold let's say. Say in the winter there was some power outage

that didn't end. Whatever could happen, let's say snow began to fall like it did on Mount Hermon and didn't stop – isn't that what they're saying now, that the weather's gone crazy? So one by one he would burn them, without giving a damn: with all the work he put into them, with all of himself, which he put into them at the time, when he wanted his wife to know how much he loved her. And in the end, if let's say everything came to an end, say if that happened, let's just say; sometimes that's what goes through his mind when he sees her, those cheeks of hers and those eyes that knock him out on the spot, melting his heart like that – then he himself would rise up there like some Indian from the soundman's stories. Yes, that's the way he feels every time he sees her, every time she laughs, every time she cries. Every time she eats, every time she plays with some toy, every time she sleeps in the bed that he made for her and from her eyelids he can tell that she's dreaming.)

The sheet was placed on the window, causing the strips and the rickshaw on the other side to glisten and blur.

(In the war, there was no question at all of them going to the kibbutz, let it take however long it takes. He didn't want to take the smallest chance: because what would he do in this life if something happened to her, what would he do? And after they went – he took them to the central bus station in the rickshaw and the bus drivers all hooted at him as if he had no right to live – after that he walked around the empty apartment like Abudi's prisoners, going from here to there and from there to here, all the time searching for traces of them. In the beginning he still picked up all the toys that she left and arranged them for her in the room, making a real lineup parade there, but the next day he went and scattered them around so that everything would look in a mess, as if she was still at home; so that when he sits down on the armchair some Simpson suddenly sticks him in the back and when he goes into the shower some rubber duck suddenly toots under his foot. And when he opens the sugar jar some badybug is feasting on a grain and suddenly takes off like a helicopter.)

"Ninety-eight seventy-four," the other prisoner said from the road.

"Go for it Ezra, why not," Weintraub answered from there, "I can see you're becoming optimistic. Just don't let it go to your head."

(One night he even slept in her bed with his feet on some chair; he smelt her smell and fell asleep right away. Just that in the morning when he got up he cricked his back: really cricked it, two days after that he was still walking bent. That's how it is, he's not getting any younger, even if the uniform conceals it not too badly.)

The nylon sheet was stretched over the window and on its edge Shechter stuck a strip of masking tape lengthwise, making a tearing sound as it peeled from the roll.

(In an old American movie whose name he's forgotten – only one of the far off Shechters would still remember it – an elderly woman sealed her kitchen window that way and the space between the door and the floor, and then went to the stovetop and turned on the gas; maybe Woody Allen directed the movie, one of those where he tried to imitate Bergman, but the name slipped his mind and his memory cannot recall any other, just as in the last war the name of the movie Bergman himself directed evaded him: an old black and white movie in which an old man bends over a corpse in a coffin, gradually leaning over it and finding his own face there.)

(Every day, but every day, no matter what, he phoned them: phoned them from this base, phoned them from the base in the south, and once phoned them from the middle of Dizengoff Street, speaking at the top of his voice; people thought he'd gone off the rails. At the time he finished early, everyone finished early then, and he went and sat in an ice cream parlor where they always sat – a month ago he even showed the little one what Red Indians do: he took a straw, put it in his mouth, stuck a toothpick in its end and poof, made it fly like some poisoned arrow and a woman shouted: "You should be ashamed of yourself!" But he wasn't ashamed – it was a lovely day and he ordered ice cream for himself just as she would have ordered, with three flavors that after a few licks she would let melt completely and still stir them with a teaspoon, all that vanilla-strawberry-banana together, and ask everyone who passed by: "Icekccm? Icekeem? No more icekeem!" And that would knock him out also. He drank diet Sprite, like his wife, and didn't feel the difference in the taste at all, not a thing, and anyway he thought that he should start taking care of himself a bit, yes: it's true he does physical work on Saturdays and that from the carpentry he's got the hands of a working man and perhaps the shoulders, but after all it was easy to get a belly from his wife's meals, with the greatest of ease. Yes, he sometimes does push-ups when she exercises next to him to music in those tights of hers, which only make her seem more naked. He had never eaten the ice cream before while it was still half frozen, and it actually was tasty. And when he finished the Sprite he went into the Center to find a toilet, it was just that his bladder was full, what can you do. The street was almost empty and there were hardly any people in the Center, not only in the toilets, everywhere, but there was someone in the toilet bent over a basin washing his armpits and for a moment the sergeant looked at how his muscles rippled on his shoulders. They were also slightly wet, the shoulders, and he was really well muscled, and suddenly the sergeant saw him glancing at him from the mirror saying: "What, it's not allowed? There's not a soul here," and after a moment said to him: "the uniform suits you." The sergeant was just opening his buttons at the time and he still looked at him like that from the mirror and said: "It really suits you, there's no shame in looking good. It looks good on you, really looks good on you, believe me." And the sergeant suddenly caught his meaning – in an instant understood – he flew out of there, really flew, he didn't need to piss anymore, he didn't need anything other than to get out of there as fast as possible.)

"Ninety-eight seventy-six," the other prisoner said from the road.

(He didn't see the shops on the way; he didn't see the ficus trees even if all their leaves had turned the color of honey. He

just flew to the square with his head to the pavement until
the post office and bought half a kilo of telephone tokens
to call the kibbutz and see that all was well with them: he
was so happy to hear their voices then! Straightaway, instead
of seeing that ugly square, which always looked to him like
some sort of humpback, he saw instead – the second they
answered the phone – all the lawns of the kibbutz whose
stalks would each be lit up by light like this, and if some rain
fell before or if there was dew, you could actually see every
drop on them, all sparkling like precious stones.)

"Ninety-eight seventy-eight," the other prisoner said
from the road and right away a stone struck the plastic and
dropped to the asphalt.

"It's gone to your head," Weintraub said to him.

(He also saw her parents' room, when his wife spoke to
him on the phone, with its mosquito net, which he himself
replaced for them with his own hands, and before that it just
lay on the floor, the net: cut to precise measurements and
filling their entire bodies with marks as they rolled over it.
Their whole bodies from top to bottom became crisscrossed.
At the time he asked her, the sergeant, when she got up and
put on her shorts and a crop top, which really didn't hide
anything, absolutely nothing, what'll she say to her parents
when they come in and ask questions. That's what he asked
her at the time because her parents still knew nothing, and
she replied – just like that, without thinking twice, not for a
moment, not a second – "that I love you, Gidi.")

Shechter stretched another adhesive strip over the
edges of the nylon sheet and cut its end. "It's not the way
you work at the Television, huh," said the sergeant, "with
assistants for everything."

Shechter stuck another strip and cut its end as well. "I
haven't worked at the Television for a long time." The nylon
protruded slightly above the bottom line and he peeled it,
stretched the sheet and stuck it down again.

"Sealed, we've been sealed," the actor proclaimed from
his chair, perhaps imitating a speaker in a Greek chorus: "To
each his own troubles, to each his own calamity, to each his

own death." He looked to the window and the shadows of
the eucalyptuses that were already merged with the darkness,
faded into it beyond the nylon.

(A thin veil covered everything and had already melded
with the pupils and the eyelids and the cheeks and the nose
and the lips and the forehead, enshrouding the entire head like
a sack whose fibers pierce the flesh. "Far away" the tall soldier
said indicating with the rifle barrel, and the dead man – they
named him Lauda after the racing driver – rolled down the
slope of the hill, his hands tied behind his back and the sack
over his head becoming caught in thorns and released from
them, caught and released, and in it the bruised squashed
smashed facial features: the pale forehead that had already
reddened slightly in the sun, the bags under the eyes that
darkened deeper, the stubble of a beard that had already begun
to grow again after it was completely shaved in the basin of a
hotel in Paris. A new Shechter got into the command car, sat
in the seat of the driver who had left, started it and put his foot
down on the accelerator without releasing it, as if by speeding
past the burnt big wheel and the mound of ash of the wall of
death and the ruins of the suburb's buildings, the smell rising
from there wouldn't cling to him. He pressed and pushed the
accelerator to the floor until reaching the mosque pitted by
bullets and the cinema whose seats were all exposed and the
promenade that the planes sprayed, not with pesticides like
this plane, but with bombs; and onwards from there – the
sea, vast blue grey green sparkling with a myriad of scales
and its smell delicately fragrant, the smell of fish carcasses
that a stray bomb fetched up just to differentiate by way of
his nostrils the dead from the dead. The communication
device called him again, over and over: "Juicy dachvan, Juicy
dachvan, your location, over. Juicy dachvan, Juicy dachvan,
your location, over," and he didn't answer. Within his body,
the stench of the dead man wrapped itself around his internal
organs, and for some moments he heard a convoy drawing
away, its steps as rhythmic as his heart; and with absolute
clarity he saw at its end the boy in sandals and short pants

whose pockets bulged to bursting point, as if all the apricot plantations and the winter rains and the summer sun were created only for yielding pits for his pockets; and in his hands he carried the aquarium that stood in his room for a month – his father tried to fix its leaks with putty and his mother would be saddened each morning by the floating fish – and in its water, between shades of flashes and bursting bubbles, hidden, transparent and silent, as yet without a smell and a name: death.)

Another stone struck outside raising a metallic sound.

(Fight years later, in a bathroom, which he turned into a sealed room, he sat in the bathtub in his clothes, on his left a bottle of anti-dandruff shampoo and on his right a bottle of white wine. The emptied glass was balanced on his trousers as he tried to sing from the depths of his throat, which had become rusty: "Riiiise up dammmned of the Eaaarth!" But nothing rose up, not in his trousers, not in his chest and not in his head. Beyond the nylon that sealed the window the next building was maybe still standing or maybe not, and beyond it the avenue stretched out or maybe not, and further on from there his parents sat in their apartment and on their heads black masks strapped to the white of their hair, and the mask fronts did not hide the age spots on their faces: spots that will soon mark Shechter's face as well beneath the fibers of the sack, even though he's not old at all, just thirty-seven all in all, but with nothing to look forward to anymore and nothing to fear anymore. And for instance, if this bottle fell from the edge of the bathtub and smashed on the enamel, he wouldn't have had the strength to pick up any of the pieces, not in order to clear them away and not in order to do something with them.)

"One hundred seventy-eight."

(And those wine stains spreading on his trousers aren't going to surprise the Russian woman in the laundry after all, and anyway the time between his visits there becomes shorter as the burden of washing gets heavier. He'll no longer be ashamed when she fixes a note to the large package and on it a few words in Russian, perhaps a nickname given to identify him: to her he was the-one-who-doesn't-use-deodorant, or the-one-with-the-weary-walk, or the-one-with-the-blank-look, like the nicknames given to children in a new country; for instance, "raw meat eaters" for Eskimos, "redskins" for Indians – in a distant room his father told him about them and about Old Shatterhand – as if there was no need for anything else to define them and they had not done wondrous deeds like taking scalps and building igloos and rubbing noses. But he, Shechter, unlike those Eskimos who called themselves Inuit – "the People" – took full responsibility for his nicknames and has but a few of the things with which he was defined: the smell of sweat, the lumbering walk, the blank look. In this sealed room, whose shower is out of working order and in whose small cupboard there is a packet of contraceptives with an expired date, his bathtub now curves around his body, not like an igloo, but like a small inverted tunnel, a white Metro station, whose rails are these two feet stretched out in front, and the drunk burping in it is he himself.)

Another stone struck and in the distance pounding steps were heard.

(It was like that station, projected from within the darkness around it, white and devoid of substantiality like the beams that would never project his films: not in the Cinematheques and not in the cinemas in which he sat like any other cinemagoer who year after year watches the magic cast upon him in the dark, until the exit door in the corner is opened; opened though from the screen magnificent and wondrous scenery is still being reflected – round hills on which cattle graze, a sleepy village from which a bell tower stretches up, wet trees dotted with yellow apples – and in the entrance the usher pushes away a squashed soda tin can with his shoe, and in the passage behind him something contemptible has been scribbled and a dingy light that will make the scenes murky from the screen to the horizon. And the angel, whom everyone feared, as he himself in his youth had feared, years before he sat in the bath with his clothes on,

perhaps isn't bony at all as we're told and doesn't hold a scythe
as we're told, but is some kind of paunchy pensioner like this
usher, in his hand just a wafer that he bought at the snack bar
before leaving, and he reaps nothing with it but only infuses
the theater with pale yellow electrical light from outside.)

"So what you doing now?" asked the sergeant.

"Making a living," answered Shechter. He passed his hand
over the nylon sheet whose edges were already stuck down.
"One has to live on something, no?"

"A hundred and two seventy-eight," Weintraub said
from outside.

The soundman brought the microphone from the corner
of the room, and the coils of the cable that connected it
came loose from the broomstick that served as a pole. The
soundman bent over the recording machine and directed the
microphone to the bed: Na'ama and Kinneret were sitting
there, the one feeling the furry ear of a teddy bear and the
other rubbing the purple shoulder strap of a dress.

"Can I help you with the microphone?" asked the
lighting man.

"First take care of your lamp," answered the soundman
and improved its hold.

"Just tell me what this soundcheck is for, just so that I
understand." The sergeant turned from the window.

"Aren't we filming in a little while?" the soundman looked
at him above his dials.

"Filming who?" asked the sergeant. "Do you see Kinneret's
parents here?"

"Anyone here see Kinneret's parents, going once? Anyone
here see Kinneret's parents, going twice?" the actor asked from
his chair, imitating a public auctioneer. Nobody answered
and through the nylon the sergeant tried to make out the
road leading to the base. In the darkness beyond him only the
light of the plane moved and drew away.

At the end of the empty road, in front of
the raised engine bonnet of the car, they
stood: a tiny silhouette of a man and the

tiny silhouette of a woman. For a moment
longer the woman looked around her and
afterwards opened the car door and got in.
"Are you coming?" she called from inside,
"if someone comes near we'll see him."
Her knee, round and white, bumped into
the glove compartment and it opened
immediately from the blow: parking
vouchers and a packet of tissues could be
seen inside it. "Aren't you getting in?" She
closed the glove compartment and in a
moment the fields turned dark in the gap
left by the car door, until she closed it as
well. She opened the window slowly and
looked into the depths of the darkness:
opposite her the fields had taken on the
appearance of a giant black lake. "Can you
hear them," she addressed her question to
the silhouette of the man, "the crickets?"
She pushed the seat back with her long
legs, reclined the backrest with her hand
and leaned her head back and closed her
eyes. The engine bonnet slammed. "The
what?" asked the man. Heavy and irritable
he got into the car and placed his hands on
the steering wheel, and in the light lit by
the door, a large ring sparkled on his fourth
finger. "What a disaster," he said, "not
even a dog passes by here at night." "The
crickets," said the woman and opened the
window further, "can't you hear them?" Her
eyes were turned to the man. "Crickets?"
he said to her, "you call a Piper crickets?"
While he spoke, slip-on canvas shoes fell
from the soles of her feet and the right
one, which had turned over, momentarily
displayed bright rope soles until the man

closed the door. "Let them wait a while
for us," said the woman, "so what." She
wiggled her toes that had been freed. "This
time it's not my fault, we left on time."
"They must be getting anxious by now," the
man drummed on the steering wheel and
his ring struck something in the darkness.
"Your daughter," said the woman, "isn't
worried about us, of that you can be sure."
The man also reclined his backrest. Beyond
his Adam's apple the distant neon sign of
the suburban mall could be made out in
his window and the letter "l" flickered in
it. The woman shifted her head until it
disappeared. "If it wasn't for that plane,"
she stretched her legs and looked at them,
"it would be like we were all alone in the
world, huh?" Slowly she slackened her legs,
and the edge of her dress fell between them
as she let them draw apart from each other,
thigh from thigh.

The sergeant kept looking at the window. "If there was
still some kind of chance they'd get here," he said to the
soundman, "you've now gone and brought bad luck."

"That's how life is," the actor clarified to all and his eyes
shone in the light of the lamp. "It's all according to the
general staff bad luck orders. Right, Gidi?" – He knocked on
the table with the spray canister perhaps imitating a judge at
court – "my transgressions are sorely remembered, according
to orders judgement has been decreed, according to orders
my eyes have been blinded so as no longer to view the
splendor of the world" – he paused for a moment – "'where
is the iron?' I shall howl and pierce the white of my other eye,
so utter is my shame."

"I see you haven't finished," said Merav.

"No," answered the actor. "Sometimes it can even take the
whole night, and in the morning it's still there."

The soundman looked at him from above the recording machine, and his suntan obscured his faded pupils even further. "Sometimes he who punishes," he said in the quiet voice of someone who has already resolved his doubts and found a path to tread, "in the end actually forgives."

"You mean him?" – the actor pointed to the ceiling in whose corner the lizard lay in wait for a fly – "but I'm talking about my girlfriend, not him."

"Maybe she'll still forgive you," the soundman said to him. The heat of the lamp made his suntan glow and when he opened a shirt button Kinneret watched him from her seat. "She won't," answered the actor and put his finger down and scraped off the last remains of the polish from his nail. "If I were in her place I wouldn't forgive either." Between his chubby cheeks his square jaw stuck out as if it had wandered in from another movie, one that also lacked a professional makeup artist to do the work properly.

The microphone pole slanted slightly toward the floor and the soundman lifted it up again. "You sure you don't need help?" asked the lighting man.

"Sure," the soundman improved its hold, "just keep an eye on the lamp so that it doesn't short again."

"What've you got drawn there?" Kinneret looked at his arm. She held an old newspaper supplement in her hand and waved it in front of her face like a fan, back and forth.

"That?" Shechter answered in his place, "that's from the days when he was still young and stupid like me." He was still gazing out between the strips of the window, and being enclosed by them it made the sagging of his shoulders more prominent. In the depths of the darkness outside, which the nylon illuminated with a milky shade, the light of the plane popped up again, advancing slowly in the sky.

"Again you make out like we're children." Kinneret blew air to the opening of her shirt and the pages of the supplement rustled, at times revealing a photograph or a section of delicate skin. "Your button's about to fall off," she said to the soundman, "the one you opened."

"If it falls, it falls," he answered her still bent down and the microphone pole in his hand. "I'll hear it in the earphones."

(And there was one who heard the fall of a bead of sweat and the formation of a grain of soot on the glass of a lantern: the gargling of the oil he himself heard and the lizard above him listened for the moths and the mosquitoes and the gnats.)

"Wouldn't it be better to pull it off," Kinneret said, "and put it in your pocket?"

(It flicked its tongue toward their tiny bodies and their wings like a stripper in Patpong flicking her tongue at the audience or bending down and licking her own lips or the lips of her girlfriend, smoke rising from them in a thousand rings, thousands, thousands upon thousands of rings of smoke. On his first trip he went there with an American on whose right arm the sign of the Special Forces was tattooed; and ever since Vietnam he lived in the train station hotel, where the thin girls pass and call out from beyond the screen door to him also: "Hey man, you want fucky-fucky?" And after they found out his name they called out: "Mister Joe, what's wrong wiz you, I can make you happy, very-very happy," and he didn't answer; but one night he went with the American to Patpong and afterwards only remembered a dark alcove concealed by a beaded curtain, and an album in which tattoos of all sorts were photographed on arms on thighs on breasts and on buttocks, and the whirls of smoke, which were not incense and not marijuana and not hashish, and how afterwards they traveled from there in a rickshaw rattling as this plane, and the American tried to stand to attention in it in order to sing the anthem opposite the masses who filled the pavements of Bangkok.)

"I'll hear it," answered the soundman and lifted up the microphone pole further.

"You sure you can manage?" the lighting man asked still trying to open the butterfly screw of the lamp tripod.

"You deal with the lamp," he said to him again.

(And on his second trip, from inside the mosquito net that had long ago lost its whiteness – the shadows of its threads were wrapped around the dragon tattooed on his skin like

cobwebs over an insect –he saw the lantern tossing from side
to side in the wind opposite him carrying the oil container
and the sooty glass to the edge of the shelf, and the flame
sprouted between the rim and quivered, not like the one on
his arm, but like the stripper's bloody uvula, and stood out
like Shiva Linga and became agitated like the palm treetops
and the papayas and the entire ocean. Through the hunger
and the heat and the commotion and the smoke, for some
moments he saw himself in the country that he had left, a lone
survivor like Manu the fisherman, sailing there, sailing on the
blazing sands of the desert in a ship whose bow was tethered
not to a fish but to a whirlwind; and he was not transporting
pairs of animals in it, but a host of clouds that floated beneath
the deck, and the rain accumulated in them like millions
of transparent fetuses ready to be born, after the fire will
annihilate all that is decreed to burn and be annihilated.)

"Don't worry about the lamp," answered the lighting man.
"It's a workhorse." The grin that before would have appeared
on his face vanished and was replaced by an involuntary hand
movement, which from time to time he repeated, rubbing his
cheek as if to check for stubble growth.

"Rather take care of that," said the soundman.

"I just wanted to help," answered the lighting man and
rubbed his stubble again.

(And until then, beyond the threads of the mosquito net
and the reeds of the door, the ocean will rage and salivate
boiling foam and bursting bubbles, and from the depths will
uproot skeletons cloaked in seaweed finery in which they'll
stroll on the cliff in place of him: he saw them strolling there
with absolute clarity. Beyond the spray of the water and the
battalions of rushing waves, for a few moments his son and
the mother of his son could be made out; on a warm evening
such as this they would watch the old couple drinking tea
on their balcony with measured sips, and his son would
make a tally of them to make sure no sip was missed. He
was not as yet engrossed in the books he received from his
replacement, and had not as yet started talking about quasars

and the Doppler effect and the butterfly effect, as if he had
not once mumbled all sorts of baby-like murmurings to his
minute fingers that he tried to open and make into a fist.
"Let's say it goes like this with its wings in Brazil," he said
one evening and beat his hands and hit the bookcase, and at
the time he saw the down of his hands, which had darkened,
and his eyelashes, which were long like her eyelashes, and the
pupils, whose color was the color of his pupils, but tiny rings
surrounded them when he calculated the grocery accounts
by heart: on the balcony a telescope, which his replacement
bought for him, stood on its tripod, a telescope in which you
could see the craters of the moon, but one evening he found
him observing the neighbors' building with his right hand
in his trousers, and when he heard his steps he shot him a
murderous look cracked by a tear and a bus below hurtled
round the bend of the road.)

"A hundred and two seventy-eight," Weintraub said again
from outside.

(Millions upon millions of waves stormed toward the cliff
on which the hut stood, and everything he had abandoned
now came upon him with a vengeance, his entire body, which
had become thin and feverish, was filled with this knowledge:
far above the unraveled mosquito net and above the thatch
and above the clouds that the lightning sliced with a thrust,
in the depths of the highest heaven, gigantic thunderous
balancing scales moved; seven degrees from the equator he
heard them with absolute clarity – in his eyes the mark of the
location was not without meaning; and in the white of a grain
of salt he could see the movement of a wave from the end of
the ocean, the blazing of the equatorial sun, the refining and
the purifying of the wave, its slow drifting toward the sky,
its slow condensing and the touch of those kneading fingers
endowing each cloud with its mark, until it ripens and falls
and billows – on one scale was this island to which he had
traveled far with all its bays and hills and masses of palm
trees, and on the other a handful of dried leaves, upon which
they had once lain: at the time a small sparrow stood on the
sill beneath the stuck shutter and whistled.)

"I'll teach you a thing or two, Ezra."

(The scales moved up and down and thundered, and in the lantern the oil bubbled; he heard it with absolute clarity as well as the wick becoming scorched and the glass becoming sooty and the smoke rising and the flame spreading to annihilate all that was decreed to burn and be annihilated: first the shelf to whose edge the lantern reaches, then the boarded floor on which the oil will drip, then the mattress filled with seaweed, and with it this mosquito net, which will instantly wrap him in a thousand threads of fire. They'll become affixed to his body and to his curses, because the love that begat them has been forgotten – in the soot a charcoal iron could not be seen being moved back and forth as he saw in the window on his first trip, nor an idle iron as in their apartment while she waited for him to sprinkle water onto his spread out trousers; he then sprinkled water onto the pockets of her blouse, until dark nipples permeated the material and he reached out to them with his hand and mouth and ate into them and lifted the material – forgotten until he was filled with regret, his entire feverish body was filled with it, and through the gurgling oil and the tossing of the mat panels, the thatch was then heard being torn to the last of its leaves. Above the threads of the mosquito net, from within a black reddish strip of the heaven of the heavens that had been shifted aside, fingers of rain reached out, a thousand fingers, thousands, thousands upon thousands: they reached toward the mosquito net, to the wooden floor, to the shelf, to the spout of the blackened lantern, to the flame, and extinguished it.)

"A hundred and four seventy-eight," said Weintraub from outside.

"You haven't got a hope against me, Ezra. What do you mean not in, it was in, and how. Ask that pilot if it wasn't."

(In the morning he opened the reed door, on whose nails his clothes were hung so as to keep centipedes and scorpions away, and before moving his gaze over the island he'll be leaving – over its sky, which had cleared and once

more covered Ko Samui as well as Ko Phi Phi and Ko
Tao and Bangkok and Chang Mai and the whole of Asia,
and subsequently over the cliff shining once more in the
sun, and over the bay in which the fishermen's boats were
already fearlessly rattling and dragging white dissolving trails
behind them, and over the beach whose restaurants were
once more serving fried barracuda and cuttlefish salad and
magic mushrooms – and before completing even one step, he
slipped on a broken branch and fell. From the ground onto
which he was thrown he saw before him a minute hollow
filled with smooth pure water, in which blue sky was reflected
with the white of a cloud, and a mosquito landed on it: with
absolute clarity he saw its slender heartwarming legs standing
on the water left by the storm, indenting the purity of the
cloud with miniscule delicate indentations, and he cried.)

"A hundred and six seventy-eight," Weintraub said from
outside. "That's how it goes, Ezra, take a lesson from Jordan.
Even on his worst off day, d'you know how many shots he
sank? No, how many d'you think, Ezra. It's easy I'll tell you.
After seven hundred and sixty-six games, d'you know how
many shots Jordan sank?"

Merav looked in the window and shifted a strand of
unruly hair back behind her ear. "Her parents aren't going
to be coming," she said, and the fingernails that appeared
behind the earlobe had been chewed to the flesh.

"You wanna go home, sweetie?" the sergeant said, "I also
want to, believe me."

Merav turned her head to the room. "It's just that with
the masks," she said, "they won't know anyway if we film
with someone else. They'll never know." With her fingernail
she smoothed out an air bubble that had formed under one
of the green masking tape strips.

"How do you mean they'll never know?" said the sergeant.
"Besides which, who you gonna put in their place? Just so
that I understand."

"Na'ama and him" – she gestured with her eyebrow to
the actor. "With a mask and with different clothes, who'll
ever know we filmed them before?" She turned again to the

window and lifted her hand to it. "In our place, someone once sat like that for maybe half the night, I mean it, half the night. Everyone thought it was the neighbor, with the mask on it was impossible to know. In the end it turned out it was some crazy woman from Tel Aviv who came all the way to us just to receive a blessing."

"From your grandfather?" asked the sergeant.

Merav gave a small nod and fixed her fingernail to the nylon. "Without the blessing she wouldn't have got through that war. His blessing is what saved her. Afterwards she even came to give him a present."

"You," the actor said to her from his chair, "only know how to mock, to make fun of everything. There's no shortage of things to mock," he imitated her and Merav did not react. "You can mock anyone, nobody's perfect, it's only when you're little you think about grownups in that way."

Merav did not answer.

"We also had a case like that," the actor said to her back. "For half the night I didn't know who it was at all, it didn't even look like a neighbor. I sat there racking my brains, until I looked in the mirror: from yonder reflected, alien yet awkward as yours truly is affected, his gaze at me mercilessly directed."

The sergeant picked up the screenplay folder from the table: just so that he understands, yes, just what exactly are they supposed to wear according to her suggestion, the ones replacing Kinneret's parents?

"No shortage of clothes here," Merav gestured with her eyebrows at the bed.

"Twenty! Twenty, Ezra, twenty!" Weintraub was heard from the other side of the window, "on his worst off day Jordan made twenty, so you wanna compete with me? What a waste. A waste of your money, Ezra, believe me. Even if you were kept in detention for a whole year, let's say you got so mad you killed Abudi, even then you wouldn't stand a chance."

The sergeant was still leafing through the folder. "Anyway," he said, "even if they change clothes and put on the masks, no matter who they are, their hair will be seen: masks don't hide hair, straightaway people will know who they are."

"How'll they know," answered Merav. "They only saw his wig, he was the welfare officer, have you forgotten? And also it was just for a minute, he was quoting Shakespeare all the time. Who will know? He'll act her father for a second, he won't speak at all."

"As for their movie," the female medic said from the telephone receiver, which transmitted the smell from his mouth back to him, the smell of his teeth that he hadn't yet brushed then and the smell of sleep whose dreams he preferred to forget, "it was pathetic, just like the whole base, everything's shoddy. Even if I'd arrived before I couldn't have helped with anything, I've barely got any plasters." And right away she carried on talking to him on the phone about burn percentages, as if his maturity in itself was enough to accord him medical understanding, and in the same breath told him – a stranger in whom she suddenly found a random conversation partner – about her grandmother, who once told her how in Russia they would place spider webs gathered from attics on burns. "Everything's so shoddy," she said again, "the sergeant had to bring another camera from home, and boy did he show off with it. He even asked his clerk to stand next to the rickshaw for a moment, he wanted to show it was possible to photograph with just the light of the indicator. I mean it, he really asked her, he swore that's how he once photographed his daughter." And on the lengthy journey, from inside his car to which the smells of his body had already clung as to the telephone receiver, he wondered for some moments if all his indicators are in working order, or perhaps their lights have worn down like the brakes and tires and pistons and the nameless thing whose stamina made him capable of traveling hour upon hour and pass by cities and towns, farms and kibbutzim and gas stations, and at traffic lights to peek at drivers whose windows frame them while they sing softly or pick their noses or place a hand on their partner's thigh or for a moment are deep in hidden thoughts; and immediately the road once again would gallop beneath him into the distance, as if kilometers were not meted out in it but rather time itself, which would all pass from one end to the other.

"They don't utter a word, just watch television."

Through the nylon sheets Shechter's blurred face could be made out and the sparkle that flickered in his one eye and moved to the other belonged to the crop sprayer. Between the strips stuck on the windowpane the reflection of the room was also seen, blurred like his face: the posters were faded there, the table faded with the actor behind it, the bed faded with its stuffed animals and the two female soldiers sitting on it. The spark crossed his head like a tracer bullet and continued in its flight.

"Na'ama's hair," he said still gazing in the window, "nevertheless, that they did see." She glanced at him from the windowpane, gathered up the hair from her neck, removed the black velvet ribbon from her arm and wound it around the bright strands over and over and over.

"What, couldn't Kinneret's mother have bleached her hair?" Merav said.

(And blow dry her hair and shout out from a dark bar smelling of eau de cologne: "what's up honey, you coming?")

"But mine's natural," Na'ama wound the velvet ribbon around once more.

"Not everyone's born that way," Merav answered. "Some have to use bleach."

(And to give honey a deep half-wink, her eyelashes were much thicker than her eyebrows, and the friend who went with her said: "they pluck everything out, above and below. To get them hot. Look, look how he's got the hots for her. Someone like that could have a stroke in the middle, that's if he can still do it at all.")

"Her hair's brown," Kinneret said, "not light brown. My color exactly." She uncrossed her legs and got up from the bed.

"Except for the grey hairs you've given her," said the actor. "Didn't you give her grey hairs? For sure you've given her grey hairs."

"She gave them to me," replied Kinneret.

Merav turned to the door and opened it, finding a widening strip of darkness there. "Wait a moment," the sergeant called to her, "how come you're going? Take the keys first." He took a large bunch from his pocket and threw it to her, and from the key ring a miniature glass shoe sparkled for a moment. Merav's back was seen from the gap left by the door as she went out the entrance hall and down the stairs and stepped on the puddle that the fire hydrant left. A faint light lit up as the door of the rickshaw opened and a white baby shoe began to swing from the mirror. Merav mumbled to herself, bent down, straightened up and got out, slamming the door behind her. On the cork board in the entrance hall the notice was lit by the light coming from the room: "Wild Party at Cliff Beach," and on the door of the clinic the poster became clear with its red heading: "An Early Examination Saves Lives." Kinneret averted her eyes from there.

"Merav-sweetie," the actor called out from his chair when she returned, "what would we do without you? Right, Gidi?" She pushed the door with her foot and slammed it; in her hands were three cardboard boxes. "The girl's irritable," said the lighting man and his hand recoiled from the heat of the lamp. Merav turned to the bed and then let the mask boxes drop there. One immediately slid off the fold in the clothing onto which it fell, and turned on its side.

"Tell me Merav," Kinneret said, "what have you got against my clothes?"

Merav swept back strands of her hair. "You're both sitting on them anyway," she replied, "and that's how it is in the script, no?" She approached the table and picked up the folder. The sergeant, who followed her brisk movements, turned around the monitor that assisted him in the filming and directed the screen to the bed.

"Room, interior: Kinneret and her parents are sitting on the bed" – across from him the actor tried to quote the heading of the scene from memory and declaiming perhaps like a member of a Greek chorus – "and watching television. From the set the voice of a female announcer – or perhaps male announcer? – is heard announcing the arrival of the new missiles from America in enormous Galaxy planes. Enormous or gigantic? Let it be enormous. Right, sweetie?"

(Not like that: they filmed the missiles in the base in the south, there was no plane there, not enormous, not gigantic nor small like this one, and after they returned and Gidi took her to the bus stop, she only saw the rickshaw staggering into the distance and the tiny shoe swinging from the mirror: even from the bus she still saw that shoe kicking away.)

"Wasn't it like that?" the actor swept his hair like her. "Bad comes to bad, the wages of disgrace – disgrace. Onwards, lead me to the gallows. Wouldn't you like a missile to fall on me, sweetie?"

("Attention!" they shouted at her from the seats at the back and without looking she knew that they were Cohen Productions' cousins and that when the bus passes by the new suburb – three-leveled houses with covered parking – they'll both clear their throats and hurl everything they managed to bring up from there at the signpost, while at the same time looking with longing at some covered parking spot whose door rises to a new car approaching. The twins would always press their faces against the windowpane, and once Pnina said in a nasal tone through her squashed little nose, "are we going to live there one day, Suzy?" And Shoshanna answered: "after New Year, right Merav?" And she replied with the words that they both sometimes used to say opposite the television: "of course we'll live there, our father's an oil *magnet*," because she didn't want to try to alter their language nor their behavior nor their dreams.)

"Would be a waste of a missile," she said to the actor.

(That oil *magnet*, who one Saturday took them all to a café on the promenade, ordered himself a beer and said: "just so that the manager won't cause any problems," and still asked the waitress if the beer came with pickles. "I can bring you pickles, no problem," the waitress answered. And right away she brought a small plate with a few olives, which they all ate very slowly as if it was candy, and opposite them the sea was smooth and glistened like the marble floor of a giant hall whose walls are too distant to be seen.)

"Do you have any idea how much one costs?"

(And when the bill came inside a small elegant leather folder, the oil *magnet* became annoyed: what, aren't the pickles included? That's what he understood from her, that the pickles were included, not just him, anyone else in his place would've understood that pickles are included. He's not paying a cent more than what the beer cost, not a cent. It's not on principle, no no, it's just that he budgeted for beer, not for pickles. That oil magnet, when a small plane like this one passed over the sea, trailing after it a long sign advertising cheap flights to New York, even chatted with the couple at the next table and said: "That really is cheap, no two ways about it." As if first thing in the morning he meant to go to some travel agency and buy them all tickets to New York, so that they could see its skyscrapers: skyscrapers and the heaven of heavens and the five heavens above them, whose angels her grandfather would summon, each by his name and according to his skills, to sway straying hearts and to open locked wombs and to annul evil eyes.)

"A million dollars."

("Pretends she doesn't see," said the Cohen's cousins from the back seat, "What's up with you, the army turned you into a snob?" When she avoided a shopping basket, on whose top the cardboard box of a gas mask was placed, and sat down, she still saw that tiny shoe kicking away.)

"And that's still without the launcher and the radar."

(The bus's brakes grated and in front of her the owner of the basket said to her neighbor: "Once? There wasn't one Saturday that they didn't come. Rain or shine they came. At ten o'clock I knew straightaway I'd hear the car, like clockwork they came. Nurit; you remember, Nurit? But now, not anymore. Maybe once a fortnight. When they can make it. But they can't always make it. That's how it is when they grow up." "How couldn't I remember, Nurit," said the woman next to her, "we went through school together, how could you think I wouldn't remember? When she was pregnant and got German measles, don't I remember that? Like it was today. Believe me I was scared. So even if I have seen something of the world, one doesn't forget. There are things that even if I wanted to forget, that I'd give my life to forget, believe me, Flora – things I keep seeing right in front of my eyes." "That's how it is," the owner of the basket placed it next to the seat so that it wouldn't move forward on its wheels, "a person without a memory isn't a person anymore. Believe me it's better to go. Yakov? That's what he was like at the end, he didn't remember a thing. Do you remember Yakov?" "Of course I remember Yakov, the way he'd sit in the backyard in the evening and you'd bring him food. I got hungry just from the smell, on my word, Flora. And in those days I wasn't someone who ate a lot, I had a figure and everything." "So now I've also got a place there," the owner of the basket said. "One has to think ahead, that's what Yakov used to say. He said lots of things, but about that – he was right. I learnt that only after he went. That's how it is. Only when someone leaves you, you realize how much he was right sometimes. I pulled some strings to arrange it, d'you know what it takes to get a place there? It's easier to get an apartment, believe me. They're all corrupt there, as much as they're religious they're corrupt. So what, are you going to fight with them? Fight with them and you can forget about a place. They'll tell you there isn't one next to him, no more – it's all taken."

"Ours cost a million," said the sergeant, "not theirs."

(In the front window, in which only a figure in the Maccabi football team uniform was swinging, the first houses of the neighborhood could be seen; low, crowded and without any charm. And nobody inside them, not only the elderly, but also the young and the children and even her twin sisters, will ever get out of there, because they're all like that Yakov in his place: they won't get out of there; not with the help of lotteries or the pools, not with the help of studies, and not with the help of angels, which her grandfather would summon one by one by name, as if they were about to land in droves in the square in front of the kiosk – in order to turn slander around as it's being spoken or to deprive sleep from enemy's eyes or to divert winter floods; when they flooded he would blame himself for thoughts brought about by the smoke of a cockscomb between barren thighs that didn't fade even when he placed his hand close to the coal grate or was locked in the toilet or traveled to Tel Aviv to a dusky bar just to rid himself of them – "come to visit, come," said the owner of the basket, "why not, maybe Nurit will come too. It's already been two Saturdays that she hasn't come, she'll definitely come this Saturday." But in front of her, as she got off the bus, the wheels of the basket mocked her on each and every step.)

"This morning as well, the airlift continued to arrive," she read the announcer's words from the script. "One after another enormous Galaxy planes landed and were unloaded by skilled teams. From here the batteries of missiles were dispatched to deployment locations prepared for them throughout the country."

(At the end of the main road, which only had two lanes, her street branched off like a split from a split: before every election the head of the local council promised to tar it, and every winter it was filled with giant puddles on which oil stains floated and glistened, perhaps oil from motorbikes that passed there in the night like a delegation of the angels of destruction. She jumped from a broken piece of tile to a broken piece of brick, and from a broken piece of brick to a building plank; and right away the plank sank and murky water bubbled up to her stockings, and with each step she heard the squelching of the mud in her shoes, mocking, mocking, mocking. In the backyard of her home, which was no different from the other homes, not in its smallness nor in its improvised extensions, ugly plants grew from the edges of a sewage pit and in the surrounding mud, small oranges that had rotted while still on the tree turned black. Every summer high thistles sprang up in the yard and every winter crabgrass; but in spring yellow chrysanthemums would suddenly pop up as if they had lost their way. And her brother Eli, before he left home – the only one who really managed to – would look at the bees there and say: "look-look, they're fucking the flowers," and straightaway she'd blush like her sister when Moshon bent over her and gave a her a sucking kiss.)

"Isn't that what I said?" asked the actor.

"Sort of," Kinneret said still fanning the opening of her shirt with the supplement.

(The gate of the building was rusted and on the door of the entrance a stripe left by the last flood could be seen. Her grandfather failed to stem it, not by his mutterings nor by his angels – perhaps from the seven heavens they still saw those red marks on his face and smelt the eau de cologne even from there. But in the living room there was already no trace of the flood; her father renewed the varnish on the legs of the sideboard and the armchairs; her mother scrubbed the wallpaper as if cracks were not branching out here and there beneath it, crack from crack, and on each wall hung a snowy peak adorned with clouds or a lake of clear blue in whose waters a small boat was reflected.)

"My memory is actually fine," said the actor. "Have you decided to give me grey hairs as well?"

"I never gave anyone grey hairs," Kinneret waved the supplement again.

> In the car, on the edge of the road between the fields, the woman's hair turned darker and fell to the other side of the seat, undone and disheveled. "Do you hear them?" the woman asked. Her head leaned back and her nostrils flared as if trying to smell them from the depths of the darkness. "Listen for a moment, can't you hear them chirping?" The man lifted his head slowly from the place where it had been to the edge of the windshield. "Doesn't it remind you of something?" With her fingers, which didn't let go of him as he got up, the woman slowly swept strands of his hair; for a moment he listened to the dusky expanse around them, a sweaty silhouette whose features were all blurred, until lowering his head again.

"That's why you didn't hear," said Weintraub from outside. Merav looked at him through the windowpane and the nylon.

(And those illustrated landscapes – the peak and the clouds and the lake and the boat – were so distant, as if they were not only in another country across the sea, but in a different heaven: in the heaven of the heavens in which there are hordes of snow and hordes of hail, or in the third heaven in which there are hordes of mist and hosts of winds, or in the fourth heaven in which there are rivers of fire and repositories of dew and in which light angels flurry.)

"Jordan doesn't sink shots from the board," Weintraub said outside. "He just drops it in, that's why you didn't hear. You trying to make fun of Jordan?"

(Or in the fifth in which there are clouds of splendor; or in the sixth in which there are hordes of honey and a place prepared for righteous souls. She once read about them all in her grandfather's Book of Enigmas, which he hid beneath the mattress, where he also tucked away notes for all those prosecutors and the bedeviled who did not come to the wedding. And in the living room, when she entered in her uniform and wet shoes, she saw on each upright chair and each armchair the mask of the person whose place it was – the boxes of the twins decorated with smilies like their exercise books, and the others just a bare carton, which suited the apartment more than its pictures did. The living room table was moved away from the couch so that her grandfather could pass through when the siren is heard – and immediately it was heard, the clamor mocking mocking mocking: rising and falling, loud as it fell too, not because they were important to someone in this country or in the local council, but because of the proximity to the water tower on whose top the siren was placed.)

"What's up with you, Ezra. Take a look, why not. See for yourself if it went in. I threw Abudi's stone. Can't you see Abudi's stone there, the one with the whitewash?"

(He could pass through there in his wheelchair between the table and the couch, and through the filter summon all the hundreds of his angels, though nobody believed in his mutterings anymore since his attack – that's what they called it at home, the attack, and they would also say: "lucky there were people next to him," or "lucky a car didn't run him over," as if he had fallen in the middle of the road and not in a bar for prostitutes — but in an instant they were in the masks, in an instant the door was sealed, in an instant a cloth was placed in the space beneath the door and they each sat in their places and turned their gaze to the television: Merav and her parents and her twin sisters, Nina and Suzy, and her sister, Smadi, and her brother-in-law, Rafi, sat watching television.)

"Take it, Ezra, take it to see with, put some light on the garbage. Just don't say I cheated you. I don't need you having hard feelings about it afterwards."

(They watched television with the woman who came to receive a blessing, but her grandfather wasn't there: a few minutes before, when nobody noticed, he left in the wheelchair and began to wheel it to the sounds of the siren over muddy potholes and over rotting planks, which float for only a moment, and over broken pieces of sinking tiles, all the way to the tower. With his hands, which once again became strong, he transported it over the neglected plot, which the neighbors hoped to sell to a contractor, over the remains of the hothouse and a pile of wavy rusted tin sheets. He sank the thin wheels and their spokes into the mud and then salvaged them from it, and behind him hung a bag that he had prepared with earthenware pots in it. He advanced slowly, his hat shedding water from the rim, his clothes darkening and his beard unkempt, an old man in a wheelchair in the rain, advancing further and further on the rise of the path to the tower, on whose top the siren sounds and from which old election posters flutter while its concrete feet are sunk in giant puddles. Only then did he stop — she saw him from afar through the mask lenses —and rested a while and moved the packet onto his knees. One by one he took out the seven earthenware pots from it, peeling away the newspaper in which each one was wrapped, and for a moment the rain sprinkled down on them. He then bent down, as if whipped by the rain, and filled vessel after vessel with clear water from seven springs, a remedy for reversing evil onto its dispatcher.

Through the mask lenses dissolving in the rain she saw how he filled them all with the water from the puddle, and how he fastened his large hands onto each vessel, and how he crushed them like the cans of embers that he crumpled in his room in order to extinguish the other fire. One after another they shattered there and he flung fragment after fragment to his right and his left, in front or behind, into the hands of the spirits of the sky whose names he knew like the names of the angels. At the foot of the tower, from the middle of the puddle rising above the shreds of newspaper that were wrapped around the spokes of the wheels, her grandfather called to the spirits – Higrit and Shrochit and Ulfa and Kırdı – to arise and gust and break the bones of the archenemy, the wicked one who dispatched evil not only to him and to his family, but to the whole neighborhood, which had ostracized him.)

"Go on, Ezra, I'll believe whatever you say."

(And evil shall not be resurrected as water cannot be returned from the dust, and it shall not be healed as earthenware cannot be healed. In the pouring rain, beneath the lightning darting from the roof of the council building to the roof of Laniado's hall – in the firmament and the firmament of the firmament and in the third and fourth and fifth and sixth heavens – beneath the rolling thunder, around his drawn in lips he cupped the palm of his hands, which were dripping mud and blood onto his beard, and pieces of clay still stuck in their flesh, he called out in a raised voice becoming hoarse, coughing cracking and flagging: "I deliver him to you angels of wrath and ire, that you may strangulate him and ravage him and disrupt his inner thoughts and carry off the very notion of him and that he dwindle until reaching death.")

"Go on, Ezra, take the lighter, it's a present. You not gonna take a present from me? It's almost used up anyway."

(While her parents and her sisters and her brother-in-law were waiting, watching television: not the announcer and not the commentators giving their accounts, and not the comedy or the thriller, which were unable to provide distraction, but the marble floor white from all the light, which perhaps was spread out in the television set like the snowy landscapes in the pictures; and all their guests enter again to the piano melody and shake hands to the piano melody and sit down at the tables to the piano melody, and no sirens no motorbikes and no planes are noisy outside, and her sister Smadi sits in the bridal chair, which was decorated like a throne, her face radiant as the face of a queen.)

"Just be careful with that, huh?" the sergeant looked at the two prisoners from the entrance. In the dusk the flame of the lighter was seen for a moment until it withdrew back into the small case.

"Don't go causing us fires," the actor called out from his place. "Hey, Ezra? So what if Weintraub's annoying you, take no notice. The pilot might think you're signaling him to land here."

The sergeant advanced another step toward the entrance and in his hand the folder, which he waved to cool his face from the heat of the lamp.

"Take it take it, Ezra," Weintraub said from the road, "just don't think I'm lying to you. The game's ruined if you don't trust me. Check with your own eyes if there isn't a stone there with whitewash on it, just don't call Jordan a liar."

"To me," the sergeant turned to the room, "the thing that really gets me down is when someone tries to lie to my face. Nothing gets me down more than that, nothing." He glanced again at the road, and in the darkness the flame of the lighter was seen again, small, yellow, bluish, until it was concealed and disappeared. "For example, once, before we had the apartment, long ago, maybe ten years, we were living with some landlord who was even an accountant-"

"What do you mean even," the actor interrupted him from his chair, "they're the biggest crooks of them all. 'Even' – he says."

"Yes," the sergeant agreed with him, "only we didn't know that at the time. I was a boy and she was just a girl, hardly out of the army. And he looked like a respectable man, a suit and everything, go figure. You can't just be suspicious of someone for no reason. But right from the very beginning he started with some story about the previous tenant's electricity bill. We didn't want to make a fuss, the apartment was actually okay, really okay. So we said goodbye to a hundred shekels, a hundred shekels are not going make us go broke."

"Check it close up, Ezra, that's how you check?"

"Only after that there were municipal rates and water, again the same story. 'The previous tenant will pay you back, take my word.' And after that the phone bill, again the same story, only what? There were never previous tenants at all, that's what the neighbors told us, before that it was his office. And what gets me down the most?"

"It's a lighter, Ezra, not a spotlight."

"That for a moment you could see how he could be one way and then another, telling you the truth and then lying to your face. Just like that, in the same moment. One way and then another. He became so so nice, smiles up to his ears, you'd think he was about to tell you your lottery number. But all that was just to lie straight to your face. It would have been better to lie from the start, less heartache."

"Why did I bring the masks," said Merav, "weren't you in a rush to film before?"

"That pilot" – the actor was still looking at the window in whose depths the red bulb was circling again – "it's no big deal making rounds next to an anti-aircraft base. They never bring down anything anyway." Shechter looked at him for a moment from the wall against which he was leaning and afterwards looked at the sergeant who turned toward the doorway again and went out to the entrance.

"What, didn't I know this would happen?" he said, his face to the road, "I could have sworn this would happen. There's no two ways about these things."

Reddish light flickered in the paint cracks on the open door, illuminating the handle.

"When bad luck comes nothing can help."

A faintly charred smell filtered in from the entrance, and on the road opposite, the side of the trash can glowed for a moment; became hidden, darkened, and after a short while a greyish pillar rose.

The sergeant took a step forward. "Not with your hands buddy, with sand," he called out, "what else is the sand for? Just don't get burned." From the back of the room the actor got up from his chair in order to see the flame, which again flickered in the can between the remnants of egg cartons and chocolate wafer wrappings, until it was strangled by fistfuls of sand.

"Now take it to the fire hydrant," the sergeant said from the entrance, "you think that's all? Put water on it so that it doesn't catch alight again. That's all you need, Weintraub. In the end I really will have a word with Abudi."

"What do you want from me?" asked Weintraub from the road. "He lit it, is it my fault that it caught alight? With you it's always my fault."

(Monday night, you, the girl with light brown hair and the velvet ribbon: I saw your hair in the firelight, glitter darted in it and my heart caught alight: please contact me through this column.)

Na'ama turned her head.

On her left, next to the wall and the poster on it, Merav still flared her nostrils and sniffed. "Shouldn't you be dressed already?" In front of her face she waved the cover of the ripped out newspaper supplement that she had folded into two, a vigorous and rustling wave. "It's just that they're waiting for him at home, aren't they waiting for you at home?" The sergeant shot her a glance from the entrance and said nothing.

"Does she call you Gidi or Daddy?" asked the soundman from the corner of the room, again bent over the recording machine.

"From the window," the sergeant answered after a moment, "just when I arrive, straightaway she shouts, 'ickshaw-ickshaw!' I can hear her from below. Small as she is, she knows how to shout. I mean that in a good way."

Na'ama, who turned toward the bed, asked what exactly she's supposed to wear as Kinneret's mother: yes, just so that she understands.

(Monday night, an army base some place: you gathered your light brown hair into a velvet ribbon and I wanted to be tied to you instead of it; you rubbed your nose on the nose of the teddy bear and I wanted to grow fur like him and to rub my nose on your nose and to gobble you up.)

"Like there's a real shortage of clothing," Merav answered. "You could open a boutique here." The newspaper supplement rustled again in her hand and she gave it another fold.

"My mother doesn't wear my clothes yet," Kinneret said. "The other way round maybe. Her dresses, her hats – any time." She turned her head to the window in between whose stripes one of the prisoners was making an effort to turn the tap of the fire hydrant on and the other trying to tilt the can and its rising smoke toward the low nozzle. In the light coming out of the room the greyish swirls were illuminated and despite all their twisting they did not stray from their upward path, as if directed toward the plane that passed by again.

"So what does she wear, your Muthah?" asked the actor. "Just so that I understand." When he leaned his chair against the wall its small front wheels spun round in the air and the nickel plating glinted in the light of the lamp. "Don't you grin at me," he said to the lighting man, though he was not grinning at all, "people are trying to set up a scene and he grins. In a month he's getting married and he grins. You take care of your lamp instead of grinning, so that you can turn it down a bit. You've fried everyone here." He lifted his hand and moved his fingers in an upward undulating motion: "Like a hell-broth boil and bubble, fire burn and cauldron bubble. Hey, Ezra? Shakespeare was writing about you. Who didn't he write about?"

"Lately," Kinneret answered quietly, still looking out at the black expanse beyond the eucalyptuses, "she's started wearing my father's old shirts, she says it reminds her of their early days. She doesn't realize that she's not twenty anymore. Flannels and things like that, also cotton ones like yours," she said to the image of Shechter reflected in the window, "I swear that's how she goes around." Beyond the windowpane one of the prisoners placed the large shovel close to the fire hydrant to collect its water.

"Now you've had it Bergman," said the actor. "And if your shirt is taken from you, give your coat too, and he who strikes you on the right cheek, turn to him the other also."

Na'ama, who turned her gaze from the bed toward Shechter, surveyed his shirt from its ruffled collar to the loose tails and right away asked Kinneret if it would suit her: green and light brown. "Think it would suit me?" she twirled a strand of hair around her finger over and over until she unintentionally touched her cheek and felt her skin.

"Your hair-" Shechter began to say.

Tiny beads of sweat caused by the heat of the lamp sprouted from his forehead and he wiped them with the back of his hand. "Your hair's really nice, it's just that my shirt's on the way to the wash. It's not worth your while." He wiped his hand on his trousers, loose jeans shortened by an unskilled hand, their edges already becoming unstitched and with white tufts sprouting.

"No excuses," said the actor.

"It's not an excuse," answered Shechter, "if you do things like that for art, all right, then it's justified, but for this?" He gave a weary look at the bed and the stuffed animals sitting on it until turning his head as if thereby concluding the argument.

"But it's your movie, isn't it?" The eyes in Na'ama's round face were fixed on him, curious and wondering, and the glow of the lamp sparkled in both of them.

"Art it's not," answered Shechter, "whatever else it may be." He averted his eyes from her and turned his head to the window again.

"Why are you so-"

"So what?" asked Shechter but did not look at her.

"Nothing, you're just a bit like someone I know, that's all."

"Know favorably?" he asked her a moment later, still looking in the window at the crop spraying plane circling there. Round sweat stains spread from his armpits to his chest and to his back and new tiny beads of sweat sprouted on his forehead above his eyebrows.

"Of course favorably," answered Na'ama. "It's just that life gave him a blow and he didn't believe he'd come out if it. But you do come out of it." Again she touched the remains of a small pimple on her cheek, and her fingers remained there until she suddenly dropped her hand. "If there are enough people around who care, then you come out of it. That way you can come out of the very worst things, everything, there's nothing that you can't come out of."

"That's what you believe?" said Shechter. The green stripes beyond the nylon could be made out behind him. His shoulders sloped downwards from one stripe to another, as if the darkness outside was laden on them and not only on the treetops, which were still sharply defined.

"My father came out of it," answered Na'ama. "And if he could then anyone could. Anyone."

"So I'm like you father," said Shechter. He turned his head to the window, and the reflection of the room, which soon became apparent through the nylon, faded and blurred in the night beyond it: for a moment the plane flickered outside until disappearing again.

"Your shirt," the actor aimed a finger at him, "or you're a dead man, maaan" – he elongated the last syllable, enunciating like a black hoodlum from Harlem – "move, man, move" – he waved his finger in front of him, and Shechter looked at it for a while and said nothing – "up-up-up," he urged him on from his seat with his drawn finger.

For a while Shechter looked at the finger pointed at him until turning his eyes to the corner of the room, at the soundman bent over there. "Do me a favor," he said, "get them to lay off me. I really don't need this now."

The soundman looked at him and when he lifted his head from the recording machine the hair of his temples brightened further in the light of the lamp. "For the good old days?" he asked, rising from his crouched position and standing up. "They could come back, you know."

"Good?" said Shechter. "We were young and stupid. Me. Not you. The main thing is to get these two off my back now."

"This one," said the actor from his chair, which was slanted to the wall again, "is someone you shouldn't threaten at all, in the East he learned to get by on little. Tea and rice, rice and tea." He blew on the tip of his finger as if to dispel the smoke from the shooting. "What did you say those ones who walk around naked are called? Don't grin at me," he said to the lighting man who wasn't grinning at all. "What are you grinning about? He's getting married in a month's time and he grins at me. The ones who put handkerchiefs over their mouths so that they won't swallow insects?"

"Jains," answered the soundman. The top button dangled from his blue shirt and he ripped it off with two fingers and put it into his trouser pocket. "They also sweep the ground, the Jains, so that they don't step on ants." One by one he undid the other buttons and took off his shirt, and Kinneret, who looked at his bare, tanned shoulders and arms, scrutinized the tiny dragon that was tattooed on his right arm. The sergeant shot him a quick glance and right away went back to busying himself with the camera tripod.

"Is the dragon from the East?" Kinneret asked. "From Thailand?" She grasped her skirt with both hands and stretched it over her thighs.

"From Bangkok," said the soundman. He too looked at his arm for a moment: it was deeply suntanned, and Kinneret, resting her eyes on it, asked if he wasn't scared. The soundman shook his head. Opposite them, between the green stripes on the window, one of the prisoners lifted the shovel, which he filled with water, to the edge of the trash can from which smoke still rose.

"I mean about diseases," Kinneret said.

The soundman shook his shirt in front of his body over and over and grains of dust laid themselves out into the light of the lamp. "There are vaccines," he said to her, "for typhus, hepatitis, encephalitis. What not. Hepatitis A, Hepatitis type B, for everything."

"Hey, Ezra, you poured it outside," Weintraub's voice could be dimly heard through the windowpane and the nylon.

"Besides which you're careful," the soundman said. "Every day you take pills for malaria, purify the water, you can't even trust mineral water. You use iodine, you use ointments. You sleep only in a mosquito net." He shook the shirt again, stirring the grains that shed.

"What a waste Ezra," Weintraub said outside, "until you got it filled."

"Not those diseases," Kinneret said. "I know you can get vaccinated. After all my brother went there."

"Well, once in all the time I was there I got food poisoning," the soundman answered, "it was from eating seafood that had gone off, in Ceylon. Seafood soup, in Hikkaduwa. It actually looked good in the beginning. At the time it was called Ceylon, not Sri Lanka, the trouble with the Tamils hadn't started yet."

"I mean from the needle of the tattoo," Kinneret said, fixing her eyes on him.

"AIDS?" the soundman asked after a while. Kinneret nodded her head.

"My dragon's already fourteen years old. When it was done there was no such thing as AIDS. In seventy-nine, who knew except for him" – the soundman lifted his eyes to the ceiling – "that some monkey in Africa was spreading it. Did anyone know? In the first place nobody had ever heard of it then." He reached out his shirt to Na'ama and she grasped it by its ends and brought it close to her body, first to her shoulders and then to her stomach as well.

"What do you think?" she lifted her eyes and turned to them with a look at once coquettish and demure, and only her chin bent on the shirt collar so that it would not fall from her body. "Does it suit me?"

Shechter, who was still standing opposite the window, turned his head and nodded. For a moment his gaze rested on the denim shirt, which slid down almost to her rounded knees, and on one of them the remains of an old scab could be seen, like on children's knees. "Blue suits you even better than green," he said to her while under his arms the sweat spread further.

"Hey, Ezra, don't give up," the voice said from outside, "try again, just don't catch alight in the meantime."

Na'ama, who was looking sideways, slowly pulled the shirt away from her body. "How would you know?" she asked Shechter, "you didn't want to give me yours." She folded the shirt along its length and then its width and held it on her arm close to her body.

"And in the second place?" asked Kinneret. "In the second place, it's a long story," answered the soundman and leaned down to the recording machine: in front of his eyes was the tiny window in which the reels of the cassette could be seen.

"It's just that I sweated in it," said Shechter, "it should have been in the wash long ago." While he spoke he folded his arms, that way slightly hiding the stains that spread from his armpits.

"Well I'm not made of sugar," said Na'ama.

The soundman touched the small button and pressed it. "You can't sum up half a lifetime in one moment," he answered Kinneret. "Let's just say in short," he peered at the numbers of the meter, which were dropping to zero, "that it's a question of your outlook on life." For a moment he also looked at the gauges of the sound level whose fine needles quivered back and forth. "Whoa," said the actor from his chair, "I didn't know that diseases are a case of an outlook on life. Did you know that, Gidi? That diseases-"

"Try, try again," Weintraub said from outside. "What, you're also no good at getting the water in?"

"Diseases," the sergeant pointed the second camera at the bed, "just hearing about it makes me feel bad. My wife already knows that, she doesn't even ask me to go to movies like that. Not AIDS, not cancer, not the elephant man, not my left foot, not my right foot. Stuff like that's not for me." He pressed the zoom button at length and let go.

"I didn't think you were made of sugar," Shechter said, after pausing to answer Na'ama.

"Well done buddy," a voice was heard on the other side of the window, just slightly faint, "a few drops outside but who's counting."

"Although sometimes one might actually think," Shechter said. Merav, who was standing with her back to him, cut in: "So what movies do you go to together?" "Think what?" asked Na'ama. "That you are made of," Shechter answered and turned his head to the window toward the spot of light that moved in it, "is he coming again? It's unbelievable." "All kinds," answered the sergeant, "the last one we saw was-" – the rattling of the approaching plane drowned out his words – "we actually enjoyed it, although violence isn't usually our thing." "No diseases, no violence, so what is your thing?" "What exactly do you mean?" Na'ama hung the shirt over her arm again. "All kinds," the sergeant said, "Walt Disney for the little one, but not only that. Do you know *Koyaanisqatsi*? *Baraka*? She took me to that at the Cinematheque. Landscapes like that, which make you want to cry, not from diseases – from the landscapes." "That you're sweet," said the actor. "That's what Shechter meant, not me." "Is that dragon also connected with your outlook on life?" Kinneret studied the twirls of the tattoo again. "The dragon?" The soundman glanced at his arm, "as a matter of fact part of it is."

"Why should I count the drops for you, Ezra, is there a water shortage in the country? The main thing is to put it out already, of course you can do it. You've got potential, take it from me; I've got an eye for things like that."

"Which part, can I know?"

"The fire coming from its mouth," answered the soundman.

Merav let the folder drop from her hand, and when it hit the table, the sergeant turned his head to her from above the second camera. "What you looking like that for; isn't your little girl waiting for you at home shouting 'ickshaw-ickshaw' from the window?" She let the felt-tipped pen drop to the table as well and the sergeant followed it with his eyes as it rolled. "Ichshaw-ickshaw," she said again and the pen rolled further until it was halted by an office clip. She picked up the clip, bent its curves and right away the pen rolled on.

"What's got into you today?" the sergeant asked. "Did you get out of bed on the wrong side?" Around his eye the cover of the eyepiece imprinted a round reddish mark, and he passed his finger over it as the felt-tipped pen fell to the floor and rolled there.

"What's it got to do with how I got out of bed?" she answered him. For a moment she looked at the pen slowing down and did not pick it up. With a finger moistened with saliva she again tried to rub out the words written on the back of her hand, and the sergeant, watching her, took a piece of flannel from his pocket and approached her. Her black eyes, which shone from her dark face, gazed at him as he offered it to her.

"Should I wet it for you with some gasoline?"

"From the rickshaw?" Merav asked after a moment. "Ickshaw-ickshaw." She pulled at a thread, unraveling it from the edge of the piece of flannel and then unraveled another one, and when the plane rattled in the distance, flickering in the darkness, it sounded as if it mockingly intensified the sound of the unraveling. For a moment and then another it flickered in the window until exiting slowly from its range.

Between the frames of the windows the eucalyptuses were not visible; neither was the rickshaw nor the trash can from which constricted smoke perhaps continued to rise. Through the nylon, between the green stripes on the panes, a blurry reflection of the room could be deciphered: the made-up bed with its clothes and its stuffed animals, the posters on the walls, the tripods of the small lamps and the tripod of the large lamp, the two camera tripods and the eight characters overfilling the narrowed space.

(As in the exit of a small cinema in the middle of an amateurish short being screened); (as inside a mosquito net); (as in a sparkling public toilet in which someone is washing his armpits in a basin); (as in a phone booth whose receiver emits the hubbub of the student residence); (as in a cellar, sitting knee-to-knee in its depths beneath all the soles of the passersby); (as in a wedding hall whose guests are few but

that is completely filled with the rattling of motorbikes); (as
in the toilet of a pub); (as on an empty plot brimming with
three thin kittens);

(As in the tiny space progressing within the vast space around it, hours
upon hours and kilometers upon kilometers, delimited only by thin metal
panels and does not touch the passing landscapes as they slip away, not the
towns being built there nor the lives being lived in them, speculated from
a distance.)

"We're filming soon," said Shechter from his spot.

He was still leaning against the wall and looking at Na'ama,
holding the shirt close to her body again while trying to see
her reflection through the nylon sheet. "Na'ama's changing
clothes and we're filming. Are you waiting for me to say it in
the tone of a father?" Across from him, between the stripes
stuck on the window, her vague reflection could be seen and
for a moment one of the prisoners on the other side was
encompassed by it like a giant fetus.

"A shirt, not clothes," she corrected him from there,
flirting like a woman and raging in a child's voice, which had
not yet lowered and deepened. "I'm leaving the skirt. Maybe
Kinneret's mother goes around in just a shirt."

> And in the dusk of the car, between the
> road and the fields that looked like a giant
> black lake, she turned her head slightly:
> the glove compartment opened again. Its
> small door swung and a packet of parking
> vouchers crept out further and further.
> Above the man's shoulder, which moved
> slowly, the left windscreen wiper could be
> seen again, sticking out like the bone of a
> wing. "You see that," she asked in a slow
> rasping voice, "how they're scared of its
> noise? The minute it comes close they stop
> chirping." Her sweaty head leaned further
> back and her eyes shut halfway once more.

An old parking voucher fell silently from the glove compartment to the floor of the car and was swallowed up there. "What do you care about those crickets?" the man asked, and their long bodies moved in the thick dusk of the car. "Are we protecting nature now?" From under him, from the small warm space dense with their smells, a strangled giggle rose, rasping, relishing, fading into the rattling of the plane.

(Monday night, you, the girl in the blue shirt: I wanted to dive down into the blue of your shirt and touch your hidden ground, never to rise up from there anymore. Please contact me through this column.)

"Not me," Na'ama said and folded the shirt in the air.

The actor, who moved his eyes from the window and the small light passing in it, turned to Kinneret. "Not that I mind that you stay in uniform," he said to her, "the uniform actually suits you, but if you're intending to change-"

"Maybe lay off her already-" said the soundman to him.

"I just wanted to volunteer," said the actor and let it go. "Again he's grinning." – He glanced at the lighting man who was not listening to them at all – "have you ever seen anything like it? Just think about your wedding instead of grinning at me. About to set up house in the land of Israel and still he grins." The lighting man did not answer.

From the bed, beneath the cardboard boxes of the masks, Kinneret pulled out a black Benetton T-shirt and black jeans. She passed between the bed and the tripod of the lamp, swinging the clothes with her full limbs until she turned toward the inner room and was swallowed up in it with Na'ama. The door remained open for a moment and one of them promptly slammed it with a bare foot.

The actor sprawled out in the chair and lifted his feet onto the table, revealing the worn out soles of his shoes. "Interior, room," he announced and examined the frayed shoelace of his right shoe, which had been broken and was tied together in the middle. "Two women undressing." He spoke softly like someone inspired, perhaps imitating some screenwriter he knew from the film studies program. "Haven't you got something like that in the script, Merav-sweetie?" Merav did not answer. "What could be lovelier than two women undressing?" He lifted his right hand to the height of his shoulder and moved it slowly in the air: "Soft music playing in the background or stormy music as they begin to dance with each other very slowly. Two women undressing. The light of the television flickers on their bodies, the face of the announcer or the snow at the end of transmission. The snow."

"No I haven't got something like that," answered Merav.

"Me neither," said the actor. "I have nothing. Oh horrid and bitter day! Oh sorrow and grief, sorrow and grief!" He recited with great feeling placing the palm of his hand close to his chest. "Though since a youth do I as a man seem, as a woman shall I weep and my deeds to my animal nature bear witness" – he lifted the palm of his hand opposite his face as if surveying his reflection in it – "a flawed faced woman in a man's image: not man, not human."

"Good that you know," said Merav to him.

Opposite them, the plane moved again in the squares of the window, drawing a fine line of light that was fragmented and then rejoined past them. The sergeant asked where to place the camera, and Shechter turned from the window, crossed two fingers of his right hand over two from his left and observed the bed through the setting he framed.

"Here," he said, "we'll take close-ups afterwards. The long shots will be from your camera anyway."

A giggle was heard on the other side of the door, stopping for a moment and starting up again, and the actor, who imitated Shechter and looked through crossed fingers at the door, asked: "Is that you, sugar?"

Na'ama did not answer (they both laughed, not just her: the girl with the ringing laugh). For a moment nothing could be heard (like in the taxi on the way from the cadet pilots', until the driver peered at them in the mirror and said: "just

don't mess up the upholstery, huh?") and right away the
rattling of the plane rose.

("We just drank," Kinneret then answered him to calm him
down, "beer-beer-beer. Tube-org," she burped unashamedly,
and Na'ama stuck her head out the window of the taxi and
right away the wind thrust fingers through her hair disheveling
it, and from the shop window of the "Mashbir" across the
way, all the mannequins standing there gazed at her, men in
suits and women in evening gowns, there wasn't a soul who
didn't look at her and wonder: is that Na'ama? Opposite the
entrance to the center a beggar slept, not the old man with
the cartons, but a young man, perhaps the other one was
already tired of Bashan cows on Mount Shamaria and of the
Lord of hoshts – she chuckled in the wind, she giggled, she
almost burst from laughing and right away was ashamed of
herself, but continued to giggle. "Put your head back in," the
driver shouted at her, "d'you want me to get a fine because of
you? You're a disgrace to your uniforms." "Eight, eight, where
are you eight," a voice sounded in the transmitter. "We're in
the air force entertainment group," Kinneret answered and
leaned back. "Tube-org." She closed her eyes. "Sure, the air
force entertainment group," the driver said to them from
the mirror, "a mile high and spaced out," and his black eyes
shone in the dusk. Only in the elevator in Kinneret's building
– there was no way she would agree to go with Na'ama to her
sister's and sleep there – she saw the two of them as the taxi
driver had seen them. She didn't smooth down her disheveled
hair with her hands, didn't turn aside her cheek with the
pimples and didn't turn her gaze away from her chubby
knees either, but directed it to the one standing opposite her
there in the mirror and said to her: "Bassan-cow" – that's
what she said to her reflection and emitted a burp from her
throat. Afterwards she ran to Kinneret's shiny bathroom and
vomited her guts out into the toilet bowl, and from there still
heard her voice saying to the cadet pilot, hearing it absolutely
clearly: "what, don't you know how to aim?" As if they aimed
that thing of theirs not from above the bowl but from inside

it, and immediately she vomited again: she, Na'ama, who as
yet had not fully loved a boy, whose sister called her Na'ama
the naïve, thoughts like that passed through her head. And
afterwards, her face washed; in Kinneret's room, in which
clothes were strewn everywhere, not only on the bed but also
on the chair and the table, she stood opposite the window,
which between the remnants of the masking tape was as clear
as if there was no pane there – "with Sano," Kinneret said
behind her, "with Sano for windows" – and she tried to see
her home and the cadet pilots' building and her sister's roof
too, with the sheets always hanging there, brandishing in her
face what was done on them at night or silent like the plucked
wings of angels – "it's one thing if you suggested going to her
place," Kinneret said from behind her shoulder, "but to sleep
like that on the roof" – and now put on the black Calvin
Klein's over her smooth long legs without having to breathe
in even a little in order to fasten them. "Should I walk in like
this," she turned to Na'ama, "without a shirt? They'd have a
stroke on the spot," but already she lifted the black T-shirt
over her head, pulled it over her large, beautiful breasts and
zipped the pants with one tug.)

"Room, interior," said the actor. "Two women are laughing.
Is there anything lovelier than two women laughing? Dimples
form in their cheeks and in other unmentionable places, out
of my reach. The record needle is stuck in the groove" – "the
disc," Kinneret called out from the other side of the door –
"over and over. One of the women is shouting." He spun
the spray canister on the table and it circled in place until
stopping opposite him. "Truthordare?" The canister sparkled
for a moment in the light of the lamp.

"What's happening, girls?" the sergeant called out and the
reddish ring, which the eyepiece cover had imprinted around
his eye, darkened.

"We're almost finished," Na'ama answered from the other
side of the door (but was still doing up the buttons of the
blue shirt with her short fingers, which she did not like; one
after another were buttoned until Kinneret bent toward one

of the pockets placing her nose close to it. She flared her nostrils and said in a whisper: "Doesn't it smell good?").

"What are you grinning about," said the actor.

("Yours is also old. I saw you eyeing him." "Maybe he was doing the eyeing, not me," Na'ama answered quietly and did up another shirt button.)

"Room, interior," the actor said from his chair. "One of the women is shouting while the other is trying to defend herself. She wants to cry but her eyes are dry and her heart is dry. Her friend pulls out a large suitcase covered with dust from under the bed and begins putting all her clothes into it: dresses and blouses and slacks and belts, what not, she pulled them out of her wardrobe together with the hangers so as not leave anything behind her. Oh horrid and bitter day! Oh sorrow and grief, grief and sorrow."

Merav approached the bed and lifted up one of the cardboard boxes. She opened it with her stained hand, overturned it onto the bed and emptied the other two as well. In the light of the lamp the large lenses of the masks glistened and the rubber straps twisted like smooth black strands down their necks.

"Room interior," said the actor from his chair. "The woman lifts the suitcase. She tells the other to get out of the way. Not to try and persuade her, because there's no likelihood of that. Not to try and stop her, it's a waste of time, just to get out of her sight. To send what's left by post. The cassette with the dubbing, yes, when he gets a copy. Not that she needs any memento of him, but in order to get work, she still needs that. By post, she can still depend on the post. At least on that. She moves near the door. She puts her hand on the door handle. She opens the door. And here they are-"

In the wide gap Kinneret and Na'ama can be seen, one wearing close-fitting black jeans and a tight black T-shirt and the other in the soundman's loose blue shirt. On their left, in the poster stuck on the wall, the female soldier continues to smile her smile in which a tooth is blacked out by a felt-tipped pen.

"Madame et Monsieur," announced the actor from his chair, presenting the two of them with his raised hand. "Damen und Herren, Ladies and Gentlemen-"

Na'ama, on whom the soundman's shirt dangled almost to the knees, hiding her skirt, asked if it looked like she didn't have anything on underneath. "Do want it to look that way," asked the actor, "Like you've got nothing on underneath?" He spun the spray canister on the table again.

"Me?" she asked (because she, Na'ama, wasn't at all like that), "no way."

(Only when she drank did she become like that, but ever since she hasn't drunk even once, she didn't even drink at the Passover meal: she had been so shocked by her behavior, by the ugliness that rose with the beer in her throat that she swore never to drink again. "I'm not even going to sleep on the beach ever again," Kinneret said to the back of her neck then and she smelt her breath, "I once did and it was enough for all time." Beyond the window the city could be seen in the distance, large and wondrous like the cities in which her parents toured on their honeymoon, when they were still young and good looking and in which their love was photographed in each and every picture: photographed in their eyes, in the closeness of their bodies, and even in the way they leaned on the rail of the bridge and the way their hair waved gaily in the wind; all the coming years could not be seen then, not the problems at work and not the slow advancement, not the difficulties of the mortgage and not the firing, not the previous wars in which her mother feared for her father and was alarmed every time the doorbell rang, and not the last one in which she sat with him on a bed, but was as far from him as if he was in another country or in his own sealed room, which he took with him everywhere.)

"Yes you," answered the actor.

(On that same morning when Na'ama went to the bank – at the time her father still feared that people would ask questions, would point at him, gossip the minute he turned his back – and waited in line, a tall woman came and stood next to her, about thirty. She stood very erect and was well groomed but her skin was tired and tiny wrinkles were furrowed in the corner of her eyes and on her cheeks, wrinkles from laughter or wrinkles from crying, that was something Na'ama couldn't tell nor did she care: because if there was one thing that Na'ama absolutely hated it was people who tried to push in front of her in a queue, because to people like that, who push in, she's just thin air, someone who needs to be bypassed in order to reach the counter quickly. Na'ama took a small step forward and right away the woman moved as well, and when Na'ama advanced forward slightly so did the woman next to her. But she was not looking in the direction of the cashier at all, but glanced past Na'ama at the young man sitting opposite the investment consultant; having completed signing a form he got up. "Oshik!" she suddenly called out as if just at that moment she had noticed him. He was taken by surprise and turned to her with the cardboard box hanging on his shoulder, and for a moment they embraced tightly alongside her, as if from the soles of their feet to the tip of their foreheads their bodies were trying to recall something that Na'ama was yet to know. "I heard you've moved to Haifa," the woman said when they took off and unwound the straps of the boxes that had become slightly entangled. "Don't look so amazed, I know everything about both of you, everything. I've got my detectives, what do you think." "Now you come back? Now," the young man said, "when everyone's getting out of here?" He was as tall as the woman and for a moment Na'ama forgot about the queue and even about her father and studied the way their features fitted each other: eyes opposite eyes, nose opposite nose, lips opposite lips.

"That's how it goes," the woman answered quietly, "we were forced by all sorts of things," and when she fell silent for a moment the din inside the bank was heard, in which everyone was rushing to finish their dealings before shutting themselves up in their homes. "But didn't you have an apartment there?" "We rented," the woman answered, "what did we have, nothing, nothing. Not that we've got anything

now, nor in the foreseeable future as well." She fell silent
again and outside the bank the dim sound of an airplane
was heard – a Boeing or a Jumbo or an Airbus, not a small
plane like this – and when the sound lessened she said: "Well,
there's no need to worry about me. It's just that I'm still jet
lagged and talking too much. A week here and still jet lagged.
I just can't control my mouth." Outside the noise rose and
after a moment the young man said in a loud voice, which
did not match the expression on his face: "It's not actually
dangerous around there now, is it?" "Not dangerous, what do
you mean 'not dangerous'?" the woman answered, "who told
you that? It's a myth. We were robbed just like that in the
middle of the day. Some black guy comes up, I had on some
chain, d'you remember my chain? With the fish? He took
it from my neck, ripped it off just like that with his fingers.
Not some tough guy, just a regular black guy." "And didn't
he do anything?" "I told you what he did!" "Not the robber,"
the man said, "Danny." "Danny?" the woman answered. "We
were both in shock. I could have been raped in the middle of
the street right there and he wouldn't have done a thing, your
friend. But enough, I've said too much. It'll be okay. You
don't have to worry about me. He'll finish specializing, start
earning a bit, life will be different. And with the child it will
definitely be different." In an overeager voice she emphasized
her confidence, and as she spoke the man put the form into
his pocket. "Well," he said "ever since I can remember he
talked about New York, even in the squadron he dreamt
about it."

"In the squadron?" the woman said. "Believe me, Oshik,
it was a different world back then in the squadron. It's as if
everyone there was better than they really were. Sometimes
that's what I think. Don't you think so?" "I stopped thinking
about the squadron a long time ago," the young man said,
and Na'ama then saw how something in the woman's stature
suddenly dwindled and disappeared in the expanse of
the bank. "Where've I got the time," the man said, "who's
got the time for nostalgia and all that." The woman said
nothing and afterwards made an effort to ask, just to keep

the conversation going: "Did you come here on business?"
"No, not on business. For the apartment. Business is actually
fine," the man answered, "really nothing to complain about."
"But you were given the apartment for the wedding, weren't
you?" the woman said. "What you looking like that for, I told
you I know everything, even in which hall you celebrated.
Argaman? I've got my sources. I've kept contact with all the
old friends, Oshik, all of them, postcards, telephone calls,
what not. You don't have to worry about me, you really don't
have to worry about me. D'you know the thing I think of
most, more than anything? That trip we made to Mount
Hermon in the winter. Out of everything that's what I
remember most. I was a kid at the time, really a kid, that
uniform still had the smell of the recruitment center. The way
you said to that driver at the time, the one who was there,
you know, what was he called, Swissa?" "Samucha," the man
said after a moment, "Eli Samucha." "You said to him, 'let's
take her with us, what d'you say, so that the guys will see a
woman first thing in the morning.' Out of everything that's
what I remember most, isn't that funny? In New York, in
Queens, with a meter of snow outside, well, you must-" "it's
just that they're waiting for me," the young man shifted his
gaze from his watch. "You're in building materials, aren't you?
Why do you look that way, I told you I know everything.
They even told me the address. I actually used to go around
there a lot once, isn't that a coincidence? Maybe we'll come
buy from you sometime, we'll be needing some . . . some-"
"Come, why not," the man said. "We'll come we'll come," the
woman said, "you'll give us a discount, no? I'll tell him to say
hello to Uncle Oshik, say hello. We'll come with the pram we
brought from America, what does he care about his parents'
troubles?" And though the plane had already drawn away and
wasn't heard like this one here, she spoke in a very loud voice
when she parted from the man, and Na'ama saw how she
slowly lifted her hand in the expanse of the bank and opened
and clenched her fingers over and over the way babies wave

goodbye and how each time her nails were further embedded into the flesh.)

"Don't make yourself out to be innocent like that," the actor said.

(And afterwards as she moved forward in the line, she thought about that baby being born without them really wanting it, and how it will grow up not understanding that it's expected to repair not only the waning love between its parents who met in the army – perhaps the woman was a squadron clerk like her mother – but also a golden chain, which a thin black man ripped from his mother's neck in another country. And afterwards when she went out, she thought about her parents and about her big sister who perhaps was born at a time when they didn't really want her and that's why she went from school to school, from one workplace to another and from one rented apartment to another, until reaching her roof – "the further away from it all the better. Also if you ever feel like jumping, where can you jump from, the first floor? Just kidding, just kidding" – and on the way she wondered if her mother too, when she was still young and statuesque, once stood in some branch of a bank and from a queue covertly peered at a young man sitting in the distance.)

"You, what are you grinning about," said the actor. "Makes out like he's not grinning, but inside he's grinning."

"Believe me I'm not," answered the lighting man. Again he was busy with the lamp tripod, trying to open the butterfly screw of one of its joints, and the side of his hand was dirtied by the rusty drizzle that trailed there.

(But all in all she was completely different, Na'ama's mother: she loved her father before he was fired and afterwards as well, loved him when his hair fell out and thinned and when he began to grow a paunch, loved him even when he would pick his teeth with a match and check afterwards what had been removed; the way he, Na'ama's father, accepted her weathered skin, and the roots of her hair showing, and her dozing off opposite the television with an open mouth wearing a tattered dressing gown. And each of these things and all of them together did not seem ugly to Na'ama, the way they did to her sister – "that's why I don't get married, why ruin everything? Even when I was still living at home it was like that, it's got nothing to do with his being fired. Sometimes I look around here, when it gets dark, and I think, let it stay like this all the time, at least it would suit my mood" – on the contrary, there's much beauty there, in their mutual deterioration and the habits rooted in it, since more love is needed to love someone that way, with all his faults.)

"I asked you something before," said the actor.

"It's not that I'm drunk or that I'd want something like that," Na'ama stretched the skirt beneath the edge of the shirt.

(Beyond both their reflections, the city could be seen in the distance, great and sparkling like the cities in which her parents were photographed years before she was born: at the foot of the Statue of Liberty and at its top, at the foot of the Empire State Building and at its top, looking in a telescope as if through it they could see not only all the other skyscrapers and the tiny people walking in the streets, but also Na'ama, whom they'll conceive on one of those nights ["did you want me to sleep on the roof," Kinneret said behind her, "it would be better to sleep on the beach, even though I swore that I'd never do it again"]: her light brown hair, her glowing eyes, and her funny ears that know how to listen to people, and also those pimples that in the end will heal, as the doctor promised, and how one night she'd bring about a reconciliation between them, when they were already not so upright and embracing: at the time her mother came running cumbersomely from the bedroom, from the bed whose right side remained completely ironed, to the sound of the siren rising and falling, and Na'ama ran to her father in the kitchen. He sat there opposite an ashtray full of cigarette butts and next to him a cordless phone, as if he'll still be asked to advise on some urgent problem that only he knows how to solve – "open your eyes a little," her sister said on the roof, "they've been like that for a long time. And him, as long as I can remember him he's been like that. It's just when he was still working you didn't notice it that much, where do you think I picked up depression from?" – "Leave me alone," her father said from his seat, "go away, the both of you." But she was already pulling his hand, the large, rough hand that had lifted her up on to his shoulders when he would begin to run with her from room to room shouting "horsey-horsey" or hoist her up to the tassels of the lightshade in her room or spin her in the air like this plane. "For my sake, and for mommy's sake come, even if you don't believe in it, okay?" That's what she said to him, Na'ama, and led him through the kitchen porch past heaters whose elements were broken, an old vacuum cleaner, a dismantled chair, towers of toilet paper, and through the bathroom in which his hairs were wrapped around the plug hole of the basin, and the passage which he trod through at night in squashed shoes that had turned into open-backed clogs. She led him to her room, to all the teddy bears, which continued to sit there fluffy and smiling.)

"You don't have to get drunk for that," said the actor. "Did anyone say you're drunk?"

(And on the chest of drawers in the corner, the collection of notes she had amassed at school, and the collection of aromatic erasers, and a piece of plaster cast with the delightful dedications that were written on it when she broke her leg. "You dragged me here," her father said when they sat on her bed, "now just leave me in peace." He still held the cordless phone, like a deposed king left with only a scepter from his entire kingdom – "before you were born, I had a parrot, not a talking one, just an ordinary parrot, she bought it for me. At night I'd put a kind of material over its cage so it would go to sleep. Well that's what it's like here sometimes, when it gets dark. In the end, after a month, it was lying on the floor of the cage, just like that, he didn't even let me bury it, straight to the toilet. He said: what's the point. I was six years old at the time, barely six years old and that's what he had to say to me" – and after a long moment in which the sound of the siren rising and falling was still heard, she reached the mask out to him. While he still hesitated she brought it close to his tired face, which suddenly seemed to her very small in its frailty, and carefully fastened the straps to his head, pair by pair. "Why are you so careful," his voice was heard through the filter, "my fringe isn't coming back." But after a short while he rose up a bit, heavy and cumbersome, and pulled out a squashed Snoopy from under him and fixed its ear, which had folded, and which Na'ama took as a sign ["I woke up with a dead fish," Kinneret said, "Mullet-mullet-mullet. Lucky nobody passed by there, they really would have finished me off."]

Beyond the nylon and the windowpane and the shutters and the dark was the street, and beyond it were other streets with buildings in which hordes of men and women sat, all the couples to which she would always listen with the pricked up ears of a small animal and the large heart of a Bashan cow: the dark girl with the pimples who said, "what didn't I try, I tried everything," perhaps someone was stroking her cheek above the black edge of the mask; and the elderly woman who said, "there's no love, none, just neediness. That's what there is," perhaps someone was hugging her; and the bespectacled woman who said, "I learned it all from books. Everything. Chinese, French, what not," she and the thin man were perhaps rubbing each other's filters in a council flat like a pair of Eskimos in an igloo; and the beggar with his pram and the cartons, perhaps someone gave him food and shelter and a new transistor, because they were all human: all the beggars and the pimpled, the elderly, the orphans and the hired workers who dreamed of building an empire, all the neighbors who knocked on the wall, all those fired who did not believe they would find work anymore, something indecipherable would make their features beautiful and endear them to the ones who loved them. ["Mu-hu-let," Kinneret said again to the back of her neck. "Wash your face," she replied to her, "it will do you good." "I don't want to feel good." "I cleaned up there," she said to her, "I vomited my guts out, but I cleaned it all up." "Have you ever done it in a toilet?" Kinneret asked {"you mean six munts you don't do dat, becoz dere is no night?" Foam fizzed in a glass and bubbles burst in it pak-pak, they flew around the pub and the

UN official nodded. "You kidding," she said, and Kinneret
sang. "So what do you do den, hunting pinguins? Pinguins-"
a pale hand moved on the softness of a dark warm thigh, and
Kinneret sang. "Dzis berd, black and white, not like dzis, az
in dzeh orchestra? Dzeh constructa?"}] And in some distant
window, in a different street or a different suburb, perhaps a
boy her age or an adult with experience looked at his parents
like her, and like her thought about all the buildings beyond
the sealed window, the tens and hundreds and thousands,
and about all the couples sitting in them, and also about a
distant window in another street or another suburb, small and
shuttered but ready to be opened at any moment, a window
beyond which she sat, Na'ama, and said into the filter in her
most hushed voice: "the middle of the night, somewhere in
the dark bombed city, you're out there beyond the window:
before I die, please, just once.")

"The ugliest things," said the actor, "can be done when
one's completely clear-headed. Believe me, I'm talking
from experience."

"If it disturbs you so much," Merav said to her, "you can
cover your legs. With a civilian blanket, not just an ordinary
one. It actually smells good."

"From Gidi's home, not just something ordinary, hey
Merav?" the actor said.

Merav did not answer. She reached the masks out to
both of them and the straps dangled black and smooth from
her hands.

The spray canister was placed upright on the table with
a thud, and the actor asked if on the soundtrack, besides
the report on the television, "viper-snake"[27] would be heard.
"How could it be without it," he asked, "adder's fork, toe of
frog, lizard's leg, bat's wing" – he listed them on his fingers
one after the other like the specifications of a cake recipe
– "double, double toil and trouble, fire burn and cauldron
bubble! That's also Shakespeare," he said, "Macbeth." Merav
lifted the third mask from the bed. "Lizard's tail, hamster's
tooth, leg of owl-"

27   Code words used on the radio to warn of an impending bomb attack

"Maybe shut up already?" Merav said.

"Raccoon's eyebrow-"

"Put the mask on already," Merav said.

"Fire burn and cauldron bubble."

"First of all you open the straps," she watched him as he busied himself with the mask, clumsy and awkward in his movements, as if someone had replaced his face and used his hands against his will: lifted the straps up, bent them, pulled and released them. "First the chin," she said to him, "like this. Now close them. Not that one, first from the top."

"Agama's eyelid, cuttlefish claw-" his voice became dim in the filter.

"Those, yes, together. Now the second ones. Tightly, not like that."

"Mouse's moustache-"

"Tighter," Merav said to him.

"Sunbird's egg, fire burn, cauldron bubble." He fastened the straps further.

Merav, who was standing opposite him, placed the palm of her hand on the filter and blocked all its holes, obstructing the air path. "Try to breathe," she said, "to see if it's sealed." The tips of her fingers surrounded the edge of the filter, and on the other side of them the actor's voice became dim; the rubber sides were sucked further into his cheeks, his face narrowed, and in the lenses shining in the light of the lamp his eyes grew and sparkled. His voice was silent. Outside, beyond the windowpane, the plane rattled, buzzed, dimmed and drew away.

"Go call the medic, Ezra," Weintraub said from the road, "tell her Weintraub's dying, dying."

Merav took her hand away.

"Go on, tell her just as Weintraub was trying to put out the burning garbage, he got a hundred per cent burnt. I'll need new skin Ezra, from her ass, tell her that."

Merav moved away to the corner of the room.

"Mask interior," said the actor. "Like a hell-broth boil. You trying to do me in, Merav-sweetie? The great Miki Le-Mic? Never mind."

"Is any as merr-y and joll-y as me – oh mask"

He stopped singing. "Back she went, he did not wait; not turning her face to look back" – he marched two fingers on the table stepping hurriedly – "oh horrid and bitter day, black as pitch."

"You make fun of everything," Merav said to him. "Is there anything you don't make fun of? You even make fun of your girlfriend who left you. Would you make fun of your own family? You'd sell them all just for a laugh, wouldn't you? Of course you would. Like you've got anyone else besides them."

"I've already sold them," said the actor. He spun the canister on the table again. "Truthordare?" The canister stopped opposite the wall and he pushed it with his finger until it pointed at him. "Truth," he said. "The whole truth and nothing but the truth. As to the selling – so did I sell, as to my life – to foulness it fell, my soul I pawned and to this day am yet to redeem. Corpus meum, sanguinis mei." – he sprayed from the canister – "What, don't you want to cover up, Kinneret?"

("Dzis singer? She doz not know how to sing. I ken sing as she doz. And to move like her also. To tell you somesing? She is just eh gerl wiz big tits. It is not a problem to hold a microphone like dzis end to move sexily" – with round movements, with rotating rear, with thigh rubbing thigh – "now she's making herself big shot, walking among dzeh audience. See? Sank God she iz not sitting on der-")

"No," Kinneret answered, "I'm not ashamed of anything."

"Well I am," the actor said. "I sent the entire acting class to my home town to study types" – he spun the canister again – "forget about somewhere like Kiryat Shmona,[28] that's what I said to them, Kiryat Shmona is right here, take it from me. They all went to the Romanian's cafe in the housing project,

28 Town whose population is largely of a low socioeconomic status

no problem finding it, from a kilometer away you can hear the backgammon. For almost a week they sat there all night and each one came back with a type. One did the Romanian, one the Salonikan, one did Rachel who does her clients while standing, one did the Persian, they all rolled the backgammon dice once next to their hearts, once next to the ear and once next to the forehead, just like the professionals. But the best part, the best part was the one who lifted his glass like that in the light as if he'll see something there, what do you mean, treasure's what he'll see there, he'll see his screwed up life and still mumble to himself: 'That's what they believe there, that's how it is with them,' he didn't stop mumbling. 'That's what they believe, just because of that they killed us, Miku, just because of that me and Jurek-' even though I wasn't there he carried on speaking to me." His eyes blinked and he lifted the palms of his hands until they came up against the lenses of the mask and after a short while wiped each lens with a finger, which went to and fro like a windscreen wiper, and promptly asked: "So what happened on Purim, who did we beat?"

In the squares of the window the plane drew a fine fragmenting line again.

"Will you help me?" Kinneret said and took a step. She stood opposite the soundman, close to his bare chest, and for a moment he looked in her eyes whose brightness was emphasized by the makeup. The tiny dragon rose up with his right arm as he placed the black mask on her face and covered the red fleshy lips with the filter. He fastened a pair of straps by pulling one onto her neck and after it the other, and also fastened the upper strap to her head. She did not blink through the large lenses; also when her breasts touched him for a moment through the fabric of her shirt.

"The Eeegyptians or the Purrsions?" the actor asked. "The Eeegyptians are actually Passover, what am I talking about."

Na'ama, who was still holding the mask in her small hand, looked at Shechter from the window in whose pane she was reflected, as he gazed outside through it. "And nobody's gonna help me?" She spoke in a pampering voice.

For a moment Shechter hesitated, until he swiveled round and took a step toward her, stopping when she turned her face to him. He was careful not to move his arms away from his sweaty armpits, and afterwards pulling slowly he fastened the pair of straps to her head, the one and then the other, and her hair was gathered beneath them, smooth and lustrous. His glance rested awhile on the remains of a pimple on her cheek, and right away he lifted his eyes and gently affixed the upper strap, taking care that her hair not get caught. A faint smell of shampoo wafted from her hair and Shechter lingered for a moment and withdrew.

"Maybe the Greeks?" asked the actor.

"Go tell her Jordan's writhing in agony, perishing – dead. Won't she pay her last respects to Jordan?" Between the green stripes of the window the second prisoner was moving, dragging the rake behind him as the rattling of the plane drowned out its sound.

Shechter pulled his shirt tails over the front of his trousers and crossed two fingers over two fingers in front of his eyes demarcating a frame within them. "Sit there," he said from below it, "next to the teddy bears. Okay?" Tiny beads of sweat slid on his forehead and sprouted within his eyebrows as well. The actor got up with the mask on his face, approached the bed and sat there leaning his back against the wall.

"Come on girls, please be seated," he intoned nasally through the filter the way he had summoned them in the scene that they filmed. Owing to their lingering he deepened his voice and called to them again with the exaggerated emphasis he used when quoting: "Wife and daughter of mine, dearer to me than life, pray return-"

Further on, beyond the eucalyptuses, between the fields, which darkened with the footprints of herons that would land there during the day, the man lifted his head and listened from inside the car. Near the corner of the windshield the parking voucher that was stuck there could be made out, barely visible in the darkness, hovering over it. "Now I can hear them," he said. The chirping rose from the fields again, rhythmic and monotonous as if it was the beat of the night. "He scared them," he said and bent his head down. "Just when he left they started." "The crickets?" asked the woman in a very hoarse voice, and the small light was still drawing away in the rear windshield, tiny and slow like the light of a weary firefly.

"Come on girls," the sergeant placed his eye close to the eyepiece.

They both turned to the bed and sat down on either side of the actor. Kinneret, who lifted her legs onto the mattress, grabbed her ankles and gathered them up to the incline of her thighs, crossing her legs in a squat. Na'ama leaned on a pillow and her shirt was pulled backwards.

"What exactly are we supposed to do?" Na'ama asked and with the blanket she covered her thighs on which bright bristles glistened in the light of the lamp, her chubby knees, and her khaki skirt whose edges were exposed. Inside the black rubber her eyes looked at Shechter and her pupils sparkled beneath the glare of the lenses.

"As father of the family" – the actor spread his hands out to his sides and rested them on their shoulders – "I suggest . . ." When they shrugged off his hands, he left them alone, but in his regular voice suggested that they should sing together: yes, singing simply helps one against fear. "Who doesn't know that? I don't," he said. "If I had only recorded myself each time I was afraid, let's say even each second time, or third, I would have cleaned up from all the records. Gold, platinum, what not, what awards wouldn't the great Miki Le-Mic have been given."

"Discs," Kinneret said, "not records." Her hands remained in her lap, resting there on the black fabric of her trousers.

"Discs," the actor said from the other side of the filter. "It's just that in the war singing didn't help that much. Nothing helped. Not singing together, not jokes, not a thing. The fear overcame everything." He placed the palm of his hand on the filter and left it there and the black sides of the mask were again sucked into his cheeks. "A washed out rag" – he dropped his hand – "was stuck under the door[29] and stank of caustic soda, what do you mean stank, it was worse than a missile with a chemical warhead, and as for the other washed out rag, he sat on the bed and stank from the sweat of fear. That's what was left of the great Miki Le-Mic, special events and happy occasions. I didn't even look at my girlfriend, from all the fear."

(Not with closed eyes, which no lenses protected, and not at her bright face, which was not darkened by the black rubber of a mask, but was very pale and completely exposed: what do you mean exposed, even during the night she wasn't exposed like that. First, he went down to the street to buy cigarettes for both of them from the blind man's kiosk, where for an entire month – when he still dreamt of playing Tiresias – he studied how he tilted his head back and listened to the approaching steps or to the rustle of a newspaper picked up from the counter or the sound of the coins placed there, and while halfway there the siren began. It rose and fell above the roofs, round and round, frightening here and frightening there and frightening from all directions, from the City Garden tower block –"there used to be lionzsh there," the Polish woman said, "in the middle of the night, lionzsh" – to the hotels on the beach front that were emptied of tourists. Lionzsh began to chase him, and tigers and rhinoceroses and bears and what not, all the animals from that zoo, that's how he ran. While running, he put on the mask and in the building went up the stairs three at a time, two at a time and one by one and opened the door puffing and sweating from fear. He opened it and still did not hear her on the cushions,

29   One of the Home Front directives in the event of a possible gas attack was the placing of a rag soaked in caustic soda under the door of a sealed room

which they bought together – "enjoy them, that's what they're for" – saying to him, in a quiet and very fragile voice, "what do you mean fragile, compared to it glass is iron." "I forgot it in the studio. Or in the rehearsal hall, what difference does it make now. I forgot it." He only heard his own breath, each and every breath, which the filter filtered, as she continued to look at him from the bed with a naked face. He only heard the inhaling and exhaling and did not dare look at her.)

"Tell him," the female medic said from outside below the rattling of the plane, "if he needs me he can come to me. But first he should think very hard about it."

(They lived together in that apartment for six months, the whitewash of the kitchen ceiling and the bathroom was peeling from the damp, but they took over the roof and installed window boxes in which they grew mint for tea and herbs for salad; and sometimes, before cutting onions, to make her laugh, over his face he put on a snorkel that still exuded the smell of sea and suntan lotion. For a while they dreamt of putting on a small show in which they'd lead the audience behind them, from the roof to the two rooms, a show for a limited-but-high-quality audience, which would play hundreds of times like Niko Nitai's shows; they also wanted to get on children's television programs, and to star in student films, which would be shown at international festivals. In the meantime they made a living from birthdays and the municipality's outdoor shows on Purim and during the summer, and from dubbing animation series as well as some softcore porn – he would be Helmut or Hans, and she would be Helga or Inga; in the middle of winter they would stand in a cold recording studio wearing sweaters and overcoats and moaning – "I'm so hot for you," Hans said, and Inga answered, "I'm so wet," and on the other side of the glass a technician was seen biting into a bursting pita bread with a drizzle of tahini flowing down onto his chin.)

"Half-dead, half-dead," said the female medic outside, "What, don't I know his games?"

"They make such a fuss about dying," Kinneret said.

("Dzere? You mean dzere? In dzeh toilet? You know
somesing, somebuddy put her panties dzere, on dzeh bulb,
I swear to you, but I am not dzis kind of a gerl. You take me
to hotel, vot do you sink I am, a cheep gerl?" – cigarettes
extinguished, saturated with saliva, brownish indentations in
the white plastic of the toilet tank flowing rising falling rising
falling – "doing it dzere? Like a hore?")

(Once every few months they would invite his father for
supper, and afterwards he would doze off in the armchair
opposite the television flickering in the dark. When they
came back from the neighborhood café she would cover him
with a blanket and not try to take his shoes off anymore – the
toenails continued to yellow and to grow into the flesh or
outwards like the nails of the dead – and one night, when
the snoring was already rising from the armchair, gargling,
gurgling and whistling, gargling, gurgling and whistling,
he saw absolutely clearly how they were killing him: not in
that city in which there were marble monuments of military
leaders on horseback and marble fountains and avenues of
chestnut trees, but on hard ground like the ground of the
Dadon brothers' plot. In the dream they held cobblers'
hammers in their hands, and between their lips large nails
like those used for building sukkot[30] and for puncturing
tires, and together they stuck them deep into the soles of
those feet and also into the palm of the hands, which for
years held nothing other than a glass in the Romanian's café
or the remote control of the television at home. And after
they had finished nailing him, the Dadon brothers, with the
same skill with which they used to attach couch upholstery
and armchairs until they won the lottery, he himself lifts his
father up on two scaffolding planks and drags him between
the buildings of the project past each and every entrance
for them to throw things at him – not only the ones who
managed to get out of there, but also the Purrsions and the
Eegyptians and the Treepolitanians – rotten vegetables and
eggs and stones and what not and shouted at him in all the
accents: "That's for your cousin, Jurek.")

---

30   Temporary structures constructed for the Feast of Tabernacles

"Big deal," Kinneret said.

(His girlfriend used to cover him with the checkered blanket, the same blanket in which she was wrapped when the siren began and still her whole body shivered. Room interior: an actor and an actress look at each other, the actor's face is covered by a mask like in Greek drama or Commedia dell'arte, and the actress waited for him to take his off. Wasn't she waiting for that? While still in the entrance he tried to make her laugh in order to buy time, "did you forget it in the studio, Inga? I'm so hot for you," and breathed in and out through the filter, and she said nothing and did not move from where she was. She just lit the last remaining cigarette, pressing the lighter with all her strength as if squashing a tick. In the mirror of the open cupboard he saw himself spread a sheet over his shoulders like some ancient Greek and heard himself saying through the filter: "the Morai wove the thread, Saddam will not sever it," and she said nothing, not moving from where she was. When the cigarette was finished she hugged her legs like a fetus, what do you mean fetus, she was already preparing to return to Mother Earth: she didn't push him, didn't block his filter, didn't spit on those lenses in which he tried to hide his eyes as he breathed in and out. And what exactly was he supposed to do, to forgo his as well? – And this city whose buildings he had already become accustomed to, each one of them stood alone, one after the other and not joined in unified blocks with numerous entrances, and he liked to stand on the roof late at night between the window boxes of herbs and recite some monologue from there, as if the whole city was listening to him from the dark, he liked his voice, which rose from the depths of this breathing chest, and also his toenails, which he treated with special ointment each summer so that they wouldn't become like his father's, and liked his mimicry, and his face in general, which didn't have a cleft chin nor high cheek bones, but just because of that he could portray a thousand and one roles when the sweat of fear eventually evaporates – "this way at least," he said to her, "if something happens-" and didn't complete the sentence. Because why should it happen, there's no lack of other places. The City Garden tower block for example, whose millionaires have all fled abroad, or the whole of Ramat Gan, where they were already used to Iraqi missiles, so over here? On their roof? On the mint and the rosemary? His voice was distorted by the filter, but he heard his breathing absolutely clearly, inhaling and exhaling, each and every one of his dear breaths. They sat like that for a very long while, a section of a sheet between them – room interior: an actor and an actress recall what they did the previous night there – they sat until the all-clear siren became silent, what do you mean became silent, next to it the Kiryat Shaul cemetery is a discotheque: only his breathing still made a noise in the room, inhaling and exhaling. Without looking at him and without saying a word she threw the blanket off her, without looking at him and without saying a word she pulled out from under the bed a suitcase that she had brought with her six months before. Without looking at him and without saying a word she took all her clothes out of the cupboard, dresses and skirts and slacks together with the hangers; pushed them all into the suitcase and looked at him for just one moment and said just one word: "scumbag." And after he got up she said, "don't even try you shithead, get away from me, get away." And when he stood in her way and tried to apologize, to make her laugh, to strangle himself with a scarf, with a nylon stocking, with what not, she said: "Let me go, drop dead," and moved toward the door and placed her hand on the door handle and opened the door and slammed it behind her. For a while he still looked at the scarf and the nylon stocking, which had fallen to the floor, and afterwards went down to the street. There were no lionzsh there and no tigers, just one thin horse beating its hooves on the road, the reins were left by his side, and behind him a wagon on which an old fridge turned white in the darkness. Without his wagon-driver the horse galloped through the empty street in the middle of the night. And on the avenue, in place of the reeking urinal on which the graffiti "Let Shamir be Elevated"[31] was written

---

31   The then prime minister Yitzhak Shamir was of short stature

on one of its walls, he saw a fountain in which marble dust intermingled with the water, and in the depths of the black sky that swallowed the echoes of the hooves, searchlights still roved – spread and crossed, but not even a small plane like this one passed – they roved here and there as he turned to one of the benches on the avenue and lay down on the hard boards and on the screws that pierced his back. Hour after hour he lay there and listened to his breathing grow calmer but noisier in the silence, until from above his head – above the low cheek bones and the smooth chin – the silhouette of a tree began to lighten and separate into its branches. And for a while the dust that covered the small leaves could still be seen, until they were replaced by others, large and red and orange and yellow continuing to change their shades according to the seasons of the year, and beneath them large ripening chestnuts whose shells darken and harden and break open as they did nine hundred and seven days before, as if nothing had happened, Miku, nothing. Absolutely nothing.)

"So should we sing?" asked Kinneret.

"Is any as merr-y and joll-y as me-"

("Doing it here? Like a hore?" – on green felt material with balls hitting and clacking, flack, flack-flack – "vot do you sink I em?")

"Do you mind holding the microphone?" the soundman asked the lighting man, "just for us to record background noise as well, so that it won't go missing in the editing later."

The lighting man nodded his head and moved away from the plug, which still emitted the smell of scorched plastic. He held the broomstick to whose edge the microphone was attached and lifted it above the head of the actor, casting its shadow on the poster on the wall: the waterfall cascaded there as before, gushing and translucent, and beyond it the young boy and girl embraced standing in water up to their hips.

"You can lower it a bit," the sergeant bent over the camera. "You're nowhere near the frame. A bit more." The microphone was lowered further and the actor looked through the lenses of the mask at the broom in whose bristles wisps of fluffy dust were caught. "Jainies?" he asked. "Sweeping the air not to swallow insects, huh?"

"Jains," corrected the soundman from his corner and looked at the gauges of the recording.

"Was that what you were trying to be there?"

"I wasn't trying to be anything there," answered the soundman, "there wasn't anything I was trying to be. All in all I understood some things about myself there." The earphones were placed against his ears again, and on his right arm, near his shoulder, the tattooed dragon coiled its flame.

"Okay no need to get mad," said the actor.

Opposite him the sergeant pressed the zoom button for a moment. "You can lower it a bit," he said to the lighting man, "a bit more, to the middle of the Eden Water. The middle, dammit! That's all we need today, for the microphone to get into the frame. Those small waves are your sign, remember that. The waves, not the waterfall." He still kept one eye close to the eyepiece while the other one remained half open.

"Evvvvrrrrry-" below the microphone attached to the pole the actor began to sing, elongating the vowel to his utmost limit.

"wa-ve carries a re-min-der-"

His voice was muffled in the air filter of the mask as he slowly moved his shoulders to his right and his left to the slow rhythm of the song.

"from h-ome and fromtheshore,
frommm the beautiful treetops and the golden-"

He became silent for a moment, still tilting his head slightly as if watching the shore with its treetops drawing away; and afterwards looked to his right and to his left and said that there was no need for putting arms around each other, it would be enough for them to sway the way you do in congregational singing, moving like waves. "Doesn't that sometimes move you to see that?" – he looked at them all through the large lenses – "people who didn't know each other at all before all of a sudden swaying together, moving like waves. What do you have to say, Kinneret?"

(Opposite a flowing toilet tank rising and falling full of beerbeerbeer on the billiard felt full of the spermspermsperm of a baby boy or baby girl)

"It's what every child does with its father," he said, "there's not a child that doesn't. Show me one. Maybe we'll also cool down a bit that way from the heat of the lamp. Hey, Kinneret?"

(Or deathdeathdeath)

"Go sway with your friends," Kinneret said.

(Every wave carried a dead fish moving back and forth, silver scales floated, fins gathered up floated: mouth to mouth the fish opened wide and passed the hook to her, the way one passes a sucking sweet. From the depths of the cliff a drain pipe emptied itself and spewed waste water murky and babbling, and high above her, beyond the thin turbid veil, a pale feeble sun flickered as if above a giant toilet bowl whose edges are in the horizon. She entered into it, moved forward in the water, further and further forward in the water. Shimmers were set off by the sun that rose from behind, and bubbles of froth fizzed on her feet, burst on her thighs, burst on her navel, burst on her nipples on her neck on her nostrils on her eyes on her hair on the water above her hair and on the water above the water above the water above the water – her dress a melting black stain, her legs bright fading stripes, her hands melting stripes – there was a shimmer on the seabed, it sparkled and subsided, sparkled, a shell, a spot of light or Bamba, sparkled subsided sparkled. And far, far away, beyond the giant waterland beyond the watercontinent beyond the waterworld with little fish clouds and a sinking seaweed sun, they shouted to her: "Ki-ne-llet!")

"You don't have to sing," Merav said. "Nobody asked you to. Just look as if you're listening to the television."

"This report's so very interesting," the actor said, "I've always taken an interest in these things, ever since I can remember. Before falling asleep – stories just like these."

Kinneret, who was not listening to him, pulled at the black T-shirt, moving the collar away from her body and blowing into it over and over in order to cool her skin. From the corner of the room the soundman continued to look at her even when she let go of the material and once more her shirt clung to her breasts.

"Are you also recording that?" the actor asked through the filter.

"Watch the television already," said Merav, "you're wasting everyone's time." The screenplay folder was open in her hand at the page whose corner was folded, and on the back of the other hand the words written in pen were still reddening. "Come on, think what the announcer is saying about the air lift from America, is that so hard? About how much each missile costs, is it a million, Gidi?" The sergeant, who glanced at Shechter for a moment, nodded above the second camera.

Opposite them, from the bed and the clothing strewn on it, Kinneret responded by bending forward, resting her chin on the palms of her hands like a tense viewer. The actor supported the elbow of his right arm with his left arm and slowly rubbed the filter with his fingers, perhaps imitating a thinker smoothing his beard.

"Pretend that you're listening, Na'ama," the sergeant urged. "We're not gonna waste time, we'll add the soundtrack in the editing." The lamp light flickered on the ceiling for a moment and the lizard walking there froze in its place. In the corner behind it a web quivered, glowed and darkened.

"There's a director here, isn't there?" Na'ama fixed her hair beneath the black rubber straps of the mask, "so let him tell me." On her right, opposite the wall perpendicular to the bed, the lighting man bent down toward the plug and sniffed around it.

"Watch the television," the sergeant ordered, "before there's another short. What, don't I know what's gonna happen? I'll take an oath on what's gonna happen. Just as we're about to film, the second I say 'camera run' there'll be a short." "Let's go home, Na'ama."

"But there's a director here, isn't there?" she insisted. "So let him direct me." Through the lenses of the mask she looked at Shechter, who all this while did not turn his head from the window, and whose shoulders sloped between the green stripes stuck there. "Why are you all taking his place? He's not a mute."

On the other side of the pane and the nylon, the light of the plane drew away again, and Shechter, who until then followed it with his eyes, turned to the room. "Na'ama, imagine you're her mother," he said in a tone of guidance, which he perhaps brought to light from the time of his studies. "How would you behave as her mother?" He leaned his back against the wall and under his folded arms the sweat stain grew even bigger.

"Tell her it's an emergency case, Ezra," a voice said from outside. "Tell her he fell in the line of duty, just as he was coming to stamp out the garbage."

The lamp flickered again and the shadows it cast faded and darkened until the light stabilized. "It's a bit hard for me to think like a mother," answered Na'ama and further tightened the straps on her light hair. "I'm not yet twenty, and of course without children. Even if you can't see my age with the mask." Her hand lingered on her head for a moment and then she slowly extended it to Kinneret and gave her a hesitant hug while Shechter watched them both from where he stood.

"One day," he said, leaning his shoulder against the wall, "you will have. And not as far off as it might seem to you. One day, when someone reminds you about this evening, you'll say: What? It was like the day before yesterday, you won't understand at all where the time flew." He turned his eyes from her toward the fluffy teddy bears, which leaned against the wall beside her. Their button noses sparkled in the light of the lamp, dimmed and sparkled once more.

"Children are still quite a long way off," said Na'ama, "a few things have to happen before that." Shechter wiped his forehead with the back of his hand, and his hand on his trousers.

"Tell her, Ezra, Weintraub's gonna get a citation, a citation, but she'll be thrown in jail. Tell her she can forget about her clinic, just forget about it, she's gonna be working with the garbage. That's what you tell her. Go on, get moving."

The actor, who was still rubbing the sides of the filter with his fingers, asked why the hell they couldn't look like a close-knit family for just one moment: finally, during the last half hour – "three quarters of an hour? Okay, three quarters of an hour" – without anyone noticing it at all, they've become a bit closer to each other. "What, haven't we become closer?" he asked. "Sure we have, and how. There're even couples, don't deny it. Isn't that touching? I find that touching. People who didn't know each other before, their hearts suddenly coming together like the movement of waves. Not me, who's talking about me. Me, Miki Le-Mic?

"Below me nana nanaaaah-"

He began to sing again moving his shoulders slowly to his left and to his right in time to the song.

Carr-y me wave, carry me wave,
to the l-aand nananaaaaah-"

He elongated the last syllable more and more until his breath became short and his voice became silent.

"Below me depths and calm," the sergeant corrected him from behind the second camera, and the lamp flickered once more, turned blue and darkened their faces. "To the land of my dreams. The Roosters sang the original." He turned his gaze from the eyepiece to the lighting man, and above their heads a lizard scurried to the corner of the ceiling, faster than the crop spraying plane, which was again seen crossing the window.

"Tell her," Weintraub said from outside, "to show some respect for her profession. That's what you tell her. She's a medic, not an electrician like Eran. She's supposed to help people, not let them die like dogs outside like Eran. Hey, Eran?" A stone hit the door and fell.

The lighting man moved the tips of his fingers toward the lamp plug to gauge its heat and the actor looked at him through the lenses of the mask.

The lamp flickered and the lighting man tapped the plug with his fist. Another stone hit the door.

"Tell her Ezra, I'm getting a medal, a decoration of honor. Weintraub the hero, not a coward like Eran. Even fiddling with a lamp is too much for him, hey Eran?" A small stone hit the window between the green stripes stuck on it and the sergeant lifted his head from the camera and shouted: "I swear to God Weintraub, I'm gonna finish you off if you don't stop that."

"You just ask Eran what a hero he was in the war," Weintraub said from outside and another small stone hit the window. "Left everything to come to the base to fight, left his girlfriend alone at residence, didn't want to speak to her even on the phone, hey Eran? Walked half the night on foot, even in the team building exercise of the naval commando he didn't walk like that – the naval commando's nothing compared to Eran. It's just that when the siren started, he locks himself in, you'd think he lived there by himself – his own private suite at the Hilton. Is it Weintraub's fault he needed to take a shit? He didn't even say to me: 'I've sealed everything already, I've taped everything down, I thought you weren't here.' Just one word, but he didn't say a thing. Even that bitch of a medic would have come out right away, but him, Eran, pretends he doesn't hear. As far as he's concerned I can die outside, right? If it had fallen here, I would have died like a dog." Another stone hit the window and fell. "What do I care if he's getting married next month, he's been saying that for a year, at the very least a year. Anyway Weintraub's also getting married. Isn't Weintraub going to get married one day, after he's screwed them all?" Another stone hit the window, larger than the ones before, and the sergeant turned to the door.

The soundman lifted his head from his gauges. "Just be careful of the cables," he said as the sergeant moved further forward, "and the legs of the lamp." But the sergeant had already hit one of the legs of the lamp's tripod with the toe of his shoe, and the embedded top section, down whose length a drizzle of spray trailed, murky from the rust, became suddenly dislodged and was implanted into the section below it. The lamp tottered and flickered.

"Eran's ruined everything for you," Weintraub said from outside. "Why not ruin everything if you can."

Another stone hit the window and as it fell the lighting man looked at it, moved near to the lamp and sniffed around it. "I'm shutting it off," he said and turned to the far wall again. "Leave it," the sergeant called out to him from the entrance, "in a second there'll be a short anyway. Don't I know? Don't bother with it." The soundman rose from his kneeling position with the headphones attached to his head. From the bed, where the folds of the clothes strewn there enlarged and diminished their shadows, Kinneret called out to him: "And you too, don't touch it-" "Did you hear her?" said Shechter and removed his shoulder from the wall. Na'ama stopped fingering the blanket's tassels. "Don't anyone touch that," Merav called from the corner of the room, and on the placards and posters the light flickered, fading and darkening their figures. "Leave it, Eran," said the actor and vapor misted the lenses of the mask, "forget about it, you're getting married in a month." The lighting man moved further forward to the plug. "Until my wedding," he replied, "everything will come right, believe me," and he reached the wall and bent down but the darkness had already covered them all like whitewash in which the wheels of an old pram are imprinted, or like the soot of a lantern tossing below an unraveled thatch and a sky pierced by lightning, or like the glass paving stones above a cellar when a body falls and darkens them, or like hordes of badybugs that fly from the tiny palm of a hand and fill the air, or like the hall of a cinema whose door the usher bolts with rounded hills at its far side and with cows grazing grass, or like a giant sheet that falls from high above in order to put two tiny wings to sleep, or like a shiny marble floor that is entirely blackened by motorbike exhaust pipes, or like water wrapping fondling touching caressing and drawing away.

In the dark window, between the green strips stuck on it, the red light of the plane was seen advancing from square to square. And further on, beyond the black shadows of the eucalyptuses and beyond the field, which has lost all its furrows, in the car parked by the side of the road the woman lifted her head and said in a hoarse voice: "Here it comes again, can you see it?" And in the front windscreen, above the folded wipers and the fields, the small light bulb grew to an illuminated globe, to a glowing lamp, to a floodlight, to an immense exploding flare.

THE DRAWER

1

"Had it not been for," the policeman will say, "did you hear him? Had it not been for, that's how, learn how to say that. Had it not been for the wine. 'If not for the wine' isn't good enough for them." He'll blow a smoke ring, purse his lips and round them, try to kiss it as it flies from his mouth. "And what would he have done without the wine?" The ring will hover in the air, expand and eventually evaporate into it like a hungry maggot that has nibbled its tail, its belly, its neck. "Nothing is what he would have done without it, nothing. After all, those types are scared of their own shadows. Not so?" He will not turn to you, but rather to his partner: the second policeman or the doctor, someone bespectacled with instruments for examining insides, not one of the ancients who heal by touch. "They only know how to talk big. Don't say anymore 'if not for her toothache I would've pumped her.' Learn how to say 'had it not been for her toothache I would have-'" He'll stop. "How do you say 'pump'?" "They don't pump," his partner will say, the second policeman or the second doctor or the angel: they will confine you with handcuffs or with sheets and sleeves or with tufts of cloud. But perhaps there will just be a nurse, or no one will be there, with stubble with wings with breasts; for a long time there hasn't been anyone whom you wished to be there.

"Had it not been for," you thought about the inspector general who resides in the heavens, and about his son who was cured of his death, and about his successor who, what was he, a fisherman? The son caused the fish to double and triple and quadruple, and his pupil spread out a net for them. One revived people with a word and the other knew how to heal with his shadow: it was enough for him to stand in front of the sun and cast a shadow over wounds, gangrenes and stumps. And what did he do at night? A large moon rose or torches were burned to cast his shadow over cuts, over abscesses, over ulcers, over cataracts, which turned pupils grey like smoke; something still burnt in their depths.

Before that – such an immeasurably long time before that – you were all looking at other paintings. The healer in his shadow was painted with a white beard, a bald head and wrinkles, but he seemed as sturdy as a farmer and was also already attached to the beams; three struggled to lift him, head down and legs up. Rope was tied around the edge of the vertical beam in order to raise it as if it was a circus tent pole, if in fact a circus pole is raised that way – you no longer had much to do with that boy who once went to circuses: from the faded photographs in the album he gazed straight at you with a blank look, as conceited as a distant family patriarch, unaware that he is already buried in a different century, or like a fattened prehistoric god in whom no one believes anymore.

There was only little that could be changed in that painting: at most, in place of a loincloth it would have been possible to dress him in a striped uniform and to write a serial number above the pocket, as if there were thousands like him waiting for their sentences and as if the trees of the forests – if there still existed forests in the world –grew from the very start with trunks and branches full of holes to make it easier on the hammers.

For a moment he seemed like some kind of acrobat whose assistants are lifting him up to a wooden trapeze, as if above him was not sky but rather a stretched canvas sheet beneath which he'll immediately begin to walk steadily or ride a unicycle, balancing the vertical beam of the cross in his hand.

But the second painting surpassed the first, and before moving over to Mantegna you all thought of working on it. "It stimulated your imaginations," the policeman will say, "how's that? Those types only fuck their imaginations. How do you say 'fuck'?" "They make love," the other policeman will say, or the doctor or the angel, whoever might be there;

even your reflection in an empty window would do, or in the water of a toilet bowl or in a muddy puddle, which has not yet frozen beneath your shoes.

There were also no angels in that painting, but after a few sips you could see them flying here and there or entering white and fluffy cloud houses and hanging their halos on a hanger. In that painting even the holy weren't holy, they were as suspicious as a jeweler to whom a hoodlum brings a diamond ring. Saint Thomas bent toward the son of God and brought his finger close to the hole that the lance had pierced, to confirm that the person who stood before him and who was breathing was in fact the one who was stabbed, who was nailed, who was buried, who will redeem you all. His finger reached out to the open lips of the wound that was already cleansed of the blood and that recalled, before you had drunk even one sip, the shaved lips of something else. And one of you said – that's what your humor was like at the time – "bringing your finger close to an open wound like that. Who would touch an open wound today? That jerk Saint Thomas should have done it with a surgeon's glove." And straightaway he moved closer to the son of God in the album, bent like one of the painted saints, but unlike him his sleeve was not open at the shoulder: in this beautiful, damned city everyone is required to be strict about his dress if he doesn't want to be arrested by policemen demanding documents in which he's still looking blindly straightforward and smiling.

It was not a bad idea, this homage, since after all you were now uncertain of everything; you could have got up in the morning and not been sure you were alive: the chest rose, but immediately fell; air entered through the nose, but immediately exited; something beat in the chest, but immediately became silent. Would the professor approve of the surgeon's glove on the hand of Saint Thomas? To hell with the professor, you said, let him be nailed, you said, a waste of nails, you said: after all you were all artists, yes-yes, and the lodgings in the servants' quarters on the seventh floor without heating and without anything besides a mattress and a blocked basin and a leaking gas burner were just a stage on the way to fame. One night you all left the bar to which the musicians go when the streets empty, and bolstered up the current drunk, accompanying him to his home; in the beginning he cried and later spewed what he had drunk. For all seven floors you were careful that he wouldn't soil your coats, and in front of his door you said: "So what. One day they'll put a sign up here: 'Here lived and cried and vomited between the years'" – Was the vomit contaminated too? The tears? – In a nature film on television, when you still watched television with her, they once showed a species of African butterfly that fed off hippopotamuses· thousands of butterflies landed on the giant eyes and fluttered until they blinked and teared up and watered them. Throngs of delicate wings beat, throngs of delicate wings fluttered, and for a moment it seemed, from the bed on which you were both lying, that they would carry the hippopotamus into the air.

At the time there was still television, and what else was there? There wasn't anything: the chest rose but immediately fell, the air entered through the nose but immediately exited, the nails continued to grow like the nails of the dead. And you did not want Saint Thomas, nor Saint Peter nor any of the other saints, you wanted God himself in all his glory, or his bastard, or his imposter, anyone: the chest rose and fell, and in front of your eyes large damp stains were drawn on the ceiling, winding like continents, but above them was only a slate and grey lice-ridden doves.

With all his tricks of light and shade, what was Caravaggio in comparison to Mantegna? An exaggerator of genius who overdid everything in order not to mislead anyone as to his intentions, yes-yes, that's what you have to understand gentlemen: believe the son of God, don't put a finger into his wound, don't put your hands in, don't put the shoulder inside and the neck and the head so that they'll all be swallowed up in there, in the hole that doubt opened wide.

On the tattered carpet, below which the neighbor would shout out with each step taken if shoes were not removed, both their albums were laid out, and on the covers the price tags could still be seen: only a third of which was paid. Gibert-Jeune[32] brought you the albums to the hotel before the end of the shift, hiding his booty in his coat and asked if they hadn't begun to miss him yet, all the hotel fleas. Eh? He had a high forehead like the character on the covers of Gibert-Jeune's exercise books, though he didn't steal the albums from there but rather from the large university shop, slipping out the workers' exit: he had a partner, an old man of eighty, who perhaps hadn't washed for half his life, and while they all watched out for the old man dirtying anything, he would put the album into his coat. "So they don't miss me?" he asked and with his finger tilted the flap of his ear, as if he'll hear them jumping in the rooms on ripped mattresses and stained sheets and blankets perforated by cigarettes. "Tell them I'm coming back at Christmas with new blood, eh?" he said and blew a kiss to the chamber maid, but she was already drawing away in the passage with a bundle of washing as bloated as her behind.

One of the greatest of them all was Mantegna, and those who saw, like the professor, only the effects of perspective, didn't understand his genius. He was no great theoretician, the professor, and definitely no great artist; had he been he wouldn't have taught you but rather shut himself up in an atelier and painted on everything that was possible to be painted: canvasses, a tattered carpet, floorboards, the hard mattress, the chest that still rose and fell.

"One day," you all said to the waiter at a late hour, "tourists will come here to see where we sat when we were young," but the waiter waited for you to pay, and when you said to him, "see you," he didn't answer. Were you not like one of those groups from the end of the century, on the brink of starting a revolution? You wanted to start one then and especially wanted to overturn the American trash can, that's what you called it, because they didn't paint people anymore, they didn't even paint poplar trees, nor the façade of a church,

---

32   Nickname derived from the bookstore chain of the same name

nor haystacks on which the light changes as if veils had been measured out on them. The room also wasn't portrayed in summer, winter or electric light when the light inside you turned dark. There they only painted replicas of tin cans with not even a squashed one amongst them, so that the fervor with which it was drunk might be seen in its creases, or the fury with which it was throttled and crushed.

"In a world in which all is art," you wrote one night with grave seriousness, on a serviette stained with coffee cup prints, "art will no longer be possible," and you kept the serviette to be used someday in your manifesto, which in a few years' time will naturally be published in some smart album that Gibert-Jeune will swipe into his coat. You all signed it in ink, not in blood; that was most dangerous, blood: it wasn't used for signing anymore, covenants were no longer sealed with it. Anyway, children who swore allegiance to each other for the rest of their lives, or at least until the end of the summer, no longer existed. There were only little people who walked in the parks holding computer games beeping digital beeps, or moved cars on the path or racing boats in the pond by remote control. Those renting out ponies and wooden boats no longer made a living: who's going to ride a pony anymore and watch the breath rising from its nostrils; who's going to push a wooden boat by hand and watch the sail, which the wind blows up like a cheek.

In a year or two – that's what you sometimes thought, not with sorrow but with malicious joy, just so no one here gets lucky – they'll also move to one of the underground tunnels or under the bridge; they'll live like everyone else in a cloud of the stench of urine that always hung there. Only the privileged came to the hotel in which you worked, when the water in the fountains began to freeze, coming with the little money they saved from begging or from petty thievery. The changes made to the hotel by its proprietor, neglect itself, they noted one by one pleasantly, like vacationers who find that the healing springs are everywhere. There were no stars on the signpost of that hotel, but its name "Excelsior" was written in ornate letters, as if the glorified name was enough to conceal the deterioration and the decay. "Did the fleas miss us?" they'd ask every year before Christmas, and at the end of February after they left, all their rooms were disinfected and the hole made in the bathroom wall didn't disturb anyone anyway: who didn't want at least once to see what people do by themselves? A heavenly delight glowed from their faces there, between the scratches of the enamel bath and the mildewed flowers on the walls; the kingdom of heaven was already in their hands.

Sometimes you could pass the entire night shift chatting and they were always glad that someone wanted to draw them: "we'll be in the Louvre one day," they would say, and afterwards they'd examine the drawing with narrowed eyes, careful not to stain it with their fingers or with their breath. You never asked them to comb their hair or change their clothes, because they looked more picturesque when they were disheveled and filthy, the expression on their faces of someone who doesn't care what anyone in the world thinks of him: features sunken even when they were not drunk, eyes shuttered even when they were wide open as well, nostrils that are no longer trying to smell, everything you could sometimes see in a mirror or a windowpane when you stood opposite it and looked out.

Were not their predecessors painted in the great works? After all, the backgrounds and peripheries were filled with them and would have lost their power without all those secondary characters: they who gathered round the manger and the radiant baby in it, they who later ate the bread and the fish from his hand, and they who assembled at the foot of his cross and shouted: "Crucify him!" "Crucify him!" They were coarse and filthy, but without them the redemption would not have come. The soldiers were just fulfilling their wishes: perhaps those soldiers were like these policemen, one silent and one talkative, and the talkative one, in breastplate armor and steel helmet, said: "'Had it not been for.' Did you hear

him? 'Had it not been for the wine,' learn how to say that."
But there was only vinegar there, and someone came out
of the masses and thrust a reed into his throat; perhaps he
climbed a ladder to reach him, after all his hands and feet
were already nailed at the time, and perhaps the ladder was
not leaned against those beams but rather on the narrow
chest rising and falling, crushed like a tin can.

The colors were rich, Gibert-Jeune took pains to write the
name of the publisher, so that they would be as similar as
possible to the original; the one that was in the Palazzo
Ducale or its predecessor who was in heaven itself: they were
distant to the same degree, the Palazzo Ducale and heaven,
only the netherworld was near and warmed the soles in every
place stepped on.

The picture you chose was called CRISTO IN SCURTO,
and the son of God was painted in it from the height of the
soles of his feet and did not look at all heavenly, but rather
like an utter corpse. He had already been taken down from
the cross and had not yet risen victorious in resurrection: he
was laid out on a bunk, and the perspective shortened his
body, making only his soles prominent. The wounds of the
nails were not the gateway to a new epoch, they were small
as if injured merely by the nails of his shoes. They had all
been cleansed of the blood; the wound created by the lance
in the chest was cleaned too, and only on the left hand a
drop of congealed blood could be seen – can congealed blood
spread it as well? – From the mattress you could sometimes
hear it slowing down in your arteries like the coaches of the
underground when the electricity shuts off, braking there
and stopping inside the long dark tunnels on whose walls
obscene drawings appeared rounded.

On the far end of the bunk his face can be seen, and
torment is painted on its features with a single-haired brush:
the quiet and restrained torment of someone who already
knows that in the entire world there is no one to hear him.
Two women were standing on his right, one drying her eyes
and the other wringing her hands. Their roles too were suited

to clochards, two of the dozens who lived in the tunnels of Chatelet, and had it not been for the filth would all have turned white there like moles. That's what you once thought, not with sorrow, but with malicious joy, so that none of the people of this city get lucky. The short one would always stare from one of the benches there and swing her legs like a child, her left leg as well, which was wrapped in a bandage and gave off the stench of rotting meat; and the other, the drinker, would sing with the drunks and pee with them behind the bench, squatting down and supported by whoever was peeing against the wall. They had no shame, no horizons lay before them beyond the glass bottom of the bottle, which they lifted against the light to coax a sluggish drop of wine, and there were no miracles but this: all the grapes of the south and the vineyards with the earth that nurtured them and the skies that ripened them, all turned into this yellowish stream.

The clochard, for whom you reserved the main role, had himself already been practicing for it for many years. For a while he lived in the tunnel with all the others – burped with them on the bench or hiccupped or yawned or crossed himself at the sight of you as if he saw a dead man in front of him – but in summer he slept in the alley, and while the album was on order you could see how once again he'll change his bedstead to the place that you've designated for him.

Beneath the electric sign of the hotel, in whose broken corner the neon is exposed like the skeleton of a phosphorescent fish, Gibert-Jeune repeated the name of Mantegna and the name of the publisher. "Half the money now, half on delivery," he said and swept his forelock back with the long fingers of a thief. And what if he doesn't succeed? He'll succeed, of course he'll succeed. Has it ever happened that he didn't succeed? Never. If a person wants to keep his clientele his word must be good. He has to keep his word. Right? Right. One winter he brought a woman with him to the hotel but the second night clerk said that only their lice were still doing it; and for a while in your room, opposite the ceiling and the damp stains on it, you could hear the tiny chitin shells beating against each other, one against the other, one into the other until they were cracked open by a nail.

Perhaps his old partner went deaf from them, from the love beats of the lice, but when his stench worsened and no shop allowed him in anymore, Gibert-Jeune replaced him with another. It had been a harsh winter; on television they said that there hadn't been a winter like this for a hundred years in the beautiful, damned city, and it's better not to think what happened to the old man under the bridge. If a person wants to keep his head clear for his own troubles he should keep his nose to himself. Right? Right.

He still maintained domestic manners, the clochard from the alley, as if he wasn't living in a cardboard box but in an apartment in the sixteenth arrondissement, even living with dignity: he didn't steal, didn't beg, but made a living from the one imitation he performed and from the inscription on his sign, and coins were thrown into his hat as with any other street performer. But anyway – you said to yourself when you chose him, and didn't say it with sorrow, but with malicious joy – he wouldn't be able to carry on making a living like that for more than a few years since he's long past the age of the man whom he imitated. That one died aged thirty-three, the son of God or his bastard or the imposter, and through all the hundreds of years that have passed since his death he hasn't aged, not even by one moment.

He could be seen in the square where he performed, in the tunnel where he slept in winter or in the alley where he slept in summer, and one night, when you were already not living in her apartment, you saw him on the way from the bar to the night shift at the hotel, standing and holding in his hands a large cardboard box that once contained a fridge, shaking it and spreading it on the pavement. He wrapped himself up in it as in a duvet and leaned his back against the lamppost like a headboard and lit himself half a cigarette, which he picked up from the pavement as if it was an open packet for his use. He then inhaled deeply and slowly expelled the smoke, reaching his hand out to a curbstone and tapping the ash over the asphalt ashtray of the road. Toward the afternoon he would move to the church square and prepare for his performance each time luxurious tourist buses slowed down there: his face was lean as required and his beard downy and sparse, the hair on his head exactly the right length – did the lice spread it by mouth or on their wings like the pollen of flowers? – And in summer he wore a white galabia, which he got from the Arabs of Belleville, a kind of desert garb that they themselves no longer wore. They all wore faded blue clothes when they gripped jackhammers and cracked open the roads that were being newly tarred; they did so without hesitation, as if beneath them were not the flames which you could sometimes feel through your soles.

The moment after the tourists alighted from the buses they would stop opposite him: Americans and Germans and Japanese, they all looked at him, not because he resembled so much the one to whom they prayed before sleep or whom they saw in museum paintings, but rather because he displayed a quaint madness, alongside which you could be photographed as with a soldier of the royal guard or the little mermaid. To those who had movie cameras he would present the trick that he learned from one of the street pantomime artists – the city was full of them, and when a person finally spoke to you, his lips would move in silence, sometimes even the man in the mirror didn't make a sound when he turned his head and departed for the wall – he took some hovering steps back and forth on the paving stones, which he colored with blue chalk to make it look like the waters of the sea of Galilee. Then he would take a bow saying "Ladies and Gentlemen" in three languages and pointing to the lettering he wrote on a piece of cardboard: "Repent thee, for the Kingdom of Heaven is at Hand." And right away he would move his finger from there to the empty hat at his feet. At the end of the square Karl the Great continued to ride his stone horse; a pigeon pecked at dry bread crumbs;

the river flowed; nothing walked on the water except for barge carriers and the transparent tourist boats.

You were all still bent over the album like the dubious envoys over the wounds of the crucified one. You were assigned to pay homage to the one whom you'll choose, Caravaggio, Mantegna or one of the others – who didn't paint him nailed or displaced or rising from the grave – and to adapt it to this century, whose last years are already linking themselves to the years of the next century one to the other like the coaches of a train. Beneath the tattered carpet and the floorboards the neighbor had already begun to snore and now it was possible to step on it, to tread with heels, to knock nails into boards until they came out on the other side; there were nights when you could imagine them there at his place, or above you, a ceiling full of nails or a sky whose clouds all shower them down.

Will you dress him in a suit? They asked, and you did not wish to reply. Will you let him fly in the sky with his cross like a giant kite? They asked, and you did not wish to reply, because in any event art students could be of no help to you. Maybe put him in a coffin of walnut wood with copper handles? They asked. And place him in the square where everyone passes by him and weeps? They asked, and you did not wish to reply, and you did not intend to put him in a coffin; a drawer would do for him. Meanwhile he still lay inside the album, a sheet covering the lower half of his body, and at the end of the bunk stood a goblet, which will be replaced by a bottle of cheap wine. And the women too can warm him there, if those people have any desire left; for a moment you pondered if it was desire that brought them into the world; and if their mothers' wombs had not opened like coaches and immediately hastened from there unshaven, hiccupping and burping.

If they had ever blown soap bubbles, landing them on the palm of their hands – a sight you still remembered, and also the touch of the bubble as delicate as an imprint that leaves a dreamed up image in the eye – immediately reflected there in the trembling, hollow crystal were the ceramic tiles of the tunnel and the urine that flowed from them. They'll be like tourists in an exotic land when they leave the tunnel: that stream there, ladies and gentlemen, you'll then tell them, is a river, and that domed endless ceiling the sky; and sometimes a rumbling that passes overhead can be heard too, but whoever travels there no one has ever seen.

The women will stand on his right, exactly as in the painting, one will wipe her eyes and the other wring her hands and both will weep for him who once lived and preached and healed and is now placed in a drawer. Would he not have arrived there in the end, to the morgue refrigeration unit? And on his big toe, a few centimeters from the hole of the nail in the sole – a hole as tiny as a burst blister from all the walking on water or on clouds – a small elastic band with a cardboard label will be wrapped around it as on all the toes of the other corpses. And in a plastic packet the few belongings removed from his body will be kept, perhaps some relative will come or a friend or a creditor: 1 loincloth, 1 crown of thorns, 3 nails: the unidentified corpse of a man on which signs of violence can be seen.

2

The school of medicine happened to be near the bar, and when someone is drunk it is of little consequence what he was doing before; whether in his hand he held a paint brush or a pair of scissors. And had a few prostitutes, a thief, an opium dealer and even a murderer entered the bar at night, they too would have been invited for a drink: "We, sir, have operated on your victim, you saved us half the work," the medical students would say to him, "but what exactly, sir, did you do with the spleen?" Curls of smoke mingled with the sounds of the cash register and the sounds of the saxophone, which some street musician brought there after earning his daily bread, and sometimes a black man would come and sing in a voice that rose from the depths, like the voice of Adam, when the Lord took it from the earth with his hands and began to mold it.

After a couple of nights of joint drunkenness you were invited to a medicine class, and it was totally different to the drawing workshops in which only the skin of the model was exposed. She was so bedraggled that only the years still took the trouble to crush her beneath them, but would remove the dress in one movement, so as not to delay the undressing and arouse someone starved or with a cataract. Sometimes in the winter the cold in the hall would make her nipples erect, but only transparent smoke fish would stop to suckle from them.

In a white coat you looked like a medical student and anyway the short lecturer was busy with his cadaver, an old woman about whom nobody inquired and whom the police were happy to be rid of. Her body was placed on a stainless steel table and came up almost to his chest; but with the skill of a butcher he stuck the knife in and instantly opened up the length of her stomach down to the white pubic hairs. All at once he broke into her like a stolen suitcase, he was eager since she was bursting with all the contents: heart, intestines, liver and spleen, the entire mechanism that put that old woman in motion until it expired. The nauseating sound made by the knife could be heard clearly and was engraved in your memory like the sound of the dragging from the arena in Madrid or Barcelona or in your dreams; it was the sound of death: trumpets did not sound then, drums did not beat, and it was impossible to differentiate between the sound of the defeated bull and the sound of a piece of furniture discarded in the street and turning into junk.

At night all the other bodies, the tens, the hundreds, the thousands, were placed in the charge of a sleepy guard dressed in a wrinkled uniform, and who sat behind the counter in the entrance staring at a small black and white television set. At midnight he would reach his hand out to the blonde announcer, touch the bottom of her cleavage and sigh. Greyish bags pulled the corners of his eyes downwards and at the tip of his nose minute blood vessels were sketched; he certainly would have been glad to down a few with some of the revelers from the street, had they offered to raise a glass with him in honor of the end of the year or the season or the minute – after all there were minutes that you could not believe would ever end: if a drop slid on the window it continued to slide endlessly on it; and if night was visible in it, you were trapped inside like a coal miner in a collapsing mine – they'll wave bottles opposite the closed glass door, and someone will lust after him from there and afterwards from behind the counter, if only one could be found who would do it for you or for Mantegna. In the room, from the mattress, you could see a woman in a black shiny raincoat standing opposite the transparent door, lazily opening her buttons from top to bottom, and you could also see the breath on the glass steamed up by her body as if it was blown from a mouth and right away a face will be drawn there or a name written.

The only one who would have agreed to do it was standing opposite the hotel in which you worked – for a while you even lived in it, after being thrown out of that apartment – and waiting there. She used to smoke cigarettes with a long holder like a lady, but the veins in her legs were becoming blue from the ankle up to the place to which they were joined. "Teachers and us," she would say to all who listened, "it's the same thing, teachers and us, on our feet the whole day long. Someone with legs like that, right away you know she's a teacher or a prostitute." And when she'll get busy with him, strip, tongue, fondle with hands wherever she'll fondle – you could feel her hand there perfectly clearly – the two old women from the tunnel will creep in with the clochard whom they are meant to be lamenting.

"Be careful in the entrance," you'll say to them, "don't bump into the doorframe," because perhaps the halos will make their heads taller like transparent top hats: with Mantegna the halos were delicate and fluttery, but with others they were rigid and pushed toward the nape of the neck or spotted with golden dots or radiating beams from their hub, and from the mattress, which was imprinted only by your body, for some moments you pondered how the drawer would close with the halo.

She held a cigarette between two fingers, whose nails were covered with polish the color of blood, and asked just what exactly she would have to do; oh yes. And for how long exactly? Yes, she has to know everything now. Everything, of course. Just to come on to him? Or after that to also go with him to some side room? No, because giving relief is one thing and all other things are completely another matter. And getting undressed is an extra, let there be no misunderstanding, not to mention that there are some who think it comes with hugging and kissing, it's not enough for them that you moan, they want love as well. So what exactly is it she's going to be doing there? That hotel, well she's never thought much of it, those types who come here in winter she wouldn't even have let peep in her keyhole, but it's one thing to breed fleas, everyone's entitled to their own taste in animals, and stealing corpses from the hospital is another matter. Not stealing? Then what is it? Painting the refrigeration unit for them? She, at any rate, doesn't want to know anything about it; to each his own as they say. Just don't let them get God mixed up in it, she doesn't bring him into her own affairs either. So then, like she says, if someone here hasn't caught on, it all depends on the amount of time. Because for example a blow job, I mean, with someone who knows how to do it well, she doesn't mean "well" for the clients, she means for herself, of course for herself: as for the clients, for their part you can bend down like that the whole year long, as if the only thing you need in this life is their teat. But someone who knows how to do it well like her, not that she intends seducing anyone here, on the contrary, anyhow nowadays you do it with only a rubber. Anyway, right away she noticed there was someone here getting along by himself very nicely; just don't let his delicate hands get blisters. From holding the paintbrush, of course from holding the paintbrush, she's only talking about his paintbrush. So with someone who does it well there'll hardly be any time to paint something, a refrigeration unit or a washing machine, whatever; she doesn't want to know a thing about it.

So if she's needed for the whole night, it's a completely different matter, completely different. And if someone here has their business near her business – okay it's not his own but he works there in the meantime, in the hotel, no? Until he becomes famous; sure he's going to be famous one day, what, wasn't she famous once? Sure she was. They came just for her from all over Paris, came even from Marseilles, not to mention the jungles of Africa, she doesn't discriminate. Just because they're in the same quarter doesn't mean anyone here's going to get a discount. Why doesn't anyone paint her? Not now. That's how you make an offer? First pay now and afterwards we'll see. And before that she wants to see some paintings, that's for starters, because does she need to be painted with one eye here and one ear there? Thanks a lot, really. As it is she's not that happy with her face; it's just that now she's become a bit used to it she doesn't want to have changes made. Yes. That's how those skinheads talk, heaven help us. Life is right here honey, what you learn in school is one thing and what you learn on the street is a completely different matter, completely different. "Get lost before you get your face slashed," that's what those skinheads said to some Vietnamese who stopped next to her once. She doesn't know how it ended and she doesn't want to know. These legs, with all their veins, know how to run very well when you need to run, yes, like when she was a girl at school and won all the races. Someone here doesn't believe her? She's not angry, no way, she can hardly believe it herself.

Which brings us back again to that guard, yes. What does the guard like? Because there are things that she won't do even if she gets paid like one from those five-star hotels. Spanking. Yes, she doesn't do that even if she's paid a million, not to be spanked and not to spank someone else. There are girls who do that, sure there are, there are girls that it's better not to know what they'll do for money. It's just a pity about that sweet face, even if someone here is trying to hide it with a beard like that. She's not trying to come on to him, no way, she's talking like a big sister. So what, who doesn't need a big sister, to teach him a few things about life. Is it too cold now? There are those who are never cold, honey. Someone here doesn't like to be called honey, okay she won't call him honey. Even if he is so sweet. Okay, he isn't. Once, she actually did have one, but ever since that she's through with it, the spanking. He was well educated, came to her with a briefcase and glasses, you'd have thought he came to play chess with her. Straightaway he started to tell her how once all people were like that, meaning were into spanking, with whips and branches and what not. And all because of their religiosity, that's what that wise guy said, solely in order to suffer the way He suffered for them. That's what he said, that wise guy. Right away she said to him, listen sir, don't bring Him into it, have some respect, besides which you don't seem at all like someone suffering, except maybe when I stop for a moment to rest.

You wouldn't believe how tiring it is, yes, even though in the beginning you feel like taking out on them all the hatred you have for them, together with all this fucked up life. Fucked up, sure fucked up. Now someone here's pretending to be interested, thinks he'll get a discount for showing some interest. It's the same price honey, with your taking an interest or not. Just so that you know she doesn't do that. Now she just wants to know exactly how she gets in, to that guard, because maybe he won't want to open? And what if he's the type that someone from the street is beneath him? Yes, because that's what she is, someone from the street, for a long time she hasn't tried to lie to herself, what for.

The type that let's say has a wife and children he fears for. Because actually the ones who look the most miserable, like porters and street sweepers, they're the ones who afterwards go home to the wife and children, even if it's in some fucked up quarter like this quarter. Fucked up, sure fucked up. It's one thing to work here and another thing to live here, she wouldn't want to see someone like herself coming out of her house, and most definitely that her children shouldn't see. Do they have to know about things like that? There's plenty of time for them to learn, no shortage. Here right next to her there's a young man, never mind how old, he still hasn't learned. He hasn't learned a thing, nothing. So it's actually those who afterwards go to the wife and children for the kind of meal we should be so lucky to have, it makes her drool just thinking about it.

Sure she has checkups, has them like clockwork, and anyway there's no getting near her without a rubber. Yes sir, she could make an advert for Durex. And afterwards she's not embarrassed to tell them: that sir, is yours, don't leave it here. Does she need their germs around in the air? Scary. Her mother didn't have any of those worries at all when she was still alive. Sometimes she really doesn't know who's got it better now, her or her mother, even if she didn't get to heaven, her mother, and that's for sure. Girls like that don't get there even by mistake. Yes, the most important thing in life is not to have delusions. Someone with high hopes finds herself in the end so low down that even ants piss on her.

There was one here once who had high hopes, she thought she'd become something of a lady, as if someone didn't have anything to do in life other than marry one of them. And how did she finish up in the end? Someone here should know how she finished up; in the refrigeration unit. Yes, she had to come to identify her, but when a person's dead they don't look anything like themselves, they don't even look like a person. So exactly how is she going to get in there? Because then the policeman let her in, they didn't even ask if she wanted to come in or not. They were so considerate to her that afterwards there was even one who tried to feel her up. She gave him such a slap that he didn't want a thing more, only that nobody should see the mark left behind on his cheek.

Sure she's got a raincoat, who hasn't? She never stands naked in the street, not even when she was young, you know a month or two ago. Now there's someone here with dimples in his cheeks; lucky his beard doesn't grow the way it should. Okay, okay, she won't touch anymore. So like she said, she never yet stood naked in the street, and neither will she ever, no sir. Because what does someone who shows it all right away at the start have left to show afterwards? This fucked up life as well, how does it get shown to you, in one go, or slowly, slowly until the soul dies out? Of course she can open the buttons that way, she'll open them so slowly that his eyes will pop out from doing it so slowly. Anyone here want an example? She actually thought he was someone who liked to look: come here, turn around, go there, bend down, isn't he one of those? All right, so he's not.

Once she even almost performed in it, she and a few other girls went to audition at some club in Pigalle; just that a week later there wasn't a club there and nothing else either. Anyhow she was just a tiny bit disappointed but one of the other girls, from doing it so slowly, managed to let the owner leave her with a baby in her belly. That's how it is with babies. They come when you don't want them and from one you don't want, and straightaway their eyes look at you as if you've waited for them your whole life. And the funniest thing? After a while it also seems that way to you; that you waited your whole life for them. They turn your head around in such a way that you begin to forget who their father was and what a son of a bitch he was, that's if you know who it was at all.

That's the way it is honey; better not to know. Better to keep yourself busy with your paintings. She could tell stories like these until the morning; but does her honey know what one could have been doing during all this time? He doesn't? – Come here, turn around, bend down, hold your purse as if it was a suitcase, look at the streetlamp as if it was a pillar drawing away in a window and at the neon sign as if it was a station signpost – you could have placed her there instead of the woman wringing her hands, after all Magdalene was also one of the girls, but you didn't want to paint a prostitute in black fishnet stockings standing next to the holes in the soles. Mantegna dressed them in simple clothing, the faces not made up, the wrinkles not concealed, there was no licentiousness nor was there holiness in them; just the sadness for a beloved dead man.

The small clochard was better suited: her hair was grey and her face completely worn out; not concealed by make-up, only her eyes were young and even childlike. But a filthy bandage was wrapped around her left leg and an acute rotting smell emanated from between each wrapping as if from the bottom of a pit. Young girl I say unto thee arise, he would have said to her, the son of God, before he was murdered, as if it was possible to arise and depart from a grave or from a tunnel, or even from a room.

A meal in the McDonald's opposite the Luxembourg Gardens was enough to entice her: she would sit there every evening until they kicked her out, and on the way out she would manage to gather a few crumbs from the tables for the birds in the park. "A Big Mac?" she asked. "Large fries? Large Coke?" She repeated the offer in a cracked voice as if she couldn't believe such happiness awaited her. She could pass hours there with tea in a disposable cup and with sugar cubes she brought with her, until the shift changed and the new person in charge shouted at her that she was driving customers away; angry as if he was the son of McDonald himself or the inventor of fries. Until then she would sit in her corner, keeping the sugar cubes in her mouth Russian style and take minute sips of tea like a bird – while there were still birds outside – for whose tiny beak alone a whole cloud was emptied into a puddle.

The second one, who lived in the same tunnel and slept on a bench alongside her, wanted a bottle of wine. "Beaujolais," she said, and for a moment you wondered if she'd insist on the vintage. But the wine that she drank straight from the bottle did not come from vines and vineyards, it wasn't harvested, not by men nor by women; nobody squeezed a cluster to parted lips nor crushed grapes on a décolletage nor crouched over to lick; flies did not buzz in the air, did not circle here and there like gentlemen strolling after a meal, their fingers intertwined behind their backs; south of the vineyards there was no sea, the wind did not carry its smell. There was no wind other than that which the Metro blew on the posters of movie stars.

When she got drunk she'd sing Piaf's songs, turn over the empty bottle and hold it by the neck like a transparent microphone and wait for the applause from anyone around: the clochards who sat on the bench, the people standing on the platform, the girl who got onto the escalator and the ceiling cut off her neck, her braid, the black man who continued to push a giant squeegee, opening wide a long furrow in the dust, which for a moment shone and immediately dimmed and was erased. Afterwards she squatted behind the bench and tried to pee into the opening of the bottle, supported by the drunk peeing against the wall. "Just be careful it doesn't get stuck there, Edith," he grinned and shook what he was holding in his hand like a horse driving away flies with its tail, if there were still meadows and green pastures anywhere from horizon to horizon and horses of white or black, grey or brown, which didn't allow flies to land on their bodies and gnaw at them.

In the alley on the way from the bar to the hotel, above the clochard whom you chose for the main role, neither flies nor angels were flying around. He sat leaning against the lamppost fixing something, concentrated on his labors like an old bachelor sewing a button on a shirt, and when you drew close you saw that he was retouching with Panda pastels the lettering on the cardboard that was lying on his knees: "Repent" in red letters, "the Kingdom of Heaven" in blue, "is at Hand" in black. Without that cardboard sign and without the pantomime steps he had learned, he would have looked to the tourists like one of those types one had better beware of or at least rotate a finger at the temple and right away exchange looks with the other tourists: we are not like him, no way no way no way, and we never will be. Thoughts that beat in our brains have yet to shatter it; nightmares that grow in the eyes have yet to rent our pupils, and mark, our breaths come out the nostrils one after another after another.

For a while you could already see the morgue's stainless steel drawer and how in the cold neon light the bottle you'll place there will glow, in place of the goblet that Mantegna painted: in places like these there were always neon lights, long, white and skeletal, as if the bones of the ceiling were revealed. It will be cold in the drawer, but perhaps he'll be warmed by the alcohol or the women's hands or their bodies or their burning tears, after all they, at least, will weep over him. You bent down by his side in the alley on your heels like the Indians in India, the Bedouin in Sinai, the Indians in the Pampas, all the impoverished of the world who did not have even a stool to sit on, but he was not at all impressed by the gesture. "So you want to paint me?" he said and inspected the cardboard sign with narrowed eyes the way one surveys a painting, which for a moment seems to be finished, but up to that point there wasn't even one that you had finished.

"What do I get for it?" he asked. Art or no art, what's he going to get? At the side of the pavement the wind rifled through the fallen leaves and read the one word written on their parchment, and promptly hastened to whistle it everywhere as if someone would still manage to be salvaged from their fate. The Panda pastels had already been returned to the crushed cigarette box and he waved a piece of cardboard to remove a few rustling leaves from his bedstead, and they promptly flew away angrily like wasps frightened from their resting place – in one of the nature programs that you watched when you still lived in her apartment, a species of wasp was filmed, one which lays its eggs inside figs and out of which only the females fly; the males fertilized them inside and lived and died there, and for a while you pondered if perhaps the entire world was not one giant fig – "I'm the star," he said and demanded the eighty-eight franc menu, that's how it was written in chalk on the board of the restaurant on the corner: a blackboard like a piece of plaster that fell from the night, but months passed and not a crumb fell from it, you counted thousands of sheep one after another after another and still not one brick from the grey bricks behind it was revealed.

Perhaps it would have been better to complete the deal with a handshake, a hand with holes in which the wind will whistle its two notes, but he had already concealed his hand inside the cardboard. "And that's without the wine," he said and demanded bottles for the whole time he'll be lying there, and right away wrapped himself up to the shoulders in the large cardboard packaging to show that in this matter too, no allowances would be made. In the drawer in which he'll be lying, a bottle of cheap wine will replace the goblet that was painted on the bunk, perhaps the Holy Grail into which his flowing blood was collected. But the goblet was not enough for the blood, a bottle was not enough, a barrel was not enough, it required the entire world.

At first the cross was laid on the ground, then he was placed on the cross, and afterwards a soldier grasped the palm of his hand so that he couldn't move it: it's easy to say "all the way" but hard to keep the hand in place as the hammer draws near. Afterwards another soldier took one of the nails that he held between his lips and lowered it and directed the point to the center of the palm. Perhaps he sunk it slightly into the flesh so that it would not slip; perhaps he had made a sign with a carpenter's pencil before.

The son of God in front of you indented a hollow in the folded coat for his head and made it deeper, as if some rusted halo will hinder him there. "Côtes du Rhône," he said and shut his eyes, "one bottle every hour," but you thought two would be enough for him and after them he wouldn't be able to tell the difference between good wine and cheap wine. Anyway with Mantegna, his eyes were shut: his pupils were concealed by delicate eyelids, which the Lord himself shuttered; millions of people in the world still heard them being slammed shut.

3

The shoes beat on the paving stones, it was good to hear them there, the shoes. There were times when the shoes were not heard and there was no knowing that you were walking and making sounds with them. The windows of the buildings were already blackened and in the darkness behind them men and women lay, a child sank into a dream, an old man awakened from a nightmare, but in the sky only the murky light of the streetlamp was visible, spreading into it like the vomit of drunks in the river. Steam filtered out around the sewer lids, greyish as smoke, perhaps mean rats were roasting inside, but their offspring still scampered between piles of garbage, licking their whiskers and burping. Chestnut branches in parks were conjoined and sealed together, a foliage of darkness grew and dark birds nested inside, hidden from the eye like the birds of the wooden cross: vultures surely circled above him waiting too for his flesh, but they were never painted, neither were the women who came to watch as if to a public hanging. They desired them all, the hanged and the crucified, to cling to and to copulate with each and every one instead of the vast vulva that gaped above to receive them.

For these two, men were just drinking partners; at the most they warmed each other on especially cold nights: the lice would then pass from garment to garment, from hair to hair; the chitin shells beat and caused a racket, cracking open skulls like miniature jackhammers. The shoes were worn out like a clochard's pair, but you still had money or its equivalent to offer them, and you still had a room in which to live apart from the hotel's rooms that you would sometimes use like a baron who sleeps in a different room every night.

At the end of the staircase the tunnel stretched out, empty as a molding cast for trains or like their death masks: there were no more trains. And from the bench the drunkard who was called Edith said: "the hotel isn't his you fool, if he had a hotel he wouldn't speak to us at all. Someone who's got a hotel doesn't go down to the Metro. Why would someone with a hotel go under the ground besides when he dies?" The tunnel gates had not been locked yet and the two of them sat on the bench and waited for you as if you had invited them to a show or a concert, and from the bench next to them one of the drunks shouted out: "here comes your admirer girls," and bristles sprouted from his cheeks like arrows shot from a blowpipe: pipes of stalk spread it, arrows, strings of bows, daggers.

The second drunk was struggling to fasten a bursting suitcase with a ragged leather belt and to tie it to an old pram laden up to the handle bar, and from the vaulted ceiling the announcer spoke again. The moving stairway ascended; used tickets floated in the gutter; a mouse's tail sprouted from beneath one of the railway sleepers, and the hidden announcer spoke again: "Ladies and Gentlemen," she said and begged your pardon and all at once the words drew away on the empty tracks and were swallowed up in the dark.

"Don't pay attention to them sir," the one who got up said and pulled your hand like a little girl eager to gain the prize promised to her, a hamburger as precious in her eyes as whale meat. "Listen-listen," the other one said, but right away got up and also stood on the moving stairway to be lifted to the outside world, a worn out handbag hung from her arm crammed full and bulging. "Wait until I tell them what you said," she said from behind, "they're not gonna like it at all, Nadia, just so that you know." The handbag swung to and fro from her arm like a metronome but the keys of the stairs already flattened at the end and were gathered up and the shoes were already drumming on the top floor their tuff-tuff, and tuk-tuk, and tupm-tupm.

The first one, who was called Nadia, held high a small grey
head on whose disarrayed bedding perhaps lice mated and
became rowdy when their mistress scratched herself. "You're
not gonna tell them," she said. You too could hear them at
night and at the time also listened to the blood being sucked
and to your nails growing in the void of the room toward the
ceiling, as if they'll succeed in removing it from above you.
"Get a load of her," the second one said from behind, "she's
gonna tell *me* what I'm meant to say or not – well really."
In the expanse of the tunnel the shoes echoed, tuff-tuff they
echoed, tuk-tuk, tupm-tupm, the barefooted and the ones
sleeping were unfortunate in not knowing whether they were
alive or dead.

The tunnel was so long, enough for thousands of drunkards
and millions of bottles that rolled in their wake like the fleet
of a retired admiral who launched miniature wooden ships
inside them. Sometimes from the room it seemed as if the
entire world, mountains valleys and clouds, had been placed
into a bottle and rolled on the tunnel floor: beyond the round
glass edges enormous trains traveled, beyond the glass edges
gigantic women ascended moving stairways and drew away,
beyond the edges anonymous musicians stood and played;
for a moment the tune was still vaguely audible, and right
away the bottle rolled further on from there and you too
rolled inside it. "Hey, Nadia," Edith called out from behind
as the tip of her shoe touched an empty one, "your bandage's
undone." The bottle rolled hastily to the next staircase as if
it meant to ascend to ground level, following the passengers
who ascended before it, a half an hour before or a year or a
decade, and did not blink when they reached there, not even
once: the electric light on the inside was stronger than the
sun, which day after day hid behind a grey blackening veil,
and at times you could not even tell if it was its face there or
the nape of its neck.

Nadia bent down to the bandage still holding on to
you with the palm of a hand wrinkled and blemished with
age spots. "She's just mean," she said after checking, "my
bandage's fine," because it was still fastened to her leg fold

upon fold, and within the filth and the smell a safety pin sparkled like a silver hairpin.

The female announcer's voice echoed again, devoid of face and body like a voice speaking in a revelation, but here she just announced the renovations at the next station; and below, the bottle still rolled, harassing everything it encountered on its way: a squashed tin can, a wall, a wrinkled up newspaper, a drainage ditch. The shoes had now already ascended with the last step and gone out to the street; your worn out crepe soles, Nadia's metallic shoes, Edith's rubber soles, and the smell of gangrene also went out, rubbing against Nadia's leg like a pampered cat or sitting on her shoulder like one of the pigeons she used to feed in the park or circling above her like a hungry vulture. Had not all the flocks soaring there stuck their beaks into the holes and unraveled his body as if it was a suitcase crammed with objects? Intestines, spleen, liver, heart, fields, forests, lakes and rivers, the entire world that spilled out from inside him.

The street was empty and just here and there in a shop entrance a man wrapped himself up in old newspapers, gathered his knees to his chest as if he's yet to be reborn one morning. From right and left the buildings with their shuttered windows were dark and silent, and on the slate roofs, which reflected a faint gleam, the night lay down breathing hushed breaths, a huge bear in hibernation. The black tree trunks emitted the stench of urine, no hearts nor names nor dates were carved in them, and in transparent telephone booths the receivers were wrenched out or swung to and fro with your steps: tuff-tuff, tuk-tuk, tupm-tupm.

But in the alley Edith did not want to go forward even one step: no sir no! No way! What, is she stupid? She kept her soles close to the pavement and would have put down roots had some rain fallen, but not even a drop fell from the black fur above: it lay over the entire city, the sleeping bear; honey being digested in its entrails or the meat of man.

"A hospital here?" Edith said. Fat chance! What, doesn't she know where the hospital is? She knows very well! Just because a person's a bit drunk sometimes doesn't make him dumb, no sir no! It doesn't make him into someone who knows nothing about life, ho-ho, she knows plenty about life! Does this look to anyone like the way to the hospital? No ambulance passed by here and that one coming toward them, that one, yes that one, doesn't she know him, that nutcase? Makes himself out like God that one, he's sick in the head.

From the end of the alley, which she thought you'd all be passing through, the bearded clochard came forward, tinged alternately by the pale orange lamplight and the dark. He was festive and joyous and already called out from a distance "good evening," as if the alleyway was opened for you all by a gatekeeper in uniform or by a maid with a headdress and apron and nothing underneath – at the time you used to see women like that at nighttime, not projected on the eyelids but on the ceiling itself and attracting the member as if it too was a thorny nail trying to push against it.

He immediately extended his hand to be shaken, and the wind did not pass through the holes of his palms and did not whistle, because there was no longer a wind, there were no longer sails that billowed in the sea, and there was no sound other than the sound of his shoes. He had on jeans and a faded army jacket and wore sneakers, which had long ago lost their whiteness. "Mesdames et Messieurs," he said the way he used to address the tourists coming off the buses in the square, "Ladies and Gentlemen, Damen und Herren," made a clownish bow and took a few hovering steps on the spot, which he learned from one of Marceau's pupils or from Marceau himself or from he who walked on the waters of the Galilee and hordes of fish tickled his soles. At nights, from the room, you could momentarily recall how the wind drew up small gentle waves like those it stirred in the fields beneath shadows of clouds; over the tops of corn stalks shadows of clouds sailed, colossal ships whose weight was less than that of a grain.

Nadia watched him with curiosity as he stepped on the spot, but Edith gripped her handbag with all her might: yesyes, a person has to look after herself! Two men with two women in the middle of the night, it's no joke sir, who knows what could happen. And if she doesn't look after herself, who'll look after her, Nadia? Nadia, who's not even capable of looking after her own self? In order to put them at ease, you outlined on the pavement with the worn out tip of your shoe, the shoe, the shoe, the painting in which they'll be painted and where each one will stand and what he'll be doing, perhaps acting as Mantegna did on the pavements of Florence when leading his models there. For a while they were silent and tried to see themselves on the pavement, between dry crumbling leaves and squashed cigarette butts smoked down to the filter, two thousand years before you perhaps the Lord himself stopped like that and with the tip of his shoe drew on the pavements of heaven.

"He'll just be asleep," you told them to calm their fears and their disappointment, because Nadia's hand became smaller in your palm and slackened, but the two of them, you said, will be doing things, oh yes they'll be doing lots of things there in that room in the morgue: she, Nadia, will be crying, yes, with tears and everything and even wipe her eyes with a handkerchief just like this. Exactly. For a moment she kept her pose as in a children's game whose name you've already forgotten, one you forgot a long time ago and perhaps never knew: that boy who played it was not you, and it was no longer possible to call him from the depths of the body as with Lazarus: you there, come forth.

"She sir," Edith said from behind, "is actually good at crying, one little word's enough and straightaway she cries." She had already let go of the handbag and allowed it to hang from her arm again and at once it began to sway above the pavement like a pendulum detecting treasure, an oil field or a diamond mine or a grain of mustard.

Do they really have to lament him, Edith said, this character? Only her eyebrow motioned to the bearded clochard, he simply wasn't worthy of Edith moving a finger for him. As for Edith, even if right now a real angel with a halo and feathers and everything landed here, she wouldn't even throw him a dry bread crumb; did anyone ever give her anything? Things were thrown at her, oh yes, just how many things it's better you don't know. For a moment she intertwined her fingers like the woman in the painting in the pose that you demonstrated for her, and beneath them were her depleted breasts, which perhaps had suckled all the drunks of the Metro or were squashed beneath their heads on especially cold nights, all the nights were especially cold: beyond the windowpane, when the wall of your room still had a window, in the depths of the black cavity that gaped there, masses of tiny yellow teeth chattered; every night from your bed you heard their chattering.

"No one laments like that," Edith said and freed her fingers. "Who laments like that, who?" And anyway, why should she put on a show in the middle of the street? Someone's going to pay for that as well? And what if someone suddenly sees her? It'll be all right there; who'll get to see her there. Whoever's lying there doesn't see anything anymore.

You explained to her that in the painting it's possible to wring your hands from sorrow, to wring, yes, that's what it's called, and that everything's possible in a painting: you could have patched up the holes of the palms or painted in them, like the holes of a fence where all at once everyone gathers to peer through, the celestial Jerusalem; but Mantegna kept the holes in His palms emptied, and through the delicate eyelids, which were shuttered, not even the last sight imprinted on the pupils was visible: the surrounding mountain tops, a shadow of a cloud that darkened their rocky terrain, a forest of pines and cypresses – you tried to remember those landscapes, but you no longer remembered, only the floral wallpaper fading into the void of the room, leaf after leaf after leaf – shadows of hawks and crows, the masses that assembled at His feet, a peddler selling them pine nuts in a packet.

In one of the dark buildings a man coughed and in another a woman groaned, and characters from a dream were perhaps beating against shuttered eyelids there: tuk-tuk, tuff-tuff, tupm-tupm. On your right and on your left the buildings withdrew step by step, the night on their shoulders, heavy, still and bloated. And Edith looked at the bearded man again, yes, that cheeky one who dared to say now that lying half-naked before two women isn't new to him and who's counting anymore?

"Someone like that sir," Edith said, "it's best to stay away from!" Yes, because does she know what someone like that's got? And he still brags about it! It's just that nowadays a person has to take care of himself, if a person doesn't take care of himself who'll take care of him? Someone like that, easy as anything to catch something from him, you can't know a thing about him, not a thing. A complete nutcase. That's what the ones from the tunnel said about him when they threw him out of there. "Believe me sir, nobody misses him, who'd miss someone like that, who."

They threw him out? Him? In the middle of the dark street he stopped and wondered. Him? Someone who's used to sleeping under the open sky in summer since he was a boy? Him? Nobody threw him out! What does he need that fucking tunnel for in summer? Give him one reason. Not two, one. In the dark of the night a few faint clouds were visible, chewed by yellow teeth of which every night one more fell to fulfill the wishes of all the gullible; from the empty mattress, whose springs pierced your back, you would look at the window and count them when they appeared instead of flocks of sheep: who still remembers the sight of sheep and how a bird would stand on a woolly back and let itself be led a step, until it flew off and with one beat of the wings passed over the entire valley.

"Ask him sir," Edith said, "since when does he suddenly like to sleep outside, huh? Just ask him that, the liar. A person wandering around outside nowadays doesn't know what's hit him, it's scary to be on the street – and he tells me

about open skies! You see sir? What did I say?" In one of the
upper windows a man coughed and cleared his throat and
withdrew inside the room with his blackened lungs, and in
the enormous penthouse above him, if the owner still lived
in it and still mourned for his son, he walked about barefoot
and silent.

"With you," Nadia slowed down, "everyone's a liar," and
in a cracked, trembling voice she told Edith she's always got
bad things to say about people, yes only bad, she never says
anything good about anyone. "That's because you're like that
yourself," she said to her in her cracked voice and stopped on
the pavement, as if you had time to listen to them talking,
and right away also said that when everything's black inside
people, they're sure that everyone else is like that, with a
black heart like theirs. Yes just like that, like some chestnut
forgotten to be taken out. There was a charred one on the
pavement and you kicked it with the tip of your shoe.

"A black leg is what you're gonna have," Edith said, "she
talks to me about a black heart. Go to a doctor already you
fool. Me, my heart's not blacker than anyone else's heart! Nice
of her to defend him all of a sudden, you're really a perfect
pair, you and he together. A spot in Père Lachaise is what
you'll be getting." She brought the handbag close to her as if
it sought to be suckled by her in the middle of the road, black
and tattered like an old African baby, one of those which
expired in their hundreds on television, ageless, nameless,
until the channel was switched with one touch.

"You're her friend?" the bearded man said bluntly as if
you had gathered them together to clarify their affairs. "Some
friend." "You and he together, believe me," said Edith, "for
once in your life maybe you'll get to lie down next to a man,
at long last you'll get the chance, on my word."

"You call yourself a friend?" the bearded man said to the
empty street. "If you were her friend you would have taken
her to a doctor long ago! Making fun of her not being able
to walk." And at once he turned his gaze for your reaction,
but you just looked at your watch: you were assigned to pay
homage to one of the great painters, you just wanted the

clochards to let you paint them one night in the morgue, in place of the son of God and the two old lamenting women that Mantegna painted.

One of them was perhaps his mother, and she too, the holy mother, everyone painted his own way. Del Prombio painted her as sturdy as a farmer, whereas Bergonia sketched her with customary delicate features. But when he painted her breastfeeding, he seated a model opposite him and from his gaze and perhaps from the paintbrush touches, a giant teat stuck out from her breast – the paintbrush hairs were fluttery and it was possible to very slowly paint the belly, the navel, the line of translucent down descending from it, the curls of pubic hair and the lips, till she groaned and pulled you toward her onto that bed on which you lay no more, not awake nor in your dreams – he also liked painting blood, Bergonia: he let it drip from every possible place, from the holes in the palms and from the cut in the chest and from the piercing of the thorns on the forehead, and around the cross he painted hosts of angels, open-mouthed, their throats parched from thirst.

"I tried," Edith said, "what, didn't I try? Ask her how much I tried. Didn't I Nadia? But she's like that bird sir, that puts its head in the sand so it won't see its troubles." For a moment she looked again at the upper windows, but the man who had coughed in one of them had already drawn away with the entire building as if on a giant crutch: tuk-tuk, he pounded with it, and others in their buildings pounded as well, tuff-tuff, tupm-tupm.

"Me sir," Edith said and you didn't react at all, "ever since I was a little girl I always heard grownups say that one's health is the main thing. I didn't know what they were talking about at all. Only now I know. It's the most important thing, health, not money, not a house, not anything. Because if someone like us sir suddenly gets sick, who's going to look after him? There was one, d'you remember him, Nadia? From drinking so much he fell asleep on the steps outside after they closed up. In the morning they found him dead sir, from the cold.

D'you think anyone cared about him? I'll tell you sir the only thing they cared about was that he got in the way of the people going in. If it wasn't for that they would have let him rot there. That's all, I'm telling you."

"So why didn't you go bring him inside?" the bearded man said, but his shoes were already beating out a rhythm in company with the women as again you marched them on with the lure of food and wine, "after all you saw that he hadn't come." Tuff-tuff, they pranced behind you, tuk-tuk, tupm-tupm.

"I didn't know where he was," Edith said and stepped onwards, "how could I know where he was! Sometimes some go and sleep somewhere else, how could I know he was on the steps? It's easy to talk. Talk is easy. What, if I had known, wouldn't I have gone to him? Of course I would have. If we don't help each other, who's gonna help us? That's why I keep on telling her all the time about her leg, even if she gets tired of me, so that the worst won't happen to her. Yessir, and then she still tells me I've got a black heart."

The rucksack on your back was heavy with bottles and vials, with paints and canvas and the edge of the folding easel rubbing against the nape of your neck as if trying to dig a hollow there. Sunday painters would walk like that to the city parks to which you didn't go anymore, and for two or three hours paint what in their eyes seemed to be a landscape: a few nurtured trees like those used for props, which only in winter, once their skeletal structure was revealed, resembled a living thing; and a lake, which only once it began to freeze over and murky water trickled between areas of thin ice on its surface, did it cease to resemble a tub. Van Gogh, whose craziness for a time you envied – time that could not be measured and could not be gauged other than according to the dulling of memory – once painted himself with an easel and a rucksack like these on his back, walking on a spring day through fields above which crows had not yet taken flight. Perhaps they were all crammed into his rucksack, inflating it like kittens yet to be drowned in the sky: tuk-tuk, bubbles

will burst there above them, tuff-tuff, tupm-tupm. Beneath
your feet the dead beat back in reply, like tunnel miners
whose comrades are drawing near to them after not having
seen each other for years.

"There was one," Edith said at the next turning, "who
threw himself onto the rails. A month later we were still afraid
to go near there sir, because of the germs, even though they
cleaned it up. He brought bad luck. Right away journalists
came and started asking questions. And photographers, the
whole time, wherever you went. Click-click, click-click, and
we're not like those who need their photos in the paper. Do
we need someone to see us? I mean from a past life? I don't
care about the people what'll see your painting sir, what do
I care about them. But those from a past life, d'you know
what they'll say sir? You see her, we always knew she'd land up
like that. Someone like that, you can tell immediately how
she's going to land up, that's what they'll say sir. I know all
about people." On your right and on your left and above you,
beyond the shuttered windows, images of nightmares clung
to eyelids, drew eyelashes apart as if they were curtain tassels
and flowed into the pupils like water into ships' portholes.

"The one that threw himself onto the tracks sir?" Edith
said and advanced forward. "If let's say we saw a mouse there
after that, on the tracks, we'd still be scared of them a month
later. Of course we were scared. We even told the inspector,
if you don't care about us, at least care about the passengers.
D'you think he cared sir? Not one bit. If he had children let's
say, then maybe he would have cared, but someone like that
hasn't got the time for children, where would he have the
time? The whole day at work, doesn't want to go home at all,
just so that he can stay and insult us some more. And she, one
little word's enough and straightaway she cries."

In the yellowish cone of light into which you all entered, the
bearded man surveyed your rucksack the way his predecessor
had surveyed the beams and the sky concaving toward him
as he wondered if it would suffice the span of his arms, and
afterwards he turned his eyes to Nadia and told her not to

take notice of the inspector, not to take notice of anyone. "They're not worth crying over," he said, "nothing's worth crying over, nothing." He's talking from experience, what do you think: he's had things like that done to him, God help us, just from hearing about it you can get depressed, and what, is he going to give somebody the pleasure of seeing him cry? "After all that's what they enjoy most, the sons of bitches, to see you cry." Beneath the streetlamp he busied himself with his cardboard signpost for a moment, straightening a corner that had bent. With his nail he scraped a glob of Panda pastel that had stuck to the "R" of "Repent" and examined all the lettering with narrowed eyes before turning it toward Edith and waving it at her.

"Him and his signpost," Edith turned her head, "makes himself out to be God, he doesn't care at all that they'll say he's crazy. He doesn't care about anything. There're such stories going around about him sir, it's better not to know, stories like that would make a person with an ounce of shame bury himself from the shame."

"Who's been telling?" said the bearded clochard having already moved out from under the cone of the streetlamp light. "The ones from the tunnel?" He waved the cardboard as he marched on. "The ones who pushed someone onto the tracks and afterwards said that he fell? All he did was lie down on someone's bench by mistake, didn't know it was his. How could he know, he had just come to the tunnel and a moment later he was already on the tracks."

"He knew it was his sir!" Edith said moving forward. "Don't listen to what he says, who didn't know? Everyone knew. He did it on purpose, right from the start you could tell he was someone who was looking for trouble. You can tell them straightaway. When he turned up with that trolley of his, you could tell straightaway. A trolley like that sir, the kind you go to supermarkets with. A children's pram wasn't enough for him, straightaway he thought he was king of the tunnel."

"They could tell," said the bearded man and advanced further. "And for that they threw him onto the tracks?"

"They got into a fight sir, that's what they were doing, fighting. That's what it's like when you fight. Even I know that, even though in my whole life I've never got into a fight, not even with my worst enemy, which I wouldn't wish upon anyone. I was the one who got hit. Sometimes someone falls. It wasn't their fault they were next to the tracks. We're always there next to the tracks. Did anyone say we want to be there next to the tracks? Someone who's got luck falls on the carpet in his house, and someone who hasn't falls on the tracks. And that one," she pointed at the bearded man, "right afterwards he wanted to go to the police, without waiting a moment. There are those who straightaway run to the police, doesn't matter how a person was once a friend and all that you did together, straightaway they run to the police. They don't think at all how it will turn out for themselves sir, because the police? They see someone like me and straightaway think the worst."

"With good reason," said the bearded clochard, and the two lamp posts before you momentarily balanced their lamps one against the other, as if they were weighing something other than the yellowish light in which no insect took an interest: not a gnat, not a moth, not an angel. "What should they think instead, good things?" he turned the signpost toward Edith again and when she averted her eyes he said he wasn't surprised: because also when he stands in the street with it, "plenty of people pretend they don't see." Sometimes he thinks he would make more money if he'd start to eat it instead, "yes why not, like the ones who swallow razor blades and glass" – bits of bottles and fragments of window, which on one side you could still see the reflection of clouds and on the other side the reflection of a room in which there was a bare mattress, wallpaper, a basin and a gas fixture, whose leak you no longer tried to fix; the air outdoors was no better than the air of the room or the air of the tunnels, a few breaths was all it took to asphyxiate the throat and the lungs and roughen the heart, making it coarse like the palms of a gravedigger in the time of plague; in the window, when the wall still had a

window, you no longer expected to see one of the things that
was once seen in it: chestnut trees were no longer standing
the length of the road below, the lights of shop windows
no longer lined the pavement, men and women did not sit
in cafés, fire blowers did not blow, fire swallowers did not
swallow; it waited under the pavement with all its flames, and
the street emptied from one end to the other apart from those
who were walking to the morgue.

On the streetlamps crows no longer stood drooling with
saliva, all of them glided in the air keeping close to each other,
a band of tailor-jugglers who sewed up the night with their
wings. Long hours passed till it unraveled, revealing a filthy
sheet that wrapped whoever lay there, swelling up above from
horizon to horizon.

"Believe me I would have earned more," the bearded man
said, "a thousand times more," and the further you advanced
the smaller Nadia's palm became in your hand as if the earth
had already begun to pull her into it by her gangrenous leg.

Others had also depicted that sight before you: Bernini
carved in marble the softness of the breasts and the thighs,
and for Hades he chiseled sinuous muscles, his Hades was
Mr. Universe and Persephone tried to release herself from his
hand as if he had not dragged a thousand others like her
to the netherworld with one finger. The netherworld was
near, just one floor below the tunnels, and you could feel it
through the soles of the shoes, through the soles of the shoes,
through the soles of the shoes, each time the trains of the
dead shook the pavement.

But it was the bottles that rattled, and the bearded clochard
listened to their sound through the material of the rucksack.
"Côtes du Rhône?" he asked while marching. "Côtes du
Rhône," you answered moving forward. From the back
pocket of his jeans he took out a red felt-tipped pen and for
a moment waved it in the light of the streetlamp and said
that this is so that no one will think he's stingy: he bought
it at his own cost, to paint the holes by himself; a Japanese

felt-tipped pen that doesn't wash off with water. Because he's a professional, not a nutcase like Edith makes him out to be.

"Makes himself out to be God," Edith said and carried on walking, "even in a joke sir, someone like that, something's definitely not right with him. Who knows what he's capable of doing." The streetlamp drew away behind with the other ones and with whoever had leaned against them like walking sticks, transparent giants who, even in their old age, could rotate their heavy soles above your heads until the whitish brain wisps spurted out.

When he heard that all the wounds in the painting were washed, he asked Edith if she's going to wash him: will she do the washing first and wring her hands afterwards? But Edith, astonished, clasped her handbag again, the black infant toward whom the crows' beaks fixedly stared: yessir, with all due respect, there are some things anyone with a tiny drop of self-respect would never do. No sir no; no matter how much you pay them, even a million. Even if you hit them and throw things at them and swear at them so that they hardly know why they're alive.

"Of course there're those who do everything," Edith said moving onwards. "What, don't I know? Those who sell their own bottoms. It's just that if a person doesn't keep his self-respect who'll do it for them, who? Because what'll they say about them afterwards, when they're not here anymore? Me, if I heard what they're saying now behind my back sir, I'd die on the spot. From shame sir. That's what shame's like. Someone sensitive can die just from shame. That's why I'm not going to wash him sir, I'm not going to wash him even if let's say there weren't any stories about him. It's enough that I'll do like this with my hands."

"Wring them," said the bearded clochard and progressed forwards.

"Whatever it is," Edith said moving onwards.

At the end of the road all the lamps crowded together, united and flowed with all the slate roofs and the buildings beneath them, together with the men and women who clung to each other on their beds, and with the boys and girls who dreamed there, and the youngsters whose limbs were filling out, and with aquarium fish and canaries and the cats who hankered after them, they all disappeared there into the vanishing point; one shouldn't live at the end of a road, one shouldn't even reach the far end of the room with the images that have not yet dulled in the memory: a long outside platform at whose end the night encamped like an enormous coal coach; an empty freight carriage whose yellow shaft had fallen; a heavy suitcase placed on the platform for a moment and on its left, faded blue corduroy on plump buttocks; a glob of chewing gum that is being scraped from the sole onto the shaft; the shadow of the suitcase as it's lifted once more.

"One thing's for sure," said Edith, "that one's not skimping on perfume." From the end of the street she drew near, swaying everything she had to sway, as if lit by a theater spotlight and not the opaque street lamps. The clicking of her heels could already be heard, the clicking of her heels, the clicking of her heels, they were ultra-thin and jiggled everything on top of them to and fro: breasts and thighs in a shiny black raincoat, a silver plastic handbag hung from the arm – move there, turn around, bend, put down the handbag as if it's a suitcase – and the light flowed onto the raincoat and was splashed from the tips of the glossy shoes clicking, clicking, clicking.

"That's one who sells herself," said Edith. "You can tell immediately. You can recognize them straightaway, they haven't got a drop of shame."

Isn't she waving at them? The bearded man asked. Even blowing kisses in the air like that, with all that lipstick. You're introducing him to some interesting types tonight, no two ways about it. Ones like that don't come to his alley. That one must be good at washing, maybe she'll be in the painting? Why not, let her come too. Soon the whole area will be in the painting, the whole city.

She spread the fragrance of cheap perfume here and there, smiled at everyone, placed her handbag close to the hip and gave you a kiss on the right cheek and one on the left and another one on the right, leaving ripples of warmth widening and subsiding like the effect of a stone in a river or a cat or a body. So how does her honey feel, just before he's going to become famous? Okay, not honey. An artist.

A famous artist, of course he's going to become famous, heading straight for the Louvre. She's just got the knack for things like that, who'll become a somebody and who won't. She could have been a talent scout, no doubt about it. That's how it is when you work with people, honey. Yes that's the kind of profession she's got, what, didn't he tell them what she does? Such a honey. For example once – have they got time for her stories? Anyway, they're walking.

On the empty pavement beneath the yellowish light, tuk-tuk, tuff-tuff, tupm-tupm, but every student year had ten like you, hundreds in a decade, thousands in the world: in thousands of cities perhaps right now three beggars and a prostitute were being marched to a morgue. All were carrying a rucksack on their backs; the edge of a wooden easel rubbed against their necks and inside were bottles and vials, canvas wrapped in an old sheet, a palette and paints and horse-tail brushes: that's what horses were created for, for that purpose fields of oats and rain were created, rivers were routed, clouds became cloudy, and the son of God walked over them there in the dark like someone trampling on grapes to make wine from them: if clouds were seen from the window of your room, they were wrung out and covered with perforated footprints and discarded at once like the remnants of grapes from a wine press.

Once there was someone, the prostitute said and clicked her heels, whom she used to hear in Beaubourg Square. Maybe they know him? Tik-tik her heels clicked. She goes there every Sunday with her little boy to hear the street singers, that's what her little boy likes best, the street singers. So, the one that performed in Beaubourg sang the way they used to, I mean just with the voice that God gave him, a voice like that we'd all be lucky to have. That's how it goes. There are those who are given it and those who aren't. And some time after that where does she hear him, the one from Beaubourg? On the radio, I mean her transistor in the hotel. Not much of a find, that transistor, but even that didn't manage to ruin the singer's voice.

But anyway, she said and walked onwards on her heels, that transistor's good enough for the hotel. It's exactly what she needs next to her head in order not to hear anything else. What, he really didn't tell them what she does? Such a honey. Not that it matters too much, she's someone who doesn't give a damn: when someone asks what she does, straightaway she tells the truth. Why lie? She's a translator. Yes. Sure, a translator. In her profession she's learned all languages. Just let him say he hasn't got dimples, one here and one here. Lucky that the beard doesn't grow there like with this one. They sleep in the garbage, so it's not the same thing. One here and also here, just where she kissed him before. Not much of a kiss, even children don't kiss like that.

There's a lady here who doesn't like her profession very much, you can tell right away from how she's clinging to her handbag, you'd think someone's going to grab it from her. But she's not a thief, just a translator. Anyway, from what you can see, you could have wrapped lots of fish with all the old newspaper she's stuffed into her handbag. That piece sticking out is yellower than all our teeth put together. That's how it is, there are those who work and those who don't. When at last they come out of the Metro, you can smell them a mile off.

The heels of her shoes beat with your shoes, tik-tik, tuk-tuk, tuff-tuff, tupm-tupm, skins were flayed and dried and became shoe uppers and changed their voices. And how does a cow go? But there were no cows anymore, no more of their big eyes into which you once could get lost until your face could also be seen in them; it's already seen everywhere, not only from the windowpane, but also from the wall against which your head was banged, right away painting there in blood a grey platform, a yellow cargo carriage, a brown suitcase, a woman's flat shoes, your shoes walking after them: tuk-tuk, tuff-tuff, tupm-tupm.

She doesn't go by Metro at all, why go down into the ground before your time? Not that she wants to go there in time, not at all not at all, but who's asking her, who. So the one from Beaubourg she hears one day on the transistor in the hotel. She takes rooms there by the hour, with all the conveniences, meaning with a towel folded in the middle of the mattress not to make stains there; you can imagine what kind of a mattress it is, really.

So she always puts it next to her head, the transistor, just not to have to hear them panting, that's what kills her the most, that panting, you'd think they're running a marathon or something, and they hardly get past the starting post. The very worst are the old ones, they also start coughing at you, you just pray they're not going to die suddenly in the middle, it's really scary. That's why she puts the transistor next to her head, because after all she can't put in earphones, how can she if there're those who like pushing their tongue into your ear and whispering how much they love you aah-aah-aah. So just as she was once lying there with someone like that panting on top of her, she suddenly hears the one from Beaubourg on the transistor! She knew his voice at once, even recognized the song! And it was so strange there between the panting and so beautiful, she thought she'd die. And the one on top of her sensed it right away, he was sure that it was thanks to him. Absolutely sure, felt like a rooster. Sure, she said to him, of course it's you. I've never ever had someone like you aah-aah-aah someone like you.

"So will the lady be washing me?" the bearded clochard surveyed her from head to toe as she advanced, lingering especially over her thighs, which swung beneath the raincoat here and there, here and there – walk, turn around, stop, put down the handbag as if it's a suitcase, scrape the sole against the chair as if it's the yellow shaft of a cargo carriage and carry on walking, glance back for a moment and look at me – but with Mantegna he was just placed on a wooden bunk and even the folds of the sheet had more life than him. They twisted above his body, rising up and slanting down like a chain of ridges, and perhaps the real ones also covered an enormous corpse beneath them whose soles only stuck out at the edge of the world.

"She's not going to wash you," you said to him, "the lady's just going to deal with the guard in the entrance." And this is how she'll do it: she'll stand opposite him under the streetlamp, undo the buttons of her coat from top to bottom, place her naked body close to the door and her breasts will be squashed against the glass like the faces of inquisitive children – to and fro they would toss when she moved on top of you in that apartment of which you remember nothing other than the floral wallpaper – nodding and nodding until they were grasped, protruding between your fingers like clown noses.

The wooden easel rubbed against your neck and the bottles rattled, and for a moment you wondered how much it would take to intoxicate an empty stomach: in the painting the ribs stretched his skin like a drum upon which perhaps drops of rain drummed afterwards, grains of hail or the beaks of birds. In the place to which you are going the cold will seep in from the holes in the palms and soles and from the cut in the chest, until it fills the entire body and turns it blue; the stainless steel drawer will reflect the pale light of the fluorescent lamps, there were always fluorescent lamps in places like that, and perhaps the drawer won't close with the bottle that will be standing in the corner instead of the goblet. It was painted next to his head like a transistor drowning out the blows of the hammer, but perhaps he actually counted them one by one like someone counting sheep before sleep or the faded floral wallpaper or the springs of the empty half of the mattress.

4

"Had it not been for," the policeman will say, "did you hear him? Had it not been for the wine. One can just imagine which wine he'd already drunk. And what would he have done without the wine? I'll tell you what he would have done." The smoke ring will fly into the air, expand and evaporate. "Nothing is what he would have done, nothing. After all, those types are scared of their own shadows, not so?" He'll turn to his partner, the second policeman or the doctor or the angel, and afterwards you thought of the one who oversees all, and about his son who was cured of his death and about his disciples: one created, one revived by saying "come forth" to the dead and one healed the sick with his shadow.

You stopped opposite the back entrance of the hospital, the bearded clochard, Nadia, Edith, the prostitute and you. The shoes were no longer heard; they stood there as they had stood before, opposite the revolving door at the front. It turned on its own, propelled by some hidden mechanism so that the limbless and amputees and cripples with their sticks and crutches and wheelchairs and stretchers could pass through. Again and again it revolved there, nobody entered, nobody exited, but it continued to revolve very slowly, stubborn as the blades of the Moulin Rouge, the translator said, before you encircled the building and went to the back entrance.

"That's what it's like when you grow up next to Pigalle," she said. What did they think, that children don't grow up in all those buildings there next to Pigalle? Of course they grow up there. That's how it is with children, they grow up everywhere; wherever they get thrown they grow up. But there, no matter where you walk with your little legs, you see those blades of the Moulin Rouge: you get sent to do shopping, they're turning around there at the end of the street, you get sent to the post office, again they're turning around at the end of the street, and if that's not enough, the whole way you've got those display windows of the clubs with all their dirty pictures. The shinier those windows are, the dirtier their pictures. The ones photographed there were dressed at the very most with a few stars, so that all the sickos can wish on them. What they'll be wishing for you wouldn't want to know.

The most irritating people, not that there's any shortage of irritating people, but the most irritating are those who want you to make sounds. I mean you'd think you were in a choir, you'd think that they can't live without you making sounds from pleasure, not even for one moment. "So listen here sir," that's what she would tell them right away, "my pleasure, sir, do you know what my pleasure is? My pleasure is only that after this I'll buy something for my little boy, that's my pleasure," usually that shuts them up on the spot. Only once she had someone who afterwards started to show her photographs, I mean of children, not what their dirty minds are thinking now. Those children of his were beautiful, a son and a daughter, dressed like children from the sixteenth arrondissement, so lovely that she couldn't understand at all what their father's doing with someone like her. His daughter had just lost her front teeth, exactly like her son, and for a moment it was possible to think they could be friends, she and her son; that's what went through her mind for a moment until a fear suddenly gripped her that he's going to show them to her in various poses, those children, but it was only birthday photographs that he took out, balloons and decorations and a cake with candles and what not. And his daughter was bent over them, she was six years old, you could see from the candles, but she hadn't succeeded in blowing them out and was crying. She was crying, yes, the tears on her cheeks and on her chin sparkled from the flash, can they imagine what that does to her? In the middle of the hotel room on the filthy mattress with that towel folded like that, in the middle of all that, a girl with birthday candles. That's how it is. They said that one with the leg cries over any nonsense. So it seems she's also like that, crying over any nonsense, but with her it's the inside that's rotten. Enough, she's spoken too much. That's what happens when there aren't clients to tire her out – go there, turn around, carry on walking on the floor as if it's a platform, sit on the chair as if it's the upholstered seat of a carriage and look through the window as if the neon sign outside is an apple tree drawing away – do they want to see now how well she does it? The striptease, what else? That's what her honey brought her for, okay, not her honey. An artist. Of course he's going to paint her after this, of course. Why not. Soon he's going to tell her that he loves her, what do you mean. Do they know what it's like when someone says that? She knows very well from experience: it's like the sun, when can you look at the sun, only when it's setting, so if someone says that to you that he loves you, even if it was once true, then it's not true anymore now. It's setting.

She moved toward the back entrance, swaying everything she had to sway above her shoes, the shoes, the shoes, and tried to catch the eye of the guard. He was sitting behind a Formica counter well within the entrance hall and watching a small television set, spellbound as if the entire world was inside it and as if there was someone who watched all of you that way from behind a cloud, with drowsy eyes, until a prostitute in a black raincoat stood opposite him. She began to open the coat from the top button, but from the place in which you were standing, next to the lot where the ambulances were parked, white and as silent as pupae whose butterflies will fly to the ground, you could not see her reflection. Through the glass door a plant could be seen wilted like the plants in the hotel in which you worked, and a few black armchairs could be seen, as if in which to wait for the dead who will arise and leave, and there was also a calendar on the wall.

"That one, sir?" Edith said, "right away I saw what she was, the moment she arrived. If she was going to be in the painting I would've left on the spot. You don't know me yet sir, but that's what I would have done." Opposite the transparent entrance door the second button was opened and between the lapels of the black coat perhaps the pure delicate skin and the cleft deepening there were revealed to the guard's eyes, if women's breasts still had a cleft between them. "Ask them all if that's what I would have done," Edith said.

"Are *them* the ones from the tunnel?" The bearded man asked, not removing his eyes from the raincoat. "You, I'm not taking any notice of you," Edith replied, "just so you know," and straightaway pushed a piece of paper into her handbag from which it had sprouted as if she could at least fool the dead. On her right, next to the lot, a stench exuded from the garbage containers; perhaps inside them were pus-filled bandages and amputated limbs, knots of intestines and placentas and aborted fetuses, and between the panels there were packs of roisterous rats, gnawing, gargling and burping.

In the dusk the stains on Nadia's smock became blurred, the gleam of the safety pin that secured the bandage dimmed as well and only her childlike eyes sparkled from between wrinkled eyelids as they were fixed on the door. "Is she gonna open it all the way?" she asked. Inside the guard had already turned the visor of his cap to the front where it hid his rosy baldpate and got up from his chair behind the counter. "All the way?" "You can depend on her," Edith answered, "there's not a thing she'll leave unopened."

Step by step the guard moved toward the door, not believing his eyes, while at the end of the counter the television still blinked. Beneath the edges of the coat, on the curve of her pale lower legs, the black panties slid and fell, stopping for a moment at the ankles where they were immediately cast off, gathered on the ground in a small dark puddle, as if in the morning the night itself will fall that way and reveal the white trembling buttocks of the skies. But above the prostitute and the guard and the entrance door separating them, there were just hospital floors with all the sick who lay on filthy beds and called for the nurse over and over, not because they believed she would come, but just to hear their voices once more.

"You see him sir?" Edith glanced sideways at the bearded man. "How he's looking at her that way? He's one who does it with anyone sir, believe me, he hasn't got a drop of shame." The bearded clochard did not reply and just put his hands into his pockets from the cold or perhaps from desire: you were not interested in the reason, because in the painting he won't sense these things any longer and won't see the prostitute in the black raincoat any longer nor anything else. "Never mind the shame now," Edith said, "but what about health? With all these diseases there are now? Sleeping under the sky because that's what he's used to. I know them very, very well, believe me sir, the biggest nitwits are the ones from the country. I've learned that from personal experience. Those?" Again she peered at the bearded man and still his hands were deep in his pockets. "They do it with everything, believe me, with everything that moves. Why should they show respect for a woman? And as for love, sir, have they heard about love at all? What do they need it for? They're not ashamed – even with cows, believe me."

The bearded man now turned his eyes with the bags of dark skin hanging below them toward her, and she turned her head from him with an expression of refinement. "With cows?" he asked and before she managed to move he had already drawn close and clung to her from behind, fastening his palms on her hands and the handbag she held close to her fallen belly. "With cows?" He rubbed against her from behind, "like this?" he asked, "like this?" But immediately he let go allowing her to extricate herself shaken and panting, an elderly Persephone in a skirt long out of fashion.

Hades – after all you had been thinking about him not only on that night but on previous ones as well – would give her pomegranate berries from the netherworld so that every winter she would return to him, the images they revealed like tiny crystal balls were enough: a platform drawing away, a bridge on which a car sprints, columns of buildings hurtling backwards, feverishly active factories only whose smoke moves slowly, a mound of earth on which a boy in a blue raincoat stands and waves his hand, pole by pole withdrawing on bare ground and electric wires arching and straining and arching, a winding path and on it a dark treetop dotted with yellow apples, they were all seen from the moving train window and above them was the rack with her suitcase, which you helped her to lift, an old bulging suitcase one of whose bolts was broken, and you wondered who the man will be, between whose clothes her clothes will be hung in the beautiful, damned city to which you were traveling.

Lights did not circle or flash on the roofs of the parked ambulances and all the red crosses on their sides gradually seeped into the darkness. In one of their wing mirrors Edith examined her face: her eyes bound by a line of soot, her ruddy nose, which still breathed heavily, her thin lips. Right away she smoothed her skirt from behind as if the bearded man had bothered to lift it, and stretched her blouse in front as if he had laid his head there, and pursed her lips once or twice as if he had kissed her, and arranged her hair at the temples as if he had bent over her and whispered love songs or sailors' obscenities in her ear.

"What are you laughing about," she said to Nadia from the mirror. "She laughs at me. Do you even know what he was trying to do? You fool, in a moment she's going to start telling me about her dogs, for sure sir, what, don't I know her? She's only got animals on the brain sir, pigeons and dogs. And the storks that bring children, right?" She was still looking in the ambulance mirror in which the reflections of stretchers taken from inside it to the emergency room or to the morgue were not yet seen.

If in the dark of the tunnels below them a stork flew under the arched ceiling on a breeze blown by a passing train, it flew there slowly with its load, wearily, with filthy plucked wings until it landed on the platform on one remaining foot, the other was chewed by the rats: one after another after another you could count them from the empty mattress in the room, hordes and hordes of rats, and still you were not able to fall asleep.

"You're crazy," Edith said and tried to check in the mirror how the kiss she wanted to be given would look; by anyone in the world, even a clochard. "If I was in your place I would have done everything, there's nothing I wouldn't have done, so that at least once in a lifetime before I – I told you sir, it takes one little word and straightaway she cries." For a moment she looked at you as if you were interested in their dispute but you were looking at your watch. "And I didn't even get to say what I wanted to say sir, I meant it for her own good, because someone who never did it in their whole life, I don't want to say what, it's like they never lived. Yessir."

Across from them, through the glass of the entrance door, the guard reached out a finger to touch the prostitute's lips and afterwards groped her between the lapels of her coat from the collar to the place in which his hand disappeared, drawing so close to her that she became blurred in the vapor of his breath. Her black bra was already on the ground and its cups stuck out there, sharp and steep as two small mountains of darkness. For a moment you wondered if one of the ants, which you used to observe as a child when they carried grains – but you never did observe ants, you weren't lulled, not suckled; and had you ever burst forth from a womb, you immediately marched between the thighs with a rucksack rattling with bottles of wine and turpentine, and the little forehead already sought a wall against which to be banged – would have climbed up and conquered them, but an old ant would have rolled down the slope. They had no names, not the young ants nor the old ants, they were of no importance to anyone unlike chicks and chickens, goats and sheep, foals and mares and certainly unlike tots and toddlers, boys and girls, lads and lasses, guys and gals, men and women, elderly gents and elderly ladies, all the masses who descended to the morgue.

In one of the workshops at art school – it at least still stood intact with its gloomy halls in which small clouds of turpentine clashed from one wall to another – there was one who started to scratch himself one day and didn't stop;

with the tips of the paintbrushes he reached every spot that itched. Instead of painting with their bristles on canvas he carved his skin with their sharp tips and for a while one could have thought he was trying out some new statement: after all Fine lay on a grate over burning candles claiming that pain purifies and Schwarzkogler castrated himself to death. But the doctors spoke of eczema or psoriasis or some other skin disease and then spoke of something mental: he scratched himself so intensely that it seemed as if he wanted to rid himself of some abhorrent filth, which no one other than he saw. When his illness was discovered, the pincers had already removed the last crumbs of flesh that still stuck to his skin. You all came to visit him in the hospital, and he was already totally bald from the radiation and older than his mother, and you saw how she leads him to the toilet, and how she washes him, and spoon feeds him, and wipes his chin, and lays him on the bed, and tickles the soles of his feet with trembling fingers, and quietly says to him, like when he was still a small boy and death was hidden beyond the cataract of years: "Tu-tu, tu-tu," without stopping, "Tu-tu, tu-tu, tu-tu," as if that tu-tu would keep death at bay.

The hospital now towered toward the low, dark sky and its upper floors seemed to be seeping into the night and being swallowed up in it with all the hundreds of the sick who were dying there. In Chinese watercolors – at the time you prized those too – sometimes a small Mandarin wearing a skein of rope on his head was painted in the corner, and when he aged and his time came to ascend to the heavens, he climbed up the rope above his head. They also had folding dragons, the Mandarins; they folded and put in a pocket one who covered the whole of Mongolia with its tail, and it was enough to reflect on it for a while, the folding dragon, for two or three hours or an entire night, and you could begin to believe that you too, if you finally get up, will cover Mongolia with your shadow or at least the floor of your room. But at the time you didn't have enough strength to even move your hand; you could only continue staring at the ceiling and seeing dragons in the damp stains. They were more easily portrayed there than a fervent ravenous vulva or lips shouting your name in the dark, when you still had a name.

Now the prostitute winked from inside the entrance hall, one the wink of an eye and the other the whole body, which momentarily burst forth and disappeared between the eyelids of the black coat. And at once, before the guard managed to lock the door again with the large bunch of keys that jingled, she pulled him by the hand to the counter. The bra and black panties remained on the paving stones outside, the pair of mountains that were placed one inside the other and the lake that poured into them: for a while you could fold a whole body that way, vulva into breast into breast into the moving hand.

"They're going to watch television together," Edith chuckled, "isn't that what you think, Nadia?" The television was still on at the end of the counter inside, and in it tiny people ran around here and there until they bumped into the sides and fell and rose and again tried to get out from inside. In the calendar on the wall blue skies could be seen, but the stalks and leaves of the plant in the corner no longer soar toward them, and in the other corner the small fire extinguisher was vermillion red and safeguarded inside it the foam or powder, you didn't know which, only a fire would have revealed its concealed contents.

"Will they do what dogs do?" Nadia's voice trembled. Perhaps she was still pondering over Edith's words about country people and their cows, but you were not interested in her musings. "Like the dogs and the cats and the bees," the bearded clochard answered her and chuckled, and right away waved his hands up and down like a large bee, rustling the cardboard sign and the patches of his sleeves, which became undone here and there. For a while he buzzed around Edith, a debauched bearded insect whose wings were powered only by the asphalt's stamens, until he coughed, rasped and spat. "Just beware I don't sting you in the end," he said to them, "like him over there," and was still panting from his awkward flight when he stopped and looked at the entrance again.

The guard was already being pulled by a naked hand to the back of the counter; you saw the entire length of that hand very clearly, its purity, its softness, its warmth and the peaked cap dropped from his head and fell to the floor like one of the plant's leaves. "Like dogs," Nadia said, as if you were leading them to a nature study class and not to a morgue, but the plant in the entrance must surely be filled with cigarette stubs and tin can rings like the plants of the hotel to which you moved from her apartment, and from which you remember nothing except the floral wallpaper.

"What did I tell you?" Edith said letting her bag swing from her arm again. "All she's got on the brain are animals. Dogs or pigeons, nothing besides that. Didn't get one ounce of sense from the time she was small, take it from me." For all that, she also spoke about dogs, those thoroughbred Russian dogs, and you no longer recalled the dog you had in your childhood: not how she'd bark over the perforated cardboard box when she heard silkworms chewing on picked leaves, and not how you spoke about her opposite floral wallpaper in that apartment, when it was still damp from the sweat of the both of you.

"Those dogs?" Edith said not hurrying. When Nadia was little, not here, of course not here, in Russia, a dog and a bitch, yes, definitely a dog and a bitch, looked to her like one dog joined together with one head here and another head where the tail is. "Yessir," Edith chuckled, "she didn't even understand what they were doing, even now she hardly gets it." Beyond the glass door the television flickered with its images, it had not yet been switched off to signal to them that the guard no longer took any interest in trespassers nor in the ball being kicked there on a lawn, dense and greyish like the stubble on the cheeks of the dead.

Above their heads the crows sharpened their beaks on the low gathering of clouds, that grindstone that used to rotate nightly above the roofs of the city. But the bearded man did not listen to its rotations; he turned to Nadia rather and asked her what kind of dogs they were.

"All of a sudden he's interested in dogs," Edith said, "you see that? That's what he cares about now, I told you sir, him and her? A real fine pair." But in order to delay the moment of entrance she mentioned their breed, Samoyeds, yes, and also mentioned other things that Nadia used to tell her in the tunnel. "Only now all of a sudden she's keeping quiet," Edith said, "she's scared because of this place. But in the tunnel at night when she feels like talking, God forbid, she doesn't care at all if I'm sleeping or not, why should she care?"

"Lovely dogs, Samoyeds," said the bearded man and removed a bit of sleep from the corner of his eye, flicking it with his middle finger, "really lovely."

"Listen to him," Edith said, "all of a sudden he's become a professor of dogs." In the parking lot the ambulances still gazed at the sky with lusterless and lidless eyes, but for the bearded man it was most important now to tell that he too once had a dog: yes-yes, maybe not a thoroughbred, that's true, but anyway a dog.

"Listen to that," Edith said, "he once had a dog. Congratulations. D'you know what she once had? Should I tell you? She could have bought the lot of us, tell them what you had, Nadia, before the bench. He once had a dog." And immediately she snickered to show him how much it made her laugh, because really, what's a dog next to what Nadia once had.

"A home we should all be so lucky to have," Edith said, but opposite all of you was just a hospital, and its inhabitants were perhaps trying to turn over in their beds and call out from there with feeble voices to the nurse or the doctor or to the one who will afterwards raise them up from the earth. "And a home's not all," Edith said, "what, didn't they have whole forests there? They certainly did, whoever doesn't believe it – that's their problem." And those dogs, didn't they catch them birds for breakfast? "Sure they caught them, what do you think, there wasn't one morning that they didn't."

In paintings of hunting scenes from the seventeenth or eighteenth centuries – you didn't remember the century, you didn't even remember things that happened a few months ago: they were all blurred in your eyes like the trees at the end of the avenue, whose branches and leaves, and the touch of their rough bark, and the trickle of sap, which she used to try and listen to by placing her ear close to the trunk, all of them were now just a fading memory like the remains of vomit in a toilet bowl above the reflection of your face – noble scent hounds were painted carrying exquisite pheasants in their mouths without damaging their decorative plumage at all, but you did not intend to paint scent hounds or pheasants. You were assigned to pay homage to one of the great painters, and you chose to paint the murdered son of God surrendering to the laws of perspective like any other corpse: of the entire divine body only the perforated soles will stand out, and beyond them the legs that once stepped on water shadowing the scales of fish will be shortened, the chest which will not rise or fall will be shortened too, as will be the tormented face of whose features only the nostrils will stand out motionless.

"I," said the bearded clochard not looking at the glass door anymore, "had a dog once, I know very well what loving a dog is. We sat together, me and him," he said glad to defer his entrance by a few minutes, "for days on end we used to sit like that at the corner of Vaugirard." With his eyebrow he motioned in the supposed direction, but the entire city was already blurred in the distance and the dark. "Anyone who once had a dog couldn't pass by without throwing a coin our way, they just couldn't. Because you don't forget a dog, sometimes you can't remember a person the way you remember a dog. She laughs at me. They just had to see him, right away they'd bend and put something down, for him, not for me. If I wouldn't have been there he'd have earned more, I swear." So he told about his dog at the foot of the hospital as if he saw it again right in front of him, but you could not see well-groomed thoroughbred dogs nor barking mongrels, but only the one staring fixedly with the red eyes of its three heads at the entrance, shining in the light of the flames: perhaps a small fire extinguisher stood there as well and a withered plant and on the ground a squashed, peaked cap and on the counter a television set still turned on.

"What happened to him?" The bearded man repeated Nadia's question as if they had the whole night ahead of them. "They wanted me to lend him to them, that's what happened to him." No, he didn't suddenly start making himself out to be God-like Edith says or to throw money away on chalk and Panda pastels and go around the street like that with cardboard signs. No Sir! They also wanted to make a profit out of Rex, that's what happened to him, like he was some whore, Rex, one who gets passed from one person to the next. "They must have given him something to make him go with them, what do I know, a piece of sausage or something, how do I know."

But he's not blaming him, no, not at all. For a piece of sausage he'd also have done anything, anything for a miserable piece of sausage. "That's how it is," he said, "don't blame anyone until you're in his place, no one. So Rex went for a sausage that they gave him, why not, another would have gone for a bitch or a cat. And me, afterwards I went through the whole city on foot to find him, and before that I didn't use to go further than the corner of Vaugirard, what did I have to look for further than the corner of Vaugirard?"

Opposite the hospital and the floor of its entrance, where the prostitute and the guard were concealed behind the counter, he told how there wasn't a public park that he didn't go to, not an underground station in which he didn't call out to him in every direction, from up and down, on the stairs, where not. "Because the thing that kills me," he said no longer looking at the glass door, "is not knowing what happened. It's better to know the worst things in life, I swear, otherwise it destroys you just thinking about whether or not they happened." For a moment he lowered his eyes, and in the silence the darkness was heard pouring from the sky, the way it was heard in your room after that grindstone wore down the roof, the ceiling, the globe hanging from it, the blanket, your skin.

"At last she's turned off the television," Edith announced. "That one's not dressed any more than how she came into the world. It's as easy as anything for them to get undressed, for me breathing isn't that easy. Those ones haven't got a drop of shame." Inside, the television was already darkened and the bunch of keys still swung from the door to and fro as if beating time for the couple with its clattering. Beneath the broken lamp you all watched it, three beggars and an art student on their way to the morgue.

"Now that one," Edith said, "the guard? He's not dressed any more than how he came into the world. Yessir yes, I've got the eyes of a hawk, from the end of the tunnel I can see what people have thrown away a kilometer from there. You just wouldn't believe sir what people throw away, believe me, we should all be so lucky. She must be putting a rubber on him sir, I don't want to say where, not to corrupt this one."

The shoes, the shoes, the shoes were approaching the glass door, the bearded clochard's running shoes, Nadia's metallic shoes, Edith's sneakers and your shoes. They advanced silently, taking neither heavy nor dainty footsteps. The undergarment, which had been blackened on the ground, you picked up with hands that had already forgotten its delicate touch. The bunch of keys sounded as you all entered, but the guard would not have heard you even had you attached bracelets and bells to your ankles and even had your shoes thundered on the platform: tuk-tuk, tuff-tuff, tupm-tupm.

The television was turned off, a small black and white television obviously bought used, but behind the shuttered screen perhaps all the little people swayed and vomited their guts out like the passengers of a ship on an ocean beneath which a pair of whales have decided to mate: yes, she said words to him, the prostitute, to drive him even crazier, how at first she was turned on by his uniform, and how handsome he is now, and how masculine he is and how hairy and how strong yes yes yes let her have it, and at the same time she looked above and winked at you. She was not at all ashamed, that prostitute, as if all in all she had covered herself with some shaggy blanket: yes yes yes yes, she said, aaah, aaah,

aaah, and according to the look the bearded clochard shot her, one moment more and he would have sent the guard to the drawer in place of him.

You had difficulty drawing them away from there, like a father whose children are watching a tiger, still uncertain of how it will pass through the burning hoop and if the clowns will reappear – one morning in the supermarket, across from a package of disposable diapers, she said to you: "they'll wait a while, our children, no?" Because then you still had faith in time, a long corridor that will open all its years one by one before both of you, with great wonders waiting beyond as from behind magicians' handkerchiefs – and meanwhile the guard was groaning on the floor. Edith put on an expression of disgust, like someone covering their eyes and opening their fingers to peek. The bearded clochard pushed her toward the corridor and when she turned her head to the counter, he unashamedly touched her sagging behind. It was wrapped in a skirt so old that perhaps it was already back in fashion, where there were still lit streets and shop windows and mannequins whose creators, like you, once dreamt of museums and statues hewn from marble or cast in bronze.

You left the bunch of keys in the door so that the guard would not find out that you had all entered, even if by then he would be tired and relaxed and anyway, it's unthinkable that the drawers would be locked: who besides you wanted the dead? Medical professors surely received all the unidentified bodies as a gift and opened at will those abandoned leather suitcases. They were as careful as airport security officers, the ones who asked the passengers if they had packed everything by themselves; if they had not recently received something to be passed on; if anyone had given them a suspicious package. Because even one memory hidden inside was enough – a moving passenger window along whose width the rain slams and the night melts, turning grey above the withdrawing round hills, and above cows grazing wet grass, and above lengthening fences whose poles are flung backwards one after another, and above the furrows of a cart filling with streaks of sky, and above the carriages advancing on and on toward the beautiful, damned city – to destroy everyone in the vicinity.

Edith no longer clutched the handbag but dragged it along the floor, open and becoming more and more tattered, and the newspapers crammed into it slipped out one by one with their wondrous and terrible events. Had someone walked behind you, the guard or some crazy person desiring to reach the morgue, he would have had to hop over a resigning government, burning lava, an overflowing river delta, serial killers, panda cubs, the largest omelet in the world, over everything that happened in Popocatépetl or Beijing or Timbuktu, all the places you would never be in: tuk-tuk, your shoes beat on the corridor, tuff-tuff, tupm-tupm.

At the time, in the window of your room there was nothing but slate roofs and the gathering of black clouds, which continued to very slowly level them out until the roofs became as thin as paper. Sometimes you imagined hearing angels beating against the ceiling like insects in a lampshade, and if you removed yourself from under the blanket and went out into the street, there would only be street lamps that continued to shower their pale light into the enormous punctured barrel of the night.

The shoes now pounded on the hospital corridor, your shoes as well, and from behind, the small television was talking again. Perhaps the prostitute turned it on so that the guard wouldn't hear your steps on the corridor, your steps, your steps, your steps. On your right and on your left doors turned white, resembling each other precisely except for their numbers, and behind your backs the commentator struggled to follow the ball and say who kicked it to whom, who dribbled it to whom, and who struck it into whom because of that butterfingers standing in the goal or because of the referee whose mother's profession and what he does with her at night all the spectators knew.

Maybe it would be better, the bearded man asked and turned to face backwards, before they get too far away, if he returned the intimate articles to the lady? Because you can't see the end of this corridor. Of course he'll take care that the guard doesn't see him, no question about it, after all he can make himself invisible: for hours, what do you mean hours, for days he stands in his square with hordes of tourists around, whole busloads, and not even one of them sees him. Never mind him and never mind his sign, at least let them see the hat he put down for the money. Because afterwards who'll help him in bad times, the municipality? The government? The one above? He lifted one eyebrow toward the ceiling of the corridor and the neon buzzed beneath it quietly like a weary fly trapped there.

So then what about the intimate articles? Okay, no. If he's told to forget about them he'll forget about the panties and the bra. He'll forget about how black they are. There's just one thing important to him in this corridor now, really, because what's at the end of it it's better not to know, and that's that Nadia shouldn't think what Edith said about him before is right: because she, as far as he can tell, is someone who takes everything seriously. So first of all he's not making himself out to be anyone, certainly not God, and second of all he's not making fun of anything, no way. Him? If he makes fun of someone it's only of himself. Yes, it's one thing to have to make a living from something, to each his own livelihood, especially after being thrown out of a job, and another thing what you believe.

Because what you believe in isn't something to make fun of, no way, he learned that from his mother from the time he was small. Believing is a great thing, really, for someone who can. Because a person, even if he's someone who says that he doesn't believe in anything, and there are plenty of big shots like that, really plenty, they're all big shots when it comes to talking, but then you have to ask that person what he does when suddenly he starts to get scared about something that's dear to him, yes, what does he do then? Doesn't he find himself suddenly lifting his eyes to the sky and saying quietly to himself, no need for big words, just "let him be well" is enough, or her. Or even his dog, whatever, a dog as well, you can only pity someone who doesn't understand how you can say that for a dog. Isn't that what he said when they stole Rex from him? When he didn't know where he was at all, if Rex was dead or alive. Sure he did. He lifted his eyes to the ceiling of the tunnel and said quietly to himself: "you up there, let him be well, please please please." That's what he said to himself at the time; it's just that he wasn't exactly heard up there, maybe the reception from the tunnel isn't good.

Tuk-tuk, your shoes beat on the linoleum of the corridor, tuff-tuff, tupm-tupm. Nadia lagged behind a bit dragging her bandaged leg, and the bearded man stopped and waited for her, as if he had the whole night before him. "In hospital," he said, he doesn't mean this one, he means when he was taken from the accident after which he stopped working, there was some Chinaman with him in the emergency room who said that their God could even hear an ant walking on a stem. Yes, that's what the Chinaman said. The whole time he shrank in his corner and didn't stop saying omani-padmehum omani-padmehum to soothe his burns; he said it so many times that by then everyone in the emergency room had learned to say it as well. As if that omani-padmehum was also good for other things, not just burns but also for broken bones and cuts and what not. Burning oil had been poured on him, the Chinaman, in the restaurant where he worked, one with a 20 franc menu where all the dishes must have tasted the same, but he wouldn't say who did it to him. He said that if God can hear an ant on a stem, he also knew who poured burning oil on him. That's what the Chinaman said.

Amongst your steps, amongst your steps, amongst your steps, and above the dragging sound, which Nadia's soles and Edith's handbag made, you could still hear the commentator's voice from the end of the corridor, angry over the center forward's missed opportunity, telling everyone that Milan knew very well what they were doing when they sold that loser. But you no longer remembered what Milan looked like or other cities, whether they were still intact; you also could not recall the feel of the ball on your shoe when you used to kick or juggle, nor the feel of it when heading, because that boy who kicked and juggled and headed was even further away than the trees racing in their bright barks at the side of the path next to the tracks, and from cows dappled with black and crusts of mud, and from a sleepy village whose bell tower stretches from it and yawns, and from the woman who was then sitting by your side, the warmth of whose body you still sometimes sensed like an amputee senses his missing leg: the organ would instantly stand out to the expanse of the room as if tightly grasped and honeyed, but all around there were just walls and beyond them nothing.

Two long iron rails were fixed to the corridor walls to support the sick or the dead when they'll arise and leave, and behind the identical doors hospital clerks must have sat during the daily hours filling out forms, making calculations, budgeting hospital fees, filing death reports, until returning to their wives and children who waved to them with a spoon dripping with apple puree.

At the end another red extinguisher could be seen and two plants whose leaves were also turning yellow, and between their square containers, which must have been filled with cigarette butts and tin can rings like the plants in the hotel, the elevator doors were already shining as they opened and closed and opened. Who will come to me who will come? They quietly beckoned to you all and opened and closed. Who will come? The fluorescent ceiling lights were reflected on the front of them, white and as long as thigh bones, and the buzzing was still heard around them as if whoever was gnawing at them, gluttonously chewed the last few grains of light.

The numbers one to three appeared on the buttons of the lower floors, black numbers around which the button was illuminated by a reddish glow, and above them on a small brass sign the maximum weight permitted to be carried was engraved: eight hundred kilograms. The bearded man instantly did the arithmetic with his fingers, which he folded one after another, each one with the filthy crescent that encircled the nail: the thumb for Nadia, the forefinger for Edith, the middle finger for himself, the fourth finger for the artist. "Four times about eighty?" he asked. "What're you getting so excited about, it's just an average." But they stayed in their places and the joy that the prostitute had put on their faces had been completely dispelled.

"So how much does that give us?" he asked, "three hundred and twenty? And that rucksack with the wine and the paints, let say ten kilos? Three hundred and thirty. And that handbag of Edith's with the few newspapers that are still there, half a kilo? Three hundred and thirty and a half."

Don't get him wrong, he was a good pupil at arithmetic, made his mother proud. Who knew he'd land up here? Who knew? So it could manage it easily according to him, yes why not, and also that lady from the entrance. Without the intimate articles, who needs the intimate articles. "What," he said, "are we the type who gets horny from things like that?" – from their color from their delicateness from their scent from the warmth, which still remained in them, or even from the window, which her naked body steamed up, blurring the street beyond it, the way previously from the carriage window it faded the stalks sprouting from the mouths of chewing cows, and the dog that lifted its leg at a fence post, and the bright barks of the racing trees: they all became shortened in the distance into cowsfencestrees, and shortened further into viewinthewindow, a backdrop solely for the brown eyes that looked at you when you got up the courage and in your feeble accent asked what the names of the trees were; "birches," she answered and right away asked you if you had ones like that in your country – "we're not perverts," the bearded man said, "it's enough that we've been screwed up by other things."

You could have also taken the cross with you in the elevator, if it could be folded like the easel, but with Mantegna it did not appear at all: from the bunk on which the son of God was laid, the beams to which he was nailed until his last breath opposite the cheering crowd could not be seen, nor the ladders used to take him down. With Rubens he was taken down by two men into a sheet, and from the height of their ladders perhaps they had harvested olives or picked figs previously – at the time there were still olives to be harvested or figs to pick or birches to look at or the curves of hills, which the cows grazed with their tongues until a bell tower hastened to gather them from the rain; and she asked you about them as well, in the same voice none of whose sounds you remembered: if there were any like those in your country, bell towers and cathedrals, are there any there? Have you ever climbed up one? And have you seen the entire city from above? And for a moment, just for a moment, felt like flying or jumping off? That's what she said in the carriage, and you recalled the branches of berries that with your thin legs you once made gallop, elated from being flung between the clear summer sky and the hard ground below you – one released the hand from the horizontal beam, and the other, an old man sturdy as a farmer, held him from the top of the cross and with his teeth grasped the edge of the sheet, which absorbed his blood.

Behind all of you the commentator still spoke about the center forward and about the half-back and the center-back and the full-back; he spoke rapidly, following the ball being passed from one to another. Rubens saw the sheet-biter in an engraving by van Groningen, van Groningen acquired it from Giovanni Battista, Battista from Lorenzo Lotto, Lotto from Giuliano Marini who acquired it from à Kempis who acquired it from Grotte. At art school, opposite the hurried slides, the professor lectured about recurring motifs in paintings of the crucifixion and about the homage that each generation pays its predecessor and about the changes in worldview: opposite the bunk projected on the screen, whose whiteness had been sullied, the whole world seemed to be a room in which an inanimate body is laid and bloats until filling it entirely.

Between the wilting plants the elevator opened its door again, and from the breeze it created, the dry leaves rustled above the stubs smoked down to the filter. Who will come to me, who will come? It beckoned. The stainless steel inside it shined even more, presenting your reflections to you as if you were all on the way to a ball: Edith hung her worn out handbag on her arm, the bearded man smoothed down his sparse hair, Nadia gazed at the old lady who stared at her, and for a moment you also looked at your reflection: after all not only was it waved at in mirrors in front of you, but also in the windowpane, the water of the toilet bowl, the stagnant water in the basin, tablespoons and teaspoons until they became filthy and remained in their filth.

For a moment the four of you were portrayed there like in a group painting, the only thing missing was a signature in its corner. But there were those who instead of signing, painted themselves amongst their characters, turning in semi-profile toward the mirror of their room in Florence, even when they were placed on the mountains of the Holy Land or on the shores of its lakes – opposite the slides in the tutorial you no longer remembered if pines grow there or how the light diverges on their needles as if each ray was etched with a nib, or how a gentle wavelet laps the shore like a paintbrush and paints a band of clouds there – Botticelli accompanied the Magi, Rosselli joined in the last supper, and Perugino was present when the keys of heaven were given to Peter.

"Which button do you press?" asked the bearded man. "This one or this one?" And again you had to say in a clear and confident voice – in a voice with which you boasted above the clattering of the train, after she told you about her window from which the cathedral could be seen, of all the paintings you would paint in her city: not its churches, not its bridges and not one of its acclaimed parks, but the sights that existed between your temples and traveled with you in that train and were afterwards unloaded in her apartment as if they would find a place there – "at the bottom, the very bottom."

The bearded clochard had already lifted his finger but right away stopped it in mid-air with the filth-crowned nail and asked Nadia if she didn't want to press it instead of him: yes, why not, maybe she never pressed the button of an elevator. "Who knows," he turned to her, as if you had the time for chivalrous gestures.

"Listen to him," Edith said, "one would think he invented this elevator." The elevator still stood in its place, a small cell that floated in the shaft between the night sky and the ground of the city, which even if covered by asphalt and buildings, they were all as sheer as a veil, which when lifted, the ground will be penetrated by the night's cool black tongue.

"He makes a big deal of elevators," Edith said, "very nice. What are elevators to her, the whole hospital could fit twice into the grounds she once had." And as if you had the entire night before you, again she said that that one wasn't born here at all, does she look like someone who was born here? Why d'you think she drinks her tea in McDonald's with sugar cubes in her mouth, for a whole hour, until they chuck her out? She's Russian, don't be fooled. This, this is just her nickname, Nadjezda's her real name – some name. But what they had there we should all have, really. "Before the Communists," Edith said, "what didn't they have. Servants and maids? Of course she had, of course, like all of them had. And a governess? How couldn't they have a governess if there were children?"

Would they look after those children by themselves like Edith, who nobody helped with her child, nobody, who helped, who? The opposite, what they did to her she wouldn't wish on her worst enemy, but this one had her nyanya. Yes, nyanya, that's what it's called there. For a moment she tasted the word in her mouth, and right away there in the elevator enumerated the carpets that Nadia had and also the armchairs and the couches and the piano and "those sorts of lamps with lots of candles." Between the stainless steel panels that were biding their time, it was of much importance to her to outline them with her hands, as if they hung above her head instead of the fluorescent light that buzzed there.

"Maybe she means chandeliers," the bearded clochard said glad of any pretext that will postpone the descent by a few minutes. "Chandeliers, yes that's what they're called." What do you mean where does he know that from? When he still worked in the department store, before the accident, before he started going around with cardboard signposts and also before he had the dog, there was a whole floor in the department store just for those, the whole fourth floor. "Actually half," he quickly corrected himself, "the other half was for electronic devices, the salesmen there stuck their noses in the air as if they'd invented electricity." And still the elevator stood in its place, a stainless steel bubble that the shaft inflated and waited for it to land and burst.

"But them," Edith said, "one who's got just a pram with rags has got more than what they were left with. Even took those dogs away from them and killed them. And after that she still says about me that I've got a black heart." She turned to you but you were not interested, not in Russia and not in the country from which you yourself came and all its forgotten landscapes: no more were there any lakes other than the stagnant water in the basin, no forests other than the wisps of dust, no valleys other than the hollow of your body in the mattress.

Above the floor buttons the alarm button could be seen with a bell drawn on it, rounded like the bell of a tower, but Nadia had already slowly brought her finger close to the button at the bottom. "Come on press it already," Edith said, "can't you see he's waiting? How's he going to pay us if we don't go down? This one," she turned to you again, "from the time she was born they could tell straightaway she wasn't quite right. Her mother must have seen it straightaway." But you expressed no interest, not in her infancy, not in her adolescence and not in her old age: you were assigned to pay homage to one of the great artists and in the painting you chose they both remained silent above the murdered son of God.

You could have painted them tickling his soles and saying tui-tui to him, like the mother of the colleague who studied with you and began to scratch his skin, or trying to feed him porridge from a spoon like her. Those acts were preposterous, there wasn't time left for the porridge to be digested and the tickling to reach the depths of the body where a chubby, chuckling baby had once sensed it. The palms of his hands were also scratched from his itching, and the scratches looked like the remnants of tattoos that his mother tried to erase with the tips of her fingers: yes, in the end he became a tattoo artist the way others became caricaturists or display mannequin sculptors, and the end you envisaged for yourself was preferable.

Afterwards, the bearded clochard said, at the end of the corridor on his floor, a black man stood in pajamas and looked from the high window at two distant chimneys encompassed by smoke like treetops whose foliage has greyed. The shirt of his pajamas was hung over his shoulders like a cloak and three little old women sat next to him waiting for him to speak to them again. Had it not been for death, which they could already see even through clamped eyelids, they would not have come near a black man or any other dark-skinned person. But he stood before them looking at the chimneys in the window, and in a soft guttural voice said to them that there's nothing God cannot do. Only a few hairs remained on their heads after the chemotherapy treatments and they were gaunt like the black man, and from the hospital wheelchairs they listened to him in silence when he asked them if God make for people one hair or many, and if he not think of everything from beginning. "God," he asked them, "make for people one hand? One leg? No, he make him two." He pointed at his hand and at his leg and afterwards pointed at his face. "God make for people one eye? One ear? No, he make him two. God make for people one body?" He then fell silent and waited for them to answer him, and right away they chirped the answer and were already waiting to be reborn in a new body while they sat there at the end of the long corridor, three old birds on an electric wire whose insulation is pealing moment by moment.

The rain beat on the large window and blurred the chimney smoke outside the way it used to blur the leaves and the petioles and the branches and the buds and the trunks and the nodes, reducing them all to *treesinthedistance*. "But God," the black man said, "he also got angel with a thousand crooked hands." He lifted his hand slightly taking care that the shirt not slip from his shoulder: "A thousand! And on every crooked hand – a thousand crooked fingers. And on every crooked finger – a thousand crooked nails," he twisted his fingers. "And in every crooked nail – a thousand crossed eyes, and in the middle of each crossed eye – a thousand mouth." He did not know how to say mouths, the black man, but from their inanimate wheelchairs, the old women could already see that angel flying beneath the fluorescent lights with his thousand hands and eyes and mouths. "And in each mouth," the black man said, "a thousand lips. And in each pair of lips – a thousand tongues, and all of them they says: thank you Bajorayo, thank you." Only then did the old women understand which god he was speaking about, but no longer did they care what his name was, he could even have been called tui-tui.

Perhaps the elevator was descending and perhaps it was standing still, there was no way of knowing. If a window had been opened in the stainless steel, their pathway would not have been visible, but rather the brown earth and the twisting of the roots and ant tunnels and mole burrows, if there were still roots and ants and moles outside.

Edith asked Nadia if she was sure she pressed because it doesn't look like this elevator is moving at all: you call this moving? And the bearded clochard asked Edith what she's so uptight about, it could be interesting to be stuck here. Really, everything's so polished here it would be like doing it in a room with mirrors on each wall, even on the ceiling. "That one in the entrance," he said, "would know straightaway what I mean." But maybe Edith as well, after all she wasn't born in the Metro or was she? Has she lived her whole life on a bench there? Hasn't she ever seen the bottom of someone having it off with her going up and down on the ceiling?

"All you're interested in is bottoms," Edith said to him and clutched her worn out handbag again, an aged infant from which all its paper entrails have been expelled and her mouth contracted between its wrinkles like a scratch. Her fingers on the handbag searched for an open clasp or a scrap of protruding newspaper but the clasps were already closed and you left the newspapers strewn over the corridor floor, as if by them you'll find the way back to the city, which from behind will perhaps still wave yellowish handkerchiefs of light. Perhaps smoke was rising there, a siren sounded and the city receded further away into the night like a shrinking platform, but none of all that could be seen from the elevator. It was still going down the shaft and compressing the dark beneath it, a coiled spring, which afterwards will dispatch it empty and shining like the drawer of a refrigeration unit.

What, said the bearded man, do they have to let this place spoil their mood? Can't a person joke a bit? Yes, especially here in a place like this. Because if you don't pay attention to the blues for a moment, not even a moment, a second, they'll grab the opportunity right away; worse than a fart. All in all, what did he say, he was only talking about reflections, big deal, okay so not about Edith, only about himself. Anyway he's been through a few things in life, after all he doesn't come from some village like Edith makes out. He comes from a city, yes. There was even a port there with ships and whores. What once was there still is there, that's for sure. It's just that he doesn't live there anymore. So as you can see he didn't become a sailor, but if he had known what a big fuss it was going to make he would have kept his mouth tightly shut. Right away he turned the palm of his hand in front of his lips, and from his beard whose ends were matted with dirt, struggled to emit a few muted sounds, just to show them all that even if they beg him he's not going to be able to talk.

"Only bottoms," Edith said and her mouth contracted again, "and nothing else. Nothing. Haven't you got anything inside here?" She placed her hand on her sweater where her heart was hidden beneath an old breast and dirty wool with thinning tufts, and immediately turned toward the elevator panel, as if you had time for their squabbles. For a moment she inspected the floor buttons, but the stainless steel showed her finger being lifted to squash a transparent louse that was bothering the pupil of the eye.

The elevator was large enough for ten people, but Edith huddled close to the rail fixed to the panel to support the sick or their visitors or the dead, should they arise from their drawers and ascend in the elevator and arrive at the counter in the entrance and open the glass door with the large bunch of keys and go out and see the sky, a sight already forgotten to them, stooping over the city to resuscitate it.

With Bosch the sky was ablaze day and night and gallows burgeoned below. Even on the return of the prodigal son the gallows appeared there – you remembered those details well – the wicker bag that he carried on his back was perhaps as heavy as your rucksack, and over the straps, which sank into his flesh, perhaps the skin coalesced like a retina over the sights quivering in it, sights of which not one detail did you remember: not the steps, which she ascended before you with the black suitcase that bumped into them; not the soft derriere, which you tried to imagine through the faded corduroys; not the brown door, which did not have a man's name on it nor any other name; not the hanger on which your two dripping coats were hung; not the opening to the bath cubicle, where a white toweling dressing gown dangled from a ceramic hook and beside it a pair of tiny black women's panties; not the kitchenette, where a small refrigerator suitable for one person could be seen and next to it an electric cooker with a blue kettle; and not that face, which turned to you after saying, "Hello house, meet," and pronounced your name in an accent, which at the time made you laugh and afterwards depressed you, and in the window the rain continued to fall on the roof slates and on the gables of the servants' rooms and on the central heating chimneys and on the cathedral steeple shrouded in greyish fluff, when she loosened her braid and said: "the whole time, without stopping, I would have gone crazy alone"; that's what she said, but you no longer recalled the clarity of the skin when the hair was spread on it, not its smoothness, not its warmth and not its softness.

When Edith pressed the button a soft sound was immediately heard, and the shoes, the shoes, the shoes all drawn downwards, and perhaps all the while were descending to the other side of the earth. When the stainless steel doors opened you could not tell the difference between the corridors anyway: there were two pot plants and a red fire extinguisher, the same fluorescent lights were turning white above, the same linoleum was spread beneath the shoes like the skin of a grey elephant whose tusks were extracted and stuck into the ceiling, and from the linoleum the shoes were heard, the shoes.

There were white doors on your right and white doors on your left, similar to the ones before, and perhaps behind them too during daily hours hospital clerks sat and worked away until returning to their homes, to their wives and children waving at them with a spoon dripping apple puree – for a while from your apartment you could see a family like that on the other side of the street, and you used to contemplate their serenity, which presupposed the schools in which the baby would study, and the journey it'll take in the mountains with friends, and the offices in which it'll work, and a wedding with a honeymoon in the south or on a Greek island, and a grandchild who too will sit on that highchair and wave a spoon – for a moment those doors could still be seen from the corner of the eye and immediately were replaced by their identical matches. Perhaps behind them during the day hospital warehousemen sat and sorted and dusted all the objects that no one came to claim: pairs of glasses and slippers, wigs combed in styles that the hospital pillows coiffured, a pile of fingered, small crosses, and heaps of other amulets that also failed to fulfill their purpose: rosary beads, stars of David, hand-shaped Arabic talismans, horseshoes, dried seahorses, marbles from when the dead were still children and did not identify the multicolored scythes of death through their transparency.

Opposite you all, at the vanishing point of the corridor's lines, the room at the end could already be made out, closed by two doors in the center of which two windows were fixed, round as portholes, as if Charon had replaced the ferry with a new model containing a one thousand horse power engine or a million, all the horses required for transferring the dead. Sometimes they were not required at all; a few hairs from their tails were enough if dipped in paint, conveying to the canvas a blue kettle that continued to expel jets of steam, an African mask blackening on the wall, the grooves in the soles of overturned shoes still wet from the rain, two sweaters whose grey and green sleeves blend together on the wicker of the armchair – on the train you already knew where your belongings would be unloaded, this was confirmed by the warmth of her responsive thigh to your own, similarly starved, opposite a mossy fence galloping backwards – squashed bra cups whose straps lie twisted on the carpet, a window melting from the rain when she draws near to it naked and stops in front of the windowpane and mists both it and the distant steeple on the other side and says: "didn't you once ever feel like it? Enough of all that, I'm over it all now."

The linoleum was still spread beneath your feet, as long as the hide of a skinned grey dragon, who if still alive would have counted your steps, your steps, your steps, instead of the sheep it set alight with flames from its mouth in order to fall asleep. On the ceiling the fluorescent lights continued to advance in a long, long convoy, albino ants that carried crumbs of fading light to their wide open burrow at the end.

They apparently reminded the bearded clochard of loaded trucks because that's just what he started to talk about on the way to the morgue, about Daf and Renault trucks, Volvo and Mercedes, and especially about the one owing to which he landed up where he landed up, on the street. When he fell silent, only the shoes, the shoes, the shoes were heard again: tuk-tuk, they beat, tuff-tuff, they daintily sounded, tupm-tupm. But actually, why should he speak about trucks now, he said after a while, rustling the cardboard carton that he held. Is a corridor the place to speak about trucks and dumb drivers? It was bad enough they were dumb, at least afterwards they could have told the truth instead of blaming you. Yes, without letting him get a word in, straightaway they found a reason to fire him, even though he was injured, is this the place to talk about it? And anyway this corridor is already coming to an end. Dumb drivers who suddenly lift the back of the truck with all the goods that they loaded there, why shouldn't they lift it if they could? And suddenly everything fell backwards, what didn't fall, tell him one thing that didn't fall, but is this the place to talk about it? Maybe half the street was filled there with their goods and from the blow he received he saw stars, you would have thought he'd already reached Mars or something, at the very least Mars, if not that Kingdom of Heaven from his signpost. That's what his mother would have said, what's written here, but then look where his mother is and look where he is.

At the end of the corridor the round windows grew larger, gazing ahead chillingly, and opposite them Edith wanted to talk a bit more about Mars. She was suddenly reminded of her son, right now, as if there was time for their reminiscences, because in the playground her son would get inside a barrel like it was some kind of rocket and wait for it to take off. Yessir yes, and from outside he could be heard counting from ten to one, and for her at the time one moment of not seeing him was all it took to become scared right away. He hid there in the barrel like he'd suddenly returned to the womb, yes, that's what went through her mind. Especially when his friends, some friends, them and their parents are just the same, started to throw chestnuts at him there, not one or two, lots, really lots, and she heard them knocking against the tin; it was really scary. Her empty leather handbag swung here and there from her hand when she looked at the doors of the last rooms on her right and on her left, and had she not moved forward along the corridor perhaps she would have turned around and removed a tear from her eye like a bellboy warding off trespassers with his fists, but another one had already stuck its transparent foot into her eyelid.

"Afterwards," she said, "even though I was his mother-" and fell silent and her shoes could be heard.

"I told you sir," the bearded clochard imitated her, "one small word is enough," and searched Nadia's eyes to see if he had succeeded in cheering her up; after all that's exactly how Edith had mocked her, like someone who cries about every bit of nonsense. Isn't that how she spoke about her before? But Nadia, taking all the time in the world, opened large eyes staring like the windows of the doors at the end of the corridor and in a trembling voice told the bearded man, be quiet, be quiet, and touched Edith's shoulder. Her fingers, beneath ashen age spots were still slender and delicate, and Edith moved her shoulder below them like someone scattering a butterfly from it – in nature films they would fly crossing tens of kilometers a day with their delicate bodies, but you no longer remembered the channel, nor the hour, nor how she would call you to watch the program – while still looking for a moment at its wings to make sure that it wasn't just something flickering in the corner of her eye brought on by weariness.

The bearded clochard was still angry about being stopped in the middle, because it's not the truck, to hell with the truck, what does he care about the truck? Was it his? His father's? His father was a shipping magnate, yes, certainly, a shipping magnate – of boats made from newspaper. So to hell with the trucks, what's important is the accident from which he lost his job, together with his one room apartment and actually all he had, even his respect. He lost it all and found himself on the street. So now is he supposed to care about Edith's son's rocket? What, he said, wasn't he once a boy flying in a barrel?

"Makes fun of everything," Nadia said and moved further forward, "you don't make fun of something like that. If you only knew what happened to her with the boy you wouldn't talk like that. People don't make fun of that, right sir? Of the war." She turned to you and you reacted with a brief nod, because that boy was not required for the painting, not his barrel and not the war – you spoke of a different war in the carriage and in her apartment afterwards, when with a shortsighted eagerness you shed light on the circumstances of your meeting: as if one had not been fought in your country other than to make you fed up with all your doings there and get on a plane and land and travel and reach the train platform, and as if all the emptiness of her apartment had not gaped wide open and her study assignments had not increased other than to make her take a vacation and return and stop next to a yellow cargo carriage whose shaft was dropped – and neither was the plant, which stood in the approaching corner of the corridor, wilted like its predecessor, needed for the painting, nor the small red extinguisher enough for one lone flame. The door windows grew larger and Nadia fell silent, and in the expanse of the corridor again one could hear the shoes, the shoes, the shoes: they marched left-right, right-left, tuk-tuk, tuff-tuff, tupm-tupm.

In the hotel in which you started to work after you left her apartment – the rain no longer fell; the grey fluff that shrouded the cathedral steeple was removed; leaves sprouted from the chestnut branches and the wind counted them like a pawnbroker gauging the watches of passersby – the American asked you if they still used flamethrowers in wars, because there was a time when one was enough for an entire village of fucking gooks: a village in the middle of the jungle, yeah just like on television, just that there it was full of fucking trenches down below. And the gooks weren't messing around with bows and arrows, they had fucking Kalashnikovs. The television with the evergreen trees in it was already decrepit from the fists that had tried to stabilize the picture, and the soft drink automat was battered too, like a suspect from whom the police had extracted a confession by kicking.

You used to watch those nature programs with her, and in one of them they showed members of an African tribe who lived in the jungle and who didn't give names to their children until they were sure they would remain alive: any moment they were liable to be preyed upon, to step on a snake or a scorpion, to be stung by a tsetse fly. It was propitious to wait with a name for a month or two, a year or two, four-five, sometimes nobody remained to give them a name apart from the black fertile earth of the jungle. Through the female announcer's voice, for a moment you could hear her enunciating your name again in a mellow tone, but beyond the entrance door, which the chambermaid had not cleaned, only the prostitute could be made out in the cone of yellowish light from the streetlamp as she shifted her weight from leg to leg and alongside you the American lit and extinguished a lighter.

The doors were already a few steps away, silent and assessing the lot of you from head to toe: they looked askance at Nadia's leg, at Edith's empty handbag, at the filth of the bearded man's clothes, and blocked their ears at the rattling of the bottles in your rucksack. They were as suspicious as porters of five-star hotels in the sixteenth arrondissement or even the ninth, in which Edith once worked, yes-yes: at the end of the corridor leading to the morgue it was very important for her to manage to say before going in that there was a time when doors like these, as well as others, were opened in front of her, and they'd say: "Please, Madame Edith, please, after you." Isn't that how they spoke to her? Sure that's how they spoke to her when she was still a concierge in the ninth arrondissement, yes-yes: if anyone doesn't know that then they should know that she was once a concierge and what respect she was given and what a building she had to look after. What do you think, they only had carpets in Russia and in her building they didn't? Sure they did, yes, from top to bottom. True, that carpet was a bit worn out, and in place of the brass poles what they once put next to the stairs, they knocked in some nails, true, not so straight, but that was long, long before her time. At the time she didn't drink, not even a drop, what did she have to drink for then? There was even an electric bell in the entrance so that not just anyone from the street could come in, and the tenants would always say to her, "hello Madame," when they would see her head peeking out from the window, or "thank you, Madame," when she would hand out the post, and they would pinch her child's cheek when he wasn't inside his barrel; at the time who knew what she'd been through in the war.

Tuk-tuk, your shoes beat on the linoleum, tuff-tuff, tupm-tupm. And where was the ninth arrondissement now? Where was Edith's child now? Where was the Metro tunnel? There was nothing other than the corridor becoming shorter and shorter until reaching an end, in another three steps, two, one step, tuk-tuk, tuff-tuff, tupm-tupm, and the bearded clochard pushed the door with his outspread fingers whose knuckle hairs had begun to grey and held it so that it would not flap and said: "please, Madame, please," and gave a little bow, as if he had opened the door to a ballroom, deftly displaying dancing couples and a pianist playing a shiny white grand piano for them: tuk-tuk, tuff-tuff, tupm-tupm.

5

Thousands of white porcelain tiles sparkled all around and the small doors of the stainless steel wall at the end shone. Beneath the shoes the grey linoleum of the corridor lengthened and expanded to the right and to the left and spread out to the distant walls. The fluorescent lights, of which one column had been sufficient in the corridor, were dispersed over the entire ceiling surface of the large room and organized themselves in threes in their white uniforms like naval sentries brought in to pay last respects to the dead. They were not yet seen, the dead, but at the end of the room the refrigeration unit towered with all its drawers. From each and every one four tiny figures were reflected as if they were already gauging your measurements, and from behind, the doors continued to flap in and out, in and out, blowing wind on your backs like the doors of a saloon.

Could not pied horses be waiting outside there? Yearning to neigh at you the moment you'll appear, the way you appeared to the eyes of the drawers. A bearded clochard in a khaki jacket and filthy jeans, an old woman in a tattered dress holding an empty handbag close to her stomach, a second old woman in a smock held together by safety pins, and you yourself with a bulging canvas rucksack from which a folding easel protruded. Its edge had already dug into your neck, but had a stray memory fallen upon it from the interior of your skull – a braid loosened on a warm, breathing unblemished back turned over to meet your hands with nipples whose softness is disappearing – it would not have moved it then more than clouds move a cliff; where there still were clouds and cliffs.

In places where there still were clouds and cliffs, perhaps there was also a hotel in whose every room a picture of a snowy peak hung, but in the hotel to which you moved from her apartment, there were no pictures other than those that were hidden in the bedside cabinet drawers: beneath the bible, which nobody opened, and the old newspapers, with which the chambermaid padded the plywood, sometimes you could discover a thumbed magazine with naked girls mounted on silk bedcovers or musclemen in tiny bathing costumes, all shiny from oil or sweat; whoever stayed in the room perhaps hoped to return someday and find those models longing for them in their drawer, pumping breasts or muscles at them as if from a dusky alcove.

Here in the morgue, there were just shiny tiles and grey linoleum and pale neon light and sparkling stainless steel. The refrigeration unit and all its drawers were not enough for the stainless steel, it needed a table as well: in the middle of the large room it shone like an altar, cleansed of every drop of blood. Perhaps the blood stopped in the arteries of the dead like the Metro trains in the earth when the ground still grew the nails of its buildings toward the covering pinned above it, a grey or black covering, which at the time never turned blue like the blues that were mixed for it, ultramarine or phthalo-blue, cobalt-blue or Prussian-blue, all the shades packed into small tubes and dried up in your room opposite the easel.

You could have painted the son of God on the stainless steel table as well, like any murdered person whose cause of death is being examined, but the drawer was more suitable for him, because it was one of dozens between which there was no difference: rows and rows were arranged opposite you all, floors and floors, sections and sections, an entire district for the dead: perhaps patrolling policeman were placed in them, bakers, secretaries, retired colonels, panel beaters, dancers, car electricians, piano teachers who were once child prodigies: the drawers concealed them all like card players waiting for the right moment to reveal their cards and trump.

Once operating tables were made of marble, and on two of them Rembrandt immortalized the anatomy lessons of Doctor Tulp and Doctor Deiman as they dissected the bodies of murderers: the skin was removed, the cranium of the skull sawed, but the murderers also achieved immortality with their parents' given names, Adriaan Adriaanszoon and Joris Fonteijn. Unlike their victims they were not forgotten, not stung, not struck, not devoured, and hovering vultures did not circle above their remains like the fluorescent lights here.

Dozens of hooks were screwed into the porcelain tiles on both sides; on the left, fresh and laundered pinafores were hung, and on the right plastic aprons washed of the spray of entrails and of the fine down of dreams, that flew from sawn skulls as birds from felled treetops.

"Don't you want to try them on?" asked the bearded man not moving forward even one step. "The pinafores." Oh yes. there's not a woman who never dreamt of wearing a nurse's pinafore, he said, show him one, just one, just like there isn't a man who never dreamt, he doesn't want to say what, because this isn't the time and place – but in daydreams you too saw her in the white toweling gown and undid its cord, and sometimes she undid it and covered you with its edges and wiped your lower back with them: a porcelain jag on which it was hung was revealed jutting out from the wall, steam thickened on the mirror and nacreous drops flowed.

"In hospital," said the bearded clochard, because he recalled his accident again, "there was one who just by looking at her made everyone's pain worse. I swear, it all ached worse. But for her nothing less than a doctor would do. Because to a nurse, what's someone who works in a department store?" And not even a salesman, at least a salesman could have given her things with a discount, but he was worse than an unqualified male nurse, same as the cleaners, "a nobody out of whom she'd get nothing." Between the wall of pinafores and the wall of aprons that nurse reminded him of the beauty consultants from the ground floor of the department store in which he worked, the ones from Estée Lauder and Lancôme and Nina Ricci who would all look through him as if he was invisible, yes, invisible. Only once in his life someone really beautiful looked at him, when he was still small, maybe fifteen; it's just that so much time has already passed since then that he's not

certain if it really happened. As for here, it's even harder to
be certain about it. Here he's only certain about bad things,
yes only about them. At the time he couldn't get her out of
his head; it wasn't only because of her that he left his city,
but also because of her. What, didn't he have enough reasons
other than that?

Opposite the hanging pinafores he began to talk, as if his
talking was required for the painting, about his city, which
he left, and about his parents, who remained there, "so young
it's hard to believe." And his parents, he said, but you were
only interested in his father – from the bed you could hear
the night sky brushing against the roof like the belly of an
enormous sinking ship whose captain still grasped the railing
of the deck – "actually had jobs, all those years they worked."
Not that he's jealous of them about that, not at all, quite the
opposite. What did he have to be jealous about? He even
swore then that he'd never be like them, "working like ants
without earning anything, they hardly went to the movies
once a month. It was a celebration when they went, I swear,
a celebration. Their biggest outing was going to church on
Sunday, as for that church, I swear the carriage of a Metro's
got more space." For a moment he looked at the cardboard
sign that he showed the tourists in the square so that they'd
open their wallets, but through his dirty beard and the skin
of his face, which already had begun to become frazzled, it
was impossible to see the son of God, whom he imitated
with pantomime steps on the paving stones colored with blue
chalk, nor the boy who lived next to the factory where the
chimney smoke conceals the sky the way the vapor of your
breath misted up the windowpane and blurred the building
across the road.

From behind, the doors had already settled and again
stared at your backs with their round eyes, and Nadia said in
her quiet voice, childish in its crackling, that everyone should
stay in their own place, yes. "That's where you should stay,
where you're born, right sir?" She requested your confirmation,
but you had already hastened to unload the rucksack from

your back – one winter morning whose sky was weighty on the roofs, after a big quarrel, it was bought from a punk shop, which also sold used surplus army equipment, but you no longer remember where that shop was, not the street and not the quarter – and you began to undo its straps. "And to thank the Lord every day," Nadia said, "just thank him."

"To thank him for sure," the bearded clochard answered her, "no question about it." Perhaps he also had to count from ten to one there, like Edith's son in the barrel? And wait there all his life for something to happen.

"Wise guy," Edith said, "thinks he can make fun of everything and everyone'll keep quiet. Don't even mention my son! That one's never been married, who'd marry someone like that, who?" She turned to you, "he only had a dog, and even a dog he didn't know how to look after! A dog sir," she said to you in front of the rucksack buckles being opened, "what's there to looking after a dog? Easy as anything. It hasn't got a thought in its head, doesn't hear what it's not supposed to hear, what does a dog understand?"

"It had thoughts just like a person," said the bearded clochard, "the exact same thing, believe me. It's just that it couldn't say them, that's all." With the tip of his finger he touched the stainless steel in order to gauge its coldness, but you had already begun to empty out your rucksack onto the table and right away the bottles and vials rang out. They had never seen a table as large as that on which they were turned out and their glass had never gleamed with so many fluorescent lights. After they were stood upright they continued to gargle with delight, this one with wine, that one with turpentine, that one with varnish, content in themselves. For a long while Edith looked at the wine as if at a long lost love met once more, in slow motion to the sound of violins, but the fluorescent lights, white as the bows of blind violinists, played above her nothing but the one buzzing sound for the dead.

"A dog?" Edith said, "What does a dog know? It only knows to eat and to pee. It hasn't got friends to tell it everything that their parents said about you, lies sir, all lies!

Even if it was long ago. One would think – the things they did then sir, their parents, the big saints. As if I didn't know what they did then, but did that help?"

The bearded clochard, glad of any delay, asked what she herself did then and just when that "then" was, but Edith did not answer. She looked at the white pinafores on the right and at the white aprons on the left, and for a moment shuddered as if they were suddenly filled out by people, surgeons with masks or nurses handing over scissors or sturdy orderlies or any other person who could burst forth from behind the porcelain tiles of the walls – in the room you rented, there were nights when the confined silence between wall to wall was so compressed that it was sharpened and stropped on your head like a surgeon's scalpel, but on other nights the walls became thin and waved like curtains in the wind and beyond them was nothing: not the gables of servants' rooms, not slate roofs or central heating chimneys and not a cathedral steeple to whose top you did not climb together, and from which you did not look at the entire city as it had once been seen through her eyes, and not at one window covered by the vapor of breath – "That one," Edith motioned with her eyebrow to the bearded clochard, when he still lived with them in the tunnel and still had his dog, what was it called? She just sometimes wondered how it didn't bark at all the people, which she used to see there at night, from her past, yes that's how it is when you don't forget anything. It all comes back, absolutely everything. She used to lie there on her bench in the tunnel and just wonder how nobody saw them except her, yes, that's how it is when nightmares come. "But besides that," she said, "the dog barked just as much as it wanted. It gave me goosebumps, on my word, goosebumps."

The wooden easel was already placed upright on the linoleum. You could have placed it upright anywhere: on the street at whose end all the pedestrians vanish, on the bridge opposite the cathedral, in the tunnel opposite the moving staircase that carried her up, in your room whose bedding is sweaty with the sweat of only your body, and also in the morgue. It was placed upright in an instant: opening the leg screws was enough for each part to immediately dangle one after another, and it was enough to attach the horizontal board to the easel and place the canvas on it for the shadows that fell there to resemble an outline, had they darkened its whiteness any further. But here they were faded from the start, the fluorescent lighting having distributed the light in equal parts like righteous nuns from the Salvation Army: they would have driven Rembrandt crazy, and Caravaggio too, and de la Tour and Gentileschi, and whoever took an interest in the war of light against darkness and in its trifling victories.

There was a gleam in the bottles and on the stainless steel, and they looked like an offering on an altar. From the ceiling the fluorescent lights watched like a band of fussy gods, had there been any god who would have been satisfied with just wine. But even the god who was mentioned in one of the nature programs, when you were no longer living in her apartment – the veteran Marine soldier who was also watching the program was trying to light himself a cigarette over and over without a lighter, so that the hotel wouldn't burn down like a village from a flamethrower – an Indian god who used to suck nectar and gather berries; it was enough for him to become hungry to immediately consume entire pastures and abandon them chewed up and sucked dry like the floral wallpaper: rows and rows of them were also painted on the walls of the room that you rented, but no scent arose there other than the smell of damp and the smell of your body turning over and over amongst them.

In the hotel in which you worked there were no fluorescent lights: forty watt globes were hung above the beds, and in the yellowish light the stains on the blankets were not visible nor the holes made by the forgotten cigarettes of whoever had been drunk there alone at night. "One day you'll all burn here," the American would say each time a scorched smell could be detected, "people just don't realize what fire is, they don't respect it." But here all the flames were folded beneath the linoleum like flowers whose time for opening had not arrived.

From the morgue, for a moment even the hotel appeared congenial, with its bare carpets and burned out globes, and the peephole in the bathroom, and the cigarette butts that lined the pot plants as the falling leaves did the ground of the park after clinging to their branches for the whole month of October like someone clinging to a window sill.

Only above the entrance was there a fluorescent light, which for a while lit up the hotel sign until the glass was smashed and resembled a bony fish skeleton. Beneath it a few of the other night clerk's bicycles were parked, fake deluxe bikes that he used to smuggle from Holland in a rickety van and sell, with no receipts, to female students who used to go down to the cellar with him. Sometimes they would close the door after them, and even though it was heavy and completely sealed you imagined hearing groans through it and through the groans her voice, so clearly heard that you would have flooded the cellar with the extinguisher hose, had it worked.

Before the hotel drew away with the entire city in a fading siren swallowed by the wind, the landlord fired all the permanent staff chambermaids. Two Vietnamese, about whom the authorities were not notified, came in place of them and used to walk daintily along the corridors, until stopping and spitting at some withering plant with the same ease with which the others put out their cigarettes on it. The American, who for the entire summer described to everyone what a flamethrower leaves in his wake, said that's the way they always are: no matter where you go you have to be careful not to get spat on, in Saigon, in Hanoi, in Bangkok, where not, and that they piss and shit everywhere, the fucking gooks, breeding even more than the mice, which they eat. But one night, after an enormous forest fire was shown on television, he went up the stairs without cigarettes and without a lighter and went into his room to check the strength of the ceiling, and from the reception desk nothing was heard other than the chair that overturned.

Opposite the extinguished sign the prostitute would transfer her weight from leg to leg and sometimes would lean against one of the bicycles or smoke thin cigarettes in a holder like a lady in an old film, a film that would become torn each time she began to cough, and from time to time she would ask you from her spot if you were not bored like her and if you felt like you-know-what – walk here, turn around, hold the handbag as if it was a suitcase and now sit here and look outside as if the building there was a bell tower; opposite the window, whose hills and villages withdrew further and shortened into *landscape* and *background*, she asked if you had climbed up and seen the whole city beneath you and wanted to fly or jump, yes, because someone who's never asked himself why he's alive isn't really alive; and the rain whipped the windowpane with a mass of delicate transparent lashings, as if trying to lead the carriages to the place toward which the hills were hurtling.

A palette, thick brushes and thin brushes, new tubes of paint and used tubes of paint were already laid out on the stainless steel table, and the bearded clochard observed everything as if knowledgeable of such things and used to them. "What do blue and yellow make?" he asked, "they make green, right? And yellow and black make brown, right?" What d'you mean where does he know that from, why shouldn't he know? It's what he learned from someone who used to paint next to him on the sidewalk, just like he learned the steps from some pantomime artist, and what was written on his sign, the repent-is-at-hand, he learned from his mother, yes, who every moment of her screwed up life believed in that as if it would help her with something, only it didn't help her with a thing. Never mind that he reached rock bottom, not rock bottom, right here, but why did she deserve that?

"He makes fun of his own mother," Edith said, but you came to pay homage to one of the great artists and in the painting that you chose she only had to wring her hands and be silent. "Never mind all the other things," she glanced at the ceiling, "but to make fun of a mother who brought him up from when he was little? And after that it's no wonder sir they threw him out, who'd love someone like that who makes fun of everything? Once they asked him for his dog, for one time, not forever, so that they'd earn a bit from him as well, he made such a fuss, you'd think they asked him for his wife. And when the poor guy fell onto the tracks," she said and you did not react, "straightaway he wanted to run to the police, he didn't wait a second. He doesn't give a damn what people say about him, a big shot, thinks he can get by on his own, without anyone."

For a moment the bearded man still tried to say to her that he's not making fun of his mother, not at all, the opposite, but promptly gave up. Across from the stainless steel table and all the painting utensils that you unpacked onto it, Edith had already begun to say everything she had to say to him, to one like that who makes fun of everything and doesn't care about anything. "Big shot," she said, "really." Because didn't she once try to go against everyone? At the time she tried to go against the whole world until she learned her lesson, oh yes, and how she learned it. "And someone who learns something like that," she said to you while you were inspecting the brushes, "doesn't forget in a hurry. No sir, no."

So now she cares what people say about her, yes of course she cares. Why shouldn't she care? Just once she didn't care, a long time ago. But after that, when she'd already become a concierge in the ninth arrondissement, when she was already sure that everyone had forgotten everything, what, hadn't enough time passed? Hadn't her life been made enough of a misery? Especially since everyone already showed her respect, not a single person entered her building without her knowing about it, not even one. So everything was really all right, that's how she felt at the time when she received that letter, the one that you had to copy out and send to ten people.

As if you were interested in letters that were not written in a slanted handwriting by a blue Bic pen – she used to leave them on the table, under the sugar bowl, which she filled for you careful not to be tempted by its cubes, or fix them to the fridge with one of the animal magnets, which also clutched memos to remind herself about groceries she needed and accounts that had to be paid. And with the same pen she listed daily tasks in her notebook according to their time, until she returned to find you watching the tenants from the building across the road through the window, which had more life in it than all the paintings you intended to paint – Edith began to tell about all the things that were written in the letter she received, "such nonsense, heaven help us."

Whoever had sent the letter won the lottery right away, "say someone found a diamond on the pavement, and then his friend In America finds oil in the backyard. Things like that sir," she turned to you and you didn't answer, "on my word, things that happen only in movies. And whoever didn't send it, straightaway something happened to his children, or his father and mother, God forbid, even if they were in good health and everything. Say someone fell from the balcony or someone got run over by a car, it was just because they didn't send the letter." They also wrote that the letter, just as it was, had already been around the world twice, and that she had to copy it out again and send it to at least ten people. Not that her name was written there, but where else would the post arrive if not to her, so that she could hand it out to the tenants? It was also written that she only had a week to do it in, meaning to copy it out and send it at the very least to ten people. And right after that anything could happen. Anything. "The shine or the shit, sir. Forgive me for speaking that way, but that's how it is, there's nothing else in the middle."

Across from the paint tubes, which you arranged according to their shades after they had become mixed up in the rucksack, she said she knew very well it was nonsense: of course she knew, she with her experience of life knows how many things are nonsense, what d'you mean, they can't fool her and not her child either. It's just that right from the start she got scared: scared, yes, almost like here, because what'll happen if she doesn't send it? She's not looking for trouble, that's not what she's short of, with all those tenants just waiting to drive her up the wall. Because that's all they're waiting for, like she's got no life of her own, like she's their slave. "Why's the stairway light burned out and why's the trash spilt next to the trash can," as if she's the one who spilt it and not they themselves. "Why's this and why's that," just so that she doesn't rest for one moment. So she's not short of any trouble. And besides that, what, is it so hard to copy and pass them out? Not that she likes writing letters, not at all, but a few lines? And after she sends them, however long it takes, say two hours, then it'll be their worry. If things happen to them, let's say winning a lottery or something falling on them, then she, Edith, will know where it came from, she'll know very well where it came from, the shine or the shit.

"And for them, all them tenants," she said opposite the large refrigeration unit for the dead that quietly buzzed opposite her, "it's no problem making even twenty copies." They'd do it easy as anything, the way she does the dishes, when she still had dishes and a fridge and an oven and everything. So first thing Sunday she already prepared herself a writing pad and envelopes – for a moment you recalled another pad with its yellow pages, but it was forgotten instantly like the sugar bowl placed on them as a paperweight and like the animal magnets, which lost not only their outlines but their grip and fell one after another and following them, the fridge to which they were fixed with the entire apartment – even though they gave her a whole week. And afterwards she finished doing some jobs in the building, just so they wouldn't say she was taking it easy, but even as she was doing them, say she was doing some vacuuming for example, that was all she thought about, as if everything she had achieved with her own ten fingers after the war depended only on that now.

Because the way she came to Paris, just a country girl still smelling of cows, that's what he said, the old man, when she met him for the first time. He was a good person, all in all. After that he gave her loads of perfume, he didn't stint on anything, not on her and not on her boy. Right from the start he told her he was a doorman in the ninth arrondissement and that those tenants are also no saints. Yes, with all their money and everything, they didn't try to hide the one who was taken in the war – in that apartment, opposite the flickering television set, you spoke together about a different war, but you no longer recalled what you were asked and what you answered and not how it was suddenly brought up opposite the screen in which dark-skinned savages were seen with blowpipes and bows and arrows – people like that, yes. All that was going through her mind again while she was vacuuming, as if everything she had achieved with her own ten fingers will all go to hell if she doesn't take care of that letter and send It.

And so Edith went down to her ground floor apartment and planned to copy the letter when her son returns from school; maybe he'll also help her a bit, so what, didn't she once use to help him with lessons when she still could? It's not because of the wine that she can't help him anymore, it's just because of those studies of his, which got harder every year, only now he doesn't come at all. She waited maybe an hour for him and he didn't come. And he had never ever made her wait! Never! She began to ring all his friends, those from school and those from the arrondissement, who didn't she ring? There's not a soul she didn't, it's just that they all told her they didn't know anything. "What d'you mean you don't know anything, you were with him at school, no?" That's how she spoke to them, she was already half crazy from worry, but they didn't see anything didn't hear anything, right away they gave the receiver to Mommy for her to put it down right in her face.

"When?" the bearded man asked. He took a large gulp from the wine bottle that he opened continuing to stare at the paint tubes that you arranged on the stainless steel, "on what day was it?"

"On the first day!" Edith said. "Not the second, not the third, the first day! Right at the beginning from being scared I wanted to write that letter, believe me it was worse than here, and from the start the troubles began, they didn't wait a day! Where didn't I phone, there's not a place I didn't, my finger was already worn out from all the dialing. By then I didn't hear who was coming and who was going at all, they could all go jump in the lake, all the tenants. I only cared about my boy." And eventually, when Edith was almost completely crazy, really it wouldn't have taken much more, if it wasn't for her experience of life she would have gone crazy a long, long time ago, eventually he comes in the door like nothing's the matter, the little prince, and doesn't want to talk to her. Makes out like he doesn't see her coming close to him, and doesn't hear her when she spoke to him, and when she tried to take him to the kitchen to eat he opened up his little mouth, which for a whole year drank milk from her tittie, what do you mean a year, a year and a half, and said something to her that at first she didn't hear, until she brought her head close and he said it again right in her face, the little prince.

The pot was still standing on the stove even though all the water had already escaped from it long ago, what, was she able to pay attention to that? How could she have – the small blue kettle was forgotten on the stove only on one occasion, on the first evening, and in the morning she scrubbed the sooty bottom as if she was mining coal from the depths of the sink; from the bed, which still retained the warmth of her body and the smell of her, you told her in the same confident voice that you had then, about van Gogh, who went down the mines of Borinage when he still wanted to become a preacher, and you heard her saying through the flow of the water that had he persevered he wouldn't have ended his life like that – and as for him, her boy, he didn't want soup anyway, he didn't want anything from her, not a thing. He didn't want her to touch him at all, that's how he stood there in the entrance to the kitchen, with his satchel still on his back, and from his little mouth said it again, as if she didn't hear it well enough, as if her ears were also worn out. He said it again and again and again and again, never mind what he said.

That all happened on the first day just when he returned from school where some foolish boy told him about it;

must have heard it from his parents. Those big saints, Edith knew very well the way they behaved in the war. It happened without any connection to that letter, without any connection to anything, just some boy telling him, some little fool. Why should she have been amazed? She could have learned long ago, from her experience of life, which she wouldn't wish on anyone, that everything happens because of people, absolutely everything: the shine and the shit. For a moment she lifted her eyebrow to the hovering fluorescent light on the ceiling, but it didn't blink even one solitary blink at her.

The entire ceiling was full of them, those whitish leeches, all the corridors that led here, and the river that flowed above as well: at the time you could see them teeming and breeding in the clouds and falling with the rain and being spewed from the faucets and the showerhead holes and clinging to the body and suckling from it like a thousand hungry puppies or like prostitutes paid not for the pleasure but for the pain: stand there, bend over, stand upright, turn around and start walking, sit: as if the floor of the hotel lengthened out to some far horizon line unto which the tracks flowed, as if the rickety cabinet, whose drawers were padded by old newspapers, was a freight carriage whose yellow shaft had dropped, and as if the small shiny handbag was a gigantic suitcase that she struggled to lift, and the hard wooden chair, which was next to the cabinet, a padded train seat, and the thighs, in which varicose veins intertwined, other thighs, unblemished plump and warm: stand there, bend down, stand upright; like a perverse peeping tom or like Degas in his old age, you wanted to see her, when you still lived in her apartment, washing, wiping herself dry, dressing, and sometimes with the paintbrush hairs you touched the delicate skin until it shuddered and the nipples were drawn out, the way she used to make your member take form by blowing or by the shadow of her body spread out.

Nadia touched Edith's shoulder and this time she allowed the palm of her hand to stay there, an aged, wrinkled trembling butterfly. "This one," Edith said suddenly dropping her shoulder, "doesn't think like that, to her everyone's okay, all people. After all they've done to her they're still okay. They didn't call her Nadjezda for nothing, to this one even the birds are okay. All those pigeons of hers." She grinned at you as if it was required for the painting and as if they were flying opposite you then, between the tiled walls, or in the park, when you still used to stroll in the park. "Didn't she see with her own eyes what they do to each other? You'd think they couldn't get by in life without her breadcrumbs. Couldn't get by, my foot." But you couldn't see them, not between the walls of the morgue, not in the breadth of the park, when there was still a park up there. "They're mean," Edith said, "the same as people. What they wouldn't do for a crumb, believe me."

At the time they weren't seen in the park, on the day that the city began to be wiped out, not the pigeons, not the statues, not the little tots, not the ponies, not the chestnut trees and not the pond and the lawn, all of which coalesced into the distance; just for one single solitary moment a few pinpointed rays of sunlight infiltrated above you like those that she once saw from the cathedral steeple lighting up all her years, infiltrated and suddenly gilded all the heads of the statues, kindled the pond's ripples, glistened the shells of burst open chestnuts, painted the shadows of each and every branch on the ground, strummed the stalks of grass on whose tips reddish leaves lay, and at the time you couldn't move your hands owing to that nameless thing that knew nothing of your existence beneath it: you were smaller than a leaf there, tinier than an aphid, but again the light promptly turned grey with the entire city.

"No matter how many of them die," Edith said, as if the drawers of the refrigeration unit contained nothing other than grey, lice-ridden pigeons, "there's no end to them. What they don't do for one crumb, with their beaks and legs and what not, one to the other like that."

Only a stray dog came up to you then in the park and suddenly licked your hand with a warm tongue, but immediately hurried off on his way. From the blunt chisel blows of the statue nearby you could imagine the dreams of the one who made them, who perhaps once boasted like you in front of a woman on a train that his creations will be exhibited in town squares and museums, and did not know that he would be just an artist-for-parks: pigeons will excrete on them, dogs will lift their legs and urinate, no one will ever know his name.

"And after that she still believes everyone's good," Edith said, "after seeing with her own eyes just how much it isn't like that, she's learned that firsthand sir, you don't have to go as far as Russia, isn't it enough what they did to her here?"

You were not even an artist-for-parks: in the room that you rented afterwards, in the depths of the jars from which turpentine has evaporated, the paint dried up on the brushes, and of all the views you told her about on the train and in the apartment not even one was painted. "Life is right here," she used to say when you described to her what was seen only in your head, and for a while it indeed was right there, life, in that room or in the kitchenette or the small bathtub or any other place where she was. "Life is right here," she once turned away from the paintings in the Orangerie to the window between them and to the park beyond it in which two tots bundled up in little coats skipped after a dignified matronly pigeon; "it's right here," in a small cinema she turned away from the greyish flickering figures of actors long dead and pressed close to your body in the darkness; "right here," she pushed a supermarket trolley in front of her, loading it with bottles of milk, cartons of eggs, a box of cornflakes and oranges, which came from your country, and when a huge package of paper diapers fell in her way she lifted them up and said: "our baby will wait a bit, no?" and replaced the package on the shelf and said: "he knows we won't disappoint him," and for a while you both believed that. In her waking hours you did not draw one of her features so as not to squander the minutes, and in her sleep you just gazed upon the limpness of the sated body, at the treacherous breast yielding to the sheet, at a curve arching toward the wall, to the extent that you wondered how it was not inclined to prostrate itself over her.

With your nails you pulled a scab of paint from the hair of the paintbrush while Edith related what was done to Nadia and her mother in the immigrants' quarter where they lived, because weren't they both hassled there, weren't they? "Of course they were hassled, no question about it. They were hassled in a way that makes a person sometimes ask himself if he wasn't better off dead, believe me sir there are situations like that, I'm talking from experience. And her mother was someone who knew how to get by, not like her, someone who kept her on her feet since she was little. They both used to embroider serviettes for the shop on their square, jobs like that. And if once they got paid, then twice they didn't."

"The sons of bitches," said the bearded man, "they should be here, that's what they deserve." He had already opened another bottle, and the cork that he threw away rolled on the surgical table until it slowed down, hesitated and fell on its side. "There are ones like that," he said and looked at the cork, "who throw money at you on purpose like that, I swear, on purpose. Not into the hat, onto the pavement, so that you'll have to run after it a bit. Not enough you put on a show for them, they also want to see you spit blood for their fucking half a franc."

He extended the new bottle to Edith and lifted his eye to the old one, peered into it and turned it over for it to trickle what was still left in it, and afterwards drew near to the canvas and began to examine it from the front and the back – it had been kept for so long in your room that its whiteness had become sullied, and on all those nights it had turned black there like some kind of additional window, as empty as the first, that had you turned a light on and stood opposite it, it would have revealed nothing but the one who placed his face close to the windowpane from outside and stared at you, a moonstruck angel weary from his flight or a man on his way to the sidewalk – "you call this a job well done," he said, to further delay that moment when he'll have to earn his meal and his wine, "that's how you attach it to the wood, with staples?" No really, that wouldn't do for their department store. "Maybe in Tati they'd allow that," he said, "if they sell things like that in Tati at all." Opposite the morgue's refrigeration unit, in whose every drawer your images were reflected, he would have spoken about anything in the world, not only about Tati but also about Galerie Lafayette and Samaritaine and BHV, if only to postpone for a while the moment in which he'll have to step toward the unit and pull out one of its empty drawers and mount it and get inside and lie down and close his eyes.

"It's just that I know good workmanship," he said while examining the wooden frame and the fibers of the material, and for a moment the crescents of his filthy fingernails fluttered, as wavy as the wings of birds in children's drawings – you no longer remembered if you ever drew like them, nor if you climbed trees, nor if you galloped on their branches, nor if you told her about that in the darkness of her apartment, opposite the window in which squares of light could be seen and in each one inconsequential routines enough to sustain a whole life, submitted themselves to your gaze – afterwards he also examined the wooden pegs that were inserted into the corners of the frame and jiggled one of them to show you how loose it was.

"What, wasn't I as good as anyone else in the store?" he asked. "The complete opposite!" Show him even one person like that, just one, not one of those who worked with him doing menial jobs, that would be too easy, he's talking in general: "all those salesmen and saleswomen, and the cashiers, and the section manager, yes even the section manager, what a dummy he was."

Opposite the refrigeration unit drawers, inside of which the dead had perhaps already begun to turn yellow like the dozens of sketches in your room, he continued to speak about that manager, how his section could have been organized a thousand times better, organized so that the people who wandered around there would feel like buying things. But him, the section manager, why should he make the effort? He got his salary and went home. Did he know about them at all? What each one was capable of? My foot. They were like clothes mannequins to him, not even that. When some part of those mannequins gets broken it's replaced right away, but them, if something just happens to them, even the smallest thing, right away they find a reason for firing them.

"Is it hard to find a reason?" he asked. "Finding a reason's the easiest thing, you can find a reason for everyone." And with him, because he's not from here, it was even easier to find one. "As if a person's not a person, just those residence and work permit papers, and besides that nothing. If something with the papers isn't in order, even if you had the accident with us and everything, out of here – to the street. That's where you belong, the street."

In the alley on the way to the hotel he used to sit leaning against a lamppost and smoke cigarette butts that he picked up from the pavement and against whose edge he tapped them, like the side of an ashtray, and you remembered how he wrapped himself up in his cardboard box, on which the symbols of the umbrella and the goblet instructing how it should be carried were still visible through the dirt. Afterwards you walked to the hotel along the same route you used to walk with her, and the railing of the bridge was paved before your eyes and became long and narrow at its end like a pier, and beyond it the river floated glints and rays of light on its surface, carcasses of crumbling lights cast from a source that no longer could be perceived. "Life is right here," she used to say opposite a caravan of street lights diminishing and vanishing at its end as you tried to tell her about Brunelleschi's laws of perspective and about the vanishing point, and her hand around your waist inserted fingers into your pocket and for a while it really was right there, life, in every place, which she touched or looked at or spoke about. "It's here," she said as you tried once again to go over the two courses that led you and her at a particular moment in time to one yellow freight carriage; drops sparkled in the yellow and you were so young that you also remembered each and every knot on the boards at the bottom, as well as the piece of apple discarded there, its stalk and its tainted core, and also the small lump of chewing gum that stuck to her shoe and stopped her there with her suitcase until she scraped her sole on the shaft. "Encounters like that," she said on one of the other nights when you both had already stopped being the-guy-on-the-platform and the-girl-with-the-suitcase, and began to tell a story which you did not want to hear, about a Greek island that she happened upon during the only winter in its history when snow fell and turned the wharf and the fishing boats and their nets white, and about the one who turned to her and suggested they raise a glass in honor of that special day. You didn't want to hear it, but one night, when she tried again to pronounce the guttural sounds of your language – from time to time you still taught each other words and their counterparts, as if in words a foothold would be found – you could hear her enunciating a Greek "s" opposite that boy, above the little table in a tavern or in a room with a large dusty fan on its ceiling, and you could see how they stick the tips of their tongues between their teeth and make sibilant sounds.

6

Rodin painted the son of God as well, but in place of two lamenting old women, he placed three vigorous soldiers alongside him: one lifted a hammer above the palm of his hand as if shoeing a horse, the other nailed the sole of his foot, and the third was still searching the ground for a nail that had fallen when he missed, due to haste or hesitation: perhaps he was stricken for a moment opposite the man laid out before him; he hesitated and then promptly regained composure. The refrigeration unit was quietly buzzing with its engine and with its drawers and with its dead, and the fluorescent lights buzzed above, a white choir that never wearied of sounding its single tone. Far below it the linoleum spread out, and beneath it was concrete, and beneath the concrete there was earth, and inside the earth ant tunnels and mole burrows gaped, and perhaps salamanders suntanned their wrinkled skins in the light of the flames from the depths: at times you imagined sensing their heat through your soles, not only when you strolled through the streets but also when walking from one wall to another in your room.

"That's just what people are like here," the bearded clochard said. "Sons of bitches. When I had the accident, you wouldn't believe the things I saw in hospital. They did someone a favor by looking after them. What I saw during that month you don't learn in a year, believe me."

"And when they got rid of her," Edith motioned with her eyebrow to Nadia, "d'you think it was any better?" But the bearded man was not allowing himself to be stopped again, and in a voice roughened by all the cigarette butts he gathered from the pavement he began to tell how they admitted someone whose hand had been amputated, some old Arab.

An Arab, yes, the first thing he did when he managed to get down from the bed was to take out a small rug from his bag.

"An ordinary rug, nothing special," he said, as if you were interested in any rugs that she did not step on with naked soles leaving wet prints gradually fading as she neared the bed, "a rug a meter long, completely worn out." And on nurses' rounds, when they came to take everyone's pulse and blood pressure and to empty out the urine, the head nurse said to him that if his feet are cold when he gets down from the bed it would be easier for him to put on slippers instead of redecorating the ward. "Pretended she didn't know what he needed the rug for. People like that."

Of course the bearded clochard knew: at the time he was still living alongside them, not right in Barbes but in Stalingrad, which is also full of Arabs and Blacks, sleeping eight in a room on two-tiered bunks, one toilet for the whole building reeking from top to bottom, and a prostitute in the entrance waiting for someone on the way home to screw her against the wall, just like that standing up.

"It's easier to put slippers on," that's what the head nurse said to him, and from the way she looked, if anything, that Arab should have apologized for breathing her air and taking the bed of someone who really deserved to be lying there. And when eventually she went out to the corridor, "it was some corridor, almost like here," the Arab began to speak about some holy person of theirs. A holy person whom the French wanted to exile to some island: "made trouble from all the things he spoke about. And even on the way by ship he put out his rug to pray, those ones pray five times a day."

On the deck of that ship, moving further away from the coast of Africa, the way you both moved further away from the city, from its streets and from its avenues, from its cafés in which you no longer sat with her and from its cinemas and apartment blocks in which men and women still made love and the vapor of their breath misted the windowpanes, on the deck filled with soldiers the holy man was forbidden to pray. "So what did he do, he asked to be lowered to the water so that he could pray from there, from the water." And the

French on the boat, which you could not picture, neither the decks nor the cabins, without the damp floral wallpaper and a night lamp casting a honey color on naked skin, all mocked the Arab and didn't even aim their rifles at him.

"And what did he say to them? He was quite right to say that to them," because he also, the bearded clochard, asked himself the same thing when he was small; because every ship in the port, even the very smallest, not only those that sail to China, that would be too easy, even the others, to him each one was as big as a factory, yes, with chimneys the same size. So what does the holy man say to them: "If God made a ship as big as this, which sails on water and doesn't sink, won't my rug sail there?" That's what the Arab told them after the head nurse had gone, how they lowered the holy man to the water with his rug, "they wanted to get rid of him, they thought he'd drown straightaway, and with all those sharks there too," and how he sailed on it back to the coast with seven dolphins, which swam around him like a guard of honor, and he told them what was there on that coast: sand without tar, and a city with white houses, and a blue, blue sea everywhere one looked.

From the hospital bed – a different hospital, which was not required for the painting, the way all the floors of the sick here were not required either, nor the slow deaths in the dark on soiled bedclothes – the Arab described the sea and moved the stump of his arm around, and the bearded man suddenly remembered, not their coast, which was always full of oil from the ships and tar and garbage, but the Bible stories that his mother used to tell him when he was little. Yes, things like that you don't forget.

And in the hospital, at the time he didn't yet know that once he'd also have to manage like that on the water, I mean for his livelihood. After all he was certain the department store would take him back, what do you mean, on a red carpet. He didn't forget even one story, with all the time that passed since his mother had told them to him. "I had a good head," he said, as if anyone was interested in his head or his childhood or his mother, "I was a good pupil once, don't get me wrong. My mother had such dreams for me, she was sure I'd go far. That I'd become someone." But through his timeworn skin and his thinning hair, it wasn't possible to see the boy he once was, nor the mimic in front of tourists taking pantomime steps on paving stones that he colored with blue chalk. In winter he would use Panda pastels so that it would not be erased in the rain, but from year to year he drew further and further away from that boy and from the son of God who was murdered at the age of thirty-three and ever since hasn't aged by even one moment. Mantegna painted him a tenuous halo, and in other paintings there were halos painted with spokes and halos with engravings and halos with adornments, but as for this one here, at the most his head was crowned with lice.

He was a complete corpse in the painting, and the name of the model was forgotten since he was just Mantegna's crucified one, as the others were Giotto's or Lorenzetti's or del Piombo's and as the bearded clochard will be your crucified one: with complete clarity you could hear the enthusing of a crowd in a museum hall and how a curious young child was scolded and warned not to touch.

"In the hospital," Edith looked at the bandage on Nadia's leg, "the time I took her when she fell down the stairs when the escalator suddenly stopped working, a steep one, not like the usual. Easy as anything to split your head open there," but you were not interested in any escalators other than the one that she leisurely ascended, and between rolling bottles you then saw how the ceiling of the tunnel cut off her braid, her hips, her buttocks. "They wouldn't look at her at all," Edith said, "for them anyone who hasn't got money can drop dead right there on the spot, all the talk of what they once used to have doesn't help at all. They only want to see the thing from the insurance, what's it called? Straightaway they made faces, like it's not their job to help people, just to take their money." Again she looked at the bandage wrapped around Nadia's leg, each wrapping had become begrimed, but opposite the large refrigeration unit for the dead the smell of the gangrene was not discerned nor the smell of the filth, nor the smell of apple shampoo given off by the loosened braid.

"We're just full up," that's what those sons of bitches said when they shoved Nadia out into the street, as if they didn't know what would happen to the leg it if wasn't treated, "they're animals, not humans. And then after that she still says that I've got a black heart." And what did they say to each other? What, didn't Edith hear what they said? She heard them very well, back from the time of her building she still had ears that sometimes made her regret what they hear; really, sometimes you're better off being deaf.

"She wants to be in hospital, very nice, did you hear her," that's what the one said to the other, "to dirty the sheets, very nice." And when Edith tried to tell them something, after all she's got a mouth on her, not like Nadia who doesn't say a word to anyone, because someone who doesn't have a mouth on them gets trampled on more than any cigarette butt. Yessir yes. But then what did they go and do, the big shots? Instead of addressing her they started to shout at Nadia, those big shots. "Crazy woman," they shouted at her, "in one moment we'll send you to a hospital where you really should be." That's how they shouted even though they were already outside and everything, "there they'll get all that nonsense out of your head with electricity. She used to be a Russian countess, very nice . . ."

"Is that the way to talk?" Edith asked, as if with electricity you could remove estates and forests and plains covered by snow, or grey platforms with yellow freight carriages or empty wine bottles. "And for what reason did they think she was crazy, for what, for some of her stories? All that they had there she learned about from her mother, not by herself. What does she know what to say? Nothing. And her mother, the way she looked after her, not that I knew her sir, just from the stories in the tunnel, but the way she looked after her! Even though right away she must have seen that something was not quite right with her, how could you not see? You can

tell everything about a child right away." And she hastened
to add, as if you were interested in her thoughts on children
or about children or about the child you yourself once were,
that's all what she meant and not how the child turned out
afterwards: "because nobody can tell that, nobody! No matter
how cute and everything he was and that you laid down your
life for him, nobody could tell what he'd say straight to your
face afterwards." Again she glanced at the fluorescent light
and still it did not blink at her not even one single blink.

"And anyway what did she tell her," she said about Nadia's
mother, which was not required, not for the bunk, not for
the refrigeration unit drawer nor for the canvas on the easel
on which you'll perhaps make a name for yourself. "Big deal,
who doesn't make up a few stories about themselves, what, is
stealing any better?" She looked at you and you didn't answer,
then immediately continued speaking. "As if he didn't just
have a child with her, her landlord in Russia, but that he
was also her husband and everything. That's what she told
Nadia and also taught her to say, that the whole house was
theirs and everything. Big deal. Who didn't make up stories
in Billancourt, you won't find one who didn't. Every waiter
there had been a general at the very least, every coachman
had been in the cavalry. Believe me sir, thank God they drink
vodka, because as soon as the bottle's finished, out comes the
truth, it doesn't wait one moment. This one was just a clerk,
that one just a servant. And her mother was just a nyanya,
which is a nanny sir. One would think that a nanny wasn't
good enough for anyone here."

For a while you still tried to think of cradles rocking
back and forth and about lullabies sung in soft voices, but
the refrigeration unit was buzzing again, and all you were
able to see were empty rooms in which the flowers on the
wallpaper fade at night as well, and in the dark you sometimes
imagined that you were floating above them, at times an
angel to whose back the bed was stuck like a pillory, and
at times a nectar-craving insect whose wings have wearied.
For some time a half-filled bottle of milk stood on the sill, a
plastic bag tied over its mouth with an elastic band, until it

too became ashen like the basin blemished by the dripping tap and like the mirror that you blemished each time you peered into it. You didn't cover the jars in the room, and the turpentine was quick to evaporate from inside them like a bottled genie; it loosened up its transparent bones, floated above the bed and sneered at its emptiness, flew opposite the wallpaper and sneered at the blooming of the mildew; and on all the neglected paintbrushes were dry scales of viridian and the vermilion of leaves, the zinc and ivory of clouds, the ultramarine and phthalo blue of skies and all the hues of the naked body.

Here in the sight of its double, standing beneath it and borne by the stainless steel, the turpentine sparkled in its arrogance. But in an instant it found itself lifted into the air and scalped, the lid removed from it like the cranium of Joris Fonteijn. And the jar now listened to the sound as he filled it by another quarter, and afterwards the glug-glug of flaxseed oil and the tfft-tfft of the varnish and the vish-vish of the paintbrush that mixed them all.

In the neon light you were still studying their facial features, which were required for the painting, and some months before you wondered whether you too will live and grow old and croak in those tunnels, perhaps even in the one in which you saw her for the last time ascending the moving stairway.

While you still lived with her and in the window the cathedral steeple was swallowed up by the sky like a nib in an inkwell, you still made plans together, and when the steeple vanished and darkness was everywhere, she was trying to imagine the window in your city, as well as the landscapes of your country, which fascinated her: the sea and hills of the Galilee, which at the time you still remembered traveling to in an old car that your father bought for next to nothing, and the dog stuck its head out the window and its ears flapped backwards. You remembered nothing of the Jordan River, and the river that flowed through your city without a single solitary stone bridge to arch above its murky waters, you did remember its banks and the reeds that grew there and the kites made from them and how they were flown to the sky like pebbles cast to gauge its depth.

In the window of the house that she described for you in the darkness of her apartment, white clouds as delicate as feathers drifted by in summer and she would search for their angels; and in black winter skies snow was woven and unraveled and she would count its flakes to fall asleep, or determine the time that passed between the lightning and the thunder in order to know if they were drawing near, or kneel down and pray with closed eyes. Their miniscule pupils were still sometimes revealed in the eyes opposite you, for instance when she would suddenly take a handful of snow in the park and throw it at you, or step in a frozen puddle and crack the covering of ice, drawing up water between its cracks and splashing it, and also when she recoiled from you in one of your bad moments, when in her window too, rows of grey bricks were being built squarely before your eyes.

She was familiar with those moments from her first years here, at the time she too was tossed between total assurance of all the enigmas that the future concealed – you imagined hearing their fingers drumming across the years, anxious to be realized – and between the complete negative; until one winter's day when she observed how a ray of sunlight descended to relieve the square below of its greyness. That's what she told you, but you could not imagine the indistinct din that she heard in the distance, nor how in that light it separated suddenly into the sound of motorcars and footsteps and chatter and the rumbling of the river, and how the tiny ants scurried down below – she felt as tiny and negligible as they were and ready to be crushed like them in an instant – suddenly in the soft light became people with coats and scarves and hair and names and nicknames and partners and children, and an eye watched over them all from within the grey sky.

She once saw the pupil of that eye in the window while dressed in pajamas that had baby elephants on them – "was there one here, and here and here?" You asked her in the apartment and touched her naked body and envied the baby elephants – and when she found it again in adulthood, the coming years were no longer a matter of doubt, but rather were already prepared for her with their great events and their trivialities, in which life was revealed to her in each and every one of them. "It's right here," she said from behind you when you pressed your face to the windowpane of a gallery to peer in at the paintings, the art school was not far from there and its students sat in small cafés, and at the time you wondered why they wasted their time on coffee and wine. She looked at the street reflected in the windowpane, a narrow street in the very same quarter in which the school of medicine was situated: in the Citroen parked behind them, a woman reddened her lips and pursed them at the car's mirror, and her daughter took her tiny finger out of her nose and with joyous astonishment examined the drop that slid down its slope and shone like a pearl; "it's right here," she said to the nape of your neck and her breast pressed against your back, soft and warm. She said it opposite the electricity meter as well on one of the first days, but you no longer remembered how she taught you to insert a plastic wire into it in order to stop its ticking, nor how she trained you to take it out should the electricity company man come knocking on the door: tuk-tuk, she knocked on the table; and also said it opposite the old television, whose channels refused to stabilize when you both wanted to watch one of the nature programs from bed, but you no longer remembered how she thumped it and immediately entire oceans and evergreen forests were squeezed into it: she thumped it with her hand, and when *thewavesthefish* or *the thicket* had already drawn away like all the sights diminishing through a passenger window, your bellies thumped against each other, and you had forgotten their sounds as well, the tuff-tuff, the tupm-tupm.

Opposite the easel Nadia stared at the canvas and pondered where she would be painted in it. Here? And where would

Edith be? And where would he be? She also wondered how all three of them would manage to fit in it, even without the huge refrigeration unit for the dead that rose up at the end of the hall with all its drawers. The canvas wouldn't cover one side of a drawer, even the small side that faced the front, behind which were the soles of feet and a toe tag with a name for one who was identified, or an empty space for one on whom no identifying signs were found other than the fingerprints that the years left on his body.

She touched the canvas gently the way she had previously touched the elevator buttons, and you led her wrinkled finger and traced her outline with it, from the aged yellowish hair to the frayed sleeves of the robe. For a moment there in the sullied whiteness it began to take shape and immediately blurred like the circles made by a pebble in water – in the park they were only made into circles after the ice covering the fountain pond melted and thawed the trickling stalactites, while the pond and the fountain and the trickles and the park could still be seen – and in order for it to remain there you had to outline it again with a pencil stub that you took out from a pocket. The stub was short, but in an instant a line curved here and a line curved there, a third twisted and a fourth spiraled, and following them the handkerchief, which she'll hold close to her eyes, folded itself over. Edith's silhouette also took form on the canvas, and the line that emanated from the pencil continued and lengthened itself like some loose thread unraveled from a sleeve: facial features were still not visible, not the remnants of makeup nor the wrinkles that her eyes spread out to her ears, as if designating their woes to them, but in the neon light it was already possible to see how she'll keep her hands close to her emptied breasts and how she'll wring them above the murdered son of God.

"No, it's really insulting!" said the bearded clochard taking another sip. What, do they want so badly for him to get into the drawer? Is it so urgent for everyone to get rid of him? And that's after he offered them wine as well? Even though they only brought that wine for him to have against the cold in the drawer. Not that he's not used to the cold, he's the world champion of the cold, what's his cardboard box in the alleyway if not the box of a fridge. Do they know who they remind him of? The way they want to get rid of him. That old woman, okay not an old woman; that lady for whom he worked after they fired him. After the accident and the hospital when for a while he still had a place to live. Actually he didn't really work for that lady – he explained to anyone interested – he only looked after her dog, that was the livelihood he found after the accident: he had to take it for a walk every day with its sweater that the old woman knitted for it and with its bowl and bottle of mineral water so that it wouldn't go near a puddle and catch germs.

"The dog itself," he said, as if it would be coming later with wagging tail to lick the bare soles cooling in the drawer, "was the size of a bug, a puppy about a month old, the whole time she had to knit him a sweater all over again" – that's what he told about that dog, but in the painting the one with the three heads won't be seen either, and anyway at the time you didn't remember it or gryphons or chimeras, which were defeated by the swords of heroes in town squares; those squares were no longer to be seen, their statues were all obliterated by the sound of steps – "there wasn't a day I didn't take him for a walk," he said, "and sometimes with the neighbors' dogs as well, they took advantage of me, right away they saw they'd found a sucker. And that," he said, "was some quarter, every third house was an embassy. Okay not every third, every fifth. Flags almost like the ones in the port where his parents lived, and every third car a cabriolet so that in summer they could drive with the top open."

"Why not," he said, "the whole of heaven is just for them, they don't have to wait for afterwards. And their children didn't play with wooden go-karts, what do they need go-karts for? Everything's electric with them. And they never had to fight for something, one peep out of them and straightaway their parents gave them everything."

"And those dogs there? Each one combed out like for some beauty competition or something, never mind that he was just taking them out to pee. In China they would have eaten ones like that for breakfast only he'd already completely forgotten about China by then, completely forgotten the ships he used to see in the port nearby him. He had become a different person, grown up, having found out at last who's who and what's what, I mean how this thing works, life: that a person doesn't get everything he wants, sometimes even nothing, and that in the meantime one has to eat."

For a whole year he walked it in the park, the little spoilt thing – you couldn't see the paths along which it ran, nor the statues against whose bases it peed, nor the others outside, not the heroes nor the monsters; neither were the thin dragons that once stood on street corners to be seen, holding bottles of pure alcohol in their filthy hooves and spewing jet streams and setting them alight with a lighter; a squashed hat laid at their feet, and if it was not filled, they had a woman who would pass it around to the spectators, maybe their wallets will be opened by that heart jiggling under her blouse, a small animal pushing its muzzle out here and there asking to be petted – "just that in the meantime it already wasn't so small, it grew so fast as if the old woman had been putting yeast in its water. Got fat from all the sweets she gave him no end, and also from the books, yes why not. It polished off their covers completely, it was spoilt and intelligent right from the start." They'd walk everyday like that; knowing all the places by heart, there's not one they didn't. Where to pee because of the dogs who'd been there before and where to shit because that was its own place, that's what it's like with them.

He, the bearded man, wasn't doing that outside yet, at the time he still had his room for a while, with a toilet at the end of the passage even if someone had ripped out the chain and you had to fill a bucket every time. He was naïve then, thought it couldn't get worse. They took walks for a whole year like that, until in the end they even started to like each other, yes, just from having gotten used to one another. "That's what it's like when you get used to someone," he said, "a dog or a person, what difference does it make, the main thing is that you've got someone."

And after each walk, when the bearded man returned
with the dog to the old woman's house, she used to ask how
it behaved, her baby, and what it made, a small one or a big
one, and if he let it go into puddles. You know what, in the
end he even started to like her a bit: that's how it goes, it
happens without knowing. Could anyone have guessed
before? Just that the old woman, after she died, she died in
her sleep, we should all be so lucky, didn't have to come to
this place. Do they know what she wrote in her will, with a
lawyer's signature and everything? She asked for her dog to
be taken to a vet and be given an injection, an injection once
and for all. I mean an anesthetic, lifelong – that's what he said
about the old woman and the dog, but for a moment you
were contemplating contaminated syringes and St. Thomas
reaching his hand out to the wound of the crucified one
without fearing all the diseases that lurked: blood spread it,
bodily juices, saturated folds of a sheet, a waning warmth,
an evaporating smell of sweat, the hollow of a head in a
pillow – the dog was so attached to her, that's what the old
woman said to the lawyer, that afterwards its heart would
break from grief: that's what the old woman wrote in the will
and she even left fifty francs for it. It cost fifty francs then.
And that dummy, that spoilt thing, that son of a bitch, which
she wanted to kill, sat in front of her slippers and howled
without end. The way it howled made you want to give it a
kick and say to him: "you little idiot, d'you know what she
wanted to do to you, the old woman? Don't you get it?" Once
it even went along with him to the cemetery and that idiot,
instead of lifting a leg and peeing on her gravestone, sat on
its bottom and began to howl like crazy. "Go figure them,"
he said, as if that howling was also required for the painting.

He didn't take it there anymore, what was the point. For a
long while its sweater had become too small for it and when
the fifty francs were gone it had to give up mineral water,
only the bowl remained for a while under the bench, until
some loony used it as a chamber pot, that's how it is with
those types in the Metro. After that it wasn't good enough

for Rex to drink from it. No matter how much he washed it, with bleach and with deodorant and what not, Rex remained spoilt until his last day. I mean until the last day he saw him, in the morning he wasn't under the bench anymore; in winter, in November. On the seventeenth of November at eight in the morning. Maybe someone gave him a piece of meat and he followed him. He's not blaming him. If someone had given him a piece of meat he also would have followed him.

"When I found out he'd disappeared," he said, "I started to pray for him the way you pray for a person, why not, you can also love dogs that way, and a dog can love you back more than a person sometimes. Without jealousy, without lying to you, without making fun of you." Yes-yes: at the time he wasn't only calling out for Rex, but to Him as well, he called out to both of them so many times that even the Chinaman from emergency, the one with the burns, didn't say his ommanipadmehum as much. He called out to them from the tunnel, from the street, from the bridge; where didn't he call from. By the end of the day his voice was gone and so he just called out to them silently to himself.

"So how much is a tube?" Suddenly he began to busy himself with the paint tubes that rolled on the table. "I mean new ones, not used ones like here." No, he's got no idea, he leaves fifteen francs behind in the shop each time just for the Panda pastels that he uses to paint his few tiles on the street; they make him buy a whole box just for that damn blue for the water. Any minute now he'll be told here again that he's making fun of everything, but he's not, really not. Anyone who was once made fun of makes fun of everything only in the beginning; afterwards he doesn't make fun of anything. After that he gets into his cardboard box and doesn't want to get out of there in the morning, even if his mother were to come and wake him, even if the whole sidewalk opposite was filling up with shoes.

In one of the far off quarters – when you still ventured to far off quarters and when they were still on the other side of the river – in a small church from which discordant singing could be heard, the children were putting on a show for

Ascension Day and you could see how their mothers were filled with content. Jesus' mother was especially proud as she clutched a big plastic bag from Tati with the clothes that he wore before he was wrapped in a sheet. A fat boy played Judas Iscariot, squinting the whole time to the right and to the left, and the little Romans stabbed him with cardboard spears each time the priest looked away. Over and over he was stabbed in the backside until all those spears with the aluminum paper wrapped around them were completely bent, and Jesus' mother began to giggle behind the bag and all the neighbors with her. Only little Judas Iscariot's mother kept silent and wiped her eyes with her sleeve, and armpit hair sprouted through a small rip, dotted with beads of sweat despite the coolness of the hall. For a moment or two compassion rose within you, until you were reminded of – things you still remembered well – the Italian genius who painted Judas with a paunch and double chin, which he copied from one of his creditors, and you remembered too that he forced out unwelcome guests from his studio with the intestines of a bull that he inflated with bellows; had you had bellows like those, then on your bed opposite the blooming mildew of the floral wallpaper, you would have inflated your own intestines just in order to fill the room with them.

"What," Edith asked, "didn't the old woman have any children who looked after her?"

"Is that what makes a difference to you now," The bearded man answered, "the old woman's children?"

"You must have seen some photographs of them there," Edith said, "people keep photographs, there's not one person who doesn't. Everybody keeps them, who doesn't? Especially if they've got their own house." She was speaking about a house inside the morgue, but opposite her, between the wall with the pinafores and the wall with the aprons, only the stainless steel refrigeration unit could be seen, and an entire building could fit into it with all its tenants and their pets: dogs and cats, budgies and canaries, goldfish and iguanas, pinned butterflies and fireflies trapped in the glass cages of lamps. You used to see one like that above you, also when you tossed and turned in your sleep; it took its revenge by filling the whole room with the darkness that it radiated.

"I actually did look around," the bearded clochard said to her, happy to further postpone the moment of having to get into the drawer.

Of course he looked around, what d'you mean, and also asked the old woman who that was, politely, listening to her with all the patience in the world. No matter how long it took, even until nightfall, why not. And deep in his heart he was even thinking then that maybe in the end it will pay off, that she'll also remember him in her will and not only Rex. Can they see just how naïve he was then? Over twenty but in life still a complete baby. And all that was after the accident and everything and him getting fired, way way after he no longer hoped to travel to all those places where the ships went; in the port where he was born and where his parents still lived. At the time he just thought, the bearded man, that if he does someone a favor it would pay off in the end. Yes that's what he thought. He'll never think that ever again.

"A boy or a girl?" Edith asked.

Her two eyes opened wide as he answered and the peacock tails at their edges spread as if both will take flight to a place much further away than the corridor outside and the tunnel and the ninth arrondissement and the arrondissement in which lived the woman you'd rather forget – you no longer remembered the number, nor its appearance, nor the route to it – but a transparent weight had already been fastened to the neck of each eye, and Edith no longer tried to untie them.

Because how that child of hers came into the world, she said, as if someone had asked her about her son, to hate her like that, how would he have got here if she didn't have that soldier at the time? "From the storks?" It was such a beautiful day when he was born, one could forget all about the war, about everything around, absolutely everything. She didn't care at all, why should she have cared? Did anyone care about her? He was born in a field, the same place where they made him, the soldier and her, even though the soldier hadn't been there for a long while. Her child, with all that he had to say afterwards, looked exactly like the photo of the soldier, "the same hair, the same eyes, the very same, like two drops of water."

Nadia stroked her hand, but even her name, which Nadia murmured in her cracked voice, was annoying: yes of course it was annoying, never mind her with the lovely name she was given, Nadjezda, which means hope in their language, someone like that they called hope. It's just that because of her leg they only said things about her behind her back, about all her stories from Russia, but as for Edith, everyone called her to her face: "Edith, Edith, Edith," the name they gave her ever since she began to drink recklessly and get drunk recklessly and sing whenever she felt like it and wherever she felt like it: when she peered out of her small window and when she cleaned the stair carpet, and when she delivered mail to Mr. Stebon, and Mrs. Bron, and Mr. Bournier, and Mrs. Gaillard. "Edith, Edith, Edith," their children would shout out at her afterwards from under the window, as if she had no feelings at all, as if everything had become screwed up from the wine and that's all there is to it.

With Mantegna she just wrung her hands, but Giotto painted even the angels crazed by grief: they swooped from the depths of the sky flock by flock, wringing their wings and sobbing; and in paintings of the Day of Judgment – Giotto thought highly of himself, the way you thought of yourself at the time – he placed himself between the righteous who would win a place in paradise, to which they would ascend in their death, or it would manifest itself to them in life like a shore, which is seen first by the sailor on the mast.

On the horizon of the room in the morgue only the refrigeration unit with all its drawers could be seen, an entire city could have fitted into it and there were only four people still standing at its foot: three beggars and an art student. A pencil stub was unraveling from your hand onto the canvas, and as the lines lengthened, more and more it seemed they were not evolving from the splint of wood but rather from the bodies themselves, and that gradually, limb by limb, you would all become unraveled like an old sweater, and the work put into it and all the years of wear – hundreds of winter days, body odor that stuck to it and the touch of fingers taking it off, they lifted the ends above the navel and above the chest and above the chin and above the braid of hair – dwindled to one spindly thread. A thought like that rose from the wine and was promptly lowered by more wine.

The stub was already in the center of the canvas and continuing to outline the son of God. It took up most of the canvas like someone taking over a bench in the tunnel, the whole platform, the moving stairway on which she went up, the street onto which she exited, the river flowing in the distance and the sky arched above it, heavy and foul-smelling as an enormous stone bridge.

"Won't he be cold?" Nadia asked and her voice quivered. "Isn't he going to be lying there half-naked?" her whole body shuddered, perhaps as during a Russian winter, of which you knew nothing and did not wish to know, when the wind sends frozen vapor clouds flying into the distance.

"That's what the wine's for," said the bearded man. And Edith, with all the time in world said that actually vodka is better for that: after all that's what they drank in Billancourt, vodka, the ones who came there from Russia. "Yes, that's what it was like there," she said, "the stories they told, just from hearing them you could go crazy. With them even a cook was at the very least a polkovnik, which is like a colonel, right Nadia?" She asked perhaps in order not to think about the building she once worked in and about her son.

"Polkovnik?" The bearded man took another sip. Afterwards he marched the two empty bottles on the operating table as if they too wished to hear the sound of marching, the sound of marching on an emptying platform or on paving stones in a street at night or on the floor of your room from one wall to another. "Attention! At ease!" He

placed them together and apart and together again until the
glass rang out.

"Commander Edith!" He saluted her with a filthy hand
– for a moment you recalled the mocking salutes of the
American in the hotel, as well as the salutes that you gave
in another country, which at the time did not exist anymore
than the gardens and squares and this whole city existed
– and right away he balanced the palette, which he lifted
from the stainless steel table, on his hand like a tray laden
with delicacies: and drops, because the anonymous person
who will be lying in the drawer is yet to be painted with its
servings; a bearded clochard or the son of God.

In the wall with the painting of "The Last Supper" in the
dining room of a monastery – you remembered that well – a
doorway was made after it was painted, but even had the
son of God and his disciples remained in their entirety it
would not have been enough for Leonardo. One morning he
captured a lizard and stuck horns he made from a fish bone
to its head, and wings he tore from a sunbird to its body, so
that there would be one creature in the world created by his
own hand. He housed it in a small box and would display
its wonders everywhere, like a father proud of his child.
Afterwards perhaps he captured a male and stuck fish bones
and wings on it too – "One here and here? And here and
here?" She asked you in that apartment and then touched
your head and your shoulders – and shut them both in a
box so that they would bear horned and winged offspring for
him. From your room he could be seen pressing his ear to the
box like you to the pillow, listening to their horns beating as
they kissed and their wings fluttering as they cuddled and to
their serenity in the morning; they lay silent and naked in the
box then, like both of you on the last mornings, they even
took apart each other's eyes.

"Nyanya?" the bearded man turned to Nadia and in
his hand a bottle whose wine was swishing, "nothing to be
ashamed of, nyanya, nothing at all. I'd also have liked to have
had a nyanya." Because his parents, he said, "are old, what

can you do?" So old that it's hard for him to look at them, I mean when he still went to visit them. So old that he couldn't believe they were once young, that they had conceived him at all. In summer, in July. On purpose or not on purpose, what difference does it make now?

"Nyanya," he said again. He visited them twice since he left, just twice. "The first time," he began to describe in detail, putting off the moment for him to get into the drawer as much as possible, the first time he was still working in his department store, he managed to save enough money to buy his mother a washing machine so that she wouldn't ruin her hands completely. He really pitied them, things like that you don't forget. He bought a good one with a guarantee and everything, he didn't scrimp on the money, why should he, and definitely not for his parents.

And the second time, he continued to go into detail, was already after he had been fired, when he hadn't found work anywhere. He went back to them like a little boy then, he thought he could stay there for a while until getting himself together or at least until getting his thoughts a bit organized; it's just that he didn't last even two days.

"Right from the start," he said, "right from the start I got really depressed, God help me." Because of her cataract his mother couldn't see the dirt anymore, which she once would clean from morning to night; his father didn't take notice anyway. He also didn't take notice of the stains that he had on his trousers next to his fly, the kind of stains that at the time made him ask himself: "Did I come out of there? For what." Yes, that's what went through his mind.

And his mother, from old age or from boredom or everything together, every time she did washing, she'd stay and watch that round window and the clothes spinning around inside it like it was some kind of television or something. "Yes," he said, "the two bits of clothing they had, that's what she looked at." As if right across from the house, far off but you could see it anyway, if only the smoke from the chimneys didn't hide it, there wasn't the whole sea to look at. A sea like that, which as a little boy he made such plans about, flying to Mars in a barrel is nothing in comparison. And he's not saying that now to annoy Edith, he's talking about himself.

Did anyone know then that he'd land up like this? That every morning he'd put his hat on the pavement and have to wait for people's favors? And not just to wait, never mind the waiting, it's just that first he had to put down some of his own coins, because without that nobody would put anything down for him. Because what do they say: if nobody put anything down for him he definitely doesn't deserve it, he'll throw it all away on drugs. That's what they say to make them feel good about themselves. So even those few coins that he put down himself he'd still have to count very carefully, to work out the proceeds at the end of the day, because sometimes he came out with a loss.

"What, aren't there ones like that," he asked, "make out like they're putting something down but afterwards there's less in it than there was? Sure there are." By now he's seen everything in his hat, there's not a thing he hasn't seen, coins from countries that you can't do anything with, clothing buttons, candy with and without wrapping, chewing gum with teeth marks, anything round that makes some sound when it falls. And when he gets thrown a real one, maybe once an hour, on purpose they don't aim at the hat.

"Let him run a bit," he said opposite the enormous refrigeration unit of the dead, "why not. Do they care what's written on the sign? Not a bit. They don't give a shit about the sign and all the kingdom of heaven put together." He also doesn't give a shit about anything. "Me," he said, "the very highest I look up to now," for a moment he glanced at the fluorescent lights with eyes whose bags darkened beneath them and bits of sleep were accumulated in their corners. "The very highest?" That streetlamp, which ruins his sleep, stuck in his eyes every night, never letting up, like some fucking policeman's torch.

"If it's so bad there," Edith said taking another sip, "what did you have to leave for?" No really, she said with all the time in the world, what does he think, that she never had any quarrels in the tunnel? "Of course I did, who didn't!" Show her one person who didn't; one person! It's just that in the end you learn to get along, that's what she's learned from all the quarrels she's had in the tunnel. Living with them? "It's like living in an apartment block, the same thing believe me. Doesn't everyone have to be considerate about each other's crazy habits? The whole time you have to be considerate."

And the dead, all the dozens, all the hundreds who lay in the refrigeration unit, perhaps they too lived there as in an apartment block: if someone made too much noise with his nails and his hair, which continued to grow, right away they'd knock on his side, and if someone tried to accommodate a memory contrary to the contract, right away his neighbor would inform on him to the landlord. There's nothing they did not hear, the dead, every mumble and murmur, like gods who hear the wool growing on the backs of sheep and a dewdrop sliding down the stamen of a rose and the rhonchial snorting of an old ant in its tunnel opposite grains of sugar from which it will not eat even one. You stood for so long opposite the dead that it was already possible to imagine them through the refrigeration unit the way one lifts one's head opposite the house of an acquaintance and speculates on how he's now reading a book or drinking a cup of coffee or she, showering her body, washing her unraveled hair, soaping her soft and heavy breasts, wetting the fine transparent line going from the navel to the privates to the pavement on which you were standing.

The bearded clochard turned the bottle upside down and shook it; through its mouthpiece he peered at the bottom to which the fluorescent lights were stuck from the other side, they too trying to suck every remaining drop. "Some apartment block," he explored all around with the bottle-telescope, until he lowered it to his shoes and tried to take a few hovering steps on the spot like in front of the tourists in the square – when she observed it from the height of the cathedral, under grey skies, he was no longer there, perhaps only the blue paving stones could be made out in the distance and perhaps she wondered what was drawn on them, as the square split into its separate components in a momentary beam of sunlight – but the wine made his movements heavy. "A bit more wine won't do me any harm there," he said, yes, it won't do him any harm at all there in the fucking drawer, in the cold, in fear. Of course he's afraid, he said, what a question. Who wouldn't be afraid in his place with all the neighbors he's got there?

"A bit more wine," he said, "one more drop?" And maybe he'll even manage to doze off there: yes, for a long while he's already used to lying down in any place, "that's just the way it is when you don't have a home anymore."

The refrigeration unit loomed opposite him, all shining, not like the house in which he once lived in the port city, but rather like a nightclub in whose entrance a doorman stands hidden in the dusk, beckoning the passersby to enter by blinking and winking – you reached places like that as well on your wanderings, when those quarters were still standing, and tried to identify there her limbs one by one – what didn't they do in those clubs, who didn't appear there.

Once a Chinese contortionist, who appeared in a small club near Pigalle, stayed in the hotel in which you worked and the second night clerk tried to woo her with cans of Coca Cola and packets of crisps, which he would obtain from kicking the automat. On the last night, she pulled toward herself the hand that reached the key out to her. Early in the morning, before the sun had yet risen, he rolled an empty can in front of him on the stairs and said that it was like doing it with a doll: one that you blow up and bend, and in the end take the air out and fold up. The television was still switched on opposite the counter and at the time you still remembered how she acceded to you on one of the last nights, how her completely motionless body drew away beneath you into the distance, *calves thighs privates navel breasts nipples neck lips and eyes*, all drew away into the distance. The eyes looked not at you, nor at the ceiling with its floral wallpaper, but further on from there, to the one who made them bloom in the parks.

"Hello Rex," said the bearded clochard addressing the
refrigeration unit, "any minute Daddy's coming." Yes, he said
sipping from a new bottle, in which neon reflections swam
here and there like tiny transparent fish, perhaps Rex can
already hear him. Or nothing can be heard there from all the
cold. Maybe, he said, maybe it's also good against the cold,
the Chinaman's method, his ommanipadmehum? The way
he didn't stop saying it in emergency, not for a second. "No
matter how much he drove the nurses crazy with it," he said,
"it didn't bother him, you'd think somebody heard him in the
skies in China."

He needed one ommanipadmehum, the bearded man,
in order to move toward the refrigeration unit according to
your instructions; but when one slipped out from his beard
it made no impression on the linoleum at all, since it only
wanted to hear the steps, the steps, from the operating table
to the refrigeration unit. Perhaps it made a bet with the tiles
as to their number, after all there were so many possibilities
– sometimes the count changed in your room as well, from
one wall to another, even when you had not been drinking
– twenty regular steps, or thirty hesitant ones, or fifteen
vigorous exaggerated ones in order to overcome the fear that
that magic word had not managed to tame.

It was impossible to know what the tiles bet on from
their gallery – no jag stuck out from them, no toweling gown
dangled, no woman's skimpy black undergarments hung
there – when they smiled their white smile to show how well
they looked after their teeth, not like the ones there inside
the drawers. Ten vigorous steps were counted as the bearded
clochard tried to tame the fear, and another six hesitant ones
as the fear growled, and one last one as it drew out its claws
– those too you knew from your room, claw after claw were
stuck into your body at night, at whose end a day was lying on
the window sill, silent and cold as a blind mole driven from
its burrow – and the sneakers he wore constantly changed
their voice like two chameleons, making it suit whoever was
walking in them: thundering like the heavy boots of a soldier

and afterwards becoming faint and treading lightly like barefoot soles, until he stopped opposite the stainless steel when in it he saw his scraggly beard and the sparse hair on his head and his dirty hand that was lifted toward the drawers.

"Ommanipadmehum," he said again, but the fear – at the time you feared that you would end your life as a signboard artist and that the canvases in your room would be painted with nothing but thickening filth – was unaffected by the ommanipadmehum, the same as for the previous one. It still had time, the fear, to sharpen its claws and hone them, when that tamer inspected the drawers and looked for a suitable hoop through which to pass. Here was a vacant one, and there too, and very swiftly he passed his hand over the occupied ones, as if their occupants would be angry at him for blocking the light. After all even through a meter of earth they still envied the living and surreptitiously pulled at their feet every place they walked, on the streets, on bridges, and even in secluded rooms.

"Pick a fight with them?" the bearded man asked. "One little smile from them is enough to give you a stroke on the spot." And all the while that more time passed, they smiled even more, whoever they might have been there: signboard artists who once dreamed of rivaling Leonardo, mannequin sculptors who dreamed of rivaling Michelangelo, violin teachers who dreamed of becoming Paganini, perfumers bloated with gas, swimmers wrapped in shrouds of shells and seaweed, pilots whose bellies are still imbedded by fragments of a window with the reflections of clouds.

Perhaps all their belongings were still being kept behind one of the doors in the corridor, and perhaps during the hours of the day there was a warehouseman who sorted article after article and placed each one into a packet. It waited there for relatives to come and claim the tatters they wore and the souvenirs they insisted on dragging along everywhere as if they were charms against death: rusty war medals, cracked marbles from childhood, a lice-filled curl from a loved one.

"Here?" the bearded man asked. Perhaps he intended suggesting drawers the whole night long like the furniture salesmen in the department store in which he worked, that one or the one above it or one of the dozens of others, after all it had to be right also for the women who'll be standing there, but you were already nodding your head and turning the easel toward the drawer. Suddenly you were filled with life: you even whistled a few nondescript notes to yourself, the very same tune you used to whistle in the hotel, a tune that sounded to the second night clerk like air expelled from a bicycle, but in the ear of another would sound perhaps like gas leaking or the flight of a bullet or the rustle of pieces of glass falling from a window on the way to the street.

The window of your room remained shuttered and the sky, which was secured to it, remained as whole as it had been, grey in the day becoming black by night, an enormous chameleon that lay on the roofs or was clung to whoever was above it. Scales and more scales piled up then on the ceiling during all the days and the nights, and sometimes your breath tried to drill a small hole toward some light beyond them or toward a gaping mouth in which to be swallowed, until the darkness was sliced by the building's saws. The few provisions you placed on the window sill lost their essence overnight and in the morning became tooth-like as well, sharp as fangs: a milk bottle, a package of margarine, an apple, all sharpened by the black grindstone that turned above the city and wore down the roofs of its buildings until they became finer than a butterfly's eyelid.

7

"Had it not been for," the policeman will say, "did you hear him? Had it not been for, that's how they say it, had it not been for. Had it not been for the wine. 'If not for the wine' isn't good enough for those." He'll blow a smoke ring, purse his lips and round them, as if trying to kiss it before it takes flight. "And what would he have done without the wine? I'll tell you what, nothing is what he would have done, nothing. After all, those types are scared of their own shadows. Not so?" But his partner won't glance at you after you are to be confined with handcuffs or with shirtsleeves or with tufts of cloud.

For a moment you still reflected on the son of God who called the dead to come out and resurrected them even before he was crucified, and afterwards you reflected on the professor and the task he assigned all the tutorial pupils, an homage to painters of the past, and you wondered if he too will be remembered thanks only to one of his pupils: Andrea would not have remained in memory had it not been for his apprentice Leonardo, who masterfully painted the pair of wings allotted to him in the corner of a painting; Domenico would not have been remembered had it not been for his apprentice Michelangelo; and Cimabue would not have been remembered had it not been for Giotto, who added a fly to a portrait that his master painted, causing him to wave his hand for a long while until realizing he had been fooled. Over time the pupils made a name for themselves, and Michelangelo, after completing the Pieta and hearing one of the spectators praise another artist, shut himself up with his statue for an entire night and carved his name letter by letter in the holy mother.

At the time, on his head he wore a cardboard helmet with a candle made of pure goat's tallow, hundreds of which Vasari had sent him on a different night on the back of his servant, the memory of whom has been preserved as well: opposite the shuttered door, beyond which the chisel thundered, he became angry and stuck into the mud all the hundreds of candles that he had hauled, and lit them all. Reading about him – you were trying to read in her language too, from the book that she bought when she still wanted to get to know those who at the time served as both your exemplary models as well as your rivals – he too with all his candles could be discerned in the marble refinement of the Pieta.

In the smile of the Mona Lisa one can discern the musicians and clowns who were brought to cheer her, in the statue of David one can discern the da Sangallo brothers who built the wooden device used to cart it, and in St. Peter's church one can discern all the donkey drivers who prodded their beasts on the escarpments that were prepared for raising all the building materials to the vaults: convoy after convoy moved inside the church in construction, some ascending and some descending: the donkeys brayed, their tails whipped, they left droppings, chewed grass and thorns that grew in their way; and at the foot of the scaffolding the donkey drivers' wives did washing and sang, gossiped about the artist and his apprentices, cooked stews over bonfires and in the evening warmed their hands over them, and each night the unfinished dome could be seen hovering above the smoke like the sky itself.

For a while you still reflected on the professor, but opposite the easel and the refrigeration unit, the crucified one and his disciple promptly returned and arose. One called the dead to come out and resurrected them and the other healed the sick in his shadow: at the time people were still healed by a word, a touch, by a shadow spread out over degenerating limbs, over ulcers, over abscesses, over eyes covered with cataracts the color of smoke; in their depths something still burned.

But Nadia, in a smock whose ends were held together by
safety pins, no longer hoped to be cured. "No sir," Edith said,
and the bearded clochard still inspected the drawers from
the outside: the whole room in the morgue was reflected
in them, and in the stainless steel each wrapping of Nadia's
filthy bandages could also be seen as they both were again
reminded, unhurriedly, what had been shouted at Nadia in
the hospital. How can you forget a thing like that?

"Get out of here or we'll send you to a hospital where
you really should be!" That's how they shouted at her, and
what was Nadia thinking at the time, she thought it was all
punishment for her stories from before. "The priest screwed
her head up completely, straightaway he saw he'd found
someone gullible. Isn't that what you said to me? That it's
better that way? I swear sir that's what she said, that it's better
to lose her leg than to lose everything after that."

"There's no shame in having faith," said the bearded man
with time to still take sip after sip opposite the refrigeration
unit. What, didn't his mother have faith? Of course she did,
where else did he know all those stories from if not from
her? "About walking on water and Lazarus and all that. Only
from her." He would have spoken about anything now, if
only to postpone longer the moment when he'll be required
to earn his wine and climb to the drawer by the handles of
the drawers below it: up up he'll climb, perhaps as he once
climbed a treetop grey with chimney soot from where to
observe the sea and the ships sailing to China on it.

As if it seemed a matter of urgency to pull out the
drawers, before it will be opened Edith hurried to say what
nonsense it was in her opinion, "that doomsday stuff and
everything." Because Edith, with her experience of life, which
she wishes on no one, really, not even on her worst enemy,
already knows very well what nonsense it is, yes: "there isn't a
soul born yet who gets further than he can spit, believe me."
Had she been standing in the tunnel maybe she would have
shown you on the tracks how far she could have got, but here
she just glanced at the fluorescent light while at the same

time drumming her sneaker on the linoleum as if she wanted to show that there was nothing beneath it. "Only someone gullible-" she arched a thin plucked eyebrow toward Nadia and did not complete the sentence. But Nadia was silent and on her cheek a strand of grey hair quivered, grimy from the filth of the tunnel benches or the soles of the passing days: each evening you heard them drawing away above the ceiling of your room, and in the mornings it was not the sun that filled the window but the yawn of the dark; for a moment an unwashed pinkish palate could be seen there and right away its giant jaws were clenched together again.

"And in the war," Edith said, "when I was still in the village and didn't know her at all yet, their quarter was bombed, half the quarter was gone, they even destroyed the cemetery there completely. For half the next day bones were still flying in the air, and after that she still believes all the nonsense the priest fed her. Isn't that what you told me? I remember absolutely everything", because in the Metro tunnel – a tunnel you remembered nothing of other than the ceiling that cut off the one who was going up the moving stairway from head to soles – she told her how she escaped with her mother on a freight train, and how the two of them lived in Billancourt, at first in a one roomed apartment and afterwards in a hotel with dissidents, and how her mother died of old age or of sorrow.

"Even the chestnut man," Edith said, "what, don't I remember the chestnut man? Of course I remember him, she used to stand there sir, to warm herself afterwards, after they threw her out of the house. She used to wait like that for someone to throw a burnt one or one that didn't peel, maybe you should thank him as well?" She glanced at the fluorescent light for a moment and right away returned her gaze to the easel and to you. "The biggest troubles," she said, "are nothing sir, if you've still got a home."

In order to grab the drawer handle the bearded man needed one more ommanipadmehum, but because of the cold, he first brought the palms of his hands close to his mouth and blew on them over and over to warm them. "It's like the worse it gets here sir," Edith said, "the better it'll be for her there, that's what she thinks, but where is there, that's all I'm saying, and when is there? Me sir, I haven't got the patience to wait like that a whole lifetime. Once I waited for someone for five years sir, five years I waited for him after all that was done to me, and after that I didn't wait for anything." Without apprehension she looked at the opening drawer and listened to the sound that rose from its tracks, a light metallic rustling, which promptly became compatible with the buzzing of the neon.

"And in the war," she said again, as if the war was required for the painting, and Nadia's dissidents' quarter or Edith's quarter or another quarter – you no longer remembered its number, not how you get there nor what could be seen behind its windows – what was so bad about the war for her? It wasn't so bad for anyone in the village during the war, not for anyone. It all started after that. At night they heard the tanks, and in the morning nothing remained other than the marks of the chains and the flags that the underground resistance had burned, yes all of a sudden everyone in the village became like saints: before that they had sold them wine and eggs and also whole chickens and what not, they just prayed that they wouldn't ever move away from them, did they care about anything except money? Not a chance. But after they left, they became like saints, what d'you mean. Straightaway the owner of the bistro erased from the board the menu in their language and wrote it out again, like nothing had happened, but Edith couldn't wipe out what she had just like that: you can't wipe out a belly like that with a rag. And neither did she want to.

What d'you think, it's her fault that people are dumb? That they kill each other like that for nonsense? Her soldier wasn't at all like all the others. He wasn't at all tidy and neat like all the others and he never left her on time like they told him to, never. He also came from a village and also knew how to milk a cow and also how funny a calf looks after its born when it can hardly stand, and how it's impossible to ever be able to tell what kind of dangerous bull can come out of that.

"It's impossible to know about anything," Edith said opposite the opening drawer, "nothing, not even what comes out of your own belly." And her soldier also learned a few French songs from her, yessir yes, like she learned a few from him, and when he used to imitate his sergeant, ho-ho, Edith used to burst out laughing, she even told him that now it's just dangerous: with this belly.

She smoothed over her sagging belly and afterwards her hair and checked it was still gathered on the nape of her neck, but when she told about the snip-snip of the scissors above her head at the end of the war, "snip-snip, the whole time, snip-snip, sometimes I even hear that snip-snip at night in the tunnel," you only thought about the scissors with which your beard was sheared one night, sheared by your own hand in her apartment after she said to you that she wanted to see your face: "here and here, here and here," she said and its cuttings dropped to the basin one after another.

"Snip-snip," Edith said, and the handbag swung to and fro from her arm, its tossing reflected in the panel of the drawer. For a moment she glanced at the fluorescent light again, it was still hovering above her, buzzing to itself the one note it knew like a sated fly traveling pleasurably in the air between one meal and another.

"I swear to you it looks better like that," the bearded man said, "like new." Opposite the half opened drawer he complimented Edith not only on the handbag but also on her reflection, to distract her from the war or to delay his ascent. Afterwards he reminded her how he clung to her before, outside, before they came down here, before the elevator and the corridors. That embrace seemed so far from here, between the refrigeration unit and operating table, that it was necessary to clarify if all those things actually happened: the parked ambulances with their turned off headlights, the glass door, which was seen from the street, and the counter beyond it, and the guard who was sitting there watching a small television set, "it's not enough that he gets a salary, he gets a television as well," and the prostitute who walked toward him in a shiny black raincoat. Remember the prostitute? For a while, opposite the refrigeration unit, they reminisced like friends who had not met in years, so far away did those events seem from this room of the dead.

All of a sudden that prostitute seemed quite nice to Edith, what with her lack of shame: in fact what did she have to be ashamed of? For whom? In her building it was enough for one like that to stand opposite it for them to call the police right away, all those hypocrites from the building, and this one covered herself with that guard like a blanket and said her aah-aah-aahs, "On my word, like a blanket, she couldn't have cared less about anything." What difference did it make that her aah-aahs were faked; she managed to get a real one out of the guard.

"She had some body," the bearded man said without going into detail, but Edith's lips were already taut.

"Of course you're an expert," she said to him, "a big hero. What wouldn't he say sir not to get inside." She turned to you, but you were still studying their facial features from the other side of the easel.

"She thinks I'm scared or something," he said, already lifting his hand again toward the drawer handle.

"Big hero," Edith answered and raised her hand to her head as if to check if all her hair was in place, perhaps not that sparse hair, but rather the thick other, which slid down her back when she was still young.

"Ladies and gentlemen," the bearded man said and with a dirty hand pulled the drawer on its tracks again.

Further and further it came out from the refrigeration unit, silent and as decisive as an index finger, a rigid and cold finger that will promptly bend two of its joints and beckon everyone to enter: please, ladies and gentlemen, anyone who hasn't visited us yet, you too, come along: bank managers and jugglers, elevator boys and telephone girls, lawyers and thieves, bullfighters and bug exterminators, who not? Yes-yes, you there! But the part of the drawer that was revealed contained just a pale neon flash and as it was pulled it slid out gently, lengthening and growing, it drifted into the expanse without sails and without oars, a silent lightweight metal raft.

With absolute clarity the stainless steel showed not only the tattered jeans and sneakers that had turned grey and the coat whose filth had hardened, but the wild beard as well and the sparse hair and the thin shoulders and the sagging belly bloated by alcohol or by flaccid muscles: is this what you'd call the son of God?

Those were the days, the bearded man said and ignored your brow urging him on, yes, before he learned those few pantomime steps of his. He was a good guy, the mime, a real good guy and had big dreams as well, he was sure he'd become well known, what d'you mean, he just hadn't reached the age when you realize that you can shove all your dreams up your ass. Anyway, there were times before he knew that pantomime artist, and before he began coloring pavement tiles and writing "repent-thee" on a piece of cardboard, when he really looked good, girls made eyes at him, not prostitutes, really good girls, even ones with money, yes-yes.

"Sure," said Edith, "who'd want someone like that."

He stood with his back to the drawer and the stainless steel revealed how worn out his coat was when he asked if he's really expected to get undressed now in front of everyone's eyes: what, hasn't he got no shame anymore, a drop of self-respect?

No he hasn't, he replied, he'll do it before everyone's eyes. If it doesn't suit someone, then she shouldn't look. That reminds him, not that this is the place to tell about it, not that it's the time or the place, but that's what came into his head; and where the hell is the place and the time? The woman with the cabriolet came into his head, yes a cabriolet. Don't they know what a cabriolet is? Where he once lived that's what they used to call wooden go-karts, but this was a real cabriolet; that's what came into his head now.

It's just that then he also got undressed, not what they're thinking, he was just a boy, okay not exactly a boy, just that at the time he didn't know about women at all, he didn't have half a clue.

"And now you're an expert of course," Edith said, "we know all about you. This one sir? At the very, very most he knows about the diseases, God help us," but the bearded clochard already continued to talk.

He was then going swimming at the beach on the other side of the port, though nobody saw him; nobody came near there because of the oil stain from the tanker. And just as he was coming out of the water, completely dripping, he saw the cabriolet on the road opposite: one tire didn't have air and the lady was looking at him so that straightaway he put his hands there and put his trousers on as quickly as possible. Shorts, like a boy's. She signaled with her hand for him to come, asked if he could help her. He nodded his head. He went up to the cabriolet, bent down next to the wheel and began to remove it for her the way they used to steal tires from cars. He saw her legs and where they went up to, even if he didn't want to. And when she bent down to give him the wheel nuts, he saw her tits as well and where they stuck out. He was feeling uncomfortable. "Whoever doesn't want to hear," he said, "shouldn't listen." Just as well he finished screwing them on, he turned around not to be seen, thought she'd give him a tip and go, like the ones he used to help with their shopping; he was just a boy then, barely fifteen. Just that she asked him if he needs a ride. He told her yes. She opened the door, he was scared he'd ruin the upholstery but she said never mind, sit-sit, are you comfortable? She adjusted the backrest for him. Have you got enough legroom? She moved the seat with the handle. Again he saw her tits and again he was uncomfortable about sitting. What they're thinking with their dirty minds is all true, she was his first woman. Cars passed all around and she wasn't fazed by a thing, she just closed the roof of the cabriolet and that was all. In the end she opened the glove compartment out of which she took a calling card; it had a rough texture, but not from being cheap, just the opposite, from being expensive. And she said to him: if you ever come to the city, give me a call, kid. You never know. For ages he used to dream about her at night, the bit of money he earned he threw away afterwards on prostitutes in the port. He put the calling card in his wallet, inside transparent plastic, like someone who keeps a picture of his girl. Two years later he left home, came to the city and straightaway called. He stood at a public telephone in the middle of the street and called. He said to her: it's me, from the beach. She said to him: what? He said to her: it's me, with the wheel I changed for you. She said to him: what? He said to her: you had a puncture, I helped you to change it and afterwards you closed the roof, you've got a cabriolet, right? She said nothing, and in the receiver he heard some music that no one would ever have heard before where he came from. He said to her: I came to the city like you said, and right after that he heard the telephone beeping, every time he'd call after that he only heard the beep.

That's how he left his mother and father, even then they weren't young. He thought at least he'd help them out a bit with money, he was an only child. Afterwards he hitchhiked and traveled once more, came here to this fucking city: thought it was a place to make money, by chance he found a job in the department store; he thanked God, he really did thank him. A year later he bought his mother a washing machine with three programs, he still thought he'd make something of himself, that it was all worth it, like he had bought them some motorcar. And if not now, then next year, why not, he'll take them traveling a bit, the old folks, they never ever left their place. A year later he had the accident with the truck and they fired him, threw him out on the street like a dog, not a dog, you don't throw a dog out like that. He still had that card in his wallet and also had a way to phone out of the country without paying, some method with a wire, he thought of telling her what happened. But by then he didn't believe in anything anymore. He stood like that in the middle of the road, didn't even go into the telephone booth. He tore up the rough textured paper into little pieces, because people like that, with their moods, you never can know what to expect.

You could see how calm changed to anger in her face, and how anger changed to joy almost in a flash: she was incensed by a crepe vendor who skimped on the Cointreau he sprinkled and instantly overjoyed at the sight of an irritable puppy barking at her leg, its ears flattened down; she frowned at a waiter who showed displeasure at the one glass they ordered and instantly was as astonished as a child at the sight of the bubbles that soared to the floating slice of lemon and were strung together beneath it, as elegant as pearls; she swore quietly in the entrance to the apartment because from the other side of the wall the neighbor was playing one of his two records again, till she pressed close to the wallpaper, waited for the end of the song and moaned over and over, and there was silence; drops fell from the edge of her coat, a few flakes were still in her hair, and their whiteness seeping into the bright brown and darkening it, until she rubbed her head with a towel and wrapped it like a turban; placing her palms together she greeted you the way they greet in India, but for her, one God, his son and the holy spirit were enough, and from the time she rediscovered them, all the upheavals that had previously upset her had been contained, as if a few ancient nails were enough to balance her entire world. She was already planning on returning to her city at the end of her studies, to work there and raise a family: plans in which you were not envisaged since you were nothing but a railway-platform-acquaintanceship, like the Greek-from-the-island and like others whom you did not wish to hear about at all. Drops fell on the glass windowpane that she stood opposite, and inside the small café, which could be seen in the corner, perhaps the dark haired boy was still trying to outdo the slot machine with his hands and his pelvis, as if copulating with it: that's what she said when you both passed by there, and you became immediately jealous: the drops on the window glowed in the electric light and beyond them the din of the city rose, faint though not silent for one moment: cars drove by, passersby walked past, a musician played on a corner; in the morning the cathedral steeple was again lost in grey fluff,

and from the sheets, which had not been sweated on at night,
you wondered about that son of God of hers, who was forced
to adjust to the dusk of churches and to their chill after the
blazing glare to which he was accustomed; a car hooted,
hooted over and over and you didn't get up.

"One would think," Edith said, "he had a thousand. Who'd
go with one like that, who? Believe me sir it's all stories so
he won't have to get in there. Big hero." Right away she too
contributed her effort in pulling the drawer, until the metallic
click was heard when it reached the end of the track. To show
that this place doesn't scare her, no way, she began to sing to
herself softly in a hoarse voice, which in spite of all the wine
she downed failed to oil even one single chord.

Did musicians not play at the funerals of friends? And did
artists not paint or bring paintings? Around van Gogh were
laid the cypresses and the wheat fields that he had painted,
until the wind they blew waved the curtain of the room and
ears were deafened by the screeching of the ravens; Monet
painted his dead beloved and the touches of light on her face
as it was when still warm and soft – turning toward you,
bringing full, fleshy lips close, or bloated from a sleep whose
dreams you were oblivious of, or rejoicing at the sight of a
toddler chasing after pigeons on a path until they suddenly
took flight: "life is right here," she once said opposite an
attendant napping in the corner of a museum as his head
began to droop; she also said it opposite the coat check who
sniffed the leather of the handbag left with her; you went out
and in the park a toddler was trampling through a puddle
and spraying water with his boots, and the light clung to the
sprays and let go. "Here," she said opposite her room window,
and in its depths for a moment the cathedral steeple turned
gold in a thin light beam that the clouds released, a fleeting
beam not enough to draw you both out of the apartment and
climb all the steeple steps; sometimes winter aroused a faint
yearning for the country from which you came and the sun
in its sky, until the memory arose of how it seared the blue of
the sky in summer, banished all the hues from the leaves on

the trees and caused the fertile earth to fade to pallid sand. "Chol?"[33] she once said in your language, when still trying to pronounce the guttural sound, and you led your hand over her contours as on curves of an arid dune, until she became moist; in the window the building opposite darkened further, but one after the other electric lights rose in its windows: in one a family sat around a table on which a box of cornflakes stood, in a another a wrinkled hand moved and ironed a white shirt, and in another a young boy was standing with earphones on his head, and in the slanted windows of the servants' rooms dark squares of sky were reflected, permeated by a rosiness from the street lamps and the cafés and the cars: everything spread it.

Opposite the refrigeration unit the bearded man had already taken off his coat and he too was humming to show that he was not afraid. He aimed the coat at the stainless steel table and lifted the ends of the sweater to his head, and for a moment he was hidden in it like a convict in a hood, paddam. He threw it to Nadia, paddam, and she caught it and blushed like a bridesmaid, paddam. He began to undo the buttons of the shirt, half of which had long been shed, and threw it onto the operating table where it prostrated itself like a praying Arab.

Afterwards he began to peel off an undershirt and revealed the sagging stomach and sunken chest on which no spear incision could be seen. Only sparse hair could be seen from the layer of dirt dark as a suntan – with Caravaggio a finger reached out to the incision and was swallowed by it, but here Caravaggio had not been heard of nor the beggar he hung by the feet in order to determine how someone crucified upside down suffers – paddam, he scrunched up his undershirt and threw it as well. It tried to reach the hooks on the ceramic tiles, but the expanse of linoleum separated it from them, entire regions of grey – Leonardo painted boys in gold before he studied their bodies, but here he had not been heard of nor his words to future generations: "You who investigate

33   Hebrew for sand

the workings of the human body, do not sink into a state of dejection having broadened knowledge at the cost of the life of another" – paddam, he swelled his chest opposite the ladies, emphasizing his ribs, Mister-Universe-of-the-tunnels, Marco-Polo-of-the-drawers. With a nimble movement he undid the buckle of his belt and pulled it from its hoops and immediately his trousers were let loose as well. Without losing a moment they fell, becoming entangled with the sneakers down below. It would have been preferable to have taken them off before, the sneakers, to undo the laces, and in the meanwhile he trampled in them on the spot, in the sneakers, in the lowered trousers, in filthy boxer shorts and with the thin legs that dwindled from them. He fidgeted and kicked until he extricated himself from his trousers and aimed them at the hooks on the wall as well, but they were separated by all the linoleum, an entire grey continent. Paddam, he tried to kick off his shoes without a care, because the fluorescent lights were high up floating in the heights like contemplative clouds, for a moment peering at his shoes like at two tiny birds who dream of pecking at them, paddam, and drop dead, paddam, midway.

Afterwards he stood the way he used to face the tourists in the square with the hat and the coins he laid down in order for them to magnetize the others in the wallets – coins spread it and wallets, hats and paving stones, asphalt roads and platforms, tracks and the arches of tunnels, a single hollow in a pillow, every glass pane swathed in steam – "mesdames et messieurs" he said, "ladies and gentlemen."

What's he got to be ashamed of? For whom? He was a working man, in a giant department store like half of this arrondissement, "whoever doesn't want to believe that doesn't have to." There were eleven departments there and twenty-eight sub-departments and over two hundred workers and never-ending branches. At the time he wasn't living in tunnels and cartons at all, and definitely not in drawers, he lived in rented rooms, like a student, where didn't he live: he lived in Pernety, in Convention and next to the Bastille, not a place he didn't, two steps from the Opera, two steps from the museum, or the supermarket or the outdoor market, or from the Algerians' bar who taught him to listen to Umm Kulthum and to play bingo every Sunday for the prostitute in the courtyard, yes, what's he got to be ashamed of? For whom?

He used to live in Belville, in Barbes, next to Stalingrad where all the North Africans live eight to a room, a double bed for every wall and one toilet for the whole building and also a prostitute who gets screwed against the wall in the entrance, only her legs could be seen on the back of the client.

"And on the other pavement?" he said opposite the open drawer, "there was some travel agency with pictures of lions and giraffes, like that's all those Blacks needed, a safari in the jungle." Where didn't he live? In the end he even lived in a minibus, a Bedford that some stoned out Englishman sold him, they haven't made them for ages and it hardly went, but you could park it in some corner in Vincennes until those sons of bitches cops threw him out of there, and that mother-son-of-a-bitch, the cold. It seemed that he left something of himself in every place he lived, yes that's what it's like; just that in the end something else gets left, yes. And without that something, mesdames et messieurs, ladies and gentlemen, damen und herren, he wouldn't dare to get into the drawer at all.

He took a few pantomime steps on the spot as if to fool the linoleum with them, with the counting of the steps, the steps, the steps, and afterwards began to climb on the shiny handles of the drawers, on this one and on this one and on this one, with bare feet, which immediately dulled the stainless steel with their dirt, he climbed like on a treetop in the poor quarter of the port city in which he was born, whose name you also did not wish to know.

At first he put in his right foot and afterwards the left, whose nails had already lengthened like the nails of the dead. He stood there upright in his boxer shorts, which he pulled and lifted above his navel, and afterwards bent his knees and sat in the drawer, one of the fleet that anchored there, the Armada of the dead.

Immediately he shivered and in the light of the neon
that the stainless steel reflected he asked if someone wouldn't
mind throwing him the sheet, the one that was wrapped
around that material before, the canvas or whatever it was,
just so he won't freeze his ass and his balls – it would be a pity.
Right away Nadia will tell him that Lazarus was told "come
forth" after he was dead and everything, but he's not Lazarus,
he's himself. Him? He's still got two or three things that he
wants to do in this screwed up life before it's over: yes, you
never know. Like the one from the cabriolet said, and after
he got out of there and put on his shorts again, he knew that
no one in the world, but no one, would believe that he once
went in a car like that, no one: very quietly the roof rose over
them and hid the sky with the smoke that still hung there
from the tanker, "it burned for maybe a whole week," rose
until it reached the front windscreen and with one click the
roof was closed.

The sky above, after you had left her apartment, lowered itself
down to the slate roofs in the mornings as well, and the wind
would then toss the treetops and extract their fingernails
as it interrogated each and every branch if they had seen
whoever it was searching for outside there, a lost child, an
escaped criminal or a god in hiding. Afterwards the extracted
fingernails festered on the ground, but you trampled them
with your shoes, raising a crunching sound until you ceased
to wander out. By that time you watched the geography
programs from the counter in the hotel, and once when the
American was watching Aztec temples from his spot opposite
the drinks automat, you heard him say that those Indians are
the same as the fucking gooks, the same methods and the
same cruelty. These deserved to be finished off by the Spanish
if they ripped out the heart of a man while he was still alive,
even for God, and those deserved to get fucked up by a
flamethrower and everything; so why the hell can't he sleep
at night, why? This little shit here won't let him sleep until he
himself will rip it out with his own hand, like this, with the
fingernails. It was in the autumn and the rich clochards had

not yet arrived to winter at the hotel, only Gibert-Jeune used
to come from time to time asking if you didn't need some
album, for a third of the price; "someday they'll make one
of yours," he used to say so that you'd invite him for a beer
from the automat, "and I'll have to swipe it from the store
for someone," but the only profit you made from art was
from portraits of tourists to whose cheeks you added a blush
of charcoal and to whose eyes a glint of chalk and whose
wrinkles you smoothed over. In the end they resembled many
and no one in particular, like an identikit on whose sight
masses from hundreds of places simultaneously phone in to
report having seen the child or the escaped criminal or the
hiding god: bearded in a café, a shaved head in a discotheque,
wearing the spectacles of the blind on a street corner, or in
the cracked mirror above the sink.

"With one click," the bearded man said, "yes." And suddenly
the smell of the sea and the oil stain and the fish carcasses
were gone, he only smelt her scent: perfume mixed with
sweat. And right away, in the metallic light, which obscured
the filth of his body, he asked Edith if she hadn't changed her
mind and didn't want to join him after all.

"Sure I've changed my mind," Edith said to him, "what
d'you think! That's all I need, really," and folded her arms on
her chest and pinched her lips together ever more: because
someone like that should thank her for agreeing to be in the
same painting, yes, he should thank her! What does she know
who'll get to see it and what they'll say afterwards? Troubles
from paintings – that's all she needs. That he's got no shame is
his problem, it's just that she takes everything to heart.

Because isn't that what they said about her all the time in
the building, about Edith, that that's how she'll land up in
the end? With a bottle in a Metro tunnel? All the neighbors,
especially Mrs. Setbon, and that one with his nose in the
air, Mr. Bron, and Gaston from the café, and Beber the
newspaper seller, and even her wicked son, yes, he must have
been happy to see that picture in the paper, today that one

fell on to the tracks and maybe tomorrow it'll be her, then he won't have to be ashamed of his mother anymore. For nine months she hauled him around in her belly, the little wicked thing, and for a year and a half gave him her milk and wiped his backside, "forgive me sir for speaking this way, one would think he was born in a three piece suit." He was conceived in a field by the soldier and her, and he was born in a field. The bird that was chirping above his head had even more hair than he did.

"Enough, Edith, enough," the bearded man said from the drawer as you corrected with your pencil on the canvas some facial features that the perspective had flattened and shortened, "let them all go fuck themselves." The port city jargon he once used had become blurred by the tunnel jargon, and anyway you were not interested in his city and not in the port, not the tanker that hit a sandbank, not the cabriolet in which he travelled, not the department store where he worked and not his getting fired.

Yes that's exactly what he said when they fired him, what else did he have to say besides that? "Let them all go fuck themselves," yes that's what he said, not to their faces, but afterwards, when he found himself in the emergency room with that Chinaman. "Does anyone here not remember the Chinaman?" That was what was funny, he said, it was just then that there was some chance for him at work, that's what he thought at the time, he was such an idiot to believe that there was some chance for him to travel abroad with their exhibits. Yes, that's what he thought. At the time it seemed completely logical, "why not, don't I deserve to get to travel?"

And right away, as if he had been asked about the department manager and his deputy ("of course they had to travel, there was no question about that at all"), he began to tell about the manager's secretary as well, whose name you immediately forgot. "She should go, sure why not," he doesn't want to say why because of the ladies here, just that besides them, didn't they need someone else there to make sure everything runs like it should? To really make sure, with all his heart, even give a hand when needed, like he always does at work. He was such an idiot then. Totally gullible. They had already begun calling him by a nickname because of all those plans of his, and at the time even McDonald's hadn't opened there, who even thought of it then, it's just that because of all those dreams of his, everyone had already begun calling him Yangtze. Yes: Yangtze. That's how it is, it's enough for one to start calling you that and straightaway it sticks. It's unbelievable just how fast. An affectionate nickname, that's what he thought at the time, that it was from affection, about how he can see them one day opening a branch even in China. And after some time, no matter where he went he would hear, "what about the shipment Yangtze," "what about the off-loading Yangtze." He was a young man then, hardly twenty, once even the decorator called him that, which showed that maybe he really did have a chance: would he call him Yangtze for nothing, when he can see what it does to someone?

"Let them all get fucked," he said from inside the drawer to the drawers above him and to the fluorescent lights on the ceiling, "the department manager and his deputy and the secretary together." And right away he lifted the bottle that he had taken with him and tilted it to his mouth. The neon light sparkled momentarily in the wine as it flowed to his throat and dribbled and trickled, causing his Adam's apple to move beneath the stubble growing on his neck. "Let the wine also get fucked," he said and stood the empty bottle next to his head as you instructed him from the other side of the easel, "even let Monte-what's-his-name get fucked, together with all the Italians." The refrigeration unit added its metallic sound to his coarse voice, as if it too resented the bottle that replaced the goblet: the one into which the holy blood was gathered, or a different goblet that perhaps was filled with wine and given to him for the journey, like to a Chinese emperor with whom the drinks and food he liked were buried, his pitchers and his plates, his cooks and his servants.

For a moment you still remembered how he used to wrap himself up with cardboard in the alley, when again he asked what about the sheet he was promised, "to cover myself up a bit, why not," and his soles stuck out in front and the dry cracks in the skin were plugged with dirt as if with putty. Once more he mentioned the sheet, and from within the drawer he spread out his hands and asked, who's coming to warm him up, who's coming? And as if he had the entire night before him he was again reminded of his mother who would do that when he was little. "I was a midget," he said, "ten of me could have got inside a drawer like this, ten I swear."

That's what he said, but from the other side of the easel you couldn't see the boy who lived in the port city, whose name you also didn't wish to remember, nor his mother who was so beautiful at the time! When he would run crying to her arms or when she would bend down to him in bed and kiss him like that on the eyes, "yes, where dreams come from, whoever doesn't want to believe it doesn't have to," she was so beautiful that he wouldn't let her leave: he hugged her so tightly then and smelt her scent and cried, yes, he still cried about things then.

"Go cover him up," Edith said from her place, "learn for once what it is to cover up a man. Go go, she's shy that one, you'd think she was told to take down his underpants." With a firm hand she threw Nadia the sheet in which the canvas had been wrapped while it was still in your rucksack, and its folds fluttered toward her like the wings of a plucked dove landing to eat crumbs. For a moment she hesitated and then drew close to the drawer and covered the clochard according to your instructions. With her small wrinkled hands she lifted the sheet from his calloused ankles to his dwindling calves; and from them to his lean thighs; and from them to his filthy boxer shorts up till almost his navel, in which with his finger the bearded man got rid of some lint.

"With us," his hoarse voice rose from within the drawer still climbing above the sides, "they used to say that when a person's in trouble, no matter what it is, it's enough for him to touch his belly button and right away his mother would feel it. No matter where a person is, no matter how old he is, right away his mother will feel it." And do they know how long he believed that? The neon light blurred the shadows on his face and softened his features. The sounds of the refrigeration unit were already mingled with his voice when he asked with all the time in the world if it would be so difficult to find him something to put under his head: yes, his hair's falling out, one less place for lice, but do the bit of brains there have to go as well? And the soles of the feet, why don't they cover them for him? Would anything happen if they covered them? "To hell with Monte-niania and all the fucked up Italians together," he said, because that one had holes to show there, and him, he doesn't even have one hole there. "Really," he said, "that's all I need, holes."

You could have added them to the painting, tiny holes, which with Mantegna looked like burst blisters from all that walking on the clouds or on the ripples that the wind raised in the water like rows of protrusions on a metal file. You still remembered how one morning you told her about van Gogh, who in the coal mines sold maps of the Holy Land with the footprints of the son of God imprinted on its inland sea like the wings of crows that he imprinted on the skies; from the bed, in which the heat of her body and its smell were still preserved, you heard the stream of water hit the bottom of the kettle that she had been scrubbing, and her voice when she asked you if all painters were crazy. You also remembered how afterwards she went into the small bathroom and washed her panties and hung them on the line, tiny balloons that will wait hour after hour for her buttocks: they swayed to and fro in her walk, and when she wore one of your T-shirts her breasts swung beneath the material, until you reached your hand out to them: the material, the water, the kettle, everything spread it.

"They can be added to the painting," you said to him. You could have painted those holes, like the holes of a fence where everyone gathers to peek through at celestial Jerusalem with all its walls and palaces, or to show with them how maggots will unravel his innards and weave the thick white thread of their bodies from them. In the room that you rented, every evening the darkness would condense and solidify, your breath made an effort to drill a hole in it like a blind worm, until the electricity switch was found and the lamp appeared, hanging from the ceiling like a drop of resin in which a primordial insect was embalmed, its eyes fixed on you, desiring your blood; and when you were still living in her apartment, you saw her open the small fridge whose light gradually illuminated her as she took from it an avocado, which came from your country, delighting in sticking a teaspoon into it. And afterwards from the window she observed the couple opposite, a man and a woman, who at the time seemed to both of you immeasurably old: they both sat at the table on which dinner was being served and a boy entered and frowned when he was told to remove the earphones from his head, but consented and brought a tickling finger close to his little brother who was sitting there, elevated on a baby chair and chuckling. "Life is right here," she said, because she had become jealous of them ever since having turned her back on all her old quandaries, and she took care with all her might not to become caught up in circumstances that would unsettle her again: not the life stories of artists, which became the stories of their deaths, not sad films, not overly quiet music; each and every object was fixed in its place lest when moved it drag the entire apartment with it, her daily agenda was painstakingly prepared as if one minute slipping away is all it would take to unsettle the very foundation of time itself; over and over she would check if the cooker and stove knobs were completely shut off, the tap handles; if the door was locked twice by both locks; if all the contents were placed in the handbag, because after all even the watchful eye that appeared to her was not bothered by such trifles; "It's right here," she said when dealing with them and shielded herself from anything liable to shake her up again, and gradually you became such a thing. In the corner of the tiny kitchenette she took out a bottle of low-fat milk and drank some from the mouthpiece, dribbling a few white drops onto her chin and her breasts, until she felt your gaze: "What are you looking at?" She asked and patted her thighs after she returned the milk to its place, "not everyone has the taste of that Rubens"; and one morning you saw her in the square in front of the university, going to a Xerox shop to photocopy some reference book with her friends, and from the opposite pavement, on the other side of the moving bus, which did not silence their laughter, you already knew that they would remain after you.

"Let the holes also get fucked," he said from the drawer and asked if he really had to keep his eyes shut like that: completely? His mother always used to say, probably just like that priest of Nadia's, that the eye is the body's lamp, that's what she used to say every night. And also that he should have dreams as sweet as his soul, sweet, yes, that's how it once was. As if he had been asked about the port city in which he grew up and about the poor quarter next to the factories, he began to tell about the youth gangs that ruled there, and how his mother warned him about them after they persuaded him once to sneak in through the small window of a shop and open it from the inside. Even then he could be persuaded to do stupid things, and then it also was the middle of the night. Only that his mother could still look out for him then, and do things, what didn't she do? Cleaning the house and going to the market to do shopping, and cooking food that made you drool just from the smell. And also calling on all her friends and doing washing by hand, she didn't need that machine that he bought her at all then and didn't yet sit like that for hours looking at that round window like it was some television or something, "as if they didn't have a whole sea there to look at."

It's just that the sea, he said from the drawer, he once even heard a captain say in some prostitutes' bar, "if someone doesn't want to listen then don't," that all in all at times it can be quite a lot of trouble. The sea, not the prostitutes' bar. Because his work, that captain said, is like managing a factory, only on the water where you can't get away from your workers for even a moment.

"Let the eyes get fucked," he said from the drawer, but immediately opened them again exposing the blood vessels that covered them and the sleep that accumulated in their corners, when he informed you that because of all the wine he drank, even though Edith almost finished half, he'll really fall asleep here in the end, yes, in a moment he'll be asleep, after all he's used to the cold. What d'you mean, he's world champion of the cold. It's just that in his alley, no matter what a mess it is, every morning he gets woken, who doesn't wake him, people leaving their homes and the hooting of cars and the pigeons shitting on him from above, what not, and who'll wake him here? Who'll bend down toward him, who, who'll kiss him, who'll say good morning to him and ask him what lovely dreams he dreamed? Who?

8

The medical school was not far from the art school and the students also used to come to the bar that the street musicians came to at the end of the night. After a few glasses of wine or small glasses of cognac or whisky there was no longer any difference between someone who previously had held a brush and painted and someone who had held a knife and cut or a violin bow and played. And the small street outside, with the cinema in which you used to watch only films that could cheer her up, did not exist then any more than the teachers of art and anatomy existed: those who assigned their students to pay homage to a great painter, and those who taught them to operate on a body.

In the lesson that you observed, dressed in a white gown, which you got from a drinking companion, with his knives and scissors the professor immediately found all that had been concealed in the double lining of the body before him, an old woman who had frozen in her room after the electricity was disconnected. Like a customs officer he exhibited all her internal organs and showed what will happen to all who, like her, conceal this and this and this, and especially this: the heart, buried deep in the corpse that had turned blue, small and as precious as a lump of opium from which minute capillaries branch out to transport the smoke in them. In an auditorium lit by a swarm of fluorescent lights he explained from the very beginning of the lesson what exactly happens at the temperature of thirty-seven degrees and what happens at thirty-five, and if someone for a moment thought he was speaking about a heatwave in the desert, he must surely have filled himself with alcohol the previous night in some bar, or in a hotel in which the drinks automat surrendered to being kicked, or in a room in which a bottle of milk turns sour on its window sill, or in a tunnel to which afterwards you used to return time and again, a tunnel that in the first moment was essentially devoid of detail and swallowed you too in its void, but afterwards to which you used to descend at the same hour, as if those entering and leaving would be enough, the black man leading a squeegee on the platform and trailing damp furrows in it, a pair of tourists with a flashing camera, two mice scurrying between the railway sleepers, the empty bottles rolling there; as if they would be enough to return the shoes from the street to the moving staircase and lower them there toward you or onwards, to the ground beneath you.

And what exactly does happen at thirty degrees, and what happens at twenty-five, and what happens at fifteen: after fifteen finito la comedia, the professor said above the old lady who had frozen, it leaves the body; life.

The stainless steel panels glistened, and above the sagging stomach the chest accentuated the ribs that were still swelling and contracting like the folds of an accordion. Perhaps the clochard was waiting for coins to be tossed into the drawer, payment for the melody played when he breathed. Nadia and Edith stood to his right, the one stuck a dirty handkerchief to her eye and the other wrung her hands, which were calloused like the soles of the feet protruding from the sheet. According to your instructions they gazed upon the son of God who was placed in the refrigeration unit like all the other dead who have nothing in the world other than a tag with the name they received from their parents or the anonymity that death bestowed upon them.

The morgue workers, when there were still people in this room other than yourselves, had to write the very same thing on the tag so many times they must surely have been sick of the lettering; never mind the tag on the big toe, all in all one word, "unidentified," but what about the list of possessions? That was the most tiring, the list of possessions: all the rags that the dead insisted on dragging around with them everywhere, all the mementos with which they hoped to hold on to the life slipping through their fingers: a rusty war medal, a cracked marble from childhood, a lice-filled curl from a loved one, a tattered hat, a crown of cardboard or thorns.

Rubens painted the son of God being crucified, not with the arms spread to the sides in surrender, but rather slanted upwards toward a beam higher than his head, to be waved in a gesture of victory. And Grunewald waited a while and then showed his fingers twisting and hardening and his skin turning green and the blotches on him mottled by death.

Gibert-Jeune also brought their albums to the hotel – you took heed of the name of the publishing house, so that the colors would match the original as much as possible – and to the American, who at the time was still watching the television from his usual spot with a can in his hand, he offered books in English, which he could steal for him by request. "Books my ass," the American said. On the television a white heron pulled a fish from a river as in the programs you used to watch in her apartment, and the American asked how someone with such a high forehead stole books from the university shop. But after emptying the can and crumpling it, he said that in fact he, who would have believed, good boy that he used to be, someone who planned on going to college and becoming a lawyer in the biggest office in New York, landed up in the jungle instead. In the jungle, yes, where mosquitoes eat you alive and the heat burns your brain even if nothing is burning under your hands, in the fucking jungle and the fucking ditches, that until you were being shot at from them you didn't know they were there at all. In that jungle where you've got nothing to wait for except a helicopter that maybe will come and take you away and maybe not, they'd sometimes be left there with the gook rats for days just to wait for the rattling of the helicopter and its gusts from the propeller, which would flatten the bushes, even had God landed there they wouldn't have honored him more than the helicopter. And with him too, he said, they would have sat on their helmets like that, protecting their balls from the shots from below.

Every time the chambermaids used to bring sheets full of holes in them down to the laundry he would say to anyone who still consented to listen to him, that even in a fucked up hotel like this, which doesn't even have one crummy star in its signpost, it's worthwhile finally investing a few dollars in a smoke detector, because someone who hasn't seen what fire can do just doesn't know anything about life, nothing: you don't need a flamethrower for that, a cigarette someone throws is enough, a match that falls is enough, even an electricity short is enough and the wires here must be crummy like this whole hotel, it'll catch in an instant. There's nothing faster, nothing. A village of geeks or a hotel, it's all the same to fire.

He also told about the traps over and over, traps covered with leaves, that whoever stepped on them fell and was skewered on sharpened bamboo reeds, two of his best friends fell in like that when they were walking in front of him. The screams, he said, he'll never ever forget. And when the village was burnt, that's all he heard, their screams, even though they hadn't screamed anymore for a long time. What could he have done at the time, try and resuscitate them? Two long breaths, fifteen thrusts on the chest, two long breaths, fifteen thrusts on the chest, he said mockingly opposite the drinks automat, two long ones, fifteen thrusts, he said and kicked the automat, it's just that the bamboo came in on one side and out the other side of their chests. His friend's chest, unlike the clochard's in the drawer, was completely crushed and didn't rise and fall even once.

A lot of white was spent on the pale neon light and on the sheet, pearl-white, titanium-white, zinc-white, and black was needed too, ivory-black, lamp-black, for mixing the silver-grey of the stainless steel with them, and besides them all the other colors were needed for the shades of flesh, you were always surprised to find how many colors were swallowed into the flesh of man; they came out the tubes joyously and arranged themselves on the palette in a half circle, brown and pink and red and yellow and even blue and purple for the shadows. They all eagerly awaited the brush, as if fields of spring flowers will be painted with them, and if they no longer exist, at least faded flowers on wallpaper. And the jar, which once contained jam, no longer remembered blueberries and forests but rather listened again to the turpentine – its predecessor gargled in the drainage hole of the operating table – and to the flaxseed oil and the varnish and the paintbrush that stirred them all together and shook in the glass, rejoicing too as if what was being stirred there was the grog that she used to prepare on your first evenings, in large cups from which someone had drunk before you and from which another drank after you. That jar had been kept for so long in the room on the seventh floor that all it remembered was its emptiness and its window: even if a moon could be seen in it on one of the nights, it was slender and curved like a hoary eyelash torn from a pecked eye.

Is there anyone who doesn't believe that he's able to fall asleep here? The clochard asked. Between the panels of the drawer he continued to talk at leisure to all who were interested in his sleep and in his dreams, dreams that perhaps were filled with an entire ocean and perhaps just with a Chinese river, which was dreamed from a port city as anonymous as he was.

Him? Not able? He's world champion of falling asleep in any place. Perhaps he meant the alley and the tunnel that served him as bedrooms for half his life, as well as the minibus in which he lived until his money ran out, and perhaps the vapor of his breath thickened into cloudlets between the sides of the cold tin walls. With a voice in whose way fumes of alcohol stood in the throat, alcohol that warmed with just a superficial warmth – in the medical school the widening of the peripheral arteries of drunks was spoken about, and the increase of the amount of blood that comes into contact with the cold, and inner cell rehydration, and circulatory collapse – he promised he'll succeed in falling asleep here nevertheless, with the greatest of ease and also without counting even one sheep.

"Are there any sheep here," he asked, "anyone seen any sheep here?" Perhaps in Edith's village there were sheep, he said, for those sons of bitches to hump, but here he hasn't

even got their wool, not that he'd be against a bit of wool
now. Even that Arab's rug, never mind how old and worn
out it was, wouldn't do him any harm in the drawer now, yes.
With his fingers, which had not yet turned blue, he pulled the
edge of the sheet under his body to separate his skin from the
cold of the stainless steel and went back into the position that
you had instructed from the other side of the easel. He lay
there quietly for a moment and promptly grumbled saying it
would have been different had the women here warmed him
up just a little bit, yes why not, but like this? This is how he
gets treated? This way at the very most he can count their
lice, when they're bending over him like that, that's all he gets
from their bending down. Nothing else but that.

"Would you listen to him," Edith said from above and
the shadow of her head was cast on the drawer, "you'd think
they threw him shampoo into the hat, what do you mean.
Like he's got a shower there in the street. Talks to me about
lice," and before Nadia could open her mouth she hastened
to add that that one, the way she knows her, in a minute she's
going to say that lice are nothing to be ashamed of, what do
you mean; that God also made them, sure. "Not just lice,
he made everything, what not," it's just that she, Edith, was
nobody's fool, no-no, and neither was her son. And she wasn't
born yesterday either, she's seen a thing or two of this world
in her time. In the middle of the war, yes, right in the middle
of it all he was conceived, because sometimes, "sometimes in
the middle of the biggest shit you sometimes find a diamond.
Yessir yes, that's how it is. For a while that's what you think."

From the other side of the easel with the wave of a dripping
paintbrush you indicated to her to return to her position,
after all you were required to pay homage to one of the great
artists. For years you wanted to rival them, as if there was
nothing more important than the canvas that would be filled
with landscapes that existed only in your head, until you met
her and for a while the entire world was seen through the
apertures of her pupils: the rays of the street lights sailed on
the river like a fleet of dinghies or a flock of rubber ducks that
in her childhood she set afloat, or pulsated like the body of a

large ticklish woman, over whose skin you hovered the hairs of a dry paintbrush until she got goosebumps and pulled you to her: and both cathedral steeples, which you did not climb the whole of that winter, rose up facing the rain like hands in surrender, or guarded the river like sentries who never tire, or trembled and groped their way in the air like two giant feelers that spread the scent of angels; other feelers, slender and small, appeared in the wire of the burnt out globe that shattered, and from the shelf on which it was placed it sniffed around and lay down on a bloated, squeaky metallic paunch, as if from within it would spawn chains of tiny globes, like the ones that adorned Christmas trees and the trees of the street, which was said to be the most beautiful in the world: just to fulfill an obligation she led you through it from one end to the other on the day you arrived, but at the time, in your eyes, every dissonant street musician seemed more important than the famous landmarks because their playing was intended for the both of you, and without any effort she persuaded you to postpone the museum visits: in the Tuileries she passed her hand over the naked trees with a circular motion, to show you that these here are not galloping backwards like the white poplars receding from the train window; she bent down and picked up a leaf and crushed it between her fingers and her nostrils widened; she felt the bark of a trunk very slowly, until your whole body envied it, and placed her head close to it as if she could hear how the sap rose within from the roots to the treetop.

The enormous refrigeration unit of the dead rattled; perhaps it was angered by the drawer dawdling in the void of the room. The wine raised to Edith's throat a song that she once taught the soldier and afterwards would sing to her son. Nadia glanced at her from above the edge of the handkerchief not moving from her position; perhaps she was contemplating the meal promised to her.

"Without insulting anyone," the bearded man said from the drawer, whose sides he padded with the sheet, "even someone who's got a nice voice and everything else, there's just no one in the world who can sing like my mother, no one," he repeated, "I mean when she could still sing."

His consciousness had not yet become blurred and his Adam's apple moved up and down leisurely as he began to speak about his mother again; his mother who used to sing to him and rock him in her arms to and fro. Like this, he showed them as if his mother was required for the painting, rocking him the way one sails in a rowboat or something, he said and didn't open his eyes. Yes, even just to the shore for the rich, which the ships never dirtied, why would they dirty the rich, they only made his one filthy.

"They had umbrellas," he said, as if the umbrellas were arched beneath his eyelids – in the medical school, over the old woman who had frozen, hallucinations were spoken about, and disorientation, and motor injuries, and the slowing down of reflexes; to each and every thing a name was given, as if the name would be enough to heal – "of all colors and also cubicles for getting dressed and undressed, and showers and taps for the feet and what not." And his mother, from whom the smoke of the chimney hid the sea opposite and blackened the washing with soot, "just a change in the wind and straightaway she'd have to wash everything all over," would rock him like that in her arms, as if he was sailing there or to China: they were just as far away, those rich people's umbrellas and the China wall.

From the drawer anchored between the tiled wharves he began to tell how he used to dig in the filthy sand to reach the other side of the world, yes, he was such an idiot then, when he was little. He would dig with an empty tin can or with his nails, he didn't care about anything at the time, neither the pieces of shell, which broke his nails, nor the tar. "What's a bit of tar," he said, "really."

From the refrigeration unit in which there were no shining shells nor black tar – no bubbly white foam like that with which she sometimes filled the bath, no little fish slippery like your fingers there, and no limp seaweed as languid as your limbs afterwards – he began to tell about his father as well, not the one hidden in the heavens but about another

one who used to walk on his hands on the beach. That's
how he described him, even though he wasn't asked to; his
father, who worked in a factory his whole life. "He worked
ten hours a day there," he said, "and in the end was bent like
a question mark, believe me." But when his father was still
young and good looking, he resembled Benfica's goalkeeper,
the spitting image, everyone said so," at the time he still used
to exercise on their beach where the children used to swim
naked until they began to get hair, and the parents just with
underpants and bras, because who had money for bathing
suits. His father used to walk to and fro with his legs in the
air like the Chinese who walked upside down on the other
side of the world.

"And there in China," he said, and as if you were interested
in any river other than the one on whose bridge she walked
– sometimes a long black barge would pass or a transparent
tourist ship in which you had never sailed, after all you had
already been given a key on the first morning: placed on a
table with a note beneath it, like the ones she placed on the
fridge door with tiny animal magnets to remind her of her
chores, so that the entire day would not be shaken from its very
foundation – he spoke again of the Yangtze river and about
what he once heard from some sailor who had been to China:
not that he spoke to him, the sailor, of course not to him, what
was he at the time, just a boy, it's just that he kept his ears open
very, very well when the sailor spoke with that fisherman. He
told him that in China they use birds for fishing.

"Birds," he said not opening his eyes from the drawer,
"yes, with cormorants, and me, I hardly knew what real
seagulls were without oil and without tar." Far from the port
city in which he was born the Yangtze fishermen used to
train cormorants and every night would tie a rope around
their necks, "yes, like a dog, when they dived for them. And
the rope," he said and touched his neck, "was tied in a way
to choke them a bit so that they wouldn't swallow the fish
completely, just keep them in their beaks like that." That's
what that sailor said, and didn't actually look drunk at all.

At the time that's all he knew about China, he said, "that's all, and also that they were champions at ping-pong because of how they held the bat," that's what he knew. And what did he know about their country? Nothing except for their wall, yes nothing except that it's huge and so far away that maybe he'll never ever get there, never. No matter how much he tries. Opposite the cranes at the port and all the garbage floating on the water, "watermelon and potato peels and girls' red pads and what not," sometimes he used to think that maybe China's exactly like that place of his mother's, the one the priest fed to her, the one it's impossible to see with your eyes, and which you have to look for only inside. Yes, that's what his mother used to tell him opposite the window and the chimney smoke that blackened the sky, speaking in an absolutely clear voice like singers on the radio, "even nicer," and putting her hand on her heart and his hand on his heart, yes like that, to feel the wings of the angels there.

His hand fell back into position, and between his ribs, which stretched his filthy skin with its hair ends, no palpitations could be seen – in the medical school they spoke about premature ventricular complex, and increased cardiac excitability, and ischemia of the digestive tract; to each and everything a name was given – when he spoke of how he once wrote those words of his mother's on a cardboard box, right after Rex was taken from him. He wrote it on two large cardboard boxes, not like the one he's got now, really really big ones, he just had to get in more words there. "The kingdom of heaven," he wrote on the back, "Neither shall they say, lo here! or lo there!" and on the inside he wrote: "for behold, the kingdom of God is within you." To this day he remembers it off by heart, every word, why not. He's got a good head, don't get him wrong. Besides which something like that you never forget, let Nadia say if he made some mistake. Did he make some mistake? No.

That's the way he went around with a giant sandwich board, like the ones that advertise something. He went around with it on Saint-Michel and Saint-Germain and Ile Saint-Louis, where didn't he go, only he scared people with it. "Them?" he said, "without some magic, their wallets won't open, at the very least put on some show for them, sweat a bit." He was so naïve at the time; you can't believe how naïve he was. He was sure that with a sign like that he'd get money for food straightaway, on the spot. It's just that Rex's eyes would have helped him a lot, his beautiful eyes, if he only knew then where he was, Rex.

Greyish whiskers quivered in his nostrils and one after another were painted with the small fine brush; and after them you also painted those that sprouted from the curves of his ears, wild as the weeds, which will rise from his cheeks. He had not yet had convulsions, still controlled his sphincter, and still spoke about his dog and its parasites after Edith suggested to him counting fleas to fall asleep. "He had the nerve to speak to me about lice before," she said from above him, "really nice," and one after another the worms of the palette were swallowed by the canvas in all their iridescence.

Maggots came to mind here, but opposite the darkening window in her apartment you saw in your memory a cardboard box, whose lid was perforated, and to the silkworms that it contained, perhaps its holes looked like stars. At the time, the sound came to mind of the nibbling you imagined hearing as mulberry leaves were bitten into by tiny silky teeth, and the barking of the dog sniffing all around; for a while the whole apartment was like that shoe box, a whole world whose total vegetation consisted of an avocado pit in a jar, and all its heaven the ceiling wallpaper; but you had already forgotten its size and colors and forms and didn't remember how she once asked you why you don't paint things like that: a dog barking at a box or poking its head out of a moving car with its ears flapping in the wind, or a grey pigeon landing on an ancient statue and gathering up its wings, or a pensive pony whose eyelashes are long and breath rises from its nostrils: "all those nice animals," she said, and you gazed at her breasts moving with the motion of lethargic camel humps, and afterwards reached out your hand to the delicate fur of her privates until she panted.

"Right here," she led you, and for a while it was indeed there in the depths of her body and her eyes; it was also there when she told about how she used to toss and turn every night, and about the depression that kept her in bed in the mornings, and also about the vocational dreams she dreamed in childhood as you did: Curie and Nightingale and Mother Teresa were to her what painters were to you, and instead of museums she wanted to go to Africa and to India and to all the other remote places seen in nature programs on television, and save all the wretched of the world like those role models. She had a god to guide her in their ways until she would become like them, and justification would be found for all the empty hours in which her room changed its appearance, and you could already imagine that room in her apartment as if you had grown up in it: the carpet with her small shoes that became nests for the preying birds of darkness, the folds of the curtain between which the snakes of darkness dangled, and also the bed fenced by a wooden railing, under which a dragon of darkness breathed heavily in its lair and growled with hunger.

And when she became an adult and moved to this city, a young girl untouched by all the recreations offered by it, the window and the cooker and the lamp and the bath, all of which you were familiar with, changed, and instead of showing her the street and its yellow lamps and warming up the blue kettle and lighting up the pages of a book and cradling her body in foam, they suggested jumping out or taking a lungful or placing wet fingers or cutting throbbing arteries with one thrust; that's what she told you one night and the din of the city rose from the window, blending car motors and brakes, the ringing of the slot machine from the corner café, the barking of dogs, a baby's cry.

In her eyes, as long as those empty hours lengthened, all the objects of the apartment became accessories with one aim, the window handles and the cooker knobs and the lamp switch and the bath shelf and the razor blades, all needed notes attached to them on which "Beware! Death" is written in large red letters, to attach and to beware each and every moment, until the watchful eye appeared to her again in a beam of sunlight.

In her eyes sparkling in the dark, you sometimes could see the eyes of a child who took oaths opposite the window in whose darkness white flakes intertwined, and you could still speculate about how she would be cheered or saddened when wishes were fulfilled or rejected, and also how in their depths it began to appear, raring to grow and as elusive as the curves of a body, that soberness through which she tried to observe everything: "there's a time for everything," she said opposite the windows of the building across from you, warding off old thoughts with all her might, recoiling from anything liable to undo the joy in which she was wrapped, not with ease but also not with great difficulty, because she really was in awe of the beauty of the trifles that suddenly revived each and every moment, if only the right gaze was turned on it.

"There's a time for searching and a time for growing up," she said opposite the lit up squares on the other side of the road – a man was reading a newspaper, a woman was looking out, a boy with earphones held the neck of a transparent guitar and strummed the air in front of his stomach – and if the repellant dreams emerged, she restrained them with a plump, warm iron fist and agreed to make do with the routine offered in those windows: having breakfast, going to work, having dinner, watching television, making love and going to sleep. She placed an insistent and fine boundary around those doubts, like the one she placed on her train journeys, one month in a year, after which she would make a complete break with people whose charm lay in their foreignness: what was concealed behind it was sometimes unbearably familiar.

"Rex," the clochard said from the drawer, and still no swelling was apparent on his body, no festering and no hardening of the muscles as he spoke also about his dog's other parasites. "Yes, why not, there's no shame in talking about ticks here."

And how he would pick them off Rex with his fingernails, "like this," he placed nail end close to nail end, filthy crescent to filthy crescent. "He actually liked having it done to him," he said and his Adam's apple moved with its stubble, "he felt like some lady in a hairdressing salon. He wasn't irritated by it, just the opposite, he liked being groomed like that."

Nobody asked him about his dog or the tunnels in which they lived – tunnels from whose hubbub the only thing your ears picked up was the tuk-tuk the tuff-tuff and the tupm-tupm of one pair of shoes moving toward the distance – nor about his mother and her beliefs, but from within the stainless steel drawer, the hair ends of his chest still rose and fell sprouting from layers of dirt, when he announced that If there isn't anyone to hold him in her arms like his mother, not even Him in who she believed her whole life long – yes, every Sunday she'd go to church with flowers she brought from the empty lot and with his old clothes as well, "not that there were that many, but she used to hand them out to everyone, and what did he give her for that? Diddly-squat, only sickness," and after that we still have to believe that he'll come to save someone or say to him "come forth", and that what's inside here are angels' wings.

So if not them, at least that son of a gun Rex, he said, to lick his face from top to bottom, like he wanted to go out for a walk, why not. Or he would suddenly start to eat his own tail, he also woke him up like that, just from that noise the teeth made.

His Adam's apple still bobbed up and down, but the alcohol had already started to slow it down and weaken his voice when he told how there was never a time when he didn't swear on whoever was out there, his mother's, or the ommanipadmehum's, whoever, they're all the same, which reminds him again of the hospital, because there, in the hospital, as if that Arab wasn't enough for the head nurse, in the next room there was also one with bands around his arm, yes, like some junkie about to shoot up.

And in the corridor, each time the bearded clochard would pass by with his small bag of glucose that eased his pain, every single time, he'd see him standing with the bands around his arm and also with a kind of small box on his forehead. Yes, a box. Not big, but a box, "they hide their biggest secret in there." That's what he was once told when he helped him out of the chair, Rex weighed more than he did; not that he had Rex then, he still thought of himself as a working man at the time.

There was no way that one was going to tell what was inside the box, not even for a million he wouldn't tell, and those ones are crazy about money. The whole night long someone shouted from the bed next to him: "call him, call to him already, call him you son of a bitch so that I won't die from pain," he shouted like that nearly the whole night, but that one, not a thing. He shot God up into his vein. But did that help in the end? Not a bit. Everyone's from the same stock.

On who didn't he once swear, the bearded clochard, on who, before he wised up and thought to put some money aside and buy Rex some flea powder, as if some pharmacy would let them come inside, him and that son of a gun Rex. Son of a gun, yes. "Lassie-come-home? Lassie's only in the movies, all those dogs that run a thousand kilometers home. That Rex, it was beneath him to even walk through one of the city's quarters, just one quarter. Yes, son of a gun, no matter where he is now, in some tunnel or in doggie heaven. No matter where he is, with those eyes, which used to look at you like people do, and those little jumps of his just like a puppy, even though he was already old and everything, he would still jump sometimes like a puppy, and also with his one thousand fleas, yes, one thousand and one, one thousand and two, one thousand and three, he had begun to count the fleas and every time his mouth opened his decaying teeth appeared, one thousand and four, one thousand and five, he counted the way his mother taught him before all the children in their quarter just so that he wouldn't end up like them, that he'd make something of himself, one thousand and six, one thousand and seven, he carried on counting

them like he used to maybe count the ships in the port and
the cranes and unloaded sacks and the seagulls dying in the
tar, one thousand and eight, one thousand and nine, one
thousand and ten, one thousand and eleven, he counted like
he used to also count the feet of the passersby in the square
and bet himself who'll slow down and throw a coin into the
hat, one thousand and twelve, one thousand and thirteen,
one thousand and fourteen, he carried on counting and the
hairs of his beard were still moving with their tiny dandruff
flakes, one thousand and fifteen, one thousand and sixteen,
one thousand and seventeen, he counted and his chest still
rose and fell and did not stop like skewered chests and not
like burnt chests and also not like the American's chest after
he went up to his room for the last time – the same bedside
cabinet was there as in other hotel rooms with old newspapers
padding the drawers, and the same scratched table, and the
same rickety chair that the second night clerk placed upright
again and climbed on and hugged the American by his legs in
order to lift him and undo the belt from his neck; afterwards
he lay him on the bed, whose cover was perforated by all
the cigarettes of occupants before him, and would not have
tried to resuscitate him even if the neck hadn't been broken,
"because someone like that, you never know what diseases
he got from the Saigon whores" – one thousand and sixteen,
the bearded clochard counted from the drawer, his voice
already weakening, one thousand and seventeen, he carried
on counting slowly,   one   thousand   and
eighteen,   one   thousand   and   nineteen,
one   thousand   and   nine   ten   one
thousand   and   eleven   one   thousand   and
two   one   thousand   one   thousand
and   three
                        one   thousand

9

"Is he sleeping?" Nadia asked after a moment or two.

Hundreds of years before her Vasari said of Michelangelo's crucified one: "a dead person resembling death more than this is unimaginable," but the bearded clochard just fell asleep. In the corner of the drawer, next to his head, the bottle placed there instead of the goblet shone in the neon light, the goblet that contained the blood that flowed from his wounds or the wine given to him for the journey, like a Chinese emperor who is buried with his soldiers and his horses and sheaths of corn and stars painted on the ceiling of the tomb to guide his regiments on nocturnal journeys of conquest.

You were assigned to pay homage to one of the great artists and from the other side of the canvas darkening like a window as evening comes, into your memory rose Kepler who was as crazy as any of the very greats. Between his telescopic observations, he devised for his patron – you actually remembered his name well: Friedrich of Württemberg – a golden domed goblet like an inverted sky in which the seven planets would move in paths and each in turn would pour out the liqueur it contained. For half a year he drafted plans and for a further two months bargained with the Duke's banker to allot a small part of his treasury for a model of the universe, until he was told to prepare a model-of-a-model from copper or other material that he's to finance out of his own pocket.

Day and night Kepler labored in his small room – you remembered it too, its smallness, the paucity of light, the stench present there – on a wooden model that he sawed and carved and filed and planed. He neglected his health, neglected his family and at the end of a year he completed a work of art whose stars moved with such great co-ordination in the wooden goblet he held that on the way to the Duke's castle he began to wonder whether all the surrounding forests, the lake with its boats and the shrieks of laughter rising from them, and the snowy mountains with the grey clouds lapping their slopes, were not all being held at that very moment in the hand of a sick astronomer on the back of an old mule that lifts its tail and empties its behind; held and being carried to a stingy Duke hidden from the eye.

"But he also had faith," she said to you, though you no longer remembered the streak of sky, jagged in the window above the central heating chimneys, nor how she mentioned the painters she had read about in her language, when you both still wanted to know every detail from previous years in which the existence of each other was not at all imagined: she read Vasari and you watched nature programs with her and heard about a kilometer of silk thread compressed into one cocoon, about butterflies the weight of half a gram that with the flutter of wings traversed hundreds of kilometers a day; it was all magnificent in her eyes, too wondrous for a guiding hand to have been absent.

"Everyone had faith," she said, "there's not one who didn't," but you also didn't remember how she told about some aunt of hers, who after her husband's death freed her canaries from their cage so that they could fly all around her: "my flatmates," she called them. In the warm darkness, opposite the window shuttered like her aunt's windows, she described those canaries swinging on a hanger as on a branch, or contemplating their images reflected in the glass table as in a puddle, and also the droppings that stained all the furniture; a price worth their friendship in her aunt's eyes. Only at night were the curtains swept aside and the windows opened, because opposite the dark rectangle the canaries would stop in midair as if opposite a wall and turn back toward the furniture that was illuminated by the electrical light.

"We're also like that," she said to you, and did not mean the both of you, but rather all the offspring of the god to which she clung with her little chewed fingernails ever since he had been found again last winter, "scared as if there isn't anything out there." Out there, beyond the windowpane you saw only the front of the building flashing in the reddish gleam cast by the hurrying ambulance below, to a birth or a burial, you didn't know; and in the window opposite, the man and the woman were arguing silently, until the woman went out to the passage and the man immediately walked behind her to deliver the decisive retort or to reconcile with her, you didn't know.

"Aren't you gonna poke him to ask him if he's asleep?" Edith said, "like you do to me in the tunnel? Of course he's asleep," she said, "together with all his fleas. The nerve! To speak to me about lice before, really nice. Me," she turned to you and her tattered handbag swung from her arm, "I had such beautiful hair once, I could have sold it for wigs, believe me sir, they begged me to sell. It's just that after they cut it it wasn't the same."

As if that hair was needed for the painting, she began to speak about her shorn hair again and about the village, but even if a train had passed by it then – from the carriage window all the landscapes became shortened and dwarfed into *gallopinghillsrecedingvillagesbelltowerstreeswetbyrain*, just a backdrop to the woman next to whom you sat and who at the time was still a total stranger, as she had appeared before, a woman with a suitcase at the end of a platform – from within it a square with a tree in its center could not be seen, nor the men and the women and the children who surrounded Edith and giggled, years before you both came into the world: giggled with each lock of hair that dropped to her feet, until a burning newspaper was thrown there.

"One second and it was burned sir," Edith said, "believe me, one second. It took fifteen years to grow and was burned in one second." But on the other side of the easel the flame could not be seen, nor could the goat tethered to a tree be seen bleating when Edith was pushed there, even more shorn than the soldier, "and half-naked too, yes, that's how they dragged me from bed, there was hardly any light outside."

Perhaps the drawer emitted the smell of alcohol toward her from the bottle or from the bearded clochard's mouth as she spoke, as if a many-branched tree was required for the painting, how she was flung against its trunk, "they treated that goat better than me, I mean it," so that she could remove the flag that was caught in one of the branches. "As for me," she said, "I was still a girl then, just with a woman's titties, and after they had gone, the locals turned into big heroes."

They forced her to climb and cling to the branches with her bare legs, the men egged her on, the women cursed, and someone had already unloosened the rope from the goat's neck, and from the branch upon which Edith crawled "with a belly showing four months sir, but they didn't care about that, the opposite, they would have loved for me to fall on my belly," she could already guess how she'd be hung there to the sound of their cheering. "All of their teeth sir, like they'd all been joined together," she'd be hung even if they let her get down in the meantime, just to see again how she rubs against the trunk: "such bastards."

Not a thing of all that could be seen from the window of the carriage nor from the easel while Edith spoke; not the flag she took down with scratched and bleeding hands nor the burning newspaper that was also brought close to it, "because all of a sudden, all of a sudden they were all big heroes, what d'you mean, big saints as well, but before that they licked their boots, just like that, with the tongue." Nor could the village idiot be seen with the rope to wrap around her neck, she was too scared to look at it, "not even for a second," until she felt the weight of the signpost that was tied to it with the words traitor traitor traitor. Because why hang her and get it over with? Really, why, if they could first make her run down the main street, "that's what they called it, one would think how many houses there were there," to make her run like that so that the signpost also hit her belly when they weren't hitting her with all sorts of rotten vegetables, "all the disgusting filth of the pigs that were shrieking like crazy, you'd think I'd taken it from their mouths," they shrieked until all of it, dead mice taken from traps and egg shells whose contents congealed afterwards, fell from her as she continued running to the fields.

"Because where could I have gone to sir, where," she said, as if you were interested in that war or another or in any fields – those seen from the train, whose furrows shortened in the distance and became *viewfromwindow*, the backdrop to a girl your age with whom you wondered if you could pass the hours of the journey in conversation until each would go his own way – "they were all against me, they wanted to show how they were saints and how they never had any dealings with them."

On and on she ran and for four days took nourishment from bulbs and berries, "because who helped me then, Him?" Until someone lifted her up onto a wagon, and another onto a pickup truck, and another onto another wagon, and another one onto a motor car that still had a mattress tied to its roof against bomb shrapnel, "he didn't believe the war was over until he saw me." And a month later she reached this city, a village girl who had never seen so many buildings and cars and buses and people.

"Not to mention the Metro tunnels," she said, "I was even scared to go in there; what am I, a mole?" And opposite the refrigeration unit she told how she preferred to walk through entire quarters on foot, "ten villages could fit into each one of them, that's what I thought," until she found refuge in a public park and slept on a bench there with her belly, "that grew even faster than before, believe me, just out of spite." And there, on the bench, the porter found her.

"And me," she said above the drawer, "I didn't give a damn about anything then. Let him do whatever he wants, that's what I thought. What was done to me on the wagon and afterwards on the pickup truck, things like that sir I wouldn't wish on anyone. And afterwards on another wagon and after that on the car's mattress, I don't wish it even on my worst enemy, believe me sir, I didn't give a damn about anything anymore."

That's what she said, and from the other side of the easel you didn't listen when she also told about how the porter led her to the ninth arrondissement, and how he took off the tatters of her blouse, and washed her from top to bottom and sprinkled her with perfume, "it's just that the bottle was only a quarter full, but what did I care, I didn't give a damn about anything," and he dressed her in a long nightgown, which gave off the faint scent of that perfume with the smell of naphthalene, and lay down on the empty side of the bed just so she would warm him from there at night.

"That's all, really that's all, he didn't want anything from me except that," she said above the stainless steel panels, "not a thing, just for me to warm him up a bit at night, and also to look at me a bit, without any dirty stuff, nothing except that. And when the child was born he really cared for it like it was his own, his blood, he didn't give a damn whose it was. He said to me, it's your child so it's also my child now. Just like that, and that He wanted it to be with him."

The fluorescent lights buzzed softly and as if in answer to them suddenly the refrigeration unit buzzed as well with its huge motor and its drawers and the chorus of all their dwellers, they all hummed for a while until becoming silent, faceless and nameless, and the bearded clochard didn't open his eyes.

"Won't you touch him to see if he's sleeping?" Edith said. "Just now he was actually okay, the way he spoke about his mother. But in the end he still had to make a joke of it. Me sir? I just pity someone who makes fun of everything. Because when something hurts me, I shout about it so that everyone will hear, yessir, why not, once I kept quiet and that was enough for a lifetime. Come on, touch him," she said again, "isn't that what you do to me in the tunnel? When she has a bad dream, then all of a sudden Edith's all right, all of a sudden we've forgotten how bad Edith is and the black heart she's got. On the bench sir, in the middle of the night, because who'll help her then, Him?"

Nadia did not answer, nor did she stray from her pose, perhaps she was afraid of losing the dinner promised to her: a large hamburger, large fries, large Coke. "Come on, touch him," Edith said again, but only the neon touched him with its light, a pale and constant light, which scorned even the sun when it was still imagined in the depths of your greyish window: He who piled up its wet twigs above and tried to kindle a fire there in the morning, at night would stomp with worn out soles in order to warm himself and indent valleys with them and crush the fingers of the plaster gripping at the ceiling: there were hours when from your bed you heard the stomping and the coughing and the cursing he uttered, so that at least they would make the clouds watching him blush, clouds indifferent as prostitutes in ports who've already seen it all.

"And what does she dream about," Edith said, "about what? You'd think she had a good reason for waking me up like that, should I tell you what it was sir? Okay if she dreamt about her leg, even I have dreams like that, it's enough to make you scared to fall asleep afterwards. Didn't I dream how I'm wheeling her around afterwards? Wherever I go sir, everywhere, and not for money, what d'you mean, only for her."

Above the stainless steel drawer, as if that leg was required for the painting, she told how Nadia doesn't even dream about how they were driven out of the hospital, and not even about the house that she once had in her country, "so what if it wasn't really hers, that's where they lived, no?" And neither about the small apartment in the immigrants' quarter, "at least about that, because for someone in the street sir, one room or ten rooms are the same thing." But for the son of God in the drawer, the dreams of a dim-witted old clochard woman were not required; and from the other side of the easel you took no interest in another quarter either, the one in which you no longer lived.

If Nadia escaped with her mother on a freight train, the two of them squashed in a corner of the carriage on filthy

straw, and if she saw sunrises and sunsets from there and
sobbed when her mother went with a border policeman, "she
did it for her, just for her, because without that he wouldn't
have let them out at all," all that was not seen from the
carriage in which the two of you traveled; and not the small
apartment in the immigrants' quarter, the small tablecloths
on which they embroidered flowers, the cheap blouses that
her mother sewed for herself from remnants of material,
the coin she kept for Sundays so that Nadia could throw it
to the man with the music box like the daughter of a lady,
all that was seen was *hillsrecedingcowslickinggrasstreesracing
anonymousuntilanamewasgiventothemthere*

Glug glug more turpentine was poured in place of its
predecessor, which had become turbid, gloo gloo more
flaxseed oil was poured and the varnish dripped. The
paintbrush stirred them all and rattled in the jar, which also
rejoiced: it had lived for so long in a room on the seventh floor
until it no longer remembered anything but its emptiness,
which was drawn into your lungs, and the window in which
no sight other than the milk bottle was seen, hesitant on the
sill, a plastic bag over its head and an elastic band on its neck.
That elastic band had been in the depths of your pocket,
attached to the carton label, and one moment more and one
sip more perhaps it would have been forgotten in the pocket
near the degenerating member, but you drew close to the
refrigeration unit until you felt its chill and bent down to
the drawer and wound it around the big toe whose nail had
lengthened, bony and yellowish. The elastic band was wound
over and over, against its will; no, it did not like the chill of
that big toe after the warmth of the pocket. For a moment it
still grumbled bitterly and tried to incite the carton label to
join it, but because the label remained silent, it just waved at
it until stopping; a weary demonstrator already waiting for
the police.

"So what if she made herself out to be more than she was,"
Edith continued, "she only did it for her, only for her. But

that one doesn't even know how to be grateful. That's how you forget a mother?" And though you didn't answer, she told how the mother wore cheap blouses year after year and how she glorified her past from above her table in the café, "wasn't it called Petersburg? Edith remembers everything, everything." They sat there, Nadia and her mother, listening to what was written in the Russian newspaper, "Nashe Slovo," about their country, which drew away from them farther and farther the way your country drew away from you farther and farther, or the way the trees drift on the slope of a river as the growing distance continues to saw them: beams into logs and logs into sticks and sticks into toothpicks, until they disappear between its teeth.

Her mother glorified her past in the café and also in the small apartment and eventually in a little room in the immigrant hotel behind a thin partition. "And this one didn't understand at all what she was saying," Edith said from above the drawer and told how one evening her mother slipped on the shower floor of the hotel, "from all the filth sir, only from that. And after that she began to limp and already stopped caring anymore how she looked. And when you're old sir, if you don't pay attention, right away hair starts coming out from here and from there, because after that what difference does it make, a man or a woman? What difference does it make when you're dead?"

Nadia still kept her pose, leaning her weight on her healthy leg and clutching the handkerchief to her eye as she had agreed to do in return for a McDonald's meal: perhaps she was thinking what a pleasure it would be without the person in charge of the shift driving her out, but her musings were not required for the painting.

"And when she died," Edith said, "just like that in the middle of the night," and told how in the morning Nadia tugged at her cold hand, and how she shook her back and forth and didn't understand why her mother didn't wake up. "Because this one, what does she know, she only knows about dogs and birds, not a thing about people. Then she was thrown out on the street straightaway, they didn't wait a second, and after that she still wonders why I talk that way."

Through the little old woman who stood by her side you couldn't see the young girl who was driven out from the hotel and worked cleaning offices and slept there at nights until she was caught and dismissed, "only before that, the one who caught her said to her, honey, just let me sleep next to you and I won't say anything, that type of person"; you couldn't see the young woman who slept in shop entrances, nor the woman who walked with her few belongings to the park and woke once when the pigeons cooed in her ear as if they wanted to console her, and a second time when the policemen shook her; you also didn't see how she went down to one of the Metro tunnels, an old woman with the innocent look of a child, alarmed also by the drunks until Edith took her under her wing; all that you didn't see, because the tunnel, like the park and the city with all its quarters, had become empty in your eyes from one end to the other.

"And everything was all right sir; believe me it was all right until she fell. In the end you just get used to everything," Edith said, "the shine and the shit, no matter what, after two days it seems like you've been there your whole life. Come on, aren't you gonna ask him if he's asleep? When bad dreams come to her then she doesn't give a damn about anything. Me sir, I don't cry over people that way, believe me my tears were finished long ago, and she comes crying to me about that."

On those nights in the tunnel – nights even longer than the tracks that you also couldn't see then – she would tell Edith time after time, out of all the things in the world about the Russian puppies in those last hours before everything was turned upside down, "there was a war there as well, wasn't that a war?" And they were still alive then and running wild on the verandah of the entrance to the house. "But she," Edith continued as if you were listening, "did she have the strength to do it? Where would she have had the strength? The gardener's son is the one who did it all, with a hoe. Would she have had the strength to lift a hoe? And right after that his father came with all his friends."

But you weren't listening to her, but rather to the weakening breathing from the drawer and you recalled what had been said hundreds of years before about a different crucified one, "never has a body been created that more resembled the body of the Savior, not amongst the bodies carved in wood and not amongst the bodies hewn in marble," and with the thin brush you outlined the big toe with the elastic band and did not feel its coldness.

"The bastards," Edith continued, "they didn't have a drop of mercy, not even a drop, and those animals, what did they do to them? It was all from jealousy. They just hated the landlord so much, and she, even though she was jealous as well, what did she understand? Nothing! She was little, not yet six years old, so what if they followed her. What, wouldn't they have found the birds and the dogs without her? And now that's what she dreams about, one would think sir – birds and dogs."

From the other side of the easel you couldn't see puppies being buried alive, not canaries squashed by the soles of furious farmers nor other ones rejoicing in their flight from room to room; not shattered furniture nor furniture stained by droppings, and also not the lips that spoke of them in the darkness impinged upon by the flickering of the television: you didn't remember if at the time you were watching sunbirds or anteaters, nor if for a while you found beaks or sniffing snouts in her body, the way she discovered an elephant trunk or a rhinoceros horn, before they flew away to suck nectar. The announcer, whose voice you both knew in all its shades, perhaps spoke about the danger of extinction facing the rain forests as well as the natives who wandered between the sides of the television set naked as you were, casting spears and shooting bows or blow pipes; one evening she told how in her childhood she used to blow tooth picks from a drinking straw, and on another evening – you were still eating opposite the television, but the crumbs were no longer gathered from the hollows of the body with fingers and tongues but remained where they fell as if all you waited for were the convoys of ants – she asked if you once shot a man in one of the wars and you answered that you didn't know: you only remembered the frantic advance and the noise heard suddenly from the thicket, some river flowed in its depths and you all took shots and moved hurriedly on further, further, further.

"A noise from the thicket," she said slowly after you, and so suddenly quiet that for a moment you imagined hearing the hidden drops of sweat flowing on her skin. In the television set perhaps the branches that would become bows could be seen, or the sinews that would become their strings, and when they were drawn you said – the desires and the beliefs of the one you were at the time had already become distant from you like *hillswithdrawinginthewindow* – that it was either him or you, whoever it was there in the thicket; and that in a moment like that moment, in which you're liable to lose everything, you can feel it in every pore, this life, isn't that what she felt from her cathedral? That's what you asked, throwing in her face the most fragile thing that she had told you. And in the darkness you still couldn't see how at the time the light had filled the empty square at her feet with groups of tourists and passersby and beggars and the statue of Karl the Great on his horse, and how the foreign din, which she heard in the distance, became clear and was identified as the noise of cars and fragments of conversations and the sound of water and the cooing of doves.

"It wasn't mine," she answered, "and I didn't kill anyone." Without looking at her opposite the flickering set you said what you said, and there would have been some truth in it had you not returned there a few days later; from a distance the smell could already be perceived. "A noise in the thicket," she said again, not with the soft pronunciation with which she once pronounced the names of trees with light bark flashing past in the window, and she gave you the same look that you both used as each veneer was peeled from the initial image, the one defined only by its backdrop: man-from-the-platform, woman-from-the-platform, at the time you knew more about the yellow freight carriage and its dropped shaft.

Nevertheless, because you had both been shaken – she had found in herself a frail equilibrium while you still wanted to be shocked, so that the landscapes that existed only between your temples would be mounted on the canvas; at the time it seemed a worthwhile price – the next day she led you to the shop that sold boots and military ranks and medals, and bought a faded army rucksack for you to put your paints and brushes in; she found the change it would undergo pleasing and still believed that you could both come to terms with the foreignness you found in each other. Opposite a spotted camouflage uniform, you didn't wonder yet when the shades of the bush and the earth in the material would be replaced by the grey of asphalt, by the white of sparkling bottles, by the footprints of shoes, which stepped in a small puddle that trickled from a smashed bottle or from the drunk who turned to the wall.

"Those ones," Edith said, "only love you for the food, only for that. Don't give them any and straightaway they'll go to someone else, what, isn't that what his dog did to him? And that's after he saved him and gave him food from his own mouth, didn't I see it with my very own eyes? And she goes and thinks that someone's punishing her for things like that, that someone cares about her at all! Who cares about you except for Edith?"

From the bench in the tunnel – a tunnel that emptied out completely from one end to the other after the ceiling cut off the braid, the hips, the buttocks – from Edith's bench, that talk was so annoying that she would immediately remind Nadia about things, which if they had happened, then for sure nobody cared about her, nobody. Because except for the fluorescent lights, "like here, exactly the same," she could see only the video camera above her, hung at the end for the engine driver – a camera that also disappeared from your eyes – "nothing besides that, but even that doesn't help at all."

From the bench she would list for Nadia all those things
one after another, but you didn't listen to her, not in the
tunnel and not in the morgue: you were assigned to pay
homage to one of the great painters, and opposite the son of
God, whose chest still rose and fell in the drawer, rose and fell
even if somewhat slowed down, you remembered how it was
noted by one of them that death should be glorified like life,
since one miraculous artist created them both.

"Let's say we aren't even talking about the village,"
Edith said as you darkened a pale shadow with the brush,
but just about the one who fell on the tracks, "when all the
photographers and journalists came it was just to throw more
mud at us, for all they care we could all fall onto the tracks so
that we won't spoil the scenery anymore. They're there for ten
minutes a day, hardly ten minutes, and we're there our whole
lives, but of course those ten minutes bother them."

And the one who froze to death there, on the steps outside?
"If he had rolled two more steps, what are two steps sir; it
would have been enough for him to get inside. If someone
had only tapped him a little, like by accident sir, with a foot,
yes, why not, wouldn't he have woken up? And the whole
time they trample on us sir without blinking an eye, believe
me cigarettes aren't trampled like that."

And that, she said, without even mentioning the village
and all that was thrown at her there, yes, did anyone do
anything to them about that? And if it would have been here
in the city with her tenants, they would have thrown some
furniture at her that they no longer need, "without blinking
an eye, believe me sir without blinking an eye, they would
have finished me off like that on the spot. And should I tell
you something?" she said, but you didn't react, also when
the lines of soot surrounding her eyes became more blurred,
"maybe it's better that way instead of it taking a lifetime. That's
what I think sometimes. At night, when I can't sleep because
of the cold. Why shouldn't I think like that sir, give me one
reason, just one. Look, now she gives me her handkerchief,
did you see her? You'd think Edith didn't have enough filth."

Nevertheless she took the handkerchief from her hand, but even as she sponged her eyes, forgoing the remains of the makeup, which she put on with a burnt match, she still murmured above the stainless steel drawer about "the birds that that one's got in her head," as if you were listening from the other side of the easel; you wanted to tackle the great artists of the past as well as the descendants of their descendants, those who shut themselves up with corpses and paintbrushes and those who never held a paintbrush but whose performances were also immortalized in the ornate albums that Gibert-Jeune used to bring you to the hotel: Beuys wrestled with a coyote, Nash slaughtered a calf on stage, Hirst drowned a sheep in a bath of formalin. And one night when the American saw you flicking through their photographs, he said that if all those fucking artists had been with him in the jungle they wouldn't do things like that at all, the very opposite. They would have sunk into the fucking bath themselves and also made sure before that to lock the door very well. Yes, he said from his spot next to the drinks automat, so that nobody would get in there in time to do them a fucking favor and resuscitate them, two long breaths, fifteen thrusts on the chest, two long breaths, fifteen thrusts on the chest, and then still feel the cold lips and hear how the ribs crack under the hands, he'll never forget that sound all his life, he still even hears it in his fingers. Outside, the prostitute shifted her weight from leg to leg, and the American got up and peered at her through the dirty windowpane of the entrance door and he said that in Saigon even her granddaughters would be too old to work at that, that's what it was like in Saigon. At first he wondered if he'd go with someone like that, barely a woman, just a pussy wrapped in a few bones and some skin, but even that's better than by hand. And if she's got diseases, better still, yes that's what he thought; at least he'll be punished for what he's doing. Not by God, but straight from her pussy.

The streetlamp left behind a pool of yellowish light and the street itself could not be seen; also at the end of the night when you returned to the room that you rented. The smell of turpentine wafted in it from wall to wall, it was quick to evaporate even more so than the alcohol and the disinfectants whose smell rose from the refrigeration unit. The remains of paint were cracked on the palette like the earth of the distant land, which had been forgotten at the time as if all your days you had stepped on the asphalt of platforms; only its map rose in your memory, the one that was sold in the depths of coal mines, and from the empty bed you could see scores of carriages being filled by their black freight, miners' lamps shedding light from sweaty, sooty foreheads, and the red-headed Dutchman, who still hoped to become a preacher and did not paint other than those maps, struggling with his voice to overcome the rattling of the wheels on the tracks and the blows of the pickaxes on the coal.

"The way she cares for them," Edith said, "you'd think they were her children, you'd think that without her crumbs they wouldn't manage, we'd all be so lucky to be that fat. The way she stands there like that going trrrrr-trrrr at them, all of a sudden she remembers how to talk. But what do they understand, only food sir, and to shit."

From between her thin lips, to which all the wrinkles of her face accumulated, for a moment she imitated Nadia and trilled to the hidden birds like her, but opposite the huge refrigeration unit of the dead – in the medical school they spoke about area formation of necrosis in the pancreas and the lungs, the spleen and the liver and the heart – you couldn't see the old woman in the tattered smock, not next to the flowing fountain nor at the end of a path padded with leaves, not standing alone nor surrounded by a band of amazed toddlers. The times when you still sat in the park you also didn't see her there, not when she called to the pigeons from all its treetops and its corners nor when they beat masses of grey wings around her as if any moment they would carry her off to one of the white nests in the sky; only an unbroken gathering of clouds could be seen above you, sewn by their wings by day and the wings of crows by night. From time to time, when it unraveled slightly, the light would resurrect the entire city, a low light in front of which the colors exposed all their shades like lonely women in a window in front of a boy in whose eyes they discern a spark, but the gathering of clouds would immediately band together, and for a moment you would be reminded of your country and the harsh light that at its zenith would annihilate and possess everything beneath it.

You couldn't see how she once wandered around there for hours from path to path, "I waited for her maybe half the day then, and in winter! I almost went crazy from worry," and from frozen lawn to frozen lawn, a small bleeding load in her hands, "and she turned it over like that the whole time, you'd think she'd find some key to turn there for it to start to fly again, what d'you mean"; you also didn't see how she considered whether to dig a hollow in a corner of the park with old fragile fingers, as if the son of God would come there and call out to the dead pigeon "come forth." You couldn't see how she went out to the street and walked down it, dragging her foot like a mute animal reconciled to its deformity, on the slope down to San Michel and on the bridge and on the Ile Saint Louis, "and she spoke to it like that the whole time right until our place, you'd think sir, it would wake up suddenly just from the talking," you couldn't see that all the streets in all the quarters and all the bridges and all the tunnels and all the stations were emptied from one end to the other.

"Sarah Bernhardt" was the name of the café in which you both sat, not one of the cafés for gatherings of great artists, but convenient for her because of the meticulous planning with which she planned her hours: she learned to attach each hour to the notebook with her chores, in her thin, needlelike writing, so that she would not fly off to nil action and nil desire to reach the next hour; the column of car roofs opposite, which extended from the traffic light, became shorter, and while still entering she asked you if it was worth wasting a whole life in the theater or in the Atelier just to

be immortalized by the name of a café, and you already
wondered if you should hasten to draw the features of her
face on one of the paper napkins; you didn't know then
that a whole packet wouldn't be enough, and that in your
room you would want to encircle yourself with pictures of
her, and in them every one of the movements that you used
to reconstruct over and over from the bed: putting her foot
into the bath like a Degas, soaping her clear breathing skin,
washing the hair of her loosened braid, drying her inner
thigh; putting a teaspoon deep into the flesh of an avocado,
drinking milk from the mouthpiece of a dripping bottle.

The winter lengthened and from the darkness of her
apartment you no longer peered at the couple in the window
opposite in order to try and decipher their small gestures, as
if you would learn some evasive stratagem from them; when
they pleased each other, when they were sick of each other,
when they were angry and quarreled; how they made up when
the man fixed a nail to a picture on the wall and opposite him
the woman exercised her stomach muscles lifting short legs
in torn tights and then spread them; and when they'd had
enough of their baby who tyrannized them from his throne
with a teaspoon dripping apple puree, and how their hearts
were touched once again as it chased after an orange ball
almost its own size; it had once all been wondrous from the
window that swallowed you up in the darkness, and one night
she passed her hand between her thighs and looked at her
finger with the same amazed look with which she observed a
white cloud of milk forming in a teacup, or at a teaspoon of
sugar whose diamond-like grains are imbued with coffee and
turn brown and dissolve, and she said: "from one drop, hands
and feet and a head and everything," but got up immediately
and after a while you heard how the water flowed over her
body, showering it, drizzling on it, dripping: everything
spread it. In front of the nature programs on television she
already knew that she would never travel to the places filmed
there to save the wretched of the world, not India, not South
America, not Africa; the announcer related how the people of
one of its tribes change their gods every morning according

to the first sight that the witch doctor sees on opening his eyes: a rising sun, a galloping elephant, a buzzing tsetse fly, or the tiny wrinkles of the sheet; for a while both of you had taken to drinking wine at night from thin stemmed glasses in front of the flickering set or by candlelight, and afterward you drank from the bottle in the electric light or in the dark, glug-glug it gargled to your mouths to cover up some quarrel for which a barrel of neat alcohol wouldn't have been enough: "Be careful you don't end up like them," she said when you talked about art school and painters and the fame lying years ahead, "be careful you don't end up like them," you said to her opposite the couple in the window; suddenly bubbles took flight from the dishwashing liquid and cheered her up, and she immediately became saddened afterwards by one wilted leaf of a pot plant, but these were fluctuations, signs of life that revived you as well, and not the upheavals by which you were shaken: "you don't need a woman," she once hurled at you, "you need a doctor, and not here, in your country"; and one night you awoke and in the corner of the kitchenette she opened the small fridge door with a sleepy motion and was lit by a low light as in the paintings of de la Tour, and it didn't light up her face but rather her clear naked body, which was imprinted by the folds of the sheet: she bent down to take out the bottle of milk and between her buttocks for a moment the delicate curls of her privates were revealed, and when she felt your gaze she stood erect, turned around and asked if you still didn't understand; and let the door close with the sound of a beat as quiet as the shutting of an eyelid.

She now would glance at her watch every so often, being in such a rush for her classes; the crumbs of the cake that you ordered she gathered up with the tips of her fingers with the same fastidiousness with which she used to attack a pot whose bottom was covered with burned grains of rice: not only were the grains scrubbed but their fields as well, of which in her childhood she dreamed of bringing to those who watered them with their sweat, convoys of food trucks or a vial with a miraculous medicine that she would concoct in her laboratory for all their diseases; she refused to partake of the slice of cake that the waiter brought since she was on one of the fasts to which she used to sentence herself at times, and to that purpose calculate amounts of calories with precise calculations so that not one of them would increase her thighs whose broadness you loved; "not everyone has the taste of that Rubens," she said to you and you wondered if her words were meant for a specific person, perhaps one of her study companions, not another random stranger and also not someone in whom your foreignness could be discerned, but someone who would be stable and induce confidence, who would be the father of her children and grow old by her side year after year, wrinkle by wrinkle; she glanced at her watch again and you both got up and left, and when she began to draw away you followed her from the first bridge and from the second bridge and from street corners – out of all the passersby you saw only one back and one braid and one pair of buttocks, and because you lengthened your stride they did not disappear from your eyes the way they disappeared the following day in the tunnel; she accompanied you then, after waiting for your clothes hanging on the line to dry and to be packed away and to let her live the life she's found, not wanting to let go of even one of its trifles: the sound of squashed snow being trodden, the shame of an umbrella whose suspenders the wind has laid bare, the casting of branches here and there like the scribbling of a child hidden in the sky; that's what she once said to you on one of the paths in the park – and from the pavement opposite the university square you saw how she joined her friends and heard their laughter: they all entered the Xerox corner shop to photocopy some reference book, and from your spot you wondered with whom she'll put her face together on the glass of the copying machine, the way she once did with you in the only picture she left you: your faces were greyish-black in it and blinded like the faces of moles owing to the dazzle of the bright light, but beyond its margins you still remembered her embracing hand whose fingers slipped into your pocket, her bag, which was placed at her feet with an edition of Pariscope in which she had marked a film of Tati, and also the rucksack that she bought you and in it the cheeses that you would eat in the park before the film, with wine that you still used to drink slowly, to savor the taste and not to cram your head with from temple to temple; you waited forty-seven minutes on the pavement for them to come out, nobody had been electrocuted inside, nobody had slipped outside and broken his neck or turned blue from the cold, and on the other side of the moving bus, which didn't drown out their laughter, you already knew they would remain after you.

In the park perhaps an old woman stood with a packet of crumbs as you sat on the metal chair, and its coldness seeped into your body, but if she was there she had disappeared from your eyes; ponies emitting a warm and sweet smell no longer walked along the paths, segments of colorful umbrellas didn't shimmer, clusters of orange and red flowers didn't flow down the stone vases; and further on from there, in the distance, old men didn't play bowls with iron balls, and a policeman in a long cloak didn't try to calm a sobbing little girl, because all the paths were swallowed up between the trees and accumulated toward the vanishing point and shortened into one clump of *avenue* devoid of detail – not trunks against which she pressed close to hear how the sap rises in them, not branches in whose depths a deserted nest was revealed and not leaves that she used to smell with nostrils spread out like those of an animal as if from their smell all the wonder of their growth, their flowering and their death could be deciphered – and stalks joined together as well, forming a uniform *lawn* that no longer had the thinness of stalks, the pearliness of glowing drops, or butts strewn on the green tips like fakirs – that's what she once said to you – and all the mothers whose faces glowed with their children rolling hoops and trampling in puddles and all the pigeons and all the dogs and all the gulls who land slipping on the ice covering of the pond, all joined together into one, and from where you were became sealed shut as *them*; *them* who were unified with the *lawn* and with the *avenue* in one universal essence untouchable to you.

10

"Aren't you gonna ask him if he's asleep?" Edith asked again. "He's asleep," Nadia answered and still held the handkerchief to her eye as you had instructed her from the other side of the easel, as she had agreed to in return for a meal at McDonald's: a large hamburger, large fries, large Coke. With her other eye she looked at his closed eyelids and his sunken cheeks, and from where you stood his whole body became dwarfed to the soles of his feet in the forefront and the cardboard label you tied around his big toe.

Whatever that label had to say was condensed to a few letters with which no name was written, and should anyone remain with questions about him they should kindly direct them to relatives. Yes, if that one had any relatives at all and whether they would come to identify him and not be scared to come close and be infected: after all one irritable flea hopping from within would be enough to spread it, one louse would be enough, one glimmer sprayed from the bottle would be enough, one yearning hiding behind his eyelids like an overgrown child behind a bush would be enough, their reflection inscribed on the drawer would also be enough, even the air between it and them would have been enough, because even after a while everything spread from molecule to molecule, like the smell of shampoo, which you continued to smell even as the staircase moved and the ceiling had already cut off her thighs, her calves, and the entire tunnel became an essence devoid of detail and swallowed you too in its void.

The linoleum flowed a deep grey below, ivory-black with zinc-white, and the legs did not sink but rather walked on it this way and that, coming close to the easel and drawing away from it, coming close and drawing away as you narrowed your eyes and widened them, correcting here and adding there, leading the paintbrush or making it gallop, turning its snout to the palette to lap up color or to the jar to drink or to the rag in order to discharge whatever it had to discharge, the remnants of cadmium or crimson and all the other colors that made the skin grow and stretched it over the ribs. It was also stretched over his eyelids, and beyond them perhaps the whole of the Yangtze River, which once he dreamed to reach, in each eyelid a dome of honeyed sky arched the way the dark ones arched in the enormous eyelid above the city.

His refrigeration unit had a special sound, rhythmic and gentle, the moderate buzzing of a group of toiling bees, contemplative in their honey and not wishing to sting anyone. It never entered their minds at all to make a noise and wake up the dead, disturbing their dreams that were enclosed with them, trapped travelers whose doors have stuck and who are beating on them with decaying fingers and cursing with disintegrating voices, after all what do they want: just to journey for a while through the streets in which they had lived and to look from below, just from the pavement, at the window that was once theirs and make sure that no light was left on, yes-yes, or to sit on the pier and swing their legs above the water or to pee their names on it, that's all they wanted. Perhaps even an elevator with buttons was enough for them now, or a corridor with doors or a counter with a television set the size of a postage stamp: does anyone here still remember that television? And the match played by the Italian losers? And the guard and the prostitute with her black raincoat? And how they left the tunnel before, do they still remember that? And how they met him in the street, this sleepyhead, and how Edith turned up her nose? Perhaps even an exposed light bulb from the ceiling would have been enough for them, how lovely it once looked with the insect embalmed inside it. They lay hidden there, all the frozen, the burned, the run over, the hung, all who waited for someone to come and give them a name. They pushed their big toes with the empty cardboard labels that were attached to them with such force that even the animals in the Garden of Eden didn't push their snouts like that toward Adam who named a doe a doe and a dove a dove and a peacock a peacock and a beetle a beetle and fear fear.

"He's cold," Nadia said. Of course it was cold. The refrigerator refrigerates, the woodpeckers peck, the butterflies fly, and how does a hippo go? In one of the nature programs, which you both watched in her apartment, butterflies drank the tears of a hippopotamus after having stimulated its eyes with their wings; they drank them as if they were nectar and not scum excreted by a giant, filthy body, and you still remembered how she stretched herself over you then and fluttered her hair and breasts and how afterwards she licked the drops from around your eyes. Sure it was cold, but as yet there was no reason for concern: in the medical school, above an inanimate corpse, the professor detailed stage after stage, exactly what happens at thirty-seven degrees, what happens at thirty-five and what happens at thirty, nobody thought he was talking about an African heat wave, and what happens at twenty-five and what happens at twenty. When the breath races, when the heart thunders like a tom-tom drum, when the blood pressure takes flight, when the arteries narrow like channels blocked with sludge, when the jaw gets stuck like a trap on words struggling to break loose, and when the muscles stiffen and the breath weakens and he no longer responds to speech and no longer responds to pain and the belly hardens and the dotted lines of the ECG flatten like trampled grass never to stand erect, but all that was still distant: he slept. His beard continued to grow, sparse and meager, his nails grew as well, and behind his eyelids perhaps some sailboats still sailed, their masts sketching lines as fine as a Mandarin's hair on the honeyed sky.

"Of course he's cold," Edith said above the drawer, "what else could he be? Were you warm in Russia? Or in the tunnel at night? Me sir, I sometimes get so cold that even my teeth start to make a fuss. Yes, no matter how much newspaper I use, it doesn't help. Not at all. So aren't you gonna warm him up?" she said, "cares for the birds – birds yes, and this person here no. As if someone would come for him, who'd come for someone like that, who? As if he'll fly off from here to heaven, straight to heaven for sure, what d'you mean."

But Edith, who for a moment surveyed the bearded man from the soles of his feet to his head, which was darkened by the shadow of the drawers above it, was nobody's fool. "Me?" she said, what's the very highest thing she could see? In the village it was that tree to whose top she was forced to climb, in the arrondissement it was the seventh floor, and in the tunnel "it was that damn camera," the video camera you could see only a long time after the moving staircases were emptied of calves, of ankles, of soles; the occupants of the bench handed you a bottle, which had not been emptied, because you had become one of them, and the blurring din of the empty tunnel began to break up into bits of conversation, into coughing, the ring of a coin falling, the clinking of bottle to bottle, the sound of a stream of urine on the porcelain tiles, into a train drawing away in the next tunnel; as if you had to finish off on a platform what had been started on a platform in order to wipe it all out, from the numerous tiny wrinkles of the sheet to the two rubber bands that you bought for the leaking faucet in the kitchenette. Perhaps they still remained there in one of the corners, engagement rings for the fluffy little fingers of dust.

"Only that," Edith said, "nothing except for that" – hard benches and curved movie posters and rows of pale fluorescent lights and people with briefcases and women with packets and tourists with cameras and tracks and railway sleepers and a black man pushing a squeegee in front of him trailing a moist furrow in the dust and erasing the footprints of soles with their sounds.

"Only that, and when you can't fall asleep, sir, from racking your brains, you can't feel your feet at all, nothing, it's impossible even to know how many toes you've got there. In the end you have to get up just because of that and jump on the spot, but have I still got the strength to jump? Where would I get the strength to jump, where?"

Sometimes, she said and returned her gaze to the drawer, sometimes she would warm herself from the air coming from inside the coat, "yes even though it's unhealthy to breathe like that, did anyone say it's healthy? But from all the cold you warm yourself even from that, why what's better, you tell me sir, to die of cold or to stink?" In the off-white constant light like the neon light here, it sometimes gets so cold that she had to get up and walk on the platform to the neighboring bench, "yes, on the same bench sir, sure on the same bench. But didn't we get along? You tell him, just so he doesn't think we didn't. Not only with her, with whomever sir, whomever. Every single one, believe me with every single one, even with the biggest nutcases you can find, just to keep warm together like that in the cold. And also not to be scared anymore."

For a moment she looked at the drawer, and then she lifted her eyes again, and the last charcoal remains around them had melted away as Nadia touched her with slender fingers, gentle beneath the blemishes that the years and the tunnels had stained.

Swiftly the paintbrush rushed after those tears, sprinted and galloped so that they wouldn't get far and suddenly hang from the end of the nose or the chin becoming ridiculous there. With Rubens, in place of a handkerchief the women held a jug in order to pour oil on the dead son of God, with van Dyk they hugged his calves to receive the last warmth, with Lorenzetti they kissed the soles of his feet. If someone else had been laid out there in his place, he himself would have come down from his heaven and said to him "come forth," Peter would have spread his shadow over him and San Geronimo and Julianus would have prostrated themselves over him not fearing the diseases he spread from his mouth and his wounds and his filth: after all one could stand on the bank of a river and be infected by someone breathing on the other bank, from the sound of shoes drawing away many months ago, from the smell of wine reached out to you from a bench.

The bottle here also needed a gleam, a touch of titanium-white to distinguish it from the shadow cast by the drawers above, all the dozens, the hundreds, whose occupants perhaps rolled over on their bellies and stuck out their dry lips and yearned for wine or a cluster of grapes or a grape or a raisin or one pip, which they could send flying to hell and gone from their mouths: one could be infected by a gust of air blown at the other end of the world, by a yawn being yawned in an apartment in which you no longer lived, and also from a bed in which only the hollow of your body was imprinted, but as you felt its frame, you could sense the trickling of the sap through the painted wood, the yearning of the water for the clouds.

"He's cold," Nadia said again and touched the hand in the drawer. Of course he was cold. One of your predecessors drew him lifting a stone tablet and coming out of his grave but showed his own enemies in hell, his creditors and those who competed with his art; that's how it was related in the book she read in her language, when you still wanted to get to know each other like explorers of lands in which no man's foot tread. "He also had faith," she said from the wicker armchair, but opposite the enormous refrigeration unit of the dead you didn't remember the yarn about his coffin that opened a year after he died and in which he had been kept intact, but rather his words during his life: that each and every moment, through the blows of the iron on the marble he heard how the chisel of death sculpts him as well.

You were assigned to pay homage to one of the great artists and brought with you a drunk beggar and two old women, and believed you could take on those who had been immortalized in marble as well as the descendants of their descendants who had been immortalized only in photographs: one, in order to make a name for himself, bathed in the blood of a calf he slaughtered on stage, one lit candles beneath a grate that she used as a bed and claimed that pain purifies, and another castrated himself to death.

Behind the eyelids in the drawer perhaps masts were still swaying to and fro and the wind blew their sails up like the rosy cheeks of children, but from the other side of the canvas you couldn't even see the sleep in the corners of the eyes. Only Edith's handbag swayed, and Nadia's dirty handkerchief trembled, its folds fluttering like the wings of the pigeon that she held over the grate of the warm air vent of the Metro. And the paintbrush also roamed to and fro, full of vigor from the new turpentine that had been poured on it, the old had already been swallowed by the drain hole of the table like the liquids of the corpses that had been operated on there. The shoes also roamed to and fro, toward and away from the easel, backwards and forwards, worn out from wandering on bridges and in streets and tunnels and inside the room from one wall to another.

The jar did not move from its place and in a flash the brush dived in causing bubbles to rise. From the palette it lifted one small lump of paint after another, a dolphin bouncing a ball on its snout – she was amazed by their intelligence, and when opposite you a species of butterfly was migrating hundreds of kilometers toward woods in which only its grandparents had flown, she could see heavenly fingerprints on their tiny brains; that's what she said between the flickering of the set as you waited for her touch – perhaps the paintbrush yearned too for a burning hoop through which to pass, to maintain the warmth of the soft grip inside the coldness of the jar. Your shoes trudged to the easel and away from it, trudged, drew near and lingered, becoming calm like the masts before they begin to draft on the dome of the eyelid, a thin straight line from horizon to horizon.

The portholes of the doors stared at your backs but you didn't see them, not the red fire extinguishers behind them, not the corridor with its dozens of white doors that continued from there to the elevator, not the elevator, not the floor of the entrance with all the floors above it, not the parking lot with the ambulances parked in it nor the entire city with its cafés and its cinemas and its bridges and its parks.

Beneath the flock of fluorescent lights circling in the air nothing of all that was seen; there was only a drunken beggar opposite you and two old women. Through the beating of the white wings it was no longer possible to hear the sounds of the shoes, through the piercing shrieks it was not possible to hear the sound of your shadow moving forward on the linoleum, a pale dwarfed shadow whose outlines are blurred, step after step toward the front of the drawer and the soles of the feet behind it, toward the yellowish nails and the cardboard label wrapped around the big right toe.

And further on, to the bony calloused ankles and the folds of the sheet winding from there to the hips, advancing and darkening the dirty navel with the sparse hair around it, and the drowsy belly and the ribs that stretch the bluish skin, and spread over the hollow of the neck and over the Adam's apple with the stubble growing around it and over the forest of beard and the multitude of dandruff flakes nesting in it and over the ravines of the cracked lips and their gorges and over the cloud of alcohol forming there toward your nose and toward your mouth, mouth to mouth, mouth to mouth, press the chest, press the chest, press, press, press, press, press, press, press, press, press, press, press, press, mouth to mouth, mouth to mouth, press, press, press, press, press, press, press, press, press, press, press, press, press, press, press, press, until the nostrils will quiver and the eyelashes will separate and his pupils will appear and the neon will shine in them above the edges of the masts or above the glowing face of his mother or above the sniffing snout of his dog or above your face reflected there, as your voice will rise from the depths of the throat and say to him: come forth.

THE THRONE

"All the researchers naturally agree on the inception, both as far as the protagonists are concerned – who indeed are the king, the high priest, the slaves – and on the yearning that deprived them of sleep at night and tossed them hither and thither on their beds, and no one wonders that their sleep was thus disrupted. Naturally there is no dissent as to the known facts although no trace remains, not of their undertakings nor of the mountain that they ordained for their yearnings; the highest of the world's mountains, to which in contrast the entire Meru range is like a hillock, which a cow leaves behind in its roaming. There is also no one who would dispute the proven fact that an entire kingdom was involved in the labor even enslaving all the nations it had vanquished – men, women and children – in order that the whole undertaking be completed in one lifetime: not only so as not to delay its gratitude to the one who brought about its victories, but also because his high priest would have no replacement, should he even in death bequeath all his plans, that were extricated from his pencil as if they had been hoarded in it from the start with no desire other than to burst forth onto paper.

"After all they are known to everyone, his previous ideas whose implementation astounded all the subjects of the kingdom from small to big; figures of the enemy kings hewn from glaciers, their crowns and weapons on them, were mounted in the central square of the capital at noon until they left nothing but a small evaporating puddle; flames of fire carved in marble, which the sight of alone diverted the enemy locust swarms from their path; and the enemy chariots, an enormous mound of glorious scrap iron coated with congealed blood, which the captives melted with their own hands forming a cloud of metal, a symbol of their fallen skies. The vast wooden sea, prepared too according to his plan and for whose sake an entire forest was felled from horizon to horizon, a trunk for each one of its waves, and in their motion a dim roar would arise from within as from the waves

of the genuine sea.[1] And he who naturally sculpted the king
as well, victor of the great war by the grace of Huan, and did
not immortalize the king as was customary, in one image all
of whose expressions were consolidated in the countenance of
the warlord, for such memorial monuments could be seen ad
nauseam even in the remotest villages; but instead modeled
the image of each and every expression and remodeled them
with the passing years until the king was surrounded and
besieged by an army of his images.[2] The argument whether
the king, seeing his arrogance rise against him, concluded at
that moment to dedicate a statue to Huan his benefactor, or
whether it was later,[3] is a subordinate argument and most
of the versions do not concern themselves with it, indeed as
is known to all, their interest lies in the place in which the
events occurred.

"Naturally one should not wonder that everyone agreed
with the well-known opening paragraph, the one that
describes how the high priest outlined the image of Huan in
a drawing of unsurpassed beauty (so beautiful that it seemed
to have been drawn by itself, not by a human hand but rather
from the depths of the paper: from the trunks of trees from
which the sheet of paper was made and from the earth on
which those trees grew; no underground water rises from
their roots other than by the force of its yearning for Huan),
and how he allocated an entire ridge for that image: not only
its mountains and their forests and waterfalls, but the herds
of deer bounding down the slopes and the flocks of eagles

1   whose sailors too, the others added, would leap into the depths
in search of its hidden mechanism there.

2   He was akin, the others added, to that unfortunate youth who
was punished in a mirror that does not erase reflections but rather
heaps them one on top of the other, until they crush the viewer
against the opposite wall; and there are those who elaborate: against
the whitewash, against the plaster, against the exposed bricks.

3   when his first born son was killed by his own hand, by his
sword, for even after the king had conquered the whole world, that
tiny heart remained sealed to him, he did not demolish its walls: they
were made of the wind coaxing languid leaves to embark along on a
great journey, and of the light that gilds the wings of gnats as if they
were cherubs, and from the gentle seeping of the night through the
pale blue from within vast and concealed clouds, like rain quenching a
mole's tunnel.

flying above the peak, so that the deer would frolic on the soles of his feet and the eagles adorn his head.

"About the modification which converted the high priest's initial idea, there too is no dissent, for indeed the reason for it is perfectly clear: had everything been left in place, might it not have been regarded by one as a measure of the greatness of Huan's dimensions, the sole of his foot supposedly being merely the length of a forest, the deer in contrast to him like ants, and eagles of the peak like lice in his hair? It is therefore no wonder that it was decided to expunge them, the cedar and the fir forests with their airborne inhabitants and their four-legged inhabitants, to expunge them to the last, together with the earth beneath them.

"That fertile ground, which covered the foot of the mountain and the lower part of its slopes, will be thoroughly dug to its foundations, the depths of the rocky ground will be delved and the rocks and the cliffs and the ice[4] will be penetrated and continued to be excavated on all sides of the mountain until the primordial stone itself is reached. And with that stone alone, the image of Huan will be modeled, and it would not occur to anyone to compare it with any object in the world.

"There is also no dissent between the versions as to the manner in which the labor was divided amongst the conquered nations, those wretched ones for whom the pain of their downfall is more tormenting than any wound: the slopes of the soles of the feet for the disdained amongst them and the mountains of the shoulders for the fearless (the head, indeed the highest peak of all, the conquerors kept for themselves, divine service whose labor they shall enjoy). There is also no dissent on that well-known moment for which everything was readied and prepared to the last detail, a moment in which all involved in the endeavor wait only for the motion of the high priest, that exhalation that will blow

4   Ice that was so hard, the others elaborated, that it seemed not to have been conceived by the water and the clouds, but rather by the rocks that the earth banished from its insides, and which were purified by the transparent pallor of the dying.

the white beard of a groundsel from the palm of his hand thereby giving the signal to commence.

"Myriads of quarrymen surround the ridge on all sides and everyone delivers his own description of them, no one passes over the sparks sprayed from the axes and mauls, from the mallets and the adzes, from the hammers and the chisels, even before they were brandished in the air. Naturally they all describe the plentiful taskmasters and their plentiful scourges; and how the air would be sliced and rejoined for just a moment, until the quarrymen were whipped again and their backs scarred over and over. Neither were the orderly and plentiful trumpeters positioned all around passed over, not them, not their trumpets nor their cheeks filled copiously with air, ample for setting sail to a fleet of three-masted ships, had they not been awaiting the sign. And they all told of the silence, a silence in which not even the very slightest noise was etched, but there was one who from his heights heard not only the blink of an eyelid and the shedding of an eyelash, but also the steps of a dreamed up figure on the pupil of a butterfly. And in the end, everyone also agrees about that high priest's motion, when he made a fist with his fingers over the beard of the groundsel because he would not yet blow it away.

"He dropped it determinedly from his hand and trampled all its wisps; and there is also no dissent about the fact that from the time he forwent his second plan and clarified his decision in his quiet voice, not only did the victors not wonder about him, they were even as tormented as he was by their previous supposition, according to which a single ridge – enormous even as this ridge – would be sufficient for the entire stature of Huan. It is only due to having been struck by the dazzle, they said, in their haste to pay him respect, even if not in fact to his image but just a miniature of it, the reflection of the-immeasurable-one mirrored in a dew drop the moment before its departure from the world.

"And behold, the researchers were in agreement about the third plan as well, veterans and novices alike, since after all its logic was perfectly clear: the image of Huan standing is not to be modeled in this ridge at all, that notion now seems singularly foolish; for even its lofty peak, soaring above the clouds and diverting stars from their path, and unraveling the night with its tip,[5] would after all not suffice, not for the height of his head nor the height of his shoulders, had even Huan remained in the world and they were stooped like the shoulders of those he created.[6] It had been a foolish idea and best forgotten as if it had never arisen at all; a new plan is to be prepared that will outline the image of the reclining Huan in sound slumber having completed all his illustrious deeds. For this plan, the third, nothing is more fitting than this ridge: indeed higher than all the ridges of the world, its base is tenfold longer, one region of the land his starting point and another his end, and that length alone somewhat alludes to Huan's dimensions.

"Consequently he shall lie there and close his eyes, and the cliffs of his closed eyelids shall hoard behind them his hidden dream of which even the remnants in the corner of the eyes are crystal clear, foretelling the future of the world to angels. Here his image will be sprawled out, the soles of his feet in the desert in the east and his head in the west, across from the sea and the fleet anchoring in it: surely he inflated its sails to the great victory[7] while simultaneously spinning delicate lace for the luxuriating rippling of the shore.

"There is also no dissent that detail after detail was drafted into the plan, the strength of the high priest had indeed not yet been exhausted. There is also no dispute as to the completion of the preparations entailed, and that the outlines of the reclining Huan were sketched out on the ridge

5   Tearing it to shreds, the others say, not to be rewoven, and ever since there has been but one solitary day stretching on to infinity.

6   Then the high priest requested to model the image of the seated Huan, the others added, and when abandoning that idea as well, he no longer attempted to model Huan but made do with his chair alone, a throne the size of an entire ridge; and this plan, they say, is what lent the surviving story its name, but this version is without any foundation

7   and to the lookout on the mast, the others added, he displayed not only the enemy's fleets but also his brethren sailors, small and so ludicrous that he desired to be bound to the mast day after day and to be waved in the wind to and fro until becoming frayed like their flag.

one after another in blood let from the quarrymen. A myriad of them are positioned there again and in their hands mallets and adzes and mauls and hammers, and in the valley at their feet scores of dancers are ready to dance to the striking of the iron on the stone, and in the lakes the whales swim here and there to spray the laborers with showers of water and cool their bodies.

"No one would contradict the moment in which the high priest surveys the ridge for the last time – he slowly passes his eyes over it with the wisps of the groundsel already aquiver in his palm, aching to be carried on the breeze blown from his mouth – there is no dissent that then, in that very moment, his fingers were again clenched into a fist, lest the wind blow away one of its wisps. They are forthrightly squashed in his palm and crushed and will no longer be fit for anything, the wind will cling to his fingers in vain and leave empty-handed.

"And indeed this time as well no one is in the least amazed by the deeds of the high priest, but rather by the supposition that they themselves held, a supposition as arrogant as its predecessors: that indeed, who in all honesty would venture to think that this ridge – be it so enormous, to which in contrast the entire Meru range is as a fly landing on a mound, which a cow leaves behind in its roaming – would be adequate for the image of Huan, should he even recline and be recumbent, the toenails of his feet in the desert and his lips imbibing the waters of the ocean to his innards.[8]

"The well-known vacillations with which the high priest was occupied afterwards for days and weeks and months, about them too there is no dissent. Indeed all remember how he abandoned the idea to model the image of the adult Huan, in whose power fleets could be set in motion and sunk, deciding to display him in his youth, even before the growth of his beard, which covers the world at night, and how he also forwent that plan and outlined the features of Huan the boy, and how he tore them to shreds as well, bits and pieces, which the wind hastened to grab. All describe too how with

---

8   His dry lips, the others elaborate; had a siren risen and kissed them, his deeds would possibly have been decidedly different.

his pencil he then outlined feature by feature Huan the baby, in front of whose eyes stars were all like soap bubbles soaring and bursting, since perhaps for that infant baby the ridge would suffice. All recall the paragraphs describing how in a fit of rage the high priest tore up these drafts as well, and how the sighs of trees from which the paper was made filled the air, and the cries of exhausted birds that have lost the last scent of their nest.

"Thus no one wonders that the continuation too is agreed upon by the majority of the narrators, since it would indeed be a deranged notion to model a dismembered limb of Huan, he-of-the-peerless-perfection: not the soles of his feet for which the entire ridge would be granted, above them the heavens of all the days and nights, crust over crust over crust ad infinitum;[9] nor a thumb, which he sucked in his mouth that was hidden in the heights; nor even a single milk tooth, which he, Huan the baby, grew ages and eons ago. It is a folly into which only fools would venture; and then the renowned plan arose by its own device, the one that in the end came into being, as everyone knows, according to which Huan himself would not be sculpted, not standing nor sitting nor lying down, not Huan the youth, nor Huan the boy nor Huan the baby, but just one minute grain that he blew, a grain the size of an entire ridge.

"Not even one of the attesters (even of the last version, the most inflammatory of them all, so inflammatory it would be best forgotten), disputes the engineering insight required for the replication of the sphere's outline onto the ridge, the magnitude of the endeavor required for it to be quarried and the organizational skill, without which the plan could not have been executed, a skill to which in comparison the most complicated military maneuver is like an offensive carried out by an ant on a biscuit crumb.

---

9   Those who subscribed to the chair-version naturally do not tell of the soles of the feet, but rather about his shoes, which he removed or let fall before taking flight into the air, so as not to be burdened by even his shoelaces.

"Perhaps as a result of this complexity there are those who relate that from the time the high priest abandoned his initial plans, he no longer wished to sculpt Huan – not one of his limbs, nor one of his belongings – but rather those laborers, all the myriads of quarrymen standing on the ridge with mallets in hand. The high priest did not intend to portray them in one uniform template, but rather that each and every one be accorded his own countenance, the contortions caused by the exertion, the beauty of his prevailing or his breaking; and above everyone's heads the stone-scourges would hover, grasped by the hands of the stone-taskmasters who will never land them, and stone-drops will flow down the slopes of their backs and stone-dancers will send forth their tongues to lick them up.

"However this version has no foundation,[10] though the task of quarrying the sphere is indeed of unsurpassed complexity: inasmuch as the treetops of the cedars and the firs have to be passed over, and the fertile ground that nurtured them be penetrated, and to also delve deep through the rocky ground at the top of the ridge where the trees have tired of climbing; and delve deeply through the snow and the glaciers and the rock as well, to the precise required measurement, after which there should be no quarrying, not even to the extent of the nail of the little finger, lest the perfection of the sphere be damaged. After all, one superfluous strike, be it of the slightest, and they would have to immediately hew around it as well; and while they are delving there one of them is liable to err and to quarry in excess, owing to not having correctly gauged the density of the rock, or to having become excited by the undulation of the dancers' breasts, and immediately all would be required to delve around, on all the other sides of the ridge, and an unspecified danger could always be expected, such as a stinging wasp, pollen induced sneezing, a blinding bead of sweat or an overly powerful jet

10   It is certain that he did not intend to carve in stone the knots of the trees gaping as terrified eyes, not their needles falling silently in their descent onto lizard tails shed in fear, nor the bud that sprouts at their feet – a yellow bud in whose eyes the sweep of a felling hand is no different to the stagnation of a rock in the solitary moment of its life in which it blossoms and in which it is beheaded.

from a whale sent to cool them and increase their striking[11] more than was necessary.

"All the researchers, each maintaining his own version as if his life depended on it, all except the juniors of whom there is no cause to speak of at length,[12] agree that the plan for the sphere, or the grain, was the one that was accepted and implemented. The argument as to the duration of the labor is subordinate; the peculiar description used by some to introduce the son of the high priest is marginal and unfounded: supposedly at the time when the trumpeters drew the air into their lungs, a gathering of clouds descended to such an extent that they became entangled in the treetops like the kite of the boy, this youth who lifted sparkling eyes to the branches and called it to return as if it was a trained bird.[13]

"Those differences did not result in the versions multiplying, and as was known to all, the issue of location alone was the cause. The conflicting descriptions of the quarrymen, contradictory as they were, were indeed easily understood as well: after all if the pale-faced people of the north told about the vanquished, who in their alarm scattered like flakes of soot, it is only natural that in the south, captives white as earthworms would be told about. In any event, afterwards everyone focuses on the extolled network of rails that were paved on the slopes of the ridge, and on the carriages constructed in order to carry the chunks of rock down, and on the ropes that were intertwined to restrain them: line upon line is dedicated to the task of their intertwining and the way that those were tethered,[14] and many also spun out

11   Or an immured memory, the others added, which too strikes with heavy axes and chisels and mallets and adzes on the sides of the skull.

12   Those who speak of statues of the quarryman; and the others who speak of a statue of a giant throne and claim it was that which gave the story its name – and even according to them the throne is not the point, but rather what ultimately took place in the throne, the purpose it served.

13   And as if its delicate fabric had not been ripped before then, the others note, and for a long time the wooden spars had come apart, and he held nothing in his hand other than a bare piece of wood shaft with not even the remnants of a shred of a thread.

14   not by the waist but by the neck, the pedants elaborated, so as to ensure that those gripping would not slacken for even one moment.

the description of the easy movement of masses of heavy rock, as if from the time they were quarried their end could be divined; since after the quarrymen and their mallets, the quarrywomen will come and smash the pieces of rock again, and after them the boys will come with their small hammers and strike the bits and pieces, and after the boys the girls will strike at the splinters, and after them will come the babies to crumble the crumbs, until all is crushed to dust.[15]

"Consequently there is no dissent other than on the extent of the success of the last plan, and this matter is what so inflamed the researchers, till each one would have been prepared to lay down his life for his belief. Because according to a few of them the labor went well and in the end an enormous perfect sphere was hewn from the ridge, a sphere whose top was in the sky and likened to a grain of sand in the palm of Huan, hovering above the clouds that yearned for the sea and above the stars that yearned for the sun.[16] However, the ending is anticipated, to the point of revulsion, leading those to the moment in which the labor is completed and the sphere is displayed and casts its shadow on the entire land: the agitation of the wind they describe in their own fashion, a wind that not only blew the trumpets out of the hands of the trumpeters and the mallets and adzes from the hands of the quarrymen and scattered the showers of the whales,[17] and made the dancers breasts stand out, breasts that had already been worn out and become tattered with all the years the labor had been endured by them; but also hugged the stone sphere itself, assessing it like an athlete testing its weight, giving it a slight push and yet another one and rolling it along the ground and the plateau. It was rolled on the slope

15   Prodigious dust, the pedants add, with which enormous leather bags will be filled in order to be exploded in front of the enemy in one of the coming wars; in front of their own faces, others claim, so that they not look on the battle in which they shall be defeated because Huan had left them to their fate.

16   For the dark, others claim.

17   They were like the trickle that the grandson of the high priest trickled, the elaborators elaborated, inscribing his name on the earth until it abated before the final letter, as if the earth itself had granted him an affectionate appellation; as if already now, others maintain, it began to bite into him.

of the valleys, according to them, and on the incline of hills; rolled over villages and cities squashed beneath it, over the winter capital and over the summer capital, whose palaces were pounded into dust, until it reached the sea and sunk in it for all eternity. Therefore, say the supporters of this version and stick to it wholeheartedly, because the water then rose and flooded the entire land, no trace at all can be found of the ridge.

"However the others are justifiably enraged by these words and by the mark of malice that the character of Huan leaves in the end. Indeed they say the desire for revenge should not be ascribed to him just because a person dared to wonder about his dimensions; not at all, they say, if indeed Huan retired completely from the world, he did so only on account of his years and his weariness, and they alone were the cause. And it should not be forgotten, they add and mention, how lofty was the mission that the high priest had taken upon himself as he surveyed the ridge and engraved its sight on his heart – not like an enemy that has to be crushed, but like someone seeking to remember the sight of the face of a cherished woman the moment before he enters her for the first time[18] – the enormity of the difficulties should not be forgotten nor the dread of the dangers entailed with all the blows of a mallet and an adze, a maul and a hammer. Of those dangers, they say one would have been enough, even the sight of two beetles mating on a stone would have been enough for a blow to miss or to go too deep and the error would bind the others as well, all the myriads encircling the ridge. It would be enough for one of them to miss his aim or to go too deep, even to the width of a nail crescent of a little finger – and even if everyone was perfectly precise, it would even be enough for the soles of their feet eroding the stone through all the years they had stood on it, it would even be enough for the winds that caress it and the rain coming through its crevices – and they would all be required

---

18   The moment before the last time, others claim, when he already knows that that touch that welds them together is transient too, and there is nothing inside her but infinite distances.

to delve deeper time after time until the completion of the mission. Therefore, also according to this version the labor was completed, and the stone sphere was indeed hewn round and perfect, except that this sphere, which had formerly been an enormous ridge, in the end did not surpass the height of the high priest's head or his navel. Chiseled and honed, that sphere too makes its way to the sea, but as is described in this version the high priest himself is the one who rolled it there to drown in its waves.[19] And the dispute whether he did it on account of anger, for the fate that befell his initial plan, or whether from arrogance, which arose in him from having laid waste to an entire ridge, is no matter of ours.

"Those who maintained the last version choose, as we recall, to dwell on the great grandson of the high priest: they who previously spun out all kinds of odd descriptions (the pebbles he skipped on the water to the jaws of the whales; his sitting in silence at the feet of the dancers, while with his finger digging a ditch for their sweat and branching out from it tributaries and tributaries of tributaries and setting sail to a stalk like a small boat; his eyes gazing at the sun beams summoned to return like children from a game; his sorrow as they are gathered to the orange cocoon in the distance, until it sinks under their gentle weight), no wonder that to them he becomes the hero of the closing paragraph. Since according to it, when from the ridge, only a stone sphere not even the height of a navel was left, just a grain the height of a grain, he, the boy, grasps it between two fingers and carefully heaps it onto an obedient ant. And if it has not yet died, they say, and assuredly it has not, then is still wandering somewhere in the world to this very day and the ridge carried on it.

"The version that was related afterwards perhaps need not be included in the count, and better it were not presented here, for indeed its insanity is too great to be concealed. If it has been quoted, it is merely in the interest of a complete review, even though it should not enter one's mind to believe it, not even for a single solitary moment. For indeed it is

---

19   Some say, with his blistered hands; others say with his bare feet, kicking it to break their nails as well.

beyond the bounds of possibility that this grain, which the great grandson grasped between two fingers and did not heap onto an ant at all, but raised to the level of his lips and blew on it, it is beyond the bounds of possibility that it is on the face of this crumb, which was blown in the air swirling here and there – and from which on occasion the scent of his breath still arises, though ages and eons have already since passed – that we live.[20]

20   On the chair whose backrest has slackened through the passing years; opposite the shutters whose slats direct thin light beams, and the little dust that swirls from one to another will not be disturbed in the least when the chair is shifted backwards. It will be dragged to the window and with it the fluffy wisp wrapped around one of its legs: there it will be placed opposite the dusty sill, and when the shutters are lifted the dimness of the room will be suffused with the light permeating from outside. The sole of the right foot will mount the seat and after it the sole of the left foot, and they will linger on it but for one single moment, and perhaps two or three moments, and perhaps four or thirty thousand and four (the light will accentuate the pallor of the feet, their nails, the isolated hairs on the joints of the toes), before the windowsill is passed by and they begin to stroll through the air.

Youval Shimoni was born in Jerusalem in 1955. He studied cinema at Tel Aviv University and first began publishing fiction in 1990. Shimoni is a senior editor at Am Oved Publishers; he also teaches creative writing at Tel Aviv and Haifa Universities. He has been awarded the Bernstein Prize (2001), the Prime Minister's Prize (2005), and the Brenner Prize (2015).

Born in South Africa, Michael Sharp currently lives in Israel where he produces radio programs for Israel Radio. *A Room* is his first translation.